LEGENDS
OF AUSTRALIAN FANTASY

LEGENDS

OF AUSTRALIAN FANTASY

EDITED BY

JACK DANN AND
JONATHAN STRAHAN

HARPER
Voyager

Harper*Voyager*
An imprint of HarperCollins*Publishers*

First published in Australia in 2010
by HarperCollins*Publishers* Australia Pty Limited
ABN 36 009 913 517
harpercollins.com.au

HarperCollins*Publishers*

25 Ryde Road, Pymble, Sydney, NSW 2073, Australia
31 View Road, Glenfield, Auckland 0627, New Zealand
A 53, Sector 57, Noida, UP, India
77–85 Fulham Palace Road, London, W6 8JB, United Kingdom
2 Bloor Street East, 20th floor, Toronto, Ontario M4W 1A8, Canada
10 East 53rd Street, New York NY 10022, USA

National Library of Australia Cataloguing-in-Publication data:

Title: Legends of Australian fantasy / editors, Jonathan Strahan, Jack Dann.
    ISBN: 978 0 7322 8848 8 (pbk.)
    Subjects: Fantasy fiction, Australian.
    Other Authors/Contributors: Strahan, Jonathan. Dann, Jack.
    Dewey Number: 823.0876608

Cover design by Darren Holt, HarperCollins Design Studio
Cover illustration by Greg Bridges
Typeset in Goudy 11/15pt by Letter Spaced

For Janeen and Marianne

Acknowledgements

The editors would like to thank the following people for their generous help and support:

Greg Bridges, Sara Douglass, Linda Funnell, Merrilee Heifetz, Howard Morhaim, Stephanie Smith, Marianne Jablon, and Janeen Webb.

Contents

Introduction:
Homegrown Legends

JONATHAN STRAHAN AND JACK DANN

We could quibble about dates and times, about which particular starting point to choose, but for the purposes of this particular book 'ground zero' happened some time in early 1961. That year an American editor, Donald A. Wolheim, spotted an opportunity. There was, he believed, a flaw in North American copyright law that would allow him to publish an out-of-copyright edition of J.R.R. Tolkien's *The Lord of the Rings*.

Wolheim's mass market paperback editions of Tolkien's classic might not *seem* to be particularly important at first glance. After all, Tolkien's trilogy had been published in England in 1955, had been well-reviewed, and was fairly well-known. But it didn't become a 'phenomenon' until Wolheim published his 'bootleg' paperback editions. In large measure Wolheim's editions turned *The Lord of the Rings* into the underground pop culture and international literary classic that it is today, with major publishers producing 'authorised' hardcover and mass market editions.

So how does all this lead into *Legends of Australian Fantasy*?

Well, we could argue the details, but *The Lord of the Rings* was the first enormously successful secondary-world fantasy that sold to young and older readers alike. Tolkien, an ageing English university professor, became the first-ever fantasy bestseller. His work directly inspired Terry Brooks, whose novel *The Swords of Shannara* — which attempted to create a more widely accessible version of Tolkien's work — became a runaway bestseller too when it was published in 1977. That book, and its many sequels, went on to sell millions of copies. That same year Stephen R. Donaldson published *Lord Foul's Bane*, the first volume in his *The Chronicles of Thomas Covenant*, a darker and more challenging book; but still an enormously successful epic fantasy.

Within only a few years writers like Donaldson and Brooks, and later David Eddings, Raymond E. Feist, Terry Goodkind, and Robert Jordan, proved that readers the world over were not only willing to, but were desperately eager to read epic fantasy adventures, and read them in enormous quantity. There's little doubt that their work inspired millions of readers, some of whom went on to become successful writers themselves.

While Australia has a long tradition of creating wonderful fantasy stories, especially for younger readers — Patricia Wrightson's stories, the work of P.L. Travers and others immediately come to mind — it took a little while for the epic fantasy phenomenon to hit our fair shores. The stories told by Tolkien, Brooks, Eddings, and Feist seized the imaginations of Australian readers; but it wasn't until the late 1980s (when Isobelle Carmody's very successful 'Obernewtyn' series debuted) that an Australian writer really attempted to create an epic fantasy adventure on a grand scale.

Novels by Martin Middleton, Tony Shillitoe and Shannah Jay soon followed Carmody's epic fantasy, but it took until 1995 for Australia to produce its first bona fide bestselling fantasy writer. That year Sara Douglass's *BattleAxe* was the first title to come from HarperCollins Australia's new *Voyager* imprint. It went on to become a runaway bestseller and was, in turn, followed by wonderful epic adventures from Traci Harding, Sean Williams, Garth Nix and many more.

Each year the fantasy and science fiction community gathers in a city somewhere around the world for the World Science Fiction Convention. The majority of readers picking up this book will most likely be unaware that it is being published on the eve of the 68th World Science Fiction Convention, which is set to be held in Melbourne for the fourth time. The last time WorldCon was held in Australia, in 1999, this book would barely have been possible, and the time before that it would have been completely impossible. Now it seems inevitable.

This book is, we believe, something very special: a collection of eleven stories written especially for this volume by some of Australia's own legends of fantasy. In these pages bestselling authors Garth Nix, Trudi Canavan, Juliet Marillier, John Birmingham, Isobelle Carmody, Kim Wilkins, Sean Williams, D.M. Cornish, Ian Irvine, Jennifer Fallon and Cecilia Dart-Thornton have created brand new short novels set in their most popular 'signature' universe ... *or* in a brand-new universe they are just starting to create. Here is a chance to settle back into the familiar worlds of your favourite fantasists ... or to sneak a 'first look' at the characters and settings that they will be creating in future.

So settle back into your armchair and enjoy these glittering jewels of magic and imagination. These stories will sing to you; they will shock, delight, and amaze you; and they will transport you to dangerous, fabulous and unknown places.

Enjoy the trip.

We certainly did!

Jack Dann & Jonathan Strahan
Melbourne/Perth, June 2010

Garth Nix was born in 1963 in Melbourne, Australia. A full-time writer since 2001, he has previously worked as a literary agent, marketing consultant, book editor, book publicist, book sales representative, bookseller, and as a part-time soldier in the Australian Army Reserve. Garth's novels include the award-winning fantasies *Sabriel*, *Lirael* and *Abhorsen* and the YA SF novel *Shade's Children*. His fantasy books for children include *The Ragwitch*; the six books of The Seventh Tower sequence; and the seven books of The Keys to the Kingdom series. His books have appeared on the bestseller lists of *The New York Times*, *Publishers Weekly*, *The Guardian*, *The Sunday Times* and *The Australian*. His work has been translated into 38 languages. He lives in a Sydney beach suburb with his wife and two children.

To Hold the Bridge:
An Old Kingdom Story

GARTH NIX

Morghan stood under the arch of the aqueduct and watched the main gate of the Bridge Company's legation, across the way. The tall, twin leaves of the gate were open, so he could see into the courtyard, and the front of the grand house beyond. There was great bustle and activity going on, with nine long wagons being loaded, and a tenth having a new iron-bound wheel shipped. People were dashing about in all directions, panting as they wheeled laden wheelbarrows, singing as they rolled barrels, and arguing over the order in which to load all manner of boxes, bales, sacks, chests, hides, tents and even a very large and over-stuffed chair of mahogany and scarlet cloth that was being carefully strapped atop one of the wagons and covered with a purpose-made canvas hood.

The name of the company was carved into the stone above the gate: 'The Worshipful Company of the Greenwash & Field Market Bridge'. That same name was written on the outside of the old and many-times folded paper that Morghan held in his hand. The paper, like the company, was much older than the young man. He had seen only twenty years, but the paper was a share certificate in an enterprise that had been founded in his great-grandfather's time, some eighty-seven years ago.

The Bridge Company, as it was universally called, there being no other of equal significance, had been formed to do exactly as its full name suggested: to build a bridge, specifically one that would cross the Greenwash, that wide and treacherous river that marked the Old Kingdom's northern border. The bridge would eventually facilitate travel to the Field Market, a trading fair that by long-held custom took place at the turn of each season on a designated square mile of steppe some sixty leagues north of the river. There, merchants from the Old Kingdom would meet with traders from the nomadic tribes of both the closer steppe and the wild lands beyond the Rift, which lay still farther to the north and west.

Despite the eighty-seven years, the bridge was still incomplete. During that time the company had constructed a heavy, cable-drawn ferry; a small castle on the northern bank; a fortified bastion in the middle of the river, and the piers, cutwaters and other foundation work of the actual bridge. Only the previous summer a narrow planked way had been laid down for the company's workers and staff to cross on foot, but the full paved decking for the heavy wagons of the merchants was still at least a year or two away. Consequently, the only way to safely carry loads of trade goods across the river was by the ferry. The ferry, of course, was also a monopoly of the Company, as per the licence it had obtained from the Queen at its founding.

The ferry, and the control it gave over the northern trade, was the foundation of the company's wealth, nearly all of which was re-invested in the bridge which would one day enormously expand the northern trade and repay the investment a hundred-fold. It was this future that made the old, dirty and many-times folded share certificate Morghan held in his hand so valuable.

At least, he had often been told it was very valuable, and he hoped that this was true, since it was the sole item of worth that his recently dead, feckless and generally disastrous parents had left him. The only doubt about its value was that they *had* left the share certificate to him, rather than selling it themselves, as they had sold all other items of worth that had been handed down from his grandmother's estate.

There was only one way to find out. The grim and cheerless notary who had wound up his parents' estate had told him the share could not be freely sold or transferred without first being offered back to the company, in person, at Bridge House in Navis. Of more interest to Morghan, the notary had also informed him that the share made him eligible to join the company as a cadet, who one day might even rise to the exalted position of Bridgemaster. Then, true to his miserable nature, the clerk had added that very few cadets were taken on, and those only after most rigorous testing which none but the best-educated youngster might hope to pass. The implication was clear that he did not think Morghan would have much of a chance.

But it *was* a chance, no matter how slim. So here Morghan was in Navis, after a rough and literally sickening three-day sea voyage from Belisaere, a passage that had cost him the single gold noble he possessed. It had been the gift of one of his mother's lovers when he was fourteen, not freely given but offered to buy his silence. The weight of the unfamiliar gold coin in his hand had so shocked him that the man was gone before he could give it back, or tell him that he had no need to bribe him. He had learned young not to speak of anything his parents did, whether singly or together.

One of the gate guards was looking at him, Morghan noted, and not in a friendly way. He tried to smile inoffensively, but he knew it just made him look even more suspicious. The guard rested his hand on the hilt of his sword and swaggered across the road. After a moment's hesitation, Morghan stepped out from the shadow under the aqueduct and went to meet him. He kept his own hand well clear of the sword at his side. It was only a practice weapon anyway, blunt and dull, not much more than a metal club. That was why Emaun had let him take it from the Academy armoury; it had already been written off for replacement in the new term.

'What are you up to?' demanded the guard. His eyes flickered up and down Morghan, taking in the cheap sword but also the Charter Mark, clear on his forehead. The guard had the mark too, though this didn't necessarily mean he was schooled in Charter Magic as Morghan was — at least to some degree. Not that he could do any magic, even if the guard decided he was some sort of threat and attacked him. There were probably a dozen or more proper Charter Mages within earshot, and many more around the town. They would note any sudden display of magic and come to investigate. A penniless trespasser would not be accorded much consideration, he was sure, and misuse of magic — Charter or Free — was a serious offence everywhere in the Old Kingdom.

'I ... I want to see the Bridgemaster,' said Morghan. He held out his share certificate, so the guard could see the seal, the crazed wax roundel bearing the symbol of the half-made bridge arching over the wild river.

'Bridgemistress, you mean, till tomorrow,' said the guard, but his hand left his sword-hilt. 'What's your name?'

'Morghan.'

'In from the ship this morning? From Belisaere?'

Morghan shrugged. 'Most recently.'

'And what's your business with the Bridgemistress?'

'I'm a shareholder,' said Morghan. He lifted the certificate again.

The guard glanced at the paper, and then at Morghan. He didn't have to say anything for Morghan to know that he was looking at the young man's frayed doublet that showed no blazon of house or service. His shirt had too few laces, and his sleeves were of very different colours, and not in a fashionable way. Even his boots, once of very high quality, did not quite match, the left boot being noticeably longer and more pointed in the toe. Both had been his father's, but not at the same time.

'You'd better see her, then,' said the guard amiably, which was not the reaction Morghan had been expecting.

'T-thank you,' he stammered. 'I …'

He waved his hand, unable to say that he'd been expecting to be kicked to the roadside.

'Don't thank me yet,' said the guard. 'If you have real business here, that's one thing. If you don't, you'll get worse from the Bridgemistress than you'd ever get from me. Go on in, across the court, up the stairs.'

Morghan nodded and walked on, past the other three guards at the gate, into the courtyard. He wove his way through all the activity, ducking aside or stepping back as required, trying to keep out of the way. It was difficult, for there were at least a hundred people hard at work. As he weaved his way through and heard snatches of conversation, Morghan caught on that the entire caravan was leaving soon, that he had arrived just in time to catch the seasonal changing of the work crew on the bridge. This was the winter expedition, near to setting off, and when it arrived the autumn crew would return to Navis and refit for the spring.

There was as much bustle inside the house as out. Morghan walked gingerly through the open front door into a high-vaulted atrium dominated by a broad stair. The room, though very large, was entirely full of clerks, papers, maps and plans. A long table stretched some forty feet from the rear wall, and was heaped with stacks of ledgers, books, map cases and rolled parchments tied with many different-coloured ribbons.

There were several people sitting on the steps, with their papers, books, inkwells and quills piled around them so widely that Morghan had to tread most carefully.

At the top landing, another guard waited patiently for Morghan to step over an abacus that was precariously perched next to a clerk stretched out asleep on the second-last stair.

Though she was at least six inches shorter than him, wore only a linen shirt and breeches rather than a mail hauberk like the gate guards, and had a long dagger at her side instead of a sword, Morghan knew that he would not last a second if he was foolish enough to try to fight this woman. The dark skin of her hands and wiry forearms was covered in small white scars, testament to a score or more years of fighting, but more telling than that was the look in her bright blue eyes. They were fierce, the gaze of a well-fed hawk that has a pigeon carelessly held, and though it can't be bothered right now, could disembowel that prey in an instant. She also bore a Charter Mark on her forehead, and Morghan instinctively knew that she would be a Charter Mage. A real, trained Mage, not someone like him who had only a smattering of knowledge and power.

'Pause there, young master,' she said, and held up one hand.

Morghan stopped below the topmost step, so that their eyes were almost level. The woman pointed two fingers towards the Charter Mark on his forehead, and waited.

Morghan nodded and raised his hand to touch the woman's own Mark at the same time she laid her fingers on his brow. He felt the familiar, warm flash pass through his hand, and the swarm of Charter symbols came close behind, a great endless sea of marks rising up to him as he fell into it and was connected with the entirety of the world … and then they were gone as he let his hand fall and the woman stepped back to allow him up the final step, both their connections to the Charter having proven true, neither one corrupted or faked.

'It pays to be cautious,' she said. 'Though it is some forty years since Bridgemaster Jark was assassinated by a Free Magic construct.'

'Really?' asked Morghan. He wanted to ask why anyone would want to assassinate a Bridgemaster, but it didn't seem like the moment.

'Really,' said the woman drily. 'What is your name and your business here?'

'I am Morghan, and … uh … I wish to see the Bridgemistress.'

'So you are,' said the woman impatiently. 'I am Amiel, Winter Bridgemistress of the Greenwash Bridge Company.'

'Oh,' said Morghan. He looked down at the share certificate, unfolded it and proffered it to Amiel. 'I … I … uh … inherited a share in the company from my parents …'

Amiel took the paper, flicked it fully open, and glanced across the elegantly printed lines, the handwritten number and the gold-flecked seal. Then she leaned forward and prodded the sleeping clerk on the top step. 'Famagus! Wake up!'

The clerk, an elderly man, grunted and slowly sat up.

'I told you everything has been done, to the last annotation,' he complained. 'A nap is the least I deserve!'

'I need you to look up a share,' said Amiel. 'Number Four Hundred and Twenty-One, in the name of Sabela of Nerrym Cross.'

'My grandmother—' said Morghan.

'Yes, yes,' Famagus interrupted. He groaned again as he stood up, and tottered down several steps to pick up a very large and thick ledger that was bound in mottled hide, reinforced with bronze studs and corner-guards. He opened this expertly at almost the right place, turned two pages, and ran his index finger along the lines recorded there.

'Share Four Hundred and Twenty-One, dividends anticipated for the next seven years, the maximum permitted, paid to one Hirghan, son of Sabela—'

'My father—'

'Care of the Three Coins, an inn in Belisaere,' concluded Famagus. He shut the ledger with a snap, put it down and yawned widely.

'This share is essentially worthless,' said Amiel. 'Your father borrowed from the company against it, and it cannot be redeemed or sold until that sum is repaid.'

Morghan's hand shook as he took the paper back. He sucked in an urgent breath, and just managed to stutter out what he had come to say.

'I-I don't want money … I want to join the company.'

Amiel looked him up and down. Though her gaze was neutral, neither scornful nor encouraging, Morghan blinked uneasily, knowing that what she saw was not promising. He was tall and thin and did not look strong, though in fact he had the same wiry strength and constitution that had allowed his father to take far longer to drink himself to death than should otherwise have been the case. His dark eyes came from his mother, though not her beauty, and he had nothing of the selfishness and cruel disregard for others that had been the strongest characteristic of both his parents.

'You want to enrol as a cadet in the company?' asked Amiel. 'The indenture is five years, and there's no pay in that time. Board, lodging and equipment, that's all.'

'Yes,' said Morghan. It was precisely the certainty of food and a roof over his head that he sought. 'I know.'

The Bridgemistress looked at him with those fierce blue eyes. Morghan met her gaze, though he found it very difficult. Somehow he knew that if he looked away, whatever slim chance he had would be gone.

'Very well,' said Amiel slowly. 'We'd best see if you are suitable. It is no small thing to be a cadet of the company. Come.'

She led the way across the landing into a roomy chamber that had tall windows overlooking the front courtyard. There was a desk against one wall, with several neatly organised stacks of paper arranged on its surface, lined up behind an ink-stained green blotter that had a half-written letter secured upon it by a bronze paperweight in the shape of a nine-arched bridge. A bookshelf occupied the opposite wall, the top shelf taken by a case of swords and the lower shelves occupied by at least a hundred volumes of various sizes and bindings.

'Do you have any knowledge of the art mathematica?' asked Amiel. She ushered Morghan into the room, and went to the bookshelf to take down a small volume.

'Yes, milady,' answered Morghan. 'I have studied at the Academy of Magister Emaun in Belisaere for the past six years.'

'You have a letter attesting to your studies with the Magister?' asked Amiel.

Morghan wet his lips.

'N-no, milady. I was not a paying pupil. I-I worked in the kitchens and yard for the Magister, from dawn to noon, and attended lessons thereafter.'

He did not mention that the Magister's lessons had been erratic and depended much on his whim. Morghan had learned more by himself than he had ever been taught, but at least working for the Academy had gained him access to the Magister's library. He had worked more regularly and longer hours at the Three Coins, where his parents were sometimes guests gand always debtors. He knew stables and cellar better than any school room. He had also learned more at the inn than from the academy. Hrymkir the innkeeper was an educated and well-travelled man, and, as a former guardsman, both an experienced fighter and a minor Charter Mage. He had passed much of his knowledge on to Morghan, in return for his work as stablehand, potboy and occasional cook. The lessons were all the pay Morghan ever saw, though his labour supposedly helped to reduce his parents' debt.

'Then we shall see what you have learned,' said Amiel. She flicked through the pages of the book and placed it open on the desk, next to a writing case and a sheaf of paper off-cuts, intended for informal notes or jottings. 'Prepare your paper, cut a new pen, and answer the mathematical problems set out on these two pages. You may have until the noon bell to finish.'

Morghan glanced out the casement window at the sun, which was already rather high. Noon could not be far off. He took off his sword-belt and leaned the weapon against the desk, hilt ready to hand, before he sat down on the polished, high-backed chair and leant over the desk to focus on the open book. His hand shook as he drew the volume closer. But the shaking eased as Morghan read, and he found that he readily understood the problems. They were not particularly difficult, but there were eleven questions, addressing various matters of practical geometry, calculation and mathematical logic, though all in practical settings, concerned with the wages of artisans and labourers, the cost and quantity of goods, the time required for works and so on. All the questions required a lengthy series of workings to arrive at the correct solution or solutions.

Morghan was halfway through question six when the great bell in the tower above the town's citadel boomed out, its deep voice sounding to him like the roar of one of the disgruntled customers at the Three Coins upon discovering their ale had been watered beyond even their low expectations.

The young man set his pen down and dropped a pinch of sand on his current paper. Four other sheets lay to the side, covered in his careful script. Morghan was fairly confident he had answered the questions correctly, but he hadn't finished, and his stomach knotted as he waited for Amiel to come in and dismiss his pathetic effort.

The Bridgemistress strode in before the echo of the bell had faded, and without speaking, picked up the papers and looked through them.

As she finished each sheet, she let it fall back on to the desk. Morghan sat uncomfortably, watching her.

Amiel dropped the last page and looked down at Morghan.

'I-I didn't finish ...' stammered Morghan.

'You've done well,' said Amiel. 'If you had done more, or shown less of your working, I would have suspected you of reading the explicatory chapters at the back. Now, your mark is true. I presume you also studied Charter Magic with Magister Emaun?'

'A little, milady,' said Morghan. 'It ... it is not the fashion in Belisaere these last few years—'

'Fashion?' snorted Amiel. 'By the Charter! If some of those court popinjays ever left the peninsula they'd ... well, you say you did some study?'

'Yes, milady, but not much at the Academy. The innkeeper at the Coins, where we lived, he was a retired guardsman. He taught me a lot of things, and my father ... my father did give me a book once, a primer of a thousand useful marks.'

'Do you still have it?' asked Amiel.

Morghan shook his head. 'He took it back, to sell it.'

'How many Charter marks do you remember?'

Morghan blinked in surprise.

'All of them. I had the book for almost a year.'

'Then you had best show me,' said Amiel. 'Not here. We will go into the inner court, and I will also have Serjeant Ishring test your skill with weapons.'

Morghan nodded, and made a curious movement with his left arm, raising and lowering it with a rotation outwards. Amiel noticed it, but did not comment. Instead she turned away to lead the young man through the house, out on to a squat tower at the back where two sentries watched. Their crossbows lay ready in the embrasures and each had a dozen quarrels neatly stood up against the wall, ready to hand.

'All's well, Bridgemistress,' reported the closer guard as Amiel and Morghan stepped out.

'Good,' said Amiel. She looked over the crenellated wall, and Morghan did likewise. The inner court was a large grassed area, the grass worn to dirt in patches, behind the house proper but within the perimeter wall. There were sentries on the outer wall as well, walking the ramparts, and more atop a taller square tower in the north-east corner.

Morghan wondered why the sentries were necessary. After all, the Bridge House was well within the town's own walls, which were in good repair and patrolled; and it was also well protected against the Dead or Free Magic creatures, being inside both the main aqueduct ring and a smaller one that encircled the Bridge House and several of its neighbours, which were also the headquarters of other major commercial operations.

'We are a rich company,' said Amiel, answering his unspoken question as they descended the steps to the courtyard, pausing at the bottom for the iron-studded door to be unlocked. 'Wealth attracts trouble, of every stripe, and lack of the same can make even the most steadfast stray. We must always be on guard.'

Morghan nodded. The courtyard was empty save for one very broad-shouldered man with a short neck. Unlike the other guards, who wore tan surcoats over mail, he had on a knee-length coat of *gethre* plates that rippled as he moved. He was chopping at a pell — a target post — with a pole-axe, sending chips flying from the tough wood on both sides as he switched his angle of attack. He made it look effortless.

'That's Ishring, my Serjeant-at-Arms,' said Amiel. 'Come on.'

Morghan followed, nervously touching the hilt of his practice sword. He was reasonably competent with swords and short blades, but he'd never wielded a pole-axe. He rotated his left arm again, trying to loosen the elbow as much as he could. A pole-axe needed the full strength and flexibility of two good arms.

As they stepped out into the courtyard, Ishring stabbed the pell at eye-height with the spear point of the pole-axe, then stepped back to the guard position and swivelled on his left foot to face Amiel and Morghan, though as far as Morghan could tell no one had warned him of their approach and he doubted their footsteps could have been heard over the sound of the chopping and striking at the pell.

'Bridgemistress!' bellowed Ishring, slapping the shaft of his pole-arm in salute.

'Serjeant,' acknowledged Amiel. 'This is Morghan, a potential cadet to be put to the test. Arms first, I think, and then I shall assay his knowledge of the Charter.'

'You know how to use that sword, Morghan?' asked Ishring.

'Ah … yes —' began Morghan. Out of the corner of his eye he saw Amiel step smartly away from him, and a more complete answer faltered and remained unspoken.

'Use it then!' bellowed Ishring, and suddenly swung the pole-axe towards Morghan's head, though not directly at it. Morghan jumped back and drew his sword, ducked under another swing and scrabbled sideways.

Ishring backed away, pole-axe at guard once more. Morghan eyed him warily, keeping his sword high.

'How do you deal with an opponent who has a longer weapon or greater reach?' asked Ishring.

Morghan gulped, and kept watching the serjeant's eyes.

'Get in close,' he said.

'What are you waiting for then?' taunted Ishring. He began to circle around the young man. Morghan circled the other way, so as not to be manoeuvred into facing the sun, and when Ishring circled back, he feinted a lunge at the serjeant's knee, which he hoped would provoke a counter and provide an opening for a proper attack. But Ishring merely stepped back just far enough to avoid this strategy, and kept his pole-axe ready.

'Nasty thing, a pole-axe,' said Ishring conversationally, as they circled around each other. 'We need them to crack open the nomad spirit-walkers, but they'll do fearful damage to unarmoured flesh and bone, shockin —'

He swung in mid-word, without any tell-tale tensing of muscle or flicker of eye. Morghan jumped back, and stepped back again as the axe blade came whistling in from the other side, then before it could come again, he leapt forward with his sword shortened to stab, and then he was lying dazed on the ground, uncertain what had actually happened other than the blunt haft of the pole-axe beating his blade aside and tapping him behind the knee.

Instinct made him roll away, a good response, as the spear-point of

Ishring's pole-axe stabbed the ground where he'd been, though it was more punctuation than an actual attack. Morghan knew it would already have been in his throat in a real combat.

'Good enough,' boomed Ishring. He stepped well back. 'Sheathe your blade.'

Morghan returned his sword to its scabbard with a shaking hand. He could feel blood trickling down his chin. He wiped it away, the slight stain of bright red confirming that it was only a graze from his fall.

'You move quite well,' said Ishring. 'But you hold your left arm strangely. You have injured your elbow?'

Morghan looked down. He had hoped they would not notice, at least not immediately, but he should have known that an armsmaster like Ishring would spot it straight away.

'My elbow was broken,' he said. 'A long time ago, and not set properly.'

'Hold out your arm,' commanded Ishring. 'Grip my hand. Hard as you can.'

Morghan did as he was told. He could not completely straighten his left arm, but he had worked very hard to make sure that his left hand was as strong or stronger than his right.

Ishring probed around his elbow joint, pushing with his fingers. It hurt, but no more than it would have hurt his other elbow.

'Old break, grown wrong,' confirmed Ishring to Amiel. She came over and prodded as well, while Morghan stood there, scarlet-faced.

'Why was it not mended?' asked Amiel. 'A simple spell, at the time, and it would have re-knit.'

'It was an accident,' mumbled Morghan. 'My mother was … was ill, and didn't mean to hit me. My father wasn't home. No one tended to it for days, and then … there was no money …'

'How old were you?' asked Amiel.

'Nine or ten,' said Morghan. He remembered every detail of what had happened, but not exactly when it was. His mother had been taking some concoction that addled her wits, and had lashed out at him with a curtain-rod, thinking he was someone — or something — else, and had then lapsed into a drugged coma for three days. She had been lucky to survive, and he had been fortunate not to lose his arm completely by the time his father returned and belatedly sought help. They had been living in a grace and favour house of his grandmother's then, on the sea cliffs near Orchyre, a beautiful but lonely spot with no near neighbours.

'It could perhaps be made new, but it is far beyond my skill,' said Amiel. 'It really should have been dealt with at the time. The Infirmarian at the glacier might be able to do something …'

Morghan nodded glumly. He knew that only a most powerful and experienced Charter Mage, one who was also a surgeon, might be able to mend his elbow. The Infirmarian of the Clayr, off in their remote glacier home, would be one such possibility. But the Clayr demanded payment for all their services, be it foretelling, research in their famed library, or anything else.

He had once thought to petition the King in Belisaere to be healed. There was a tradition that the ruler of the Old Kingdom would consider such petitions on certain feast days, but Morghan had found that in modern times, putting the petition into the hands of the right people who would convey it to the King cost far more money than he had ever had. Besides, the King, though a powerful Charter Mage, was not a surgeon.

With his weak elbow known, he supposed that Amiel would now decide he was unfit to join the Bridge Company, and he would have to come up with some other plan. The only problem was that he couldn't think of anything else. Joining the company had seemed the one possibility that might lead to decent work and regular meals. If he failed here then he supposed he could try to gain employment in an inn or tavern. He knew the work, after all. But such relatively unskilled jobs always had many takers, and he had seen enough beggars in the walk from the docks to know that there were few prospects in Navis, and he had no money for the return journey to Belisaere. It would be a long and hungry walk back to the capital, if he had to make it — though with winter coming, he would probably die of cold before he had the chance to starve.

Morghan stood and tried to be stoic, preparing himself for the bad news. Perhaps he could begin his begging here, and ask for a loaf and cheese, to see him on his way. They were certainly loading provisions enough in the front courtyard.

'Try the pole-axe,' said Ishring unexpectedly. Amiel said nothing.

'Uh, on the pell?' asked Morghan. He took the pole-axe, forehead knitting as he felt its weight. It was much heavier at the head than the axe he had used to split wood at the Three Coins, but the shaft was also longer and had a counter-weighted spike, so its balance was far superior.

'On the pell,' confirmed Ishring. 'Three strokes to the left, three strokes to the right, and finish by jamming the spear into the middle, hard as you can.'

'Hard enough to stay there?' asked Morghan doubtfully. He had done little spear work, but the old guard who had taught him had been insistent that you thrust a spear in only as far as you could pull it out, to avoid disarming yourself in the middle of a battle.

'Aye, for this test,' said Ishring. 'But it is good you asked the question.'

Morghan took a deep breath, stepped forward, and swung, rapidly delivering three hefty chops to the left side of the pell. As he had expected, they were not quite as powerful as they would be if he could straighten his left arm, but a satisfying number of wood chips flew from the timber.

Reversing the momentum of the pole-axe was also tricky, but Morghan managed it, rolling his wrists and pivoting on his foot to address the right side of the pell. But his first swing was weak, and at a bad angle, so that the axe-blade was almost pinched, caught in the tightly-grained wood. Desperately, he wrenched it free, though it put him off-balance. He almost panicked and swung back immediately, but all the lessons in the inn courtyard had their effect. He almost heard Hrymkir bellowing at him to calm down, that balance was more important than sheer speed.

Morghan regained his focus, delivered two more forceful strikes, then rammed the spear-point of the pole-axe as hard as he could at the very middle of the pell. The impact jarred his hands and he felt a savage jab of pain in his bad elbow, but he held on long enough to make sure the weapon was firmly embedded before he let it go, the shaft quivering as it slowly leaned toward the ground. But the spear-point did not come out.

'Good,' said Ishring. 'Now draw your sword with your left hand. Take guard.'

Morghan grimaced with the pain, but he drew his sword. His elbow felt like it was burning up inside, but it hadn't locked up. He could fight left-handed, after a fashion, but Ishring only needed a few passes to disarm him.

'The elbow *is* a weak point,' pronounced the serjeant-at-arms while Morghan bent to pick up his blade. 'If we used longbows I would say we could not take him. But we don't, and a crossbow should present no difficulty. He can wield a sword well enough and can manage a pole-axe. He can be trained to be considerably better with both. Is he a useful Charter Mage?'

'That we shall presently see,' said Amiel. 'Come, Morghan.'

'Yes, milady,' Morghan replied hurriedly. He nodded thankfully at Ishring, who inclined his head a fraction in return. The serjeant had a hard, scarred face, but his eyes showed considered thought, rather than anything else, and Morghan felt none of the fear that other such faces had provoked in him, back at the Three Coins. Eyes showed true intent, and he had learned young to make himself scarce when he saw the glint of need, anger or just plain madness in a gaze, usually intensified by too much drink or one of the more vicious substances you could buy in the alleys behind the inn.

Amiel took him to the very centre of the courtyard, as far from the wall and the house as possible. There was a large flat paving stone under the dust there. It was some ten feet square and had a bronze grille set in the middle, above a sump or drain to the town sewer.

'Stand next to the grille,' instructed Amiel. She walked away from him, off the paving stone. 'Now, I am going to ask you to cast some basic Charter spells. If you do not know the spell, do not attempt it! Simply tell me that you do not know. Similarly, if you begin a spell and lose your way or the marks begin to overwhelm you, stop at once. I do not wish you to kill yourself, or me, for that matter, by attempting magic beyond your knowledge or skill.'

'I understand,' said Morghan. This was also a basic principle that had been drummed into him by Hrymkir, and he had a dim memory of the consequences of over-reaching with Charter Magic. His grandmother had tried to be-spell his father to make him stop drinking and become responsible, but it had completely failed. She had been struck blind and dumb as a result, and had died soon after. Morghan had been six, but he still remembered her withered hand clutching at him as she tried to tell him something, her voice no more meaningful than the cawing of a crow.

Morghan was very careful with Charter Magic.

'Make a small flame, as if to light a candle,' called out Amiel. She had retreated another dozen feet. Morghan briefly wondered just how catastrophically other potential candidates had fared with such a simple spell, but forced himself not to dwell on that. Instead he took a deep breath, and reached out for the Charter, immersing himself in the endless flow of marks, visualising the two he needed, reaching for them as they swam out of the rush of symbols. He caught them and let them run through him, coursing with his bloodstream to the end of his index finger. He held that finger up, and the marks joined and became what they described, a small yellow flame that did not burn his skin, though if he touched it to wick or paper it would set them ablaze.

'Good,' said Amiel. 'Dismiss it.'

Morghan stopped concentrating on the two marks. They retreated back into the great body of the Charter, and the spell instantly faded. A wave of tiredness passed through Morghan as the marks fled, a kind of weary farewell. It must have shown in his face or perhaps he shivered, for Amiel immediately asked if he was able to continue.

'Yes,' answered Morghan, as strongly as he could. He felt that his voice hardly reached Amiel, but she nodded.

'Call forth water from the air, to cup in your hands,' she instructed.

Morghan knew this one well. It was a simple spell, but could save a traveller's life. It could be difficult in a very dry place, but the air was moist in Navis.

Once again he reached into the Charter, summoning the marks he needed. This time, when he connected with them, he sketched them in the air with his fingers, completing the tracing by cupping his hands under the glowing signs that hung in the air before him. They turned to sweet water, which trickled through his fingers. Morghan found himself thirsty, and drank.

As before, the conjuration made him tired, but the drink helped a little. He wiped his face with wet fingers, took a breath and looked to Amiel, signalling his acceptance for the next challenge.

'Call a bird to your hand, from the sky,' said Amiel.

Morghan hesitated. He knew some of the sequences of marks that identified particular birds, and he knew some marks that could be used together to call to someone, to let them know that the caster wanted to see them. But he did not know any specific spells for calling birds.

'Uh, I don't … I don't know how to do that, milady,' he said. Better to confess it, he thought, than to accidentally summon a thousand birds, or perhaps something far more dangerous. There were Free Magic creatures that could fly, and were not deterred by running water. Sometimes such creatures slept beneath cities, or had been imprisoned in bottles or jars, and a slipshod Charter spell could help them escape their confinement.

'You are wise,' said Amiel. 'Do you know the spell of the silver blades?'

'Yes,' answered Morghan. This was a very old, much-used spell for combat. He could feel the three marks already, rising up from the swirl of the Charter, pressing to come into his mind and mouth.

'Cast against the pell,' said Amiel.

Morghan raised his hand and pointed at the wooden post. It was already almost hacked in half by the attentions of Ishring and Morghan's own efforts. The serjeant had left it now, and the space was clear around it.

'Anet! Calew! Ferhan!' roared Morghan, the use-names of the marks flying from his mouth, leaving the burn of power against his lips. The marks became silver blades as they flashed across the gap between him and the pell, and then the timber exploded as they struck, the top of the post bouncing across the yard in a cloud of dust and wood chips.

'That will do,' said Amiel.

Morghan blinked, wiped his sweating forehead and tried to suck in air without making it too obvious that he was absolutely shattered. His legs felt weak and barely able to support his weight and he wished there was something he could unobtrusively lean against.

'You have done well,' said Amiel. She surprised Morghan by taking his arm and helping him walk back towards the house. He tried to not lean on her, but found he was too exhausted. In any case, she seemed to have no difficulty holding him up.

'I have tested many a cadet who has fainted after their first spellcasting,' said Amiel as they slowly ascended the stairs in the rear tower. 'Few manage three spells in so short a time with no allowance for rest, and I think on only two occasions has a cadet candidate managed four.'

'Will you … will I … may I join the company?' croaked Morghan as they came back out on the main landing, above the grand stair. It was much as they had left it. Famagus had not returned to sleep on the step, but instead was sitting up and writing in yet another large, metal-bound ledger.

'Yes,' said Amiel. She sat him down on the top step, next to Famagus. 'You are accepted as a cadet of The Worshipful Company of the Greenwash & Field Market Bridge.'

'Sign here,' said Famagus, balancing the open ledger on Morghan's knees.

Everything was already written out, in neat lines of script, indenturing Morghan son of Hirghan and Jorella, to the Company for the next five years in the position of cadet, one share of the company to be put in trust as a surety for his conduct and application, a further share to be issued should he on the completion of four years be commissioned as a Bridgemaster's Second.

Morghan took the pen, signed with a shaking hand, and passed out.

Though he had been allowed to sleep on the step for an hour or so after he signed his indentures, his awakening marked the beginning of Morghan's training. Even before he rubbed his eyes, a passing Bridgemaster's Second whose name he missed thrust a book called 'Company Orders' into his hand, with the instruction that he was to read it before he next saw the Bridgemistress, as amongst many other things, it detailed the comprehensive duties of a cadet. He had barely opened this small but thick volume, printed very clearly and precisely on onion-skin paper, before a different Bridgemaster's Second took his elbow and led him away to another part of the main house, where he met someone he initially thought was called Sutler before he realised that was her title, as she was in charge of a veritable treasure trove of clothing and equipment.

Before he could protest, Morghan was stripped to his underclothes by the Sutler's assistants, one of whom was a woman not much older than he was, and when the Sutler saw the state of disrepair of the undergarments, though they were clean, those came off too.

Morghan almost lashed out at his helpers as they stripped him, but just in time he realised that they were not trying to humiliate him, they were just trying to get on with their jobs as quickly as possible and that the Sutler herself was piling up new undergarments and other clothes on the table, ready for Morghan to put on immediately.

Newly attired in the livery of the Company, Morghan was loaded up with more new stuff than he had ever had before, the assistants piling things into his outstretched arms as the Sutler wrote them in her ledger. When the pile of five undergarments, three leather tunics, six sleeveless shirts, six pairs of sleeves with laces, one pair breeches short, two pairs breeches long, one heavy greasy wool cloak with enamel Company badge, one light cloak lined with silk, two leather jerkins, four belts, one pair doeskin boots, one pair metal-heeled leather boots, one pair woollen slippers, one broad felt hat, one cap, six pairs assorted neckerchiefs and one sewing wallet reached Morghan's chin, he was tapped on the elbow by the first Bridgemaster's Second, back again, and led out of the Sutler's store to yet another part of the house, this time a long, high-ceilinged room that had to be a wing all on its own. It was lined with trestle beds, forty along one wall and thirty on the other, each of them with two chests at the foot of the bed, a large one and a smaller one with leather straps.

Morghan was told this was the barracks, which was usually about half-full as the greater majority of the company's people lived in private accommodation in the town, and the senior officers had their own chambers above. But when on guard duty, this was home for a week at a time, and for their first year at least, the cadets were required to live in barracks.

'Not that you'll be here long,' said the Second, whose name Morghan still didn't know and didn't want to ask. 'You're joining the Winter Shift, under Bridgemistress Amiel, and you move out tomorrow at dawn.'

'How many Shifts are there?' asked Morghan. Under the Second's direction, he chose a bed, even if it was only for one night.

'Four, of course. I'm in Summer, under Bridgemaster Korbin. But I was loaned to Winter, under Amiel, last year. She's a tough one.'

Morghan must have looked worried, because the Second added, 'She's just, mind you. Or, not exactly just … I mean she's …ah … just do what you're told willingly and you'll be all right. Now, get your things stowed. Your small chest will go with you, so make sure you have everything you'll need in it. I'll be back to take you to the armoury for your weapons and hauberk, the refectory for supper and then the Bridgemistress wants to see you before her evening rounds.'

Morghan muttered his thanks, and immediately packed away all the things he had been given, carefully sorting and inspecting them. Everything went into the smaller chest. He had nothing personal to put in the larger one, and he belatedly realised that the Sutler had not returned his former clothes, his ill-fitting mail shirt or his blunt training sword. He supposed they might be sold, and that would be part of the business of the company, or perhaps the Sutler's personal perquisite. In either case, he didn't care. They were a reminder of a life that he hoped he had left behind forever.

After a final, satisfied look at his well-packed travelling chest, and mindful of the Second's parting comment about the Bridgemistress wanting to see him, Morghan tried to read as much as he could of 'Company Orders' before he was led away again.

He managed thirty-six pages before he was hustled out of the barracks to become re-acquainted with Serjeant Ishring in the Armoury: a large, split-level room that opened out into a smaller courtyard of yet another wing of the main house. It held more weapons and armour than Morghan had ever seen in one place before, including the large swordsmith's that had been near the Three Coins and was supposed to be one of the best in Belisaere.

Ishring explained that while he was Serjeant of the Winter Shift, and so would be training Morghan on the road and at the bridge, command of the house had been formally handed over to the Spring Shift just that past hour, and thus it was Serjeant-at-arms Corena who now ran the armoury. So it was she who carefully measured him for a hauberk of ringed mail that would be adjusted and ready for him to pick up after he saw the Bridgemistress that evening, a promise made concrete by the sound of the smiths working at the forge in the courtyard outside the armoury.

Morghan was also issued a pole-axe; a sword, a proper long hanger with a rounded point; two daggers, thin and merciless; a knife of more general purpose and rougher make; and the number of a crossbow that would be his to use and care for, but, when not in active use would be stored in the armoury wagon or, when they reached the bridge, in the fort on the northern bank or the mid-river bastion, depending on his assigned station.

'You can ride, I suppose?' asked Ishring, as he helped Morghan back to the barracks with his gear.

'Yes,' said Morghan. 'I … I worked a lot with horses.'

He did not say that this consisted mostly of mucking out the stables, cleaning tack, and wiping down and brushing the mounts of guests at the inn. But he had been taught to ride properly when he was very young and his grandmother was still alive, and though he had not ridden far since, he had plenty of practice taking horses across the city.

'We walk, mostly,' said Ishring. 'With the wagons. But there's always a mounted patrol as well, and cadets and guards alike take their turn.'

'How long does it take to reach the bridge?' asked Morghan.

'You mean, "how long does it take to reach the bridge, *serjeant*",' said Ishring. 'You're a cadet now, not a visitor. Don't forget.'

The serjeant's tone was formal, but not aggressive.

'Beg pardon, serjeant,' said Morghan. He felt his back straighten by reflex as he asked again. 'How long to reach the bridge please, serjeant?'

'Sixteen days, weather permitting,' said Ishring. 'Twenty or more if there's snow. Now, in barracks, your pole-axe goes across behind the bedhead, you see the brackets? You wear sword and knife at all times, and daggers as well when mustered to the guard. When you get your hauberk and gambeson, you will wear them at all times, except when you're asleep, when they go on the stand here, half-unlaced and ready to put on. When I think you're used to the weight, you can wear leather and cap when not on duty, but not until I say so. You'll learn more about your duties and service on the march, from tomorrow. Understand?'

'Yes, serjeant,' said Morghan. He spoke softly, as he usually did, a habit born of not wanting to draw attention to himself at the inn.

'I can't hear you!' roared Ishring. 'Do you understand me?'

'Yes!' Morghan roared back, surprising himself.

'Good,' said Ishring, in conversational tones. 'Ah, here comes Second Nerrith to show you to supper. Welcome to the company, Cadet Morghan. Good evening , Second Nerrith.'

'Good evening, Master Ishring,' said Nerrith, who was the first Bridgemaster's Second who had rushed him hither and yon. She didn't look much older than him, but had far more self-assurance. 'Cadet Morghan.'

Ishring departed. As he strode away, Morghan relaxed a little, but not too much. He remembered Hrymkir's stories of life in the Royal Guards, and though he didn't fully understand the hierarchy of the company, he'd read enough in his new book to understand that the Bridgemaster's Seconds were junior officers, and could not only give any cadet orders, but also subject them to a long list of punishments for any perceived infraction of courtesy or duties. He had not read about the status of the serjeants-at-arms, but it was clear they were to be obeyed. As for the Bridgemistress herself, she had already attained a status for Morghan as a figure of vast authority, who was not only to be obeyed, but worshipped.

'Have you read the Orders?' asked Nerrith.

'Ah, some of it,' said Morghan. Belatedly he added, 'Bridgemaster's Second.'

'Just call me Second,' said Nerrith. 'The Bridgemistress is milady or Bridgemistress. Cadets call the serjeants 'serjeant'. The guards you address by name, or 'guard' if you absolutely have to. You'll need to learn everyone's names as quickly as you can. I'll get you a copy of the full roster, but you'll need to try and fix the names in your head as you meet people. Do you have any questions right now? We have a few minutes before the first sitting for supper.'

'Are there many cadets?' asked Morghan. He was a little anxious about how he might get on, particularly after his experiences at the Academy. Working in the stables was not conducive to good relations with the mainly noble students and their highly inflated views of their own standing and how it might be affected by deigning to even notice, let alone befriend, a stableboy, even if his family had once been important at court.

'You're it in the Winter Shift,' said Nerrith. 'Didn't you know? Each Bridgemaster only takes on one new cadet each season, and only then if they're short of Seconds. You were lucky the Bridgemistress only has two Seconds right now and she didn't care for the cadet candidates we've had these past months. I thought she might have to borrow a Second from one of the other Shifts, which is what happened to me last year, but I suppose she always knew you'd turn up.'

'How?' asked Morghan.

Nerrith gave him a look that he supposed was one of kindly scorn.

'She's a Clayr of course. You don't see those blue eyes and that dark skin on anyone else do you? And her hair was all gold before, so they say.'

'But the Clayr live in the Glacier,' said Morghan. 'They See the future there, in the ice. What's she doing here, with the company?'

'Maybe she'll tell you one day,' said Nerrith, with the air of someone who already knew this secret, though Morghan doubted that she did. But he did believe Amiel was a Clayr, though he had never heard of one that had permanently left the Glacier. He had seen Clayr, from time to time in Belisaere. But they were only visiting, and always travelled in groups, on the business of their strange community.

'Where are the Bridgemistress's Seconds?' he asked next.

'Gone on ahead, to check the road and the waystations,' said Nerrith. 'They're all right. Terril, the senior, will probably be a Bridgemistress herself in a few years, and Limmie, I mean Limath, he was a cadet till only last summer, so he'll remember what it was like and not be too hard on you.'

They're often the worst, thought Morghan pessimistically. *Keen to pass on whatever horrible happened to them.*

His thoughts were interrupted as Nerrith announced it was time for supper. On the way to the refectory, she told Morghan that there were usually two sittings and that it was important to be on good terms with the chief cook and the stewards or else one might be served more gristle than meat, and that at some time, he would spend three months working in the kitchens and the refectory, as part of his training.

Morghan did not mention that he already knew this kind of work well, though he quickly discovered that the food in the refectory was better than that of the Three Coins. He had to force himself to eat slowly. If he'd been alone, he would have bolted down everything in sight, and tucked half a dozen of the small brown-crust pies under his shirt for later. But the refectory was crowded, and Nerrith sat next to him and talked and talked, so he ate slowly but steadily, and listened

Nerrith told him he would have an unprecedented three meals a day, including breakfast, luncheon and supper. She detailed the travelling rations they would draw, and what the food was like at the bridge, and where he should sit, or more importantly not sit, some tables being reserved by custom if not actual regulation for particular officers of the company. For example, Famagus the chief clerk, who after the four Bridgemasters was the most important officer, had a favourite table and a particular chair. On no account must a cadet ever sit on his chair, for as the keeper of all records he was a very important figure in the lives of both cadets and Seconds. Though he did not leave the headquarters in Navis, Nerrith said it felt like he was always around, because his letters fell upon them like arrows. There were dozens each day, always wanting some count of equipment, a tally of goods or an explanation of work, and replying was always the work of the junior officers.

'I hope you have a good writing hand,' she added. 'And you can spell. If a report is untidy or misspelled, Famagus sometimes makes us write it out again, three times.'

'You mean when you were a cadet,' suggested Morghan.

'You're in for some disillusionment if you ever make it to Second,' replied Nerrith. 'We get paid and all, but no one thinks we're worth much more than the cadets.'

'Sometimes with good reason,' said a voice behind them. Nerrith choked on a mouthful as she hastily stood up, and Morghan almost fell backwards over his chair as he followed suit.

'I said I wanted to see Cadet Morghan before my evening rounds, not at the commencement of them,' said Bridgemistress Amiel. 'I am not pleased, Second Nerrith. Please let Bridgemaster Korbin know that you have let me down.'

'Yes, milady,' said Nerrith. She turned on her heel and left.

'I expect my cadets and Seconds to be punctual, within reason,' said Amiel. 'It is now a quarter after the hour. Did you not hear the town clock strike, Cadet Morghan?'

'No, milady.'

'Here we take our time from the town clock. At the bridge, horns are blown in the North Fort, the Mid-river Bastion and the Work Camp, on the hour, every hour. Doubtless you will be responsible for such timekeeping at some point. You have been provided with a book of Company Orders?'

'Yes, milady.'

'You will find a section on timekeeping between pages eighty-seven and ninety-one. Do you possess one of these timekeeping eggs the artificers are making in Belisaere?'

'No, milady,' said Morghan. He was about to add that they called them 'watches' now, but decided against it.

'You can tell the hour from the sun? Or the moon?'

'Yes, milady,' said Morghan. He hesitated again, but this time he did speak. 'And ... and from the Charter, milady.'

Amiel looked surprised.

'Good. That is an old spell, not often known these days, save amongst folk who need careful count of time.'

'My grandmother taught me,' said Morghan. 'It is the only spell that I had from her that I can remember. I was six and ... and wondering when I would get my dinner.'

It had been one of the last of the regular dinners. His grandmother had attempted to 'fix' his father not long after she taught him how to find and recognise the marks that spun in time with the passage of the sun, and waxed and waned in keeping with the hours of light and darkness. She had said it could sometimes be very important to know how long it would be before the sun would rise.

'It is the first small part of weather lore,' said Amiel. 'Do you know anything more?'

'No, milady,' answered Morghan.

'I have some small knowledge of weather lore,' said Amiel. 'If time permits from your regular instruction, we may look into it. Speaking of such, as doubtless you already know from your reading of Company Orders, part of the regular duty of cadets and Seconds is to accompany the Bridgemistress on her rounds, whether at house, bridge or camp. As my two Seconds have gone ahead to scout the road, this privilege is solely yours this evening. Follow me.'

Morghan learned a lot about the company and the Bridgemistress in the next hour and a half as he followed Amiel all over the house, as she called the whole sprawling array of buildings. Though preparations had been underway for more than two months for the Winter Shift to move to the bridge, and everything had supposedly been done, Amiel checked into everything. On nearly every enquiry she was satisfied with the result. The one occasion where she was not satisfied, and the nature of her dissatisfaction, made Morghan very thoughtful. He had been beaten, shouted at, spat on and worse on numerous occasions by his supposed superiors and customers at the inn, by older students at the Academy, and by his own parents when they were drunk or drugged. He had nursed his wounds alone, and swore that one day he would be richer, and more powerful and important than his tormenters. Their dominance over him was only temporary, a fleeting moment that would be forgotten.

Amiel did not swear or use force. On discovering that one of the wagon drivers had not replaced a broken axle with a new one, but had had repairs done instead and presumably pocketed the difference, she merely looked at the axle, then at the driver, and had said, 'This is the second infraction, Werrie. There is the gate.'

Werrie had fallen to his knees and begged and pleaded for another chance. He'd sobbed out a story, made incoherent by his tears, something about debts and family. But Amiel had merely pointed at the gate again, and then when Werrie grovelled at her ankles, she gestured to summon two of the gate guards, who picked him up and dragged him out. Morghan made particular note that they tore the company emblem from the sleeve of Werrie's coat and unpinned the enamelled badge from his hat.

'Cadet Morghan,' said Amiel conversationally, as she continued to the next wagon, 'you have seen a very rare occurrence. This company looks after its people well, but we expect much in return. While you may err out of stupidity, or weariness, or simply make less than ideal choices, if you intentionally put the company's goods, persons or premises at risk, you will be warned once only. The second time, you will be expelled, your share or shares forfeit and your name published across the Kingdom as an offender against the company. In some very few cases, we take even sterner action, as we may under our original patent from Queen Hellael the Second.'

Morghan thought about that later, as he lay in his narrow bed and tried to sleep. There were many people in the barracks, a lot of them still preparing gear, or talking, but it was not this busy noise that kept him awake.

It was pure amazement that forestalled sleep. He could not believe how much his life had changed for the better, a wonderment that was accompanied by a deep-seated fear that something would happen to take it all away again.

Finally, Morghan did sleep, but he felt like he had only just closed his eyes when he was roused again, by a rough shake on his shoulder.

'Come on, lad! The day won't wait for you.'

The next few weeks were a golden time for Morghan. He wasn't necessarily happy, as such, for he did not really know that such a state existed, or how he might reach it. But he was content and busy, a combined state that he was equally unfamiliar with, the result of finally finding a respectable place among a well-ordered community, rather than the confusion of never knowing what the next day would hold, apart from the petty miseries that were his lot at the Three Coins, or the arbitrary actions of his parents.

The company's wagons travelled the Royal Road north, and had right of way over almost everyone, so they rarely had to leave the paved and well-drained highway for the muddy shoulder. They were lucky with the weather too. To begin with the days were cold but fine, and the morning frosts light, not much more than a tonic to wake up a tired cadet.

He *was* tired, for his every waking hour was occupied, mostly following the Bridgemistress everywhere or dashing off at her orders, usually to discover something she already knew but Morghan did not. She also set him passages of Company Orders to memorise, and showed him Charter marks that he had to summon for her the next day, with the promise that in time he would also learn how these marks could be combined with others to become useful spells.

Amiel did not sleep very much herself, which made things even more difficult. By the fourth day he was very tired indeed, so tired that he could not even summon the energy to be nervous about the imminent arrival of the Bridgemistress's two Seconds, who were due to arrive that evening, having already been to the bridge to check the road and discover anything unusual, before doubling back.

The two Seconds rode into camp at dusk, the hails of the sentries alerting Morghan before he saw them. He was holding a washing basin and an ewer of warm water for Amiel in her tent, for her to wash the dust from her face and hands. She heard the calls too, and gestured for him to set basin and ewer on their stands.

'Go and meet my Seconds,' she instructed. 'Tell them to report when they have taken some repast.'

'Yes, milady.'

'For your instruction, if they have anything urgent to report, they will refuse and come straight to me,' added Amiel. 'As you will do, if returning from a similar task.'

'Yes, milady,' repeated Morghan. He bowed and went outside into the orderly camp, and walked between the rows of tents to the horse lines. The guards there nodded to him.

'Good even, Romashrikil and ... Kwor ... Kworquorakan.'

The guards smiled and nodded again. Morghan walked past them, still unsure if they were playing tricks on him. They had told him their names themselves, but they were like nothing he had ever heard before, and they did not look as if they were from so distant a country as to have such names. He had yet to hear anyone else address them, which in itself suggested it was all some kind of elaborate joke to play on the new cadet.

The Seconds were taking off their saddles. Terril was a slim, serious-looking woman easily eight or nine years Morghan's senior. Limath looked to be much the same age as himself, Morghan reckoned, though he was considerably broader in the shoulders and sported a rather splendid beard as jet black as his hair. He was also much more mud-splattered than Terril, some of it above his belt, though Morghan noticed neither of the horses was particularly dirty, and not at all above the knees.

Limath saw him first as he turned around with his saddle and gear over his shoulder.

'Terril!' he cried. 'By all that is marvellous! A cadet!'

'A cadet indeed,' said Terril. She inclined her head.

Morghan bowed, not quite as deeply as he did to Amiel.

'My name is Morghan,' he said carefully. 'The Bridgemistress desired me to inform you that you need not report to her until you have taken some repast.'

'I am Second Terril,' said Terril. 'This rag-bag is Second Limath.'

'Rag-bag is rather extreme,' said Limath. He clapped Morghan on the shoulder. It was a companionable touch, though the younger man had braced for a testing blow. 'I fell off, if you must know. There was a storm, and bandits, and ...'

'Perfect calm and an empty road, in truth,' said Terril. 'Limath just isn't a very good rider.'

'True, true,' sighed Limath. 'But perhaps the luck that has given us a new cadet will also allow me to walk to the bridge, and I need not ride till ... oh damn ...'

Morghan turned his head to see what had stopped the flow of Limath's speech and instinctively braced as he saw Serjeant Ishring.

'Need not ride until tomorrow morning, Second Limath, I think you were saying?' asked Ishring. 'To the seventh milepost and back, perhaps you were about to say?'

'Indeed, Master Ishring,' said Limath. Morghan was surprised to see him smile, as if perfectly happy at being caught out. 'I daresay I could use the practice.'

'I daresay,' said Ishring. 'I beg your pardon for my intrusion, Second Terril.'

He turned his attention to Morghan. 'Cadet Morghan, the Bridgemistress has decided that now the Seconds have returned, she can spare you from tomorrow for additional arms drill. You will have the first hour after dawn and the first hour from the halt with me, for pole-axe and other work.'

'Yes, Serjeant!' bellowed Morghan.

Ishring nodded, and stalked off past the torch-poles, out into the darkness toward the nearest of the outer guard posts. Morghan had already been taken around the outer ring of sentries, learning where they all were so that he could, at least in theory, find them in the dark. In this careful preparation, as in so many other things the company did, the young cadet saw the very real expectation of trouble.

'Show us our tent and the refectory wagon, then,' said Limath. 'I could eat a horse.'

'You'd probably do that better than you ride them,' said Terril.

'Ah, I shall miss your wit when you are made Bridgemistress,' said Limath. 'Now, Morghan, is it? Was the watch list for the bridge made up before you joined?'

'I don't know, Second,' said Morghan.

'Ah, you would know, because you would have been writing out a dozen copies if it had,' said Limath with great satisfaction. 'Fortune smiles upon us, Terril.'

'I suspect that rather you should say the Bridgemistress knows her business,' said Terril drily.

Morghan was unable to stop a flicker of puzzlement wrinkling his brow, though he did suppress a question. Terril saw it pass across his face, like a swift cloud across the sun.

'Tell Cadet Morghan why you are so pleased to see him … or rather, any cadet … and the associated matter of the watch list.'

'Ah, it is simple!' roared Limath, clapping Morghan on the back. 'You know that the Bridgemistress must always be accompanied about by a Second or a cadet? We must buzz about her like bees around the queen of the hive, ready for anything, to sting or fly at her order. You follow?'

'Yes …' said Morghan cautiously.

'But unlike bees, who only work under the sun, the Bridgemistress moves by night as well as day. You see now?'

'I'm not sure …'

'It is simple! You comprehend that the day and night is divided into four watches?'

Morghan nodded.

'With only two Seconds, we must divide all four watches between us, to follow the Bridgemistress about and do her bidding. But there is also weapon work, and writing work for Famagus, and all manner of other works that must be done, and if we must serve the Bridgemistress watch-by-watch, it leads to a terrible lack of that wonderful thing that we know as sleep.'

'Ah, I do see now,' said Morghan. He paused for a moment, wondering if he should admit a weakness that might be used against him. 'I admit that I am a little bit —'

'Tired?' interrupted Terril. 'That is the lot of cadets, and even for such exalted beings as Seconds. But you will be more tired still by the time we reach the bridge. It is in many ways a test, Morghan.'

'A test! But I have been tested …'

Morghan's voice faltered, and stopped for a moment, before he resumed.

'I see. I shall not fail.'

'That's the way, young cadet!' boomed Limath. 'Let's get this gear cleaned up, Terril, and then … food!'

'You'd best go back to the Bridgemistress,' said Terril. 'If I were you, I'd run. The Bridgemistress does not make much allowance for the chattering we have just done. We will not be far behind.'

'Yes, Second!' replied Morghan. He turned and raced back past the tents, jumping over guy ropes rather than taking the time to go around them.

'Keen,' remarked Terril.

'Yes,' said Limath. 'I hope he makes it to the bridge. I confess that I do not fancy watch-and-watch for the whole winter.'

Morghan did make it to the bridge, though he was battered and scratched from his daily practices with Serjeant Ishring and other guards, and weary beyond reckoning, for he had never walked so far for so long, and had so little sleep.

None of that mattered as he stood on the hill top, and looked along the road that wound down to the river valley. The Greenwash ran there, in slow curves, at its narrowest more than two thousand paces wide. But the river, for all its majesty, did not hold Morghan's eye. He looked at the bridge, the greatest bridge he had ever seen. Nine vast arches sat on piers the size of houses, their flanks extended by cutwaters that divided the river's flow into nine swift channels. Though the stone deck was not yet laid, it was clear that when finished the bridge would be wide enough for four carts to pass abreast.

The Mid-River Bastion, built on an all but submerged islet that underpinned the middle of the bridge, was complete, barring all passage along the temporary boardwalk or the side parapets. A square tower, eighty feet higher than the bridge deck, which was itself forty-five feet above the water, the bastion's gates were shut, and guards walked along the battlements, the company's banner flying high above them.

As Morghan watched, a horn sounded on this tower. It was answered a few moments later from the castle on the northern bank. Morghan switched his attention to that, noting that while a relatively small fortification of only four towers around a single bailey or courtyard, it was built on a rocky spur that rose from the river, and a small stream wound about it before rejoining the Greenwash. The castle was thus protected by swift water, and sat on the highest point for at least a league, till you reached either the southern hill where Morghan was, or the slowly sloping land to the north which led to the high steppe, somewhere beyond the far horizon.

Ahead of Morghan, the Bridgemistress raised her hand in the air, and a single bright Charter mark flew into the sky. It whistled as it sped, a single pure note that was louder and clearer than the horn-blasts of the two fortifications, loud enough to be heard for leagues. Morghan wondered what mark it was, for he did not know it, and wished he did.

'Onward!' ordered Amiel. 'Let the Winter Shift take possession of our bridge!'

Three months later, Morghan felt it was indeed his bridge, as much as anyone else's in the company. He had walked and climbed every accessible inch of it, slipped on its icy stones, been bruised by it, and almost drowned shooting the rapids under its arches in a too-flimsy craft. He knew every nook and cranny of the North Fort, the Mid-River Bastion, and the work camp on the southern shore. He had learned and even understood Company Orders and could recite any part of it. He had grown a fingerwidth in height and a fraction broader in shoulders and arms, though he was still thin. He had come to know several hundred new Charter marks, and forty-six particular spells. Though his elbow held him back from reaching the standard Serjeant Ishring expected with a pole-axe, he had been graded as very good with a crossbow, and the Serjeant had once hinted that another year or two of constant practice might — just might — make Morghan a worthwhile addition to the company's fighting strength.

It was more difficult to tell what the Bridgemistress thought about his value. She was not generous with praise, but did not criticise unduly either, not unless it was deserved. Morghan had made his small mistakes, and had taken his punishments without complaint, which were usually designed to ensure that he learned whatever he had got wrong the first time.

But he still worried that he might not be considered good enough, a fear that slowly grew as the winter waned and the first signs of spring began to show in sky and field. Eventually, he broke his habit of caution and on one of their last evenings spoke to Terril about it. They were on watch in the Mid-River Bastion, Terril commanding the small garrison, while Limath was off with the Bridgemistress, inspecting the southern ferry station which was a league to the west, far enough away to avoid the rapids created by the bridge. With the Field Market only a week away, the ferry was very busy, and there was a line of waiting wagons, trains of mules and even footsore pedlars that stretched from the ferry station to the bridge and then halfway up the southern side of the valley.

'Second Terril, may I ask a question?' Morghan said, as he stood at her side on the top of the tower.

'You may, Cadet Morghan,' said Terril. She was always formal and deliberate, unlike Limath, who treated Morghan as something of a cross between a pet dog and a little brother, with great enthusiasm and friendliness, but not a lot of thought.

'I have been wondering,' Morghan said carefully. 'I have been wondering if cadets are often dismissed.'

Terril turned her complete attention to him.

'Very rarely,' she said. 'Only in circumstances of incompetence, or gross turpitude. Selling our secrets, for example. Or weapons or something like that.'

'What exactly might comprise incompetence?' asked Morghan. He swallowed and thought of his elbow and Serjeant Ishring's frowns at his pole-axe work.

Terril put her head on side and looked Morghan in the eye.

'You have nothing to worry about, Cadet Morghan,' she said firmly. 'You have worked well, and I am sure that you will get a very good report.'

'I will?' asked Morghan.

'Yes,' said Terril firmly. 'And if you keep on as you have, I expect that one day you will make an excellent Second, and in time, will be a redoubtable Bridgemaster yourself.'

Morghan nodded gratefully, unable to speak. He had not been able to think past their return to Navis. But to one day be a Bridgemistress's Second, and then ... to reach the impossible peak of becoming a Bridgemaster!

'Now go and get some sleep,' instructed Terril. 'I expect we'll swap watches a little early, when the Bridgemistress comes back tonight, and you go with her, and Limath takes over here.'

'But the dusk rounds, shouldn't I go with you?'

'Not tonight,' said Terril. 'I'll go in a moment, and Farremon will keep watch here. I'll wake you in good time for the Bridgemistress, have no fear of that. We won't see her much this side of midnight.'

'Thank you, Second,' said Morghan gratefully. He bowed, and climbed down the stairs to the guardroom on the second floor, where everyone off-duty slept. The bastion was garrisoned by a dozen guards and an officer, and six of the beds were occupied by variously silent or snoring guards. Morghan found his own, wearily shrugged off his hauberk and hung it and his weapons on their stands, and sat on the bed. He thought about taking off his gambeson and boots, but before he could decide one way or another, he fell sideways and was instantly asleep.

Morghan awoke from the grip of a terrible, frightening dream to find himself in total darkness, and immediately felt waking panic too. There should have been a lantern lit, as per standing orders, and the Bridgemistress might be there at any moment. He leapt up and felt for his armour and weapons, dressing and equipping himself with practised speed, despite the absence of light.

It was only when he fastened his belt that he fully woke up and realized something was wrong, much more wrong than one unlit lantern.

He couldn't hear any snoring, or even the soft breath of his companions, and there had never been, nor could there be, a guardroom so quiet.

They've been called to arms was Morghan's immediate thought, and panic choked him. *I've slept through an alarm! I'll be dismissed after all!*

He caught a sob in his throat, choked on it, and coughed, the sound harsh and loud in the silence. With the intake of breath after the cough came a sour, nasty taste, as if the air itself was tainted with something like the hot, metallic air of a forge …

'Free Magic,' whispered Morghan, and a different fear rose in him and washed away all other fears. Instinctively he reached for the Charter, and found that it was already there, that he must have reached for it in his sleep. A faint, almost extinguished mark glowed feebly just below his heart, and it was joined to other marks that ran in a chain around his chest. Morghan touched them one by one, and remembered a spell that he had forgotten that he knew, a spell his grandmother had taught him when he was too young to know what she guarded him against. But somewhere deep inside, the child within had remembered in the time of need.

Morghan called the marks again, and rebound them to himself, winding them around like the armour they were. Armour against spells of ill-wishing, that if strong enough might still a beating heart, or close mouth and nose against the life-giving air.

With the new marks came light, but not enough. Morghan reached into the Charter again and found the one he sought. He drew it in the air, and it hung above his head, a companion brighter than the best of candles. In its light, Morghan surveyed the room.

Wisps of fog, thick and unnatural, oozed in through the shuttered arrow-slits and clustered around the beds. One quick glance across the silent, still figures and the winding fog was enough for Morghan to know that all his sleeping companions were dead, even the three who also had the Charter Mark.

Morghan picked up his pole-axe and ran down the steps.

The five guards below were also dead, but though their chests were still, they were moving. Four of them were clumsily unbarring one of the northern gates, while the fifth kept walking into the wall, bouncing off it and walking into it again. The reek of hot metal was stronger than ever, and the fog flowing in under the gates was as thick as wool.

Morghan did not immediately recognise the guards were no longer alive.

'Stop! Stand!' he shouted. But they did not stop, or stand still, or even turn. They had one end of the bar lifted out of its bracket, and he realised they would have it off entirely in a minute.

Morghan shouted again, then dashed forward and struck the closest man across the back of the legs with the shaft of his pole-axe. Bone cracked, but the man did not turn. Still he lifted the beam, and Morghan belatedly saw what he was dealing with.

The pole-axe swung, and a head rolled on the floor. The decapitated body kept at its work for a few seconds, then lost coordination and began to flail angrily at the gate.

Sobbing, Morghan swiftly beheaded the other guards, and beat the headless bodies back from the gate. The Dead tried to keep opening the door, but without heads they could not see, so they crashed into each other and fell over, and felt about blindly and worked at cross-purposes.

For a moment Morghan thought he was done with them and could take a moment to think. But then he heard something from outside, something that at first gave him heart, for it was the pure, sweet sound of a bell, before the sound was overlaid with something else, something he felt rather than heard, that made his stomach cramp, and bile come flooding into his mouth.

The dead guards, headless as they were, answered the bell as if a guiding intelligence had occupied them all. They came at him together, hands grasping, trying to bring him down, and he swung and bashed and cut and kicked at them with everything he'd learned from Serjeant Ishring and in the alleys behind the inn, but it was not enough and at last he had to jump back to the stairs.

He was only just able to slam shut the heavy door as the Dead charged against it. One dead guard's hand was caught in the doorway, and severed. It scuttled at him as he swung down the bar, and he had to stomp it to pieces before it lay still.

Morghan stood for a moment, trying to regain his breath. He could hear the Dead going back down to unbar the gate. There had to be a necromancer there, maybe more than one, or several Free Magic sorcerers. There might be an army of the Dead …

Morghan stopped that thought. There would not be an army of the Dead. They could not cross fast running water. In fact, it was only because the bastion was built on a rocky island that the Dead below could survive. The necromancer outside could only use those people in the bastion that had already been slain with Free Magic to raise the Dead —

Like the sleeping guards upstairs.

The thought had barely formed in Morghan's mind before he was running again, jumping up the steps four at a time in a desperate race to get above the guardroom and bar the next door. If he could make it past, then there would only be the sentry above … and Terril.

Maybe Terril's alive thought Morghan. *Please, please, let Terril be alive!*

Kworquorakan stepped into his path, eyes still half-shut as if he merely slept, but his skin was pallid and blue around the mouth and eyes. He held a sword in a weak and clumsy grip, for the Dead spirit within him was not his own, and was too new to the body.

Morghan swept the sword to the floor and hammered the Dead guard to one side, rushing past before it could get up. He caught a glimpse through the open guardroom door, of the other Dead shambling from their beds, arming themselves slowly and stupidly.

Morghan shut the next door, and barred it twice. This door was almost as heavy as the lower gate, but he had no illusions about how long wood and iron alone could hold against the Dead and Free Magic. Despite his lack of breath and the wave of shock and weariness that threatened to overwhelm him, he calmed himself and found the Charter. For a moment he almost lost himself in the welcoming sea of marks, before training and desperation asserted control. He found the symbols he needed, cupped them in his hands, and pressed them against the door while he whispered their use-names.

Warm, soft light spilled out between his fingers and ran through the tight grain of the wood, swirling round and round as it sank deeper, strengthening and binding. Rivulets of gold ran from wood to stone, like tree roots seeking water deep underground. The iron hinges spewed rusty flakes as they took on a deep, yellow glow that was sunlight and gold and a comforting, well-banked fire.

Morghan turned away from the door and fell over, momentarily too weak to support himself. He jarred his bad elbow on the stone, but the pain helped, the old familiar sensation cutting through his exhaustion. He got up and picked up his pole-axe, only to see that the axe was notched and there was a crack in the shaft. His fight against the Dead below had been desperate indeed.

Morghan left the pole-axe where it lay and stumbled to the rack of crossbows on the wall. He took down his own, and the cranequin and quarrel, and quickly wound back the string and loaded a shaft. Then he thrust four more quarrels through his belt, and slowly began to climb the stairs.

He tried to be as quiet as he could, but within five steps this became unnecessary, as the Dead below attacked the door he had spelled shut. He heard the deep boom of heavy timber against timber and assumed that they had made a battering ram from one or more of the beds. Beds which should be made less sturdy so as not to be used against us, Morghan thought. Something to be noted for the Bridgemistress, and if she approved, a memorandum sent to Famagus for the other shifts.

Morghan slowed near the top. The battlements were reached by a ladder through a hatch, and this was open when it should not be. Tendrils of fog came spiralling down through the hatch, as if some hideous, tentacled sea creature of mist and dark vapour was squatting on the tower.

His crossbow held ready, Morghan moved underneath and looked up. But he couldn't see anything but the fog, and he couldn't hear anything, either, apart from the repeated crack and boom of the ram below.

Morghan started to climb the ladder with the crossbow at the ready, and found that he could not. He could not pull himself up or balance with his left arm. It would not support him, the elbow locking up or giving way, all flexibility lost. Morghan cursed under his breath and put the crossbow down to take up one of his thin daggers in his left hand. He could barely manage even that slight weight, but at least he could climb with his right hand.

But I won't be much use in a fight, Morghan thought. *When I stick my head up through that hatch, there'll be … there'll likely be two Dead on me right away … I can't win … I can't do any good … but I have to try … whoever is attacking us, they mustn't cross the bridge … they will not cross the bridge … my bridge …'*

Morghan took a breath, and began to climb. Slowly at first, then as he neared the top, it became a sudden, scrabbling rush and he burst out onto the battlements like a startled pheasant from the heath, sending the fog swirling in all directions.

Two bodies lay near the hatch. The guard Farremon was dead, pale and blue. But Terril's chest rose and fell slowly. Morghan put his dagger down, ready to hand, and quickly pushed Farremon's body through the open hatch, slamming it shut afterwards and locking the bar. Then he turned to Terril. Her eyes were half-open, but she looked drugged and insensible. Her hand was on her breast, and there were three faint Charter marks drawn there, pulsing in time with a very slow heartbeat.

'Terril!' said Morghan. 'Terril!'

There was no answer. The death magic that had come with the fog had not claimed Terril, but it had left her fighting for her life. Perhaps the spell was weaker, higher up, Morghan thought. Not that it mattered.

He reclaimed his dagger, drew his sword, and went to the northern battlements to look over the side. All he could see was thick, white fog, completely cloaking the bastion, hiding it from the Northern Fort and the southern shore. He couldn't even see directly below, though he could hear the clank and jangle of armour and weapons on the boardwalk, in between the booms of the ram on the lower door. There were a lot of enemy out there, scores of them, if not more.

But the continued booming was oddly reassuring. It meant that the door, or more likely at this point, the spell alone, still held. When he didn't hear it, but heard instead the clatter of feet on the stair, that would be … well … the end.

I'm not thinking straight. I need to warn the fort, and the ferry … and all the waiting merchants …

Morghan's head hurt, almost as much as his elbow, and he now knew that it was possible to feel even more exhausted than was the usual lot of a cadet on the bridge. It took a supreme effort to prise himself from the embrasure and walk over to the great horn that hung between two iron posts.

He leaned forward to set his lips to the horn, ready to blow the alert, when he saw that it was split at the mouth, riven in two. At the same time, he tasted hot metal that blistered his tongue. The horn had been split by magic, and that was no mean feat, unseen from below.

Or was it done unseen? Morghan thought. *Is there someone else up here, in the fog?*

Morghan stepped back and almost fell over before he managed to spread his feet and steady himself. Despite his pain and weariness he was thinking faster now, aware that he might have very little time.

One of the several hundred new Charter marks he had learned over the winter was the one that was the scream of the saffron-tailed kite, only the Bridgemistress wound into it another mark, one of magnification, that made the scream louder, more than a hundred times louder.

But they were difficult marks, not old familiar ones that he knew well. He might well meet the death of his grandmother, seeking to find and wield such marks when he was already so weary.

So be it, thought Morghan. *Better to die here than in an alley in Belisaere. I have had my winter, and it is enough.*

He knelt down, and rested his hands on the hilt of his sword, setting the point deep in a crack between the flagstones. Then he went into the Charter once more, knowing it was one time too many, that his weary body could not bear to harness the power he sought. Not and live to speak of it.

The first mark, the cry of the bird, he found easily, and he let it slide from his hands into the sword. The second was more difficult, and his vision swam and his breath grew ever more ragged before at last he pushed through a swarm of too-bright marks and caught the one he sought, and sent it into the blade too.

With the spell ready, and his strength fading fast, Morghan left the flow of the Charter and brought himself back to the foggy battlements. Slowly, ever so slowly, he rose to his feet and prepared to lift his sword, to send his signal flying to the night sky above the fog.

But the blade was stuck. Morghan pulled at it, and almost had it free when he saw that he was no longer alone. Someone … or something … was slipping over the battlements. It stopped to fix its gaze upon him, and then came stalking towards him.

Morghan knew what it was at once, for it was part of his lessons. It was why the company's guards carried pole-axes, to fight such a thing of stone, impervious to lighter weapons. Carved from solid rock to match the fetish of one of the tribes of the far steppe and infused with a Free Magic spirit to make it live and move; this was a Spirit-Walker.

It moved towards him, not lumbering as one might expect a statue to do, but more like a stalking insect, all sharp starts and flurries. It was man-like in the sense that it had two legs and two arms, but the legs were long, and the arms jointed backwards and ended in wedges of sharpened stone.

One cruel wedge shot forward. Morghan twisted aside, too slowly, and his hauberk was sliced open as if it were no more than thin cloth, and he felt the sudden pain of a deep wound. At the same time, he wrenched his sword free and thrust it forward in riposte, though he knew no mere blade could harm a spirit-walker.

The riposte missed, but drawing back, the very tip of the sword touched the Spirit-Walker on its backward-jointed elbow.

Morghan felt the connection to his very bones. He felt the ancient, malevolent spirit inside, striving to do as it was bid and slay him, and he felt the stone that it inhabited, and at once knew every fissure, every faint crack and weakness.

'Go,' whispered Morghan to his spell, and he fell backwards, all strength gone.

The marks left the blade, and not hundreds but thousands of saffron-tailed kites screamed their hunting scream inside the Spirit-Walker's stony flesh, the sound resonating and echoing along every crack, growing and expanding, fighting to get out.

The Spirit-Walker took one further step, then exploded into powder as the distress call of the bastion echoed through the river valley, to the North Fort, and the ferry stations, and up the road and beyond the hills, to Navis and even to the very walls of Belisaere.

The great scream blew away the fog, and under sudden moon and starlight, a necromancer cursed and hurried back along the boardwalk. His Dead bashed once more at the door, then fell, the spirits too weak to sustain themselves in Life without their master. Hundreds of nomad tribesmen, spread out along the bridge, heard what they thought was the death-cry of their Spirit-Walker. They saw their necromancer flee and turned to run with him. The great raid upon the southern lands, so long in the making, had failed before it had really begun.

At the Ferry Station, Amiel cast a spell that sent a night-bird of dull Charter marks flying faster than any bird to the Glacier of the Clayr, and then another, like as a twin, winged south to Navis. But even as the magical birds left her hand, she was running for her horse, and shouting orders, with Limath at her heels, spitting out the over-large mouthful of cake he had just wedged in his mouth.

Atop the bastion, Morghan looked at the stars, now so clear in the sky. They looked welcoming to him, something he had not thought about before. If he'd had the strength, he would have raised a hand to them, but he'd could not. Besides, he could feel the river calling to him, could hear the roar of the Greenwash — or perhaps it was some other river, for it did not sound entirely the same …

'You are *not* allowed to die, cadet,' said a voice near at hand.

Morghan slowly moved one eye to see who was speaking to him.

It was Terril, who was crawling over to him. Her hand moved across his face and climbed to his forehead, and two fingers touched the Charter Mark there. He felt some small spark of power flow from her, a faint thread that nevertheless was strong enough to arrest the pull of the unseen river and lessen the attraction of the distant stars.

'I said you are not allowed to die, Cadet Morghan! Do you understand?'

'Yes, Second,' whispered Morghan. He did understand, and in that moment, he knew that he would not die. Terril held him back, and Terril was the company, and the company was the bridge, and he was part of it, and always would be, and one day he would be a Second and a Bridgemaster too, for he had not failed the test.

He had held the bridge.

AFTERWORD

I often find it difficult to remember the genesis of a story, or sometimes there just isn't any identifiable spark or catalyst that sets everything in motion. Also, often the basic idea doesn't end up being related to the eventual story at all, it is like a booster rocket that falls away, while the story speeds on without it.

However, in the case of 'To Hold the Bridge' I can pin down the source of inspiration, and the basic idea ended up being very much part of the narrative. As with many of my ideas, the spark came from history. I was reading a most excellent book called *Power and Profit: The Merchant in Medieval Europe* by Peter Spufford (Thames & Hudson, 2002) and was particularly fascinated by a chapter called 'Helps and hindrances to trade' which focuses on bridges, roads, rivers and all the means by which medieval goods got to market.

From that book, and from real history, I got the idea of a long-lived company involved in constructing an important bridge, and in turn I set that in the established realm of my Old Kingdom novels. All I had to do then was to find a story to tell against that backdrop, and as I often do, I began with a character who would discover the world of the Bridge Company with me, and then with the reader.

— *Garth Nix*

Trudi Canavan lives in Melbourne, Australia. She has been making up stories about people and places that don't exist for as long as she can remember. Her first short story, 'Whispers of the Mist Children', received an Aurealis Award for Best Fantasy Short Story in 1999. When she recovered from the surprise, she went on to finish the fantasy novel-that-became-three, the bestselling *Black Magician Trilogy: The Magicians' Guild*, *The Novice* and *The High Lord* followed by another trilogy, *Age of the Five*. Last year the prequel to the *Black Magician Trilogy*, *The Magician's Apprentice* was released and she is now working on the sequel, the *Traitor Spy Trilogy*. One day she will write a series that doesn't contain three books.

The Mad Apprentice:
A Black Magician Story

TRUDI CANAVAN

The sumi pot rose in the air seemingly of its own volition, tilted and poured the hot drink into her cup. Indria looked at her brother. He grinned, and she rolled her eyes.

'I see your magic training is coming along well, Tagin,' she observed.

Tagin waved dismissively at the pot as it settled on the table again. 'That was nothing. First year exercises. Boring.'

Sipping the hot drink, Indria considered her brother over the rim of her cup. His eyes were bright and he had fidgeted constantly since arriving. This usually meant he was in a good mood. When he was hunched and glowering she had to be doubly careful what she said and did, as his temper was much easier to spark. But something was different about him today. Though he was cheerful, there was a hint of tension in his movements, and his eyes kept darting about the room.

'Is what you're learning now more interesting?'

'With Magician Herrol teaching me?' He sniffed derisively and looked away. 'Hardly.'

Indria suppressed a sigh and put down her cup. Tagin had been an apprentice magician for over two years but, like with most of his obsessions, he had grown impatient with his training and teacher. Usually he found something new to engage his brilliant mind. But magic was no hobby or pastime. It was supposed to become the source of his income and place in society. If he ended his apprenticeship, rather than remaining until his master taught him higher magic and granted him independence, he would not receive income from the king, or attract work from the Houses.

'Perhaps if Magician Herrol moved back to the city — to the Guild — it would be better. You'd have a greater variety of teachers.'

Tagin sneered. 'He suggested it, but what's the point? All the Guild magicians are like him: stuffy old men. I'd rather be away from them, but close enough to visit you.' He smiled. 'You wouldn't want me to leave you all alone with *Demrel* for company, would you?'

Indria grimaced. Lord Demrel was an excellent husband, according to her family. He'd improved their connections among the Houses, earning them valuable favours in trade. He was wealthy and generous. But he was also a boorish, possessive man, and old enough to be her father. Growing up with her volatile brother had taught her how to handle difficult men, and Demrel was a lot less troublesome than Tagin. But she hated how Demrel treated her like a child and an idiot.

Tagin may be a handful, but he doesn't think I'm stupid, she thought. *And at least he loves me — in his way.*

'When we rule the world, I'll build us a palace in the city,' Tagin said, his eyes flashing. 'We'll get rid of Demrel and all the boring, old magicians.'

She smiled at this familiar game. They had played it since they were children.

'When we rule the world, Demrel and the Guild will search all the lands for gifts to lay at our feet,' she replied.

He grinned. 'When we rule the world ...' He paused as his attention was drawn elsewhere, toward the windows. Indria listened, and heard the sound of galloping horses.

'Visitors,' she said. 'I wonder who it could —'

She faltered as Tagin leapt to his feet and hurried to the windows, stopping a few steps short and peering down at the courtyard below.

'Ah. Rot them,' he said in a sullen, resigned tone. 'I have to go.'

'What is it?' Standing up, she moved to one of the panes of glass. Directly below them three horses milled. Their riders — wearing the uniforms of higher magicians — were handing their reins to the servants who had greeted them. One looked up at the house and saw her. In the corner of her eye she saw Tagin duck back out of sight. She glanced at him, then down at the magicians, and felt her stomach sink.

They're here for Tagin, she guessed. *And this is no social visit.* But she knew from long experience not to speak such thoughts aloud. If she was right, Tagin might jump to the conclusion that she had already known they were coming, and perhaps even betrayed him to them.

'Who are they?' she asked.

'Magicians,' he told her.

'I can see that from their robes,' she said crossly. 'What are their names? Why are they here? Do they want to see Demrel?'

'They want me. They want to kill me.'

As she turned to stare at him, he smiled crookedly. Sometimes Tagin believed everyone wanted to do him harm. Even herself. She shook her head.

'Why are they here, really?'

His smile faded. 'I did something bad.' He turned away and strode toward the door.

Indria rolled her eyes. 'What this time?'

'I killed Magician Herrol,' he told her, without looking back.

She stared at his back. *He's joking.* Tagin might have a temper, and a cruel sense of humour, but he was no killer. He had beaten servants and horses and, when a boy, had been inclined to torment her mother's pets, but he'd never *killed* anything.

He opened the door. From beyond came the sound of voices and footsteps, growing louder. He closed the door and cast about, his gaze suddenly flat with terror. 'Help me, Indria,' he said helplessly. 'I've got to get out of here!'

Her heart twisted. He truly believed they meant him harm. And when he was in this mood it was better to let him run away and hide than try to reason with him. He'd calm down and return later. If the magicians believed Tagin to be a murderer they might try to kill him before he had a chance to calm down, explain himself and prove his innocence.

She beckoned and started toward a side door. As they passed through it into a narrow corridor she considered whether she'd be punished for helping him. Surely not. If she claimed to be too frightened to do otherwise, the Guild would see her as more of a victim than an accomplice.

But is there still some truth to that? she wondered. *Am I still scared of Tagin?* She thought of the bruises he'd given her, before she'd learned to avoid rousing his temper or to calm him down. After she'd married he hadn't dared hurt her, lest Demrel notice and stop him from seeing her.

Yet if I thought I could turn him over without either of us getting hurt, would I?

Probably not. He was her brother. Beneath the temper there was a fragile, lonely boy with a clever mind. She would not want to see him imprisoned. He'd go mad — madder than he already was — if he was ever locked away.

They reached the door to her husband's study. Tagin's footsteps were loud behind her as they entered the room.

'You're lucky Demrel's away. He'd never let you in here,' she told Tagin as she moved to a large wooden cupboard. 'Open this for me, will you?'

He narrowed his eyes at the lock and she heard it click open. She pulled the doors apart and slid aside the bolt locking the inner doors.

Cold air rushed in from the narrow cavity beyond. 'There's a ladder. I don't know where it comes out — and I don't want to know — but it must be safe or Demrel wouldn't use it.'

His eyebrows rose. 'Why doesn't it surprise me that your husband has a secret way out of his own house?'

'I only know about it because he got stuck one day and nobody else heard him shouting for help. He wouldn't let me get any of the servants. I had to pull him out all by myself.'

Tagin's lip curled in disgust. 'You should leave him and come with me.'

She shook her head.

'But you hate him.'

'Yes, but I'd also hate being homeless and hunted.' She gave him a serious look. 'And I'd slow you down. I'll be more able to help you if I stay here.'

He stared at her and opened his mouth to speak, but the sound of footsteps in the main corridor outside the room reached them. 'Hurry!' she hissed. 'Get inside and lock the door behind you.'

As he climbed in she felt her heart starting to pound. She closed the doors and heard the lock click. A scuffling inside the cupboard followed. The footsteps outside the room grew ever louder. Her heart raced. If Tagin didn't stop making noise soon the magicians would hear him and investigate the cupboard. A knock came from the study door and her heart lurched.

The sounds inside the cupboard finally stopped. Taking a deep breath, Indria wiped sweaty hands on the sides of her dress and walked slowly across the room. Opening the study door, she forced herself not to flinch at the wall of masculine, uniformed power that stood before her.

'Welcome, my lords,' she said, with as much dignity as she could muster. 'If you are after my husband I'm afraid he is absent. Is there anything I can help you with?'

The magicians stepped into the room. The first was tall and quite handsome — nothing like the way Tagin had described the magicians he'd encountered The second was as grey and stooped with age as her brother had described. The third was of an age somewhere between his companions and wore an expression of disapproval and disappointment.

'I am Lord Arfon,' the tall magician said. 'This is Lord Towin and Magician Beller. Is your brother, Apprentice Tagin, here?'

'He was, but he has left.'

Arfon frowned down at her. 'Do you know where he is now?'

'No. What is this about?'

'He has committed a terrible crime. He has murdered Magician Herrol.'

She feigned shock and surprise. 'Murdered?'

'Yes. You brother told you nothing of this, I gather.'

'No.' She looked away. 'He said something about being in trouble. He didn't explain.' *That is close enough to the truth.* She turned to regard him closely. 'Are you sure Tagin is the murderer?'

'Yes,' he replied returning her gaze steadily. 'I read the mind of a servant who witnessed the crime — and other, earlier, crimes. Did you know your brother had learned higher magic in secret, against the king's law?'

Indria shook her head, not having to fake her shock this time.

'He's been taking magical strength from the servants for months, no doubt in preparation for dispatching his master,' the scowling magician said with unconcealed disgust.

'But ...' Indria finally managed. 'Tagin wouldn't do that. Well, I can imagine him learning something forbidden out of boredom. But he's not the murdering type.'

Lord Arfon's eyebrows rose. 'Are you saying you've known enough murdering types to be able to tell them from non-murdering types?'

'Don't mock me.' She raised her chin and met his gaze. 'He's my brother. I know him better than anyone.'

He pursed his lips thoughtfully, then nodded. 'Forgive me. That was tactless, and this is a serious matter. Can you guess where your bother may have gone? A simple read of your brother's mind would confirm or disprove his guilt.'

'No,' she said, honestly.

He nodded. 'Then I'm afraid we're going to have to take you with us.'

Record of the 235th Year.

News arrived today of the death of Magician Herrol, family Agyll, House Parin and of a terrible crime. A mind-read of the servant who reported the death revealed that Magician Herrol had been murdered, the strength drained from him with the use of higher magic, by his very own apprentice, Tagin. How this apprentice came upon the knowledge is unknown, but it appears he was able to overcome his master by first strengthening himself by draining servants, who were kept silent through threats. His crimes are threefold: first in learning higher magic before being granted independence by his master, second in applying it to commoners to strengthen himself, and third in using it to kill.

Lord Arfon has been given the task of finding Tagin. He has taken Tagin's sister, Indria, into custody as the siblings are close and the apprentice may emerge from hiding in an attempt to free her. He has informed me that she is cooperating with efforts to detain her brother.

Gilken, family Balen, House Sorrel, Record-keeper of the Magicians' Guild.

Gilken wiped the nib of his pen and set it down next to the old leather book. Moving over to the tower window, he looked out over Imardin, capital city of Kyralia. The high wall of the Royal Palace rose to the left, facing down the mansions of the rich and powerful Houses. He could not see the King's Parade leading down from the Palace to Market Square and the docks, but his memory supplied images of it willingly, along with the remembered smells and sounds of the busiest parts of the city.

If he listened, he could hear a constant hum, but a wide stretch of gardens separated him from the bustling metropolis, keeping the noise and hustle at a distance. Two hundred years ago, after the magicians of Kyralia had defeated invading forces from Sachaka, King Errik had granted them a generous area of land and ordered a Guildhall to be built to house their newly-formed Magicians' Guild. The Record-keeper's Room, Gilken's domain and responsibility for the past twenty-three years, was in the highest room of the southwest tower.

While he had never grown tired of the view, he was liking the long climb up to it a lot less as the years passed. He had never gained the mental control necessary to levitate himself around and around and up the staircase, and the only way he could have gone straight up — on the outside of the building, then somehow crawling in through a window — would hardly be a dignified way for a magician to behave.

There are worse things for a magician to be guilty of than being undignified, he thought, and his mind turned back to the ill news he had recorded that day. *Murder. Blackmail. The unauthorised learning and use of higher magic. Surely no apprentice would abandon his training and future by committing such crimes without good reason? What could have driven him to do it?*

Gilken knew little about the apprentice. Only that Tagin had a sister and that his family was of a weaker, less favoured House. It was unusual for the only son and heir of a family to be given magical training, since magicians were forbidden, by law, to act as head of a family in political matters. The law was meant to stop power in Kyralia shifting entirely into magicians' — and the Guild's — hands, though it was by no means entirely successful. By allowing Tagin to become a magician, his father had put future control of the family and its assets into the hands of his daughter's husband.

Lord Herrol must have known this when he took on the young man as his apprentice. Gilken considered what he knew of the magician. Herrol's wife had died ten years ago, and his five children were grown and married. He had been a good-humoured, intelligent man.

Having grown up in the country, Herrol had returned there a few years ago. His home was a day's ride from the city. And a few hours' ride from Tagin's sister's home. Herrol, knowing how close the siblings were, may have taken that into account when he made his decision to move.

If he had, then Tagin chose a terrible way to repay that favour.

Gilken looked out over the Guild grounds to the city again. Herrol had been well liked in the Guild. Many were upset at his death, especially his ex-apprentices. Magicians had been alerted across the country. The docks and borders were being watched day and night.

Wherever Tagin is, he'll not evade the Guild and justice for long.

* * *

Lord Arfon lifted a glass jug and poured clear liquid into a matching goblet. He handed the goblet to Indria. She sniffed at the contents, then sipped.

'Water?' she said, surprised and a little disappointed. She'd expected an exotic and expensive liquor that only royalty or the Guild could afford.

'There's a spring in the Guild grounds,' he told her. 'The water from it is the purest you'll ever drink. It is piped only to this building and to the Royal Palace — and in the Palace it goes first to the king's rooms.'

Taking a larger sip, she swirled the water around in her mouth, then swallowed. It had almost no taste to it. Perhaps a faint suggestion of stone and rock. Arfon poured himself a glass.

'Tell me more about your brother.'

She shrugged. 'What haven't I told you already?'

He gave her a level look. 'The servants at your family home say he was prone to violent tantrums, and that he often struck you.'

She looked away. 'Not often,' she corrected, figuring there was no point denying the truth when it could be confirmed by a mind-read. 'Just … when he was frustrated. He's smart, you see. Too smart. People don't understand him, and he's not good at explaining himself in a way ordinary people understand.'

'Did you understand him?'

'Not always. That's why he loses his temper with me.' She waved a hand. 'But I see his frustration and his …' *His loneliness*, she was going to say. But Tagin would not have liked her to speak of him as if he was weak or pitiful.

'You want to protect him?' Arfon observed.

'Of course. I'm his sister.'

'Would you still want to, if you knew he'd murdered Lord Herrol? Would you still hide his location, if you knew it?'

She looked at him and smiled crookedly. 'Probably.'

'Why?'

She sighed and turned away. 'He's the only one who ever cared about me. Mother and Father never did. And Demrel certainly doesn't.'

Arfon said nothing. The silence stretched between them and

eventually drew her eyes back to him. He was looking at her intently. His expression was not disapproving. It was unfathomable, and yet it sent a shiver up her spine.

Stop it, she told herself. *It's not right to fancy the man who wants to catch and possibly execute your own brother.* Then, belatedly, she added to that *and you're a married woman.*

She could not help liking Arfon, though. He'd treated her so differently to her husband — as if he not only saw that she had a mind but was interested in its contents. He had been gentle and apologetic the few times he'd had to physically force her to co-operate. The only time she'd seen him angry it had fascinated her to see how he'd held the anger back, and how quickly it had faded away.

And it doesn't help that he's so good looking. She sighed. *I guess that's part of the Guild's ploy to get information out of me. I might give more away if I wanted to impress that person. Fortunately I don't have any information to give.*

Arfon drew in a deep breath and stood up. 'It's late. I'll take you back to your room.'

My 'room'? she thought as she followed him up the stairs. *My 'prison' is more accurate.* Though the little bedroom the Guild had set up for her in one of the Guildhall towers was comfortable, she had not left it or the room below it for two weeks.

Arfon left her as soon as she was safely locked away. It did not take her long to change into her nightclothes, and she fell asleep as soon as her head touched the pillow. The next thing she was aware of was the patterns of light and shadow the moon had cast on the ceiling.

Then she frowned. *I'm awake and it's still night. Why am I awake?*

Something interrupted the pattern. She raised her head and stared at the window. A shadowed face was pressed up to the glass.

That's impossible. This room is three floors up and there are guards outside. She let her head drop back onto the pillow. *I must be dreaming.*

'Indria!' a muffled voice hissed. 'Get up! It's me. Tagin.'

Her heart skipped. She wasn't dreaming. Someone really was there, and that someone was Tagin. *The fool! They'll catch him for sure!* She scrambled out of the bed and stumbled to the window. Cold air surrounded her. The paper screens had been pushed aside and the frame of mullioned glass hinged outward. Tagin was outside. Below his feet was something flat, hovering in the chill air. It looked suspiciously like a piece of the paving from the Guild gardens.

'How are you …?' she asked.

'Same way I move a pot of sumi,' he said. 'Only this time I'm standing on it. Took some practice to keep my balance, though. Don't worry. I'm used to it now. I won't drop you.'

'Drop me?'

He grinned. 'I've come to rescue you. Can't have my sister in prison because of something she didn't do.'

'I don't need rescuing,' she told him. 'When they realise you're not coming to get me they'll give up and let me go.'

'But I *have* come to get you.'

'And take me where?'

'Away from here.'

She shook her head. 'They'll find us, Tagin. Listen, I believe they won't harm you if you give yourself up. They'll give you a chance to prove that you're innocent. Once they read your mind they'll know you didn't kill anyone, and they'll let you go.'

He smiled crookedly. 'But I *did* kill Herrol. And most of his servants. And …' he looked down and shrugged.

She followed his gaze, past the floating stone beneath his feet, and caught her breath. Three men lay on the ground below, their eyes open and staring. Dead. Had Tagin killed them? *Of course he had. To save me.* She felt guilt welling up, but pushed it away. The Guild had set a trap for him. If it had gone badly then it was hardly her fault.

But it did mean her brother had killed. And once again admitted to killing his master.

'Oh, Tagin,' she heard herself say. 'They'll definitely execute you now. And me, if I come with you.'

'They won't find us,' he told her, extending a hand.

'But …' *But I don't want to leave and become a fugitive*, she wanted to say. His eyes narrowed. She could see the first signs of suspicion and anger. His anger was always worst when he thought he'd been betrayed. *Only this time he's killed people. But he won't kill me.*

Still, he might take his anger out on others. He'll blame the Guild and my husband for turning me against him. She felt her heart sink. *If I go with him, I might be able to persuade him otherwise. Steer him away from further trouble. From murdering people.*

It would mean leaving her life of comfort and safety.

But he's my brother. I'm the only one who can save him.

Sighing, knowing that he did not comprehend what he asked her to sacrifice, she climbed up onto the window sill and took his hand. His face was transformed by a grin. Pulling her forward, he steadied her as she stepped onto the slab. She looked down as they began to descend.

Lord Arfon was going to be so disappointed in her.

Record of the 235th Year.

The rogue apprentice has rescued his sister, killing two guards and Lord Towin in the process. Lord Towin's death is a shock and loss to both his family and the Guild. He had so much potential, and his innovative study of the application of magic in shaping metals will be left unfinished.

Towin's death has roused and united the Guild. Apprentice Tagin has shown himself to have little moral character, willing to use higher magic as cruelly as the Sachakans did before the War. We cannot leave him to roam the world unchecked and unpunished. Lord Arfon believes that we must capture him and find out how he learned higher magic without the assistance of a teacher, but many of the others feel Tagin is too dangerous and must be killed at the soonest oppor

Gilken let his pen hover over the page for a moment, listening to the expectant silence that came after the knock at his door. Then he finished the sentence, wiped the pen and set it aside. Rising from his chair, he sent a little magic out to the door to nudge the latch open and then tug the door inward.

Lord Arfon nodded politely at him. 'Record-keeper Gilken, may I speak with you?'

'Of course, Lord Arfon,' Gilken replied, waving to the comfortable chairs he kept in the room for visitors. 'Would you like a drink of water?'

'No, thank you.' Arfon sat down, his gaze distracted and a crease deepening between his brows. 'I thought you should know that Lord Valin, Magician Loral and Lord Greyer haven't been seen since last night's meeting. You know they volunteered to search for Tagin, but I didn't choose them?'

'Yes.' Gilken nodded to show he understood Arfon's alarm. The young magicians had been friends of Lord Towin, the magician who had been guarding Indria, and were so outraged at the murder it was clear to all that if they'd found Tagin it was unlikely there'd be an apprentice alive to question and put to trial.

Would that be so terrible? he asked himself. He considered how conflicted his feelings had been the previous night, at the meeting. While he felt the same sense of loss and anger at the murders as many of the magicians, he had been disturbed by the fierce, unquestioning drive for revenge raging among the magicians. *We are supposed to be examples of calm and reason. And justice. Tagin deserves a trial.*

'You fear they will kill Tagin,' Gilken said.

Arfon looked at him. 'Or in attempting their own search they will upset our arrangements for capturing him.'

Gilken nodded again. *He wants me to put something in the record, so that if the trio upset his plans and Tagin gets away, Argon and his helpers won't be blamed. It is a pity that he feels the Guild might react that way, but he is no fool. If things go very wrong, people always look for someone to blame, and leaders always fall first.*

'I should make note of their absence,' Gilken said, rising from this chair.

Taking the hint, Arfon stood up. 'Thank you. I will distract you no longer.'

Gilken smiled. 'Receiving information for the record is more necessity than distraction. And you are always welcome, Lord Arfon.'

The young magician bent at the waist in a half bow, then left the room. Gilken sat down at his desk again and considered the last sentence he had written. Then he picked up his pen and resumed writing.

Though she wanted to look away, to flee from the scene before her, Indria forced herself to look at the five bodies. Three magicians and two apprentices lay sprawled around the campfire — three men and two boys a few years older than Tagin. They looked as if they had fallen into a drunken sleep, but she knew better. Each bled from a small cut, through which her brother had taken their magic and their lives while they had been drugged. She wrapped her arms around the simple commoner's tunic Tagin had brought for her as part of her rescue and disguise, and shivered.

It had been her idea to let the magicians catch her, convince them she had been Tagin's prisoner, then drug them so she and Tagin could gain some distance or even get them off their trail. She had bought the tincture at a market, pretending to be suffering from insomnia and women's pains but wanting something that didn't taste foul. As the herbalist had recommended, Indria had mixed it into the magicians' wine, taking care not to make it too strong and risk poisoning them.

But Tagin had decided it was too great an opportunity to pass up. He'd taken their power, and in doing so he'd killed them. And now he was dancing around the fire, crowing with triumph.

'Too easy!' he exclaimed. 'And all it took was *this*.' He slipped a hand into the pocket of his jacket and brought out the little bottle containing the drug. 'Not a bit of magic wasted — none of mine, none of theirs, and now it's all mine!'

He grabbed her hands and whirled her about. Her foot caught on a fallen branch and she stumbled, so he stopped and steadied her. 'Did you hear me?' he asked. 'Do you understand?'

She nodded. 'Not a bit wasted,' she repeated. 'And now they're off our trail. We've gained … how many days? How long do you think it'll take before they're found or missed?'

'A few days.' He shrugged. 'More if I burn their bodies.'

'Long enough for us to make it to the border, if we take their horses. We'll have to hope the Elynes aren't waiting for us.' She looked at the dead magicians again and forced herself to see the situation with cold practicality. 'Are they carrying any money? We could buy passage on a ship. Head for Vin. Or Lonmar.'

Tagin shook his head. A familiar mad gleam came into his eyes. 'We're not going to Vin, sister. Or Lonmar. Or Elyne. We're going to Imardin.'

'The city? But …'

His grip on her hands tightened. 'Think of all the times we pretended we'd rule the world one day …' He laughed as she opened her mouth to protest. 'Yes, I know it was a game, but I think … I think it's possible. We *could* change the world. We could make the Guild see that their rules and restrictions are wrong.' He looked at her and his expression became serious. 'It would be a way to make up for what I did. Which is all their fault, really.'

'But …'

His face darkened suddenly, and he flung her hands away. 'You don't know what it was like, Indria. Every night, Herrol taking all my strength so I could barely do anything he'd taught me.' Tagin flushed and turned from her, his head dropping so she could not see his face.

'That's the secret, you know,' he said in a quieter voice. 'The secret of higher magic. Masters take the strength from the apprentices, supposedly in exchange for their teaching. It seems fair at first. Strength in exchange for knowledge. But Herrol kept holding me back. When I started teaching myself — things in his own books — he was angry. He started taking extra power so I couldn't try anything. I couldn't learn anything.' Tagin looked up at her, his gaze tortured and his face older than it had ever appeared before. 'It doesn't have to take ten years for an apprentice to become a higher magician. They hold us back — stop us from learning at our natural pace — so that they can take magic from us for longer.'

Indria felt her heart twist. That might not be so bad for any ordinary apprentice, but for Tagin it would have been intolerable. He was clever. He learned quickly, and grew bored even faster. Herrol should have realised that. Should have rewarded Tagin for his initiative, not punished him.

'But I'm going to reveal the lie,' Tagin continued, straightening as determination filled him. 'I'm going to make the Guild tell everyone the truth.' His gaze shifted to the distance and he was silent a moment. Then his eyes snapped to her and he smiled. 'We're going to change the world, Indria, and this time it's not a game. It's real.'

Record of the 235th Year.
We now know that the three burned corpses found yesterday are the remains of Lord Valin, Magician Loral and Lord Greyer. They were identified by the charred scraps of their clothing brought back to the city.

Today our minds have been buzzing with mental communications as magicians here and there have reported more terrible news. Nine of Arfon's searchers and two apprentices had stopped at a Stayhouse for the evening. By the morning they, their servants, the Stayhouse owner and his wife, and many of the staff and customers at the Stayhouse, had perished. Most died in the fire that burned the building to the ground, but we suspect the magicians were first killed by Tagin and his sister as the pair were identified by those lucky enough to escape the blaze.

All here are shocked by this tragic loss of life.

Gilken paused. His mind crowded with questions, but he always tried (and often failed) to keep speculation to a minimum in his reporting. Records should be strictly factual. Had the searchers come upon Tagin and his sister, and if so, was their attempt to capture them a catastrophic failure? Why did none of them report the encounter to the Guild via mental communication before they died? He could not help but think the location of the two groups of perished magicians was significant. The bodies of the three young magicians were found further from the city than the Stayhouse. Instead of fleeing after the first encounter, Tagin and Indria had turned and headed toward the city.

Almost as though Tagin is hunting magicians, not the other way around.

But he couldn't write that in the record. With a shudder, he wiped his pen, set it down and went to bed hoping for a night uninterrupted by mental calls reporting ill news, or nightmares.

When Indria had turned herself in to the first three magicians, they'd decided not to tell the Guild in case Tagin heard their mental conversation and their intention to sneak up on him. It had surprised her to learn that any mental communication could be overheard by all other magicians. She'd wondered why they bothered to use it at all.

The second group had no reason to contact other magicians — they had fallen asleep from the drug Tagin had forced the innkeeper to add to their drinks, and never knew they'd just eaten their last meal.

However, the third lot of magicians to fall foul of Tagin's grand plan did not die silently.

To Indria's relief, Tagin hadn't told her to approach and drug the four magicians they'd seen at the village. Instead they'd watched the men buy food and a bottle of wine, then followed them at a distance. The four did not have any apprentices with them, she'd noted. As dusk greyed the landscape, the magicians had stopped to eat their meal, though they remained on their horses. Tagin and Indria had tied their own horses to a fence post out of sight, then crept closer, hidden by a stone wall.

Bringing out the bottle of poison, Tagin had somehow taken a large drop of it out of the bottle with magic. The drop floated up in the air to hover above the magicians. Indria had watched, heart racing and wondering how they could not have noticed it.

Then one of the magicians had brought out wine to share around. The droplet had shot downward and into the wine bottle so fast that none of them had seen it. The magicians had begun taking it in turns to drink straight from the bottle.

It had seemed a needless risk to keep peering over the wall at the men, so Tagin and Indria had slipped away to reclaim their mounts. That had been their mistake, Indria realised. The magicians had ridden on for several minutes before the drug began to take effect. As they began to fall from their saddles, Tagin confidently rode up to them, grinning widely. But one magician did not fall. One magician hadn't drunk from the bottle, or else had drunk too little, and that magician had attacked Tagin. The strike had knocked Tagin from his horse, and the animal had raced off down the road. 'Get out of range!' Tagin had shouted to Indria, so she'd raced off to shelter behind a copse of trees.

It was hard to tell what was happening, watching the battle from a distance. Night was advancing, and she caught flashes of light and booming noises, but only glimpses of her brother and the magician. Her heart pounded, and she felt sick.

Don't kill him, she pleaded silently at the magician.

Suddenly all went black. For a long moment there was only darkness and silence, then a figure appeared, lit by his own magic. It waved at her, beckoning. She felt a rush of relief as she recognised it. Guilt followed as she realised the magician must be dead. Then something else stirred. Something darker.

Dread.

Tagin was alive and well, but so were his plans. Until she could talk him out of them, more people would die. Sighing, she urged her horse out of the copse toward the site of the battle. The dust was settling now. Tagin was crouching beside one of the unconscious men. Perhaps she could talk him into letting them live.

But before she had moved far from the trees a flame suddenly shot up from the ground, twice as high as the trees, and she felt heat on her skin. Her horse started and she clung to its back, heart pounding. *What was that?* Tagin shouted — though it sounded more like a curse than surprise or pain. Another flash of light burned the night. She felt her horse tense, ready to leap into a run, and quickly hauled on the reins. It danced in a circle, slowly settling at she talked to it soothingly. She looked toward Tagin to see him standing near where the flames had come from. He turned away and started toward her.

When he reached her, he frowned up at her.

'Are you sure that's the same poison you bought last time?'

She nodded, then shrugged. 'It smells the same.'

Tagin scowled. 'Two of them died from it before I got a chance to take their power. That's what the light was — the last of their magic released from their bodies when they died. Good thing I was shielding.'

A shock went through Indria, despite knowing that he would have killed them anyway. She thought of the size of the drop of poison Tagin had put into the wine. Much bigger than the single drop per person she'd used before. Had he used too much?

'Maybe it's stronger,' she suggested. 'Maybe the ones we drugged before this would have died too, if you'd been delayed this long.' *The herbalist was very insistent that I not use too much.*

He nodded. 'I've used too much power in the fight.' He looked up at her, his expression thoughtful. 'I'm a strong magician, so as my sister it's possible you have strong powers, too.'

She frowned. 'But I'm not a magician.'

He smiled. 'No, but you have the potential. You can't use any of your magic, but I can.' He beckoned. 'Get down.'

Reluctantly, she dismounted. He took her hands and looked into her eyes earnestly. 'I know I said that having power taken from you is awful, but it isn't if it's done gently. If you aren't drained dry you hardly know the difference. Will you let me take your strength?'

She stared back at him. He wanted her to endure the same thing that he'd killed Lord Herrol for.

'We need to do this,' he told her. 'Or the next time we meet any magicians they'll kill us.'

After what he's done, of course they will. But his expression was so direct and anxious. Not a hint of crazed ambition, or deception. He looked far more sane than she'd seen him in weeks.

She nodded. He smiled briefly in thanks, then became serious again. From somewhere in his clothing he produced a knife. The blade touched each of her palms. She felt a pressure, then a slowly growing sting. Covering her hands with his, he closed his eyes.

First she went a bit wobbly as a feeling of weakness spread through her, but somehow she stayed on her feet. Then she felt languid and passive. After a time the feeling eased, and she felt normal but for a tingle in her palms. Tagin grinned and let her hands go. The cuts he'd made were gone, healed away with magic. He reached out to touch her cheek, his eyes warm with affection.

'Thank you. How do you feel?' he asked.

She considered. 'Fine. It was a bit draining, at first.'

He nodded. 'Took me a while to judge the speed of it. I'm not used to having to do it slowly.'

'How do *you* feel?' she asked.

He frowned and looked at the ground, then he shook his head. 'You're strong, but you're only one person. I need more magic.' He turned around, stopping as he faced the road to the village they'd just left. Tiny lights glinted in the distance.

'Stay here, hidden behind the wall,' he said, taking the reins of her horse. 'I'll be back in an hour or so.'

Record of the 235th Year.
Our worst fears have come to pass. Apprentice Tagin, now being called 'The Mad Apprentice' has turned on the common man and woman in his pursuit of power. Lord Telkan, on his way to the city after a visit to Elyne, found the entire village of Whiteriver dead and left to rot. All victims had

been killed with higher magic. Even the locals' enka, gorin and reber had perished. Only small children were spared.

After informing the Guild of the tragedy, Lord Telkan continued on his way only to encounter signs of a magical battle, and the bodies of Lord Purwe and Lord Horet. The two deceased were not even on Tagin's trail, instead, misfortune brought them in contact with their killer. Fortunately Lord Telkan was not so unlucky, and has this evening reached the Guild safely.

Looking down at his entry, Gilken shook his head in disbelief.

'Nearly a quarter of Kyralian magicians have died at Tagin's hands. I'm beginning to find my opinion swaying toward those who believe he should be killed as soon as possible, rather than risk further lives in the attempt to catch him.'

Lord Arfon sighed. 'You are not the only one, if whispers in the Guildhall corridors are any indication.'

'But you still feel strongly that we must find out how he came to learn higher magic without assistance?'

'Yes. And it is less likely Indria will be harmed if we capture him.'

Gilken looked at Arfon closely. The man had spent several nights talking to Indria while she had been held at the Guildhall. Had he grown fond of her? While the general opinion of the magicians was that Tagin's sister was guilty of helping a murderer, Arfon had pointed out many times that she may not have any choice. But when her husband, who had been found in Lonmar visiting his trading partners, was told of her involvement in her brother's crimes he had all but disowned her, and many in the Guild had taken that as proof of her bad character.

'What will you do now?' Gilken asked.

Arfon frowned as he considered. 'He's so unpredictable. First he runs, now he attacks. I've instructed the searchers to report his position if they see him, but to avoid approaching or confronting him. Once we know where he is, we can gather together and decide how best to corner him.'

'You don't have any idea how strong he is, do you?'

'No.' Arfon's expression was grim. 'Only that, now he has taken to attacking commoners, he will grow rapidly stronger. The longer it takes for us to find and subdue him, the stronger he will get.'

'Do you need my help?'

The younger magician looked at Gilken in surprise and gratitude, and shook his head. 'The Guild needs a record of these events,' he said. 'Hopefully only as a warning to those who come after us. But thank you for offering.'

Gilken smiled and shrugged, feeling a mixture of relief and frustration. If only there was something he could do to help. But he was old, and perhaps the best he could do was the task already in his hands.

Exhausted, Indria sat down on a low wall and stared at the ground. She did not want to see the bodies of the villagers around her. Despair and guilt would only drain the last of her energy — though deliberately avoiding the sight brought a wave of shame anyway.

Every night Tagin took magical energy from her. He said it not only kept them strong and safe, but it would help her sleep. He was right: she all but fell unconscious and only woke when he shook her the next day. She would have been grateful for the lack of dreams, if her waking hours had not become so nightmarish.

He insisted she come with him each time he attacked a village, afraid that the magicians would find her and use her against him. When she had seen what he did to the people she had protested, too tired to care what he might do to her. But she had been too worn out to argue convincingly, and he had obviously been expecting and preparing for her reaction. He wore her down with his reasoning.

Or maybe it was the sheer madness of his reasoning that left her unable to speak or resist. *He has gone so far past the point of ordinary human boundaries, so beyond my reach, that there is no use in me arguing with him.*

Still, she clung to hope. Perhaps he would return from his delusion. If he did, she must be there to steer him back to sanity. The right word at the right time, and she might persuade him to flee Kyralia and hide somewhere remote and safe from the Guild.

Either that, or turn him in. But even now, that was unthinkable.

A movement caught her eye and she reluctantly looked up. A figure was approaching her. Tagin.

'We'll have magical company soon,' he told her.

She frowned. 'What do you mean?'

'I saw it in the mind of the village leader. The local Lord told him to send a messenger if we turned up. Once he knows we're here, he'll call on five other country magicians for help. They'll come after us.'

'Oh.' She stood up with an effort.

'Rest, sister,' Tagin said, his voice growing gentle for a moment. 'We're not going anywhere.'

'We aren't running away?'

'No.'

'Are we going to poison them?'

'No. No more poison. No more tricks. It is time for good, honest battle.'

She felt her heart start to beat faster, and suddenly felt a little more awake. It was not a pleasant sensation. 'How many magicians did the man say there were?'

'Six.'

'But ... you're ... one.'

'Yes, but they are weaker.'

'How do you know? Don't they take power from their apprentices?'

'Yes. One apprentice, once a day. I have taken magic from many hundreds, and you would not believe how many commoners have as much latent power as a trained magician. I can see why the Sachakans have slaves ...' His voice faded, then he shook his head. 'Guild magicians aren't allowed to take magic from anyone but their apprentices. Not unless there's a war.'

'Do ... do you know anything about fighting?'

He smiled. 'A lot more than they do. It's been over two hundred years since the Sachakan War. Kyralian magicians have forgotten how to fight. There's been no reason to, since the wasteland ruined Sachaka.' He frowned. 'Herrol had a big library, most of it inherited, and I don't think he'd read all of it. I found books on strategy. Books all about fighting and planning battles. I've practised as much as I could, trying different kinds of barriers and strikes. It wasn't as good as real fighting practice, but it was more than what the Guild teaches.'

'But … if you attack them … does that make it war?'

He looked at her and smiled. 'They're already in a war, they just don't know it yet. And by the time they realise it, it will be too late.'

Record of the 235th Year.

It is difficult to believe that any man could be capable of such acts of needless violence. Yesterday's attempt to subdue him appears to have sent him into a passion. The last reports say he has slaughtered all in the villages of Tenker and Forei. He is beyond all controlling and I fear for the future of us all. I am amazed that he has not turned on us yet — but perhaps this is his preparation for that final strike.

Gilken, family Balen, House Sorrel, Record-keeper of the Magicians' Guild.

I definitely should not include my suspicions in my entries, Gilken thought as he finished re-reading his previous entry. *Whenever I do, they prove to be correct in the most unpleasant way.*

He sighed and dipped his pen into the bottle of ink.

It is looking more and more likely that the confrontation between Tagin and the country magicians was a deliberate move. Most here now believe he was ridding himself of the threat of attack from the rear in preparation for his advance toward the city.

Today, reports have been arriving every hour of villages and towns emptied of life, the luckier citizens having fled on Tagin's arrival, and of country magicians found dead in their homes or searchers perishing on the road.

The only benefit to this is that Tagin is no longer hiding. Today Lord Arfon left with twenty-three magicians with orders to kill, not capture, the Mad Apprentice and his sister, Indria.

A sound in the stairwell leading to his room made his heart skip. Had Lord Arfon returned? Had he been successful?

The steps were slow and dragged with weariness. Gilken wiped his pen, set it down, and hurried to the door. As he opened it, the man climbing the stairs looked up. Arfon's expression was grim, but it softened as he saw Gilken. By the time he had entered the room and collapsed into a chair his face was drawn and strained.

'It's not good news, is it?' Gilken said, taking the other chair.

'No.' Arfon covered his face with his hands, drew in a deep breath and shook his head. He looked up at Gilken. 'He defeated us. I only survived because … Indria suggested Tagin let me return to the Guild to deliver the news and suggest we surrender.'

Gilken felt his heart sink down low in his chest. 'How is that possible? How could we have got to this point in a few short months. How can we fall to one crazed apprentice?'

'Because we have underestimated him,' Arfon replied. 'He is no apprentice; he knows higher magic, therefore we should have treated him as a higher magician. And because we are fools, too slow and arrogant to consider we could ever be challenged, too split by politics to cooperate when we were, and too proud to foresee that one of our own might turn on us one day.'

'You could not have predicted any of this,' Gilken protested. 'How could anyone have guessed that Tagin would dare to attack us?'

'We should have considered it.' Arfon shook his head. 'I should have considered it. But there is no point arguing about it now. We can argue all we want, but it won't undo our mistakes.'

Gilken regarded the young magician with dismay. He'd never seen Arfon so resigned and hopeless.

'What will your next move be?'

Arfon shook his head. 'The hunt has been taken out of my hands.'

Gilken's stared at Arfon in disbelief. There was little wonder Arfon looked so defeated. 'But surely Tagin has been weakened by the fight. He is just one magician. Another attack will surely —'

'If anyone wants to gather a force to confront Tagin now it has to be at their own arranging,' Arfon told him. 'But the Guild may not approve it. When I left the meeting room talk had turned to bargaining and negotiation.'

'Do you think Tagin will be willing to negotiate?' he found himself asking, not quite ready to abandon the future he'd always assumed would come to pass.

Arfon shrugged. 'I've given up guessing what he will do. Maybe there will be no Guild left to negotiate with. I suspect those of a less optimistic outlook will have gathered their most valued possessions and found somewhere else to be by tomorrow morning.'

'Can't we ... can't we call upon the people of Imardin to give us their strength?'

'That was also discussed, but I have to agree with the prevailing opinion: the people are unlikely to agree to it. This has happened too fast for them to comprehend the danger. There is no army at the gates — no foreign enemy. There is one man. One of our own members, who we are responsible for dealing with. They don't understand how one apprentice could be such a threat. Even if we tried to explain ... they don't trust magicians like they used to, and this king is hardly the type to stir love from his people.'

Gilken looked away. *So they weren't even going to try to persuade the people to help? Or confront Tagin one more time, while he was weak?* He pushed himself to his feet.

'I'm going down to this meeting. There are other options they may not have considered.'

Arfon looked up at him in surprise, then nodded.

'I'll come with you,' he said.

Gilken smiled in gratitude, then led the way out of the Record-keeper's room to talk some sense into what was left of the Guild.

Indria had lost all sense of feeling, apart from a numbness that frightened her. It had been hard to justify the deaths of the magicians that had pursued Tagin, but she'd managed it. Watching her brother strip the life from one person after another, sparing only the youngest of the children, she had found she could not reason it away, so she stopped reasoning at all.

He is a monster. My brother. A monster, the shreds of her conscience told her.

But if he is, then the Guild made him so.

They may have used their apprentices badly, but did they deserve this in return?

She ignored the question. Once more she told herself that, once all this was over, the monster in her brother would go and the old Tagin would return. It was madness to hold onto this hope, but she did. Stupidly, stubbornly. There was nothing left but that hope. It was all out of her hands. Never had been in them to start with.

He never listened to me before all this started. Why did I think he would if I came with him?

She had been a fool to think she could keep him out of trouble and stop him from killing more people. Nothing she had said or did had turned him from this path.

But at least she had tried.

Not hard enough. You could have refused to go with him. You could have neglected to slip the poison in the wine that first time. Look at what your cowardice has brought about.

She looked up. The road before her was littered with the bodies of magicians.

As the last of the magicians fell, Tagin turned to grin at her. He beckoned. Obediently she followed him into the city. The people of Imardin shrank back, watching the lone figure and his sister. Indria thought back to the apprentices who had sought her brother out, traitors seeking to join him and thereby save themselves.

'You would give your lives to my cause?' he'd asked.

'Yes,' they'd assured him. So he'd taken what they offered, wiping their blood from his knife onto their robes.

As he turned into King's Parade a chill of foreboding shivered through her. He was not heading for the Guild, he was heading for the Palace. Somehow that realisation stirred up an emotion deep within the emptiness and she faltered. It briefly pushed away the numbness and after a moment of confusion she realised what she felt was anger.

'When you and I rule the world …' he had said to her, playing their familiar game. *This was his plan all along. All the talk of changing the Guild has been a lie.*

No. He was merely heading to the Palace because he knew that was where the magicians would be. Tagin looked over his shoulder at her. His eyes gleamed with mad eagerness, but as he looked at her it faded and changed to concern.

'Are you well, sister? Am I walking too fast for you?'

She felt her heart lift a little. There was still good in him. She managed a smile. 'I'm fine.'

As he turned back she let the chill in her heart numb her doubts and held onto a hope that had shrivelled and shrunk, but somehow refused to wither away entirely.

Record of the 235ᵗʰ Year.

My worst fears have come to life. Today Tagin killed Lord Gerin, Lord Dirron, Lord Winnel and Lady Ella. Will it end only when all magicians are dead, or will he not be satisfied until all life has been drained from the world? The view from my window is ghastly. Thousands of gorin, enka and reber rot in the fields, their strength given to the defence of Kyralia. Too many to eat, even.

Thousands of people are leaving the city while Tagin is too occupied with establishing control in the Palace to stop them. The Guild is all but empty. Aside from a few brave magicians, we have all fled to safer locations to wait and observe. Some are planning to leave Kyralia. I am undecided. Should I leave the country and take this record with me, or stay and continue in my duty to document these events? Some would reason that the Guild is finished so there is nothing more to record. But we are not all dead yet.

Gilken, family Balen, House Sorrel, Record-keeper of the Magicians' Guild.

The carriage bounced and swayed as Gilken put aside the record book. The driver had been instructed to get them all as far away from the city as possible, as quickly as possible so, once the vehicle had passed all the people fleeing the city on foot or in carts, it had sped up. The combination of speed and the rougher country roads made writing impossible.

His fellow passengers, two female magicians and one male apprentice, were silent. *Along with me, a grey-haired old man, we are hardly a formidable force.* He thought of the rest of the Guild members, now scattering across the country: mostly the older or younger magicians, a handful of women — and far more apprentices than magicians, since so many had lost their masters.

Though two hundred years had passed since the Sachakan War, the Guild's Kyralian membership hadn't reached the number of magicians that had existed before the war. Now, even if Tagin was somehow defeated and all surviving magicians returned to the Guild, it would take many more years to replace those that had been lost to the Mad Apprentice.

Not to forget the emptied villages and towns. And however many Imardians Tagin killed in future to keep himself in charge of the country. *But I suppose he'll have to keep some alive, otherwise he'll run out of people to take power from. He'll keep the ones with the greatest latent magic as slaves, most likely.* Gilken shuddered. *Maybe it is better that I am leaving. I not sure I'd be able to bear recording it all.*

'They have *what?*'

The old servant flinched at Tagin's anger.

'Left, my lord.'

'Where did they go?'

'I don't know. They took carriages and headed in different directions. Some to the south, some to th —'

'Good,' Tagin declared. 'If they've split up, they won't be coming back to fight me any time soon.' He moved back to the throne and sat down. 'I want a list of all the magicians that left.' Tagin narrowed his eyes at the man. 'I know you'll try to hide some. For every magician I learn you've left off the list I'll ... I'll kill a member of your family.'

The man nodded. 'I understand.'

Tagin looked away, his expression thoughtful. 'I also want everyone in Kyralia to know that any magicians that are found are to be sent to me. And their apprentices. Let it be known that no magician is allowed to use higher magic to strengthen themselves.'

'I will summon the street callers,' the man murmured.

'Thirdly, I want all the books in the Guild sent here.' Tagin pointed to one of the courtiers he'd selected, after reading their minds, to serve him. 'My assistant will go with you to make sure you don't hide any.' He waved a hand. 'Go.'

The man bowed and backed away. Tagin ignored him, reaching for his glass of water.

Indria watched from a chair that had been placed beside the throne for her. As Tagin drank, a memory flashed into her mind of a glass goblet full of clear water that had tasted faintly of rocks. A memory of Lord Arfon.

'There's a spring in the Guild grounds,' he told her. 'The water from it is the purest you'll ever drink. It is piped only to this building and to the Royal Palace — and in the palace it goes first to the king's rooms.' She had told Tagin about the spring, but not about its location in the Guild, and he had decided to drink only from this safe source.

'Oh, that's right.' Tagin looked up at the retreating man. 'Stop! I have another instruction. Send me the Guild records. I want to know what's been said about me.'

The servant bowed again, then hurried out of the entrance to the audience chamber. Indria felt a pang of sympathy and sighed.

'Are you well, sister? You look pale.'

Indria looked up to find Tagin looking at her, and shrugged. 'Just tired.'

He considered her thoughtfully. Since taking over the Palace he had insisted she stay by his side. She told herself he was being protective, but sometimes she detected an old, familiar mood of suspicion and distrust. Worry grew like a tangled knot inside her. She knew that mood. It had always been a dangerous one. In the past it had led to accusations of imagined slights against him and, when she was younger, beatings. Now that he had grown accustomed to killing with little hesitation, what would he do if he imagined she was betraying him?

Suddenly he smiled. 'Go on, sister. This has all been exhausting for you. Rest and return when you feel better.'

Somehow she forced her weary legs to take her to the rooms Tagin had chosen for her. The beauty of the decorations and furnishings within the Palace only made her more melancholy. As she reached the door to her apartment a guard held it open for her. She all but staggered through to the greeting room, relieved when the door clicked shut behind her. Then she froze.

A man stood in the centre of the room. She blinked at him stupidly for a moment. He was not a servant. He was familiar, but for a moment she didn't recognise him because he wasn't wearing his robes.

'Lord Arfon?'

He nodded. She glanced back at the door. Had the guard noticed the intruder? Surely if he had, he would have said or done something. Or did the guard know Lord Arfon was here and was helping the magician?

'Tagin will kill you if he sees you,' she warned.

Arfon nodded again. He gazed back at her, saying nothing but looking hesitant. As if he wanted to say something, but didn't know where to start.

'Why are you here?' she asked.

He swallowed. 'To find out if there is anything that can be done.'

She looked down at the floor, realising only as the feeling faded that the sight of Arfon had lightened her heart a little.

'Nothing. Even if there was, it's too late.'

'He trusts you.'

She looked at him. His eyebrows rose suggestively, even while his expression remained grim.

'I can't do that,' she told him. 'I can't kill someone. Least of all my own brother.'

Arfon nodded, then sighed and sat down on the edge of one of the chairs. All the determination fell from him and he shook his head.

'I wish the world could have heard you say that. It is such a strange thing, that the sibling of the worst killer in history has the gentlest of natures. It is too hard to believe, for most people.'

She frowned. 'What do they believe?'

He looked away. 'That you are his ally. You are, aren't you?' His gaze returned, and his eyes were now hard and judgemental.

I tried to stop him, she wanted to say. But that was a lie.

'I was never able to stop him, once he got something into his head,' she said instead. 'Not when we were children. Not now.'

Arfon nodded, then rose and walked to one of the large paintings. To her astonishment, it hinged away from the wall like a door. Behind was a square opening. He paused and looked back at her.

'If you decide to do something, I will help you.'

Then he stepped into the hole, reached back and pulled the painting-door closed behind him.

Indria stared at the painting. She felt a strange disappointment. *I wanted him to stay and argue with me*, she realised. *He accepted my excuse too easily.*

But she *had* tried to stop Tagin. In her mind she heard the argument begin again. *No. You haven't*, the quiet voice in the back of her mind replied. *You could have stopped him many times. But you were afraid of what he'd do if you failed, or he escaped. You were a coward.*

But he was her brother.

And your responsibility. What would have been worse: betraying him to the Guild when he had only murdered a few, or letting him kill again and again until he became the monster he is now?

Her head spun. There was no point acting now. It was too late. Tagin was on the throne. Things could not get any worse.

Oh, yes they can.

He would have to keep killing to stay strong enough to repel attempts by the Guild to rescue the city. Or else he would enslave people so that he could take power from them, over and over.

Slaves. We'll end up like the Sachakans. Only there'll be just one master, my brother, and all Kyralians will be slaves.

There was nothing she could do.

Oh, yes there is.

Her mouth went dry as she thought of it. The solution had been there right from the start. She only needed the courage to use it. She walked slowly to the cabinet that held the few possessions she had carried these last months and took out a small vial, paper, ink and a pen.

Nothing stopped her. She resolved to keep going until her nerve failed, or her conscience stopped arguing with her, and stilled her hands.

Some time later she found Tagin digging through a chest of dusty books in the middle of the audience chamber.

'Look!' he said as she approached. 'Books from the Guild.'

She grimaced. 'They smell old.'

'They are,' he told her. 'This one is a record of the Guild magicians who ruled Sachaka after the war.' As he dug through them dust billowed up and he coughed. He waved a hand. 'Get me a drink, sister.'

Her spine tingled as she picked up the goblet beside the throne and moved to the back of the room. The spring water was clear and cold. She filled the vessel and returned to Tagin's side. As he watched, she raised the goblet to her lips and sipped.

Satisfied, he took the glass, drained it and handed it back to her. She refilled it. He selected a book and returned to the throne. She watched as he began to read. Then, as his eyes closed and his head began to nod she set the goblet aside.

Moving to the throne, she leaned close as if to look at the pages. He swayed as he looked up at her.

'Sister,' he said, his eyes slowly closing and opening again. He let the book drop. 'I am very tired.'

'Brother,' she replied. 'I am, too. Lean on me. Don't worry. I'll take care of you.'

She caught him as he fell and held him as his eyes closed. Slowly his breathing slowed and his lips turned blue. Reaching out to take the glass and drain it, she marvelled at how the taste of the drug was barely noticeable in the clear water, even when strong enough to kill.

Then her eyes were assailed by a flash of intense white, and a sensation too brief to register as pain.

A few weeks' absence had not made the tower steps any easier to climb. This time Gilken had a burden to carry, too. The record book and writing equipment felt heavier than they had when he'd taken them out of the room. Finally he reached the last step, and the platform before the door. He stopped to gaze at the plain wood and the plaque stating that this room was for the 'Record-keeper of the Magicians' Guild'. For a moment he was overwhelmed by emotion.

Taking a deep breath, he pushed into the room beyond.

There were a few signs of disturbance. Cupboards had been opened. A glass water jug had been smashed. The bed was at an angle, suggesting it had been moved. But the small, high table on which he always worked remained whole and in place.

He put his burden down on the table, then moved to the window. What he saw made his breath catch.

Though he had seen the ruins of the city as his carriage had passed through to the Guild, it had been a confusing jumble of stone and wood. Now, from the higher position, he could see patterns in the devastation. The explosion that had levelled so many buildings had fanned out from the Palace. It had missed the Guild, instead smashing everything between the throne room and the docks. It was a terrible sight, but it stirred a guilty relief.

Tagin was dead.

So were thousands of people. Magicians and non-magicians. Lords and servants. Men and women. Adults and children. Either murdered by the Mad Apprentice, or killed when all the magic he had stolen had been released on his death.

Gilken stared at the view for a long time, until he could no longer bear the sight. He turned from the window and moved back to the high table. Taking the record book out of its wrappings, he placed it on the sloped surface. He returned the inkpot to its place and removed his pen from its carry case.

He wet the nib.

And began writing.

Record of the 235th Year.

It is over. When Alyk told me the news I dared not believe it, but an hour ago I climbed the stairs of the Lookout and saw the truth with my own eyes. It is true. Tagin is dead. Only he could have created such destruction in his final moments.

Lord Eland called us together and read a letter sent from Indria, Tagin's sister. She told of her intention to poison him. We can only assume that she succeeded.

Did she know that killing him would release the power he contained? Did she know it would blast the Palace and much of the city to rubble? Why did she support him despite all he did, only to turn on him at the end?

We will never know. It is likely we will see more stringent rules governing apprentices and the teaching of higher magic. Some have even suggested higher magic be banned altogether, though that would leave us foolishly vulnerable to attack. Still, Sachaka is no longer a threat and we are on friendly terms with our other neighbours.

One suggestion gaining support is to encourage magicians to dedicate themselves to learning and using magic for fighting and warfare in the same way that some of us do with magical healing. Perhaps then we'll be ready for the next threat, and not repeat the many mistakes we made in dealing with the Mad Apprentice.

Change is certain. I suspect the effects of this tragic story will haunt us for many years to come, but I am starting to believe that we will grow stronger and wiser as a result.

Good things can come from awful events, so long as we learn from our mistakes and record what we have learned for future generations.

Gilken, family Balen, House Sorrel, Record-keeper of the Magicians' Guild.

AFTERWORD

The story of Tagin was a little runt of a tale that sprang out of creating history for the Black Magician Trilogy. Unlike the story of the Sachakan War, which turned into *The Magician's Apprentice*, it was not substantial enough to fill an entire book. Yet it had too much substance to comfortably squeeze into a short story. I always considered it good novella material, but it is hard to justify taking time out from book schedules to write a novella when there isn't as great a market for them as there is for short stories. So when Jack told me of the *Australian Legends* anthology, I had the perfect excuse to tell Tagin's tale.

While it had begun as a lesson in the destructive potential of black magic in the wrong hands, the story had to be more than that as a novella. I could have written it from Tagin's perspective, and enjoyed a black ride seeing the world through his mad eyes. But when I came up with the idea of writing it through his sister's perspective I knew it

would be more than a lesson or mad ride. It would be about family, loyalty and the pain, denial and dread of being related to someone with a somewhat shaky grip on morality, reality and his temper.
— *Trudi Canavan*

Juliet Marillier was born in Dunedin, New Zealand and now lives in Western Australia. A graduate of Otago University, she worked as a teacher and public servant before becoming a full-time writer.

Juliet has written ten historical fantasy novels for adults and two books for young adults. Her books have won a number of awards including the Aurealis (three times), the Sir Julius Vogel Award and the American Library Association Alex Award. Her most recent novel is *Heart's Blood*, published in November 2009.

Juliet is a member of the druid order OBOD. She shares her home with a small pack of needy dogs and a sweet-tempered cat.

'Twixt Firelight and Water:
A Tale of Sevenwaters

Juliet Marillier

CONRI

A fair maid in the wildwood lies
A raven pecks her sightless eyes
Then wings into the heavens again
To shriek his song of death and pain.

I have a tale to tell. I would recite its verses while playing the harp, had not a sorceress long ago robbed me of my capacity to share my story. That may be just as well, for my tale would only make you sad. I was a bard then. I brought tears to the eyes of my listeners, made them hold their breath in anticipation, gasp in wonderment, cheer as the hero won his battle, cry as the fair lady lost her true love. In those days, I contrived happy endings. Folk like to see lovers reunited, challenges met and overcome, good triumphant over evil.

If ever my voice is returned to me, I will sing only sad songs.

I listen as my companion instructs a clutch of green novices.

'In the land of Erin dwell three races,' he tells them. 'First are the Tuatha De Danann, commonly known as the Fair Folk, proud and strong, noble and wise.' *With a few notable exceptions*, I add in my mind. 'They dwell in hollow hills and in deep forests,' the druid continues, 'though such sanctuaries are shrinking with the coming of the new faith. Second are the Old Ones, the Fomhoire, whom I should perhaps have placed at the start, since they have prior claim. Their shapes are many, their attitudes inscrutable. Long time and endless patience provide their solutions. They blend; they wait; they observe. The Old Ones are survivors. Last, human folk, late come to this land, short-lived, unsubtle, as moody and changeable as a Connemara shore in autumn.'

Up speaks a bright young fellow, all bony wrists and eager eyes. 'Master Ciarán? There are surely more than three races here. What of leprechauns? Clurichauns? What of the *bean sidhe?*'

'What about the Sea People?' another novice chimes in.

'And there's those wee things that drink the milk straight from the cow,' pipes up a red-cheeked lad who, from the looks of him, has but recently replaced his hayfork with a druid's staff.

'True,' says my companion, unruffled as always. 'There exists a fourth race, a fifth, a sixth; perhaps more than we will ever know. Set them aside for now and consider another variant. Ask yourself what may ensue when the pure blood of the three races is mixed and blended, creating something new. Imagine a being with human passions and frailties combined with Fomhoire endurance, say, or human stubbornness alongside the pride and craft of the Tuatha De. Imagine an individual with the Old Ones' long memory and the Fair Folk's facility in magic; picture a warrior of superb skill and courage, who possesses the ability to become rock, water, earth, tree in a heartbeat.

'Such blends are not common. The three races of Erin seldom have congress with one another, and such alliances rarely produce children. When there is a slipping across boundaries, a union between old enemies, and an infant is born of that coupling, chances are the child will be something exceptional. The bravest heroes and the darkest villains are oft products of such unsanctioned pairings.'

The tutor pauses, his mulberry eyes seeing something beyond this grove, beyond this forest, beyond this summer day. I, too, contemplate. Hero or villain? If I still had my human tongue, I could answer for him. My companion walks the path of light. Here in the nemetons, his vocation is to teach, to guide, to set the feet of the young on right ways. His choice brought him some peace of mind. Some. He has suffered losses as painful as my own. The shadow of death lingers in those dark eyes even as he leads the young brethren in a prayer.

Hero or villain? It depends. I was once hero of my own tale, loved by a girl with star-bright eyes and hair like a soft shadow. I had youth, talent, a path before me. And then … and then … Had I a human voice, I would turn the fresh faces of these young druids pale with horror. I would shout and scream my story to the treetops, I would sit by the pool and let my tears fall into the still water, one and two and three. I would whisper her name to the wind, I would teach it to skylark and thrush, to sparrow and nightingale, and they would sing it abroad, an anthem, a lullaby, a love song, a dead march. Oh, if I had my voice again, there would be such a tale to tell. And in that tale, perhaps I would be hero and villain both.

> *I glimpsed her first 'twixt lake and fire*
> *My heart took wing; soared high and higher*
> *Lóch was her name. The moon above*
> *Smiled down, pale witness of our love.*

Ah, that night! She stood reed-slender, the fire's glow warming her face, and behind her the bright moon danced on the waters of the lake. My heart gave one great leap and I was changed forever. But I get ahead of myself. First I must tell of a day some years earlier: the day when I watched my mother bringing her new son home to the Otherworld.

I was hiding. At thirteen, I was in more fear of her than I had been as a little child. By then I'd begun to understand the darkness she carried within her, a weight of bitter resentment so tightly woven into the fabric of her that it was plain nothing would ever shift it. She'd been away. Three years it had been, three wonderful, peaceful years without her. I'd spent them making verses, practising the harp, and hoping beyond hope that she'd never come back. With her gone, folk had begun to befriend me. I had started to believe it might be possible for one of my kind to follow the paths of light. Yes, even a son of hers.

I was hiding high in the cradling branches of an oak. I watched her pass below, every part of me on edge, willing her to be only a phantom, only an evil memory. But she was real, as real as the little boy she carried in her arms, a red-haired mite of perhaps two summers. I knew at a glance that he was hers. Her son. My replacement.

It was her habit to summon me after one of these trips out into the human world, and her summons came as soon as she'd left the child with a pair of local cottagers, then returned to our own realm. She stood in the shadow of the oaks, eyes cool as I approached. 'Conri,' she said. Her tone hardly differentiated me from a grain of dust under her foot.

'Mother.' I knelt before her, since that was the way she liked it, making my voice respectful.

'I don't suppose I can hope you spent the time of my absence working on the elements of your magical craft.'

It was not a question, and I did not offer an answer, merely gazed at the ground, wondering how she would punish me.

A sigh. 'I've had a reversal, Conri. A serious reversal that needs attention. Look at me!' Her voice suddenly sharp as an axe. I raised my head. She was young today, auburn hair cascading over her shoulders, figure shapely in a gown of soft green. Her mouth was set tight. Her eyes probed deep inside me. I could think of nothing to say that would please her.

'You've wasted the time fiddling about with your music. Yes?'

'Yes, Mother.' I set my jaw firm and held her gaze as my belly twisted in fear.

'Pah!' An explosion of annoyance, then a click of the fingers. Pain shot through my arms and hands, crippling, crushing. I crumpled, screaming. Around us in the high trees of the Otherworld, a host of birds echoed my cry. 'Stupid boy! With your parentage, you could have amounted to something. You are useless! Useless! A weakling!'

I forced myself back up to my knees. The agony was fading. I glanced at my arms, half-expecting that every bone would be broken, but they looked much as usual. My breath wheezed in my chest. I said nothing at all.

'Never mind that.' Mother's tone had changed again. 'It's of little account now. Despite the reversal, I have not returned empty-handed. I have a weapon. A fine weapon. Or so it will become, when suitably polished. Conri, I have work for you.'

'Yes, Mother,' I croaked.

'There's a child. A boy. I've left him with human folk, right on the margin between that realm and this — you know the cottage in the forest, close by the place they call Hag's Head in the human world?'

I did not tell her I'd been watching as she passed her baby boy over to strangers. 'Yes, Mother,' I said.

'Folk might come looking,' she said. 'Human folk. The child is too small to be brought to our realm as yet; he requires a tiresome degree of feeding and cleaning. He'll stay with these cottagers for a year or two. I've set a ward over him, of course. But you will watch, also. There will be a certain degree of ill will towards me, I imagine.'

'Are not human folk too weak to break these wards, Mother? They have no magic.'

She smiled thinly. 'These are not your everyday human folk,' she said. 'They'll be rather determined, I fear. Conri, you must tell me immediately if you see anyone loitering close to the cottage, or in the woods nearby. And I need to know if my son's guardians become at all careless. I don't anticipate that will happen. They understand the importance of this task, and the punishment that will befall them if they do not fulfil it to my expectations.'

'Your son,' I said, making my tone suitably surprised. 'So I have a little brother.'

'Hah!' There was neither affection nor amusement in the sound. 'A half-brother, but you'd be wise not to regard him as kin. You will not approach him, Conri. The child is mine only. As soon as he can listen and obey, I will commence his training. He will be subtle; clever; powerful. Ciarán will be my sword of vengeance.'

It sounded ridiculous. That little scrap, not long out of swaddling clothes, the instrument of her fell power? Time passed. I watched as his carers tended to him, as he learned to run and to climb, as he began to talk. I watched him solemnly investigating all he discovered. I saw him gazing into tranquil pools; I observed him sitting so quietly the birds came up to perch on his toes. He was still a very small boy when I saw him bring a ripe plum down from high in a tree, right into his hand. Not long after, he sang a fox out of the bracken to lie down by him, obedient as any pet dog. My brother; my clever little brother. The cottagers tended him well, but they had no time for play. I wanted to show him how to catch a ball; how to make a little house in the woods; how to tease minnows into his hand. I wanted him to know he had a brother.

I reported regularly to my mother. 'Nobody has come looking for him. Nobody at all.' Of the magic, which Ciarán explored further with every passing day, I said not a word.

In time, inevitably, she discovered to her fierce satisfaction that this second son possessed all the potential the first had failed to exhibit, and she began his training. My job as overseer was at an end. I found myself at once relieved and saddened. I was free now to pursue my music. I did so within both worlds, for I could pass as a talented human bard provided I was careful not to reveal my eldritch gifts. Those were meagre enough beside my tiny half-brother's.

I was selfish to step away from him. I knew how cruel she could be; I had experienced her training at first hand. She would not understand the frailty of a small child. She would not care what damage she inflicted. I told myself I could do nothing about it. She was a sorceress, powerful and without conscience. I was a half-and-half. My only assets were a good singing voice and nimble fingers. I reminded myself of this when occasionally I chanced upon my mother and the child working together. My brother's small face had become pinched and pale; his eyes, so like our mother's, were smudged with a bone-deep weariness. I saw her punish him. He took it stoically and tried harder to please.

The joyous, instinctive magic he had used as an infant was quite gone. She taught him other skills.

Yes, I was both selfish and a coward. I avoided the clearing where they were accustomed to work, an Otherworld place beyond the eyes of Ciarán's human guardians. I tried to be blind to what she was doing to him. In the human world I found a master harper, a solitary man who made time for me, and I stayed long months with him, learning new skills and sharpening old ones. Ciarán was a prickle on my conscience, but I ignored him. Any attempt to intervene would see us both punished.

I was nearly seventeen; my brother would be four or five. I went to a Beltane fair and played my harp for dancing. At dusk a great fire was lit on the lakeshore. All knew the forest nearby held portals to the Otherworld. On such a night doors might be left ajar, and lovers who wandered into the woods for a little dalliance might find themselves on a longer journey than they'd anticipated. A perilous spot. Still, that was the traditional fair ground, and there we were, a little merry with good mead, a little dizzy from dancing, a little amorous, as befitted Beltane. At least, the human folk were — I remained detached, concentrating on playing and singing. I reached the end of a jig, looked up and across the throng, and there she was. The firelight glowed on the perfect curve of her cheek; it put a warm glint in her lovely eyes. The breeze blew strands of her dark hair over her brow, and she pushed them back with a graceful hand, smiling. Behind her, the moon shone on the trembling waters of the lake. She was looking at me.

In a heartbeat my life was changed.

With arms entwined, all summer long
We danced to our own secret song
We shone with love's transforming flame
And then — oh, then — the autumn came.

I forgot my mother. I forgot the small shoulders that now carried the weight of the sorceress's expectations. Lóch loved me, and I was new-made. We wandered the forest paths hand in hand. I made sure we kept away from portals to the Otherworld.

We were young, but we made plans. I could earn a living as a bard. Thanks to my maternal line — who would ever have believed I might gain some good from being *her* son? — my skills were already superior to those of human musicians, and I would have no trouble finding work. Lóch wanted a baby. We imagined her, a girl, always a little girl, with dark wisps of hair and eyes the colour of lake water. We would travel north. Lóch's grandmother, who had looked after her since she was an infant, could come with us. We would be a family.

There was no need to spell out my ancestry. My sweetheart had sound instincts, and she saw from the first that I was something unusual. I would not talk about my mother. I would have spoken of my father, but I knew nothing about him. When I'd asked my mother, as a child, she'd said, 'It doesn't matter who he was. He fulfilled his purpose. Not especially well, as it turned out.' I had seen in her eyes that I must not ask again.

'We'll live wherever you want,' I told Lóch as we lay on the grass one warm afternoon. 'Just not here.' The tide of desire was strong between us, the denial of it a painful pleasure. Her fingers traced delicate patterns on my arm; mine rested against her stomach, the soft sweetness of her body only a thin layer of fabric away. We had sworn we would not lie together until we were married.

We planned to be hand-fasted at Lugnasad, after the prayers of thanks for the season's bounty. Once wed, we would go, away, away, free of the burden of my mother, free of the anxiety and fear and pain she seemed to bring with her no matter how obedient I was to her commands. The freedom that beckoned was not only the opportunity to be with my love as her husband, and to tread a new path with her beside me. It was my chance to be unshackled from my mother's dark ambition.

'Conri,' said Lóch, raising herself on one elbow to study my face. 'You look so sad sometimes. So troubled. What is it, dear heart?'

'Nothing,' I said. 'I'm trying to remember the words of a ballad, but the rhyme's eluding me.' I sat up and tickled her nose with a blade of grass until she was helpless with laughter, and the shadow was forgotten.

*　　*　　*

Lóch's grandmother liked me, but she wanted us to wait. We were so young, she said, too young to see anything but an easy future. The prospect of leaving the cottage where she had brought up her orphaned granddaughter, and the friends she had in the district, and everything familiar, was frightening to her. Well, she was old by human standards, and I almost understood how she felt, but I knew we must leave. If we stayed close to this forest we would be within my mother's reach for all of our lives.

My musical skill was not the only thing I had inherited from my mother's line. I would live far longer than Lóch; I would continue to look young as she gradually aged. I dismissed this, certain my love for her was strong enough to withstand any test. Like many folk of mixed heritage, I had the ability to turn the minds of human folk one way or another — charm, one might call it, though not a charm in the sense of a spell, more a gift for choosing the right tone, the right words, the right look of the eyes to persuade a person to a certain way of thinking. I never used it on Lóch. She chose me for myself, for the man I was. I shied away from all magic, for I wanted to be human, not fey. But when Lóch's grandmother put her foot down, determined that we should wait at least a year to be sure of our minds, I used it on her. It was not long before the old woman was saying the plan was a fine one, and of course we were old enough, at seventeen, to be wed and journeying and thinking of a baby. So the hand-fasting was set for Lugnasad. We'd be married as soon as the harvest ritual was over, and straight away we would head north to a place where there were some cousins of Lóch's dead father. We packed up the cottage; there was little enough in it.

'What about your things, Conri?' Lóch asked. 'Clothes, tools, all your possessions?' She had never asked me where I lived. I thought perhaps she did not want to know. Of recent times I'd been sleeping at the cottage, chastely on a bench while Lóch and her grandmother shared the bed.

I was about to reply that the only possession that mattered was my harp, but I realised it was not quite true. I had a little box, back in the Otherworld, with objects I had collected through the uncomfortable years of my childhood, treasures I had taken out at night after the day's failures and punishments were over. Holding and stroking each in turn, I had been comforted by their familiarity. I did not want to leave that box behind. Besides, Lóch was right about clothing. In the human world one had to consider such activities as washing and mending. Before I was quite done with the Otherworld, my mother's world, I must make one last trip back.

Ten days before Lugnasad, on a morning of bitter wind, I slipped across the margin and fetched my box from the cave where I had hidden it. I took a cloak, a pair of boots, a favourite hat. I spoke to one or two folk, not saying I was leaving, and discovered that my mother had gone away to the south. Nobody knew if it was a short trip or a long one. I breathed more easily. With luck, she would not return until Lóch and I were far away.

I emerged into the human world close by the cottage where Ciarán and his keepers lived, a low, secluded place nestled at the foot of the crag called Hag's Head, and surrounded by rowans. Why did I choose that way? Who knows? As I passed the place I heard a sound that stopped me in my tracks. It could have been me weeping like that, in little tight sobs as I tried to hold the pain inside, so nobody would hear me and know how weak I truly was. I found that I could not walk on by.

He was scrunched into a hollow between the rocks, arms wrapped around himself, knees up, head down. The bones of his shoulder, fragile as a bird's, showed under the white skin, through a rip in his tunic. His hair was longer now, and the hue of a dark flame. He heard me coming, soft-footed as I was, and every part of him tensed.

'Ciarán?' It was awkward; he did not know me.

The small head came up. The dark mulberry eyes, reddened with tears, fixed their stare on me. He was like a little wild animal at bay, quivering with the need for flight. And yet not like, for there was a knowledge in those sad eyes that chilled me. My brother was too young for this.

I squatted down at a short distance, putting my belongings on the ground. 'Did she hurt you?' I asked.

Not a word. She had threatened him, no doubt, to keep him from speaking to passers-by.

'Ciarán,' I said quietly, 'my name is Conri. We both have the same mother. That makes us brothers.'

He understood; I saw an unlikely hope flame in his eyes. Impossibilities flooded through my mind: *we could take him with us, we could hide, perhaps she would never find us.* And then, cruellest of all: *I should not go away. I should stay for his sake.*

'Conri.' Ciarán tried out the sound of it. 'When is my father coming?'

The hairs on my neck rose. Surely he could not remember his father. I'd seen how little the boy was when she brought him here: too young to understand any of it. But then, this was no ordinary child.

'I don't know, Ciarán.' *Don't ask if you can come with me.* Already, so quickly, he had a grip on my heart. Why in the Dagda's name had I passed this way? 'I have to go now.'

'Will you come back?'

I drew a shaky breath. There would be no lying to this particular child. 'I don't know.' It was woefully inadequate. 'Ciarán, I have something for you.' I reached across and picked up my treasure box. My brother edged closer as I opened the lid. It was a meagre enough collection, but each item was precious to me. What to give him?

'Here,' I said, picking out a stone with swirling patterns of red and grey, a secret language ancient as myth. 'I found this up in the hills beyond the western end of the lake. Earth and fire.'

His fingers closed around it. 'Thank you,' he whispered. 'Goodbye, Conri.'

'Goodbye, little brother.' Morrigan's curse, tears were starting in my eyes, and they trembled in my voice. The longer I stayed, the worse this would be for the two of us. I gathered my belongings, turned my back and walked away.

Eight days until Lugnasad and our wedding. There was no point in looking backwards. I could not save Ciarán. Even if Lóch had not existed, even if I had been prepared to sacrifice my own life for my brother's sake, and stay where she could find and torment me daily, the sorceress would never have allowed me a part in his future. If Ciarán was to be her tool, she would not want his edge blunted by weakness, or his true metal tarnished by love. I could do nothing for him.

So there was a thread of sorrow and regret in the shimmering garment of our happiness. All the same, Lóch prepared for the ritual with bright eyes, and both she and her grandmother professed themselves ready for the adventure that lay ahead. Lóch and I embraced under the shelter of the trees, our bodies pressed tight, desire making our breath falter. Our hearts hammered one against the other. Our wedding night could not come quickly enough.

Six days until Lugnasad, and both Lóch and her grandmother had gone to the far side of the lake to bid farewell to an old friend, a crippled woman who would not be coming to the celebrations. They would be gone all day. I planned to spend the time practising the harp, for we'd been busy of late and I had neglected my craft. With the two of them to support, and perhaps soon a babe as well, I'd need to maintain my technique and keep on making new songs. Folk soon weary of a bard who repeats himself.

I worked all morning and by midday I was growing thirsty. I decided to go down to the local hostelry for a cup or two of ale. While I was sitting there minding my own business, a man came in. I looked at him once and I looked twice, for there was something familiar in that face. The fellow was quite old, with many white threads in his dark hair. His face was a map of experience. Despite his years, there was a strength in every part of him, like the tenacity of a wind-scourged tree. He was clad in plain traveller's garb, a grey cloak, well-worn boots of best quality. A broad-brimmed hat; a dagger at his belt. No bag. I studied the face again, and this time knew where I had seen it before.

The traveller looked around, then approached the innkeeper.

'Ale, my lord?' The innkeeper had sized up the newcomer and was greeting him accordingly.

'Share a jug with me,' I put in quickly, indicating that the traveller should come to sit at my table. 'I'll pay.'

The traveller's grey eyes narrowed, assessing me. My mother's words came back to me, sharp and clear: *These are not your everyday human folk. They'll be rather determined, I fear.* Then the man walked over and seated himself opposite me.

I waited for the ale to come. I did not ask any of the questions he might have been expecting, such as *Where are you headed?* and *Where are you from?* Instead, for the time it took for the innkeeper to bring the jug, I let myself dream. What if this strong, sad-looking stranger was *my* father, come to fetch me? What if he had been looking for me all these years, seventeen whole years, and now he was going to bring me home, and I would meet my family, and Lóch and I could live in a place where I truly belonged?

'Are you from these parts?' the man asked diffidently as I poured the ale.

'Close by.' I wondered if he glimpsed my mother in me. I wondered if he was as good at guesswork as I was.

'Been here long?'

'All my life. My name is Conri.'

'Mm.' He acknowledged it with a courteous nod, but did not offer his own in return. After a moment he added, 'Why would you buy me a drink, Conri?'

My heart thumping, I said, 'You're a stranger in these parts. I imagine you may be here for a particular reason.'

'You imagine correctly.' I could almost see his mind working. He needed information, but speaking to the wrong person might put his whole plan in jeopardy. 'What kind of trade do you ply?' He glanced at my hands.

'I'm a musician. Soon to be wed. We'll be travelling to live with kinsfolk in the north.'

He nodded. This answer seemed to satisfy him. 'Know all the locals, do you?'

'Most. Are you looking for someone?'

'A child. A boy.'

'I see.' I traced a finger around the rim of my ale cup, thinking he must indeed be tenacious if he thought to pit his human skills against her uncanny ones, his honest strength against her overweening ambition. 'A small boy or a bigger one?'

It was in my voice, no doubt: the knowledge. The fear. When he spoke again his tone was hushed, so nobody else could hear, and there was an edge in it. 'He'd be five years old by now. Red hair; pale skin; unusual eyes, the colour of ripe mulberries.'

'Your son?' I kept my own voice down.

'Never mind that. Have you seen him?'

I thought of my mother's wrath. I thought of Ciarán with my gift in his hand and his eyes full of shadows. 'There is a child who meets that description living nearby,' I whispered. 'But there are … risks. High risks, my lord.' Oh, how his eyes came alight as I spoke! The selfsame look had kindled on my brother's small face when I told him we were kin, and died when I bade him farewell.

'How do I know I can trust you?' Ciarán's father asked.

'I might ask you the same question,' I said. 'But I will not. I think the two of us want the same thing: for the boy to be safe. Where would you take him? How could you keep him out of danger?'

He looked at me. I saw the strength written in his face, and the suffering. 'If I tell you,' he said, 'those who seek to harm him can get the answers from you and hunt him down. So I will not tell. But there is a place where he can be protected, and I will take him there. His father and his brothers will keep him safe.'

'Brothers?' I echoed, somewhat taken aback to think there were more of us out there.

The stranger glanced towards the unglazed window of the inn. I had thought this a solitary journey, a father's lonely quest to claim his lost son. But this man was no fool. He'd brought reinforcements. The two of them were standing out the front waiting for him, youngish men made very much in his own mould, with pale, intense faces, keen eyes, unsmiling mouths. Weaponry of various kinds hung about them. The father hadn't needed to carry a pack; each of his sons bore one. His sons, but not hers. There was no touch of the uncanny on these hard-faced warriors.

'Half-brothers.'

It was not a question, but I thought it needed an answer. 'I only have one half-brother,' I said. 'Promise me he will be safe, and I will show you where he is.' Fear dripped through me like ice water. 'But understand the danger, for all of us.'

'Oh, I understand.' His voice was like iron. 'You are her son?'

I would not answer so direct a question. 'I will show you,' I said. 'The best time is early morning, not long after dawn. You must be prepared to leave quickly and travel swiftly. At present she is not here, but she may return at any time. Weapons such as those your sons bear will not help you in this struggle.'

'Come,' he said, rising to his feet.

The two sons were wary; everything about them spoke distrust. I bore some resemblance to my mother, and while I did not know their story, I imagined she had wrought havoc amongst their family. Unsurprising, then, that they did not warm to me. But they did their father's bidding and a plan was made. We would camp out in the woods overnight, close to the cottage. We would move in before dawn and take him. They had horses stabled nearby, and could travel swiftly. And they had one or two other tricks, they said, but nobody told me what those were.

I prayed that my mother's visit to the south would be a lengthy one, though I knew Ciarán's training would call her back soon; her methods required that the student not be allowed time to mull over what she was doing to him. If she discovered this plan, all of us would be caught up in her fury. By Danu's sweet mercy, it was a risk indeed.

'We must make a pact of silence, Conri,' the nobleman said when the four of us were out of doors, under the trees, working out how it would unfold. 'Neither I nor my sons here will mention your name, whatever pressure is applied to us. None of us will say how we found the boy. In return, you will not speak of what happened. You will cover our tracks as best you can. You will do all in your power to avoid laying a trail. If you love your little brother, and it seems to me that is so, you will do what you can to ensure he is not hurt.'

Not hurt? Ciarán had already been hurt so badly the scars of it would be with him all his life. 'I will honour the pact,' I said. 'As I said, I'm to be married at Lugnasad. We won't be making our home here.'

'I wish you joy,' he said quietly. 'Now take us close to the place. We must remain in cover until it's time.'

I wondered what Lóch would think when she came home and found the cottage empty. I'd have to invent a story to cover my overnight absence. It felt wrong to lie to her, but she could not know the truth. If this worked, if Ciarán escaped, my mother would be brutal in her efforts to track the perpetrators down. The thought that her touch might reach my sweetheart curdled my blood and froze my heart within me. *Let the sorceress stay away. Let us be gone when she returns.*

I think Ciarán knew. His eldritch abilities were exceptional. As the first dawn light touched the leaves of the rowans, a small form slipped out the cottage door, a hooded cloak concealing his bright hair. He moved across the open ground as swiftly as a creature evading predators, which, in a way, was exactly what he was. I glanced at the father's face, just once, and saw the glint of tears. The nobleman squatted down as the child approached us where we stood under the trees. Ciarán stopped two paces away, a tiny, upright figure, preternaturally still.

I think the father was intending to re-introduce himself, to reassure, to explain quickly the need for silence and flight. After all, his son had been a baby when they last met.

'Papa?' The small voice was held quiet. The child understood that this must be covert.

'I've come to take you home, Ciarán.' The grimmest of warriors could not have kept his tone steady at such a moment. 'We must go now, and as quietly as we can. Shall I carry you?'

Ciarán shook his head. He put a hand in his father's, as if they had been parted only from twilight till dawn, and they set off side by side. At the rear, uneasily, came the two brothers and I.

It felt as if I scarcely breathed while we made our way out of the forest and along the lake to the place where their horses were stabled. I waited at a distance while they retrieved the beasts; the fewer people saw me in their company, the fewer could make a link if my mother came asking. They mounted. Ciarán was seated before his father in the saddle.

'Thank you,' the nobleman said gravely. 'I understand what you have risked for him. I am in your debt.'

'Ride safely,' I said. 'I don't suppose we will meet again. Goodbye, Ciarán.' I saw, looking at him, that while he was my mother's son, a child with more than his share of the uncanny, he was also a human boy of five, scared, excited, almost overwhelmed by what had happened. 'The blessing of Danu be always on you, little brother.'

He allowed himself a smile. 'And on you, Conri,' he said, and they rode away. Perhaps Ciarán's father did not understand that an ordinary human man could not break a sorceress's protective charm, however strong and determined he might be. But I understood, and I recognised in that moment that without the innate talent of the child himself, this rescue mission could never have been accomplished.

Lugnasad morn: the dawn of our wedding day. The cottage had been promised to a local family down on their luck; they had paid only a token sum for the use of it. The grandmother had traded her house cow for a creaky cart and an ancient horse. I doubted either would last as far as our destination, the place where these cousins lived. Nonetheless, as soon as the hand-fasting ritual was over we were heading north. We would make camp by the wayside, and our wedding night would be spent under the stars.

Lóch sent me out of the house while she put on her finery. It was a surprise, she told me with twinkling eyes. I had seen her gown already. In a tiny cottage, there is little room for secrets. But I kissed her and went outside anyway. We had a small supply of good hay we'd kept aside to give the horse a strengthening meal before we started out. I'd take that down to the field, not hurrying over it. By the time I got back Lóch would be ready.

One moment I was standing by the dry-stone wall, feeding the horse by hand. The next I was flat on my back, held immobile in the grip of a spell. I could not move so much as my little finger. I looked up and into my mother's eyes.

'Where is he?'

There was only one feeling in me, and that was terror — not for myself, not for Ciarán, who should be well away by now, but for Lóch. I didn't make a sound. I couldn't have told my mother what she wanted anyway. The charm she had set on me made every breath a mountain to climb. Speak? Hardly.

'Where is he, Conri? Tell me! *Vanished in the night,* his keepers said. A child of that age does not wander off on his own.' Her face was a spectral white, her eyes wine-dark. Her voice scourged me. 'Speak, Conri! What did you see? Who came? Which way did they go?'

I lay mute, staring up at her like a dullard who cannot understand plain words. With a very small part of my mind, the part I was able to shield, I willed Lóch not to come out and look for me.

'What is the matter with you, wretched boy? While you tend to horses like a feeble-minded farmhand, and no doubt waste day after day on your endless hummings and tinklings, my son has disappeared from under your nose! You fool, Conri, you stupid, treacherous fool! Tell me! You must know! Tell me who has taken him!' She relaxed her spell a little; she wanted me capable of speech.

If I lied, she would recognise it instantly. If I told the truth she would be off after them in the blink of an eye. My silence could win them precious time. I lay there, looking up at her, and spoke not a word.

'Come.' My mother clicked her fingers. Now I could move. I could move in one direction only, and that was after her. A good thing. She led me away from Lóch, away from the grandmother, away from the cottage and into the forest. She led me, a dog on an invisible chain, across the margin and into the Otherworld. We stood in the shade of the oaks, the sorceress and I, and in my mind I offered an apology to my little brother, and another to his father, and my regrets to the two hard-faced men who were Ciarán's half-brothers. I had not particularly liked them, but I had respected them. I had seen the bonds of family there, a phenomenon previously unknown to me. I hoped those bonds were strong enough to withstand a sorceress's fury.

'Very well, Conri.' My mother's face was calm now. She knew I could not run, not with her spell on me. She knew how easily I had bent and broken before her punishments in the years of my growing to a man. 'I can ensure you never set your fingers to the harp strings again. I can turn you into a twisted, crippled apology for a man. I can do this between one breath and the next. There is one way you can save yourself, and that is by telling me what you know. Now, Conri. Right now.'

My heart thudded like a war drum; my skin broke out in cold sweat. She didn't know about Lóch. Somehow, all summer long, she had been so engrossed in her new project, honing her human weapon, that she had taken her eyes right off me. She had not seen that I had fallen in love. She had threatened my hands; she had threatened my body. She had not used the threat that I most feared. Oh gods, if only I could be strong, both Ciarán and Lóch might be spared my mother's wrath.

I drew a deep breath. 'I know nothing,' I said. 'Nothing at all.'

I expected pain, and she delivered it. I put my teeth through my lip; I bloodied my palms with my nails. At a certain point I lost control of my bladder, ruining my wedding clothes. The sun rose higher. The Lugnasad ritual would be starting, and Lóch would be cross with me. I tried not to think of her. The most probing, the most penetrating charm my mother could devise must never find the small, safe place where my dear one was hidden, deep in my heart.

My mother must soon come to believe I had nothing to tell her, surely. I had never held out so long before. Always, eventually, I had delivered what she wanted once the punishment reached a certain level. Back then, I had not had Lóch to think of. Or my brother. I was starting to understand about family. As I writhed, I allowed hope in. *Soon she'll give up on me. She'll leave me here and head off to wherever she gave birth to him, and I can creep back over the margin. Lóch will forgive me. We can be wed tomorrow …*

The sun rose higher still. The harvest ritual would be over; the folk of the village would be celebrating with mead and games. Lóch would be upset, worried.

Through the tears and blood and sweat I saw a change in my mother's eyes. She became very still, so still that only a person familiar with all her moods, as I was, would have realised what fury possessed her. 'You know something,' she said. 'You have lied to me; you have held something back. I cannot wait any longer, Conri. Someone's taken my jewel, my treasure, my son. Not his father; I left that man fit for nothing but dribbling into his beard. It will have been one of the brothers. They'll have taken him back to Sevenwaters, thinking to hide him in the nemetons. Fools. Not one of them can outpace me, outride me, outwit me.'

I thought of Ciarán. Might not my exceptional little brother and his formidable kinsmen stand strong even against her? *Hold your silence, Conri.* I was almost beyond speech anyway. My lip was split; my jaw was on fire. Every part of me hurt. I was glad Lóch could not see me.

'I knew you'd never amount to much,' my mother said, and one elegantly-shod foot came out to deliver a casual kick in the ribs.

And then, ah then, when she might have headed off on her quest and left me lying, a pathetic bundle of rags and bloodied, filthy flesh splayed amongst the hard roots of a great oak, I had to open my mouth, didn't I? I had to speak. Fool. Bitter, hopeless fool. 'In the end,' I whispered, 'Ciarán will turn against you. He will defeat you. I know it.' And I did, though how, I could not have said. Not magic. Not the Sight. But deep in the bone, I knew.

Looking in her eyes, beyond terror, I believed she would kill me. I was wrong. I believed she would find Lóch and destroy her. I was wrong there, too. What my mother did was set a *geis* on me.

'Conri son of Oonagh,' she said, raising both hands so the full sleeves of her robe spread out like wings, the fine blue fabric rippling in the forest breeze, 'you will pay the price for your disobedience!'

I was starting to feel very odd, as if the aching in my joints, the nausea, the burning and stinging and tearing sensations had been only a prelude to the grand tune of the day. Now I itched all over. My skin began to sprout like a field of new-sown wheat, save that this crop was night-black. My lips pushed forward, tightened, hardened; my throat began to close up. My limbs shrivelled. *A twisted cripple of a man …* She was doing it. She would make me a man unfit to wed, unable to earn a living … *Lóch loves you, Conri. Hold onto that. She will love you no matter what kind of monster you become.* Gods! I was shrinking, changing, my clothing falling off me, my feet becoming … my feet becoming … claws …

'From this day forth, Conri, take the form of a raven! You will live in this bodily shape, but your mind will remain that of a man. Every moment you will understand what your life might have been, had you not chosen to defy me!'

Raven. I was a raven. A dazzle of colour assaulted my eyes; all was light. Tiny sounds came clear to me from high in the canopy: chirp, rustle, whisper. I turned my head one way and the other, and the dizziness made me stagger on my splayed bird-feet. No wonder my skin itched so. I had sprouted feathers.

'Fifteen years will you live thus, as a wild creature. When those fifteen years are done you will regain the form of a man. You'd best live solitary, Conri. For should any man or woman know who you are, should anyone at all recognise you as the man who dared thwart me, or as my son, or as Ciarán's half-brother, or as the fellow who used to play the harp in these parts, should anyone know you and call you by your name before those fifteen years are up, you will be condemned to stay in that form —' She paused, the word *forever* trembling on her lips. Perhaps the knowledge that we were kin stopped her; or perhaps she simply wanted to make this more entertaining, as is the nature of *geasa* generally. She was nothing if not inventive. 'Until a woman agrees to marry you in your bird shape,' she said. And after a pause for reflection, 'A woman of *that* family. The Sevenwaters family.' There was an unpleasant smile on her lips, a smile that told me how likely such a means of salvation must be. 'None of them would ever agree,' she added. 'Not after what I did to them. The shadow of it will hang over generation on generation. Make sure nobody knows you, Conri. Fly away, foolish musician, fly far, far away. *And never meddle in my affairs again.*'

> *Cursed to remain in raven form*
> *I left Lóch on our wedding morn.*
> *No word could speak, no story tell.*
> *My life became not heav'n, but hell.*

My mother could hardly have pronounced a crueler *geis* if she had known all about Lóch and our plans for the future. Fifteen years. In fifteen years' time, Lóch would be well past the safe age for childbearing. In fifteen years, her grandmother would be gone. For all that time I'd be incapable of providing for anyone but myself. Worse still, I had no way to explain to Lóch what had happened; why I had vanished on our wedding day with not a word, not a sign, not a clue. I could not even watch over her. There were only two people in the world, barring my mother, who I believed might recognise me in the form of a raven. One was my clever little brother. The other was the woman who loved me. If I were ever to be a man again, and if Lóch were ever to be my wife, I must keep out of her sight for fifteen years.

I stayed close, but not too close. And so I watched as it unfolded, the disaster I had brought down on the one I loved. The cottage was already promised; the cow was already sold. Lóch and her grandmother waited a while for me, relying on the hospitality of friends. The grandmother thought I had bolted, suddenly frightened of the responsibilities of marriage. Lóch refused to believe it. Some harm had come to me, she said; but I was strong and courageous, and eventually I would make my way back to her. I would have wept at that, if I could.

When others were growing weary of housing the two of them, they took up the old plan and headed north. I followed, unable to do more than keep an eye on them, but finding it impossible to leave. Lóch looked sad and tired; the grandmother was stoical, tending to the horse, finding firewood, saying little. I made an error, coming too close one day when I saw Lóch weeping by the fire, her head in her hands, her lovely shining hair lank and lifeless across her shoulders. She had taken off her boots. Her feet were red with blisters. Perched on a branch nearby, I was startled when she raised her head suddenly and looked straight at me.

'You again,' she said, and smiled. I was possessed by the longing to wing down and alight beside her, to feel the gentle touch of her hand, to offer what comfort I could. But I saw in her eyes that I had already come too close. My broken heart cracked anew as I spread my wings and flew away, away, where there was no chance that she would see me. I could offer her nothing at all.

Fifteen years. Lóch and I were seventeen when the *geis* was set on me; its term was almost our whole lives again. My imagination, trapped inside my bird form, ran riot with what could happen in such a time. I was a bard; I conjured up tragedies of a grand and entertaining nature. Well, I have said already that my tale was a sad one, and that much was true. Grand and entertaining, no. Just full of helpless, useless tears.

From this point on, it is short enough to tell. The early years passed. Lóch's grandmother died within two winters of my transformation, carried off by an old people's sickness, a cough, a loss of appetite, a quick fading. They had given up the search for their kinsfolk when the horse could not manage the distance, and had instead established themselves in a tumbledown hut abandoned by earlier tenants who perhaps feared the encroaching forest with its shadowy strangeness, its mysterious night time noises. Lóch eked out a living. She turned her hand to whatever tasks the season demanded, helping local farmers with haymaking or pear-picking or minding children. I could not leave her; it would have been like cutting out half my soul. I lived in the woods near her little house, making sure I saw but was not seen. I learned the habits of a wild creature. Sometimes it seemed to me I was losing myself, becoming more raven than man, until I saw Lóch coming home, a slight, purposeful figure, thinner now, the gentle curve of her cheek turned to a sharper line, her gaze watchful. On her own, living so far from other dwellings, she had an eye out for the perils one might expect in such a situation, and once or twice I saw her drive off a foolish fellow with her pitchfork. She was waiting for me. Four years on, five years on, she was still waiting.

I never saw my mother. I tried not to think of her, but bitterness grew in me with every passing season. I wondered if she had found Ciarán, or whether my silence, maintained at so great a cost, had won my little brother freedom and a place in the heart of his family. I felt some pangs of jealousy. Under the circumstances, that was not unreasonable. I began to understand how resentment and fury could drive a person mad. I did not want any insights into my mother's mind, but they came to me anyway. If I had possessed the means to destroy her I would have done it without a second thought. The wide-eyed bard who had fallen in love with a girl between firelight and water was no more. The raven was a different creature. With every passing year, some of my mother's darkness crept into my spirit.

You could imagine, I suppose, various endings to the tale of Lóch and Conri. I have said already that it did not follow the path of *happy ever after*. I watched her; she waited for me. By the time ten years had passed, Lóch had cleared a good-sized area around her cottage and established a garden, in which she grew not only vegetables for her own use, but a variety of herbs. She had taught herself certain healing skills, and received frequent visits from folk in search of simples.

My love had a circle of friends and was no longer alone. She had admirers, too, men whom I hated for the way they looked at her, but she refused every offer of marriage. I dared not come close enough to hear what she said to them, but I imagined it. *I will not wed. I'm waiting for my sweetheart to come home.* After ten years, folk must have found this more than a little odd.

It happened in summer, late in the afternoon. Lóch had been working in the garden, and I watching her from a position high in the boughs of an oak, well screened from her sight. I loved the lines and curves of her body in the practical homespun she wore. I could see how time was changing her, but for me she would always be the perfect creature I had seen that very first night, the fire on her face, the moon at her back, the woman who had looked at me and made my heart hers in an instant.

Lóch had a work table outdoors, a place where she could enjoy the sun while preparing vegetables for the pot or herbs for drying. I gazed down from my branch, and it seemed to me every movement she made was a poem, and every glance from her weary eyes was a song. She lost her balance, her ankle turning as she trod on a stone. The knife in her hand slipped. I heard her cry out, and I saw the blood flowing from her arm, a crimson stream, welling, spurting … Lóch snatched up a cloth, pressed it against the red tide. The cloth filled with blood, the stream dyed her gown, her face went ashen pale. She fell to her knees, too weak to hold the staunching rag in place. So quick, oh, gods, so quick …

I flew to her, bird-heart rattling in bird-breast, dark wings beating a panic song, shock driving the *geis* right out of my consciousness. I tried to help her. I tried, I tried. Where were my human hands that could press the cloth hard against the ebbing life? Where was my human voice that could shout for help? Where was my human strength, so I could pick her up and run to the nearest house? Gone, all gone. Nothing I could do would save her.

Lóch lay where she had fallen, her sweet features filmed with sweat, her skin pale as moonlight. With a fold of cloth held in my beak, witness of my futile attempt to stem the flow of blood, I stood by her right shoulder, my bird-eyes fixed on hers. *Beloved. Oh, beloved.*

She tried to speak; her lips moved, searching for words. I remembered the *geis* then, and cared nothing at all for it. Lóch was dying; I could not help her. I had failed her. If she was gone it mattered nothing whether I lived or died, whether I was bird or man. Without her I had no life. In that moment, all I wanted was that she look at me and know me, know that I had kept faith all these years, as she had. Know that I had not deserted her; know that I loved her still.

A film was creeping over her eyes; her breath faltered. *Oh, Lóch. Don't leave me. Don't leave me all alone. I love you. More than the moon and stars, more than the pure notes of the harp, more than the whole world. Lóch. Lóch, my love.*

She snatched a rasping breath. The dying eyes turned on me, sweet and steadfast as always. 'Conri,' she whispered. 'I knew you'd come.' And she was gone.

There was a long time in the wilderness. Heedless of danger, caring nothing if I lived or died, I came close to starving myself, and closer to killing myself by other means, but the fey part of me made that a harder task than it might have been. As for the *geis*, it was no longer of any significance. I'd be a bird forever. What did that matter? I had nothing. I had nobody. I was less a raven than a festering mass of bitterness and sorrow, and if I became a man again, I did not think I would be a man worth knowing. So I wandered, and the years passed. I never took a mate; I never kept company with other ravens, for wild birds shunned me, sensing my difference. All feared me: man, the predator. Hah! If only they knew what a helpless, hopeless creature I truly was. If Lóch had not loved me, she would by now be happily wed, with children half-grown. She'd have a man who could warm her bed and provide for her. Loving me had destroyed her.

I do not know what changed in me. Perhaps it was visiting the hill where once I had picked up a stone patterned in red and grey: fire and earth. Perhaps it was seeing a man with his two little sons, walking on a lake shore and laughing. I remembered that I was not quite alone. If my sacrifice and Lóch's had not been in vain, somewhere in the north I had a brother. Ciarán would be a man now, close to the age his sombre half-brothers had been when they came for him. I remembered the name Sevenwaters. I considered the bitter, cynical, hopeless creature I was now, and knew I could not bear to live on like this, summer after summer, winter after winter, for all the lengthy span allotted to a half-and-half like myself. If I did not manage to make an end of myself, I would live far longer than the lifetime of an ordinary man. So would Ciarán. I went to find him.

'Ready to go?' he asks now. So lost have I been in my reverie that the lesson is finished, the novices have departed without my noticing, and Ciarán is watching me quizzically, his travelling bag strapped up and ready in his hand. Today we head off into the forest for a few days' solitude. It is our habit to make these quiet journeys from time to time. Ciarán gathers herbs, prays, meditates. I keep him company, making myself useful when I can.

We've been together many, many years. His father brought him safely to the nemetons but died not long after, and Ciarán was raised by the druids. A choice was made to let the boy forget what little he knew of his origins. He grew up unaware that his father had been lord of Sevenwaters. In time, that proved costly indeed.

Ciarán became a fine man; a better man than I ever would have been. He had his own share of sorrows. Love drew him away from the druid path awhile. What our mother did to him and his sweetheart was crueller than the punishment she meted out to Lóch and me. Ciarán rose above it. My brother; my strong, clear-headed brother.

'Come, then,' he says. I fly to perch on his shoulder, and together we walk off into the forest of Sevenwaters.

AISHA

'Go,' my father said. 'Go and find out for yourself.'

It was fair enough. I was a woman grown, and though there were certain expectations I had not fulfilled — by my age, a woman was supposed to have a husband and children — my life so far had contained more than its share of adventures. I could always rise to a challenge. I was my father's daughter, wasn't I? He'd done both, the adventures and the family. It was family we were discussing now, the shadowy, mysterious part of it that was away to the northwest in Erin. I'd travelled to many places, but never there.

'I will,' I replied. 'And you can come with me.'

Father laughed, his eyes crinkling up. He had my smallest half-brother, Luis, on his knee and was whirling a wooden rattle. The baby reached for it, shrieking with delight. 'Me? I'm an old man, Aisha.'

In years, perhaps he was. He didn't look old, save for the touch of snow in his dark hair and those smile lines on his sun-browned skin. 'Is that what Mercedes says?' I asked, knowing my stepmother said nothing of the sort. Mercedes was a few years my junior: my father's third wife, and mother of his youngest children. Ours was a noisy, busy establishment that saw a constant stream of visitors, mostly folk from the village wanting Father's advice on matters of law or religion or the care of sick animals. He had become a father to all of them since we settled here. His seafaring days were done; in that sense, perhaps he was old, but there was a vigour about him like that of an aged olive tree, hardy, tough, his roots sunk deep in the land. And fruitful; the children kept coming. The place was full of toddlers and animals — Father had never learned to resist the pleading eyes of a homeless dog.

'Never mind that,' he said now. 'You go. Sail on the *Sofia* when Fernando next takes her to Dublin. You're an enterprising girl, Aisha; you can make your own way from there.'

'And what do I do when I get to Sevenwaters? March up to the front door and say, Good morning, I'm your — what, great-niece? Second cousin? Sorry my father couldn't come; it's only been forty years.'

'Closer to fifty,' Father said, lifting Luis up against his shoulder. 'Just as well I taught my children Irish. At least you'll be able to introduce yourself. Tell them your father's a doddering ancient who has trouble hobbling as far as the front door. Tell them whatever you like.'

I wondered, for the hundredth time, why the bonds of family had not drawn him home in all those years. With his ships loading and unloading in Dublin regularly, he could easily have gone. Sevenwaters was not so very far north of that port, provided one could negotiate the borders between Norse and Irish territories, which were under ongoing dispute. But while Father had a hundred stories of his boyhood, and a hundred more about heroes, monsters and warrior women, he never talked about what might have become of his kin since he last saw them.

'I don't want to know, Aisha,' he said, reading my thoughts on my face. 'Every time I got news, in those first years after I left, it was bad news. My brothers dying, one after another, all uselessly. The borders shrinking; war and madness. Besides, I like the sun. It's always raining in those parts. And I'd miss Mercedes and the little ones.' After a moment he added, 'I suppose Conor may be still alive — your druid uncle. It's been a long time. And my nephew may still be chieftain at Sevenwaters; he was only a lad when my eldest brother died. But they'll be strangers to you, despite the tie of blood.'

It was hard to think of my father's family as strangers. They were in the most enthralling of his stories, the one that told of a disaster that had nearly destroyed them all. It included a wicked stepmother — when I thought of Mercedes, this made me laugh, for my father's rosy-cheeked, smiling young wife was as far from that figure as I could imagine — and a transformation wrought by magic, six brothers turned into swans and saved only by their sister's courage and endurance. My father had been one of them. I knew those boys from the inside out. I knew the intensity of their anguish; I felt their terror; I understood their guilt. I knew them up till the point when the ordeal was over and my father, Padriac, who was the youngest of them, decided to walk away from Sevenwaters and never look back. And yet they were not real. They were characters in a story, like Cu Chulainn the great hero, or Emer who was turned into a fly. The notion of meeting them in the flesh felt very strange. They would be old now. But perhaps they were like Father. I only had to look into his eyes to see the boy there, the same who had once splinted the legs and salved the wounds of injured creatures in Erin, and who still did it here in Xixón, far from the shores of home.

'You must miss it sometimes,' I said. 'You must miss them.'

'My life is rich, Aisha,' said Father, patting his son rhythmically on the back. Luis was hungry; the rattle of pots and pans from the cooking area told me Mercedes was preparing a meal. 'I've made my home wherever I travelled. And you are your mother's daughter, my dear. A restless soul; an adventurer. So go, and go with my blessing. When you come back, I'll be ready to hear the tale.'

I owed it to both of them, to Father who had always trusted me, no matter how wild an adventure I attempted, and to Mother who had perished at sea while working as his first mate, to go ahead with the plan that had sprung from nowhere. Two months later, I was stepping off the *Sofia* in Dublin, where my general appearance caused bystanders to gawk and whisper behind their hands. What went relatively unremarked in Galicia was clearly the height of exoticism in this city of wheat-fair, pale-skinned Norsemen and slight, dark Irish. I'd offered to give Fernando a hand with the unloading, but he'd declined, saying I'd only attract crowds that would get in his way. So I wished him well and headed off on my own, telling him I'd pick up a lift home when next he made landfall here.

There were one or two incidents by the wayside. Not every traveller in Erin is respectful of womenfolk, but I'd had plenty of practice at fending off advances of various kinds; there were years and years of dented skulls and bruised privates behind me. At a wayside inn I arm-wrestled a local farmer for a jug of ale and ended up sharing it with him and his friends. I didn't talk any more than I needed to. Demonstrating my fluent Irish would only mean all sorts of questions, and idle curiosity bored me. With Father's map in my head and a sailor's sense of direction — I'd captained the *Sofia* for Fernando more than once — I headed north to Sevenwaters.

I reached the edge of the forest at dusk. I had seen plenty of forests in my time, back home in Xixón and in other parts of the world on one voyage or another. Hot, damp forests full of bright birds and howling creatures. Cold, crisp, empty forests where snow bent the boughs of fir and spruce, and bears lay in winter dreams. This was less forest than blanket of darkness, lying over hill and valley in mysterious, shadowy silence. I decided to camp overnight and go on by daylight. It wasn't just the brooding quiet of the place, the sense of its being somewhere out of ordinary time and space. There were guard posts to north and south, well-manned even at this hour. Likely the whole forest was ringed by them. I didn't suppose those guards would put an arrow through me first and ask questions later. But they might well try to apprehend me. I hadn't decided yet how I would introduce myself to my father's long-lost family, but I knew I didn't intend to walk into their hall with a spear shoved in my back and some man at arms announcing that he'd caught me spying.

It was a cold night. I made no fire, but slept rolled in my blanket. Soon after dawn I packed up and set out into the forest. Somewhere in these woods there was a lake, a big one. Beside the lake was a keep, and in that keep lived the family of Sevenwaters, my father's kin.

Father had warned me about the paths through this forest, both directly, when he knew I was coming here, and indirectly, through the stories he'd told over the years. I'd never been sure whether to believe the implication that eldritch folk made their homes here alongside the human ones. In the tales there were two other races of people in Erin, both of them ancient. Understanding between the various groups was quite unusual in other parts of the land, but at Sevenwaters they all lived more or less side by side. When a person told tales about cows with wings and giant serpents that spewed up precious stones, it did lead one to assume that he was given to flights of the imagination. On the other hand, Father was the most practical of men, whether removing a thorn from the foot of a dog or talking over trade matters with Fernando and me. Besides, there was one especially uncanny story in his past that I had come to believe must be true, the one about him and his brothers being turned into swans. So perhaps he was right about the paths through the Sevenwaters forest changing of their own accord from one day to the next. It was to keep out strangers, he had explained. Many was the traveller who had gone astray somewhere in this tangle of pathways, only to come to light years later as a little pile of bleached bones. But I would be all right; I would find the way. I was family. For me the paths would lead where they should.

I considered this as I headed further into the dense and murky woods. It was all right in theory. The difficulty lay in the fact that I looked nothing like Father. Since stepping off the *Sofia* in Dublin I had seen no woman, and few men, as tall as I was; I had seen nobody, male or female, with skin as dark as mine. My features were not those of an Irishwoman. I took after my mother's side of the family. How would these uncanny forces — supposing they did exist — pick me out as my father's daughter when all the outward signs suggested I was as out of place here as an olive in a bowl of grapes? It was supposed to be less than one day's walk from the forest's edge to the keep of Sevenwaters, depending on where one started. Since I was heading for a lake, I'd find a stream and follow its course. I'd watch out for markers — rock formations, notable trees, ponds, clearings — and with luck I would reach my destination before nightfall.

It was a pleasant enough walk, for the main part. The woods were not as empty as they'd seemed in that odd dusk light, but full of birds and other creatures about their daily business. I saw no uncanny folk, but I spotted a deer, a wild pig and a wary fox. I found a stream and, after refilling my water skin, I followed its course as best I could. Here and there the waterway lost me, gurgling among tumbled rocks netted with brambles. The day passed, and the massed trees stretched ahead. By morning light I had admired the myriad greens of their foliage, the patterns of sun and shade, ever-changing; I had enjoyed walking to the sound of rustling leaves and calling birds. Now, in late afternoon, they were starting to look more like guards, an army of dark trunks blocking my way. I found I was longing for open ground.

I walked on, sure I was heading due west, yet uneasy, for there was a sameness about this row of leaning beeches, this stone somewhat resembling a toad, that suggested I had passed this way before. I was not the kind of traveller who walked in circles. There was a true direction in me; I had never been lost. Under my breath I uttered one or two choice epithets, keeping to Galician, though with only the poxy trees to hear me I might just as well have cursed in Irish. This was ridiculous. If I didn't find a better path soon I'd be spending the night in here. All right, I had a blanket, I had food and water, I had slept in far less comfortable places in my time, but I grappled with the sense that the forest of Sevenwaters was shutting me out. Or in.

'My grandfather was a chieftain of Sevenwaters,' I said aloud, finding myself faintly ridiculous. 'If I can't come in, who can?'

I expected no reply and I got none, save for the mocking *kraak* of a raven as it flew to alight on a branch nearby. The creature turned its head to one side, assessing me. Was I imagining things, or did it have a particularly inimical expression in its eye? As I looked up, it flew a short distance away, then alighted and peered at me again.

'Would I trust a bird with eyes like those to show me the way?' I muttered. 'Not for an instant. But as I'm headed in that direction anyway, by all means tag along.'

The light was fading fast. The thick canopy and the filtered sun had made me misjudge the time of day. With hardly a clearing to be found and the broad, leaf-strewn paths of this morning completely absent, the wise choice would be to make camp the next time I came upon some rocks that might provide shelter, and accept the fact that I would not reach the keep today.

There were, of course, no rocks. I was starting to believe Father's stories now, and wishing I had asked him for better directions. As for the wretched raven, I didn't like the look of it at all. It seemed altogether too knowing for a wild creature, and it wouldn't go away.

'Rocks,' I said, slithering down a muddy incline bordered by stinging nettles. 'An outcrop, perhaps a cave, that's what I want.' I eyed the bird with distaste, wondering if ravens made good eating. I suspected this one's flesh would be as tough and bitter as the look in its eye. I slid to a halt, digging my walking staff into the ground. 'Or then again …'

We had emerged at the edge of a small, circular glade. It was a patch of light in the dark forest, and in its centre the stream flowed into a neat pool circled by flat stones. A campfire burned on the stones, and by it sat a man, cross-legged. His back was as straight as a child's, his hair a striking dark auburn, his eyes a peculiar shade of mulberry. He looked around my own age, and was clad in a long grey robe. As I stood at the edge of the clearing, waiting for him to speak, the raven winged its way over and landed on his shoulder. I winced, imagining those claws digging in.

The red haired man rose gracefully to his feet. His garb seemed that of a religious brother of some kind, though I saw neither cross nor tonsure. All he wore around his neck was a white stone strung on a cord.

'Please, warm yourself at our campfire,' he said courteously. 'We see few travellers here. Have you lost your way?'

I moved forward, feeling not only his gaze but that of the bird. 'Thank you,' I said. 'Lost my way? Not exactly.' I studied the pair more closely, wondering if there was anything uncanny about them. I wasn't sure how one could tell. There was a neatly strapped bundle over near the trees and a blanket spread out, as well as cooking gear and some other items — corked jars, a little book, a bundle of rowan twigs, a sheaf of herbs. I saw no weapons. 'I'm heading for the keep of Sevenwaters. It can't be far from here.'

'Less than a mile as the crow flies,' the man said. 'But dusk is close. I'd advise you to wait until morning, then we can walk on with you and show you the way. You're welcome to camp here, if you wish.'

Not a word about who I was or the nature of my business. I liked that. On the other hand, it showed a remarkable lack of caution. What was to stop me from sticking a knife in the fellow's back and making off with all his worldly goods?

The raven gave a *kraaa*, which I interpreted as: *Don't flatter yourself, we can overpower you with our eyes shut*, or something to that effect. I shot the bird a look of dislike. 'Unusual pet,' I commented, putting down my pack and lowering myself to sit beside it.

The red-haired man almost smiled. 'Fiacha is an old friend,' he said. 'Far more than an ordinary raven, as you can perhaps see for yourself. My name is Ciarán.'

That startled me. I scrutinised his features anew, seeking signs of my father. This was a handsome man, strong-jawed, the planes of his face well-defined, the eyes deep and watchful. Ciarán. There was a Ciarán in the tales of family, a half-brother born of a sorceress, who had been spirited away from home and had not returned until after my father was gone. The sorceress had been one of those others, the ancient races I was not quite sure I believed in. If this was the same Ciarán, his mother had come close to destroying my father's family. But no, this could not be the man; he was far too young.

'I'm a druid,' he said. 'The nemetons where my kind live and work are not far from here. Fiacha and I are spending a few days alone in quiet meditation. A respite from my teaching duties. I am responsible for the novices.'

'Then I've interrupted your time alone.'

'As to that,' Ciarán said, organising a cook pot, water, beans, herbs with a deftness obviously born of long practice, 'my visions have been troubling. I want no more today. I would welcome your company, if you wish to remain with us.'

I asked no questions until the supper was cooked and we were eating it by the fire. Night was falling in the forest around us; birds sang their last farewells to the fading light. The raven, Fiacha, sat hunched on a tree stump nearby, his unnerving gaze following every mouthful from bowl to fingers to lips. If he was hungry, why didn't he fly off and catch something?

'Do you know the Sevenwaters family well?' This seemed a safe way to broach the subject.

Ciarán glanced up from his meal. 'I do.'

'You mentioned that you are a druid. Can you tell me if there is a man called Conor among your number? He would be old, over sixty by now.'

A silence. Then he said, 'Why do you ask?'

There seemed no particular reason to hold back, so I came right out with it. 'My father's name is Padriac. He's Conor's youngest brother. I would be interested to meet Conor, and perhaps the current chieftain and his family. That's if I get to the keep. Father told me family can find their way in this forest, but I can't say it's been easy.'

'You are Padriac's daughter?' A smile of delight and wonderment transformed Ciaran's sombre features. 'Then you will most certainly find your way. In any case, Fiacha and I can guide you to the keep, as I said earlier. No hurry. For now, let's enjoy our meal and the quiet of this place, and perhaps exchange a tale or two. I did not know your father. He left Sevenwaters when I was an infant. But Conor is still here. My brother is chief druid, in excellent health despite his years, and much respected. He will most certainly want to meet you.'

My mind was working hard. *My brother.* 'Forgive me,' I said, 'but does this mean you are indeed the same Ciarán who was born to the chieftain of Sevenwaters and a … a …' I seldom found myself short of words, but this was delicate.

'I am that Ciarán. My father was Colum of Sevenwaters. My mother was one of the Fair Folk.' He spoke plainly, as if this knowledge were in no way extraordinary.

It went some way to explaining why he looked so young. Father's tales had taught me the Tuatha de Danann were a long-lived race and kept their youthful looks into old age. Observing the calm expression on Ciarán's face, the relaxed, graceful hands as he passed me a chunk of bread, a wedge of cheese, I considered the likelihood that along with her longevity he had inherited his mother's facility for magic. A druid. Were druids something akin to mages?

'You spoke of visions,' I said. 'What kind of visions?'

'It is part of our discipline to practise the use of still water — a scrying bowl, or a pool — for this purpose,' Ciarán said. 'We may see past or present; we may see a possible future. We may be shown what might have been. Or nothing at all. Some folk have a latent ability. Several in the family have a strong natural gift. We do not always use water. Images may be present in the smoke from a fire, or we may see them after fasting, a vigil, a time of bodily denial. Unspoken truths may visit us in sleep.'

I shivered. He sounded so matter-of-fact. I watched him as he passed a slice of cheese to Fiacha, who snatched it from the outstretched fingers and swallowed it in a gulp. 'How long has the bird been with you?' I asked.

'Long. Fiacha has seen me through many trials. Folk think him ill-tempered. He has his reasons for that. Time after time he has aided me in the cause of good. He has worked with me to battle the forces of darkness. And indeed, to quell the darkness within. Our mother … never mind that. Let us exchange a tale or two. May I know your name?'

'Aisha. It is a name from my mother's country. He brought her here once, he said, when his sister was dying. But they didn't stay. Father was changed by what happened to him when he was young. He wanted to live his own life, far from this place.'

Ciarán nodded gravely. 'I, too, went away,' he said. 'I made a choice to return. I have my brethren. I have the family, though I do not dwell among them. I have Fiacha. I have my memories and my visions.'

He was a man of such controlled demeanour, it was only the slightest break in the mellow tone, the very smallest change in the eyes that hinted at suffering, regret, a depth of sorrow I had no hope of understanding. As Ciarán spoke, Fiacha flew across to perch on his shoulder again, almost as if offering comfort.

'Clearly your father wed and had at least one daughter,' Ciarán said, entirely calm again. 'Is he in good health?'

I grinned. 'Robust health. Thrice married, and a father of many children, the newest a babe not long out of swaddling. Beloved in his home village; owner of a significant trading fleet that is mostly managed by my half-brother these days. My stepmother is a woman of four and twenty. She loves Father dearly. He made a good life for himself.'

'And taught his children to speak Irish like natives.'

'He said the stories wouldn't sound right in Galician.'

We sat in silence for a while. I felt suddenly edgy. I had plenty more questions to ask, but it seemed to me there was something unspoken, something weighty that the druid knew, and the bird knew, and I didn't. I held my tongue. Ciarán had been perfectly courteous and open, and there was no reason at all to suspect him.

'What of you, Aisha?' he asked. 'Have you a family of your own, a husband, children?'

Kraaak. The sound conveyed a desire for the conversation to take some other turn, or to cease so we could all sleep.

'It's uncanny,' I murmured. 'That bird speaks a language I can almost understand. No, I have neither. I've never felt the need or the wish for a husband, and as for children, the kind of life I lead hardly has room for them.' As I spoke, I thought of Mercedes and her many sisters, cousins and aunts. At all times of day and night there tended to be a bevy of women in our house. If I had produced a child or two, there would have been no shortage of doting substitute mothers. 'I don't really want them,' I said, making myself be honest and thinking, not for the first time, that darkness and a campfire encourage all manner of confidences between strangers.

Ciarán nodded. 'A child is the most precious gift of all,' he said quietly. 'But you cannot understand that until you have one of your own.'

This idea was familiar from the little talks I got from Mercedes and her kinswomen, lectures that had become increasingly frequent as I approached the age at which I might as well give up thoughts of motherhood. I had not expected it from Ciarán. Nor had I expected him to say it the way he did. 'But you're a druid,' I blurted out.

'I was not always a druid. Nor was Fiacha here always a raven.'

This was getting beyond the acceptable borders of oddity. 'What did you say?'

'That is a tale for another day,' Ciarán said. 'Let us have something else instead. Has your father told you the saga of the clurichaun wars?'

He was an expert storyteller. While I had heard the clurichaun tale before, Ciarán had his own version, droll and witty, and I was soon captivated. I told a tale in my turn, about a princess and a drowned settlement. He told another, and all too soon it was time to settle by the campfire for the night. I fell asleep still smiling. The raven roosted above us, a deeper patch of shadow.

The next day we struck camp and walked on, and as we walked we told more stories: the voyage of Bran, Cruachan's cave, the dream of Aengus. The prince who kept his dead wives in a closet; the spurned lady left to starve in a tower, her ghost thereafter scratching at the window every night and keeping the household in terror. Fiacha punctuated our tales with his hoarse cries. Time was not softening his evident disapproval of his master's new travelling companion.

Dusk fell on the second day, and we still had not reached Sevenwaters.

'I thought this was only one day's walk,' I said as Ciarán stopped in a comfortable camping spot. A rock wall sheltered a patch of level ground, and there was a pool among stones, much like the one by which we'd camped the previous night. 'I'm sure that's what my father said.'

'Sometimes it takes a little longer.' Ciarán was calm. Out came the cook pot, the bunch of herbs, the flint and tinder. 'Could you gather some dry wood while we still have light?'

I busied myself collecting fallen branches and piling them nearby. I watched him building a fire, and after a while I asked, 'Will we reach Sevenwaters tomorrow, do you think?' He seemed a good man, but I could not help being a little suspicious. If he had told the truth about his identity, he was half fey. What if he was guiding me, not to the home of Father's kinsfolk, but down one of those tracks spoken of in the tales, leading to the Otherworld? There were stories of people getting trapped in that uncanny realm for a hundred years. I might relish adventures, but the prospect of such a journey was a little too much even for me.

'Perhaps,' Ciarán said in answer to my question. 'If not tomorrow, then the next day. If not the next, then the one after. Are you in a hurry, Aisha?'

'No,' I said. 'But I'm perplexed. *One mile as the crow flies*, I think you told me. It seems you've chosen quite a circuitous path, Ciarán.'

He smiled. 'The path is as long as the stories we tell,' he said. 'It is as long as it needs to be. Don't concern yourself; we'll reach our destination at the right time.'

I could think of no appropriate answer. It would be sheer folly to strike out on my own; I had no choice but to stay with him. The evening passed. We sat by the fire and told more tales, wondrous, grand, surprising and silly in their turn. I achieved a minor miracle by coaxing Fiacha down from his branch and onto my shoulder. I could feel his claws through my woollen tunic.

'Come, then,' I murmured, holding my lure — a piece of the cheese the bird so liked — between my fingers. 'Come on, I'm not so bad.' The raven sidled down my arm, step by cautious step. I thought he would snatch the prize and fly off, but I kept talking to him quietly, as I had seen my father do with wild creatures, and he stayed there long enough to eat the morsel from my fingers. I reached slowly across with my other hand; brushed the soft breast feathers. The bird fixed his bright gaze on me, and my heart went still with the strangeness of the moment. Then, in an eye-blink, he was gone back up to his perch.

'Ciarán?'

'Mm?'

'Do I remember correctly, that you told me Fiacha was not always a raven? What did you mean by that?'

'Ah.' My companion settled himself more comfortably by the fire.

'I imagine your father has told you many tales of Sevenwaters. You know what I am and can guess, perhaps, what my mother's line has given me. I could tell you a story, a remarkable and sad one. You might find it easier to believe if I did not use words, but showed you instead.'

My skin prickled. 'Showed me? In pictures?' I could not imagine how this might be achieved by night, in the middle of the forest.

'In a vision. If you are open to it, I can reveal the story to you in the water of this pool. Indeed, that would be entirely apt, since the tale begins between firelight and water.'

Fiacha ruffled his feathers, moving restlessly on his branch.

'Why is he doing that?' I asked, eyeing the bird. 'Does he not want the tale told? Or is he merely complaining of hunger or a sore belly?'

'He thinks he does not want the tale told,' Ciarán said, apparently taking me quite seriously. 'But there is no doubt that this is the time to tell it. I would guess you are afraid of very little, Aisha. There is no need to fear this. The challenge lies not in the tale itself, but in the choice it reveals.'

'A choice for whom?' I was intrigued. I had always prided myself on meeting whatever challenges came my way.

Ciarán did not answer my question, but moved to kneel by the pool, stretching out a long hand towards me. 'Will you try it?' he asked. Fiacha turned his back on us. He could hardly have made his disapproval more plain. 'You'll need to sit beside me, here, and keep hold of my hand. Fix your gaze on the water, and you will see what I see. It may take some time. Be patient.'

It did not take long at all. Images formed on the surface of the pool and in its depths, and while I held Ciarán's hand I could see them quite clearly. I thought I could hear voices, too, though here in the glade all was quiet. Perhaps they spoke only in our minds. It was indeed a strange tale, and a sad one: a big brother and a little brother; a malevolent mother and a courageous father; true love turned to sorrow and loss; an ingeniously cruel curse. It was a tale that fitted neatly around the one I already knew of Sevenwaters, the story of the Lady Oonagh, who wed my grandfather and turned his sons into swans. Conri's was a tale fit to bring a strong man to tears. When it was done, and the pond showed no more than a ripple or two, we sat for some time in complete silence. Glancing at the bird, trying to imagine what might be in his thoughts, I met a glare of challenge. *Don't you dare feel sorry for me.* It came to me that I had been told this tale for a purpose.

'A choice,' I said flatly. 'You're offering me the choice to marry a raven.'

Ciarán stretched his arms and flexed his fingers; he had become cramped, sitting so still to hold the vision. 'Offering, no. Setting it before you, yes. I thought it just possible you might consider it.'

'No man would want a wife who wed him out of pity,' I said.

The raven — Conri, if it was indeed he — gave a derisive cry. The sound echoed away into the darkness under the trees.

'Is it pity you feel?' Ciarán asked.

'For the bird, no. He's a wary, prickly sort of creature, and I wonder what kind of man he would be, if it were actually possible to reverse this — *geis*, is that the word? — by going through with a marriage. Who would perform such a marriage, anyway? What priest could possibly countenance such a bizarre idea?'

'The one you see before you,' Ciarán said. 'Performing the ritual of hand-fasting is one of a druid's regular duties.'

I felt a chill all through me. He could do it; he could do it right now, tonight, and if the peculiar story proved to be true, I could free a man from a life-long hell set on him simply because he'd wanted to protect a child. And I'd be saddled with a husband I didn't want, a man who'd likely prove to be just as irritable and unpleasant as the raven was. I wondered if I had in fact fallen asleep in the forest, and would wake soon with a crick in my neck and the nightmare memory fading fast.

'What possible reason could I have for agreeing to do this?' I asked, then remembered something. 'Wait! Did you actually know I was coming? Did you guess who I was? He came to find me. Fiacha. He led me to you. Don't tell me —'

'Nothing so devious, Aisha. I did not know who you were until you mentioned your father. I had seen you in a vision, earlier, approaching this place. I sent Fiacha out to find you, thinking you might need help.

Perhaps some other power has intervened to aid my brother here, for your arrival seems almost an act of the gods.'

I thought about this for a while. Reason said I must give a polite refusal. A small, mad part of me, a part I recognised all too well, urged me to be bold, to take a chance, to do what nobody else in the length and breadth of Erin would be prepared to do. That impulse had led me into some unusual situations in my time. I'd never once failed to extricate myself safely. I considered the story itself and the odd bond between these two half-brothers. 'I have some questions,' I said.

'Ask them.'

'First — is it safe to speak his name now? To acknowledge that I know who he is?'

'Quite safe. That part of the *geis* died with his beloved Lóch.'

'Then tell me, how did you learn Conri's story, and when? Was it like this, in a vision?'

'Some of it was revealed to me in that way. But I knew already what had become of him. She told me. Our mother. There was a time when I went back to her. A dispute with my family drove me from Sevenwaters. There were aspects of our mother's craft I wanted to learn. She welcomed me, little knowing the depth of my loathing. She gloated over what she had done to Conri; she thought herself ingenious. It was another reason to destroy her.'

'She's gone, then?'

His mouth went into a hard line. 'She is no more.'

'Ciarán ...' I hesitated.

'Mm?'

'What she did to Conri — it was very long ago. Haven't you tried to undo the *geis* before? There must have been other unwed girls in the family over the years.'

He grimaced. 'It seemed too much to ask. As you can see, he himself has mixed feelings on the matter.'

'Can you ... can you communicate with Conri?'

'You mean speaking mind to mind, without words? Alas, no. We have an understanding; it has developed over the years and has served us well enough. But I cannot ask him what he wants, Aisha.

I can only use my own judgement. He needs to do this. And I want it done. He's my brother, and I owe him. I cannot put it more simply than that.'

'Then why now and not before? If it seemed too much to ask those other women, why is it all right to ask me?'

Ciarán regarded me with his dark mulberry eyes. 'You seem … formidable,' he said quietly. 'A woman travelling all alone with perfect confidence; a woman of wit and intelligence, balance and integrity. Strong; brave; whole. If anyone can do this, I believe you can.'

'You don't even know me.'

His lips curved. 'You think not? We've exchanged many tales as we walked, Aisha. We've passed through the forest of Sevenwaters together. Besides, I am the son of a sorceress; I have abilities beyond the strictly human. I believe my assessment of you is accurate. If I did not, I would never have suggested this course of action. Would I trust my brother's future to a woman who was doomed to fail?'

The situation was nothing short of ridiculous. I considered the possibility that Ciarán was actually completely mad, one of those wild men who are supposed to wander about the woods and commune with the trees, and that the next thing he might do was strangle me or have his way with me, or both.

'Why do you smile?' he asked.

'I'm wondering what he's like now,' I said. 'Conri. In the vision he was just a lad, barely become a man. He hadn't even —' I broke off as a new thought struck me. Conri had been transformed into a raven on his wedding day. If I did what Ciarán wanted, I'd be acquiring a husband who was not only elderly, but also inexperienced in the art of love. The prospect hadn't much to recommend it. 'There would be rather a large gap between our ages,' I said. My mind quashed this objection instantly with an image of Father and Mercedes dancing together by lantern light. Tenderness. Passion. Complete understanding. A pang of some hitherto unknown emotion went through my heart. Longing? Yearning? That was crazy. My life was a good one, a complete one. I did not need this complication.

'He was a goodlooking boy,' Ciarán said. 'He's likely to be a well-made man. And he is the same kind as I am: my half-brother. I expect that in physical appearance Conri will seem no older than five and thirty.'

'And he'll come complete with an ill temper and a load of bitterness on his shoulders.'

'It's not as if there's been no cause for that,' said Ciarán mildly. 'And once he is a man again, it may change. You could change it, Aisha.'

'And if I can't bear the fellow?'

'A hand-fasting can be made for a finite period. A year and a day. Five summers. Whatever is deemed appropriate.' After a moment, Ciarán added, 'I must be quite honest with you. To be sure of meeting the requirements of a *geis*, one might need to make permanent vows.'

'I need time. Time to think.' By all the saints. Was I actually considering this? What had got into me?

'Of course.' Ciarán looked as if he'd be quite content to sit here by the fire all night if necessary. 'You'll be tired,' he added. 'Take all the time you need. He's waited many years; a little longer can make no difference.'

A little longer. Or much, much longer. If I said no, Conri might be condemned to stay in bird form more or less indefinitely. The raven seemed bitter and warped. What would he be like in another twenty years? I began to realise what a patient man Ciarán was. A good brother. They both were.

'You may prefer that we lead you straight to the keep in the morning,' Ciarán said now. 'I can introduce you to Sean and his family: his wife, two unwed daughters and a very small son. And Conor; I could take you to meet him.'

There was something he wasn't saying.

'But?'

'It just occurred to me,' Ciarán said with unusual hesitancy, 'that if we performed the hand-fasting *before* you went to meet the family, your explanations would be much easier. You arrive with your husband, the two of you receive a delighted welcome. Conri is accepted as a member of the family without question. There would be no need to speak of his past or of his parentage. It seems you have travelled widely, Aisha, and met many folk from different lands. The fact that you were wed to a man of Erin would hardly provoke questions. Appearing as a single woman travelling alone, then suddenly acquiring a husband more or less from nowhere, surely would.'

'Do these people know about Fiacha?'

'They know him only as a raven.'

I stared into the fire, trying to imagine how it would be to walk into the keep of Sevenwaters as a married woman. I could not picture it. Instead, I saw young Conri facing his mother, holding his nerve against the onslaught of her cruelty. That boy with the lovely voice, losing himself. And the raven by Lóch's side, watching her die.

What Ciarán had just suggested would be too much for Conri. It would be too soon. Once the transformation was done, he'd need time, space, quiet. I'd seen the way Father tended to abused animals, how he gentled them, waiting until they were ready to take the first steps forward. Gentle was not a word folk used when describing me. But I supposed I could learn.

'If I agreed to this,' I said, 'I wouldn't take him straight to meet the family. It's been a long time for him. We'd be best on our own awhile. He needs to mend. Until that's begun, he should see only you and me, I think. I know how to fend for myself in the woods, Ciarán. All we'd need would be shelter and quiet, until he's healed.' Out of the corner of my eye, I saw that the bird had turned around. He was looking at me.

'You have the time for this?' Ciarán asked.

I had told Fernando I would catch up with him next time the ship came into Dublin. It could equally well be the time after, or the time after that.

'There's no point in agreeing to something if I'm not going to do it properly,' I said. 'I'd be foolish if I expected a man to step out of such an ordeal with no damage at all. And if I'm to be his wife, it's up to me to help him get over it, I suppose. I should make it quite clear' — I glanced over at Fiacha, who had gone so still he resembled a carven effigy of a bird — 'that I never planned to settle in these parts. That doesn't change. I can stay awhile. As long as he needs. Then he'll be coming back to Xixón with me. He should meet my father.' It was quite difficult to surprise Father; in that, he was like me. But I was sure, *Here's my husband. Not long ago he was a raven,* would startle even him.

Ciarán had gone rather pale. I think that up until now he had not given real credence to the possibility that I might say yes.

'I suppose,' I added, 'it's not so much a husband I'll be getting as an adventure.'

CONRI

My frail bird body shudders. I watch my brother as he readies himself for the hand-fasting ritual, and there's so much in me I think I might split apart. Lóch, sweet, lovely Lóch, forever lost. And this woman, this tall black woman with the clear eyes and strong jaw, a woman like a shining blade, a woman as unlike my sweetheart as anyone could be; why is she doing this? She almost frightens me. *Lóch, dear heart, I'm sorry. It should have been you by my side. Lóch, don't hate me for this.*

'Are you ready?' Ciarán asks.

I cannot answer, but the woman — Aisha, her name is — nods her head. At the last moment, she reaches up and tweaks a corner of her elaborate head-cloth. The cloth unwinds; a cascade of hair descends, black as night and glossy as silk. Even my ascetic brother gawks at her. Suddenly, despite her height, her garb that might be a man's — long tunic, woollen hose and boots — despite the strength and challenge in her gaze, a warrior's look, Aisha is all woman.

She turns her dark eyes full on me. 'Conri,' she says, quiet as a breeze in the grass, 'I'm sorry your hand-fasting cannot be as you once dreamed. I did not know your Lóch, but I am certain she would not want you to spend the rest of your life this way. I can never replace her. But I can offer you a new kind of life. I can offer my best effort.'

Sheer terror churns in my gut. I don't want this! Why would I want my life back without Lóch? If this works, what will I be, so many years on? A wrinkled greybeard with the mind of that young lad who thought himself man enough to wed and be a father? What if Ciarán speaks the words and I become a creature with a man's body and a bird's mind? What if I turn into a monster? I never asked for this, I never expected anyone to do it, I don't want it …

'Are you ready, Conri?'

I look at Ciarán's face, high-boned, steady-eyed, calm as still water. I do not look at Aisha; there is no need. I feel her presence beside me, strong as oak, fearless as Queen Maeve herself, beautiful as the keen flight of an arrow or the piercing cry of the pipes. I want this. I want it from the bottom of my heart. I want it as the parched earth wants rain. I want it as a man wants sunlight after long winter. I want it with every wretched, bitter, cynical corner of my body.

I cannot give Ciarán an answer, so I stretch my wings and fly to Aisha's shoulder. She flinches, then straightens, ready for the challenge. Her strong mouth softens into a smile.

'We're ready,' she says.

Ciarán paces steadily, casting a circle in the clearing. He greets the spirits of the quarters, asks the gods for a blessing, then moves to stand before us in the centre. We are on the stones between the campfire and the pool. Aisha and I face north, Ciarán south. The star-jewelled night sky forms our wedding canopy.

As my brother begins the hand-fasting, a deep stillness seeps through me, a peace I have seldom known before. It is something like the sensation a bard feels when a song is done; when the music lingers on the air and in the heart long after the final measure.

'Under sky and upon stone,' the druid says, ''twixt firelight and water, I ask you, Conri, and you, Aisha, to make your solemn vows of hand-fasting. Aisha, repeat these words after me.' The mulberry eyes meet hers and I feel the smallest shiver run through her body. I edge along her shoulder until my wing feathers brush her cheek, black on black. And she says it, phrase by phrase, word by sweet word, she says it.

'By earth and air, by fire and water, I bind myself to you. Until the stars no longer shine on us, until the earth covers our bones, until the light turns to dark, until death changes us forever, I will stand by you, Conri, my husband.'

She does not shiver now. Her voice is the note of a deep bell, strong and steady.

Ciarán draws a breath. Looks at me. His eyes are suspiciously bright. 'Conri, best of brothers. Repeat these words after me. *By earth and air, by fire and water …*'

Oh gods, oh gods … The change is quick. My heart has barely time to hammer a startled beat, my wings hardly manage to carry me down from Aisha's shoulder before my body stretches and lengthens and thickens, my features flatten, my vision alters with sickening speed, pool and flames, man and woman, stars and dark branches swimming and diving all around me. Stone under my cheek; stone under my chest, my belly, my limbs … a man's limbs.

Aisha is kneeling beside me; I feel her hands, sure but gentle on my back, my shoulder. I have forgotten how to use this body. I cannot move. *Repeat these words after me* … I struggle to my hands and knees, Aisha helping me. I think I might be sick. I am sick, retching up the meagre contents of my belly onto the stones. Aisha scoops up water, cupping it in her hands. I drink. The skin of her palms is lighter than the rest of her, the hue of fine-grained oak. Her fingers are long and graceful.

I stand. Her arm rests lightly around my shoulders, supporting me. I draw breath, open my mouth, utter a croaking sound.

'Take your time,' says my brother quietly. '*By earth and air …*'

I understand, through the nausea, the dizziness, the utter wrongness of this clumsy man-body, that the *geis* cannot be fully undone unless I can play my part.

'By … by … ah …' A paroxysm of coughing. The two of them wait for me, quiet, confident. 'By earth … and air …'

'Good, Conri,' whispers Aisha. 'You're doing fine.'

'By *fire and water*,' says Ciarán, and I see that he has tears rolling down his cheeks.

'By fire … and water … I bind myself …'

It comes more easily with each word. A harsh voice, for certain, no bard's honeyed tones, but a human voice. I stumble through the vow. I owe it to my brother for his long care and for his belief in me. I owe it to this woman, this stranger, to honour the sacrifice she's making for me. So, turning to look into her lustrous dark eyes and seeing not a scrap of pity there, only joy at the remarkable feat we've accomplished tonight, the three of us, I finish it: 'Until death changes us forever, I bind myself to you, Aisha, my wife.' *Dearest Lóch; goodbye, my lovely one.*

Ciarán takes a cloth strip from his belt. Aisha extends her right arm, I my left. We clasp hands, and my brother wraps the cloth around our wrists.

'By the deep, enduring power of earth; by the clarifying power of air; by the quickening power of fire; by the life-giving power of water, you are now joined as husband and wife. By the mysterious, all-encompassing power of spirit, you are hand-fasted until death separates you one from the other. I give you my solemn blessing, Conri, my brother.' He touches my brow with his fingertips and I feel a thrill of power run through me. 'I give you my solemn blessing, Aisha, my sister.' He touches her in her turn, and I feel her tremble.

My knees are weak. I'm still dizzy and sick, my eyes unwilling to accept the change. Aisha holds me up while Ciarán speaks the final prayers, closes the circle, then moves to add wood to the fire and get out his little flask of mead. My knees give up the struggle; Aisha only just manages to stop me from falling. She settles beside me on the stones, her arm around me in comradely fashion. It feels good.

Ciarán pours mead into cups. For a while, the three of us sit in utter silence.

'Don't look at me,' I say eventually. 'This was your crazy idea; yours and hers.' I glance from the sombre, pale Ciarán to the silent Aisha. Before either of them can speak a word, I burst into tears. I sob and shake like a child, my head clutched in my hands. Aisha kneels up and wraps me in her arms, cradling my head on her shoulder and humming under her breath. *Gods, oh, gods …* The worst of it is to be so helpless, so feeble, so unmanned before this woman, this extraordinary woman who surprises me at every turn.

'Weep now, Conri,' she says in a murmur. 'Weep for Lóch; weep for your young life lost; weep for what could not be. Weep all night if you need. Weep until those sad tears are all gone, husband. And in the morning, know the good gifts that you have. The most loyal of brothers. A wife who will stand by you forever and always tell you the truth. We will not long be strangers, Conri. Family, at Sevenwaters and in Xixón. When you are ready, we will go to meet them.'

Still the tears flow; I cannot stop them. This does not mean I do not hear her.

'The sunrise and the moonrise,' says Ciarán. 'The forest and the lake. The stars in the sky. The flight of birds; the secret paths of fox and badger. The company of friends. The wisdom of elders. The laughter of children; perhaps, in time, your own children.'

'We'll see about that,' Aisha puts in dryly, but there's a smile in her voice.

'A song by the campfire,' says Ciarán. 'The notes of the harp.'

That stirs me to speech. 'No,' I hiccup against Aisha's shoulder. 'Not that.'

'Hush, Conri,' says my wife. 'Hush, now. It's a long road ahead, and we must learn to walk before we can dance. I've one more thing to say to you.'

I manage a sound of query.

'You're a much finer specimen of manhood than I was expecting,' she tells me. 'I think it possible my father may approve.'

Ciarán splutters on a mouthful of mead; he's a man who rarely laughs. I lift my head. Before I can wipe my streaming eyes, Aisha's fingers come up and brush the tears from my cheeks, sweet as a mother tending her child. But different. Quite different.

'I might see if I can keep a sip of mead down,' I say in a whisper. 'Long time since I …'

'Here,' says Aisha, holding out the cup. 'Tomorrow is a new day. A new dawn.'

I can barely speak, but I must. 'This is a gift beyond measure,' I say, taking the cup. She knows I'm not talking about the mead. 'I'm not up to much just now, and I may never match it. But I'll do my best.'

Raven no more, I came to rest
Then set forth on another quest.
What might I be before the end?
Brother, husband, father, friend?

My brother's patience shielded me
And Aisha's courage set me free.
'Twas hope that saw me come at last
Out of the shadows of the past.

As I take up my harp again
I do not sing of death and pain.
In my song, love and courage rise.
These are the gifts that make us wise.

Afterword

'Twixt Firelight and Water

''Twixt Firelight and Water' ties in with my *Sevenwaters* series, of which the fifth novel, *Seer of Sevenwaters*, will be published in December 2010. Thanks to the remarkable longevity of the Tuatha de Danann, the story of Conri and Ciarán spans almost the entire time frame of the Sevenwaters books, which cover three generations of the (human) family. Two of the most commonly asked questions about the series are: What exactly is Fiacha? and: What happened to Padriac? This story answers both those questions. I was finishing ''Twixt Firelight and Water' when I was diagnosed with breast cancer. The story's triumphant happy ending reflects my vow to stay positive in the face of challenge. It's a tale brimful with courage, hope and love. The story's title comes from a folk song, 'The Tinkerman's Daughter', written by Mickey McConnell.

— *Juliet Marillier*

Isobelle Carmody is an award-winning speculative fiction author, with many books and short stories to her credit. She won a Golden Aurealis for Best Overall Novel for her book *Alyzon Whitestar* and an Aurealis award for Best Short Story for 'Green Monkey Dreams' from the short story collection of the same name. She received a White Raven and an Aurealis award for her book *Greylands*. She won the peace price and was joint winner of the CBC children's book of the year for older readers for *The Gathering* and she was shortlisted for both *Obernewtyn* and *The Farseekers* in her Obernewtyn series. She won the NSW Premiers prize for *Angel Fever*, a talking book of the year award for *Scatterlings* and an industry design award for *Little Fur* and *A Fox called Sorrow*, both of which she illustrated. She is currently working on the last book in the Obernewtyn series, *The Sending*. She lives with her daughter Adelaide and her partner Jan, who is a Jazz musician and poet, between their homes in Prague in Eastern Europe and on the Great Ocean Road in Australia.

The Dark Road:
An Obernewtyn Story

Isobelle Carmody

For Min

Hannah had walked so many days that it felt as if all else had been a dream, and yet she saw no end. The road stretched before her, dark as had been foretold, though not in any way she had imagined, and all around it sand flowed away to the horizon in every direction.

Sometimes it covered the road in a pale grainy tide, or mounded up over it in great mute stubborn dunes, so that keeping to it was not always simple. She must sweep the sand off it with a rough broom she had made up for that purpose out of her store of foraged wood, or burrow through sand hills, for while the road went straight for days at a time, it had three times turned inexplicably as if whoever made it had suddenly changed their mind about where it ought to go. Hard to imagine the mind that had commanded the making of such an indelible thing, being uncertain of its destination.

But the road was the product of a world dead and gone. The desert might not even have existed when it was made and the rare sudden turns might once have served some purpose that time had erased. There was a chilly thought, for it might easily be that the road would come to nothing. Certainly nothing seemed more likely than something, let alone a city.

Yet what else was she to do but go on? She had run out of water a day past, and food three days before that. If she turned back, she would not survive the journey without food or water. Nor would she survive much longer going forward without them.

As well as being hungry and thirsty, she was very weary and one of her knees had begun to ache in an ominous way. That was old age for you. Things wore out. She would have liked to stop, but dusk was the goal she had set herself and it was only middling afternoon.

You can always go on longer than you think you can.

That had been one of Mellow's sayings and it came to her now in his slow, soft voice. It was the first thing he'd said to her. She'd thought herself footsore back then when they had met on another road, long ago, though in truth she had been more heartsore than anything else. She had felt herself to be old then and to have walked far, though she had only been twenty-four and walked a mere sevenday or so and some of the time she had ridden in carts.

Mellow had come behind her, herding some goats up the road; coddling them along before him with soft taps of his stick. He had walked so quietly that when the goats had surged soft and warm and musky around Hannah, just as she slowed to a weary stop, she had thought them wild.

'Hello goats, I think I have to stop,' she said, made a bit stupid from the hot sun and the long walk.

'A body can always go on a bit further than they think,' their master had told her kindly as he stepped around her. 'You might stop here, only there is a place up ahead where there is a stream. I'll water the goats and then make a fire and tea there. You're welcome to join us.'

She was too weary to be haughty, and besides she felt foolish having been caught talking to his goats. The young herder did not press her to accept his offer, which would have put her back up and made her wary. He just nodded and went on in his slow quiet way, walking heavy and gentle at the same time like one of those greathorses they bred in Murmroth.

She'd had no intention of stopping. She was still angry-hearted at the way Evander had ordered her away, and sorrowful at the things his mother had said to her, for they had been too much of duty and the future as her mother's words had always been. But most of all she was aching because of her mother's letter burning a hole in her pocket. Too many contrary things to feel, to leave room for fending off the amorous advances of a stranger.

Almost an hour on, she found Mellow sitting over a nice little fire between the road and a stream. The smell of tea and bread toasting floated to the road and crooked an inviting finger at her. Stomach rumbling, she went over the damp tufty grass. He told her his name and asked hers, then matter of factly he asked if she'd a mug of her own or would share his. So she got out her blue mug. He took it from her hand.

'It's a pretty thing,' he murmured, admiring the glaze pattern with his fingers before filling the mug with tea. She blushed with pleasure, for while she'd never mastered the sculptor's hammer or chisel, nor been over much of a potter, her glazes and designwork had been a matter of pride.

Later, he told her he'd guessed it was her work by the way she held it. He said little and saw a lot, Mellow. He was the utter opposite of handsome, dark-haired, copper-skinned Evander with his unexpected two-coloured eyes and gloomy, complex moods. Mellow had soft brown floppy hair, shy, watchful, smiling eyes and a quiet gentleness that had won her friendship. But it was his kindness that won her heart, all the more because it did not stop at humans. He was kind to beasts in general, though he had a special fondness for goats, which many farmers sneered at keeping, calling them wayward and difficult.

After the tea and a bit of inconsequential talk, they'd put out the fire and gone on walking slowly up the road together. Mellow said very little, but his company was soothing and later that night when he stopped to make camp, she accepted his invitation to stop as well, for he was right when he spoke of the dangers of the road to lone travellers. Nevertheless she had stayed sitting up stiffly by the fire, saying she would not sleep. Mellow did not try to reassure her, but only said goodnight and wrapped himself peacefully in his blanket, telling her there was no need to set a watch as the goats would let him know if any thing came near, human or beast. He closed his eyes and soon snored softly. She watched his eyelids twitching after a while, and wondered what he dreamed.

Near morning, she called herself a fool and lay down and slept too, though not deeply and not well. When he woke her, they ate some porridge she made and went naturally on together. Three days later they reached the turnoff to Arandelft. Mellow said he must go that way and asked if she would want to come with him. He was visiting his brother's farm to drop two of the goats. He'd stay a night and be up to Guanette village just beyond the mountains by the next night. His own place was between Guanette and the Darthnor mine. In those days there was no Darthnor village and the miners camped out or went home to lodgings in Guanette.

But Hannah's mother had written of Guanette village and of the strange birds for which the village was named, and hearing it was just beyond the range of mountains ahead, she was eager to get there and so refused his offer. They'd taken a friendly leave of one another and she had gone on alone, finding to her surprise that she missed the farmer's unassuming companionship.

A few weeks later, she'd seen him in Guanette. She had taken work at an orchard, fruit picking, and had come to town with some of the other women to the Moon Fair. His face had lit up at the sight of her but there was no surprise in his expression. This told her that he had known she was there, which meant he had asked after her. The realisation made her blush but it was dark and he only asked if she had heard any news of her mother.

'She lived here for a while,' Hannah told him, grief making her curt, for she had truly thought to find her mother here. 'She was the beekeeper at Tarry's farm.'

'The old woman they called the moonwatcher,' Mellow said, eyes widening a little. 'I saw her a few times when I was a boy and roaming, She had a way with bees. You could have sworn they did as she bid them.'

'I was told that she left when she was ill,' Hannah told him. 'They would have kept her on but she would not stay when she could not do the work. She said the old ought to take themselves off like beasts do when they are near to dying. She was last seen heading up to the high mountains.'

'I can ask about for you,' Mellow offered gently. 'See if anyone took her in.'

'She would not have let them,' Hannah said.

Mellow let it go at that, and invited her to have some mead and pie with him. He had not offered meat from the spit because he remembered she did not eat it. One thing led to another and when the picking season ended, she went to work on Mellow Farm where there was a wheel and a kiln and a few tools left over from when there had been a pottery. It was a small farm but well cared for, and the beasts and men and women that worked there were all contented. Hannah found contentment among them, living out the simple rhythms and hard rewarding work of farm life. By the end of wintertime, she had replaced all of the rough pottery in the household and there was a little over to sell at the Moonfair so that she could buy cloth for a dress and a few bits and pieces she needed.

At the fair, she sold the pots and then walked with Mellow to see what was on offer. She spotted a cat and its kittens in the back of a Travelling Jack's wagon and slipped around into the shadows to croon at the pretty things. Mellow reached out and petted her hair as if he couldn't stop himself. And when she set down the kitten she was holding and turned to look at him they were eye to eye for she was tall. He was red and she felt her own cheeks hot, and that made her smile. Seeing it snipped some thread holding him back and with a soft sigh, he gathered her into his arms and kissed her tenderly, then with gathering hunger, until she found herself winding her own arms about his neck.

By the end of spring he asked her to bond. They did not speak of wiving or wedding in the Land. Love had been an unexpected gift, for she'd never seen herself as lovable. The only one who had loved her, other than Cassandra and her mother, who had both gone away, had been Evander, and his love had more to do with wanting what he could not have. He always wanted things that were out of reach, ever since he was a baby. But Mellow was how she had imagined her father might have been. All kind humility and gentleness; never seeing his own worth.

In time Hannah had given birth to the two daughters her mother had foreseen for her. Bonny and sweet they had been and all three of them had wept together when Mellow died of a fever after rescuing a goat from a half frozen bog in the bitter wintertime.

'Those goats,' Nell laughed through her tears. 'I always said he loved them to death.'

Hannah had been tempted to read the rest of her mother's letter then, but she resisted and in time both girls were wed, Nell to a farmer's younger son, Dace, who'd come to work Mellow farm after its master died, and Ivory to a clever dandy of a scriber from Arandelft, with a little house not too far from Mellow's brother's farm. Then came the first grandchild, Daisy. Looking at her, red and wrinkled and fresh as her mother had been before her, Hannah had a sudden memory of seeing her own mother gazing up at a moon hanging full and ripe over a red desert. She had not known she had developed the habit of gazing at the moon herself until Nell, seeing her looking up one night asked, 'Will you go up into the mountains when you are old, like grandmama did?' Nell had only been seven at the time, and a solemn and acceptant child, unlike pretty, demanding Ivory.

'Not while you and your sister need me,' Hannah had answered her solemnly.

In the years before Mellow died, Evander came several times to the farm. The first time, he had searched her out to apologise for the way they had parted. He told her that his mother had been taken by Gadfian pirates as she walked along the shore one night not long after Hannah left. He was now leader of the Twentyfamilies. He was only twenty-one but the weight of the responsibility had steadied him and ground the sharp edges of his arrogance. His apology had been sincere and she had liked the earnestness with which he swore to do all his mother had asked of him. He told her somewhat wearily that although the Councilmen had been forced to honour the safe passage agreement his mother had wrung from them for the sake of a rich annual tithe, they had contrived to turn it into a ban on gypsies having any permanent home.

'In the end it matters not,' he had said. 'We are looked upon with doubt and distrust by other folk.'

'What of Stonehill and all your mother's sculptings?' Hannah had asked, for Cassandra had possessed a true and rare gift.

'Many of the sculptures are still there simply because they would be near impossible to move safely, but no one lives in the buildings, for I have ensured that the place has an uncanny air. That stopped the treacherous Councilmen profiting from their perfidy. We call there often enough in our wanderings to tend the stone garden.'

'Do you know why your mother bargained so hard to turn you all into homeless gypsies?' Hannah had asked. It was a thing she had never understood.

Evander had given her a long look before telling her, with his new seriousness, that he did know, but could not explain it to her since it was connected to promises her mother had exacted of his when they were in the Red Land, before he was born. He was permitted to tell no one but the son or daughter that would one day take his place as Director of the Twentyfamilies gypsies. That hurt. Perhaps he saw it, for he told her he was to take a wife that summer, since he must have an heir. She had seen then that his feelings for her had not changed.

She told him quietly that children were a great comfort in life. She had Nell then, a quiet babe in arms.

'Your Mellow is a good man,' Evander said, when they were walking back to the house.

Hannah knew he saw that in the way he had always had of seeing those sorts of things, but she only said, smiling to take the sting out of it, that she did not need telling.

'Do you mind if I call in from time to time?' he had asked, but it was Mellow he looked at as they walked him to their front gate.

'Some of my neighbours say gypsying folk need watching, but you are Hannah's friend and as she tells it, your mother mothered her, so you come when you like. Pasture here in winter if it pleases you.'

'That's kind. We might,' Evander had said.

'He loves you,' Mellow murmured that night.

'Yes,' Hannah said. 'And I love you.'

That had been all that needed saying. They had always spoken the truth to one another and where something could not be said, nothing was said and that was all right, too.

Hannah had a sudden stabbing sorrow for the loss of such a man, and yet they had had a good long life together and he had died in his bed with his women weeping about him and his workers sorrowing honestly for him. The beasts had lowed and howled, too, though that was because of Hannah's grieving, which they felt, save maybe for the goats that had loved him.

Evander had come back several years running after that first visit, though his troop, as they now called themselves, never did winter. Then one day Evander's woman came riding up, red-eyed and stormy with sorrow, a little boy with two-coloured eyes like Evander's riding behind her. Both were as dark-skinned as Cassandra and her son and many of those who had made that first journey with them. She told Hannah that Evander had died after a fall from a horse. He had been taken on his own command to be buried on Stonehill, but his last wish had been for her to be told of his passing.

'He loved you,' the woman had accused.

'He was my brother and I loved him too,' Hannah had answered calmly, Nell hanging onto her skirt now and staring wide-eyed at the strangers.

'He asked if we would go on calling to see if you had any need,' the woman said, with less anger. 'This is his son, Rally. When he grows he will be D'rekta of the Twentyfamilies.'

'Come as you like,' Hannah answered, smiling at the little boy. 'Pasture in winter if you will.' Much to her surprise, the troop had come to Mellow Farm to winter the next year, and from time to time thereafter even when the Twentyfamilies came to have a wild and infamous name and gave up breeding with any but their own. But the visits stopped after Rally came of age and his mother died of plague one year when the troop was on the West Coast.

All that had been long ago when Hannah woke the morning after Daisy's tenth birthday, having dreamed of the yellow-eyed cat that Cassandra used to weave and send to play in her dreams, pretending she had nothing to do with it. In the dream, the cat was older like her, and he had lost one eye. It glared yellow as the cat told her in his imperious crotchety way that she must go to the high mountains, for it was time to walk the dark road.

'A dream,' she insisted to herself, but whether a dream or a sending from Cassandra, wherever she was, Hannah took out the letter and read it again to the place where she had been bidden to stop reading so many years before.

'Read no more of this, for your heart's sake,' her mother had written, 'until your first grandchild turns ten.'

Now, Hannah read on, and her heart sank, for this next section of the letter again bade her follow, which meant she must travel up into the high mountains. A chill flickered through her as she read that on no account must she remain at Mellow Farm, for death would come soon for her here if she did, and she would not be the only one it carried off. Hannah wanted to scoff but the words frightened her as she wondered what her mother had foreseen for her and her family if she stayed. To go up to the high mountains was surely another road to death, for it was common knowledge that the pass and the high mountains were tainted with deadly poisons left over from the Great White that had destroyed the Beforetimers world. But at least Nell and her family would be safe.

At length, Hannah came again to a place where her mother bade her cease reading, this time until she should see the Beforetime city at the end of the Black road. She was not tempted to read more. She folded the read and unread pages together and wiped the tears away before getting to her feet. She stretched her back to get the kinks out, dressed and took out the pack she had borne when she met Mellow. She put into it a few clothes, several water gourds, some food that would keep and then she pulled on her stout walking boots. Dace had gone out already to see to the milking and Nell who was quiet and watchful like her father, had observed her preparations in silence.

She cooked up a pot of porridge and served it with dried fruit and honey from Tarry's bees. That seemed an omen and Hannah slipped the rest of the pot, well corked, in a side pocket, for luck.

They ate together from the good bowls that had come out of Nell's last glazing, for she had taken up her mother's craft. Replete and finding no excuse to linger, Hannah rose with a sigh and let her daughter help her on with her pack. She had explained that she wanted to see if she could learn the truth of her mother's death. Maybe talk to someone who had seen her walking higher up. She would like to carve a stone with her name on the grave, if she could find it.

'Steer clear of that new settlement at Darthnor,' Nell said. 'They have a priest there now and he is full of fire and brimstone, Dace heard tell.'

'I will,' Hannah said, taking up Mellow's old goat staff and they walked side by side and hand in hand to the gate, Daisy holding Nell's hand and the two dogs flanking them, wanting to know where Hannah was going and if they could come.

'*Not where I go,*' she had told them silently. '*Stay and watch over Nell and Daisy.*'

Nell had given that sideways look she always got when Hannah spoke telepathically to beasts, making her wonder if her daughter, too, had a touch of the same ability. But Nell never mentioned it, and it was better not spoken of in these times with the Faction priests growing bold and striding about the towns with their bald heads and fierce scouring eyes, calling it a sin to be different.

Well it had been the cause of woe in her mother's time, too, from what she had heard, she thought, embracing Nell and Daisy. Nell had held her tight for a moment before releasing her and Hannah had known that the girl understood that they would not see one another again.

Was it any less cruel for a mother to go off and leave her children grown than to leave them when they were young? Hannah wondered as she set off. Her own mother had left her at Stonehill when she was a child and Hannah had suffered, for all Cassandra had loved and cared for her as a daughter. But as a woman, she understood that a mother might not always have a clear choice. And for all her own sorrow at leaving her daughters and her grandchild, a part of her rejoiced in setting off on an adventure and leaving all domestic duties behind her. No more washing dishes or mending clothes or making beds or listening to Dace lecture about the Councilman of Guanette.

Just the road stretching away into mystery.

Her mother had spoken of the Black road for as long as Hannah could remember. She even had a dim recollection of her arguing about it with the tall handsome bronze-skinned warrior who had fallen in love with Cassandra and wed her with the blessing of his blazingly beautiful sister, Aquilla. Luthen — that had been his name — had asked why his wife should travel the dark road that Hannah's mother foresaw for herself.

'I did not say that Cassandra will walk the Black road with me,' Mama told him in her cold way. 'Only that our paths have marched side by side for a very long time, and that they will not diverge in this land.'

'She is my wife,' Luthen said.

'She is more than that, and the son she will bear you and all the children your sister bears will serve the future even as Cassandra and I are sworn to do.'

At these words, Hannah reached up to touch the hand of her formidable mother, and when those rose-brown eyes looked down at her, she said, 'And me? Will I serve the future too, Mama?'

She had seen that her mother had been about to shake her head, but instead her eyes had widened and she had become so pale that Hannah had become frightened.

'Hannah?' Luthen had asked softly, all the anger gone out of him, for he and his sister and their people revered those who could see the future almost as much as they revered those who could commune telepathically with beasts. Luthen had not meant her in speaking that name, Hannah had known, but Mama, for their name was the same.

Mama turned back to the tall warrior and Hannah saw pity in her face. 'Your wife will travel from this land with me, Luthen. She will bear your son in a distant land, and leave him in that land when he is grown, to go to another. She will never return to any land where she has been before. Her way is always onward as she prepares for the one who will come. But she will never walk the dark road. It is my daughter who will walk on the Black road with me, as my husband did before me, and as the Seeker will do after us.'

'If Cassandra will go from this land with you, then I will go too,' Luthen said, softly.

'You will not leave this land with her,' Mama said, but only after Luthen had walked away.

Mama had spoken the truth. Luthen was killed in battle with the Gadfian sea pirates that plagued the waters about the Red Land only a few weeks later, and soon after Cassandra and Mama and Hannah and most of those that had come with them to the Red Land years before, had begun to prepare for the difficult sea voyage across the perilous Clouded Sea first to the Spit, where it was said that a wave of stone reared up from a seared black land, and thence to a distant part of that same land, where Mama said they would come to the place where she had been made. Obernewtyn.

Hannah had thought often of her mother's words to Luthen on the journey that followed. The thought of walking along a dark road with her grim, powerful mother thrilled her as much as it frightened her, and after they had been blown ashore on the Land she had waited eagerly for the day when her mother would tell her more of the journey they would make together. But she had never done so.

Hannah spoke of the dark road often enough, but only in mutters to herself, and those words had seemed part of a great and endless story her mother had been telling herself for as long as Hannah remembered. But it was Mama's story and all Hannah got of it were overheard scraps.

'Oh, don't blame her, little one,' Cassandra said, having drawn Hannah onto her knee after Mama sent her out. Cassandra had always made excuses for Mama's distracted coldness, which had grown worse rather than better after they came to the Land. Cassandra, by sharp contrast, had always made time for Hannah. Even nursing Evander, or in the midst of the drawing or the sculpting and honing of stone that was her love and her passion, she had been willing to stop and stroke Hannah's cheek as she explained that Mama's moods rose from grieving over Hannah's father whom she had left, never knowing they would not see one another again. Hundreds of years, maybe more, and the end of a world lay between their parting, and yet Mama grieved and grieved. Hannah had been too young to be able to say that she wished only to have a share in that grieving, even though her father had died long before she was born. Because sharing the grief would bring her closer to her mother.

'She was not always like this,' Cassandra said another time, laying aside a chisel to brush away a scatter of tears. Combing Hannah's wild dark tangle of hair, she told a story in which Hannah's jade-green eyes and dark hair were given to a princess in a thorny castle who had slept an enchanted sleep as she and Mama had done, when Hannah had lain in Mama's belly. Once Hannah asked Cassandra why she was not hard and cold like Mama, since she too had lost a husband and served the future.

Cassandra's answer had been very serious. 'I serve the future, it is true, little one, but I do not *see* it as your mother does. It is she who must swim the currents of time to learn what I must do to prepare for the Seeker who will ensure that what was done will not be done again. Sometimes she has shown me glimpses of futures that froze the blood in my veins.'

Hannah had not liked it when her beloved Cassandra was so stern, and so she asked, 'Tell me how it was when you met Mama.'

Cassandra had smiled at the familiar question; a curving display of the perfect white teeth that she shared with Mama but not with Hannah or Evander who had come to life in a world without the uncomfortable magician doctors Cassandra called dentists.

'I wrote to your mother,' Cassandra always began the story of her meeting with Hannah's mother in this way. 'I wrote to ask if there were truly powers of the mind, for it was my belief that I possessed them. I could speak to the minds of other people and animals and sometimes make them do as I wished. Your mother was a scientist known as having an interest in the paranormal, though in that time few believed in the existence of such things because they were rare. Your mother wrote back and invited me to meet her.'

'You met in Newrome the first time,' Hannah prompted, knowing this part of the story.

Cassandra nodded. 'I had never been there and it was a marvel to me. Your mother was waiting for me at the Reception Centre of the Reichler Clinic, which studied paranormal phenomena, but little of any note was shown to me there and the tests I was given showed I had no particular ability. I would have been disappointed, save that your mother had used telepathy to tell me the place was a façade to fool the government warmongers interested in developing paranormal abilities as weapons. Very soon, she promised that she would take me to a true refuge for people with special abilities like mine and hers.'

'Obernewtyn,' Hannah said eagerly. 'How I wish we could go there.'

That was where the telling usually ended, for the mountains were tainted by the poisons of the lost world and could not be crossed. The history had been told many times and both Hannah's questions and Cassandra's answers had the formality and familiar cadences of a response song. But one day Cassandra had answered that last rhetorical question. 'Your Mama believes the mountain valley of Obernewtyn is not contaminated. She intends to go and see if she can find a way up.'

Hannah had not known what to say to that, for she did not want to leave Cassandra and little Evander nor the glazes and tools that had been allowed her. She thought of their departure from the Red Land after the special memorial chamber had been built for Luthen. Cassandra had carved his likeness on the wall because there was no body to put in a grave, since neither his body nor his sword had been recovered from the sea. Aquilla had refused to allow them to leave when it had first been mentioned, for Cassandra was carrying her brother's son. But after Cassandra and Mama spoke at length to her in Luthen's funeral chamber, she had gifted them with boats marked with her own sigil, and on the day they left, she summoned porpoises to guide them safe across the Clouded Sea. Hannah had not known how she could reach the minds of sea creatures, for her own ability to commune with beasts did not extend to anything that swam or lived in water.

The sea had been still and the currents steady and they had not once fallen foul of the multitude of shoals and hidden reefs for which the Clouded Sea was infamous. But the porpoises left after they reached the Spit, and Hannah sometimes had nightmares even years later of the storm-wracked nightmarish journey from the dreadful Spit along endless lifeless Black Coasts till they were washed up in a storm more dead than alive on the shore of the Land. Evander had been born very soon after that desperate landing, and Hannah had shivered and cringed hearing Cassandra's screams of pain during the birthing.

'I will have no children,' she had told her mother.

Mama had looked at her, eyes suddenly flickering and milky in the fluttering lantern light. 'You will have two daughters, Hannah, and they will have two daughters apiece and their daughters will have daughters and so on until a son is born in the time when the Seeker will come. When that son is grown, he will make Obernewtyn his own.'

Hannah had wanted to ask if that unborn boy far in the future would also have to walk the Black road, for she had always believed that it was the road that led to Obernewtyn. But before she could frame the question, there was a groan and a slap and the sound of a baby wailing in the night. Evander had cried all night long and for days following, for Cassandra was too thin after the loss of Luthen and the terrible hardships of the journey from the Red Land, and had no milk. It was Mama found a wet nurse for the wailing child and nursed Cassandra.

Sometimes as a woman grown, with Nell suckling contentedly at her breast, Hannah had wondered if those first hungry days were the key to the yearning that had made Evander such a wearisome, demanding boy. And if that was so, how much of her own nature had been shaped by her birth in the midst of the deadly ruins of a dead world, to a mother racked by sorrow and loss?

They had feared Cassandra would die after Evander was born, but Mama said it would not be so. She had been right, Cassandra's fever had broken, and weak as a kitten she staggered over and scratched her son's name on the stone face of the gargantuan Tor rising up from the edge of the land, which formed the back wall of the rough hut built to house her. Hannah got goosebumps when Evander told her, years later, that he would be buried under those carved words when he died.

She had been happy in those early days on Stonehill. They had all been, maybe because they had come so close to dying on the terrible journey to the Spit. After they got established, they began trading to the nearby settlement of Halfmoon Bay and it was not long before Cassandra's work with black Tor stone, not to mention the work resulting from the skills and arts that had been taught to the others by the artisans of the Red Land, had made Stonehill famous. Soon the demand for Cassandra's work was nearly equalled by requests to be taught. They had set up a modest school and before long they had a waiting list of students and a thriving community.

But most of that had happened after Mama left. They had not long lived upon Stonehill when Hannah had found her mother packing. Cassandra had told her Mama's intentions only days before, and she had complained bitterly, saying she did not want to go.

'You will not be going,' Mama had answered without looking at her. 'You will stay with Cassandra.'

Hannah had been aghast for, while she moaned at having to go, she had never imagined being left behind. 'But I am to walk the Black road with you! You saw it! You said it!' she had shouted.

'I must go,' her mother had answered harshly, brown eyes dry, brown hair streaked with grey. A brief hard embrace and then a push away and Mama went out. She spoke a moment to Cassandra, giving her the letter, Hannah realised years later. Another hug and then Mama went off along the road leading to the switchback trail the men were making so that bullocks and horses could go laden up and down Stonehill. She had not looked back, and Hannah had stood at the edge of the Tor, tears drying on her cheeks as she watched until her mother appeared doll-sized far below and set off in the direction of the main road that would bring her to the Suggredoon River ferry.

There had been letters from time to time over the years. She had got work in a village. The pass to the high mountains was badly contaminated with radiation but she was looking for another way up to Obernewtyn. In another letter, she spoke of a vegetable garden, and added that she was trying to find a way into Newrome, where a contamination suit might be found that would let her walk safely through the pass. Hannah had stood stonily while Cassandra read the letters out, glancing sympathetically at her. She only cared that her mother never asked for her to come.

Once, Cassandra drew her close and said it was hard, with mothers. She had spent her life hating her own mother, only to regret that she had not found some way to reach her, ere the end. 'Don't waste time hating, love,' Cassandra whispered.

Hannah stayed with Cassandra for the rest of her childhood and into womanhood. She potted and glazed and tended house and pumped water and dug vegetables and helped care for Evander until he was old enough to be a playmate and then a companion. All the while Cassandra's fame as a sculptress grew. They now called the Tor stone Cassandra-stone, because its gleaming darkness resembled her skin, and her students all but worshipped her. Councilmen came from afar to beg her to make a piece for them. So much was created that gradually a stone garden was built, filled with Cassandra's work and the work of her students. She carved Evander and Hannah several times over the years at different ages.

The last carving Cassandra had done was of her long dead husband, Luthen. That had been the centrepiece of the great bribe to be paid to the increasingly powerful Councilmen, whose soldierguards now patrolled the roads and demanded to know who and where and what of every traveller.

'It will get worse,' Cassandra had told Evander. 'Hannah's mother warned me of it years ago. Soon permits will be required for anyone wanting to travel. But this bribe will ensure that we are allowed to move about the Land freely.'

'But why offer a yearly tithe as well as the bribe?' Evander had protested. 'You have offered them king's ransom in goods and coin as well as that statue of Father.'

'It is not for them but for us that I offer a tithe,' Cassandra told him. 'It will be a reminder and a desirable reinforcement of the bargain I have made. Whenever the councilmen contemplate setting the safe passage agreement aside, and they will, greed for what is to come that year will stay them. That is why they must be offered the best and most lavish of our work.'

'That is why you ceased taking students outside the Twentyfamilies,' Evander had said.

His mother had nodded. 'The time of students and teaching is over. The things we offer in tithe must be able to be obtained only in this way — by the faithful keeping of the bargain I have wrought.'

All this Evander had told her on one of his visits to Mellow Farm after his mother vanished, and Hannah had listened with only half an ear, remembering that it was the night Cassandra finished the carving of her that Evander kissed her. She'd had an inkling of how he felt about her before that, but she had refused to think of it seriously. He was only seventeen and her brother. She fought him but only after she got over her shock at being kissed so thoroughly.

'I am not your brother,' he had said defiantly, when she got free. 'There is no blood tie between us. We could wed.'

'I don't think of you like that!' she had told him truthfully.

'You let me kiss you for long enough if you didn't like it,' he said slyly.

She had felt herself blush, but she said as evenly and gently as she could, 'Vander, I love you but not that way. You are my brother and you are only a boy. When you grow up you will see it properly.' She had tried to be kind, and maybe that had angered him most of all.

In answer he had grabbed at her and kissed her again, pressing his body the whole length of hers so she must know that he was no child.

She had spent her childhood protecting him and coddling him and it was her instinct, even now, to protect him. But feeling him against her like that shocked her, and she pushed him harder than she meant to. He overbalanced and hit his temple when he fell. There was a trickle of blood and when she reached down to him, as he got to his feet, he struck her across the face and told her in a voice that shook with rage and humiliation that he would be the king of Stonehill and the Twentyfamilies when his mother was gone, and that she might have been his queen, but since she had spurned him then she must leave.

His harsh words hurt her as they were meant to do, and yet Hannah would have stayed, knowing the words spoken and the blow came out of pain. But Cassandra had come to her with a cloth for her bruised cheek after he stormed out.

'My darling girl, it hurts me to say it, but he is right in one thing. It is time for you to leave Stonehill. Evander is young and frightened of the burden of leadership that I must lay upon him much sooner than he knows. You think his feelings for you are those of a child, but they are not. He loves you, but I know that you do not love him. And that is well, for your future is not with the Twentyfamilies gypsies.'

'You will leave?' Hannah's eyes filled up with tears.

'Your mother foresaw it, and I told Vander of her vision just a few nights past. Now I will tell you this much of it. A Gadfian pirate ship like the one that took Luthen will come to this shore and I must let myself be taken by it, for the next place the pirates go is a Beforetime place where I must go to obtain something the Seeker will need.'

'The Seeker,' Hannah had echoed bitterly, almost hating the shadowy woman in the future who had stolen her mother from her and now Cassandra as well.

'Listen to me, Hannah. I send you away now because this quarrel with Evander will make your parting easier for him to bear. You see, your mother bade me send you to the mountains before I am taken. I do not know exactly when the pirates will come. It may be days or weeks, but not more. I have a letter Hannah gave me to give you when this moment came.' She drew the letter from her apron pocket and kissed Hannah, then left her to read it.

My daughter, it began. My Hannah. I have not been a good mother to you. So much of me was swallowed up always by visions of the future. Terrible visions that I scarcely understood, and which commanded things of me that seemed impossible. I refused your father to begin with, because of the long and difficult duty my dreams and visions laid upon me. But when he asked again I loved him and could not hide it. Once he saw that, he would not accept no for an answer. 'The end of the world is coming, my love,' he said. 'You have seen it and I believe in your visions. I am not as you and the others are. There is no special thing about me save my wealth and that is already yours.' How wrong he was. I have never known a man more fair and kind and steady hearted. I wish you could have known him, Hannah. I called you by my own name because he said if we had a daughter I must give him that one thing. It hurts me and has always hurt me that he never knew about you. But I did not know I was pregnant when I left him that last time. I ought to have done, but I had felt myself too old for children. And for all the visions that had come to me, not one had shown me your face.

Always it seems to me, I have failed to see the things that mattered most to me personally. When I left my own Antipoda so very long ago, I knew my destiny was in Uropa, for my visions showed it to me. I thought to find those like me, never knowing it would be me who would form the secret place to which others with paranormal abilities would come, never knowing that I would see the end of one world and the birth of another. In those early days William Reichler was my hero, and I thought not of love. I did not see Jacob in any vision. I did not know him when I met him and thought only to win him as a patron. I had no idea that he would come to be so dear to me. Never once did any vision show me that I was coming to love him as a man. Nor later, when I lay with him, did I see that we would have a daughter. Both of you came to me in that blind spot in my vision and more than all else, it has confirmed for me that my visions are not to serve my own dreams or to enhance my life or the lives of those I love. They are given me to serve the world, and so I have done as faithfully as I could.

Yet do not doubt that I have loved you. I knew of your existence only at the end of that age before this one. It was a machine that told me, before it cast me into a sleep that would trick time. The machine did not know what coldsleep would do to a fetus, but we had no choice. I had to submit to that long sleep, never knowing if I would wake or if you would survive. I had foreseen only that Cassy would live and it was she who mattered because she was to prepare the way for the Seeker. Then I woke and you lived and you grew in me even as we sailed across the devastated world seeking the place where my visions showed me life had survived. To feel you inside me was a joy and yet a terror too, for I did not know would come of a baby who had slept lifetimes in the womb. But born you were amidst the ruins of the past, and perfect you were to my eyes. How I loved your serious, gentle nature that was so like your father's and how it pleased me that you should be able to speak to beasts as I could. How hard it was to hold back from you so that I could do what I must.

I hurt you when I left you, I know, but less than I hurt myself. And now, if you are reading this, the time has come for you to follow me. Come up to the high mountains. There is a village where there is a rumour of Guanette birds. That was my destination when I left Stonehill. Come thus far, and find the future I have foreseen for you. It is my gift to you. Read no more of this letter until your first daughter bears a child and that child is ten. Trust me that it will be better thus.'

She had stopped reading, obedient as ever. Her face and bodice had been wet with tears shed out of a painful joy at knowing that her mother had loved her, had thought of her, had sorrowed at their parting. That letter healed a bitterness that might have twisted her, and she went to Cassandra and showed her the letter and they wept together, then she went and packed her things and left, regretting that she could not say goodbye to Evander, but eager for news of her mother. The argument with Evander seemed to have happened years before and it startled her when she touched her cheek that she could feel the bruise where he had struck her.

'I was not too old for an adventure back then, but I am too old for it now,' Hannah said, trying to grumble, but the foreboding and sorrow she had felt leaving Mellow Farm a week before had sloughed away. Birds were singing and the sun was shining and when a breeze blew, the air was sweet and white with blossom. She went up on the made road as far as the turnoff to Darthnor mine and saw few folk on the way, and no one at all on the overgrown track that ran on towards the mountains from there, passing as it did between the firestorm ravaged wilderness of the White Valley on the one side and a dark, dense pine forest frequented by bears and worse on the other. Now she was following a track that brought her in the afternoon to the steep pass that ran aslant through the high mountains. The sky was clear but queer storms roiled in the pass that never stopped or went anywhere else. Hannah had heard talk of them but they were unsettling to see and she could not imagine what caused them. The static in the air made all of her hair stand on end.

Her mother had said in the letter that a person could not go safely on foot through the pass without a contamination suit but by the time she came there a horse going at a gallop might manage it and keep itself and a rider safe. Hannah had camped the night then sent out a call. A shaggy mare answered it, a frayed tether rope about her neck. Her bones stood out and the marks and scars upon her coat wiped away any guilt Hannah might have felt at calling her, though she was not sure the poor thing would have the strength to carry them both through the eerie pass at a flat gallop.

However, she must trust the beast, whose name was Willing. In those days in the land, there was a fashion for the naming of children and beasts after virtues, hoping the former would beget the latter. Sometimes it was so. In Willing's case it was, for despite her poor condition, they flew through the terrifying pass at a gallop. The mare had been panting like a bellows, wild-eyed when they passed out of the queer storms and into clear air, but she soon calmed, for the valley they found on the other side of it was very fair and green and quiet. Hannah had climbed down from Willing and they went side by side up the remains of an ancient road, until they came at last to the ruins that had been fabled Obernewtyn, where her mother and father had once lived and worked. The walls that once surrounded the grounds had all fallen as if a giant hand had thumped the ground, but the walls of the building were mostly intact. The roofs had long rotted away though, and the inside was all grown over with moss and creepers, but the maze her mother had talked of planting with her father thrived, though it was so knitted together with weeds and brambles that it would have been impossible to go through it.

Willing grazed contentedly on the rich sweet grass and moss, nourishing herself and the foal she had told Hannah she carried. Hannah picked over the stones, searching for some chord in herself that would resonate with this place where she had been conceived. But it was just a stony ruin, beautiful and desolate in the way ruins always are when left to nature. After a time, Hannah found the little hut built up out of fallen stone, resting against a bit of the wall that had once surrounded the maze. There had been a vegetable garden planted beside it, she guessed, though there was no sign of it now. She did not need to go inside it to know this was where her father had lived out the long lonely years of his life before he left Obernewtyn to walk the dark road.

She found her mother's bones laid out by a crumbling stone bench overgrown by a wild rose bush with scarlet blooms and ferocious thorns.

Do not fear my bones, her mother had written. *I will lay me by the bench your father made so we could sit and talk at the end of a day, and smell the roses he planted for me … What is left of my flesh will nourish the soil and the beasts and birds and insects that kindly pick them clean. Not far from the bench is a crypt with Jacob's name upon it. Do not trouble yourself over it for he is not inside it. The grave was built before I came to understand all of the visions I had seen, and it serves a purpose that is no concern of yours or mine. Take up my bones in a sack and carry it to the highest mountains above this valley. Pass the horned mountain and travel North until you find the ruins of an ancient tower. There will be an old road going down from it to the black and blasted lands. Go down to it and walk directly towards the setting sun. Wear the contamination suit which I have foreseen myself finding and which I will leave for you in the hut Jacob built, along with packages of food and water and eliminatory bags I will find in the laboratories as well. There will be instructions on how to use them with the suit. They are none of them comfortable or pleasant to use, as you may remember, but used correctly, they will ensure that you need not take off the suit. Do not remove it until you reach the white plain and the Black road that runs across it.*

We will walk that road together even as I foretold, though I did not warn you that I would be dead. You were too young for such a grim truth. The Black road, followed to its end, will bring us to a city and your father's true grave. One warning. Keep to the road once you have set your feet upon it, for I have seen that if you lose it, you will never find it again. Do not read past this page until you see the city, then stop and read the rest of my letter. It will tell what must be done to bring me to your father's grave.

This difficult and lonely duty I give you now is not to serve me or your father but for the world that we humans have so battered and diminished. What you do will ensure that what was done can never be done again. If you fail to lay me with your father, all that Cassandra and I have done, all that your father did, will be to no avail. The Seeker will fail too, and the world will come to a final dreadful ending.

But I do not think you will fail the tests ahead.

I use the remainder of this page to tell you that I love you, my daughter. My only regret is that I did not say it often enough to you. And yet if I had done so, if I had let myself feel that love or looked too much at you, I would not have been able to leave you. Never in my life was anything so hard to do as to do so knowing I would never see you in this life again. I might have kept you with me all the years between my leaving and my death here at Obernewtyn, but I wished for you to have the life I foresaw for you, with love and children of your own; Not only because, in time, your descendants will claim Obernewtyn and rebuild it, but because you deserved it. That would not have come to you, if I had kept you with me.

Hannah stumbled slightly over a crack in the Black road, and blinked away a mist of tears that had come up at the memory of those words cramped together to fit into the end of the page, and at the thought of her mother living out her life with only bees for company, all so that her daughter could have a husband and children. It hurt and salved Hannah at the same time that all of her mother's hard choices had not been for the future of the world and the Seeker to come.

She thought of making camp and staved off stopping with Mellow's words, but her knee was bad enough that she had begun to limp. She would bandage it when she stopped and she told herself that she was lucky to have been able to abandon the wretched contamination suit, for aside from being uncomfortably hot and difficult to manoeuver, it had stunk and she had stunk in it. Nevertheless she had bundled it up and tied it to the bottom of her pack with her sleeping roll, because

Mama's letter had not bidden her abandon it. She might very well come across another stretch of poisoned Blacklands before she reached the end of the dark road or maybe she would have need of it, in the city at the end of the Black road.

She stumbled again and this time her bad knee gave way under her. She fell half on the Black road and half on the soft hot sand. She had not the strength to lever herself up, but mindful of her mother's warning to keep to the road, she rolled over onto her back until she lay wholly upon it. She was startled to see the moon riding above her. Was it true what Mama said of the moon, she wondered, half delirious with thirst and dehydration. The people of that lost time had been magicians and miracle workers by all accounts.

She tried to get up, but she had not the strength.

'I promised,' she said through gritted teeth. The words croaked out for her mouth was dry as a bone. She gave a shivering laugh and then lay back and slept until panic woke her and gave her strength and clarity for a moment. She levered herself over and reached for the sack containing her mothers' bones, weeping with relief to find she had not spilled them out into the swallowing sand. Or would have wept if there had been any moisture in her to weep out. She lay her face against the sack of bones and wondered if someday the Seeker would walk upon the same road and find her bones clutching a sack of bones. What a mystery it would be. But the Seeker would fail in her quest if Hannah failed to bring her mother's bones to lie with her father's in his grave. She thought of the unread pages of the letter, but she did not take them out.

You can always go on longer than you think you can, Mellow coaxed.

Hannah closed her eyes and slept. Cassandra's cat came and looked at her with his one bright yellow eye. '*Get up, funaga, or you will die and be meat for the crows. Get up or the efari will come and if they take you, you will die a captive and the world will die with you.*'

Hannah had woken with the clear memory of the honey pot she had pushed into the side of the pack. With trembling fingers, she found it miraculously unbroken, and she undid the lid and licked the sweetness and the wetness from her fingers. It was too sweet and not wet enough, but it strengthened her.

She sat up.

She must have slept for hours, for though it was dark and stars glittered overhead, the moon had set and she could see by the sword of light along the eastern horizon that it was nearing dawn. She stood somehow, using the goat staff to lever her up and ignored the pain shooting through her knee. All around her the undulating dunes had a greenish look, as if they were ripples underneath the water. It was then, as she stood swaying on her feet, that she saw the city. It was so far off that she could not have seen it save for the lights, and they would not have shown in the daytime or even when the moon was up.

The city at the end of the Black road.

Hannah's heart trembled at the realisation that she was going to make it after all. Mama had been right. They had journeyed along the Black road together, and they would come to its end, together.

She sat down again and took out her mother's letter in readiness for when the sun rose, so that she could read the last of it.

AFTERWORD

When you create a world, it can be so enticing and interesting and delicious a place to inhabit that you keep going back and back until no corner is unexplored, no map name unplumbed. This results in the sort of unfortunate series that goes on and on with no true end in sight. But a book or even a series is a journey, and so it ought to plot the same narrow course through an invented world as our lives do through this world. Having said that, I loved revisiting the world of Tehanu in *The Other Wind*; and in the exquisite collection of stories, *Tales of Earthsea*, Ursula Le Guin returned to that invented world. The foreword to that collection, explaining the enticements of a world to its creator, is profound and beautiful and wise, and reading *Tales from Earthsea* made me think how wonderful it would be to write another story set in the world of Obernewtyn. Not a story that was a continuation of Elspeth's story, but a tale by a character who might catch only a glimpse of Elspeth and her time.

Then serendipity and morphic resonance conspired and Jack Dann wrote to ask if I would like to write a story set in a world I had invented for a collection he was putting together. Aside from uttering a resounding 'yes please', a dozen possibilities bubbled to the surface of my mind, for I had created lots of worlds and the idea of visiting many of them was appealing. For a time the creative cauldron was a seething mess. But when it, and I, cooled, I came back to my original idea.

So here is the story of a character who is almost completely invisible in the Obernewtyn Chronicles, unless you know where to look for her. Her story reveals a secret that readers of the Obernewtyn series cannot otherwise discover.

— *Isobelle Carmody*

Kim Wilkins was born in London but grew up at the seaside near Brisbane. She has degrees in literature and creative writing, and teaches at University of Queensland. Kim has published more than twenty books, in a variety of genres and for a variety of age groups, though her heart belongs to fantasy.

Crown of Rowan:
A Tale of Thyrsland

KIM WILKINS

I was cruellest to him whom I loved the most.
— *Laxdaela's saga*

I. BLOTMONATH

There are seven kings in Thyrsland. My father is one of them, and my husband is another. In my belly, perhaps, I carry a third.

It is blood month, and outside my bower window I hear fear-moaning cattle on their way to slaughter. Every night this week, I have smelled blood on the wind: faint but unmistakable, worming under the shutters. And I've turned my face to my pillow and held tight to avoid retching.

My sister's hands are cool, pressed against my belly, sliding down hard towards the bone. Ash hasn't seen me naked since we were children, when we shared the same bath before midsummer feasts. Her face is a mask of concentration: her eyebrows are drawn together, which makes her look cross. And yet Ash is never cross. She is as bonny as the sun.

She lifts off her hands and smiles, smooths my skirts down again. 'You are definitely with child,' she says, leaning in to hug me, her long dark hair becoming caught in my mouth. 'Darling Rose, I'm so pleased for you.'

Even though I was expecting this answer, the world swings away from me a moment and I see myself from afar. Small and soft, a snail without a shell. Then I am back, and it is hotly true: a child grows within me, somebody who will one day think and speak and rule over Netelchester when my husband, Wengest, is gone.

But Wengest is not the child's father.

Ash has turned away. The afternoon light through the narrow window catches the side of her face and she looks so very young. Too young to be away from home and studying; but she has gathered my fate, just as I gathered my older sister's. Bluebell, as the first daughter, should have been married off to Wengest, to weave peace between Netelchester and Ælmesse. But she flatly refused; she threatened to cut out her guts if pressed. Father's eyes could tell him that no husband would lament not having her. She is six feet tall, all long limbs and jutting bones. Her nose was smashed sideways in battle practice when she was eighteen, and each arm wears a sleeve of scars and tattoos. Which is to say, she is formed for war, and not for love.

So I was sent to Wengest, and Ash was sent to the Study Halls of Thriddastowe. She is learning to be a counsellor of the Common Faith. Part of her role is to tend to women in childbirth.

'When will the babe come?' I ask her, pulling myself up into a sitting position with my arms around my knees.

'If you last bled in weed-month, then the babe will come in milk-month.' She laughed. 'It won't just be the cows making milk, then.'

I think about my breasts, the faint blue veins that appeared on them eight weeks ago. I knew then, of course. I had counted back the days. Wengest was away, meeting with the king of Lyteldyke. He had been away a month and four days. He hadn't been in my bed for nearly a fortnight before that.

I know that he has not subsequently noticed those tell-tale lines on my breasts. He prefers to couple in the dark, believing somehow that passion reduces us, strips us of our dignity. But Heath had noticed them. Out in the fields far from my husband's hall: sunlight white and and warm, caught under the ears of wheat as they shook in the breeze, dazzling in Heath's pale gold hair, bathing my bare white skin … He saw the veins, he traced them with his fingers, but he said nothing. I said nothing. The memory comes upon me fresh: my belly grows giddy, my heart pinches. Many say that love is a blessing; but to love a man one cannot have is surely a curse.

'You will be here for milk-month?' I ask Ash, aware now of my body's vulnerability, of what childbirth can do to women. Our mother died delivering twins. 'You will deliver the child?'

'I will ask my elders at the study hall for permission to come.'

'You are a king's daughter,' I say, 'you can surely do as you please.'

'My loyalty as a counsellor is not to any king. It is to the horse god, to the great mother. In their eyes, no family is more important than another.' She reads the anxiety on my brow and she shifts to sit on the bed next to me. 'I will do my very best, Rosie. But even if I can't make it, you aren't to worry. You will be perfectly well, and your baby will too. She'll be bonny and strong, you'll see.'

'*She*? You think it is a girl?'

Ash smiles, but I see her eyes flicker like a person about to tell a lie. I know that expression; I wear it often. 'There is no way to tell, no windows to the womb.' She shakes her head gently. 'With four sisters, it's hard to imagine a baby boy. Forgive me. It might as well be a son as daughter.'

My daughter. I have never been fond of children, but this creature embedded in my body is not just any child. It is *my* child. And his.

'Wengest will be pleased,' Ash continues. 'Will you tell him soon?'

I cannot answer. I am thinking, instead, of telling Heath what he surely already knows.

*   *   *

160

The wide Wuldorea divides my husband's kingdom from my father's. The river snakes through Thyrsland from its mouth on the south-west coast, up towards the great lakes of western Netelchester, on the border with tiny Tweoning, a little kingdom that has seen much war. The Wuldorea is brown today, engorged with a week of rain. Heath owns twenty hides of land bordered by her banks; five miles downstream from Wengest's hall and the rest of the town. When I stand at the western edge of his land, I can see Ælmesse, the kingdom of my birth. On a clear day, I sometimes imagine I can see the steep hill upon which my father's hall is built, the gleaming ruins of the giants' halls at Blicstowe — my home town, the most beautiful place on earth — though I know it is an illusion.

Heath's fields are dark and smell of earth and rain. I make my way up the line of elms between fields to the thatched round-house where Heath lives. A crow sits on bare branches above me, watching. I don't like to be watched; frost creeps over my skin. The crow clicks its beak against the branch, spreads its wings, and takes off into the white sky. Its wake shivers across the branch.

Inside, Heath is sitting by the fire. Smoke catches in my throat and stings my eyes. The hewn carcasse of a cow is hung from the rafters to smoke for the winter. The shutters are closed against the cold, so the room is dark as it will be until the sun comes back in summerfull-month. The weak light from the open door shows me Heath's back and shoulders, his long gold hair. Then I close the door and only firelight illuminates us. He turns and smiles at my arrival, shifts over on the bench to make room for me. I slide into place and he catches me in his gaze.

Heath does not wear a beard, as most men in Thyrsland do. But it isn't true that he can't grow one. How many times have I heard that insult whispered? Even Wengest has said it to me. 'My nephew must not be fully a man at twenty-five summers old and still no beard.'

I know Heath's secret. He shaves it from his face with a warm knife every morning, because when it grows it is bright coppery red. Heath is part Ærfolc; he is the half-breed bastard son of Wengest's wayward sister. The Ærfolc, who were driven deep into the north-west and across the sea a hundred years ago, are regarded by the people of Thyrsland with suspicion, hostility. Some of us, in the south of

Lyteldyke, still use them as slaves. Their coppery hair and pale green eyes mark them. Heath, beardless, could barely be recognised as Ærfolc except if one is looking for the signs: threads of copper in his golden hair that are only visible in bright sunlight; an undercurrent of sea-green in his eyes.

'I wasn't expecting to see you today,' he says, bringing rough fingers to my chin, running his thumb gently over my lower lip to coax a smile.

'It's so hot in here,' I complain, unpinning and shrugging out of my cloak. It falls in a puddle behind me. Heath's home is small. The only furniture is this bench and a straw mattress. We have made love many times upon that mattress; the straw ticking scratching our bare skins softly through the thick blankets. My husband's hall is far grander than Heath's home; my father's is a hundred times the size. But I have known unutterable happiness in this warm room.

He sits and waits for me to say what I must say. Ever-patient Heath. The fire cracks and pops, the smoke catches my throat. Finally, I say, 'I am with child. It is certainly yours.'

His face softens; I have no idea what he is thinking. 'What have you told Wengest?'

'Nothing.'

'And you intend to keep the child?' he says, almost fearfully.

'I do,' I say.

Heath rubs his chin, and I see he is hiding a smile. And now I am crying, because we made a child and he is glad, even though he knows he will never be recognised as the child's father. An image skids into my mind — a small boy at Heath's side, helping him load the sheaves on the cart, laughing in the autumn sunshine — and just as quickly I banish it. It will do me no good to harbour such fantasies and, in any case, Ash says the child will be a girl. And Ash *knows* these things even though she shouldn't.

I press my body into his arms and weep warm tears against the rough fabric of his tunic. 'What is to become of us?' My voice is husky from smoke and from crying.

Heath kisses the trail of tears from my cheeks, and even in this dark moment the desire that arrows through me is bright and urgent.

He pushes me gently away so he can look at my face, and he opens his mouth and says, 'Rose, we could …' But then he stops, and I am glad he has stopped, because I know he is going to say, *we could run away: we could find my father's family in the wilds of Bradsey, we could raise the child as our own and have six more and always be happy.* But we both know that such a sunlit scene blinds the mind's eye to darker truths. Ælmesse and Netelchester have been at war since the giants left Thyrsland, centuries ago. My father and Wengest's father were the first kings to bring peace between the kingdoms; and all of it rested on the marriage promise my father made to Wengest. If Heath and I ran away to raise fat babies in the wilderness, the sure result of our indulgence would be war. Thousands would die; many of them would be children. I want to shout and shake my fists and proclaim how unfair it is that I should be in such a position, forced into marriage, the fate of kingdoms weighing on me. And then I remind myself — as I always must — of my sister Bluebell on the fields of battle with my father, stained in blood and slipping over the spilled intestines of her fallen friends. A king's daughter knows duty. Bluebell would sacrifice her life for Ælmesse; how selfish I am to complain about sacrificing my womb.

Heath stands, pulls me up next to him. Then he takes my hands and kneels, his hands around my hips. He kisses my belly, and I can feel the heat of his lips through the cloth. I close my eyes and turn my face upwards. The mingled smells of meat, smoke, and mud seem stuck in my throat. He rests his cheek against my body, and I turn my gaze to him, tangle my fingers in his hair. And then the first bolt of true panic comes.

In the firelight, I see the red glimmer in his hair. It is suddenly clear to me that should my child have the faintest trace of the Ærfolc colouring, we will be undone.

Her hair or her eyes may tell a tale that should remain untold.

II. MOTRANECHT

Wild snowy wind rattles the branches outside, battering the shutters, howling down the hill and plucking at the thatched houses of the village. Snow lies in uneven layers on the empty market square, on the roofs of barns where animals stand still and close together, on the bowerhouse and the blacksmith's forge. But here in Wengest's great hall, the freezing damp seems impossibly far away. The fire is huge and hot and bright, the smoke hangs thick in the air until it escapes, little by little, into the black cold outside. The occasional bold snowflake falls through the smoke-hole and melts in a hissing half-moment. All around me are the sounds of people shouting and laughing and drinking, the smell of damp clothes and roasting fat. It is the night we celebrate the great Mother, the deepest point of winter, the day when the sun rises the latest and sets the earliest.

I am wearing my best red dress for Mother's Night and, fittingly, it is strained across my waist as it never has been before. A loose pinafore pinned over it disguises my belly; but it won't be long before it is apparent to everyone who sees me that the king's wife is with child. Perhaps it is time I told the king.

Wengest is holding my hand loosely as he turns away to talk to his ageing uncle Byrtwold, who sits at the head of the table with us. My gaze travels the room. Beyond our table, other groups are arranged around the fire. The hall-staff work at the hearth, carving deer on spits, slopping gravy and parsnips onto plates. By the far door, a tale-teller is performing. I cannot hear his words, but I can see his exaggerated actions: an invisible sword, a dragon with hands for jaws. The warm, sweet ale has made me flushed and happy.

Of course, I am looking for Heath. Wengest has seated him at a far table, with a duke from the deep west of Netelchester. The duke's two daughters are with him; sullen skinny things. Neither of them great beauties. I think not.

Wengest's whisper is in my ear, his beard is rough against my skin. 'Save us.'

I look up. Uncle Byrtwold is holding forth at length, and under the influence of too much bog-myrtle ale, about the right way to knacker sheep. Wengest's closest retainers are silenced and glazed. I swallow a laugh.

'Uncle Byrtwold,' I say in a sharp voice, 'have you seen the way the hall-staff are carving that deer? I'm sure it is not right.'

Byrtwold sits up, alarmed, peering towards the fire. 'You are right, my dear. If they cut across-wise, all the fat will end up on the first twelve plates.' He is on his feet in a moment, unsteadily. Wengest's hand shoots out under his elbow.

'You need to explain the process to them in detail,' Wengest says, using his leverage now to propel Byrtwold away.

Then he is weaving off through the crowd, and restrained laughter blooms at our table. Wengest smiles at me, the firelight reflected in his dark eyes. 'You are as wise as you are beautiful, my Rose.'

This is surely the worst aspect of my betrayal: my husband does not deserve it. He is a patient man, and he loves me. The first time we met, I was struck by how handsome he was, how strong. He is not yet forty summers, and has thick dark hair and smiling eyes. The cold has made his skin florid, and his cheeks above his beard are dry and cracking. But he is by no means an ugly man, nor an unkind man. Had I not met Heath, I may very well have fallen slowly in love with him, as I expected to when our marriage was arranged.

I am overwhelmed by strong pity and lean up to kiss him, and he quickly pushes me away, glancing around. 'Not so everyone will see, Rose. People do not like to think of their king as a man. Men desire, and desire saps judgement.'

Such ideas about what kings and men should be is no doubt at the very root of the long-standing differences between my father's kingdom and Netelchester. For my father thinks that a king is first a human, and only through our shared humanity can we be a strong kingdom. Wengest believes kings are separate, different. Better.

I playfully put my arms around his neck and blow softly on his hair, and he looks cross for a moment and then laughs.

'Look you at my nephew, Heath,' he says, his gaze going over my shoulder.

I turn, probably too quickly, my hands still linked behind his neck. I see nothing unusual. Heath is listening to the tale-teller, the duke and his daughters are eating their meals.

'I have been watching him all night, and I am suspicious,' Wengest says.

My face grows hot. 'You are?'

'I put him there with two women who would be perfect for marriage, and he looks at neither.' Wengest frowns, disengages himself from my arms. 'He cannot grow a beard, he does not enjoy the company of women. I hope he is not a cat-paw.'

At that precise moment, a wooden trencher piled with meat and vegetables is dropped at my elbow. I become aware that the noise in the room has been dampened as people eat. Wengest has not invited me to reply, so I do not. But of course I am the person who knows best that Heath is far from being a cat-paw. Back at Heath's table, the tale-teller is finished and people around are clapping and cheering. The tale-teller turns and Wengest beckons him forward. He is a small but sprightly man with a wispy beard and a pronounced crook to his right shoulder.

'My lord,' the tale-teller says as he approaches our table. 'I have a tale for you.'

'Tell on,' Wengest says, breaking his bread to sop up gravy. 'I could use some entertainment. Let it be a tale of adventure and men's courage.'

But before the tale-teller can speak, a man dressed in white at the end of our table stands and, in a bold voice, says, 'I can tell a tale.'

The man, whose name is Nyll, is a pilgrim. I do not like him, but that is not his fault. He is friendly enough. But he is of the Trimartyr faith, a woman-hating death cult. Wengest is fascinated by this faith, but resists converting. Out of some strange pity or fear, he gave the pilgrim a half-hide near the river as book-land, and there Nyll has built a little house with a grass roof, where he writes his strange letters on his stretched calfskin and counsels those who have questions about the Trimartyrs. Winter has come, and he is still here. I know by this that he intends to stay until he achieves his object, which is my husband's soul and the souls of his people.

'You have a tale, pilgrim?' Wengest says, sitting back in his chair and swirling the drink in his cup. 'I did not know pilgrims did such frivolous things as telling tales.'

'Ah, my lord, but the Trimartyrs have the most glorious tale of all. That of the courage and sacrifice of the three martyrs so that we may all one day stand in the hall of the great god Maava.'

The tale-teller retreats, bowing his head. Wengest shrugs his broad shoulders. 'Go on then.'

Nyll the pilgrim spreads his hands and clears his throat. 'Listen,' he says, straining to be heard over the noise in the room, 'for Maava's word is great and good.' A good tale-teller needs a strong voice, an ease with his own body. But Nyll does not know how to project his words, nor what to do with his hands. They clutch and unclutch in front of him. Undeterred, he continues. 'Maava is the one god, the only god.'

Already the group around him has divided. Those who are already sympathetic to the Trimartyrs are nodding, urging him on. Those of the common faith mutter to each other, they frown or roll their eyes. Some look murderous: to preach such nonsense on Motranecht seems evil. One god? When there are so clearly two? A mother: for growth, love, harmony, family; and the horse god: for war, diplomacy, thought, action. One for birth, and one for death: the two poles between which we all wander.

Nyll clears his throat again, and this time manages to imbue his voice with volume. He slips into verse, letting the words lead him.

Listen, the Lord Maava: mighty, good and great,
A message for men, cast off customs wilful and wild.
One god, only god, mortals must hear him,
For fate awaits all at end of life's lease,
Some in the Sunlands, the bad in the Blacklands.
Do not deny this told tale, and wail for wrong,
Listen, the Lord Maava.

At world's warm middle, moist garden of good,
Beyond before: the giants' grandfathers' times and tales,
Maava made two; twins proud to prophesy,
Babes in the belly of the loving Liava, who knew no men:
Virtuous virgin, birthed the babes, tended those twins,
In the honoured hall of the King of kindness, victorious Varga,
At world's warm middle.

I stifle a laugh. Perhaps if Wengest can believe that a virgin can get with child, then I need not worry about being discovered in my affair. I turn away from the pilgrim, and hum a tune in my head so I need not listen to the rest. I have heard the story before, and it is a cruel and sad one, of two little boys — the child prophets — and their mother, all cast alive upon a pyre as punishment for preaching the teachings of Maava. Nyll recites this verse with spittle-flecked relish. I try not to think about the mother, lying down and taking her children in her arms, knowing that she can no longer protect them from pain and death. When did I become so vulnerable to tales of cruelty? Since this child lodged itself inside me, I am a different person. I know not myself, I know not my future.

Nyll ends his tale by holding out the golden triangle he wears on a strap around his waist; the symbol of the three martyrs, of their pyre, of their bones standing among the cinders of their flesh. 'Listen you, for those who take Maava as their god will travel upon their deaths to the Sunlands, where happiness is eternal; and those who do not will find instead the Blacklands beyond the clouds, to fall forever in fear and ice.'

Everybody has stopped listening, even Wengest. Nyll tucks his triangle away on his belt, and returns to his seat, his elbows crooked awkwardly against the indifferent noise of people eating and talking, and not listening. The tale-teller leaps into the space vacated by him, launching into a tale of two brothers fighting over a dragon-maiden. Maava's fear and ice are banished by the return of firelight and laughter.

It is not simply the avid interest that the Trimartyrs take in cruelty that irks me; it is their law that women cannot rule. Four years ago Tweoning's queen, the mighty Dystro, was deposed and beheaded by the tide of the Trimartyrs. I wonder if Bluebell ever muses on Dystro's fate. I touch my belly lightly, unthinkingly. My own daughter, if Wengest converted, would not be queen. The thought lights up all my veins with a sense of injustice. A misplaced one, I suppose.

I become aware that Wengest is looking at me. Closely. Watching my hand moving softly over the outside of my pinafore. I drop my fingers quickly, he meets my gaze.

'Rose?'

'I am with child,' I say, willing myself not to blush with guilt.

His beard splits with a grin. 'Oh, my.'

I cannot help but smile, his pleasure is contagious.

'When will it come?' he says eagerly.

'Ash says on midsummer,' I lie. An early child is not unusual; he will not suspect.

Wengest stands, knocking over his cup. He reaches for mine, holds it aloft. The tale-teller falls silent. Wengest booms, 'Listen you, all of you!'

I feel my face grow hot. I know Heath is looking, but I cannot meet his eye. Instead, I stare as hard as I can at Wengest, and a tunnel of blurred darkness forms around him.

'Let it be known,' Wengest says, when the room has fallen quiet except for the whoosh of the fire, 'that my wife Rose, the daughter of King Æthlric of Ælmesse, is with child.'

A loud cheer goes up, and my eyes are stinging from staring so hard and from unshed tears.

'We expect the child on the very day of midsummer,' Wengest boasts among the cheers and shouts. 'An auspcious time for a king to be born.'

'Or a queen,' I say quietly, but he does not hear; or if he hears, he does not answer.

I do not know how close the dawn is when I finally slide into my warm bed. I let my head fall onto the soft lambskin and close my eyes. My mind still whirls. I feel the weight of Wengest's body as he lies down next to me. He often does not sleep in my bed, but tonight his excitement about the child has made him affectionate. He rests his warm hand on my belly and is silent for a long time. I am almost asleep, when his voice wakes me. It seems very loud.

'Rose, are you asleep?'

I open my eyes. In the dark, he is just a shadow. 'What is it?'

'I need to ask you about your father. You know him better than I do.'

I sit up, craving sleep. 'Go on.'

'Last time I spoke to Æthlric, he predicted he would soon be asking me for a hundred good warriors, to take up to the border of Is-hjarta in summerfull-month. I have had an idea, but I wonder how your father will take it.'

'What is it?'

'Heath.'

'Heath?' My heart beats a little faster.

'He shows no inclination to marry, so I shall put him to war. He has a strong arm and a good mind. It would be the making of him, as a man. But would your father object if I sent him an army led by a half-blood?'

My tired mind is so overwhelmed with thoughts and feelings that it freezes my tongue.

'Ah, I have offered you insult, too —'

'No,' I say quickly. 'My father would not object to Heath. My father does not harbour prejudice to Ærfolc — half-blood or full-blood.'

Wengest's voice grows quiet, as though he is ashamed. 'It is perhaps wrong of me to be partial towards my nephew. I loved my sister, so dearly.'

'Heath is a good man,' I say, guardedly. 'But can he lead an army?'

A pause. A gust of wind hammers the shutters. 'Ah, you are right. He has had only basic training for war. It is too soon to put him in such a position.'

I relax, the black imaginings of the northern raiders' famed cruelty temporarily retreating.

'I will send him as second-in-command, behind Grislic.' Wengest kisses my cheek. 'Good counsel, my Rose. I can sleep with a clear mind now.'

But my mind is not clear. I am a fool. I should have said, *no, my father does not want a half-breed.* I should have said, *you are wrong to send a gentle man such as Heath to war.* I should have begged for Heath's safety; but I said none of those things, too concerned with protecting my secrets from discovery.

I turn over on my side, then my other side, then my back. The wind rattles the shutters, threads of snowy cold creep through. Hair works loose from my plait, and tickles my face and ears. I cannot sleep,

I cannot sleep. I tell myself, perhaps my father will change his mind. Perhaps he will not ask for an army, after all. But these thoughts are small comfort in the face of the awful fear that my lover may soon meet his death, far far away from me.

III. SOLMONATH

I watch him from my bower window. Mud-month has come and the snow has turned to brown slush. Rain falls on every cold inch of Thyrsland. And every day for the last six weeks Heath has been out in the war field with Grislic and a hundred other men. They throw spears at straw targets, they heft their great swords, they raise their wooden shields, they roar. From this distance, they are all small, dressed alike in mail shirts and iron helms. I recognise Heath only by where he is standing: at the front, beside enormous Grislic. Wengest has come down to the field today, in his rarely worn battle gear. My husband is not a warrior king like my father; or, indeed, Wengest's own father who was slain by raiders in his sixtieth winter.

It is too cold to have the shutters open, and my fingers have become ice on the window frame. Yet I watch a little longer, as I do every day. Now he is at Wengest's hall daily, I see Heath more than I ever have. But there is no private time for us. I have not had a chance to tell him how afraid I am for him. I suspect he is afraid too. Once I entered the hall to find him standing there, talking to Wengest alone. My heart caught on a hook, though it ought not have: Wengest is his uncle; he is partial to Heath. It is of no consequence if they speak to each other. So I joined them, and his eyes travelled to my belly and I know he was thinking what I was thinking: what if he never sees the child?

And I had the most despicable of thoughts. If Heath is away when the child comes, nobody will suspect. Should the child be flame-haired or sea-eyed, there will be disquiet, yes. But nobody will point to Heath, for Heath will not be there. He will have dropped out of mind. People may see her colouring as dependent on the way the sunlight falls: an autumnal glow in fair hair, a blue gaze like my older sister's.

I banish the thought again. To see any benefit in Heath's deployment is to beg for special misery should he fall to the ice-men. I watch him a little longer: his grace, his strength.

A flash of colour in the distance catches my eye, and I peer into the misting rain. Riders are coming, and they are carrying the king's standard of Ælmesse. My father has sent them. My heart hollows, for it can only mean that Wengest was right to predict Ælmesse would ask for an army; and that Heath is surely going with them in only a matter of days.

I close the shutters and return to the fire. I pull up a stool and hold my hands out to the warm flame. My fingers ache as the ice melts out of them. I condemn myself for my selfishness. If I had not entered into this love affair with Heath, he might have married and Wengest would have left him alone on his farm. He would be happy and safe. Outside, I can hear running footsteps, people calling to each other. *Riders are coming. King Æthlric sends an envoy.* Tension and excitement infuses their voices. War is terrifying and thrilling: a hundred of the town's men — sons, brothers, lovers — are soon marching out to meet it. I close my eyes. My bower, with all its fine wall hangings and carved beams, disappears. Now I am just a woman, not a queen. The baby squirms inside me, pushes tiny limbs against the wall of my womb, then settles again. She knows no fear, she anticipates no loss.

More voices outside, the shouting on the war field has stopped. I open my eyes and return to the window, crack the shutter. The riders have pulled up their horses. The first rider is talking to Wengest. She wears no helm and her long, blonde hair is unbound. My heart leaps. It is my sister. It is Bluebell.

I fly from the room, forgetting my cloak. I am running, my heart thundering, all woes temporarily forgotten. Pregnancy has robbed me of much of my grace, but I hurry on, down the uneven road out of town and into the cold sludgy fields. She looks up and sees me and breaks Wengest off half-sentence with a sharp hand gesture. She has no love for him, and he none for her. He believes women do not belong in battle; she believes that kings do.

Bluebell dismounts with athletic strength and no elegance, and stalks towards me. A moment later she is bending to embrace me as the rain deepens. Her body is bony, the mail is cold and hard. Then she stands back, laughing at my swollen belly, reaching out a tattooed hand to touch it.

'Why are you here?' I ask, breath held against the answer.

'I'm here to fetch you and take you back to Ælmesse for summerfull-month.' She tries to smile but it arrives on her face as a grimace. 'Our father intends to marry.'

The drinkhouse on the village square is warm, and flooded with sweet cinnamon steam and the pungent smell of fermenting yarrow. The rain intensifies. Bluebell's retinue sit at the hearth and order bread and meat. I take Bluebell to the king's table — a carved table with high-backed benches, tucked away from the noise in a corner of the room — so that we can talk uninterrupted.

Bluebell has few manners. She spends most of her time with warriors or with my father, so hasn't had the opportunity to learn niceties. She sits with her knees spread wide and her big feet lolling in the walkway, wipes her damp nose with the back of her hand, then raises her fingers and shouts to the young man with the tray of drinks, 'I'm starving! Bring me food and beer.' In height and colouring, she is my father's copy. In almost everything else in the world, she is my father's favourite. The rest of us have always known it and have each managed our jealousy silently. The idea that Father is to marry again is shocking to me, but to Bluebell it would sting like a betrayal. They are bone-achingly close. He makes no decision without her counsel; he enters no battle without her at his side.

'Who is she?' I ask, almost the moment we have sat down. 'Is she a good woman?'

'I hate her,' Bluebell growls. 'Of course.'

'But how did they meet? I didn't know Father had any thoughts about remarrying.'

The shutter next to us leaks, a slow trickle of water runs down the wall and pools under the table. Bluebell half-stands and slams the shutter with her shoulder. It crunches tightly. No weak light can make its way in. The small, close room is dim except for hot firelight. It could be morning or midnight.

Bluebell sits. 'She came with a retinue down the river from Tweoning, on her way to visit her sister at the far coast. Her boat sprang a leak two miles from Blicstowe.' She leans forward on her elbows, resting her chin in her hands and mutters, 'Would that it had sunk.'

I assess Bluebell as the rain thunders on the mud outside. I cannot trust her opinion; her jealousy skews her judgement.

'In any case, she made her way to town and Father offered her a place to stay,' she continues. 'It turns out that she's the widow of an old friend he knew in his youth. Her name is Gudrun.'

'She's a widow? Any children?'

'A son. Wylm. A spotted eel, not yet fifteen.' Bluebell's food and beer arrive, and disappear down her throat alarmingly quickly. As she chews loudly and slops her beer on the table, she describes to me our new stepmother. Gudrun is a pretty, soft-spoken woman who has lived among the Trimartyrs but retains the old ways of our common faith. I am curious to meet her, to see how far Bluebell's resentment of her is justified.

Finally, my sister slaps her hands against each other to wipe them clean, and indicates my belly. 'Can you travel?'

'Blicstowe isn't far.'

'A day and a half. Can you ride?'

'I … I don't know. I'll never fit into my riding clothes.'

'You can't ride a horse in skirts. Two days then. You'll have to take a covered cart.' She says the words as though they taste bad.

I feel weak and damnably feminine. Yet I am as relieved by the idea of a covered cart as I am ashamed to accept it. 'Yes, that might be for the best,' I admit.

The corner of Bluebell's mouth twitches in a smile. 'I'm not riding with you. My men wouldn't look at me the same again.'

I burst into laughter. The idea of Bluebell on an embroidered seat in a covered cart is entirely wrong. The baby responds to my laughter by squirming. I press my fingers against a tiny foot, poking me hard.

'What is it?' Bluebell asks.

I reach for her hand and pull her to her feet, holding her palm against my belly. The baby obliges by kicking her soundly. Bluebell's face is overcome by childish wonder.

'Is that the child?'

'Yes. She kicked you.'

Bluebell presses her hand hard against my stomach, waiting for another kick. She knows not her own strength. The baby has gone quiet now, and eventually my sister sits again. 'It was a foot then?'

'I don't really know. I think so.' For a moment I feel sorry for Bluebell. She has no knowledge of the giving of life, only the bringing of death. She has often declared that she will never marry and bear children; though Ash and I suspect she has had lovers. I know that she is a fine warrior, a great leader, that she is addicted to the bloodrush of battle. But does she not deny somehow what the earth mother formed her for? So few women go to war, far fewer lead armies, because women are created for another purpose. As Wengest always says, crudely, *women have sheaths, not spears.*

But then I shake off my pity. She wouldn't want it. She has known glories and sorrows that I cannot imagine; she would consider me — trapped in the bower — to be living only half a life.

She raises her cup to her lips and drains the last drops from it. Turns and shouts for more. Then fixes me in her steely blue gaze. 'You said *she.*'

'Ash said "she",' I reply warily.

Bluebell's eyebrows arch. 'I see.'

'Though she tried to deny she meant anything by it.' I shrug. 'We ought not to talk of it.'

'I don't see why it should be a secret. If she has the sight, it will make her a better counsellor. Many counsellors in the faith are sighted.'

'After twenty years of practice maybe: not in their first year of study. She might be thrown out of school. Nobody wants to be around a wild latent.'

'She should be proud of herself.' Bluebell drops her voice anyway. 'I go to her, if I can, before every battle. She sees, she knows what will happen.'

'Truly?'

Her voice becomes urgent. 'Before we went to Skildan Bridge, back in winterfull-month, she told me to strike while the tide was still low. I marched my men for two days with barely a pause to get there at low tide, and praise the horse god that I did. The raiders had war ships waiting to come down the river on the next high tide. We had already spilled their blood before the other half of the army came. We picked off the reinforcements quickly and raided their ships.' She thrusts out her arm and pushes up the heavy mail sleeve, to show me a gold armband — two fish eating each other's tails — jammed hard over the blurring blue tattoos on her forearm. Then she leans back, toying with her empty cup. 'Ash is far from me now. Too far. As are you.'

Outside, the rain has eased and the wind has begun to gust. I contemplate Bluebell's words. I had no idea that Ash's sight was so strong. But instead of feeling anxious for her — untrained latent sight can take a heavy toll, especially on young women — I am only anxious for myself. When Ash felt my belly, declared I was pregnant and accidentally told me the child was a girl, what else did she see? What else does she know about me, and about Heath?

'Something troubles you, sister?' Bluebell says.

I shake my head. 'I am tired, that is all.'

Bluebell rises, stretching long legs. With quick movements, she pulls her long hair back and winds it into an untidy knot. 'We'll stay two nights and then head to Ælmesse. But first I have to speak with Wengest. Will you come? I find him so difficult to talk to.'

'Surely. Though why must you speak with him?'

She doesn't blink. 'Father needs an army. A hundred men to go with us up to the northern border of Bradsey. The raiders are pushing hard against the people there. We're going to go and crush them, send them back into the heart-of-ice. Where the dogs belong.'

But I hear nothing beyond, *Father needs an army.* Because this is the news I have dreaded to hear. Heath is going away. To war.

Silence draws out uncomfortably. 'Will you be going?' I ask at last, aware my voice is tremulous.

'Of course.' Her chest puffs proudly, almost imperceptibly. 'Father is staying home for the first time. I'm in charge.'

A small comfort then. Bluebell will be there. Bluebell will look out for him. But, of course, she doesn't know he is important to me. I want to cry: I am so full of spidery fears and hot secrets.

Bluebell misreads the anxiety on my face and slings an arm around me, roughly pulls me close and slams her fist into her chest. 'You need not worry, sister. No raider will cut out this heart. I'd cut it out myself first.'

And I cannot tell her: it is not for her heart that I am anxious. Selfishly, it is for my own.

I wake earlier than the sun. Bluebell sleeps beside me, snoring softly. Wengest has given her his bed for the night, and he sleeps at the other end of the bower house. He has decided not to come to the wedding, because he must get his army ready for marching north. I know this is an excuse, that he trusts Grislic to prepare his men. But he is all too aware of Bluebell's disdain for his lack of involvement in war. He is trying to impress her, because she is so famed a warrior. And yet she remains unimpressed. I almost feel sorry for him.

I lie, stuck awake, for a long time. Outside, the darkness leeches from the sky. The wind has blown all the clouds away, leaving the world shivering unprotected under the stars. We are leaving this morning, after breakfast. My father's wedding feast will last a week, perhaps two. All my sisters will be there, clamouring for each other's company. Bluebell will ride early for Is-hjarta, but I will not get away before the end of summerfull-month. I will not see Heath again before he goes.

This thought throws itches into my belly. I sit up quietly, feel around in the half-dark for my clothes, and dress quickly and quietly. Bluebell sleeps hard, as does anybody who works vigorously and has a clear conscience. She doesn't hear me leave the room or the bower house; I doubt she will wake before the full rising of the sun. By then, I will have said my goodbye to Heath.

I walk, through the town and out the gate-house, calling good morning to the guards there. They are used to my long absences. The king's wife, it is well known, likes to walk and think. Perhaps, in whispers, they talk about how my father allowed his daughters to be too independent, far too clever for their own good. Yet they seem to have accepted my ways now, and I believe there is genuine fondness for me in the town. The birth of this child will be welcome and happy news.

I take the main road out of town and then cut across fields and skirt the edge of the wood. I see cows and sheep in the distance, farmers taking their first steps, yawning, into the day's work. The long walk warms my blood; I don't feel the morning cold anymore. I arrive at the edge of the river and follow it, staying in the cover of the trees. Finally, I am at the edge of Heath's farm and I make my way up towards the house. His fields have been freshly ploughed, and he is moving between the furrows, throwing handfuls of lime around him. The fields will be ready to sow soon, but he will likely not be here. Wengest will send a caretaker to watch Heath's farm in hopes he will be back for harvest-month. I pause, to burn the image of Heath into my mind. He is so beautiful, with his wide shoulders and his golden hair. He turns and sees me, half-lifts a hand in a hopeful wave.

I hurry towards him, and he catches me in his arms. I breathe in the scent of him: smoke and straw and faint sweat. He stands back and admires my belly, dusting his hands on his pants.

'You are growing apace,' he says.

'There are just three months to go.'

Sadness crosses his face. 'I will not be here.'

'I know.'

We fall silent a while. Then I say, 'I came to say goodbye. I travel to my father's hall at Blicstowe today. He is marrying a second time.'

'I had heard it from Wengest,' he replies. 'But I had not guessed I would be so lucky as to see you a last time. Come inside, where it is warm.'

He leads me into the house. The fire is hot but he doesn't go to the hearth, he sits on the mattress and I kneel, leaning on him. I am crying before I can promise myself not to cry.

'Hush, hush,' he says, his warm lips moving over my face. 'Your tears alarm me. They say you fear I will fall to the raiders.'

I take a deep shuddering breath and stop myself. 'My sister leads Ælmesse's army. Look to Bluebell. There is not a greater warrior in all of Thyrsland. In all things, look to Bluebell.'

'Hush,' he says again. 'I won't speak of it.' His lips are on my throat. I climb onto the mattress beside him. Lying against each other, we trace familiar patterns on each other's bodies. My belly is in the way, so I turn on my side and Heath presses against my back, his hot skin against me, his fingers gentle on my breasts, his kisses in my hair. The harder we chase desire, the more it seems that passion's tide cannot move us. Instead, I turn against his chest and cry a little more and this time he lets me. I am warm, I am tired. I drift to sleep. We both do.

The next thing I am aware of is a loud voice at the door.

'Heath? Are you there?'

My heart jumps into my throat. Heath is scrambling for clothes, throwing the wool blanket over me and calling, 'Who is it? What is it?'

'Grislic sent me. You are past an hour late for training.'

I hear the door open, only a crack. 'I slept late,' he says. 'I will come shortly.'

'You will come with me now,' the voice says. 'Grislic insisted.'

'I … very well.' Then I hear the door close and I know that I am alone, that Heath has left immediately so no attention could be drawn to the figure hiding in his bed.

He is gone and I didn't say goodbye. I didn't say, *I love you.*

IV. Summerfylleth

Seven hours from home, my bones are aching and my ankles are swollen. The covered cart bumps along the rutted path and no matter how I sit I cannot get comfortable. Added to this, a miserable drizzle is falling so that I cannot even part the curtains to see outside. I hear voices from time to time, Bluebell laughing with her hearthband, but I am stuck in here with a sagging cushion and nowhere to put my feet up. Added to this discomfort, I am desperate to relieve myself but too embarrassed to ask because it is not yet two hours since I last stopped the riders for the same purpose. Travelling while pregnant, I now see, is a form of torture. My father should not have expected me to come. The very thought of having to get through another day of this, and then take the return journey after the wedding, makes me want to sob.

I have with me a wooden box packed with edible treats that Cook prepared for me: mince pies and sugared fruit. I am not hungry, but I pick at it and eat too much, until my stomach feels blocked and queasy. I am a lump, glued to the seat, the hours carrying me along in uncomfortable monotony.

Just before dusk, the retinue stops. I pin back the curtains to peer out at the fading day. My knees are sore and my thighs are numb. The rain has cleared, and I see a nearby copse with sufficient privacy. My legs thank me for stretching them, my bladder thanks me for emptying it. When I return, Bluebell is nowhere in sight. Her retainers are gathered on the muddy road, arguing among themselves.

'Brygen is only two miles. If we don't stop there, we will not reach the next village before nightfall,' one man says.

'I am not afraid of nightfall,' another man says.

'And yet you are afraid of Brygen.'

'The horses are tired. They need to rest.'

'It will only be two hours more.'

I glance around, searching for Bluebell. Two hours more! I cannot bear the thought. I need to convince Bluebell to let us stop in Brygen. I need a soft bed. There is my sister, slouching out from behind a tree, straightening her riding pants. I hurry over, but the men have spotted her too and are already calling, 'Brygen or Dunscir, my lord?'

'Brygen is —'

Bluebell raises a long hand. 'Dunscir.'

Immediately the arguing ceases. Nobody is willing to disagree with Bluebell.

Except for me. 'Please, Bluebell. I can't travel another two hours. I am raw. I must rest.'

She turns to me, brows drawn down. Even I am afraid of her for a moment. 'Rest? But you have been resting in the carriage.'

'I cannot make myself comfortable. I am too big.' I pat my belly for emphasis. I see that the expression on her brow is wavering. 'Please.' Her retainers are shifting from foot to foot. Even the horses seem nervous with anticipation.

'Very well. We will take the road up to Brygen.'

'But, my lord —'

'My sister's comfort is all I care to hear about.'

Silence.

'Let's go.'

I deduce the reason for their reluctance to stop in Brygen almost immediately. The little village is dotted with empty, sagging buildings, the forest around seems to encroach on the hill upon which it is built, every third tree appears to be blighted with perpetual winter: leafless black branches raised against the whitening sky as the sun sinks somewhere behind clouds. Our inn is draughty and the food has the texture of sawdust. But when I climb into bed — leaving Bluebell downstairs drinking with her hearthband — I think of nothing but the soft lambswool. I drift to sleep within three breaths.

It is much later that I wake. A prickling in my bones. Bluebell is asleep next to me. I have no reason to feel unsafe.

But sleep will not come. A chill creeps under the shutter. My cheek is frozen. I sit up, but can see the the shutter is closed tight. I rise, and find myself opening it and peering out into the dark.

The clouds have dissolved and a pale half-moon lights the scene. Down the hill, on the side of the road, a woman kneels next to a pile of dirt. Her figure is traced in shades of midnight and moonlight. She looks dreadfully familiar.

'Mother,' I gasp.

But it cannot be mother. Mother has been dead for twelve years.

Bluebell rouses. 'Rose? Is everything well with you?'

I turn, words falling from my tongue in a tangle. 'A woman, outside on the road. She looks like mother.'

Bluebell is out of bed faster than an arrow, but as I turn back to the window I can see already that there is no woman. That the road is deserted but for the skulking shadows of bare, sick trees.

A moment of silence passes between us, then Bluebell touches my hair. 'It was a long journey, Rose. Come back to bed. Rest.'

'I did see her.'

She closes the shutter firmly. 'Come back to bed,' she repeats, tugging my wrist.

I follow her instruction and lie down next to her. I tell myself that Bluebell is right: I am tired. I cannot distinguish between sleeping and waking. And yet my heart stammers and my eyes will not close, even after Bluebell has let go of my hand and turned on her side to sleep. My bones are still prickling. Quietly, careful not to wake my sister, I return to the window.

She is there again, the figure that looks like my mother. And I know that this sending is for me. Not for Bluebell, or she would have seen it too. Despite the depth of the night, the cold of the moonlight, the eerie emptiness of the forest, I dress warmly and leave the room.

The front door of the inn creaks as I open it, and again as I let it fall closed behind me. The figure has not moved; she is hunched over the shape on the ground and I realise now that she is crying. I can hear her harsh sobs over the breeze rattling in the trees.

'Mother?' I say, but my voice is a tight, fearful whisper. I steel myself and approach. The shape on the road is a mound; a triangle — symbol of the trimartyrs — glints dully in the weak moonlight. A grave. My mother's spirit is bent over a grave. My skin shivers.

'Mother?' I say, louder now. Closer. She looks up. I stop in front of her.

'She will never be queen,' she says.

'Who? Who is buried here?' Mortal dread flares in my heart: it is a presentiment of death.

'Nobody is buried here. Just her crown.'

The flame of fear subsides a little. 'Whose crown? Bluebell's? Will she be safe?' I glance over my shoulder, back to the inn, wondering if Bluebell still sleeps. When I turn back, it is not my mother at the side of the road, but a creature formed of sticks and mud, glaring at me. A mudthrael. I yelp, and back away.

'Wait!' it calls in a voice scraped from the bottom of a murky pond. It reaches its uncanny hands towards me, and distaste slithers over my skin. I see a dead branch on the ground, scoop it up and take aim —

But the creature flings up its muddy fingers and something gritty and darkly sparkling enters my eyes. I am instantly dislocated from the cold, wet road in Brygen: there is no mudthrael, there is no stick in my hand, there is no road, nor any trees. I am inexplicably *elsewhere*.

On a vast plain. A million miles away, there are mountains perhaps, beyond the fiery horizon. Wind buffets me, whipping my hair around my face. I gulp against the shock, pressing my toes hard into my shoes to ground myself. The mudthrael has thrown me under an enchantment, I must try to remember who and where I am.

The earth shudders, and I know that something terrifying is approaching. Sunset colours burn the sky. I am horribly aware of how open and exposed I am out here. 'Bluebell!' I call, my throat raw with fear and effort. 'Bluebell!'

But then I remember, I am not here at all, I am ...

The shaking underfoot intensifies, and my whole body resounds with the movement. A scant ten feet in front of me, a fissure appears in the ground. Paralysing fear turns my limbs to stone. I try to lift my feet, but they are part of the juddering ground. I am caught, heart and bones, in the thundering fear. Inch by crumbling inch the ground disappears in front of me and, from the black depths, a twisting firedrake rises.

Its eyes are bigger than my skull, its golden hide is spiked with bronze. The smell is fish and sulphur, dirt and old blood. It is the three-toed firedrake: the writhing shape on my father's standard, the symbol of Ælmesse's power. The drake spreads its jaw and spews curling fire above my head. My heart slams. I struggle against the glue that holds my feet to the ground, feeling the reflected heat of the firedrake's breath singeing my hair and stripping my cheeks bloody. I throw my arms up and call out in fear.

Silence, stillness, cold.

I open my eyes. The light has bled away. I am still on the plain, but it is late — so late. Past time for sleep, past time for death. My eyes search fearfully for the dragon, but it is now just a blackened skeleton in the distance. The churning sky is visible between its ribs. An icy wind creeps across the ground, tumbling ash over its gaping skull. Movement catches my gaze. A hand extended out of the ground, fingers spread apart. Ghostly white. It beckons slowly.

I move towards it. I have long ago forgotten that I am actually standing on the road in Brygen, under the influence of mudthrael magic. This dream is sharper than truth. The dragon bones are still and cold. Three feet from the tip of its tail, a dark pit of soil has been dug. A woman, buried in it except for her face and hands, glares up at me with icy blue eyes. I know this ritual of partial burial: it is a magic ritual of the underfaith, that shady cult that exists below the common faith and has been all but driven from Thyrsland. Her eyes terrify me; they seem to know my soul better than I know it.

'Who are you?' I ask.

'I am your father's sister.'

'My father has no sister.'

'He has a sister, and I am she. You may not know me, but I know you, Rose,' she says. Her hair is mostly buried, but I can see that it is silvery-brown around her brow. 'My name is Yldra. You know I am of your family, for I called the three-toed firedrake.'

Shivering cold is eroding me inside. I cannot stay here; it will mean my destruction. And yet, I cannot remember where I am from. 'How do I get back?' I ask.

Her mouth moves and no sound comes out. She tries again, and this time it seems as though her voice is far away. Reality glimmers back into my mind. This *is* a dream.

'You must kill Wengest as soon as you return from your father's wedding,' she says. 'Or Rowan will never be queen.'

'Who is Rowan?'

'Your daughter. Kill him before the child is born.'

'I am no killer.'

And then it all dissolves, just like one of cook's sugar mice under hot beer. I am back in Brygen, mid-swing. I cannot stop my arms, the branch crashes into the mudthrael's sodden body, and the creature cries out and flies backwards, coming to rest in a heap in the middle of the road.

'Rose?'

It is Bluebell, running towards me, taking the branch from my hand and grasping my wrists. 'What happened? What are you doing here?'

'I …' I point to the mudthrael, but it is just a pile of twigs and soil. 'I have been … somewhere.'

Bluebell looks closely at me. 'Your eyes are wild and black.'

'Mudthrael,' I manage.

She glances around, alarmed. 'This forest is known for bad magic,' she says. 'That's why my hearthband didn't want to stop here.'

Bad magic. The kind that everyone is afraid of, the kind that is brewed within the earthen huts of the underfaith. Mudthraels are fashioned and controlled by its devotees, and somebody sent this one to me: disguised it as my mother to tempt me out of my bed and throw visions in my eyes. But who? Bluebell is herding me up the road towards the inn, but I stop her.

'Bluebell, does our father have a sister?'

'No.'

'You are certain?'

'I am certain. He has no sister. Come, inside.'

I allow her to lead me, but I am awash in confusion. I will sleep no more tonight.

My first glimpse of home comes late the following afternoon. I feel bruised all over from the journey, but when I see the hill — the town, my father's hall, the red and yellow flags fluttering on the gate house — I forget my pain.

The giants once lived here; they raised buildings and monuments made of some dazzling stone, the like of which has never been seen since in Thyrsland. Their buildings have fallen into ruin, and nobody alive knows how to fix them. And so the tall white ruins wait out the centuries, catching the sun to give the name to our town. Blicstowe: the bright place. Laid out in front of the ruins are the thatched roofs of the town itself. I know each building and its inhabitants well: the weavers, bronzesmiths, carpenters, bone workers, their wives, their muddy-faced children, the mad war-widows and the sane, bakers, potters, fishermen, lenders, counsellors of the common faith, the faithless, the homeless, the adolescent boys who dream of bearing swords alongside my sister. The roads are lined with wooden planks so that traffic may move even in muddy weather, and move it does. Carts, horses, pigs, chickens, and everywhere people. My father's people.

The town has been decorated for the wedding. Russet ribbons are wound around pillars and flutter from gable finishings, but it is too early in the year for white daisies. Our retinue thunders over the echoing bridge, up the hard-packed dirt road between the lines of oaks, and finally past the gatehouse and down to the stables. Bluebell helps me out of the cart and I stretch my legs gratefully. I glance up at the ruins: they are stained with sunset colours. My father's hall — a hulking, wood-shingled building — is stark black against the giants' stone. And there he is, standing between two of the pillars that he carved himself, smiling at me.

'Father!' I call, and he strides lithely towards me, catching me gently in his arms. His long yellow hair is streaked with grey, and age has made his blue eyes pale and his strong hands knotted. But he is still tall and handsome; he is still the first man I ever loved.

'My Rose,' he says, standing back and admiring my belly. 'It is wonderful to have you home, but doubly wonderful that you are here for such an occasion.' He turns to Bluebell. 'You spoke with Wengest?'

'Yes, Father. They will be ready to march.'

A slight frown crosses his brow, but then he dismisses it. 'Come inside, both of you,' he says, leading me by the arm. 'Gudrun is waiting to meet you, Rose. Ash arrived yesterday, and Ivy and Willow have been here a fortnight.' He talks a little too fast, and I realise that he is nervous. My father — the man who sometimes comes home from battle with other men's blood embedded under his fingernails — nervous. I am caught between good-hearted amusement and pity.

We round the front of the hall, and here on the massive beams that support the doors are two carved firedrakes. My vision in Brygen returns to me. I pause to run my hand over the creature's back while Father lifts the beam and pushes the doors open. I have gone over the vision many times on the long journey today, turning the images and words over and over the way the tide turns over seaweed. Whether or not my daughter is one day queen is still an abstract thought; at the moment, she is just a bundle of squirming limbs in my belly. I will not kill Wengest, and that is the most important thing. I do not know if I have the ability to kill any man; perhaps we all do when tested. But I know that I cannot kill my husband. I like him, he is a good man. And should my crime be discovered, that would plunge his kingdom into war with my father's. So I have not spent another thought on that possibility. Instead, I have pondered on why his death now would ensure my daughter's ascension to the throne, on what could happen between now and milk-month. Of course, the handful of anxious ants in my stomach tells me that somehow Heath and I will be discovered. Other possibilities have not occurred to me and so, despite the fact that I need to ask my sister Ash about the vision, I am terrified to speak to her. Her second sight is too alert. My secrets may be uncovered.

'What is it?' Father asks, turning and seeing that I haven't followed him inside.

I smile as though nothing is wrong. 'I have missed home, that's all,' I say.

He takes my hand. 'Home has missed you. Come. Supper is about to be served.'

I hurry after Father. Bluebell stalks, sulking, four steps behind us. I am wholly prepared, on her behalf, to dislike Gudrun. We cross the vast hall, where Father's hearthband is loosely gathered, lying on benches, stoking the fire, talking softly, enjoying supper. A number of them call out to Bluebell and she breaks off to talk to them. Father drops my hand and opens the door to his state room — really just a small room with a table for private meals — and ushers me through.

The room is cosy, crowded with firelight and faces. Tapestries plundered from battle adorn the walls; some are shot with golden thread or are bordered with the fur of exotic animals. Along the wall beams are lined other treasures: cups and armbands of gold, pots and statues, ceremonial swords. The firelight is caught on the gleaming surfaces. The long carved table is laid out with baskets of fresh-baked bread, wooden bowls of pickled vegetables and strips of dried fish. I am suddenly ravenous. Around the table, on wooden benches, sit my sisters. Ash is at the far end, smiling at me. I smile in return, but move no closer. Instead, I sit between Ivy and Willow, the twelve-year-old twins. Ivy, with her magpie eyes, is pointing at my belly with a spoon, making some rude joke. Willow is shushing her. Ash is asking me how I endured the journey. But all I can pay attention to is this woman who is not one of us, Father's new wife. Gudrun of Tweoning.

She is nothing like I had imagined. I imagined somebody, I suppose, like my mother. Noble, dark-haired, eyes that betrayed steel in the spine, light in the brain. But Gudrun is softly pretty, with pale brown hair, round cheeks and bovine eyes, a gentle smile that she has turned on me.

She leans across the table and places a soft, white hand on mine. 'Hello, Rose. It is truly a joy to meet you. I've heard so much about you.'

How on earth can Bluebell object to this woman?

'This is my son, Wylm.' Gudrun leans back and puts an arm around the middle of the boy who sits next to her. He is on the verge of manhood; his limbs seem to be growing before my eyes, straining at clothes that were probably comfortably sized just a week ago. His dark hair is lank and his hazel eyes are sullen. He manages a grudging smile, his knuckles half-hiding his mouth.

'It is a pleasure for me, too,' I say. 'I am very happy for my father especially.' As I say it, I realise I mean it. Twelve years without my mother. He must have been so lonely, and if this woman with her soft edges and white hands can provide him the company he needs, then I cannot join Bluebell in her dislike of the situation. All things change. I touch my belly. I *know* that all things change.

A moment later, Bluebell is at the door. 'Father?' she says.

'Come in, Bluebell,' Father says, taking the seat between Gudrun and Wylm. 'It will be our first meal as a new family.'

Bluebell's eyes flicker like flame. She can barely keep her mouth from turning down. 'I'm going to eat with the men,' she says. 'Sighere wants to discuss the march up to Is-hjarta.'

There is a space of time — no longer than three seconds, though it feels longer — where tension infuses the room. Father locks eyes with Bluebell. It is a challenge, and he recognises this and, as a king, his chest expands ready to demand his will. The insult Bluebell offers is not only to him, but also to his new wife. But then he softens. Of course he understands Bluebell's resistance; he understands everything about her and his partiality is legendary: he cannot help but forgive her everything. 'Very well, Bluebell,' he says, glancing away.

She withdraws quickly, closing the door behind her. Gudrun studies her hands, blushing. Wylm gazes at the door with unsheathed hostility. My pulse quickens. Perhaps this is the stuff of any family disagreement, but for us it has the makings of much more significant conflict. I can see with my own eyes that one day Wylm will be a tall, strong man. The last thing a potential queen needs is a half-brother who hates her.

'Let us eat,' Father says brightly.

And we do. We eat and talk, and I get to know Gudrun a little. Ivy asks me dozens of questions about babies, about Wengest, about life in Netelchester. Willow is quiet, almost shy, which makes me sad. The twins have been raised by my mother's brother and his wife, far south, since birth. My father was grieving my mother's death, Ash and I were too young to raise them, and Bluebell, frankly, would have made a mess of it. So they are our sisters, but they are also strangers. I have met them, perhaps, a dozen times.

The evening wears on, and weariness infuses my poor bones. I need to lie down. Ash catches me yawning and says, 'Time for bed, Rose? I am tired too. Would you come and share with me?'

My blood tingles with ice. I cannot lie next to Ash all night: she may read my dreams. I shake my head. 'No, I am fine. You go on ahead. I will wait for Bluebell.' Even though Bluebell snores and her elbows invariably end up in my ribs.

'I will share with you, Ash,' Ivy says, springing to her feet. 'Is there room for Willow too?'

Ash looks pleased. 'Of course. We may have to squeeze in, but three bodies are warmer than two.'

I am falling asleep into my hands, but I stay while goodnights are said. Gudrun takes her leave, Wylm following. Father kisses her softly, murmurs something in her ear. I stand and stretch, peer out the door into the smoky hall for Bluebell. She is deep in conversation with Sighere.

Father's arm is around my waist. 'You are tired, don't wait for Bluebell.'

But Bluebell has looked up, seen me. She lifts her hand in a gesture that says, *wait just another short moment; I am coming.* I smile.

I turn to Father to say goodnight. I realise in a sudden hot rush that I am alone with him. It may be the only occasion for a long time. I form the question too quickly, and nearly stumble over it.

'Yldra? Do you know her?'

He flinches, almost imperceptibly, but it could be because of the abruptness of my question. 'What name?'

'Do you have a sister? Or a half-sister? Yldra?'

Then he is shaking his head. 'I have no sister, Rose. I know nobody of that name.'

I want to say, 'Are you sure?' because I sense too polished a veneer on his answer. But if he hasn't told me now, he won't tell me later. That is the nature of secrets. They do not emerge on repeated questioning; rather they burrow deeper as more lies and denials are thrown on top of them.

'I must sleep,' I say, instead. 'I must sleep for a hundred years, I am so tired.'

'Yes, and the feast starts tomorrow.' He leans down and kisses my forehead. 'Goodnight, Rose.'

I beckon for Bluebell, and we head for the bowerhouse.

My father is blessed with a perfectly blue sky, perfectly warm day for his wedding feast. Everyone says it is a sign from the great mother. He throws open the doors to his hall so that the sunshine can slant in on the scrubbed wooden boards and fresh rushes. Winter is over. The ceremony itself took place in the state room earlier this morning, presided over by Byrta, who has been my father's counsellor for nearly forty years. She delivered me and all my sisters, and buried my mother twelve years ago. Now solemnity is behind us, and the rest of the afternoon is given over to noisy carousing. The first full moon of the summer will rise tonight, and I have no doubt that my father's retinue will be sleeping drunk on the grass under its glow.

It is hard to be sad or anxious when all around me red and white streamers dance in the breeze. I feel light, as though my worries have drifted away a while, and I am determined not to dwell on them on this happy day. Ivy and Willow are sitting on a bench just outside the door, and I join them with a cup of spiced honey-wine and chat a little while. The smell of roasting pig rises from the hearth and circles the building, making stomachs rumble. Many of the townsfolk come up to the hall with gifts for my father and Gudrun — pots, baskets, charm dollies, cotton flowers, lucky stones — and I gather them with smiles and good wishes. My father and Gudrun move from group to group of friends and well-wishers. He barely takes his eyes from her face. Bluebell comes outside into the sunshine with two of our young cousins, who battle her with wooden swords until she pretends to be defeated and theatrically throws her long body onto the grass. Ash is safely inside with Byrta. All is well, for now.

But then the day grows cooler, dimmer. Blue washes from the sky, shadows lengthen, the scent of damp earth rises. All at once, it is too cool to sit outside, and I am starving. The noise and chatter withdraws into the hall and the great doors are hefted shut, the shutters sealed and the fire stoked. I am one of the last to enter, because I want to see where Ash is sitting. So I can choose the furthest seat from her. I end up with my one of my distant uncles and his much younger wife. She is pregnant too, though barely out of childhood herself. She tells endless stories about women whose bodies were torn to pieces by childbirth, and how she hasn't slept for fear since midwinter. I grit my teeth, stealing glances at the table where all my sisters are now congregated, eating and laughing. Ash catches my eyes, beckons. I pretend not to see her. My young companion rattles on, barely stopping to put food in her mouth. With the coming dark, the morbid company, and the growing noise, my sense of contentment frays around the edges and then begins to unravel. I am so tired. I want to go somewhere dark and quiet and close my eyes. And think about Heath, even if thinking about him makes me feel desperate and frightened.

A warm hand on my shoulder. I look up, then flinch as though a snake has touched me. It is Ash.

'Rose?' she says, alarmed, pulling her hand back. In that brief touch, did she sense something? Did she read my thoughts?

I am on my feet in a moment. 'I ... Ash, I'm sorry. I'm not ...' I intend to tell her I'm unwell, that I have to go immediately, a lie that would not convince even a child. But in that same instant the doors to the hall burst open and a man is standing there, ragged and muddy, calling for the king.

Ash turns; her eyes widen and seem to go black. The blood drains from her face.

'Ash? What is it?'

'They have underestimated the ice-men,' she whispers.

Father is on his feet. Bluebell is at his shoulder. A curious, frightened silence takes hold of the wedding feast.

'My lord,' the ragged stranger says, falling to his knees at my father's feet. 'I have ridden night and day to pass on some grave news. The raiders are already inside the border of Bradsey. They have burned six villages, all outposts of our allies. They spare nobody, not even children. We have left it too late to slow them down. We have …' He trails off, exhausted. 'Forgive me, my horse could go no further. I have run nearly all the way from Dunscir. They are butchers, my lord. Butchers.'

Gudrun, her face lit by fire, sits at the table where a moment before she was a happy newlywed. I see she is terrified. Father said he would sit this campaign out, that it was a small matter, that he needed to be with his new wife and Bluebell needed her chance to lead the army alone. But now Gudrun thinks he will go away, and make her a widow again. She catches my eye, and I try to smile to offer her comfort. But I know precisely how she feels.

'We will march tonight,' Bluebell says to him, and it is not a question.

Father strokes his beard. 'We can be ready by —'

'You are not coming.'

Sighere, one of the war chiefs, joins them. 'My lord,' he says to Father, 'Your wife sits there quaking; you have been married only a day.'

Father looks from one of them to the other and, horribly, he looks old and confused. For the first time. My heart catches. Then he gathers his bearing and turns to the assembly, raising his hand. 'Forgive me, my friends. I have a matter of state to attend to. Gudrun?' He beckons her and she is under his arm in a second. Ash runs after them. They leave the hall, a hundred dull murmurs in their wake.

I pace the confines of my bower while a greasy candle sputters next to the bed. I know Bluebell will come here before she leaves; her sword is still tucked under the lambswool on her side of the bed.

Outside, the wedding feast continues, the revellers have spilled out of the hall under the full moon and the cloudless sky. I clutch my hands together as though to catch myself before I fall deeper and deeper into a dark place. It is really happening; Heath is really going to war. *They are butchers.* Morbid pictures have colonised my imagination. It is as though I can already feel the flush of searing heat, the hollowing out of my stomach, the unhingeing of my knees as I hear the news: *Heath is dead, he has fallen to the raiders.* All my nerves have come loose, I am helpless.

The door slams open, letting in a blast of cool evening air. I jump. It is Bluebell. As though she hasn't seen me, she strides to the bed and pulls out her sword. She is already dressed in mail, her helm pushed down over her head so that her broken nose is hidden and her mouth looks grim under the iron's shadow.

'Bluebell?' I say.

'It is decided,' she replies, without looking up. 'Father is not coming.'

I notice that her hands shake.

'Are you ... nervous?' I ask.

She freezes, catches me in her frost-blue gaze. 'Oh, no, Rose,' she says, slowly, passionately. 'I am on fire.'

She sheathes the sword and turns. I call out, 'Wait.'

'What is it?' she says, still half-turned from me.

'There is a man ... Wengest's nephew. He will ride with you from Netelchester. You will know him because he is fair and has no beard.' My heart is thundering. 'He is special to Wengest — his favourite nephew — and I do hope that he ...'

She is impatient. She cares little for Wengest, and even less for his beardless nephew. 'I have only two eyes in my head, and they must look direct in front of me. I cannot look behind for a —'

'His name is Heath,' I say quickly, softly. 'And he is special to *me*.'

A caught breath. She turns slowly, tilts her head almost imperceptibly to the left. She blinks slowly. 'Rose?'

Say nothing, say nothing. And yet, even as I scream these words in my head, my lips are moving and tears are spilling out of my eyes. My voice is thick, almost guttural. 'He is the father of my child, sister.'

The helm creates such shadows on Bluebell's face that I cannot read her expression. Ugly regret clogs my throat. I have surely doomed Heath, myself, the peace between Ælmesse and Netelchester.

Bluebell's voice remains even, almost cold, but not unkind. She says, 'Then I will protect him so that one day she may know him.' And she is gone, the door clattering shut behind her. The gust helps drown the candle flame, and I am left standing in the dark, crying with relief and cursing myself for saying anything at all.

It is morning, not yet warm. The sun still lingers behind the rocky hill and I am walking among the giants' ruins above my father's hall. I have not slept, I have only thought. So many thoughts that they all twisted up together and made no sense. The ruins are calm and white. Here and there, brave saplings struggle against the stone foundations. The spaces between fallen stones are brimming with leaves and twigs, and captured rain that has turned brown and rank. I find a fallen pillar and I sit down and slide onto my side, allowing my temple to touch the cool stone. Willing such coolness, such implacable and ancient calm, into my poor, tired brain.

My eyes are closed, but there are random impressions of colours and shapes on my eyelids. I try to watch them, but my mind skips from one hot thought to another, shattering my focus.

'Rose?'

And my skin is alight again with fear. I jolt, sitting up and opening my eyes. Ash stands a few feet away, and she looks eight years old and worried that I might shout at her. But what does it matter anymore? I told Bluebell. I no longer have a secret to hide.

'I'm so sorry,' I say to her, and my voice breaks and I begin to cry.

Ash is next to me in an instant, and I press myself against her and my face twists with sobs. She rubs my back, rocks me as though I were a child and not a mother. And she says, 'Rose, I already know. I've known all along.'

The tears seem to fall forever.

V. HRETHMONATH

Seven weeks have passed since Heath marched for Is-hjarta, and I know not whether he is alive or dead. Sometimes I believe it possible that I would sense if he had died. But I have no second sight; I have nothing but a desperate heart.

And yet the fields bloom as though hope is everywhere. The first two full moons of the warm season have come and gone: red and yellow wildflowers stretch in every direction, tight buds curl on branches, and lambs chase their mothers as though slaughter's shadow will never fall. Two nights ago, we held the hearth-month feast, to celebrate life's renewal and the great mother's benevolence. My belly has grown so full that it is an effort to put my feet on the floor in the morning. Wengest hasn't been in my bed since I returned from Blicstowe. If I were to guess, I might say that he finds my swollen body distasteful. In truth, I am glad not to see him. I am less anxious when I am not always examining his expression for knowledge of my secrets.

It is an hour before evening's fall, and any moment I expect my sister Ash to arrive. I paced at the gatehouse for two hours this afternoon, until my ankles grew tired and fat. I lie in my bed now, waiting for the gate watchers to call me. I should have remembered that Ash is often late, that she has little concept of time and its passing.

Ash will stay for three full moons; as a companion, an advisor, and to deliver my child. I have not spoken with her since she bid me farewell at my father's hall, when her soft eyes reassured me that all my secrets were safe, that she loved me and did not judge me for what I have done.

Faintly, I hear the signal from the gate. They have spotted Ash's retinue in the distance. I struggle to sit, put both feet on the floor and heave. And I am up: a festival trick involving cows and coaxing. I take a breath and start to move, open my bower door and peer out.

It has grown cold. I put my hand on the threshold and sag, admitting that I will not be walking to the gatehouse. I will not wait there for Ash, nor will I bound out to meet my sister. I will stay right here in the bowerhouse, where she will come before taking me to the hall for supper.

As I turn to move back inside, I see on the stones a small wooden box. It is tucked up against the wall next to the door. I brace my back with my hand and bend to scoop it up. My name is written on it in charcoal. Black smudges transfer themselves to my fingers.

Perhaps it is a gift from one of the villagers. I have been given many warm swaddles; though usually the giver sees me in person, wanting to speak and receive a thank-you.

I close out the late afternoon cool, and return to my bed with the box. I sit with my legs crossed in front of me, and pick open the knot on the string that holds the lid on. Inside is a clay figure of a woman, no bigger than my hand. She is roundly pregnant, and wears a tiny silver knife on a thin ribbon around her neck. I am part curious, part apprehensive. It is so strange. I turn her over to look for a mark, anything that would indicate who has sent her, where she has come from. But there is nothing. The knife is set with two very small gems, and I pull it close to my face to examine them.

When I touch the tiny silver blade, I feel the first cold bolt of magic. It races up my arms and through my shoulders, and in a gasping moment is spinning in my brain.

The vision is very clear. I hold a knife, the real-size version of the miniature with its two gems in the handle. Around me is a winter's landscape. Pure white snow, and a huge spreading rowan tree with leafless branches casting skeletal shadows. Underneath the tree sits Wengest, fat and merry, drunk and hung with jewels and gold. His sword has been discarded a few feet away, and is rusted from never being used.

'I do not want to be here,' I try to say, but my jaw is clamped shut and the knife is finding its own path towards Wengest's heart. My whole body lurches forward as though someone else is inside me, controlling my limbs. I strain every muscle against it, but it is no use. The knife plunges into his chest. I scream, but the sound is just an echo in my mind. Blood begins to pulse from him, staining the snow and then melting it. Steam rises, the rowan tree creaks to life. In moments, leaves are sprouting, buds are unfurling, fruit ripens fatly and drops. The profusion of life is almost grotesque, feeding on my husband's spilled blood. I know what this vision means: only with Wengest's death can my daughter flourish, can she be queen of Netelchester.

A blast of cool air hits my face. I blink slowly and the vision dissolves. I am looking, instead, at my sister Ash.

My mind lights up and, without greeting, I press the figure into her hands. 'A sending,' I say. 'Who is it from?'

Ash's face is confused a moment, but then her fingers scrabble to grasp the object. She focuses, her eyes flutter closed. A few moments later they open again, and she shakes her head. 'I tried to chase her, but she withdrew the instant she sensed me.'

'She? A woman sent this?' I lean forward. 'Is her name Yldra?' Even as I say this, I realise it must be true. Yldra, whoever she is, trying to convince me to kill Wengest so that my daughter will thrive. The daughter she thinks I will name Rowan.

'I had no sense of a name,' Ash replies. 'But it was odd …' She bites her lip, then smiles apologetically. 'I'm afraid I am sometimes not so in control of this gift of mine, but she was familiar somehow. And unfamiliar, too.'

I frown, trying to discern her meaning.

'As though,' she says, 'she might be related to us, but distantly.'

My *father's sister*.

Ash is stroking my hair. 'Are you well, sister? Was it a sending of ill news? Heath?'

I shake my head, the old sad longing welling up again. 'No. I have no news of him,' I mumble, profoundly uncomfortable with speaking of my love aloud. 'It was nothing. Confusion. Trees and snow.' I have not told Ash or anyone about the message these visions are sending me. I cannot bear even to say the words, *kill Wengest*, next to each other. Nor do I want to alarm my sisters about the possibility that my daughter — whom I have never considered naming Rowan — will not rule Netelchester. This possibility still fails to strike my heart strongly. Becoming a queen is, after all, not a kind thing to wish upon innocents. All I can think is that I must be in danger of being discovered, for how else could my husband's first child not succeed him? I vow to stay well clear of Wengest until the child is born.

I smile weakly at Ash. 'I'm glad you are here.' It is the truth.

Ash's presence brings me great joy. As summer deepens, I sleep easier at night with her beside me. I try not to think of Heath, or, at least, I try not to worry about him. I tell myself Bluebell will keep watch for me and I can ask for no greater assurance. We begin to plan the midsummer feast, raising the polite ire of Nyll and his small band of curmodgeonly trimartyrs, who grow more vocal with every seasonal festival. The predicted date of my child's birth comes and goes, and I am both glad — for a late birth will mean less suspicion directed at me — and horribly disheartened. I am so very, very tired.

VI. TRIMILCEMONATH

Sleep does not come easy in these last days of pregnancy. Some reasons are material: it is simply impossible for me to get comfortable. But some are immaterial: I feel lost somehow, and guilty all the time. The dark of early morning is not a betrayer's friend. Something has woken me and I strain my ears into the dark to hear what it might be.

Voices. From the king's bower. Muffled through the wall, but voices nonetheless. Wengest is talking to somebody in his room, very late. My first thought is that he has a woman in there, and my heart grows indignant. But the second voice does not sound like a woman's. I listen for a while, trying to make out words but there are none clear enough. There is occasional laughter, but then there is quiet. The quiet stretches out. Ash breathes softly next to me. Sleep doesn't return.

I rise, curious about the voices in Wengest's bower. Is it a woman? If so, would I have the courage to confront him? I pull on a shawl and go to the door, out briefly into the starry clear night, then back in through Wengest's door. The fire is low in the hearth, just enough light for me to see that he is asleep now. His dark features are shadowed. He does not flinch when I come in, and I see that there are two empty cups on the chest of drawers. He has been drinking, but now his companion — whoever it was — has gone.

I move to back out, but my eye is caught by the dull gleam of steel. His sword.

My gaze moves, as if outside of my control, between the supine figure of Wengest and the hard blade.

Kill him before the child is born.

And I allow myself to imagine it. Not the act itself, not the resistance and gristle of his body to the blade. But the aftermath, where I am queen of Netelchester and Heath is my consort. My blood rushes with it, my good sense is in danger of being swept away.

But then I feel a strange pain in my back, down very low, and water splatters onto the rushes between my feet. Wengest stirs, so I know that I must have groaned with the sudden pain. He opens his eyes and says, 'Rose, is that you?'

'The child is coming,' I say.

He sits up. 'Return to your sister,' he says, fear and anger infusing his voice. 'Men should have nothing to do with such things.'

I want nothing more than to hurry back to Ash, but another pain grabs me and I have to stop and lean forward, groaning. As I do, my eye falls on a folded vellum book on the end of Wengest's bed. Wengest cannot read, and the book is clearly marked with the triangle of the trimartyrs. Nyll has been here. Nyll has been laughing with Wengest until the early hours. With the sudden clarity of anybody pulled forcibly out of her self obsession, I see why my daughter will never be queen. It has nothing to do with Heath; it has everything to do with faith.

'Go on, off with you!' Wengest exclaims. He is out of bed now and helping me — thrusting me — towards the door. 'Ash!' he calls as he slams the door open. 'Tend to your sister.'

All thoughts of Nyll, of Wengest, even of Heath flee from me as the pain grasps my body again. I am as confused and terrified as a pig being led to the butcher's block. I try to catch my breath and clear my mind, but the pain is far worse than I had imagined and Wengest hands me over to Ash with a barked order that he wants to hear and see nothing until the child is born and wrapped in clean linen.

At least I am back in my own bower, near my own bed. Ash bustles about me, unfolding clean cloths and offering soothing words. 'Make yourself comfortable,' she says.

I almost laugh. An unforgiving monster has fastened sharp jaws around my back and groin and is squeezing harder and harder. I had heard that there should be a rhythm of pain and relief, but I have no relief. Ash is concerned enough by this to feel my belly carefully. She frowns and says, 'The baby is facing the wrong way. Her back is against yours.'

'Is that bad? Will she die?' *Will I die?*

'No, no,' Ash says, brushing my hair from my face. 'She is safe, you both are. But it will hurt, Rosie. I'm sorry, but it will hurt and it will be long.' She helps me onto the bed, arranging me so I am kneeling over a pile of cushions. I fear the unremitting pain, the long night ahead. I want to cry, I want to be a young virgin again who never thought of the passions of the body and all their black consequences.

The night unfurls, the sun returns and climbs high into the sky, and finally the child slides from my exhausted body. I sob with relief, and Ash sobs too. The child — hot and squirming — is a girl. A dark-haired, slate-eyed girl. I bundle her against me and offer her my breast as though I have been preparing for her arrival for my whole life. There is a pause in life, a moment of still, warm silence. A moment, perhaps, of pure happiness.

Then Ash asks me, 'Do you want me to get Wengest?'

I clutch the baby jealously. She has settled to suckle. 'No.' She is not his, anyway. He would be a stranger in here.

'I think it would be wise to show him the child,' Ash says carefully.

I gaze at her. She has dark rings under her eyes, and I realise she must be tired too. She is looking back at me with eyes as dark as mine, eyes as dark as I suspect my daughter's will be. Of course she is right. Wengest is likely in the next room. He will have heard the moaning stop, he will have heard my daughter's keening cry. He will be waiting for Ash to tell him to come, that the bloodied sheets have been piled away and that the child and I are cleaned and covered up.

We prepare ourselves and the room, and Ash goes to fetch my husband.

In the few moments remaining, I study my daughter's face and hands, her impossibly soft cheeks and ears. She is purely mine in this last sliver of time before the king — the man who will be her father — comes to meet her. If I wasn't so exhausted, I would consider running away.

No. I would not. I know what duty dictates. The door opens and I apply a smile. Wengest looks young, but almost afraid to show his excitement. I realise that we have spent too little time together in these last few months, and we have grown strange to each other.

'It's a daughter,' I say. 'I hope you aren't disappointed.'

'No, of course not,' he replies, approaching and sitting next to me on the bed. 'There will be other children.'

I do not remind him that my father had five daughters and no sons at all. He is gazing at the child with soft eyes. 'She is pretty like you,' he said. 'Dark like me.'

'Like both of us,' I say, hoping that I do not sound as relieved as I feel.

'I should like to name her after my mother,' he says.

In an instant, I remember that his mother's name was Rowan. 'No,' I say. 'Must we burden her with someone else's name? Can we not give her her own name?'

Wengest arches an annoyed eyebrow. 'Queen Rowan was much loved by her people. You cannot deny them the joy of remembering her in the image of her grand-daughter.'

I cannot resist him. Under any other circumstances, I would like the name Rowan. The rowan tree has long been associated with power and mystery.

'Come,' Wengest says, his voice growing soft. 'You have had her all to yourself these past nine months. Allow me one small mark of ownership.' His eyes drop to her face. 'She is beautiful, is she not? Perfect?'

I say nothing, imagining this serious dark creature growing into a little girl named Rowan, into a woman who will never be queen. I decide to ask Wengest directly. 'You are considering taking the Trimartyr faith, are you not, Wengest?'

He studies me a few moments, a puzzled smile at his lips. 'You are terribly astute, Rose. I thought you had nothing in your head but thoughts of babies.'

'Nyll has you …' I do not say, *in his thrall.* 'He has you interested?'

'I like the faith well enough, though it is a little gruesome. But a king in the trimartyr faith is appointed by Maava. No man can take his kingship without offence to the one god. It is a decision of strategy more than faith, Rose. It will make me more powerful, cement my position in my people's estimation.'

I stroke Rowan's soft head. Her eyes are falling closed. 'Then Rowan will never be queen.'

'If she marries a king she will. We will make an advantageous match for her. Put your mind at rest.'

I do not have energy for protests. In truth, Rowan is not Wengest's child so has no right to his throne. Perhaps the next child will.

Wengest kisses my cheek softly, his beard scratching my skin. 'Are you happy, Rose?'

I shake my head, teary now. 'I am so very tired, Wengest. Send my sister back in. I am sorry to send you away, but I must sleep now.'

He rises, tracing a soft line on the baby's cheek. 'Very well,' he says. 'When you are feeling better, we will consult with Nyll about an appropriate feast of welcoming for the child.'

I nod, crying now. My tears do not unnerve him. He merely turns his back and walks away.

Rowan is eight days old when the messenger comes. He has ridden from Is-hjarta, but not in the hard, urgent way that a bearer of bad news would ride. When he appears at Wengest's hall, he looks well-rested, cheerful, and he sends for me directly.

I leave Ash folding swaddling clothes in our bower, and take little Rowan in the crook of my arm to the hall. She has been fractious today, unable to settle to the breast or the crib. She seems happiest in motion. I rock her idly, tired beyond measurement and yet stupidly happy most of the time.

Wengest and the rider wait between the carved columns that line the outside of the hall. The doors are thrown open and inside there is the bustle of dinner's preparation, the smell of roasting meat and baking pie. When I see Bluebell's standard, my pulse quickens.

'I have news from your sister Bluebell,' he says, before I have a chance to greet him.

My heart is caught up high in my chest, waiting. 'She is … well?' It is news of Heath, I know it. Wengest is standing right next to me. How on earth will I hide my fear, my hope?

'Yes, she is. She wanted to pass on that the campaign goes well, she is unharmed and looks forward to a swift end to war in Bradsey. She wanted me to pass on, too, news that she has taken your husband's young nephew as third-in-command.' Here the messenger turns to Wengest and nods his head deferentially. 'You would be proud, King Wengest. He is by her side at all times.'

Wengest smiles and shakes his head. 'Is that so? I would not have imagined it.'

I allow myself to smile too, but for different reasons. This is Bluebell's way of telling me Heath is alive, he is whole, he is by the side of the greatest protector I could wish for him.

'I thank you for your good news,' I say to the messenger. 'Will you stay for dinner?'

He shakes his head. 'No, I will start the return journey immediately, for I have family in Dunscir who are expecting me by nightfall. Have you any message to pass on to your sister?'

I choose my words very carefully, feeling Wengest's presence close to my elbow. 'Tell her I am delivered of a daughter named Rowan.' I glance down at my daughter's face, and notice that she is finally asleep. 'That she is a perfect beauty and a compliment to the loving bond of her parents.' Here, Wengest touches my arm tenderly, assuredly; and guilt touches my heart with just the same finesse. 'Tell her I am happy,' I finish. 'But that she and her army cannot come home soon enough.'

'As you wish,' the messenger says, nodding and turning. 'Farewell.'

'Farewell,' I say.

Wengest takes my free hand and I hold it for a moment, then pull away as gracefully as I can, crossing my arms over the baby. He does not notice this small act of defiance; and we stand under the colonnade and watch the rider wind back down the hill, on his way to deliver my message of love.

204

AFTERWORD

'Crown of Rowan' is my first journey into Thyrsland, a country where I look forward to spending much more time. Thyrsland is based on Anglo-Saxon England (around the 8th century), and the backdrop is meant to be vast and epic; but the stories are meant to be intimate, human, and draw very close to the five sisters at their centre. Look for the first volume of my intimate epic, *The Garden of the Mad King*, in coming years.

— *Kim Wilkins*

Born in the dry, flat lands of South Australia, #1 *New York Times*-bestselling author Sean Williams has been described as 'the premier Australian speculative fiction writer of the age' and dubbed the 'King of Chameleons' for the diversity of his output. He writes for young readers and adults, and is best-known internationally for his award-winning space opera series, such as *Astropolis*, *Evergence* and *Geodesica*, and his work for the *Star Wars* franchise. 2004's *The Crooked Letter* was the first fantasy novel to win both the Aurealis and Ditmar Awards in history. 2002's *The Storm Weaver & the Sand* was recommended by *Locus* alongside novels by Neil Gaiman and Isabel Allende. In 2009, *The Changeling* and *The Dust Devils* were nominated for three Aurealis Awards between them. Sean lives in Adelaide with his wife and family, and is still dreaming of new stories to tell about the magical land around him.

The Spark (A Romance in Four Acts):
A Tale of the Change

SEAN WILLIAMS

ADITI SABATINO

The young man lay cool and unresponsive on Adi's bed. She had undressed and washed him, and in the process thoroughly examined his body for any sign of injury. She knew him now much better than she ever had, but not in a way that satisfied her.

His eyes were open and they did not see her. She lay next to him in the hot room, wearing only her underclothes, and he made no move to touch her.

'What do I do now, Ros?'

He gave no sign of hearing.

'Tell me what happened and I'll do whatever it takes to fix it.'

His expression didn't change, not even when she rattled him by the shoulders like a vat of settled ale.

'You're supposed to be my husband, not a corpse!'

Roslin of Geheb lay quietly beneath her, lungs steadily breathing and heart steadily beating.

Adi bent forward and wept onto his hairless chest.

A day earlier, she had checked into the Lost Dolphin Hostel under the name Hakamu, an alias they had used on their last journey together. As a boy, Ros had bested both the Bee Witch and the Golem of Omus, and had saved her life no less than twice along the way. Adi had saved him too, that last time, and stories of their deeds had spread like locusts across the land. Everyone knew Aditi Sabatino and Roslin of Geheb, or thought they did. For some years it had bothered her that people told tales by firelight that amplified or decreased her role, or ignored her entirely to focus on the farmboy-made-good. Then she had learned that it was fine for business, and discovered that she wasn't above using the weight of storytelling to drive a harder bargain.

On this occasion, she didn't avail herself of that opportunity. She happily took the hostel's going rate and hid her Clan markings behind a veil. She had come to finish a story that no one but she and Ros knew anything about.

Despite this resolve, her hands shook as she unfolded her pack on her bed. The precious brassy charm lay within, nestled carefully among wadded clothes and her toiletries, worn smooth by years of careful examination — dented too by being occasionally hurled into a wall — but it still functioned. At one end was fixed a crystal that glowed red when she pointed it at the south-east corner of the room.

She shuttered the windows and tested it again. The sunlight reflecting down crystal chimneys to the underground thoroughfares of

Ulum was not a patch on standing under the naked sky, but her eyes had become used to it, making subtle gradations of shade in the crystal difficult to tell. Swinging the rod from side to side in the gloom, she confirmed her first impressions. South-east it was.

Caught between impatience and dread, her empty stomach festering, Adi waited until nightfall before putting the promises she had made to the test.

The charm was a limited thing. Its crystal glowed only when it was pointed in the direction of Roslin of Geheb. That simple trick had sustained her for five years of separation. Many, many times in the years they had been apart had she taken comfort from it. No matter how far away he was, the charm would seek him out and tell her where he lay. South, north, east, west — on lonely nights, he could have been on the far side of the world or just outside the walls of her wagon.

She never once opened a window to test the latter hope. Until his apprenticeship was complete, she knew it was bound to be dashed.

One hour after sunset, when the halls of Ulum were as dark as they were going to get, she dressed and placed the veil across her features once again. Tightly clutching the charm in both hands, she left the room and headed into the warrens outside. Still south-east, the crystal said. Ulum was cramped and crowded, a city squeezed into caves that were forever too small, no matter how much the civil miners dug. At the highest points of the underground city, curving towers reached for the ranks of luminescent algae that dotted the night 'sky' like stars. Elsewhere, winding roads fought with buildings for space, and people squeezed in where they could.

Even after nightfall the city was busy. Traders mixed freely with locals once the markets were closed. Accents varied, as did clothes and skin colour. Adi's skin was darker than most to the north, her hair and eyes with it. With her Clan markings covered, she could have passed for an emissary from the Strand — perhaps even a Sky Warden, had she the torc to match.

The charm led her deep into a maze of lanes and teetering buildings. For seven days, according to the charm, Ros hadn't moved. She didn't expect him to move now. It was a sign, she told herself, a sign from him. It had to be. He had never before stayed so long in one spot, and the charm had never pointed her so surely to a city like Ulum — a natural meeting place if ever there was one.

Her nostrils breathed with easy familiarity the comingled scents of perfume, spice and camel shit. It wasn't lack of air, then, that made her feel light-headed. Roslin of Geheb was in the city somewhere. She wouldn't sleep until she found him.

The charm led her truly, but the ways of Ulum were ever crooked. Straight lines, like the flagstones underfoot, had long been worn into curves or cracked entirely. When she wanted to go left, every road tended right. Crowds of people and flocks of animals frequently blocked her path. It took her half the night to travel a mile.

Tired and on edge, she arrived at a tiny, hexagonal courtyard that was lit by reddish glowstones and greened only by weeds growing through the cobbles. The charm pointed to one of two doors on the far side. Plunging through the doorway, she collided heavily with someone emerging from within.

The charm went flying. She clutched at it, caught it just as it made contact with hard stone. Something *tinked* within its metal casing. A cold feeling rushed through her at the knife-sharp thought: *broken.*

She spat a word she only used when negotiations took a particularly atrocious turn. The man she had run into didn't stop. He was moving too quickly, already disappearing out of the courtyard. She flung another harsh word at his back, and let him go.

With faint hope, she raised the charm and pointed it south-east.

The crystal was dark.

Sickness rose up in her, physical and existential. There was only one course left to her: through the door, with momentum regained; trusting in the charm's last flicker just as she trusted Ros to be there, waiting for her.

The building was a doss-house, cramped and stinking. Every door was open, every screen pulled aside. People came and went freely, muttering and cursing in the fashion of the broken-minded. She stumbled through their filth and refuse, thinking that this wasn't the life Ros had set out to find. What had gone so badly wrong? Or was it possible that the charm had been malfunctioning all along, and he was no closer than he had ever been?

Then through the darkness of her thoughts she saw him — a pale shape sprawled partially-clothed across a filthy narrow mattress. Dark, lank locks hung in lazy spirals across his brow. Half-open eyes cast deep shadows across his cheeks. His lips were slack. He was older, larger, manlier — but it was him.

Him. Truly, truly him.

She ran to him and cupped his head in her hands, lifted it as she would a child's. The weight of it surprised her, as did the tears that came on seeing him. They dripped unchecked onto his face and she called his name in relief.

He neither moved nor spoke. His eyes saw right through her, if they saw anything at all. He didn't register her presence, no matter how she implored him, then shook him, then slapped his face lightly, hoping that would bring him back to himself.

'Won't do no good, miz,' said a wild-bearded man from outside the room. 'He been like this a full week.'

At first, she had no response. A small crowd had gathered, watching her with wide-eyed curiosity. She suddenly saw herself as they did, and wondered at the determination that filled her.

This wasn't how the story was supposed to go, but that didn't mean it was over. It was only beginning.

Her tears vanished. Her spine straightened. She put Ros's head down gently but firmly. Whatever had done this to him — a golem, perhaps, or a charm backfired — she would fix it.

'You'll help me,' she told wild-beard and his friends. 'I'll pay you to carry him.'

Shrugging, sceptical, but convinced by her coin, the city's under-dwellers were as compliant as she needed them to be, and no more.

The manager of the Lost Dolphin had seen stranger things, no doubt. His right eyebrow might have risen a fraction on seeing the strange procession coming up his steps, but it was soon restored to its proper location. Once Ros was installed in Adi's room and the grubby entourage despatched, he provided all that courtesy and custom demanded. The staff entered only when asked to bring tubs of warm water and clean towels, and food that only Adi ate. Ros drank drops of water at a time, when she tipped his head back and forced him to. She spoke to him, telling him how they had come to be together again, then asking him how he had arrived in Ulum. He hadn't necessarily been injured in the city, she thought. He might have been brought here by persons unknown, rescued from the desert, perhaps, in which he would have quickly died. If such a benefactor existed, Adi wished she could track them down and press the questions that burned inside her on them.

Ros said nothing.

'You're supposed to be my husband, not a corpse!'

Ros said nothing.

She wept because she had to. Powerful emotions were like sparkling wine: a vessel could contain them only so long before shattering under rising pressure. If she shattered, that would do neither of them any good.

The moment she regained control, she washed her face and dressed, moving swiftly but calmly. She rolled Ros onto his side and covered his nakedness with a sheet. A maid appeared at the door the moment she rang. Adi paid her to watch him while she was gone. She doubted he would be going anywhere.

Back out into the city she went. Dawn light was beginning to filter down the chimneys, pouring a brighter shine on the dirty streets. Adi's hopes of a quick solution had evaporated during that long night, but she hadn't given up yet. A physician was the next step, the best the city could provide at short notice. She had money in the form of coins and credit, the latter backed by the wealth and reputation of Clan Sabatino.

The third physician she called upon was willing to leave his bed and return with her to the hostel. Doctor Rishard, a hale-looking fellow of middling years with a crest of greying hair that stood up like a galah's no matter how he tried to plaster it down, walked with long, sweeping strides, and to keep up Adi had to take two steps for every one of his. She responded positively to his haste, though, feeling as though he was giving her strength just by taking her plea seriously.

'And you say he has been like this for how long?'

'Seven days, I suspect. Perhaps longer.'

The physician nodded and went back to lifting Ros's eyelids and poking at his flesh. He employed crystals, hammers, and needles, all without response. He passed a sample of Ros's breath across a mirror and tested the consistency of several bodily fluids. Ros had soiled himself during Adi's absence, and the maid's half-hearted attempt to clean the mess proved to be a blessing in disguise.

Last of all, Doctor Rishard took a small bell out of his bag and rang it softly next to each of Ros's ears. The tone warbled oddly, as though it was being sounded underwater.

He nodded.

'What is it? Can you tell me what's wrong with him?'

The physician bundled all his instruments back into the bag. 'He was a Change-worker. That much I can tell you.'

She felt her ears growing pink. 'How does that make a difference?'

'It means I can't treat him. I can only guess what might have put him in this state.'

She nodded, even as disappointment filled her. 'Go on, then. Guess.'

'It's not a physical thing like a drug or a disease, but Stone Mages talk of it. They call it the Void Beneath. It eats minds. Dissolves them.'

'How?'

He shook his head. 'There, I'm of no use to you. The Void doesn't appear in any of my textbooks. You'll need another Change-worker if you want an answer.'

She did. Thanking Doctor Rishard, she paid him and sent him back home.

A Change-worker. She was on quicksand now, and she knew it. This was Ros's world, not hers. If he had got himself into trouble that way, she might not be able to get him out of it.

She briefly considered calling his teacher for help. Master Pukje was a strange being, though, part-dragon and entirely capricious. It was his demand that Ros be trained in the ways of the Change that had led to their long separation. Any help he offered would be coloured by that history. She soon decided to do what she could on her own before following that path.

Her first step was not the obvious one. The Stone Mages who ruled the Interior would recognise Ros immediately, and she wasn't ready yet to cast off her cloak of anonymity. Adi was sure they weren't the only Change-workers in the city. Illusionists, charm-makers, and seers all gravitated to the light of respectability, even if they were themselves denied a place within the brazier. With the markets open more than an hour already, she would have no trouble finding someone to talk to about her problem. The quality of the answer was the only variable.

This quest took her considerably longer than had her search for a physician. Carefully worded enquiries and bribes led her slowly up the ranks from tricksters and fakers to the genuinely talented. Along the way she received advice she had no intention of following: ensuring that the foot of Ros's bed faced exactly north; daubing his skin with a salve made from wolf spider venom; chanting a series of nonsense words over him at every dawn and dusk; tattooing complex symbols at key points on his body, so the grace of the Goddess would be drawn to him, and restore him to himself. The procedures were offered with all appearance of sincerity, but she doubted even the practitioners believed in them. She was no more a Change-worker than a physician; nothing she did would make any difference, beyond finding the right person.

She came at last to a stately home in a relatively quiet corner of the city. Cubical and blunt, the house even sported trees at each corner — spindly, sick-looking things but trees nonetheless. They were the first of any size that Adi had seen in Ulum. It struck her as strange that a Change-worker should live in such opulent surrounds, but that wasn't the mystery she had come to solve.

She knocked on the door and asked for Samson Mierlo. The house boy led her to a book-filled study and invited her to sit. She waited patiently, feeling very little by now but fatigue and desperation. Elsewhere in the house, doors opened and shut, and floorboards creaked. A woman coughed, long and throatily. On a plinth in the corner of the study, the bust of a high-templed man turned its head to regard her more closely.

She stared calmly back at it. Man'kin bothered some people, who saw in them nothing but falsity, a parody of life, but she was untroubled. They had their uses.

'Now, Lady Hakamu,' said a voice from the doorway behind her, 'what is this grave matter of which you speak?'

She stood and shook the hand of the man she hoped would bring Ros back to her. Samson Mierlo had been described as something of a maverick, courting controversy and condemnation from the establishment he criticised, but he looked like nothing so much as a lawyer. Instead of robes he wore a grim, grey suit. His eyes were cool and grey, but weren't without warmth.

Once again Adi explained the situation. This time, however, she went into greater detail. Mierlo was the city's foremost expert in the Void Beneath. From him she hoped to gain a greater understanding of Ros's condition, at least.

He waved for her to resume her seat, but didn't rest himself. Pacing the room as she talked, he nodded and uttered short phrases that conveyed no actually meaning but encouraged her to continue.

'Yes.'

'Indeed.'

'How so?'

'Quite.'

The man'kin's granite eyes tracked Mierlo smoothly as he walked and listened.

'Naturally.'

'Well.'

'Hmmm.'

Only when she had finished did he take the seat opposite her and fold his long-fingered hands into a steeple.

'The physician you consulted would have been no help at all, Lady Hakamu. This is quite beyond his understanding. Be thankful for his honesty, though; a less scrupulous surgeon might have insisted on treating your friend regardless, and done him more harm than good. Nothing in the world of medicine can help him now.'

'Can you help him?'

'No. But I can tell you this: your friend is where he is because of something he did, not something that was done to him. To use the Change one must reach into oneself. Reach too deeply and the Void awaits. I've seen many promising young talents overbalance and fall, out of pride, perhaps, or fear of failure. Either way, there's no coming back. The Void Beneath devours all who enter it. How, exactly, we don't know; it is a mystery we may never solve. But please don't take hope from that admission. Every case history points in one direction. Your friend's body may be perfectly sound, but his mind is gone.'

Adi stared at Samson Mierlo, certain he was telling her the truth as he understood it. It was, however, an understanding that she couldn't accept.

'There must be something —'

'The Void Beneath is not a place, Lady Hakamu, that you can enter,' he said, brusquely cutting her off. 'It is not a foe that you can challenge. It is nothing — a nothing that takes everything in a person and grinds them back to nothing in turn. Such is the foundation of the world; there are no certainties but this one.'

Her right hand crushed her left. She was unable to speak.

'I'll leave you now,' he said, standing. 'I'm very sorry for your friend, and for you, since you care for him so deeply. When you are able, Ugo will show you out.'

She nodded, wanting to offer her thanks but unable to trust her clenched throat to issue anything remotely like a word.

His crisp footsteps led from the study, deep into the echoing house.

'You will go to Madam Van Haasteren.'

Adi's head jerked up. The voice wasn't Samson Mierlo's, and she had heard no one else enter the room.

The man'kin was looking at her.

'Magda Van Haasteren,' it repeated. 'The seer.'

She stood too abruptly. 'What?' she asked through a wave of dizziness. 'Are you talking to me?'

'You will go to her.'

It froze as the house boy appeared in the doorway.

'Did it just speak?' he said incredulously, crossing to the plinth and staring hard into the stony eyes. 'Did it say something to you?'

She shook her head, unsure why the man'kin wanted to keep its animation a secret but deciding that she was willing to go along with it in exchange for its help. 'I didn't hear anything. Did you?'

'I could've sworn ...' The boy shook his shaved head as he guided her to the front door. 'That old thing's been in the family forever. If it ever woke up, the mistress would have a fit.'

'It's probably for the best, then, that it doesn't.'

'I guess.'

Adi could tell that the house boy had already put the mystery from his mind. She had no intention of doing the same.

Magda Van Haasteren. The name meant nothing to her, but it was known in the city's underbelly. Within an hour Adi had an address, and even a word or two of warning. For a mere seer, Van Haasteren had a surprisingly dark reputation. The rumours were light on details, though, and quite possibly inspired by envy. It was often the way with the genuinely talented, Adi thought, that they should be downplayed and reviled. Were Samson Mierlo correct in his opinion, it would take all the talent in the world to find Ros and bring him back.

Before returning to the dark side of the city, Adi returned to the Lost Dolphin to check on the man whose mind she was trying to save. He hadn't moved beyond breathing or drinking the water dripped into his mouth by the maid. She was bored, Adi could tell, but she would have no respite. The manager assured Adi that the maid would attend Ros faithfully throughout the night, if necessary.

Adi stood for a moment, staring at the covered form of the man she had promised to take as a husband, so long ago. What had happened to that dream? The charm was in her bag, broken like him. How could either of them have been so careless?

It wasn't as if she hadn't taken risks down the years. She was human, and forgave herself for being so. There had been other young men she'd had feelings for, and even one she had given herself to as a lover — in the desert port town of Lower Light, with complete anonymity. If she was to be anything in life, bride or otherwise, she would do so in the full light of the knowledge available to her.

A promise was a promise, though. A deal was a deal. That was a philosophy trading Clans took seriously. Her life had been built on it.

Your friend is where he is because of something he did, Samson Mierlo had told her.

If Ros ever spoke again, she would ask him what had been so important that he had risked throwing away their life together. She doubted, in the weary heat of the moment, that any answer would be sufficient.

Back through the constricted streets, back into the filth. Adi was retracing her steps in a very real way, for Van Haasteren's closet-sized stall was only a handful of blocks from the doss-house where she had found Ros. Where the charm had been broken. At that place, in that moment, everything had gone wrong.

An unwarranted thought occurred to her then: that if she had arrived one minute earlier, events would have unfolded in a very different way. The charm would have led her truly, and Ros would have greeted her with open arms. Was it so unlikely? The man she had collided with — he had been fleeing the scene as she approached. Could he have had something to do with Ros's condition? Could he, in fact, have been the one responsible for it?

She struggled to remember his face. At most she had glimpsed him, for her attention had been almost entirely on the falling charm. Long hair pulled severely back from lean features, crisscrossed with thin lines that weren't tattoos but might have been scars …

She forced him from her mind. Lichen stars were coming out above as the chimneys fell dark. She hadn't slept at all since arriving in Ulum the previous day, and it came to her then that she wasn't thinking as clearly as she ought to. She needed her wits about her when dealing with Magda Van Haasteren — for fear of deception, or further disappointment.

'Come in quickly,' the seer said when she rapped at the stall's flimsy portal. 'There is a chill in the air that gives me the bone-ache.'

Adi did as she was told. There was no sign above the door, but it matched the description she had received, as did the seer's disposition. The air was no chillier than normal; the fans that stirred the cavern's otherwise stagnant air turned with their usual velocity.

Madam Van Haasteren was a shapeless, slouched woman in a faded blue smock. Her face was heavily lined, with a down-turned mouth, and eyes that glittered in the light of a single, squat candle. One large-knuckled hand rested on a three-legged table to her side; she clutched a stinking cheroot in the other. Her voice was full of oil and gravel, like gears that had broken years ago, but ground on regardless, without respite.

Adi offered the woman her fake name, and it was accepted with a knowing stare.

'You're looking for someone,' the seer said. 'Such is the state of all who come to me — at their wits ends and desperate, more often than not.'

'I'm no different, to tell the truth. If you can help me, I'll pay you well.'

The seer waved at a second stool, more rickety than the first, and instructed her to sit. 'Give me your hand, girl, and mind your tongue. I don't do this for money.'

Adi felt five years old, and fought a sudden, surprising urge to weep. Her mother had died when she was a young girl, and her father had followed ten years later. For a time she had despaired of the attentions of her well-meaning aunts, but now she missed them, and her mother, and everything that family represented. She had left all that behind to come in search of Ros. And gained nothing.

Leathery old fingers clasped Adi's left hand and pulled it close. Sharp eyes inspected back and front, and her fingernails too. They were bitten to the quick.

The seer grimaced. 'Does he have a name?'

'Sovan,' she said, still unwilling to reveal their identities if the seer hadn't already guessed them.

'Tell me about him.'

'He's lost,' Adi began, 'fallen into the Void Beneath —'

'Not that. Why do you want him back? If he's gone, why not let him be gone and move on? Is there something special about him that you can't find in any other man?'

Adi gaped, feeling slightly scandalised. Something special about Ros? Of course there was! She wouldn't have come this far if there wasn't.

'Put it in words, girl. If you can't define it, maybe it's not there at all.'

She tried. Her voice shook as she talked of their first meeting. Ros had run away from home and her family had given him temporary shelter on the road. Adi had been promised to a boy from another Clan, and she had convinced Ros to take her with him when he left. She had trusted him more in that moment than anyone else, for reasons that she now found hard to capture.

The seer seemed to understand well enough. 'You're talking about the spark,' she said, nodding gravely. 'When two people meet who are … not destined or connected, but complementary — yes, that's the word I'm looking for — when that happens, you get the spark. You feel it with your whole body and in all your thoughts. It's like a little bit of lightning, and it too can start a fire.'

Adi stared at the old woman, amazed as much by the passion that suddenly filled her voice as by the aptness of her words.

'There's more to the story,' Adi said, thinking of monsters and death and the nightmares she still had, sometimes, 'but none of that matters now.'

'No, it doesn't. That's why I don't need to know where you think he's gone. What's important is that he's not here, or that he doesn't recognise you, or both. That's where it begins, but it doesn't end there. You want him to know you, to be here for you, and you're afraid that you can't make that happen. Maybe he's forgotten who you are. Maybe he doesn't want to come to you. You can't read his mind, and he won't talk to you, so the uncertainty eats at you, eats at your faith in him. That leads to the questions. Did you do the right thing by letting him go? Would things be better or worse now if you had not? What will you do if you can't get him back? Who changed — him or you? And the most important question of all: do you even want him back any more?'

Adi felt as though the seer had reached into her chest and clutched her heart in a tight grip. She could only stare at the gnarled hands still holding hers, and hope that those sharp eyes didn't see any deeper.

'Answer my question, girl.'

'Which one?'

'Do you want him back?'

Adi thought of the doubt she had entertained on the way to the seer's stall. Could anything Ros said now undo the damage that had been done to the faith she had in him? She saw in her mind his lifeless and impotent form. He had once been so strong. Was it his strength that had given her love for him such vitality? Could she love him now in weakness? Was that a weakness of her own, to even ask that question?

Her breath came in gulps. She barely noticed that she was crying.

'Yes,' Adi managed. 'Yes, I do want him back.'

'That's a brave answer,' said the seer, 'after all that see-sawing. The cloth you're cut from is strong as well as fine. Remember that, when you need to — because although I can help you, the cost will be high.'

Adi found herself released from the old woman's tight grip, and she sat back, blinking. The single candle flame, which seemed to have become much brighter in recent minutes, dimmed now, casting thick shadows across the dingy cubicle. Someone in a hovel nearby was shouting, but she couldn't make out the words.

Adi wiped the tears from her cheeks and breathed deeply of the smoky air.

'How much?'

'I'm not talking about money, girl.'

The seer gestured with her right hand at a wall hanging that might once have been quality work. Ill-served in its lifetime by smoke and neglect, it barely warranted a second glance, but for the significance it had now been given. Faded thread picked out the figure of a Stone Mage in full armour, his iron plates painted ochre with ceremonial rust. The figure stirred slightly, as though someone had moved behind him.

'The understanding you seek lies through that curtain.'

Adi stood, and shivered, feeling the chill the seer had complained of earlier.

'All right,' she said, telling herself to see it through. She had faced worse fears and survived. 'Thank you.'

The old woman shook her head. She had slouched down even further on her stool, so she sat splay-legged, like a man, and stared despondently at the muddy ember of her cheroot. 'No need, Adi. No need.'

Adi was halfway through the curtain before she realised that the old woman had used her real name. By then, it was entirely too late to turn back.

ROSLIN OF GEHEB

The young woman ducked into an alleyway. Ros shouted at her to wait, and when she did not do so he set off in immediate pursuit. He had caught only a glimpse of her, but he was certain this time that it was her, the woman he sought. There was no mistaking that long, thick hair, bound up in whirls and streams — or her rich, dark skin, against which the colourful fabric of her dress stood out so vividly — or the confidence in her walk and the almost capricious glance she cast over her shoulder as she vanished from sight.

By the time he reached the corner, the alleyway was empty. He ran ten steps along it, checking doors and fences as he went. They were secure. A clutch of women appeared from the nearest intersection, and he hurried to them, studying their faces carefully in turn. All of them were strangers. The side roads were clear too.

He turned in circles at the crossroad, unsure which way to go. That was the fourth time he had lost her in an hour. He was running out of both options and patience. Everything she asked him to do he had done, so why was she still playing games? What did she want from him?

'Don't do this, Adi,' he called to the winding streets and the indifferent crowds. 'I came for you like I promised. Show yourself, please!'

A flock of sparrows danced under Ulum's buttressed ceilings, casting shadows from the light-chimneys that came and went, came and went.

With fists tightly clenched, Ros lowered his head and returned to the doss-house alone.

He had been in Ulum a week, asking around after Clan Sabatino at Adi's usual haunts, guided by his memories of her letters and little else. Civilisation seemed a strange thing to him now. Five years with Master Pukje had left him accustomed to empty spaces, rigid routines, and arcane forces. The ebb and flow of ordinary people confounded him. Sometimes he felt that they spoke an entirely different language, one he might never be able to understand.

He did learn that Adi's Clan was on its way back from a long, north-western haul, and, to his regret, that Adi's father had died a year ago. Ulick Sabatino had been a bluff, honourable man, who had placed his faith in Ros under extraordinary circumstances. That Ros had saved his daughter's life hadn't hurt, of course, but it took more than that to earn a permanent place at the Clan's table. Marriage was the only sure-fire way, and even then it could be withdrawn.

That Adi supposedly wasn't in Ulum surprised Ros, for his gut told him she was close. His gut had led him to the city from the depths of the desert, and he trusted it still. Persistence would prove the attempt worthwhile, he was sure. The veil of strangeness surrounding him would part before him, and reveal the one he sought.

He only hoped success would come soon, for his material means were limited. In the desert, he could survive for years unaided, but here he needed money, or a job, or some other means to support himself. The trials of a mad dragon were not recognised in the city as a valid qualification for anything — and besides, Ros was reluctant to reveal his true name. The power of his reputation had almost entrapped him once before. That wasn't a road he wanted to follow again.

For several days he did nothing but walk the streets, trusting not only his instincts but the paths he carved out through the city over the course of time — ornate, sprawling charms for the finding of lost things, the binding of hearts, the uncovering of secrets. He left cryptic messages employing aliases they had assumed in their youth, requesting rendezvous, return messages, or signs ranging from the subtle to the overt. He visited and revisited each location, but never once did Adi leave a response. His messages went unread, or at least unanswered.

He searched the face of every woman he passed, hoping for a flicker of familiarity.

He searched his own face in his shaving mirror, wondering what she would think of him when they met. There was no denying that he had changed. Sometimes, catching his reflection in a window or a doorway, he barely recognised the man he had become. But was he more or less handsome? Would she think the cost of his training too high?

'Staring'll make you no prettier,' mocked the wild-bearded man who inhabited the cot across from him. 'And if the mirror cracks, you'll be worse off still.'

Ros ignored the cackling half-wit and resumed his search.

On the sixth day, he received a note. It was delivered to the doss-house during one of his extended searches and left upon his bedroll to await his return. He unfolded the stiff paper with eager fingers and scanned the single line it contained. A place and a time. No more.

She had neither addressed it to him nor signed it, but he was sure it was from Adi. Holding the paper to his nose, he imagined that he could detect a faint residue of her scent upon it. His heart beat a little faster at the knowledge that they were one step closer to reunion.

The rendezvous was scheduled for dawn the next morning. Ros barely slept that night, imagining how his life would change. The stories told about him ended with the defeat of the Scarecrow five years earlier. For him, the real story was about to begin.

He arrived one quarter of an hour early, and waited exactly where the note had specified. Even at that early hour, the market was busy, and he craned his neck to catch a glimpse as she approached. As the appointed time neared, he could barely keep still. His jostling and pacing attracted the attention of more than one trader, but he rebuffed their sales pitches with steadfast cheer.

The hour came and went, and Adi did not appear. Ros told himself to be patient, and waited another quarter-hour, then a half.

A full hour after the time specified in the note, he left, a pale approximation of the man he had been earlier that morning.

There was another note on his bedroll, equally brief. The second meeting was on the far side of the city with bare minutes to spare. Ros didn't question the need for haste. Adi must have been delayed, surely, and all explanations would be rendered unnecessary by her presence. Barely stopping to draw breath, he sprinted along the dusty thoroughfares and carriageways, dodging and weaving when crowds failed to part before him.

He arrived almost punctually, breathing heavily and casting about for her in the halls of the city library. It was cool and quiet within. Too quiet: his urgent calling and searching were not welcome. Undaunted he peered into every nook and cranny and through every door, pushing books aside when faces were obscured. He left only when certain that the chambers were empty of the one he sought. He had missed her.

Furious at his ill fortune, he hurried back to the doss-house in case another note had arrived.

It had, but this time he did not immediately open it. He held it gently in his hand. Like a dead moth, it could be crushed in an instant, and for a dozen breaths he was tempted. This insubstantial yet weighty thing could lead him on another fruitless quest. Without proof that it was from Adi, he would be unwise to hurry anywhere.

With new circumspection, Ros opened the letter. It contained the same as before, only this time there was even less opportunity to make the rendezvous.

No, he told himself. He was not at anyone's beck and call. This test of loyalty, if such it was, would be answered by a test of his own.

Folding the note into halves and slipping it back onto his bedroll, he exited the doss-house and made as if to follow the route required.

When he was certain he wasn't being shadowed, he doubled-back and procured a vantage-point atop the building adjacent to the doss-house, from which location he could clearly see the entrance. There he would wait until the next note arrived. When it did, he would follow it back to the source.

Night fell, and with it his spirits. Master Pukje's final test — surviving the same, at any rate — had left Ros feeling prepared for anything. There had been no graduation ceremony, just the assumption of knowledge, of responsibility, of adulthood. He was his own man now, or ought to be.

Not that he hadn't already experienced a large measure of doubt on his way to the city. He had little experience with women, having met barely a dozen since his apprenticeship began and known none of them intimately. He couldn't guess what might be going through Adi's mind, just as he wasn't entirely sure what was going through his own.

He didn't want to think that she was behind this strange sequence of events. After all, hadn't she encouraged him to come to her the moment his apprenticeship was finished? Why would she take advantage of his gullibility like this? He was sure now that it couldn't be her. It flew in the face of the memories he had treasured for so long.

Numerous people passed through the six-sided courtyard off which the doss-house lay. None of them were Adi; none of them came bearing notes or displaying any signs of conspiracy against him. As the night deepened, he began to feel foolish and upbraided himself for his paranoia. Master Pukje would have harsh words to offer if he ever learned of this. And so would Adi. She tolerated neither untimeliness nor inconvenience, and he had offered her nothing but both, so far. He looked forward to the day when they could laugh about this together, as they might many other anecdotes from their long betrothal.

His back was getting sore and the steady stream of passers-by had slowed, if not ceased entirely. He dropped with light feet into the courtyard and went into the doss-house. Too tired to bathe, he unrolled his bed and flicked out a bug or two that had made a home there during the day. There was no fourth note, of course.

On the way back from the primitive toilet, he stopped in mid-step, every imaginable sense alert. A certainty that Adi was nearby coursed through him. Without hesitating, he ran to the entrance of the doss-house and peered carefully outside. For all his theories concerning anonymous culprits, part of him remained alert for games of any kind on her part, and he wasn't about to drive her off by pouncing too soon.

There was a woman in the courtyard, hurrying his way. She wasn't Adi; no Sabatino would dress that way. His eyes were instead drawn into the shadows. Through the Change he detected several rats and one alert cat, but no humans. If she was there, she was artfully concealed.

And so she was. Her skin was black against black, but the whites of her eyes stood out — one of them, anyway, around the edge of a ragged brick wall. Their stares locked for an instant, and in that instant he saw her pull back, realising that she had been spotted. The eye winked out, and he set off in pursuit.

Later he would remember the wild fever of those hopeful moments as he shouldered past anyone in his way, calling Adi's name and imploring her to reveal herself. He glimpsed her many times, stepping out into darkness from under streetlamps, through archways, down alleyways that would inevitably turn out to be empty when he arrived. How she did it, he didn't know, but his darkest, most convoluted fears were confirmed. It was her, and she wasn't as he remembered.

All night he chased her, across all quarters of the city.

'Don't do this, Adi,' he called. 'I came for you like I promised. Show yourself, please!'

She offered him nothing in reply.

It came to him eventually that he wasn't thinking clearly. He was chasing phantoms and they weren't leading him anywhere. He needed to be calm and find another solution. Adi was somewhere in the city. He could find her if he tried.

He returned to the doss-house only to discover that his property had been stolen. That didn't improve his mood. The wild-bearded man and his foolish collaborators professed no knowledge of the theft, but Ros could see more than the usual fogginess to their eyes. Sold for ale, he presumed. Everything he owned was drunk and gone.

There was no point railing against it. Stalking back out into the streets, he found the closest thing to a quiet corner in Ulum and scrawled complex charms about it, cocooning it and himself in silence. He closed his eyes and sought the vital heart of himself, as his master had taught him to do. That was all he had left. Every other certainty had evaporated.

In that tiny island of calm, he viewed his emotions with something approaching objectivity, and was even able to shed them for a moment. Anger, fear, embarrassment, and loss were the least of his problems now. He was the victim of an elaborate prank, and the first step to rising above it was to regard it from the outside.

Almost immediately he realised something that should have been obvious all along. Adi's prank relied on talents Adi herself didn't possess. Not that she wasn't talented in her own ways; Ros was sanguine about the fact that she was certainly smarter than he was, and cunning with it. But she lacked any kind of predilection for the Change, and to his knowledge had never pursued an understanding of it. How, then, could she be cloaking her presence so effectively and running him in such ever-widening circles?

There were two possible answers: one, that it wasn't her at all; and two, that she had hired someone to do the work for her.

The first possibility was attractive because it absolved her of all responsibility, but offered no hint as to the identity of his antagonist. He decided to pursue the second possibility simply because it gave him something to do, and offered a small chance of success. Finding Adi's Change-worker-for-hire might prove easier than finding her, if only because Ros might approach the prank sideways rather than head-on.

Although his direction was now clear, he stayed within his bubble of silence a while longer, to double-check his thoughts, in case he had missed something else equally obvious, and to establish an appropriate emotional balance. The decision to be with Adi had been an easy one five years earlier. To dishonour it now would be cowardice of the highest order. He would see it through if he was allowed to, and he would do his best to keep hope alive.

In theory, the Stone Mages had the city stitched up. Every child with the slightest whiff of the Change about them was sent off to be trained and ultimately inducted into the country's elite, from which few ever emerged into independent practice. Ros's utter unencumbrance was frowned upon and, in some quarters considered actually dangerous to society at large.

Master Pukje had been quick to instil in Ros the understanding of the true purpose of theory, which was simply to be tested, and so he went with confidence into the city once more, sure that he would find an exception before long.

And so he did. First one, then another — both Change-workers known for shoddy work, but at least acting independently of the country's masters. They were jealous types, reluctant to let a potential customer fall into a competitor's orbit, but Ros had mastered more techniques for extracting the truth than they had ever forgotten. Not effortlessly, but at least painlessly, he learned what he needed to and moved on.

The black market for Change-working grew in extent the more he picked at it, like a loose thread pulled from an expensive rug. With keener eyes than he had had before, he saw charms that bore no relation to any grammatical system he had studied. He found dealers in potions using ingredients unknown to anyone but their discoverers. He studied significant tattoos in books whose reason he could not tell from madness. All of it was wonderful and strange, and utterly incapable of catching him in any kind of web. The prankster, whoever he or she was, had attained a higher degree of mastery than these crazed dabblers.

From one he learned a name that he mentally filed away for later pursuit. The name was repeated two interviews later, as a person Ros should contact should he wish to procure the expertise he required. The person thus identified was not a Change-worker herself, but a business-woman from the quieter side of town. Her customers resided outside the populous caverns, so she did not advertise locally. Word inevitably spread, though, and Ros was keen to follow it. Through this woman Adi might have hired someone from outside the city, and therefore someone more difficult to trace.

Twice Ros caught glimpses of Adi in the crowds of the marketplace. Once he saw a jewel she had worn hanging around the neck of another woman. Ros ignored all such instances of recognition for fear of being entangled again. He had to focus on the trail he had found for himself and not be led aside, no matter where it led him.

'Explain to me again, young man,' said Jenfi Mierlo, 'exactly what kind of charm you think this might be.'

Ros did his best, although their surroundings discomfited him to an extreme. He felt utterly out of place among such finery. There were books and relics from ancient times, and works of art so delicately formed that light itself seemed gentle with them. Everything about him — his shabbiness, his demeanour, his smell — was alien to this world. There was no denying it, and little that could be done about it.

The hard, keen gaze of a man'kin on a plinth didn't help much, either.

'What do you think, Mawson?' the mistress of the house asked it when Ros had finished. 'Does this sound like the work of anyone we know?'

The man'kin didn't reply, but she nodded as though it had.

'No,' she said. 'I didn't think so either. In fact — in fact —'

She broke into a series of deep, hacking coughs that turned her glassy skin purple and bent her almost double.

Jenfi Mierlo was a woman old enough to be Ros's grandmother, but as slender as a teenager. She wore a silk gown, dyed black and white in geometric patters, from which her wrists and throat emerged like fragile stalks. Her hair was steel-grey, and her eyes deep-set. The line of her jaw stood out like a knife, almost as sharp as her fingernails.

Ros half-rose to offer her assistance, but she waved him away. The house-boy rushed into the room with a glass of water, which she accepted with gratitude and sipped from as the fit subsided.

'Please pardon me,' she said, returning to something approaching a healthy colour. 'The trials of age are as vexatious as the trials of youth. I was about to announce that your predicament, this glamour or spell or whatever you wish to call it, seems more like hallucination to me than conspiracy — for after all, where is the evidence? You can't produce a single note you said you received. And as for either mechanism or motive, both remain obscure to me. But it is foolish ever to write off the inventiveness of people, particularly where torture is involved. And you do seem tortured, young man, if you don't mind me saying so. Would that be a fair observation?'

Ros allowed that it was.

'Tell me more about the woman you suspect to be the mastermind.' Jenfi Mierlo folded her wrists in her lap and leaned forward. 'I am unfamiliar with your Lady Hakamu.'

'I cannot,' he said, unwilling to reveal anything that might identify either of them. 'She is unknown to me, except by name.'

'It seems odd to me that she would thrust her illusory form upon you yet remain herself in the shadows. Are you sure there could be no other agent at work here?'

The phrasing of her observation —'in the shadows' — reminded Ros of the moment he had first seen Adi's face. There had indeed been another woman present at the time. It wasn't inconceivable that she had triggered the charm then, although he remembered no such thing. He could barely recall her at all. Had she said something as he hurried past her? Had he bumped into her, perhaps?

'I'm as sure as I can be,' he said.

'And you feel that you have done nothing to earn such a plight?'

'That is the case, yes.'

'You don't surprise me there,' Jenfi Mierlo said. 'Young men rarely do.' She leaned back. 'I fear that I have little help to offer — except for the prospect of employment. You're new to the city, clearly, and in need of friends. I could make an introduction or two, if you liked.'

There was a predatory cast to her face. Ros had seen such before, on traders who recognised a bargain and sought to claim it before its true price became known. Clearly his imposture as a victim of a Change-worker, rather than a practitioner himself, was thinner than he had hoped.

'Thank you,' he said. 'I'll keep that thought in mind.'

'You'll do better than that,' she said, rising suddenly from her chair. 'Wait here. I'll be back in a moment.'

He stood, wishing now that he had never come. Instead of rescue, he had found himself swept out to deeper water still. One of the many reasons for studying under Master Pukje had been to defer the attention of sharks who, like Jenfi Mierlo, were drawn to his talent.

Many times in his childhood he had been exploited, unknowingly and cruelly, and he would not suffer such again.

'You will go to Madam Van Haasteren.'

He glanced around in surprise. The man'kin had spoken.

'I know that name,' he said. 'Magda Van Haasteren, the seer?'

'You will go to her.'

'Why?' He frowned. 'Can she tell me where Adi is?'

The man'kin didn't answer.

At the sound of Jenfi Mierlo's heels clicking in the hallway outside, Ros turned. She was holding a trinket that was part charm, part business card, which she pressed upon him with irresistible insistence.

Desperate to return to the subject he had come to pursue, Ros indicated the man'kin and said, 'Is your friend here always so reticent?'

'Mawson? He hasn't spoken in a hundred years. If he ever does, the roof will probably fall in.'

She burst into another coughing fit, and Ros took the opportunity to leave her presence. The man'kin's advice had taken on a new significance in the context of its usual silence, and he wanted to avoid another sales pitch. The trinket he kept, though. It was harmless. Apart from the clothes he wore, it was also his sole material possession.

Night had fallen. Ros had almost lost count of how many he had been in the city now. Eight, he decided. He wouldn't spend this one chasing phantoms. He would take the man'kin at its word and pursue the mystery to its conclusion.

Even from the outside, Magda Van Haaasteren's stall reeked of smoke and the murkier applications of power. The Change was neither good nor bad; like air, though, it could be befouled. He hesitated before knocking on the door, irrationally convinced that nothing good would come of it. His senses were muddled. Adi could have been standing right next to him and he wouldn't have known.

To its conclusion, he reminded himself, knocking firmly upon the portal.

'Finally made up your mind, did you?' came the croaky voice from within. 'Come in before you change it again, and shut the door fast behind you.'

Ros kept his first impressions from showing as best he could. The place was crowded, dirty, and worn, and the seer herself fared little better in his assessment. But for the aura of potency swirling around her like a cape — thick and dark, as reptilian as a snake — he would have walked out in an instant.

'You're chasing someone,' she said, heavy-lidded eyes sweeping down and then up his frame. 'What's the matter? Has your face frightened her away?'

That same face betrayed him while he considered how best to answer. Blushing furiously, except for the white of his scars, he could only think of the wild-bearded man mocking him in the doss-house. It was true that there was nothing to be done about his appearance. He could only try to put his fears behind him and trust that Adi would see beyond the mask, to what lay beneath.

'Neither of us is going to win any beauty pageants,' he said, not about to have that fear reinforced by a creature like this.

'Indeed we're not.' She waved imperiously. 'You're crooking my neck, making me look up at you. Sit, sit, and tell me about your elusive girlfriend.'

'What do you need to know?'

'How much can you tell me?' Her eyes slitted fractionally. 'No, really — how much?'

Ros gave the matter the attention it deserved. How much did he know about Adi any more? It had been five years since he had last seen her. And even then, had he known her well? They had been kids, really, in exceptional straits. It had been easy to let the stories dictate how the rest of their lives were supposed to go. Should he be so surprised that their poorly-laid plans had gone awry?

'I thought so,' the seer said as the silence dragged on. 'Yet there was something about her, something that transcends knowledge, requiring no words or explanations. Wasn't there?'

'Yes,' he said, the answer tugged out of him almost against his will. 'I thought — I thought it would be easy. All we had to do was grow up and become — become whoever we needed to be. And then we could be together. Why hasn't it worked like that? I know it was wrong to think she'd drop everything for me, but I've come back for her as I promised, and now she —'

He stopped, unable to speak past the lump that had grown in his throat.

'Perhaps she's testing you,' the seer said. The candle that burned on the table at her side filled the deep lines of her face with shadow. 'Not just you, but the legacy of your first meeting. Has the spark you originally felt survived the passage of time? Sometimes it may not, and they fare badly who try to draw on a power that isn't there. You know that much; you've felt the Void at your feet; you know what awaits us all, in the end. The death of love is no different, and the fear of it drives people to strange exploits.

'You feel that you must prove yourself,' she went on, 'yet in that very attempt you trap yourself anew. Why is the burden of proof solely upon you? It's like being an apprentice with a master who never speaks. You can only guess at the lesson and bear the punishment when you get it wrong. And what about her? Is she not also required to do as you do, to demonstrate her faithfulness and determination as well?'

'Yes,' he said, springing to his feet and circling the tiny room. 'I'm not just tested — I'm trapped!'

'And what are you going to do about it?'

'I'm doing it, aren't I?'

'Don't round on me, boy. If I solve this puzzle for you, doesn't that make me more worthy of your girlfriend's hand than you?'

'Well, damn it, what?'

The seer smiled. 'Tell me what it's worth to know.'

He sagged, emptying of anger as suddenly as a water-bladder stabbed with a knife.

'I have nothing of value to give you,' he said in the candle's flickering light.

'That's not true,' the seer told him. 'Not true at all, Roslin of Geheb.'

He stared at her, wondering how long she had known. The whole time, perhaps. 'What do you want?'

Her smile widened. 'I'm trying to ask you the same question.'

'I want Adi,' he said. 'That's all. I have no family, friends or future without her. That's the truth of it, so —'

'So the choice is easy. Go through the curtain. You'll find the answer you seek on the other side.'

He glanced at the dirty wall-hanging with disquiet. The squat armoured figure, picked out in tatty thread, stared back at him with eyes as cold as a man'kin's. A woman's gasping sobs came from beyond the cubicle's thin walls. The air was thick with grief, and power, and warning, too. No ordinary doorway lay beyond the curtain. Yet where else did he have to go? The trail ended here.

Ros stood straighter and found a clarity of thought that had eluded him earlier. Whatever awaited him, he would face it head-on. Golems and witches hadn't bested him in the past, and neither had dragons and machines from the dawn of history. He might lack money or prospects, but what need had he of them? Maser Pukje had taught him to be strong and sure on his own. If this was a test of more than his faith in Adi, he would pass that as well.

Filling his chest with smoky air and ignoring the old woman's potent stare, he stepped forward, through the curtain, into darkness.

THE THRALL

Adi's outstretched hands found a brick wall ahead of her. She stopped walking and felt to either side. The wall was curved, and would form a circle roughly four yards across if it met itself behind her. There was no light at all, and therefore no quick way to check. The air was entirely too close and warm. Claustrophobia struck her like a fist to the gut, and she turned to find way back to the door through which she had come.

The sound of an indrawn breath brought her up short. She wasn't alone.

'Who's there?'

The sounds of the city vanished the moment Ros walked through the curtain, leaving him wondering if he had been struck deaf. At the sound of a woman's tremulous inquiry, he knew that was not so. He also recognised her voice.

'Adi?'

'What's going on? Where am I?'

'Hold on.' He reached out with his senses and found the wall. Grateful for something concrete to deal with, he chose one brick at random, pressed the palm of his hand against it, and flexed his will.

Adi blinked as pinkish light flared into life. It brightened and whitened as the man who had cast it removed his hand from the source.

'You!' she gasped, recognising his scarred face immediately. It was the man she'd collided with the night the charm had been broken. He was the last person she had expected to see. Magda Van Haasteren had promised her understanding. What did he have to do with anything?

Ros was no less surprised. The woman spoke with Adi's voice but looked like the stranger he'd seen in the courtyard by the doss-house. So much for finding answers.

'How is this possible?'

'You tell me,' she said through tight lips. 'You got me into this.'

'Me? No,' he protested. 'It wasn't either of us. It was —'

Ros looked behind him, and for the first time they realised that the door they had come through was invisible. Worse than that, as a quick patting down and thumping of the wall soon revealed, the door was no longer there at all.

'A Way,' he said, remembering everything he had learned about such space-bending passages from Master Pukje. 'The curtain must have hidden it. And now it's closed.'

'We're trapped?'

'We certainly appear to be.'

Adi looked up, then down. They were caught in a chimney or well that vanished into shadow at either extremity. A heavy metal grill was all that kept them from falling.

Heights *and* tight spaces, she thought grimly to herself. What next? Crabblers? Ghosts?

She caught her fellow prisoner staring at her oddly. He turned quickly away.

'I think,' Ros said, suppressing the impulse to bring his hand up to his face, 'I think I can get us out of here. A Way leaves a dimple behind, even when it's closed. It's like a flaw in glass, and if I can find it —'

'You're babbling. What's wrong with you?'

'Nothing. Just hold on for a moment —'

'No, you wait.' She clutched his arm and pulled him around. 'How do you know my name? What kind of trick is this?'

'Trick? If anyone's tricking anyone, it's you.'

'Oh, please. You can't possibly expect me to fall for that one.'

He wrenched himself from her grip and backed away. For a moment they just glared angrily at each other. Then his face softened.

'Take off your veil,' he said.

'No.'

'I already know your name, so what difference does it make?'

'What difference *does* it make?'

'I want to see your face.'

'Get back to finding that door,' she said, 'or by the time I'm finished with you you'll have no face at all.'

He winced at that, but this time didn't turn away.

'Adi, look at me properly. I'm not hiding anything from you. You can see my face perfectly well. The scars are new, but the rest is all me. Just me. Don't you recognise anything?'

He moved around the well so the light caught his features better. She edged away, unable to tear her gaze from them.

'I'm Ros.'

'Yes.'

'And you're Adi.'

'Yes.'

With numb fingers, she pulled the veil aside.

He physically sagged with relief. Behind the Clan Markings, it was definitely her. Tired and paler than he'd ever seen her before, but her all the same. Adi the girl had become Adi the woman, and he hadn't known her — just as she hadn't known him. The familiarity they had felt in their minds had betrayed their senses, leading them badly astray.

'But if you're you,' she said, 'then who ...?'

She recoiled with a hand over her mouth, remembering the flaccid form she'd left wrapped in her sheet at the hostel.

'What is it?'

He reached for her, but she wasn't ready to be touched yet.

With shaking voice she explained about the comatose version of him she'd struggled with the last day and a half. He responded with a short account of his own trials.

'Someone's been toying with us,' she said, revulsion becoming anger, and fast. 'I'll have that someone's hide when you get us free of here. And you —' She poked him hard in the upper arm, right where his nerve was. 'You really thought I'd put you through a dance like that? How could you?'

Ros could find no good answer to her question. He returned to the task of finding the Way in the hope that it would cover his confusion. 'I'd been looking for so long. I was getting frustrated.'

'Well, that makes two of us. It's crazy to think we were so close and never knew.'

'Maddening. And it did drive me a little mad. I was helped, remember? We must have been, both of us. I can't believe you mistook that imposter for me.'

Her features darkened. He hadn't seen Adi blush for five years. It was distracting him from the task at hand.

'Well,' she said, glancing away, then back again. 'I guess this is what Magda Van Haasteren meant by sending us here.'

'I guess so.'

She touched his shoulder and was amazed at the muscle she felt there. 'It really is you.'

'Yes.'

'And I guess I'll get used to having you around again.'

'I hope so.'

Her fingers moved up to his cheek. 'Will you tell me what happened to you?'

The Way was entirely forgotten now. 'I'll tell you everything,' he said, cupping her hand in his and stepping closer.

*　　*　　*

It happened so fast there was nothing either could do. To Ros it seemed as though a ring of blue flame blossomed beneath their feet and rushed upwards past them with the speed of a dragon at full stretch. To Adi's eyes, it was a fiery dust devil, spinning with furious energy, that was born at the invisible bottom of the chimney and whipped up around them, tangling their hair and clothes as it swept up to the heights above.

That it was difficult, afterwards, to place their impressions in accord, was the least of their problems.

The force of the thing's passage blew them to opposite sides of the well-like space. Ros's ears blocked, as they had some times when Master Pukje ascended with unexpected swiftness. Adi felt a rush of vertigo, and relied on the wall at her back to keep her balance. Above them, the apparition writhed and spun, growing smaller with distance until it vanished entirely. The silence it left in its wake was almost supernatural in its intensity.

For a second, neither spoke. Something had changed, something difficult to define but impossible to deny. It was clear that the flame or dust devil hadn't been a random happenstance. There had been purpose behind it.

The clanking of metal broke the silence. The grille beneath them jerked downward an inch. Adi gasped and clutched the wall even more tightly than before. Ros looked around with wide eyes. What new trial was this?

A second racket came, as of rusty gears turning. The grille dropped again, then froze at a canted angle. It was clear now that it was turning, rotating — and that if it continued the two of them would be tipped to their deaths in the depths of the well.

A third time it turned, further than before. Adi dropped to her knees and put her fingers through the rusted metal slats. Could she hold on as it went? What exactly would that achieve? Better to fall quickly, perhaps, than to remain suspended in terror until the strength in her arms gave out.

Despair rose up in her. It was impossible to conceive that just moments ago she had been happy.

Hadn't she?

Ros loomed over her, scarred and strange. He who had seemed so familiar now looked alien and wild. His hair stood out about his head. The air prickled, making her feel as though another apparition was about to burst around them.

Instead it was the world itself that tore. She screamed as the grille seemed to lurch beneath her and she was suddenly weightless, falling.

With an explosion of brick dust and mortar, the Way opened in a place far from Magda Van Haasteren's stinking hole. Out of it burst Ros first, then Adi, tugged by his arm on her wrist. Filthy, shocked, and grateful to be alive, they staggered away from the gaping rent in the wall behind them. The boom of their arrival echoed and re-echoed through the halls of the city, and this portentous announcement did not go unnoticed.

Ros blinked his eyes clear and took in his surroundings. It was dark, but not so dark they couldn't see. They appeared to have emerged into one of the city's industrial quarters, near a tannery by the smell of it. Numerous vehicles rumbled along a major thoroughfare not one block away.

He craned his head back to inspect the rising cloud of dust silhouetted against the living lights in the ceiling. The Way had closed the moment they'd passed through it, but the after-effects were still spreading.

'We should move,' he said, 'in case anything follows.'

Adi coughed and spat. She had staggered off to find her own bearings, slowly recovering from the suddenness of their escape but still feeling a nag of worry. If anything, the nag was growing stronger, not weaker. She felt as though she had forgotten something important. The more she reached for it, the further it pulled away.

'It took what it wanted,' she said, understanding that much with certainty. 'That's why we were going to be dumped. It didn't need us any more.'

He nodded and put both hands to his temples. The exertion of opening the Way had left him dazed. He would recover, but until then his thoughts moved like slugs. 'So much for what lay behind the damned curtain. Do you think she knew this was going to happen?'

'How couldn't she? It was a set-up, and we walked right into it.' Adi was tired, more tired than she had ever been. 'We're idiots.'

He had no humour in him, but attempted a joke anyway. 'A perfect match.'

She stared at him as though he had said something utterly incomprehensible.

'Are you all right?' he asked, alarmed by a sudden, new intensity to her.

'Quite the opposite, I think.' She shook her head and looked away. 'Ros, it's gone.'

'What's gone.'

'The spark. I don't feel it any more. When I think of you …' Her eyes returned to his. 'I feel … nothing.'

He took a step backwards, rocked as though from a physical blow. Her words pained him, stung even through the dense fog in his mind, but reaching into himself he found exactly the same yawning absence. What had been so strong and clear just moments before was now missing entirely. It had evaporated.

'That thing,' she said with dismay on her face. 'It took it.'

Ros shook his head, reaching through coldness like a drowning man at a rope.

'Let's not jump to any conclusions,' he said.

'What other conclusion could there be?'

'I don't know. But we can't just give up.'

'Do you think we can fix this?'

Tears painted dark streaks through the white dust in her face.

He had no answer for her.

'I'll see if I can flag someone down,' she said, heading at hast for the thoroughfare. 'If we're quick, if we come to her in time, maybe we can get it back.'

The cab was cramped but fast. Fuelled by a mixture of alcohol and the Change, the growl of its engine only added to the pounding in Ros's head. The pain paled in comparison, however, to the feeling that his heart seemed to have died in his chest.

They endured the journey in silence. Although they were crammed together on the back seat, they felt as distant from each other as they had at any point during the previous five years. Adi's thoughts returned constantly to that moment when hope had turned to horror. How could neither of them have seen it coming?

She was conscious, also, of the cab driver glancing at them in the mirror. It was well within reason that he should be curious about the dust-covered pair who had hailed him with such urgency, but it was more than that. Only midway through the journey did she realise that she had forgotten to replace her veil. The driver had clearly noted her Clan markings and, if not already certain as to the identity of his passengers, was at least speculating wildly.

The only way to stop him talking was to keep him close by.

'Wait here,' she said when they pulled up outside Magda Van Haasteren's dive. 'We'll need you afterwards.'

The value of the coin she gave him was out of all proportion with the request. He understood immediately. 'Of course, miss,' he said. 'I'll not go anywhere.'

They left the cab and warily approached the portal through which they had both entered earlier that night. The magnitude of the charm that had enveloped them boggled Ros's mind. Not only had their paths crossed, but they had also come to this very place practically on top of each other. How was it possible that they had not noticed, that Magda Van Haasteren had talked to both of them simultaneously, *that he had not seen her*? He was angry at himself for letting the broader illusions distract him while a deeper treachery unfolded. That was a lesson he would not forget in a hurry.

You feel it with your whole body and in all your thoughts, Adi was thinking as she stared at the door. *It's like a little bit of lightning, and it too can start a fire.*

Ros too was remembering what the seer had told him about the spark. *They fare badly who try to draw on a power that isn't there.*

The hovel was empty, but only recently so. That Magda Van Haasteren had fled in a hurry was left in no doubt by the cheroot still smoking in an overflowing ashtray, and the many possessions she had left behind. Even in the absence of candlelight they could make out the curtain still hanging on the wall before them.

Ros tore it down and threw it aside. A featureless wall stared back at them.

'She heard us coming,' Adi said.

Ros nodded. 'We'll never find her. She could be anywhere.'

'So where to now?'

Separately, they reviewed the path that had brought them here. It couldn't have been entirely illusion, unless the entire city had fallen victim to it. Furthermore, man'kin weren't easily influenced …

Ros pulled the business card from his pocket and held it up for Adi to see.

Facing each other in the study two couples sat, one old, one new — if they were a couple at all — and on the floor between them rested the bust of the man'kin, Mawson.

'You say he spoke?' asked Jenfi Mierlo. 'To both of you?'

'Without question,' Adi replied. 'He told us both the same thing: to go to Magda Van Haasteren.'

'You will go to Madam Van Haasteren,' the bust obediently repeated, like a parrot.

'You see?'

Jenfi Mierlo gaped first at Adi, then at Mawson. Then she started coughing, and Ros thought would never stop.

'The trouble is,' said Samson when his wife's fit had subsided, 'that Mawson didn't in fact tell you to go anywhere. He simply said you were going to.'

'I hardly see the difference,' Adi retorted. 'We wouldn't have gone if he hadn't brought it up.'

'And therein lies the problem with man'kin. They don't experience time the same way we do. They see it all at once, so as far as he's concerned: you will go, you have gone, and you are already there — all at once. The notion of intentionality is quite foreign to him. Sometimes, dear, I think it'd be better if they never spoke at all.'

'Yes, yes,' his wife said, tipping her birdlike frame to the right and then straightening again, 'but we're missing the point. Mawson isn't the culprit. It's that wretched Van Haasteren woman again.'

'Again?' Ros asked.

The elder couple exchanged a look. It was clear that neither wanted to be the one to explain.

'If we'd known who you were —'

'If you'd told us about Mawson —'

They cut each other off. Jenfi waved for her husband to continue.

'I mean to say,' he said, 'that you fit her requirements perfectly. The pair of you, not as individuals. She of course knew your history. She had years to study you and to prepare the trap. First she lured you, Ros, to the city, thus ensuring that Adi would also come. Once you were both here, she redoubled her efforts. She took your feelings for each other and turned them around — and did so quite expertly, I must say. You were hopelessly entangled. There was no chance of seeing your way out of it.'

'What he's trying to say,' said Jenfi, 'is that she played on your worst fears: that you wouldn't be recognised or respected for who you were. And of course you played along with those fears, albeit unwittingly: you *were* both hiding; you both *had* changed. All Van Haasteren had to do was set the ball rolling. You did the rest.'

'But why?' asked Adi.

'Why would she want to do something like this?' Ros echoed. 'To us?'

'You mentioned the spark,' said Samson, taking his wife's hand in his. 'That was what she wanted, as you have deduced, and everything she did was designed to magnify its existence. You enjoyed it in your youth, and you might have reawakened it naturally simply by being reunited — but the fact that you didn't even recognise each other the first time you crossed paths suggests otherwise. Your spark therefore had to be nurtured — by anxiety, by doubt — and by hope too, for without that the spark never catches.'

'She primed you for that meeting behind the curtain,' Jenfi concluded. 'For the moment in which you truly recognised each other. That was what she wanted. Not just a spark, but first-class ignition.'

Ros and Adi remembered that moment well. What power their spark had had! Now it was harnessed by another, the value it might have had to them was irrelevant.

'We would have warned you off,' Jenfi repeated, 'if only you'd told us.'

'How could we have known?' Adi rose suddenly to her feet. 'You make it sound like it's our fault. But it's not.'

'No one's saying that. Are you?' Ros asked the Mierlos.

Adi didn't wait for an answer. With fast, angry paces, she walked from the room.

'Wait here, Ros.' Jenfi Mierlo hurried after her.

'There's something else,' said Samson Mierlo in a grave voice, leaning forward to look Ros in the eye. 'There's something else you both need to know.'

They received much the same addendum in much the same words, Ros in the study and Adi at the front of the Mierlo mansion, where Jenfi had caught her before getting into the cab

'Magda Van Haasteren doesn't work alone,' the Mierlos told them. 'She's in partnership with something else, a creature that's named in the bestiaries but barely described. No one knows what form such creatures take or where they come from. No one knows where she found this one or why she tamed it. All we know is what it does.

'Van Haasteren is the procurer in the arrangement. She finds the lovers and lures them into her trap, pair by pair as you were lured. At the heart of the trap lies the creature, which thrives on the offerings she brings. They are a meal to it, you see. It has no hunger for flesh and blood, for it isn't a material thing itself. Like eats like. This being has no physical presence, and has a hunger to match.

'It eats the spark. That's all. And that's how we know what it is. Stone Mages have examined a rash of deaths in recent years — all pairs, all mysterious. Their bodies showed death by falling, but there were other signs, hints of a more sinister rupture before death came to them. We followed the investigation, for it touched on our own interests; we noted its conclusion. The Stone Mages can't convict Magda Van Haasteren of anything, for she herself has done nothing wrong. The lovers came to her of their own free will; her pet does the rest; and she is canny enough to leave no evidence. Since predators are not disallowed in the city — for if they were, the markets would be forced to close forever — all we can do is warn people away, and hope that they'll listen.

'But lovers rarely do. They're caught in their own world. That's the great tragedy of it all — that the situation wouldn't be possible without desire and dreams, those things that normally make us flourish. The dark side of the spark, if you will.

'The bait in the trap was set by you yourselves.'

'Not all stories have the happy ending we desire,' Samson said, putting an avuncular hand on Ros's shoulder, 'but that doesn't make them bad stories.'

Jenfi told Adi: 'It's not entirely hopeless. The Mages can tell when a Way opens up outside the city, so they'll know if Van Haasteren is still here, somewhere.'

Neither Ros nor Adi was soothed.

'You said it has a name — the thing that ate our spark?'

Jenfi and Samson Mierlo told them, knowing the value of naming an enemy even when the fight has been lost.

'It's a trystophage,' said Samson.

'It's an amavore,' said Jenfi.

Both said, 'Its common name is the Thrall.'

'What now?' Ros asked as they took their leave of the Mierlos, no happier but at least better informed.

'I don't know.' Adi's exhaustion was total. 'Your things are back at the hostel, if you still want them.'

He wasn't sure, but said nonetheless: 'Perhaps I can help you get rid of that doppelganger, while I'm there.'

To the Lost Dolphin they went, where they found the hostel in a state of restrained panic. The doppelganger had dissolved in a shower of fiery arcs an hour ago, startling the maid and setting fire to the bed. The fire had been extinguished before serious damage resulted, but the place remained in an uproar. To this was now added the revelation that Lady Hakamu might be none other than Aditi Sabatino, judging by her Clan markings — for Adi had forgotten once again to replace her veil — and if that were the case, then the long-haired, scarred stranger could only be her legendary betrothed, Roslin of Geheb.

The whispers as they surveyed the damaged room were impossible to ignore. Adi knew she wouldn't be able to bribe the entire staff, as she hoped she had silenced the cab driver when they finally let him go.

'Just give me one night,' she begged the manager and the staff. 'That's all I ask. Then I'll release you. Tell the world then, if you must.'

'There's nothing to tell, anyway,' said Ros, misunderstanding the situation completely.

'If you do it for us,' Adi added more persuasively, 'you will become part of the story. You'll have given us sanctuary when we most needed it.'

The hostel's manager, sensing an opportunity for free publicity, took the matter into his hands. He swore that the staff would be discreet, on penalty of his own job. Threats were issued to all in his presence and solemn oaths undertaken. Furthermore, he said, the hostel's other guests would be moved elsewhere — the smell of smoke had given them the jitters anyway — and new arrivals would be carefully vetted before gaining access to the building.

'Thank you,' said Adi. Ros echoed the sentiment wholeheartedly.

And so the room was cleared.

They checked their belongings without talking. It didn't seem to Ros that any kind of words were possible between them now. The Thrall had taken them too. There was just emotion, raw and red, too painful to pick at.

Among Adi's scattered effects, none of which appeared to have been burned, she found the broken charm. The wave of grief she felt then was so powerful that she lost all strength in her legs. She let herself fall into a chair and cradled the charm in her hands. What good had following it brought her? All those dreams, all those hopes, shattered like workings of the charm itself.

Ros walked past her, and the crystal flared bright red.

They both stared at it in surprise. Had it fixed itself somehow? Had it too been afflicted by Van Haasteren's web of deceit?

More likely, they both realised, it had been working all along. When Ros had brushed past Adi by the doss-house, he had gone from being in front of her to behind her. If she'd turned and pointed the charm his way, it would have glowed as normal. But she didn't. Instead she saw the doppelganger and thought she'd reached the end of her quest. She stopped looking.

The pain on Adi's face was awful to behold. Ros assumed his looked much the same.

'I guess I should leave,' he said, hefting the pack he'd thought lost forever.

'Don't be ridiculous. I'm not sending you back to that horrible place.'

The suite was far more comfortable than the doss-house, even with the scorch marks on the bed. Ros appreciated the offer.

'I can sleep on the floor.'

'No. You take the bed.'

Fresh linen had been left, but neither of them made a move towards it.

'Are you sure?'

'Positive. You need it more than me, and honestly, I could sleep anywhere.'

'Well, all right.'

Ros replaced the sheets while Adi arranged cushions in one corner, diagonally opposite from the bed. They didn't look at each other as they undressed. They didn't talk, not even to say goodnight. The light was extinguished, and they lay for an eternity, listening to each other breathe.

A shaking of the bed woke Ros from a nightmare in which his face and hands were being scarred anew. Adi crouched motionlessly beside him, barely visible in the darkness. Her eyes caught every faint trace of light in the room and sent them, refracted and concentrated, right at him.

'I want to stop her,' she said. 'No one deserves to feel like this.'

'I agree. We'll do it tomorrow. Together.'

'There's no together any more, Ros. We can't think like that.'

'Then we'll ask for help. Everyone'll know we're here by breakfast anyway, so let's get the whole city looking for her. Use the stories to our advantage for a change.'

Adi didn't confess that she'd already been doing that, when it suited her.

'I want revenge, too,' she said, lying down next to him.

Ros put his arm around her. They stayed that way as sleep claimed them again, and they didn't wake until dawn.

KEEPSAKE

Word spread like fire through tall grass. Where the rumour started wasn't clear. The light-chimneys had barely delivered the distant sun's first rays when its source was obscured behind a wall of friends-of-friends and cousins-in-the-know. Once the news hit the markets, it took on a life of its own. Roslin of Geheb and Aditi Sabatino — he who vanquished the Golem of Omus and she who walked the Weird — were in Ulum, and in trouble.

Once released, the story accrued strange new details: that a monster walked the city streets, devouring children; that an explosion the previous night heralded an invasion from the depths of the earth; that the pair were impostors whose real selves had been disposed of days earlier. Among the elaborations and fabrications, however, lurked enough of the truth for the message to sink in. That which the famous lovers held most precious in the world had been stolen by a seer.

Every one of the city's innocent seers — if such existed — closed shop for fear of reprisals against them personally or the profession as a whole. Some declared themselves to the authorities in advance of wrongful accusations. A description of the culprit in question circulated, passing from hand to hand and via the more exotic means available to those talented in the Change. Officially, the Stone Mages played no role in the seer-hunt; they could not until the ruling Synod had issued an order to that effect. Unofficially, a growing cadre assembled in the city's Grand Minster in order to lend their weight to the search.

Hastily constructed charms scoured the underworld for clues, while ethereal images and messages wafted along the streets. Regular commerce ground to a halt. Of those with a choice, only the most churlish abstained from the city-wide effort. Some grumbled about the jammed thoroughfares or the delays in some services, but all pitched in somehow. Reports flooded in of suspicious-looking characters, most bearing no resemblance whatsoever to the missing woman. Boarded up spaces were exposed to daylight, some for the first time in decades. Panic spread through the city's rodent and insect populations as previously safe haunts were overturned. Birds and lizards headed for roosts out of reach of human hands.

The day wore on. Crowds gathered in wait of news, hopeful too for a glimpse of the famous couple. Whispers spread of sightings as leads were followed and dismissed, one after the other. Opportunistic merchants set up stalls and manipulated rumours to direct crowds their way. As night approached, a carnival atmosphere set in, complete with music and impromptu dances. Families and neighbours set up camp on corners, sharing wine, beer and food, and any news that happened to pass through. Not all was merriment and joy, of course, for the reason for the holiday had not been forgotten by anyone. Fights broke out in places, among the poor-tempered and those who found the tension too much. The people of the city were waiting for an outcome, each in their own way. Ulum, as a whole, held its breath.

From behind the curtained windows of their hostel room, Ros listened to the crowds moving through the city. They had barely left the building all day, relying on runners and other means to convey messages back and forth. Only twice, when particularly strong evidence had pointed to a near-certain location, had they gone out in pursuit of a resolution, and even then only by a back entrance, secure from the public eye. The hostel had hunkered down around them, the manager enjoying his role as their protector and confidant. Adi dreaded to think what the bill might tally to.

'What if she's gone?'

She looked up from double-checking the stack of information that had already been gathered. 'Do you think it's possible?'

He doubted it. The city had been physically sealed all day, as well as blocked against the Change. If she had made a dash for the outside the very moment her latest lovers had been kidnapped, maybe then she could have made it out in time. The still-smoking cheroot haunted that theory like a ghost; it wouldn't be laid to rest, and made a mockery of the attempt.

'She has to be here somewhere.'

A team of volunteer Stone Mages had gone over every inch of her abandoned stall. The Way Ros and Adi had followed was now firmly shut, and the room clear of any other exit. Van Haasteren must, therefore, have had another escape route secreted nearby. Neighbouring buildings had been searched from top to bottom, without success.

Adi pushed the stack aside. 'What about *why* rather than *where*? That's what I'm stuck on. What's in it for her? She fed the Thrall, but she must've gained something in return.'

'Not wealth, that's for sure,' he said.

'Or fame.'

'Look where they've got us.'

'My point's the same, though. She's a criminal. Her motive has to be more than just cruelty.'

Adi remembered the passion with which the seer had spoken of the spark.

'Maybe her own spark died,' she said, posing an answer to her own question, 'and she doesn't want anyone else to be happy.'

Ros felt the thought coming long before it arrived. Something Adi had said had collided with a detail considered irrelevant, and together they prompted another question.

'What about *how*?'

'The Change,' she said. 'All that.'

'But where did she learn it? Even rogue Change-workers have teachers, and I've never heard of anything like this.'

'Maybe she invented it herself.'

'Not from scratch. That's impossible. She would've burned herself out, most likely, or at least attracted serious attention before now.' He tapped his chin. 'No, there had to be someone else. Someone who helped her at least part of the way.'

The thought was still coming. He gave it time while she watched him, wondering what was going on inside his head.

Suddenly he was heading for the door and scooping her up along the way. 'Come on,' he said. 'I know exactly how to find her.'

'But we've already searched here,' said Adi when the convoy they were leading pulled up at the seer's hovel. 'Over and over.'

'Not well enough,' he said, fairly bounding from the cab and approaching the entrance. Armoured Mages recognised him barely in time and waved him through a split-instant after he had passed.

Adi dragged herself after him, reluctant to return to that awful hole no matter how excited Ros appeared to be about it. He had kept the secret to himself the whole way, saying that he wanted to be sure. She told him not to worry about getting her hopes up, since they were as low as they could possibly go, but he had stayed silent, fairly vibrating with energy.

Before she could reach the door he emerged again, holding something heavy and shapeless in his arms.

'Take one end,' he said. 'Turn it over.'

Together they unfurled the curtain through which they had walked to their spark's doom. The threadbare Stone Mage stared up at the unnatural stars. By their light his indifference looked entirely calculated.

'Lay it down, right here.'

Adi did so and took a wary step backwards.

'Watch,' Ros said.

This was the first time she had witnessed his new skills with the Change. His movements were economical and assured. There was no urgent fumbling, as there had been in his youth or when in the grip of the Thrall passion had ruled his head. Here he was cool and confident, utterly in command.

The world flexed around them.

Adi and the small crowd that had gathered watched to see what would happen next.

Ros stepped lightly onto the carpet and dropped out of sight into Magda Van Haasteren's hidden Way.

*   *   *

Immediately he stumbled, made clumsy by an awkward tangle of geometries. He had wanted his revelation to be dramatic. He had wanted Adi to be surprised. Too late he realised that they should have fixed the curtain vertically, as it had been originally placed, so he could simply walk through instead dropping out the wall on the other end of it.

He was the one caught off-balance. His right foot came down awkwardly, twisting his ankle. Pain shot up his calf and the leg gave way beneath him. He tumbled forward and landed heavily on his side.

'Get ready to catch your girlfriend,' growled a familiar voice.

Ros rolled onto his back with his hands upraised as Adi hurtled through the Way after him. Lighter and more sure on her feet, she merely staggered two steps and came to a halt, standing still before him with both soles firmly planted.

Behind her, the Way snapped shut with a whip-crack, silencing a growing clamour from the far side.

Ros gathered his strength to punch a hole back through.

'Do it,' said the seer, 'and I'll kill all three of us.'

Magda Van Haasteren was a shapeless mass sitting in the centre of the rough-hewn chamber, hunched over a candlestick holder as though for warmth. The candle was lit, casting a flickering yellow light across her walnut features. Adi helped Ros to his feet, watching the seer closely and taking the measure of the place in which she had sought refuge. It was far below the city's deepest extent, that much Adi was sure of, with no physical entrances or exits, windows or exhausts. The air was clammy, hot and foul, and apart from the candle the only light came from tiny glowstones embedded in the ceiling like jewels. Water dripped in a far corner, and trickled elsewhere, leaving gleaming paths and stalactites in its wake.

The seer's hidey-hole wasn't a comfortable space by any human standards. The more Adi saw, the less certain she became that it was intended for human habitation at all. A series of makeshift shelves lined the chamber's walls, and on those shelves were things that hurt the eye to look at.

'Do that too,' said the seer at some plot of Ros's that Adi couldn't sense, 'and I'll lock you down here forever. With me.'

Ros sagged backwards, favouring his right leg.

'Are we trapped?' Adi asked him, sotto voce.

'No. I'm sure I can get us out.'

'How sure?'

'As sure as he can be, girl,' the seer said with a cackle at their expense. 'You're asking the impossible and he's failing to deliver it. Or he's showing off and you're not being a very good audience. I forget which.'

Adi's fury rose. 'We should leave you to rot.'

'I'm rotten enough as is.' The seer put the candlestick to one side and stood up with a grunt. Her shape didn't appreciatively change. 'As are we all, on the inside. See that one there?' One twisted finger stabbed at the nearest shelf. 'That's all that remains of your spark.'

Ros stared at the thing she indicated, aware of Adi's hand painfully gripping his arm. It, like the others filling the shelves, was black and twisted, seeming both thorned and half-melted at the same time. Some grass seeds had the same look, seen up close, but this held no vitality or beneficence. It was entirely malefic.

'What did you do to it?'

'I did nothing — and what was done would have been done anyway. You would've killed your spark without the Thrall's intervention.'

'Never,' said Adi, sure that the aching void in her heart had once held something of great permanence

The seer hobbled to the shelf and picked up the hideous object. 'The surety of youth is a brilliant thing. It takes a brighter fire still to burn it out. You'll see soon enough that I did you a favour. I've seared your soul against the wound of disappointment; the deeper scars of loss and regret you'll never know. You should thank me rather than rail against me.'

'You would've killed us,' said Ros, 'like the others.'

'Yes, but don't you see that would have been a blessing too?' The seer clutched the thing in her hands, not heeding how its wicked points cut her, or at least not minding. 'Where there is life, there is hope — and hope makes us do terrible, terrible things.'

'You're done now,' said Adi, repulsed by the mixture of self-pity and triumph displayed before her. 'Ulum has had enough of your "blessings".'

The seer uttered a sound that might have been a laugh. Blood dripped in heavy splashes to her feet. 'So you plan to kill me. I thought you came to take back what you have lost. What if I told you that I could return it to you? Would you let me go, if I did?'

Ros knew she was lying. She had to be, for such a claim was preposterous. The spark had been eaten. All that remained was the waste, the excreta, of a being that thrived on the dreams of others.

Yet he was tempted. To recover what had been taken — to reclaim the future he had spent five years planning …

'And then what?' said Adi. 'We don't have much in common, Ros and I. That's why our story was so popular. We were the odd couple, the mismatch made good. Look at how we tested each other when you gave us the chance to. Look at the wedge we drove between ourselves. You didn't create that wedge; it was already there. You just wielded what we would've wielded against each other, in time.'

The seer's lips curled. 'You're not so dense after all. Congratulations.'

'That's what you'd have us believe, anyway.' Adi had let go of Ros and was moving slowly to her left, widening the gap between them. 'You spared us the lie of the spark and an agonised life when it's gone. You tell yourself it's a good thing because you wish someone had done it to you. You don't have the courage to end your own pain, so you end the pain of others instead. You create it, and then you end it. You're your own little industry, aren't you?'

'Stay back.'

The seer's eyes danced between the two of them. She was beginning to feel hemmed in: Ros could see that much. He wanted to warn Adi to be careful, to be wary of pushing her too hard, but he was unwilling to interrupt the tide of words. True or not, Adi's insights were having a profound effect on the seer.

'Stay back, I said!'

'Who did this to you?' Adi pressed, feeling her fortunes turning at last. 'Who did *you* lose?'

The seer's face broke out into a snarl. With surprising strength, she hurled the wicked thing at Adi's head. Adi raised her hands to ward it off, but the barbs dug deep. She fell backwards with a cry.

Ros was already reaching for the Change when the seer turned to him. They were surrounded by stone — stone wedded hard to the bedrock by virtue of its depth. He was surrounded by power. All he had to do was channel it.

So too the seer, and she had blood and territory on her side. Their wills locked in strange and deadly shapes in her secret hideaway. Light flared through all colours of the rainbow. Flashes of heat seared their skins. The floor beneath them buckled, and showers of dust and rock rained on them. The black shapes lining the walls exploded like ghastly black rockets, filling the air with soot.

Ros knew within seconds that he had the measure of her. It wasn't in his mind to end it quickly, though. He needed to know the source of her knowledge. He had to be sure his guess was right.

And thus it turned out to be, for behind her wild improvisations and baroque peccadilloes he did recognise a philosophy, a method of teaching that was different from his own but at the same time familiar to him, as it would have been to any Change-worker raised in the Interior. A Stone Mage had taken her part of the road towards mastery — a Stone Mage much like the one depicted on the curtain.

The battle of wills had achieved its purpose. Ros bore down as Master Pukje had taught him, forcing his will upon her so that she could hurt no one else. His intention was not to kill her, but to bind her long enough for the authorities to take her captive. His desire for revenge only went that far.

Movement to one side caught both their attentions. Adi was up and moving, groggily but purposefully. Somehow, despite all the commotion, the candle was still burning. With one bleeding hand she reached for it.

Ros reeled back at a wild attack from the seer. Driven by surprise and panic, she rushed for Adi. From whence the sudden surge came, Ros didn't know. It was all he could to slow the vicious outpour and prevent Adi from being riven in two.

For herself, Adi was aware of a terrible conflict waging over her, buffeting her from side to side, but she couldn't let it get in the way of what she had to do. She had guessed the source of the seer's tortured motivations. There was a hurt in Magda Van Haasteren's past that matched Adi's own, and she maintained it still, perversely nurturing it just as she nurtured the Thrall. The two, therefore, the pain and the Thrall, had to be connected by more than just metaphor. If one wasn't literally the other, then perhaps they shared the same origin.

The Thrall had rushed at Ros and Adi like an ascending bubble of flame, sweeping their spark off with it. Adi didn't understand what kind of creature it was, but she did understand the nature of human desires and needs. When Magda Van Haasteren had sensed that Ros and Adi had escaped, she had taken just one thing from her stinking hovel. That one thing was the candle, and she had been cradling it when Ros and Adi had found her.

Adi's right hand was slick with her own blood. Thumb and forefinger hissed when she closed them tight about the flame. It squirmed and writhed, as slippery as a slug, and it burned her as badly as her dead spark's barbs. Pain lanced up her arm and assailed her body and mind. She fought it with fury and maintained her grip. It felt good to reverse the flow of ill-fortune. The Thrall would die just as all of Adi's childish hopes were now dead and gone forever.

The Thrall howled as the fire of its existence was slowly extinguished. Adi felt a lifetime of guilt and entrapment burn through her, and knew that she had guessed correctly. The source of the seer's despair and power were one and the same. Had he betrayed the young woman he had been teaching? Had he used her love and thought to throw it away? Either way, the seer had taken her revenge on the man who had wronged her, forcing him to kill in order to live on as a captive, and to feed by taking that which he had taken from her.

The storm intensified in direct proportion to the fading of the flame. When the latter died, so did the other. All resistance collapsed, and Ros and Adi fell to the ground, stunned by the sudden silence, spent.

Ros could barely crawl. The glowstones shone fitfully and the air remained thick with ash. He could hear Adi breathing — or did he simply imagine that he could? — and by painful effort was able to follow the sound to where she lay huddled on her side, cradling the dead spark tenderly with all of her body. He touched her hair, and she rolled over to face him, leaving the awful thing behind.

'Is she dead?' Adi asked.

'I think so. By her own hand.'

She winced, but there was triumph in her eyes, too. 'We managed it, then.'

'We did. Together.'

They lay side by side for a long moment, holding hands tightly, unsure exactly what this meant for them.

'I suppose we should go soon,' he said, thinking with no great joy of the crowds that would be waiting for them.

'I'm taking it with us,' she said with iron in her voice.

He understood, and lacked the strength to argue.

The closed cab that whisked Ros and Adi from the scene was the talk of the city's night-owls, for its import was ambivalent, perhaps even ominous. While it was good news that the pair had survived, the fate of the treacherous seer and the great romance itself was not known. A new kind of anxiety gripped the darkened streets. Was seeing justice done better than seeing damage undone, or vice versa? If one couldn't have both, who could possibly choose between them?

The Mierlos guided them into the mansion, trusting in the cloak of night and a torturously complicated route to keep prying eyes at bay. Adi was shaking, and Ros felt as though every bone in his body might spontaneously shatter. A physician was on hand to tend their ailments, both physical and otherwise. Adi's wounds were bathed and bandaged; Ros's twisted ankle was bound. Both were given clean clothes and all the food they could stomach. No one asked about the ebon crystal that rested on Mawson's former plinth in the study. That it was to be guarded and not touched was the only instruction issued, by both of the Mierlos' guests.

Shortly before midnight a small gathering convened in the study. There a senior Stone Mage presented his conclusions on the matter of the Thrall and its patron, Magda Van Haasteren. Her body had been recovered from the underground redoubt. An autopsy had confirmed Ros's intuitive diagnosis: her heart had literally burst from the application of her own will. Neither Ros nor Adi were to blame for her death, although if they had been they would surely have been exonerated.

Few doubted Adi's interpretation of the creature's origins, and several candidates were put forward to account for the man the Thrall had been. No one accused Adi of killing the Thrall too quickly, but it was apparent that the lack of an opportunity to test the hypothesis seemed a shame to some. Perhaps all such creatures had undergone the tragic birth and endured the grotesque symbiotic life as this one. Until another appeared, there was little way to tell.

A representative of the city's administration officially apologised for the damage done by one of its residents, and expressed a sincere hope that the incident would not affect relations between Ulum and the trading Clans, who were, after all, the lifeblood of the Interior. Adi assured him that it would not, and went on to profess her profound gratitude to the people of the city for lending their aid when need had been greatest.

'On that matter,' Jenfi Mierlo began, but her husband nudged her silent.

There followed several other declarations, clarifications, and interrogations, all of which began to take on a slightly surreal nature until, finally, the hosts declared the convention over and ushered the officials to the door.

'You're welcome to rest here the night,' said the mistress of the house when its halls were quiet once more, 'but there's something we want to tell you first.'

'Your spark was powerful, yes,' said Samson Mierlo, pacing awkwardly about the sealed study. His tone was the same as it had been the day he had informed Adi that Ros was lost in the Void Beneath. He indicated the twisted, black thing: 'There's nothing to be done for it now, though. You have to move on.'

'What are you suggesting?' Adi asked, her face taut and pinched. Inside, despite the ministrations of all those who had tried to help, she felt the same.

'I'm suggesting that we are not so different, Jenfi and I. That is, we *are* quite different from each other, but that's what makes us the same as you two. We can serve as an example, if you need one.'

'You must feel that all is lost,' Jenfi said, turning violet with the effort of restraining her relentless croup. 'But it isn't. If a spark was all it took for love to survive — not just survive; thrive and grow — Samson and I would have parted years before now. Not one couple in the history of the world has ever been perfectly matched, and not one spark has lasted the length of a marriage. Sparks come and go — that's the secret your twisted friend neglected to learn.'

'You're rather fortunate, after a fashion,' said Samson.

Ros stared at him as he had stared at Magda Van Haasteren, who had suggested the same awful thing.

'This is the worst it will ever be,' Jenfi explained. 'You've seen what happens when expectations aren't met. Hopes dashed, dreams unfulfilled — and that was before the spark was taken.' She waved a hand expressively. 'How much better to move forward with eyes unclouded in search of a new spark, one you brought into being yourselves rather than one that owned you.'

'Because you have all the raw materials,' said Samson. 'You have a history — as anyone can tell you — and now you have shared something else too. Several equally important things. A common enemy and unity of purpose; grief — and a keepsake to remind you of everything that happened here. Sparks have been born from significantly less than that, in my experience.'

'But what if that's not what we want?' Adi interjected. 'What if everything we now have in common —' She couldn't keep the bitterness from her voice. '— the pain and the suffering, the memories, the exhaustion — what if that becomes self-perpetuating? What if we just want to leave it behind and go back into hiding again?'

Jenfi Mierlo folded her hands in her lap. Ros recognised the fiduciary gleam that returned to her eyes.

'I'm afraid,' she said, 'that isn't an option just yet.'

*   *   *

Dawn crept down Ulum's chimneys and cast the beginning of another day in a muted golden light. It had been a long night for all in the city, and an especially dark night for some. An atmosphere of apprehension had settled in like fog, making restless even the most stoic of dreamers. Rumours continued to fly, if more sluggishly than previously without fact to back them up. Roslin of Geheb and Aditi Sabatino had not been seen for hours. Some said that they were gone and would never visit the city again. Had all of Ulum's help been for nothing? Would the markets ever re-open?

That morning's crowds were simply waiting for answers. Wild-beard was among them, with a mazed look and a leer for any who caught his eye, along with the cab driver who had whisked Ros and Adi to safety after escaping the trap and the maid who had watched doppelganger-Ros decrepitate. They knew as little as anyone else. Those who did know were, for the moment, not talking.

Ros dressed with a calm he would have though impossible just hours before. Adi helped him fold the fabric, which came in a style that had risen to prominence during his long apprenticeship. The terror of the everyday was for the moment deferred, thanks in no small part to her good example. The world of the Thrall and the seer — *his* world — had been no less challenging for her, and she had excelled in it.

They had spent the night at the Mierlos, who had, without any obvious dissemblance, explained that only one guest-room was available. Although they had chafed at the intimacy at first, later they been glad for the opportunity to talk through everything they had been told — for a telling-to is what it had certainly amounted to. And later still, with the advice of their benefactors still clear in their minds, they had stopped talking altogether, feeling as though they hadn't any choice in the matter but not in an inordinately negative sense. The truth of it was that it had been a relief to let go of the expectation that they *should* choose. The head couldn't stand in for the heart, when it came to such matters. The moment decided, if anything did, and in that moment all had been well, and something of a release for both of them.

When the folding and tying was done, they held each other tightly and cried for a while. There was nothing shameful or wretched in it. The time for that had passed. New challenges awaited them, deserving all their attention. They could still grieve, but at the same time they could also move on.

Ros looked uncomfortable in his finery. Adi wished he would relax into it, but supposed he would in time. He had been so powerful, so potent, in Van Haasteren's subterranean cave, and she was prepared now to give him the benefit of the doubt. For herself, she had chosen something absurdly impractical from her own wardrobe, recovered from the Lost Dolphin before souvenir collectors could claim it. She was aware that a large part of her took comfort from the familiar routine of dressing and the novelty of preparing someone else's dress, and although it wasn't a habit she wanted to encourage, for now she would embrace the task.

'True stories don't have endings,' said he in a contemplative tone. Mawson had broken his silence for the third time to deliver that gnomic fragment, which she supposed gave some insight into his stony motivations.

'Indeed,' she said, quoting in turn Jenfi Mierlo's opinion on the importance of the people around them, not merely as customers who spent more when they were happy: 'And love doesn't thrive in isolation.'

Hand in hand, they went to pay their respects to the city.

AFTERWORD

'The Spark' sits midway along the timeline of the ten linked fantasy novels in my Change series — the Books of the Change, the Books of the Cataclysm, and most recently the Broken Land. Inspired by the landscapes of my childhood rather than European or indigenous Australian mythologies, I had no conception when I set out on this journey that the places I revisited would become such an enduring obsession. The people who occupied them, also.

My young protagonists Ros and Adi were left somewhat hanging at the end of the Broken Land trilogy, as had Sal and Shilly years before them, because the conclusion to their story lay beyond the purview of a series for young readers. I always intended to return, to see their knot tied, but the deeper I dove into their story the less, perversely, it became about them, or even about the landscape that originally inspired their world.

Yet in a very real way, 'The Spark' is the capping stone on the entire series. All the characters I've loved are present, in one form or another, and all the motifs too. Loss, the passage to adulthood, the nursing and healing of old wounds — for me, that's always what these stories have been about.

And love, too, with which all can be endured.

— *Sean Williams*

An illustrator by training and a deeply unrepentant word-nerd, D.M. Cornish is old enough to have seen the very first *Star Wars* (the now unhappily titled 'Episode 4'). From such flights of delight and fancy he has developed an almost habitual outlet for his passion of word conjuring through the invention of secondary worlds. A fortuitous encounter with a children's publisher gave him an opportunity to develop these ideas further. A thousand words at a time, this has lead to the writing (and illustrating) of the *Monster-Blood Tattoo* series — *Foundling, Lamplighter* and *Factotum* (yet to be released). Rumour persists that he possesses a life outside of these books, but it is a vague and shadowy thing.

The Corsers' Hinge:
A Lamplighter Tale

D.M. CORNISH

Corsers' Hinge, the ~ *(noun) the vernacular and long-standing policy of conduct supposedly governing the behaviour of corsers — that is, grave robbers (a corse being a dead body, of course) — stipulating such ancient customs as how frequently a single boneyard or crypt or surgery may be plundered, disallowing such foul practices as employing murder to fill a toll (quota) and providing the modes of etiquette when corsers meet over a coincidentally prized tomb. Adherence to the hinge is, of course, entirely voluntary, but its existence helps a corser to hold to a certain illusion of respectability in their ignoble trade. Ashmongers — dealers in dead bodies and their parts — do not of course hold* themselves *to such missish restrictions.*

The first spring month of Orio had been especially poor for Bunting Faukes, corser and perpetual wayfarer; one of those times to bring a weaker soul to despair of the path of their life and to stoop to consider an early exit from under the world's wearying weight. The cause of such disconsolation?

Money.

Forever money, Faukes reflected glumly, drawing out his long iron corse-pole to prod Hammer, then Anvil, his brace of donkeys drawing the rattling cart, as if the dogged beasts were to blame.

As was the way of his profession, winter with all its maladies, its early gloom and low flesh-preserving temperatures was typically a boon. Yet this year's frosted months had brought an inexplicable increase in the want for corses of all ripenings. Bunting could not account for it. *Perhaps necromancy or some other fabercadavery has become all the fancy among high-flown society?* Yet, what he knew all too well was that a multiplication of orders had made for a multiplication of work, bringing corser all too close to corser, contact that left only one with the prize and the other with … well, amongst bruises and shovel wounds, potive burns and bullet holes, an empty order. In added insult, fresh-plucked spring was proving to be especially cheery, its balmy promise of a fine summer ripening ripe flesh all too quickly, inviting a torment of flies and making fraught the already chancy traffic of corses; its shortening of the nights denying him time to work.

For only the second spell since his clumsy, best-forgotten start so long ago as a boneman, Bunting was enduring a genuine crimp in his career. As of late, no matter how excellent the money that came as a necessary recompense for such odious and dangerous labours, Bunting always seemed to have none and owe much.

Only a fortnight gone, in the mighty mercantile city of Brandenbrass, Weakleefe Spleen — that infamous money-lending shaky benchman — had called in his debt. Accosting Bunting while he sipped a well-earned knuckle of Ol' Touchy in the drinking room of the *Mother's Nudge*, Spleen along with his terrifying malodorous scourge, Welkin Mull, and a quarto of sturdy roughs had left the corser in no doubt as to his *responsibilities* — as the master benchman liked to call it. Pressing Bunting painfully and making crude insinuations to his scourge's flesh-melting skills, Spleen had demanded on point of death payment by a month; an entire season's necessary living all due Newwich next — a mere seven days.

Bunting *did* have money: oscadrils — debased Imperial coin, long held to be made of inferior metal despite their golden twinkle. Spleen had proved in no mood to accept such stuff, the cold dull gold of common sous was his whole desire. After conversion by the only money changers who took the business of those of his ilk — and their high tellage fee — Bunting was left with scarce enough to eat once properly each day and fit himself for his current venture.

To compound poor Bunting's woes, Master Pypsquïque, ashmonger and the corser's usual agent, was being especially punctilious about this newest order. Typically Bunting would fill as much of his toll ticket as he could with corses of the required states of category and decay then meet the rest with odds and sods dug from any old plot and with this what in the trade they liked to call *windfall* — bodies found beddened, that is, newly dead, on gallows or Catherine wheels or the sides of roads. Though most ashmongers did not like it much, such a practice was only disallowed by the hinge in as much as it threatened good relations *betwixt a corser and their usual agents*, as Bunting's properly printed and much treasured edition of the hinge read. Yet, little matter how Bunting might consider himself an honourable fellow — *as honourable as one of my ilk might be*, he thought wryly — in lean times such ambiguous ploys were within his habits.

Haphazard bits and sods, however, would not do this time.

Master Pypsquïque, ever alive to his suppliers' ploys, had been pointedly *un*ambiguous in his insistence for this most recent order. 'Fill the toll full and properly, Mister Faukes!' the ashmonger had declared imperiously when presenting the list. 'The *whole* toll, that is — our client waxes impatient with shortcuts and if he don't get every corse as he wants it, he has said he won't pay me … and if he don't pay me, *I* won't pay thee!'

The toll was fairly typical:

2 of the male kind, adult of young or middling years, wormed;
1 innards only of the female kind, adult, young or middling, decadent;

1 of the male kind, adult middle-yeared, tanned;
1 of the female kind, a child of elder years, scarce beddened.

… typical, but for that last item. Such fresh ashes were rarely called for but by the worst ash-dabblers. Still, the principles of those upon the other side of the transaction with Master Pypsquïque were not of Bunting's concern. His labours were trial enough without fussing with such mewling niceties. He — and most corsers with him — prided and consoled himself that as long as he kept to his iniquitous yet necessary work, the need for kidnap and murder by lingerlaces and other bodysnatching wretches was diminished.

Be that as it might be, his current cause had not been aided by the fact that his usual rivals, the Micklethwart brothers — always desperate to make good themselves — seemed to be beating him to every patch within easy journey. The one time he had got to a plot ahead of them, they drove him off violently in blatant disobedience to the hinge and against common decency among fellow wayfarers too.

Not all are honour, Bunting reflected bitterly.

Keenly sensitive to any lapse in her master's attention, Anvil the smaller donkey — fit as she ever was — slowed in an attempt to feast on a few wilted thistles struggling through the mat of russet needles on the verge of the ill-kept path. Flicking the left rein irritably, Bunting prompted her on. Probably a near-forgotten mine or woodsman's road, their course had kept tenaciously and somewhat disorientingly to the north-western flank of a convoluted valley, snaking right then left then right again amongst the young and murky wood.

Peering higher to the low, leaden sky, Bunting breathed a long draw of stagnant, resin-scented air. *At least the weather is turned cold again.*

In grasping anxiety he had resorted finally — despite the ban on such conduct — to chasing the Micklethwarts off in turn, firing all *seven* barrels of his heptibus at them, only to find he was left scant pickings of the new plots. Moreover, hinge prevented him from revisiting Spelter Innings necropolis — his favourite necropolis and ever a source of fine fresh corses. He had been there not more than a month ago and, obliged by the hinge, was compelled to leave an interlude of two months — half a season — before returning. Yet,

Spelter Innings was too far away anyway regardless, if he was to go and dig and be back in Brandenbrass by the 5th of Unxis. Steered by desperation, he delved far to parts of the Brandenfells he had once promised himself never to tread, trundling amidst the infamous black hills of half-mad boar-swains and violent backwards bumpkins seeking their private humegrounds in the baffling warren of gullies and combes.

Bunting stared warily at the tall crooked pines, gaunt turpentines and lichened boulders a brooding sullen grey, the perfect hide for rabid men clotted with filth and gore or worse, a slavering bogle fit to eat whatever it could lay its hand to. There had been talk in a woodsman's ham down south, Whittle Sawsly, of some giant hobnicker stalking the hills about — especially in these more northern hills.

Yet despite all the obstacles, our man — avoiding bumping with even one wild bumpkin — had managed to find much of what he needed in these secluded plots, disinterring the right and proper ashes of every item on the toll.

Every item, that was, but that last …

1 of the female kind, a child of elder years, scarce beddened.

The plethora of plots of Brandenbrass would surely hold such rare ashes. Yet in fear of tempting the short mercies of Weakleefe Spleen and his stinking bandage-wrapped scourge, Bunting did not dare return to Brandenbrass early, not even to spoil the boneyards of that city. Even if he had, such an endeavour would have been futile, for the city's deadpatches had, after a winter of especially heavy plundering, been bounded for the spring by common accord between corser and ashmongers alike. Moreover, ever since that *misunderstanding* last year with the corse of the Archduke's cousin's youngest daughter and a prominent ashmonger, the mortigriphers of the city — responsible for the rites, burial and recording of the dead — had shut their doors to the dark trades. The only recourse had always been the usual remote plots; but when these did not yield the necessary *harvest* and the city was out of bounds, what was a fellow to do?

Short of abducting some girl from her dear mother's bosom —

embed, or kill for himself, a soul who dead would fit the toll, and present them after some treatment with the necessary chemistry as if legitimately exhumed — he had no notion how he would fill it. For a breath in the darker regions of his soul, such a grim notion was beginning to hold merit ... As much as many ashmongers would be perfectly at ease with such murder, the hinge held it *expressly forbidden, serving not the posterity of our ancient and necessary trade* — or, as his father had put it, 'just cause we're part o' the dark trades dun't mean we 'ave to behave darksomely'.

Aside from guilty, vaguely lofty notions of honour, Bunting was not sure he had the courage for such an act. Messing about with the members of some long dead soul was amusing enough, but killing cold and calculated was a whole other dastardly stripe of deed. Should he truly consider such a deed it did not matter anyway: deep in the Brandenfells now, he was too remote from properly settled places to find anything so fresh and civilised as a young girl. Yet times were waxing so desperate so quickly, should he find such a creature, he could not rightly say which way he might decide.

My neck or another's ...?

Abruptly he was brought out of his reverie.

Was that a shout?

Someone — or *something* — had cried out.

Bunting listened but heard no repeat of that first cry over the light clatter of his cart. He shook his head as he leant back on the reins, Hammer and Anvil only too eager to halt and chew upon drooping weeds. Reaching back from the small bench of his cart, the corser patting searchingly for a green glass bottle of vin settled between four long, burlap-wound bundles. Disturbingly suggestive of a human form, they were lain side by side in the cart's tray beneath the folded framed of wooden struts that made the simple sheer he used to haul prizes from the mould, and over this several great obscuring stooks of kindling. A scent of myrrh mixed with rot rose from them, though Bunting found it neither unpleasant nor overpowering, in part for the skill of their wrapping, in part the censers of sweet powders fixed to rods on either side of the cart's bench, and in part because he was numb to such odours. Like vinegarroons in their rams treading the acrid vinegar seas, corsers possess a measure of dumbness to all manner of bad airs. *A most necessary qualification,* he smiled sardonically at himself. Swatting at a knot of flies hovering about his ears, he took a toss of sharp sweet vin and set the cart in motion.

A startling boom, like the discharge of a mighty cannon, cracked through the narrow defile, reverberating over and over like the whole wood was about to collapse on itself.

Bunting near dropped his bottle.

Though there was no reckoning where such a heavy sound came from in these frowning furrowed hills it certainly seemed disconcertingly near. Soon this was followed by the flat popping of what could only be musket or pistol fire. Ducking instinctively though the threat was surely some way off, Bunting reached for his heptibus and quickened the pace of his donkeys.

Coming easy as he could about a sharp right-hand crook in the road, he peered ahead to see if the road was threatened. Cut into the hillside, the road bent around a short precipice of rust-stained stone little more than the height of two tall men. Shouts and the tell-tale popping of flintlock fire seemed to sound from directly above.

Bunting scarcely turned in time to witness a figure dressed in dim grey and black, head and shoulders swathed in brilliant red appear suddenly directly above him. Face hidden behind an all-seeing sthenicon box, the figure looked down at him for a mere breath before launching itself from the blunt crag. Even in his fall, the red-swathed lurksman twisted to plummet back first, a pistola pointing in each hand back up to where he had just left. *Crack! Crack!* the pistols fired as at that very instant two strangely pale heads rushed into sight at the summit of the overhang. One ducked nimbly from view, the other simply slumped, hat tumbling, pierced through the brow with a leaden ball even as the red-swathed fellow landed with a great jarring rattling crash of kindling and groaning joints, and a gust of dust, right into the laden tray of Bunting's creaking cart. Hammer and Anvil bellowed and brayed in dismay. Striving to keep the beasts from bolting, the corser instantly thought his cart ruined and the man dead — *I might find a buyer for him,* a cool and ever-present calculation inwardly turned — but with a quick jerk, the red lurksman sat up.

'Hurry on, man!' he cried to Bunting, voice clear despite the impediment of the simple oblong sthenicon box, its single optic hole swivelling rapidly from Bunting to ledge-top.

Without a second thought, the corser obediently flicked his poor donkeys to start, the two creatures only too keen to be on their way.

'Petulcus Sprawle,' the lurksman introduced himself with the tone of an educated man as he hastily reloaded his irons. 'My chief will be shortly ahead at the bridge … You may take me there.' He turned abruptly and let loose with a twin of pistol shots at the foe still chasing them atop the rolling precipice. Under the bulky folds of his red cowl, Bunting could see this Sprawle carried a hefty wad of dark cushioning cloth strapped in a bundle to his upper back, as if to soften many a backwards fall. Such acrobatics were common for this fellow it seemed.

Hammer and Anvil took them as fast as they might on such an awkward path over the spur of the hill, the cart-axles rasping with stricken groans Bunting knew had not been there before. The crook in the road straightened and began to bend back to the left as the land rolled down to a shallow gully rising steadily on the right. Only a couple of fathoms ahead stood a neat crossing of arched and ancient stone traversing a small runnel bubbling its course down the needle-thick gully between root and rock and tree. Climbing steeply on the other side, the gloom beneath the black pines was hurrying with white-faced shadows. Looking quickly Bunting could see that they were grubby fellows in mixed proofing stalking amongst the dark trees, their pallid faces grubby white blanks. In a nonce, he could see that they were masks bearing one or two horizontal red bars across their dials.

'Fictlers!' Bunting hissed.

Falsegod worshippers, fictlers were the worst fashion of backwards hill-dwelling nincompoops, filled with delusions of a world ruled by their deep-dwelling masters, the slumbering idiot falsegods.

'Indeed …' Sprawle proclaimed, his boxed face an unnerving blank.

Balls spanged and slapped about them as Bunting whisked his team to a brisk trot, one striking Hammer on the well-proofed petraille that covered the startled donkey's back and flanks, another knocking his master's tall hat from his crown. So astonishing was this blow that Bunting did not notice a stout gent in costly proofing of luxurious blue stooped behind the cover of the high stone abutments upon the further side of the bridge until he was nigh upon him. The corser hauled hard to slow their scampering pace.

That very moment there came a mighty flash high up the slope, quickly accompanied by a crackling roar. A great gush of debris and orange and clearly toxic smoke engulfed half the height of the gully, flinging fictlers down with implacable force, overcoming them in a thick, dirty fume.

'The timing of your fuse is as excellent as ever, Mister Sprawle!' the short thickset gentleman in blue called with grim cheer to Bunting's passenger, the red-wrapped lurksman leaping lithely from the wreck in the cart's tray to the wall of the bridge. 'I see you have brought a jaunty fit to extract us from this stouche,' he added, reaching up to halt Hammer and Anvil without any reference to the cart's proper owner.

At first Bunting thought this fellow was still bent for cover, but he quickly discerned that though he was hunched, he was standing at his full height as he gripped Anvil's bridle, barely taller than some middling child. 'Hoy! I ain't your champion, old muck,' he retorted hotly, trying to provoke his donkeys to keep going away from all this danger. 'I'm not here for your saving!'

'No,' the stunted, blue-harnessed gent returned rapidly, the intent in his gaze hidden behind murky spectacles. 'But you're a humble, hucillucting soul who'll help his fellow wayfarers in their need.'

Bunting frowned, feeling utterly exposed sitting high on his cart bench. 'If it isn't the hinge it's the cordiality of the road,' he muttered bleakly and stared nervously up the gully.

For now, threatening silence ruled.

Beyond the squat blue fellow crouched a third figure, hidden behind a hefty boulder that jutted near the bridge. Clad in a heavy black weskit over his clean white shirt, he was taking aim with a prodigiously long long-rifle up the left flank of the gully. The weapon spoke, offending the hush with its violence, the bark of its deadly voice crackling back to them through the convolutions of the gullies. After the great blast of before, Bunting could not see who there was to shoot at, but the fellow set to reloading with great yet practised haste: powder from a horn, already-patched ball from a pouch, all rammed with steady alacrity. The corser thought this oddly old-fashioned — waxed cartridges had been about for near as long as he could recall — until he saw that this fellow, too, wore a sthenicon, no doubt to give him a franker aim yet preventing him from biting a cartridge, as was necessary.

With a queer shriek, a new figure dashed down the left slope of the gully, coming at them through the residue of fume. Dressed in closed-fitted proofing, this one too wore a mask, though instead of a dirty menacing blank it was the clean white of a regal egret with sharp yellow bill. Here surely was a sagaar, a skipping tempestuous dancer of the dread dances of war, the many hems of long protective skirts flying behind like madly fluttering wings of moonlit night.

Bunting reckoned them undone. *Why does he not fire!* he thought, watching in rising horror as the black-proofed franklock set aim on the rushing dancer but no more.

Taking up his heptibus, Bunting resolved to act. Set to fire all seven shots at once, he levelled it on the charging foe when the cluster of barrels was abruptly seized and the weapon near wrenched from his unready grasp.

'Rather you didn't, friend,' Sprawle smiled thinly while the gent in blue declared to him mildly, keeping hold of the firelock, 'She is rather valuable to us,' clearly meaning the egret sagaar.

She? Bunting marvelled darkly. *What stripe of crank panto-show have I met with?* Eying the man dismally as he let the heptibus go and turned to welcome the return of his weird egret-faced comrade, the corser's next thought was for flight. *I'll leave these uppity lurksmen to their fate,* he determined when his attention was arrested by a young lady.

Fair-haired, perhaps a third his age, she sat huddled and very still beside the busy black-clad franklock. Draped by an overlarge cloak covering the shame of her too simple slip, her eyes were round and terribly solemn, yet she appeared indifferent to her immediate danger. Darker thoughts possessed her attention.

An impulse deeper than a conscientious notion of honour or habitual obedience to the hinge made Bunting stay; indeed, it moved him to pull his cart to halt beside the great boulder and clamber down ready to proffer any aid required to the frighted young thing.

'Well done, sir,' the gentleman in blue said, his expression tight, even grief-stricken, and he stepped now to Bunting. The fellow was truly short, the top of his three-cornered thrice-high barely coming to the corser's chin. 'Atticus Wells, sleuth and theoretician,' he added, presenting first a courtly bow that provoked a sour reaction in the corser's proudly simpler manners, then a manly hand. 'How come you to this fine neck of the world?'

It was then that Bunting realised this one called Atticus Wells was actually moving by aide of a sturdy walking cane. *What by the precious here and vere ...?* he cursed inwardly, but said, 'Fetching stooks,' tossing his hand evasively to the broken kindling still masking his true load, his eyes glassy with a what-do-you-reckon stare. 'How is it *you* are here, my chum?'

Wells peered at Bunting a moment. 'We are *here*, sir,' he declared with a flourish of his hand towards the girl as the big fellow in black weskit put her into the cart, 'to rescue her ...'

On the low streets and rear lanes of any city in the Soutlands — or the Half-Continent or even the entire Harthe Alle, for that matter — the disappearance of some reduced or destitute girl is regrettably common and goes largely ignored. A hazard of moll potnies, goodday gala-girls, posy vendors, snugman snitches and songbird beggars are routinely snatched from benighted streets by sinister souls; the disappeared typically unmissed but perhaps for a meagre and equally powerless collection of needy relations and impoverished acquaintances. Such folk as these can do little to prevent their rough darlings from being carried off on secretly-fitted vessels to distant lands and there to be auctioned into marriage or servitude; or set to hard labour in some impossibly remote mill or mine; or worst yet, delivered up to an ashmonger and on-sold to anthropists, massacars, parts-grinders or the transmogrifying surgeons of Sinster and other notorious butchering cities.

Yet though they keep their operation to the fouler districts of the city, occasionally these malevolent abductors unwittingly misstep and pinch some lass who is actually in possession of superior connexions;

and these superior connexions almost always send shrewd and doughty fellows to restore their missing damsels to them.

It was for this grievous and dismal reason that Monsiere Valentin Pardolot of *the* Pardolots of the suburb of Steepling Oak, Brandenbrass — receiver of the Garland of Courtesy and chief senior indexer at the Grand Plus Banking & Mercantile — had shifted himself to seek the apartments of one Atticus Wells, the city's most illustrious, indeed celebrated, sleuth. If asked, Valentin would readily confess he was not the kind of gentleman to run with such sneaking and clandestine fellows, however fine their reputation. Yet the complete and suspect vanishment of the wayward eldest daughter of Grey, his dear wife's much admired and hardworking housekeeper, pressed him to such extremes. *Need,* as he had put it to himself on the quarter-hour journey by day carriage from his townhouse in Steepling Oak to Bankers Lane in Risen Mole, *makes beggars of us all.*

And so it was that this vaunted mercantile clerk ventured up the narrow flight between a fine-cut poulterer and a violin maker to the upper-storey rooms of the vaunted sleuth. Shown by a blank-faced servant from the small pristine vestibule to a sparse but tastefully furnished upstairs drawing room, he was greeted by a tall, profoundly capable-looking man in a silken bagwig. Introducing himself as the great Atticus Wells, the fellow offered Valentin to join him and sit on gilt and velvet armchairs before an alabaster hearth. Here, comforted by a tott of malmsey thinned with a little water, Monsiere Pardolot poured out the whole sorry story.

Viola Grey, a defiant child barely in her majority and — as with many city girls thinking in their misjudged adventures to follow the steps of the such fighting women as the Branden Rose or Epitomë Bile — determined to make herself a spectacle. Breaking free all too frequently from lock and window, she sought to live it high in the make-merry districts of Pantomime Lane and the Fairerside. Always, she would return the next day, either of her own accord or fetched back from her favourite haunts by one of Pardolot's stablery men. But on Midwich last, she had absconded one final night, never to return, and the house staff unable to find any tell of her for the past three days.

'Mother Grey is the finest keeper-of-house I have ever employed,' Pardolot concluded soberly, almost to himself. 'My wife — and I too, of course — would hate to see her permanently distempered by her daughter's non-return.'

'As would any employer worth the service, sir!' Wells returned with frank concern.

The chief senior indexer passed over a large pane of paper. It was figured with a rather skilfully executed spedigraph of poor Viola Grey, drawn by one of the many nameless struggling fabulists; creative folk of irregular trade who, along with many other night-merchants, do hover about revelling high-society crowds like gulls for an opportunity to make a little money. 'This is a most excellent likeness,' he said, 'done only a day before her last outing …'

The sleuth regarded the image with pursed lips, glanced for a moment to the far end of the room but said nothing.

'I can pay *very* handsomely, Mister Wells,' Pardolot offered at last, sitting straighter as he reached into his waistcoat pocket, giving a hearty clearing of his throat. 'Whatever is required to secure Viola's restoration to the embrace of her good mother's bosom.' Money, he was sure, was the most compelling incentive for such fellows as sat before him — however smart their clothes or sturdy their frame — and he was prepared to part with a considerable sum … though decency proscribed excess.

'My fee, most generous monsiere, is the same come peer, peltryman or pauper,' the sleuth replied smoothly, lifting his well-defined chin gallantly. 'The best recompense is the job done well.' For but an instant he seemed to glance quite pointedly to a great storied weave hanging at the far end of the room.

Pardolot went to look too, but before he could get a good view, Wells returned his keen attention to the chief senior indexer and declared, 'We accept your mission, sir.'

Nobility, manifest with such fine address and fine bearing, were always fit to impress Pardolot most, and he could see plainly the why of this man's high reputation. Smiling gratefully, he returned his wallet to its usual deep pocket. An interview followed — as extensive as the little he knew could provide — during which his attention was continually drawn to the huge tapestry. He could not say why, but he held the distinct impression that the near wall-high figures playing out a moment of history upon it were in truth watching *him*. Clearing the notion with a shake of his head, the chief senior indexer answered every inquiry as best he could, which after many, many questions did not amount to much more than her last known position: *Ratio's Swing*, a rowdy drinking house of low reputation found on the barely accessible fringe of the slums named by its mucky denizens as the Alcoves.

'I shall need some manner of weargild from the young lady's person, something truly her own and bearing her true scent … It will help us to locate her.'

Pardolot frowned but with only the slightest arching of his brow, agreed.

It all seemed such paltry evidence, but this Wells fellow exhibited such verve and confidence that — after paying the retaining fee to an impressively efficient clerk in the small file attached to the drawing room — Pardolot left the unremarkable narrow-fronted apartment on Banker's Lane with a bill of receipt most properly filled and spirits greatly improved. He had expected to return to his wife with little more than a lighter purse and shuffling excuses but here he could bring the happy report to Lady Pardolot that housekeeper Grey would see her daughter again, he was certain of it.

For the *real* Atticus Wells the prospect was in truth not nearly so clear, though such doubts would never do to be made plain to clientele. Indeed, Wells did not make *himself* plain to anyone at first interview and often not beyond. 'A sad and vexing yet all too common set of circumstances, 'tis sure,' he proclaimed as he shuffled out from behind the very tapestry that had aroused Pardolot's sensitive curiosity. While it was a very striking hanging, its main function was to screen a recess in the wall from where the real sleuth could sit and watch unseen while others would play his public role. For short and stocky strong, with an oddly long face and a large nose like a smashed fruit, Atticus was a most unimpressive fellow at first glimpse. Yet under his thick, melancholy brow peered glitteringly intelligent eyes, quick to see for a mind yet quicker to perceive, their irises stark cerulean blue in orbs a complete and bloody red. These were the eyes of a falseman, washed in painful potent chemistry so that Wells might see speciousness in people's words and treachery in their deeds. These eyes gained him a respect his own filial connexions had never done, causing some to reconsider his stunted frame and ugly dial. Yet the curse of all such power was a strange disconnected loneliness, surrounded by people but never properly engaged with them. Mentored by that eminent falseman, Nestor, telltale to the illustrious Duchess Pymn, Wells himself well knew that when pressed or in genuine dread every person might dissemble or lapse in truth. He himself relied on trickeries and sleight of language daily — by the hour even. Yet only those in possession of a mostly clear conscience or the constant self-ease borne of a forthright and uncomplicated soul were able to remain in his company for long.

Still slouched in the highback, the noble — nay, leonine — man who had played him in the interview, was one such soul. Petulcus Sprawle was his name — tall, lithe, dangerous-looking; a man of action and the precise opposite of his chief. This surrogate 'Atticus Wells' cocked a handsome brow and promptly removed the powdered and beribboned bagwig from his crown. Glad to free his natural flaxen thatching, he let out a long puff of breath. 'I do wish you'd have Mister Door do this more often,' he carped. '*He* does not mind the itch of this scratchbob,' he added, tossing the wig around and around upon his finger.

'Indeed, Mister Sprawle,' Atticus returned, 'as you say every time; and as I ever reply, *security* and *fine impression* are most necessary; my notoriety is problematic enough without every man-jack knowing my face, and my ... *awkward* condition,' he flourished his sturdy cane, tapping his legs, slightly bowed and somewhat stunted, 'is unhelpful for introducing properly placed confidence in prospective custom.'

'Fie and dash to prospective custom and their misjudgements,' Sprawle swore faithfully.

Wells smiled vaguely and took up the thin sheaf of papers that constituted his aide's notations of the interview to peer at them closely. 'Beside this, Mister Door does not possess your eloquence, and is — as you well know, my man — better for ... *humbler* clients.'

Staring long at the cheap spedigraph of poor Viola Grey, he sought to fix the visage of the girl in his thoughts.

The faint scrape of fiddle being tortured into tune yowled from the shop below.

'Did you mark my line about "peers, peltrymen or paupers"?' Sprawle grinned, stretching complacently to stare at the high pale ceiling divided into ovals and oblongs of convoluted moulding. His face abruptly contorted in a lion-like yawn that distorted his voice as he continued, 'Heard you pronounce that one last week to a patron — I thought it very convincing. Seemed to please our present chap some too.'

Nodding absently, the senior sleuth stepped to the rightmost of three long windows that stared east over the great stretch of suburbs hiding the city's teaming civil mass, his regard shifting out to the pallid grey sliver of Brandenbrass' harbour and the high dome of wan sky. The sun was barely at the 10 o'clock. 'Call Mister Thickney' — by whom he meant that impressively efficient clerk in the adjoining file —'for the coach, the day is yet young and time is scarce for the truly disappeared. We have a darling young daftling to find.'

Busy with people of every station moving in this margin of decent society and desperate poverty, the outer districts of the Alcoves were safe enough — during the day at least. In this city where money moved more quickly than conscience, the anonymous affluent governors of all the illicit trades came down from their fine suburbs in undisguisedly fancy lentums, arrogantly riding the squalid streets in flashing carriages as they rushed to sponsor the next venture of profitable darkness. Thus Wells' own glossy lentum was perfectly commonplace as it drew over the Falindermeer trickling its malodorous way thickly to the harbour, and eased before the *Ratio's Swing*. Built mostly of grey brick and murky white stone, the drinking-house was a remarkably well-kept establishment, surrounded as it was by mouldering houses built as quick as could be — and often without permit — upon the ruin of any previous structure. Under the see-all stare of Atticus Wells and the striking glower of Petulcus Sprawle, the *Ratio's* portly sour-eyed boniface did not recognise the likeness of Viola, no matter how much he wanted. He did, though, make out the style of the spedigraph.

'It's the hand of a certain Mister Peltfelt,' the fellow offered, staring down Atticus with peculiar, unwilling yet anxious fascination. 'I — I have several by him of my wife. H-has a room down at Mother Wrist's common lodging house … on the Scramble Street.'

In thanks, Wells bought the boniface a jug of his own best stingo, the fellow mumbling something approaching fidgeting gratitude, keen for them leave.

Deeper into the Alcoves, inside the tottering third-hand edifice of Mother Wrist's, the shrewd-eyed lady herself informed them that the fabulist Peltfelt was not in but had stepped out for some necessary or other. Deciding to shift themselves to a dingy tomaculum conveniently situated directly across the road and down in a half-cellar with slippery steps the sleuth and his agent sat to wait. Wells keeping a weather-eye through the grimy lights of squat arched windows for their mark's return, Sprawle ordered early lunch: pullet and ramsin broth and vinegar pie for them both, sluiced down — though it was before midday — with pitchers of the best Patter Moil beer. It was an aromatic combination and they spoke little as they ate.

Brow cocked and mouth bent wryly, Sprawle finally uttered, 'She's as likely to have eloped with some gambling-debted naval captain.'

'And if that is so then that is what we shall find and that is what we shall report to Monsiere Pardolot. Ah! Our man cometh!' Wells, draining the dregs of his beer, stood and hurried up the tomaculum steps with the surprising nimbleness he possessed when fixed entirely on his current prize.

Accosted at the door, Peltfelt blearily confirmed the drawing as of his own execution, but who the girl *was*, he could not recall.

'I scrawl so many dials it gets so I cannot tell one person from next.'

There was no lie in him, Atticus could see it easily enough, just hunger and a craving for forgetfulness.

Returning to the vicinity of the *Ratio*, they attempted some simple canvassing, asking all they passed if they had seen the girl in the sketch. It was remarkable how often such a seemingly haphazard method succeeded in unearthing important traces, but by midafternoon their endeavour was proving to be little more than finding the pin amongst the needles.

'I guess its down to my box-bound nose, now,' Sprawle said lightly as they rattled home aboard the lentum.

'We shall see what inklings Messrs Door and Thickney have mined,' the sleuth returned, 'but yes, as I presumed it would always be, your facility with a sthenicon may once again be the only key to our success.'

'Let us hope then that her trail has not gone too stale,' his companion countered, serious for the first time that day.

Leaning chin on hand, Atticus covered his smile under a suede-gloved hand. It was always a great satisfaction when Petulcus Sprawle grew serious.

Things happened.

Good things.

Back in Banker's Lane, the two found Door and Thickney also returned, having achieved some better success interviewing two of the four girls who claimed themselves as disappeared Viola's friends. It turned out that the initial tale told to father Pardolot had been thin *in extremis*, but between Mister Thickney's dour gaze and Mister Door's amiable half-smile a fuller account emerged.

The five girls had been dancing the vinegar's jig with a group of lively, heavily-tattooed vinegarroons, ticket-of-leave men from some Gottish main-ram. After some addling drink the girls did not know the name for, they were taken — near dragged — to some night-cellar not far from the *Ratio's Swing*, where the vinegars promised the waters were harder and the fun with them. It is here that Viola's friends finally applied some wisdom and left. Alas, the eldest Grey, thinking she found at last her moment for complete infamy, remained and would not be prevailed upon to do otherwise. That was their last sight of her, so small and careless among all those huge, sweating men.

'Do you have the name or location of the night-cellar?' Wells inquired when Mister Thickney's accounting was done, standing again by the drawing room window to watch the city in the latening light.

'No,' Thickney returned, chin thrust into his copious neckerchief as he thumbed rapidly through his several notations. 'They did not notice. Miss Amfibia Pardolot — our client's daughter and Viola's chief inducer and ally — did say that she might find it again by sight.'

'I suppose it might be too much to hope the sweet lasses cared to mark what vessel those coarse vinegars served aboard.'

'It is, sir ...' the clerk looked up. 'I have already sent to Mister Settlepond at the Harbour Governor's for the necessary vessel lists. It should be arriving any moment now.'

Wells suppressed any exhibition of weariness or dismay; it would never do for his assistants and fellow sleuths to see him burdened or flagging no matter how head or body ached.

'Might have been good to have this tale clear at the first,' Sprawle murmured grimly from the further end of the room, the lurksman pacing his usual track on the fine Dhaghi carpet that near obscured the floor. 'A day wasted ...'

Exhibiting admirable efficiency of his own, Pardolot had — by way of messenger sent from his palatial file at Grand Plus Banking & Mercantile — furnished them with the required keepsake. Delivered by one of the man's servants in a plain flat box of card, it was rather startlingly a petticoat assured by way of a brief sealed note with it, to have been frequently worn by the young lady, and to have been rescued from the fuller's basket before it could be cleansed. For all his swagger, Sprawle blushed when he discerned exactly its nature.

'Well — I —' he tried.

'What ails you, good sir?' Wells spoke goadingly over his shoulder. 'You are forever goosing about the faintness of the smells typically provided you, yet here a proper odour is presented and you are complaining still. As good a slot-trace you'll never get.' He took in a long breath and turned abruptly. 'Come, gentlemen! Put on better proofing and arm yourselves discreetly. We shall have dear Miss Pardolot show us this night-cellar.'

At first dear Miss Pardolot proved predictably reluctant. Yet with a few dashing smiles from 'Mister Wells' and the timely return of her father, Monsiere Pardolot himself, she agreed finally to retrace the night as best she could. After some tears, gentle cajolery and even a dark prediction of Viola's possible fate, she proved her worth, directing them to a dangerously cramped part of the Alcoves. While Mister Thickney returned the young lady to her home, Wells, Sprawle and Door found themselves at the top of what locals satirically named 'gullies' — narrow sunken channels between the towering, tottering houses. As much cloaca as laneway, the 'gully' bending slightly right ahead of them was rank with sewer-stink, mixing with the reek of the harbour coming on the gentle evening breeze.

''Tis surely faint, but I can smell that Viola was here,' Sprawle muttered through his sthenicon box and hared down the gully-way, sending a pair of rabbits nosing unseen amidst the refuse fleeing ahead of him.

Wells — Door at his back — came as quick he as could, ignoring the resentful observation of a pair of surly locals peering from their inadequate apartment window above.

Slowing some to let his chief catch him, Sprawle soon halted at a stony stair on the right that lead down deeper than a cellar stair ought to the entrance of a sinister establishment with a tiny marmorine — false-marble — sign quietly pronouncing the unseemly name of *The Empresses Bosom*. Little doubt it was a lewd reference to ancient Dido. 'She went in, but there is no slot of her coming out again ...'

Here insisting on taking the lead, Wells trundled laboriously one step at a time to the bottom, ignoring the deep ache of hip and knee. Keeping his tall-brimmed, three-cornered thrice-high with its inner proofing band firmly upon his crown and, setting the murky glasses that hid his eyes more firmly upon his nose, he stepped within.

Perched on a highback chair and flipping lazily through an out-of-date copy of *Military and Nautical Stores*, the greasy doorward showed scant interest in this trio of heavy-harnessed gentlemen; every sort of fellow came for a visit with the *Empress*. His role was not to stop them going in but, when required, prevent them leaving. With scarce more than the merest look, he gave Wells and his assistants a darkly knowing nod and returned his attention to last year's news only to find a well-drawn spedigraph thrust in his face. Did he recognise her? He drew back his head like a turtle might retract into its shell, blinked languidly at the image and shrugged.

Without the fellow speaking another word, Wells could fathom from the shift of humours beneath his skin that this was true — just as with the boniface of *Ratio's Swing*, it was a case of too many faces. A variation in the hue of the door-clerk's temper gave Atticus a moment's warning as the fellow made a strangled kind of bark.

A pair of hefty doorwards emerged from handy nooks in the walls, the biggest standing over the stunted sleuth to bend menacingly over him.

'Get thee lost!' he breathed stinkingly into Wells' face. 'No fluffs allowed!'

Neither Sprawle or Door, immediately behind, moved to intervene.

Mistaking this as reluctance born of fear, the big vinegarroon seized the short sleuth before him by the arm. Quick as an asp Wells struck, dropping his cane to drive the nose of this fellow into his face, snatching a second doorward by the wrist even as the rough lunged and threw a swipe. Twisting the fellow's entire frame about, the sleuth pressed his assailant's hand down, thumbs pushing on knuckles, pinning him entirely with pain so that the lout was forced bawling angrily to his knees.

'Awrigh'! Awrigh'! I knows when I'm beat!'

'I wish an interview with the procuress of this *fine* establishment,' Wells stated matter-of-factly.

'Deglubius!' the pinioned rough hollered to the clerk blinking a little stupidly at the doorward writhing with broken nose on the cold stone flags.

The clerk snapped to like a foot-slogging pediteer in the Archduke's army.

'Tell the Empress some f —' Wells gave his arm a smart bit of pressure, 'fine gents wants to see her in-personal.'

The clerk hastily went and hastily returned: they could meet the Empress.

Wells let his adversary free, standing back and ignoring resentful glowers as the two doorwards guided them to their interview.

Peculiarly sweet narcotic fumes wafted about the over-warm

common room lit by little more than the enormous hearth in the left-hand wall. Under the low, ponderously-beamed ceiling sozzled men representing the entire human catalogue of Soutland citizenry lounged amongst genuinely exotic cushions and falsely exotic women of hard faces. In fluffing dresses like sombre subterranean flowers, these predatory lasses were uniformly thick with pastes and rouges that went some way to obscure the falseman's reading.

Wells was almost grateful for it.

Everyone looked more stark and bizarre to him, their skin shifting, flushing, nigh oh crawling at every turn of thought, every falter of soul, every unspoken cruelty. The almost corpse-like distortions that flushed across a person's visage as they concealed or deceived, growing ever more grotesque with the increasing convolutions of their lies was for him a daily and ghastly spectacle. Despite half a life with such singular lucidity he yet remembered the pasty blank a face presented to usual eyes and was glad sometimes not to know the turnings of another fellow's mind.

Punch-drunk, brawling, howling or throwing lots, patrons and ladies alike ignored them entirely as the three were taken deep within the night-cellar.

What desperate nadir one must reach in themselves to call on such a place for amusement, the chief sleuth marvelled quietly, hobbling by grimy amorerobes — love-cupboards — holding half-concealed displays of depravity, their suggestion perhaps more shocking than the reality. Not all these men would make it out again tonight, Wells was sure of it — but there was little he could do to prevent the fate of men so given over to dissipation, and his current mission must come first.

The *Empress* turned to be one of the many hard-faced, over-painted ladies dwelling here, dressed in a full-bosomed dress of wide-flaring scarlet taffeta. Settled in a tall elbow chaise of ruby-red leather, she sat in a cheaply plush boudoir, fanning herself and making show of her apparent unconcern.

It was only skin deep.

Wells could well tell the disturbance of her spirits. Still hot in soul after the scuffle, he wasted no time revealing his telltale eyes to this madame.

Deeply unamused at the persecution of her own, the woman regarded him evenly from her lustrous couch. Cold comely eyes rimed in thick black flicked to Sprawle lithe and dangerous with his red hood and boxed face; to Door well harnessed, and barely able to fit through the gleaming red portal to her chamber; and finally to the pair of sturdy roughs hovering tensely behind them. A brief calculation passed across her gaze. 'Fetch in Caspar,' she finally called to her uneasy wards with a voice so jaded Wells nigh felt sorry for her.

'Our girl was brought in here,' Sprawle murmured in his chief's ear as they waited.

The Empress sipped at a flute of dark purple vinothe and made show behind her beauty plaster of indifference, while bloody-nosed, the taller rough shuffled.

A small neat man in a worn but well-mended coat of silver-grey silk emerged from some back chamber. Wells closely observed his detached face blatant with ugly and habitual dishonesty as the fellow stopped by his mistress's wide desk and paled by the merest degree when he saw that there was a falseman before him.

'These men have lost something, it seems, Mister Caspar,' the Empress said in dangerous hush, glaring at the fellow, thought clear in her eyes, *What quandary have you got me in now!* 'Answer them as best you can where they might go to find it and leave us to peace.'

Caspar recognised the image of Viola, though he did not say as much. Indeed, upon seeing the spedigraph he peered at Wells as if to say, *Do I truly need to tell you what you can already see …?* His expression turned dogged, as if expecting some retributing blow. 'She seemed a ripe cherry, so little an' bright amongst all them rowdies. So I plucked 'er away from 'em, an' I — I … *passed* 'er on to a … more deservin' gent …'

'*Passed* her on …' Atticus repeated like the pronouncement of a Duke's Bench magistrate. This fellow was a chattelman — a vile stealer and seller of people as mere goods. It was such *people* as these that kept the sleuth in constant work — how hard it was not to lash out and destroy this deliverer of misery where he stood. *I shall return perhaps and shut this place down,* he promised himself.

'Ah,' Caspar glanced uneasily at his mistress. 'Aye … I soporified 'er an' carried 'er down the trap right below yer feet, sirs,' he nodded to the imitation rug upon which the three questers stood.

Clearly furious with her employee, the Empress struggled to suppress her dismay at such an admission.

'To who?' Wells persisted with the fellow, ignoring the woman's poorly hid discomfort.

'Um' ... a nervous chappie I 'ave done trade with from time to time ...'

'WHO!'

'One Mister Emptor Settlepond; he owns a whole bunch o' tallowbellies and is constantly seekin' sturdy souls to work 'em on account of 'im always openin' more. Money must be good in th' fur business, I'd say ...'

'There is more, sir,' Wells persisted, bizarre blue-on-red gaze narrowing. 'Your eyes might have been blinded with a bribe but *I* can still see.'

Caspar baulked a little. 'J-just that yesterday a fine chappie comes in looking for a body just as her. Not a-feared of any old body, that one, has the Enigmatic Mouth of Sucathës cribbed on neck an' 'ands, clear as a bum in a bath-'ouse.'

Sprawle caught an involuntary draw of breath.

Wells simply blinked.

The Enigma of Sucathës was the allegory — the cult-sign — of a particular group of falsegod worshippers.

Emboldened by even slight dismay, the chattelman smiled wickedly but hid it hastily behind a cough. 'Called hisself Monsiere Jack.'

Wells simple sniffed at such an obviously fake appellation

'Was set fast on a girl of such a one as this'un, so I obliged him with Settlepond's address and beyond that I am done.'

'You shall furnish us with this man's particulars too, of course.'

The chattelman nodded impatiently, wrote an address upon a fold of paper and passed it over.

'There you are, man,' the Empress said frostily. 'You have all we can give. Go now and bully some other poor soul trying to make his way.'

'Thank you, madam, I shall,' Wells said blandly, with a tight bow first to the procuress then the chattelman Caspar. Pivoting on his heel, the sleuth and his two allies departed, the chief sleuth remarking as he passed the doorward with the pummelled face, 'Sorry for your nose, man. I am sure you and your social life shall survive it; I have a perfect mess of a proboscis yet my friends are devoted to me still.'

Orotund and utterly bald, Emptor Settlepond — owner and master of several tallowbellies and other sweatmills beside — sweated nearly as much as his desperate or impressed workers endlessly treading tallow into new-skun fur. While the work he offered was by no stretch pleasant, it was for some the only thing keeping them from a empty stomach and death. Settlepond was more than happy to provide such indigent souls with the necessary labour to keep them from such an end, and that perfectly efficient Caspar fellow seemed to have an endless supply of the wretches.

Looking down from his third-storey file over the bustling convergence of Mole End Circuit, the owner congratulated himself on avoiding such misery. Below him a fine-looking lentum drew to a halt and disgorged three fellows, one remarkably and misshapenly short, all three possessing the faces of men with set, serious purpose who would brook no obstacle. *Hate to be the sod who has to deal with them,* he smiled to himself as he watched the short chap and his fine-looking friend enter the building while the biggest fellow waited by the coach. Sipping long at his warm morning saloop, Settlepond extended his delight to the warming sun peeping low through early clouds.

A sturdy thump at his file door gave him a sharp start and he span about to see the very same dangerously determined men from below sweep into his very own comfortable file. Well, one swept, the other shambled.

'Who are you?' Settlepond finally mastered himself. He was inclined first to be impressed by the sweeping fellow — tall, brawny, flaxen-haired. Yet it was the stunted shambling fellow who arrested his attention most, peering as if right through him with the blue-in-red of a falseman's stare.

'Are you a gnosist, sir? A fantaisist?' the shambling gent pressed accusingly, ignoring this very fair enquiry and forgoing any introduction as he and his tall, impressively-set comrade barged up to his very table. 'Someone who believes themselves supplied with the secret knowledge of the falsegods?'

'I — n-no not I, sir!' the owner half stood, expression switching rapidly from ire to fear to complete befuddlement. 'Just a gentleman attempting to make his place in the usual mercantile setting.'

'By selling and buying souls,' the impressive younger man said in aside, through gritted teeth.

Empty of excuses Settlepond's mouth gaped, shut, gaped again. Completely absorbed with the function of his business and faced with such grim-looking men — one of them a lie-seeing falseman into the bargain — he quickly confessed under their close questioning to knowing the girl, if only to get these two froward fellows to leave. 'What did you say her name was again?' he asked, glistening head ducking forward obsequiously.

'Viola Grey,' the short fellow answered, adding portentously, 'a ward of Monsiere Valentin Pardolot, Companion of Courtesy.' For all his stunt stature he was patently the leader of the two.

'Ah ...' The owner's innards leapt with dark dismay; this was the name of a man whom he greatly admired, of great means to which he greatly aspired. 'Well, the problem is that I — I have *on-sold* her, sir.'

'To who!' the short gent glowered while, with equal measures of exasperation and infuriation, the fair one bristled frighteningly beside him.

'I — I — it was some strangely marked chap with excellent address and his quiet servant,' the owner stammered. '*Master Jack* it said on his card. He seemed exceedingly pleased with the girl — Viola, you said her name was?'

Mister Short nodded gravely.

'He paid a dazzling amount for her, enough for me to replace her ten times over, so I am afraid I passed her to him ...' Settlepond could hear his voice trail to nought as he realised what he was admitting. He wiped with a large kerchief at the sweat dribbling on his dimpled crown. 'This Mister Jack bore the oddest patterns on his knuckles, like — like a series of lesser case e's ...' He obliged them by attempting to draw one on a blotting sheet.

'No doubting it's fictlers now,' the impressive fair chap muttered despondently when he beheld the fully-formed sign.

'Are you in the possession of this Mister Jack's whereabouts, sir?' the short man pressed.

'Uh … no — no I am not …'

'Of course …' the fair-haired one continued his grim mutter.

'And his servant?' the short man pushed yet more.

'I — he seemed a simple lad … with big wet eyes and a much-itched ginger beard,' Settlepond shrugged — normally a gesture he despised as insufficient in good company — and smiled weakly. *Please just go*, his mind kept repeating.

This final revelation seemed to appease the short man. He gave a brief, barely meant apology and the two left poor Mister Settlepond to call his maid to bring a draught of Dew of Imnot and calm his over-exercised humours.

Returned to their carriage and well on the way back through bustling streets broad and narrow to Bankers Lane, Atticus pinched his brows, knuckles pushing into perpetually aching dents of his upper eye-sockets.

For folk supposedly seeking creatures who dwelt in the vinegar-washed depths of the sea, fictlers did not do anything so predictable as live near oceans, where regular patrols of landsgarde rams might spot them. Amongst the most despised of all the idiot fringe, neither did they dare to meet or remain in numbers in the city for the Archduke's constables to find and apprehend them. Rather — as rumour told it — they kept themselves hidden in the backwoods and far recesses of the Brandendowns, avoiding prosecution and though often small in number, thriving.

Yet not all their adherents were so shrewd …

'Brother Scritch,' Wells thought aloud.

'The brother does what?' Sprawle frowned quizzically.

Sitting across from him, Door, as always, said nothing but waited with mute and steady intent.

'The simple fellow with the wet eyes our Mister Settlepond spoke on,' Wells returned. 'Brother Scritch is the only name he answers to; we shall find him sitting atop the Veil where it runs through

Oghbourne Sunt Gage. He is a confirmed adherent of Lobe and one of the few fictlers who dares remain in the city. Sits by the harbour all and every day, watching and waiting for his chosen *god* to emerge from the water. He will appear to you a wretched fellow — unmotivated and useless, but he is remarkably well connected amongst his category. He aided me once with some morsel of information regarding his fellow fantaisists. Oghbourne Sunt Gage, Mister Thickney,' he cried through the fine grille at the head of the lentum cabin. 'Take us to the sea!'

Pulling easy beside the squat seawall of the Sunt Veil, Wells pointed from the lentum window at a lone figure perched atop the poked and corroded barrier.

'There's our man!'

Avoiding the eel-vendors and tunymongers —'Five goose a brace o' unsweetened tun!' they called, 'A cob, a coil of fresh-hiked maraine, saps sniggled straight fro' the wine!' — they drew to a halt and alighted.

Peering at the precipitous climb offered by a scale of iron rungs, Wells knew there was no way up for him but on the ample back of Mister Door. The sleuth sighed long-sufferingly, called for his assistant and tried to ignore the shame and the quizzical watchers as he was bodily carried to the summit of the seawall. Finally set safe at the top of the Sunt Veil, Wells marvelled at the spreading vista of thousands of busy boats, self-important cargoes and prowling rams moving across every yard of Middle Ground, Brandenbrass' main harbour, all its minor anchorages and the waters beyond.

There on his left a mere handful of fathoms sat his intention, Brother Scritch, a gaunt, malnourished man cross-legged between the row of foot-tall thorns blackened with monster-slaying aspis that crowned the ponderous rampart. Muttering through scrawny beard, he stared longingly out to sea as if all his satisfaction might spring bodily from the milky waves. Drawing close, Wells could make out the blue spoors that corked the man's jowl, like the rounded figure of a '3' — the allegory of Lobe the Listening. Slowly the fellow became aware he had company, large limpid eyes blinking almost torpidly then narrowing in sharp comprehension. Half-standing, he turned clumsily to flee, completely untroubled by the precarious narrowness of the lofty perch in his intent to escape. Sprawle clambered into view from a scale on the further side, smiling ruefully as he blocked Scritch's exit. The haggard fictler's shoulders slumped in all too common defeat and he sat again, hugging bony knees now drawn up under his chin.

While Door waited at the scale, Wells negotiated the slight and thorny path, feeling the breeze pick up and tug at him as if to throw him to the flags and the bustling mongers. 'Who only seeks truly the overthrow of the interminable monstrous plague?' he intoned sombrely.

Brother Scritch brightened just a little. 'The seekers and the knowers, the sons of the deeps,' he returned with equal solemnity.

'And bring the ruin and damnation of the domain of men with them!' Sprawle murmured and looked out to sea, thereby avoiding Wells' quick warning glower.

'There is no damnation for the properly blest, sir, grant me …' Brother Scritch returned coldly.

'Indeed,' Wells nodded in a show of continued gravity. '*Beluae nunquam superarum* — may the monsters never get you,' he added, mimicking a fictler's cantric phrase.

The wizened fellow stared at him searchingly. 'I ain't playing muttering mouse for ye, Mister Wheel. No matter what good turns ye have done fer me, grant me, I'll not speak out ag'in a brother like you had me that other day …'

Wells could well see that nothing short of harm would make this simple searching fellow say what was needed and the sleuth already had a tally enough of regrets. 'Fair is fair, Brother Scritch,' he returned. 'Is there some other help you might give us, nothing specific mind, just some broad advice.'

'Well …'

'Come now, sir, you know I can see you avoiding an answer.'

Scritch fidgeted, but kept his attention on the endless industry in the harbour. 'I got me a silver counter, from one knowing brother to another, grant me, for me help,' he said finally.

'You are ever the obliging chap,' Wells smiled. 'They should call you Brother Help, I understand.'

Scritch grinned blandly. 'Master Jack said so, too …' he murmured.

Ahah! Wells kept his voice even. 'But Master Jack is brother to Sucoth,' he let his words linger. He did not know much of the falsegods — or even believe them true — but what he did ought be enough to draw this fellow out. 'I thought you were brother to Lobe. Sucoth never listens like Lobe …'

'Aye, Succoth does not listen, he only eats … Only eats …'

'But …' Wells trod now with care. 'But you helped a brother of Sucoth?'

'I'm no follower of Sucoth, grant me! Vile destroyer.' The simple fellow gnashed his teeth then muttered incoherent imprecations. 'Now Lobe — he's the Listener; he listens, see.' Scritch tapped his forehead. 'Everyday I talk with him and he listens to me. He'll know I alone have held to him and he'll keep me safe …'

'May I see this silver counter, sir?' Wells asked in continuing amiability.

After an agony of indecision, Scritch finally relented and produced the smudgy sequin coin from the little used fob of his equally smudgy weskit.

'How about I swap this single dull silver for a shining one,' the sleuth offered, pulling a new-minted sou from his own pocket.

The larger coin glinted in the misty high-noon light.

No small amount, it was probably enough for someone of such rudimentary needs to sustain him for a whole season. Yet Wells could easily compass it. He had been shrewd enough to make the modestly substantial inheritance left him by his loving, long-dead parents grow to one thousand sou a year; enough to keep him, his under-sleuths, clerk and housestaff in roof, board and wages. Nevertheless, a small, continuingly calculating part of his thinking ruefully acknowledged the wrestle of conscience he would later have over its inclusion in the bill of expense that would be passed to Monsiere Pardolot once Viola was restored.

Scritch licked his lips.

A mollyawk glided above, the midday sun casting the scavenging bird's thin hovering shadow over the cripple and the simpleton.

Realising there was no food to be had here, it gave voice to a churlish croak and glided away on the piquant airs.

The simple fictler put out his hand, the dull sequin lying there.

Wells duly passed the sou over.

If falsegods were real then such a bribe was in support of a tiny but genuine menace; if not, then it was adding to the corruption of a vulnerable soul. Ignoring this dilemma, the sleuth quickly took up the dirty sequin in an unscented kerchief and wrapped it in his fist. He took little joy from beguiling such a harmless man for his own ends — however noble — especially one who trusted him so completely; whose soiled face was so rarely distorted by the truly unsettling deformations of falsehood.

'Where did he give this to you?

'*The Bird*,' Scritch nodded. 'Outside *The Bird* where I put that girl, grant me, aboard a lenty-coach. They want to use her to sing the proper cantricles to Sucoth ...'

Wells' neck prickled. His innards griped cold. He shot the merest glance to Sprawle who watched on with hawkish expectation.

'Them Seven-Sevens, they want to be Emperor of it all. They say their cantricles from Case Nigrise and reckon the Great Devourer will make them lords but he eats, he only eats ...'

'You would never ... *sing* with the *Seven-Seven* at *Case Nigrise*, would you, Brother?' Wells asked in a manner most concerned.

Scritch looked at the sleuth sharply and eventually shook his head. 'No, grant me ... You sing up Sucoth and may bid goodbye to — to ...' he cast about, his distant gaze beholding imagined scenes of horror, 'to all this living and eating and sleeping and boats and fishermen.' He took a deep breath and returned his attention to the milky waters of the harbour. 'You'll never get me out to the Witherfells neither, too far from the sea ... far too far ...'

The fictler continued in his rant but Wells and his compatriots did not remain for it to play out; all that was needed Brother Scritch had divulged, whether he wanted to or not.

'There you are, Mister Sprawle,' Atticus declared without a mite of satisfaction as deposited back onto surer ground by Door, he passed the bundled kerchief to his aide, 'another weargild to sniff out our quarry.'

*   *   *

Three storeys of venerable grey stone and stone arched windows, *The Bird* by Madam Nutkin Cloth proved to be a fine little hostelry in Steepling Oak, a mere handful of streets from Viola's own home.

'This Mister Jack is a cultivated soul, it seems,' Wells observed as he negotiated the three short white steps to the blue front door.

'All this chasing over the city and we might have just jinked over here from Pardolot's house and saved ourselves the trouble,' Sprawle returned tartly.

Madam Cloth, the proprietoress, met them in the clean, sky-blue vestibule, Sprawle — playing Wells — dazzling her with his handsome dash and air of natural authority. Having already determined with his chief that openness was most politic, he told the blank shocking truth upon the nature of their call. Astonished and patently aware of the great sleuth and his good repute, Madam Cloth burbled out her evidence.

'He did have some young creature with him,' she explained, her face wide with dismay, 'said she was his niece. The little lass seemed very poorly. I offered to fetch him a physician or dispensurist but he said no, he was about to take her to the hills for some better air.'

'And that was all?' Sprawle-come-Wells pressed.

'That was the all of it, sir. He was scrawled all over with markings like some teratologist but his coin was true and his manner even, so I asked no more of it.' Eyeing the true Wells — playing quiet assistant — a little uneasily, Madam Cloth allowed them access to the room their quarry had occupied not two days ago, the proprietoress insisting upon accompanying them.

'You've cleaned, I see,' Sprawle-come-Wells declared flatly, peering about at the glaucous walls, brow arched unamusedly.

'Of course I have, Mister Wells,' the proprietoress bridled. 'What common kind of bunk do you think I run?'

Fixing his sthenicon over his face, the lurksman spent much time still in the middle of the room, the faint hollow sounds of snuffling coming from the round cavities upon either side of the dark wooden box fixed over his face. After a while he began to rove about, bending down to sniff at corners, behind the simple walnut commode, under the washstand, beneath the long narrow bed, then returning his attention to the coin nestled on its kerchief in his palm. Pressed by needs of present guests, Madam Cloth was forced to leave them, promising to presently return.

With her gone, Sprawle straightened. 'I thought she'd never go!' he hissed as he slowly removed the sthenicon, eyes squeezed shut and only opening slowly, trying to avoid the disorientation that would sweep over him even after so short a stint in a sensory box. It did not work. Swooning for a moment, he sat upon the bed, creasing its perfect folds.

The true Wells waited patiently.

'There is definitely a scent of the same slot that is on dear Scritch's coin,' his companion soon recovered and confirmed. 'It was nigh unperceptible on the coin but now I have found it a little stronger in here I can say they match. Even had they not,' Sprawle added, 'Viola has been here. Her slot is everywhere …' the lurksman trailed off severely.

Madam Cloth returned, cheeks bustling rosy, and blinked at the two sleuths as if to say, *Surely you are done …?*

'*How* did he go?' the true Wells asked — meaning by *he* of course, Mister Jack, and forgetting himself for a moment in the rapid preoccupations of his thoughts.

The proprietoress gave him a look as if he was a most impertinent fellow, but after Sprawle-come-Wells did not rebuke this apparently overweening servant, answered, 'He left by morning post departing the quarter of six from the Knave & Post for Coddlingtine Dell and Pour Claire.'

Without another word, Atticus departed, leaving Sprawle to make a gallant goodbye.

Wherever this Case Nigrise that Brother Scritch had spoken of might be, Coddlingtine Dell would be their next port.

Now was the time for adventure well beyond the city's many curtain walls.

Now Wells would need help.

*　　*　　*

When pressed with the need for some fighterly stripe of person, most folk choose the Letter and Coursing House — or the Knave & Post — found on the Spokes in the midst of the oldest innermost part of the city. Here in its cavernous hall you can charter from one of its many knaving-clerks an entire catalogue of bravos, from monster-battling teratologists to life-guarding spurns. Prices are fair, operation efficient, prizes and recompenses are paid promptly and in full, and its register includes many pugilists of high reputation, especially surgically-altered lahzars. Yet, for all their vaunted power, Atticus Wells did not trust the mind-bending wit or the lightning-throwing fulgar, reckoning them too clumsy — too apt to kill — for the *fine work* he typically required. Moreover, a bad incident between a scourge in his hire and a patron left him wary too of an exitumath's extreme smokes. Unfortunately, the regulations and practice of the Knave & Post did not allow for one to easily choose who it was who answered your call for a fighter. Consequently, Atticus habitually sought a small agent knavery, Messrs Prighmy & Till on the Knot Street, in the shadow of the second curtain wall in Higher Brandt, faithful representatives of the more mundane pugilists he preferred.

There were three enterprising sets of bravos he regularly engaged when such strength was needed, every one of them commonplace in regards to surgical improvement or employment of chemistry: the Double Irons, a brace of pistoleers and their holstermen for when dash and pith were the order; Mister Ptolemis, a franklock with impeccable aim for when accuracy from afar was necessary and Mister Door alone was not enough; and the battle-dancing sagaar sisters, Cilestine and Paraclesia Pail, subtle, fearless, patient. With each of these there was no chance of a misthrown potive bringing instant death or the ill-directed puissance of a lahzar, just flashing weapons and cool professional deference … And of them, the Pail sisters were his foremost preference. Stocky and somewhat plain of face, both wore bird-masks as was the inclination of their particular school of dance — Cilestine the regal egret, Paraclesia the noble heron — and both fought like wild things. Wells had witnessed them singly subdue men twice their mass — ferocious men cornered and fixed on tearing their way free — with nothing more than their armoured hands and the sublime skill of their steps. What is more, Wells knew that the Pail sisters had contended with fictlers before and would be happy — even keen — to do so again.

Happy fortune, Mister Prighmy, chief knaving clerk of the Knot Street, informed his valued client that the pair had returned only the week before from hunting nickers in the southern wilds of Chessers' Gall. 'In fact they have only just put themselves back up for hire this very day,' Mister Prighmy declared with modest clerical cheer. 'I am sure they shall be most delighted to know you are hiring again.'

Filling a certificate of assignment and taking out a Singular contract, Wells returned to Banker's Lane to continue the multiplicity of preparations required to venture forth: harness, weaponry, clothing, the necessary chemistry to ward off monsters — however rare they might be in the long-inhabited hills — wayfoods and water and other less necessary but more toothsome liquids, travelling papers, and all the rest. After so many years, Wells, Sprawle and Door knew just how little could be taken and a certain degree of comfort still maintained. Their plan — as always — was to remain in civilised regions for as long as practicable as they followed the indications of the evidence, eating wayhouse fare and sleeping in wayhouse bunks until they had no choice but to leave known or populated paths. Hoping to leave within the next day or two and including travel time, Wells reckoned on their return by a fortnight.

The following morning the sleuth sent a note by footman to his physician, Doctor Ganymede, then ignoring the growing qualms of knee and lower back, stepped out alone. On Green Lady's Walk he hired a takeny coach to Foursdike athenaeum where fledgling concometrists learnt how to record, to fight and to measure the world. Entering the grand institution with its high sombre walls and paved, tree-shaded quadrangles, he called on his old, age-ed friend, Grimwood, Undermarshal-Archivist at Foursdike's great library. With the aid of the librarian, he hunted for most of the day amongst the numerous documents — ancient and new — on this mysterious den of fictlers, Case Nigrise. In a dusty shelf of obscure facsimiles of historied records he finally found the tiny glimpse he needed. Scribed by Imperial asseyors — the forefathers of the concometrists — in their multiple assessment surveys of the then newly-conquered lands, each held great tallies of the figured worth of ever-increasing territories, the Brandendowns included. For all their fine high-flown Tutin they were basically the ledgers of a man counting his coffers. Yet in these tedious lists was a single mention of an unconquered fortalice made by the native Pilts. Built from swarthy stone, it was named rather derisively by the invaders as the 'Black Hut' or — as recorded by the learned Tutin-speaking asseyors — *Casa Nigrum* ...

'Or Case Nigrise!' Sprawle declared brightly and with no small measure of self-satisfaction when Wells had returned in the waning of the hour to explain his find.

'Perversely,' Wells elaborated, sitting heavily on a favourite turkoman squatting by the green-grey hearth of his cluttered yet properly ordered file, 'as a purely numerical record of estimated value, the facsimile contained no map, so the location of this Case Nigrise was little more than vagaries; somewhere northeast beyond Coddlingtine Dell.'

'Put me on the proper heading,' Sprawle proclaimed, without any false showing away, 'and I will smell our way to our despairing damsel!'

'Well, I hope you can smell quick, Petulcus,' the sleuth returned seriously. He passed a marked book Grimwood had allowed him to take away. 'I have been able to clarify Brother Scritch's dark hints on the nature of her ultimate abductors ... and I fear that the wedge is getting perilously thin for Miss Grey.'

Sprawle took the small yet hefty duodecimo bound in a humble red cloth and peered at its hard-to-read title:

A Continuing Survey of Marginal Cults in the Grumid States, with Especial Attention on those deemed Dangerous to the Continuing Harmony of our Most Pacific Empire.

He turned to the marked pages and found the following lightly indicated with the even silvery pale lines of a stylus:

Septs are the many and various obfusc collections of people whose membership name themselves helots, but universally are named fictlers or fantaisist (for they believe in fantasies). On either hand, these helots are the willing thralls of those reputed yet barely encountered 'beings', the *falsegods*. Mentioned often in rare and dubious text, these *falsegods* are supposed to lurk in the deepest parts of the oceans, imprisoned there by some unknown force and desiring above all things the rule of dry land and all the creatures dwelling on it; yet they are so seldom seen that ascertaining their true nature, or more fundamentally, verifying their proper existence has proved impossible (and, in the reckoning of this pen, supremely unlikely).

Regardless of my opinion or that of sensible rational society, the septs believe the *falsegods* (or *alosudnë* as is their supposed proper appellation) real enough to attempt *summonings* at certain propitious junctures in the seasons (times understood only to the higher members of each sept), employing many peculiar and loathsome techniques to draw their chosen 'god' from the lightless pits of the oceans where they are legended to be interned (if such stories are to be countenanced). Among the more benign customs is a quaint practice known variously as *grammar*, *cantrics* or *cater legite* (there are meant to be distinctions between each, but these are lost on this pen) whereby the helots sing through some manner of amplifying device into the water, hoping to wake their trammelled and slumbering 'god' and excite them enough to throw off their fetters and rise to take their place as lords. In the grip of such luxuriant fancies they use these 'songs' to call on the supposed servants of their chosen 'god', *famuli* they called them, (or *pseudotheons* in some learned manuscripts), beslimed, often massive things who become the 'mouth-pieces' for the helots to commune with their 'god' and if some Phlegmish texts are to be believed, the 'god' communicates with its thralls in return (what a reportedly slumbering idiot beast might have to say this pen cannot pretend to conjure) …

Sprawle's eyes skipped impatiently over continuing verbose elaborations of one baffling practice to another until his gaze was arrested by sentences darkly and double lined …

… Of all these exercises the most extreme is the 'sacrifice' of life to their master. Typically this will be an animal, something to give the 'god' a *taste* of vitality they are said to crave but cannot get for themselves. At its worst expression the life will be that of a person, for the falsegods and their famuli are said to crave everyman meat above all else and most of all the delectable flesh of the very young. As the adherents of the falsegod Sucoth (so named the Devourer), the Seven Brothers of the Seven-Mouthed Lord or simply the Seven-Seven (also the Sucathene), are among the more malign and degenerate of all the septs, and it is this final wretched practice that they to their unmitigated shame, employ most often …

There was more — of course — but the underlining ceased here and so did Sprawle. He did not need to read anymore had he even desired to. The cause for his friend's solemn urgency was clear enough: scant as it was, the evidence they possessed told that Viola was in the clutches of the Seven-Seven and that — if not already — she would soon be slain in the worship of a crude and fabulous notion.

'I see …' was all he said in pointed conclusion. 'Do we know much of this Sucoth — this *Devourer* character, other than this and what Brother Scritch uttered?'

'No, not really …' Wells answered, distractedly kneading his often paining shins.

The lurksman peered through the tall windows out on the great grey city spreading out low under the leaden mantle of louring water-logged sky. It was all so quiet and usual. He could not quite conceive that somewhere out under the milky waters might dwell such powerful embodiments of enmity and horrific all-devouring ambition.

'Anything of your own to report?' Wells inquired.

'The Pail sisters called by in person to accept your Singular,' Sprawle replied. 'They could not remain, though; needed to pack so as to be ready to depart on the morrow.'

'Most excellent!' said Wells, brightening some. 'I am sorry to have missed them,' he added, a little too lightly.

'Indeed,' Sprawle returned, cocking a brow. Despite clear apprehension of the futility of such an action, his chief had spent the better half of a decade trying to foster a deeper association with these noble sisters — especially the elder Cilestine. To little avail. They were certainly amicably acquainted, as best as one could be with taciturn women who rarely ceased motion as they pursued the Perpetual Dance.

'And the packing?' Wells asked through a heavy sigh, rising to pour himself a double draught of watered obtorpës for the pain. Moving to a tandem, he sat and stretched out his crooked panging excuses for legs.

'Door and Thickney are doing splendidly.'

'Excellent …' Wells returned muzzily, head lolling, eyes drooping under the rapid influence of the draught. 'Will … will you be returning for a final night of conjugal bliss with your wife?'

'Not tonight, good sir, I have said my goodbyes to my dear Flymmsia and shall stay here with you tonight so that we might be off a promptly as possible the morrow morn …'

… But snoring ever so slightly, Wells was no longer listening.

Perceiving more of his friend's struggle than he knew Wells would find comfortable, Sprawle smiled to himself a little sadly and went carefully from the room to help in the final preparations.

Soon after, Doctor Ganymede made his call, prescribing the usual rubbing ointment — salve varante — to apply before the start of each new day, and slake of subvenire, one of a new strain of restorative scripts called alleviants, said to dull pain without the drowse. After so many quackery salves, Wells was gratified to find subvenire seemed actually efficacious, bringing his various algias down to a blunt throb.

'I am sorry I cannot do more for you, my friend,' the physician apologised in parting. 'Short of you climbing back into the womb to re-emerge more properly knit,' he added with his usual gallows humour, 'I do not fathom what is to be done.'

Wells knew this all too well. He strove to keep self-pity bayed, yet there was always the lingering wish to walk fast and free like others did and without this constant pain. He had heard unsubstantiated whispers that the surgeons of Sinster, who make people into lahzars, could help him into a better pair of limbs. Such was their dark reputation, however, Atticus did not want to go upon the shanks of some poor dead man or worse, those of a mule or other brute beast.

For the thousandth time, he dismissed the notion, ignored the lingering pain and returned his attention to immediate need.

In the grey and brilliant pink-shot dawn of the following day — barely four days since Monsiere Pardolot's first approach — the quest to extricate Viola Grey set out aboard a pair of privately hired lentums, a profound sense of the rightness and urgency of their cause beating in each bosom. In the chilly hush of the waking city they clattered through clear streets, sending many loping shadows of mangy rabbits retreating in to the fog, a mere glimpse of the great multitude of rabbits reputed to inexplicably haunt this city more plaguingly than its rats, dogs or cats. Wells smiled at the flash of their retreating tails. These were creatures just like he, thriving where they ought not and despite himself, he regarded them as a good portent.

Through the Moon Gate, the last bastion port in the northern arc of the city's outermost curtain wall, the five were taken as rapidly as six-horse carriages might through dew drenched upland pastures. While Door and Sprawle travelled in the first fit, the necessary day-bags and linen packets beside them, Wells went aboard the second lentum accompanied by the Pail sisters, 'To explain details,' he had said to Sprawle before boarding.

The lurksman was not convinced. 'If only I had your eyes,' he had muttered mordantly.

As it was, they changed seating after a change of horses and middens meal at the *Plum & Apple* wayhouse nestled at the leafy feet of the Brandenfells proper. Mister Door — all blushes and mumbles — joined the laconic dames, while Atticus and Petulcus sat together to continue their own discussions of their next action.

'Wonderful sincere damsels,' Wells elaborated when teams were changed and they were on their way again, 'but one can only compass so much ponderous silence, meaningful half-avoided glances and slow, endless sagarine restlessness.'

Well acquainted with the peculiar cross-legged poses and measured elegant contortions of the limb that marked a seated sagaar committed to the Perpetual Dance, Sprawle knew well enough that *this* was not the problem. 'Indeed ...' was, however, all he said.

By the time cold twinkling evening descended and Phoebë lifted her august lunar face early over the rim of the world to shine it full upon all the scurrying souls below, all plans had been discussed, all conversation exhausted. It was silent, travel-weary souls that clambered tail-sore and hunched from the lentum cabins, across the coach yard and into the cheery welcome of the *Green Mile*, finest wayhouse in Coddlingtine Dell.

Since before the first peep of sun, Sprawle had been up on the wooded slopes about the town, sthenicon strapped to face, sniffing, sniffing, sniffing, while the wagtails warbled to each other in the shrinking dark and the branches cracked and snapped with frost.

Yet he found nothing.

None of the goodly locals nor the boniface of the *Green Mile* asked the next day knew of any such place as Case Nigrise, Casa Nigrum, or Black Hut; neither were the clerks or officials of the town willing to spare their time.

'If it is an account of property yer after,' one friendly clerk offered as Atticus made inquiry in the town's small but fine civic hall of lofty pillars and glowing coppered dome, 'then I'd recommend ye seek the temporal registers kept at the Fallenthaw in Pour Claire.'

With a rare genuine smile, Wells said that he most certainly would and hurried as fast as cane and crooked leg would allow to tell his comrades of this lead. Soon enough they were back aboard their lentum-and-sixes rumbling through increasingly steep woodlands that rang with the chock of axe and rasp of saw, making good time to reach to the remote city of Pour Claire by nightfall. Slowly they trundled across its long, heavily fortified bridge, Wells staring almost hungrily at the high white walls before him, white towers and dark spine-like chimneys climbing behind, all built upon the summit of an utterly enormous pinnacle of rock that split the flow of a ravine-running river. The trail had better go on from here, because time was running short and *he* was running thin of clever notions ...

Above the clatter of the carriage he could hear the roar of tumbling waters far far below.

*   *   *

At the beginning of a fresh day — while Sprawle and company made inquest of their own in other parts of the city — Wells made his way by planquin-chair to the administrative focus of the Fallenthaw. Standing in the small space granted common folk in the expanse of the main file, he asked gracefully for access to the temporal registers. At the first, thinking he was come in answer to a singular their civic masters had sent to the city seeking to be rid of the monstrous night-prowling horror named the Gutterfear, the clerks had greeted him most cordially. Yet, upon discovering he was not there to rescue them, they became stiff and aloof. No, he was told, only to be informed that such a thing was only granted to proper representatives of state or empire or high-placed mercantile league, or someone bearing a proper Notation of Release from the Inland Ordinance Board back in Brandenbrass would induce them to change their mind. Neither a sincere recounting of Viola's terrible abduction nor the dropping of Monsiere Pardolot's name moved these stony-faced adjuncts.

These were not stupid men before him, in their powder bagwigs and sleek clerical soutanes, but they were what the sleuth liked to call *over-efficient*. However much Wells might usually enjoy the chase of paper and a good clerical stouche, ever mindful of slipping time and the girl's life, he was growing swiftly impatient of this delay.

A tight bow and Wells bid them good day; yet he was not to be thwarted. Returning to the common hall of dark beams and wide stretches of white walls hung with portraits of generations of the city's lords, he took out the spedigraph of Viola folded, blank side outermost, and clutched it like it was a document of import. *One can do anything in a file as long as you have a piece of paper in hand,* he reflected wryly, and began to stroll about the attached passages as if he was meant to be there. At the end of an extended passage hung with the likenesses of the hall's long line of bureaucratic masters, he found what he was looking for, a plain door helpfully signed:

Catalogues, Registers & Annals

This door was locked.

Without hesitation or any suspicious casting about to see who saw — thereby drawing attention to himself, Wells produced his faithful tumblerpicks from the small padded case he ever carried on him, quickly had the lock released and was through. Down a cold stone stair he descended to a wide cellar chamber filled to the broadly arched ceiling with filecase upon filecase of swarthy wood. Here he sought among the chilly rows for items sharing the vintage of the clue gained at Foursdike library, and following the clearly dated labels on each long filerow found himself in a seldom visited part of the archive. Supping on a paltry cache of wayfoods he had brought in a satchel with him — ox charcut, nine cheese and an apple — he quietly, carefully rifled the efficiently filed papers gathered in the great avenues of vertically slotted shelves. Often he was forced to struggle up stepscales that slid conveniently on runners, nearly tumbling as his rebellious legs failed to lift high enough. Finally, perched high on a scale, he found the one scrimp of knowledge needed to unlock the next step. In the loose-sheeted record of one of the many ancient mining ventures out in the darksome hills, the Emperor's faithful long-passed registrars had dutifully reported of a hidden fortress. Calling this place the Widdenhold, it was from here that the wild Piltmen of old — the Widden, they named them — did launch their frightening ambushes upon the mining surveys. All rather standard stuff, but there in the margin notes Wells barely discerned a time-faded scrawling ...

Dunnbyre.

It was Old Pilt; which he was versed in enough to know meant *dark cottage* ...

'Or *black hut!*' the sleuth muttered in fatigued triumph.

They had found their place.

Equipped with such local knowledge, they soon engaged a swain well acquainted with the hindermost parts of the Brandenfells who knew of such a place as Widdenhold, finding him through advice from the common room of the *Spout & Hearth* and other drinking places. Younger Pemple was this fellow's name, come in to town without his pigs on a point of business. Born of a line of hog- and goat-herds long-lived in the district, he wore a sagging, well-used tricorn upon his crown and was clad in a long herdsman's smock over which was buckled a sturdy lambrequin of proofed hide. Smelling strongly of the pigs he tended, he had excellent repute amongst his fellow drinkers and, more importantly to Wells' unnaturally percipient gaze, possessed a natively honest soul. Declaring that he was venturing near that way himself, Pemple readily accepted the offered imbursement, though Wells could tell that there was a caution in him.

'Them Piltfolks were right proud of it once,' the swain said of the isolated fortalice, 'or so I'm given to understand. They used to cause no end o' mayhem from it, afor the Tutins came.'

'Then why is it so obscured to universal knowledge?' Wells returned loudly over the rattle of their progress.

'Cause I reckon usual folks — and our masters most — don't hold that the Pilts is got much t'say nor do that's worth taking ken of,' came the sagacious reply.

'Do people live there now?' Cilestine Pail asked one of her rare questions.

'Not so I know of,' Pemple answered, 'though some speak of floating lights and fearsome hoots coming from it. P'r'aps hobpossums have taken their home here,' he shrugged easily enough but underneath his bold show the sleuth could see he was nervous. 'Still, it bain't a place with a wholesome reputation at either stretch,' the swain warned, 'and with the Gutterfear loose and unchecked about them parts, if ye won't be minding, I'll take ye but be on me way again right quick. Best to be indoors by night.'

'Most certainly, Mister Pemple,' Wells gladly agreed. The last thing he desired was involving another in dangers not of their own choosing or perhaps more truly, have some curious bumpkin hovering and foiling the entire enterprise.

All settled and arranged they set out under Pemple's guidance at day break, myriad weapons cleaned and oiled, each member of the party dressed in full harness and ready for daring exploits. Almost immobile when he rose with stiffness from all yesterday's climbing in the stony cellar chill, Wells reluctantly let himself be lifted in to the lentum that they were to take to the site of their rescue. The carriage was drawn by a six-horse team of stout well-proofed beasts —'The better to make a hasty exit,' as Wells said to Cilestine — Door driving now and Pemple acting as his sidearmsman, directing the way from his seat, Sprawle and the Pail sisters stayed in the cabin.

Initially they took the main way back south again towards Coddlingtine Dell. Yet Pemple soon went right onto an ambiguous path possessing barely enough width for the carriage. On this they went south-westwards further and further into the strange tower-like hills and pinnacles of rusting stone so distinct to this part of the hills proclaimed on maps as the Witherfells.

Wrapped in his usual thick scarlet hood and sthenicon on his face, Sprawle sporadically drew forth a stick knotted with a wad of porous cloth from a leather-sealed cylinder about his belt. With this he would lean dangerously out of the cabin window to daub the dark scabrous trunks with scent — a *trail* to follow back to safer paths. Should Pemple get them lost, *he* would find them out again. As the day grew to full and the sky more sombre, the lurksman began to speak of faint clues on the wind and several times called for a halt, so that he might take care to discriminate between a real slot and teasing hints that promised a lead but led to nought.

Occasionally they passed through ramshackle settlements huddled behind a sagging palisade of high thorny wood; wooden hovels crouched on uneven foundations of stone as tall as two tall men, keeping their dwellers high from the reach of night-prowling monsters. For as close as this region was to the wide-reaching influence of Brandenbrass and technically held to be safe parishland, such a maze of vales and ravines hid hobpossums and skulking nickers as easily as it did its many degenerate rebellious citizens. As they passed through, narrow regard was ever on the party, jealous heavy-lidded gazes lingering upon the fine harness and glinting weapons of these strangers. Once Wells gave a wry tip of his thricehigh to one especially curious denizen. The soiled sullen fellow snarled, considered violence, but let them be.

Winding a convoluted route along steep-sided gullies through young pines and bent turpentines marching up on either hand to shadows, the vague path Pemple picked carried them deep into untenanted lands haunted by little more than muttering crows and whistling choughs and small azure-headed snakes. Several times they eschewed perfectly serviceable roads in favour of the increasingly obtuse and crooked route, traversing sudden cracks in the ancient stone upon wooden bridges of uncertain construction. These were often so narrow, the passengers were forced to alight and walk behind while Pemple coaxed the team of six and their lentum across. The further they went, the more an ineffable heaviness beyond mere internal abstraction began to weigh on the party, enough to dampen even the swain's simple cheer. It was with something akin to relief when Pemple called a halt and through the coston's grate in to the cabin, invited his temporary masters to alight.

'There's yer pointy place,' he declared, pointing up and away to their right with a nod and a poke of his ivory-ornate heirloom musket. 'An ne'er a more unrote establishment will ye find.'

Out of the black trees rising now row upon row to their right, upon a heel of corroded orange rock thrusting from the slope of a higher summit, stood a high black tower flanked by two smaller keeps. Case Nigrise — the black house, lair of the Seven-Seven, cult of Sucoth, looking all the more dismal under the heavy grey of a lowering afternoon sky. Where the mighty blocks of its jet-black walls might have come from was a mystery, for all the rock about it and upon which it grew was rusted sandstone. It was built so cunningly upon its perch that Wells could easily see a mere company of determined souls might preserve it indefinitely from an entire army railing at its feet. Now that they beheld it so brooding clear, the adventurers wondered why the melancholy fortress had not been remarked by one of them earlier. Yet such were the contortions of these forsaken combes that only when a traveller was under the very caste of its long shadow would they see the Black House looming.

A lonely wind seemed to descend from it, a frosty sigh that brought with it brooding fear and a promise of doom.

Sniffing, sniffing, Sprawle quickly set to work and soon found a trace, the thinnest sandy trail in the needles, snaking and switching back upon itself, disappearing in the dull shadows of the higher woods.

'It's our *Master Jack*,' he hissed through his box into the creaking hush of the dry shadowy woods.

'Bless your accurate senses, sir!' Wells enthused, then turned to the swain climbing down from his high seat at the front of the carriage. 'You have done admirably, Mister Pemple.'

'Thank'ee, sir,' the swain becked. 'Will — will ye be needin' more of me?'

Wells smiled graciously. 'No, Mister Pemple, your labour is complete — as agreed. Go your way, sir, and may your path be always clear.'

'And yours, sir,' the swain smiled in open relief. Giving them all a final deeper bow, he went quickly back along the way they had come and going about a gloomy bend, soon ambled out of sight.

Hanging until this moment at their backs, the Pail sisters now fixed their avian masks over their faces, their aspect instantly becoming warlike.

'And now to getting in,' the egret-faced Cilestine declared, her voice thick with irony and her eyes twinkling grimly through the slots in her mask as she peered up at the stronghold and swayed like a viper set to strike.

Wells stared up into the gloom of the precipitous woods. There was no means for the lentum to ascend among the threatening trees and knuckled boulders to the dreary bastion's stony feet; time was running too short to search for a possible hidden entrance. Their path had come — as the sleuth had expected it might — to a difficult climb. As much as his curiosity might burn within him to look within the den of a fictler cult, his clumsy legs would only be a liability where speed and lithliness and all fashions of physical cunning were best. Wells had got them to this juncture, but now was the moment when Mister Sprawle came most fully into his own.

'My curiosity can wait,' Wells proclaimed stoutly. 'Your safety and Viola's rescue are paramount!'

'I shall as always give you as full a description of all I see as I can when this is done,' Sprawle declared gently to his resolute friend.

Wells smiled gratefully and, relegated to mere spectator, wrestled with the bitter all-too-familiar frustration — his old *friend* — that threatened its own darkness whenever he was forced to such a choice. With Door as guard and bridleminder beside him, Wells shoved the rising melancholy back down to the pit of himself from whence it rose and fixed his attention on his comrades as Sprawle and the Pail sisters alone climbed.

Following the zigzag route of the path — a mere sandy scrape switching back and forth between the creaking whispering trees, the scent of Sprawle's quarry became clearer and clearer to him with every step of their cautious yet rapid ascent. Just the once when the lurksman was about halfway up, while the Pail sister leapt and stalked weirdly ahead, did he allow himself a glance down to Wells now far below. In the weird washed-out sight granted by the sthenicon his friend was a small yet clearly pallid blot among the shades of the trees, the larger blot of Door and the duller heavier blemishes of the six horses near obscuring him. No other lurid shapes showed themselves in the trees of the valley. Sprawle always loathed leaving Wells behind, in part because he hated to see his ally so dismayed, but also that he felt somehow exposed and ... well, *limping* without the sleuth's sharp mind working away beside him.

Near the summit the three adventurers found a dim channel of steps hand-cut into the stained and lichen-splotched rock. Grotesque statues made of the sandstone of the cliff stood at the end of this stony conduit, effigies depicting a squat figure clutching at its own head and covered in gaping mouths. Should he care to count them, Sprawle was sure he would find seven sets of orifice upon each form. Coming slowly through this carven lane they found the great black footings of Case Nigrise proper and were deposited at last at the base of the dour stronghold. They were in a closed and weedy yard, the leadening sky above, the beetling cliff to back and the inky walls of Case Nigrise on the other three sides.

Waiting in the cover of the statues, the three kept themselves hidden, listening; Sprawle peering into every cleft and shadow above and about, the Pail sisters strangely still next to him, the constant motion of the Perpetual Dance an allowable sacrifice for the cause of safety.

Nothing but tiny furtive wall-dwelling skinks moved here.

All else was silence.

The drag of Mister Jack was so strong now Sprawle could near see it leading to a mighty black gate in the wall of an attached annex to the main tower. As high as the annex itself, it was out of proportion with the structure of the keep it sat within. By the evidence of hewn and patched stone work about its arched frame, it had clearly and more recently been enlarged for some unguessable reason. Indeed, the longer they observed it the more the masonry about the arch looked like jagged teeth, rendering this ponderous door a perversely gigantic mouth.

'The Devourer …' Sprawle murmured to himself as the three carefully approached. Checking the priming yet again in his pair of twin-barrelled pistola, the lurksman sniffed and peered in the quiet for any sign of his allies' progress or of a foe.

For long moments hidden in the mouth of the channel, they observed and waited, yet the walls were too thick to peer through and beneath the obvious scent of Master Jack, the smell of occupation general. All seemed clear enough; people lived here certainly, but they were not currently present. A bent wandlimb grew before the very front of the gate, showing that it had not been opened for some years. Typically there would be some smaller sally-port in the base of such a gate, but close examination did not reveal it.

'There must be some hidden way in,' Sprawle muttered as he stepped carefully up to this impossible portal to pace to and fro before it. 'The slot brings us right here …'

Without a falter in their subtle dance, the Pail sisters went to the wall, each upon either side of the gate, and abruptly, began to climb. Finding sufficient claw holds in the uneven slabs of the keep wall, they hauled themselves adroitly upwards, scaling the swarthy surface with astonishing ease while their skirts fell clear by their ingenious cut from the women's proof-stockinged legs. Near the acme of the wall ran a row of loopholes, mere slits from which to ply fire down upon thwarted and milling attackers, yet with abnormal twistings of their frames, the Pail sisters each found a loophole to their liking and wormed a way through and inside.

'Well, well …' Sprawle exclaimed softly, hands on hips as he watched the two sagaars disappear into the black bastion. He never tired of the resourcefulness of these two fighting ladies.

Before long and with a hollow *thunk!*, a thin vertical fracture appeared in the overlarge gate, instantly widening to the sought-after sally-port. Cilestine and Paraclesia stepped gracefully out, eyes twinkling with self-satisfaction.

'I understand you wanted in, sir ...' the elder sister offered with a slight curtsey.

Within they discovered a great hall made from the removal of the original floors and mezzanines clear up to the aging beams and rafters, an echoing untenanted space hung about with vast woven and painted fabrics depicting nigh-orgiastic scenes of destruction.

At their feet, the rescuers beheld a great e-form — the Enigmatic Mouth of Sucathës — painted in white upon the flagstones in the centre of the chamber. On the right from the door stood a monumental image carven in swart stone, yet another seven-mouths monstrosity formed with unnerving clarity, its oddly crooked arm holding aloft a tiny, clearly struggling figure dangled over a hungrily waiting maw.

'It appears that no one is here,' Cilestine declared, peering about cautiously.

Sprawle nodded in confirmation, his box-augmented senses revealing that though this place was usually — and until recently — occupied, its current residents were at this moment elsewhere; no sentinels, no guards, no milling idlers, all were absent.

But where? Sprawle surveyed the hall in brief bafflement.

Upon the left of the wall of what must have been the flank of the main tower, there was spread an immense tapestry woven with a complex scene of a thousand figures of ever-decreasing size gathered in clear groups. In the centre of them all stood a man-sized figure, its comely ruddy frame ringed about with an aberrantly murky light, its thickly-haired head set with seven mouths: one where it ought to be, one for the nose, one either side for the ears, one each for the eyes, and above them one set in the very middle of the smooth forehead — all full-lipped and disturbingly pretty.

'A heirarchograph,' Cilestine explained gravely, the beak of her mask pointing up at the bizarre piece of fabulary. 'In the middle is

Sucoth in his human form, and all about him in diminishing importance are his servants, man and bestial.'

Despite all the dark and dreadful deeds Sprawle's adventurous life had forced him to witness, he could not help a shiver of disgust and felt Paraclesia beside him also shudder. Suddenly something caught his attention and with a flash of relief mingled with a kind of dogged consternation realised what it was.

'I smell *her*,' he hissed. 'I smell Viola!'

It was faint but it was unmistakable amongst the miasma of older male odours. Lifting a mere corner of the disquieting arras, the lurksman discovered that the wall had been mined, almost entirely removed, the great gap opening onto a conical vacancy rising to the grey heavens and sinking to incomprehensible gloom — an enormous gaping emptiness from which seemed to emanate an oppressive pall.

This must be the inside of the tower proper.

'Here …' the lurksman confirmed.

Before him a slender stairway coiled down into darkness and this the three now vigilantly descended, Sprawle leading the way with his perspicuous, pit-fall seeing sight. Rain set in, falling through the yawning rooflessness above and making the steps perilously slick. On they declined, the rain becoming a diffuse drizzle then ceasing entirely as they climbed deeper and deeper. Water dripped with conspicuous plops, the echoes bringing an insinuation of some other almost melodic muttering.

Still they went down.

Finally the descent terminated in a cavernous hand-hewn grotto, and though Sprawle could see easily enough, the sagarine sisters were forced to unhood a small mosslight to see by. All about them was the same lustrous black stone from which the tower above was fashioned, somehow cut and hauled by ancient, rude-living Pilts, all the way to the light.

Though there were many small openings, the slot of Viola and Master Jack went through the largest, an exit of massive height and girth, the tunnel beyond like some mighty throat that whispered and mumbled with what for all the gird sounded like distant choral music. Though far below the round peaks of the shunned hill, air seemed to shift and move in that throat, bringing along with the drag of their quarry, the tangy stink of the sea.

'The Grume!' Sprawle muttered. 'Can you smell it?'

Cilestine nodded.

As the three wended through dripstones hanging like carnivorous teeth from the hewn ceiling or rising from the paved floor, Sprawle could well imagine them descending into the very gullet of Sucathës himself.

If one can believe such things, the lurksman scoffed inwardly.

Yet whatever massive bulk was meant to come along this mighty passage, it had clearly not yet done so.

Ahead the choral murmur began to resolve itself into definite singing and soon enough into tangible words …

> *Hi O! Shiggeloth! Hyr thy pegen sop!*
> *Haeg to thee aenlig famuli of Suthas!*
> *Harken as thy cynn sange dethe*
> *ofer thou afaerende wepan welas,*
> *Of Maegan Sucathene!*
>
> *Hi O! Shiggeloth! Hyr thy pegen sop!*
> *Gripan them gast and mod in fyrht*
> *And aefter don wael abeodan*
> *of us to thou maegen dryht,*
> *O! Maegan Sucathene …*

On it went in bizarre tongue, a song at turns strident and demanding, at turns plaintive and beseeching, reverberating over and over upon itself in the mighty chamber until with each pace closer it became an almost painful booming. Pressing on into this clamour, they spied a small doorway on the left and Sprawle quickly ascertained that Master Jack had gone through this lesser way, while Viola had continued on.

This was the path they kept.

All too soon the three met another massive portal, oblong and opening out to the most profound foreboding. Here the chanting song resounded in full and pounding volume, and suddenly, over it, the single high voice rang clear:

Succedere, O! Sigilot Magni! Succedere!
Vos offa dulcis ego deferre!

This Sprawle understood well enough. It was Tutin, the old language of erudition and the Empire, droned indelibly into him at the hands of Master Tope through the long afternoons of young years at the juniary, and he grimaced at the import of the words. *Come up!* had been the cry, *Come up! O Mighty Shiggeloth! I have brought a sweet morsel before you!*

Shiggeloth? Sprawle wondered briefly. *I thought these fools served Sucathës …*

There came a sudden flash, some manner of flare launched from well above them, lighting the murky scene starkly as it trailed down in a lazy arc that struck the chanting dumb and near blinding Sprawle in its abrupt glare. Clutching at the wood over his face, blinking rapidly to clear his dazzled sight, he was grateful when the flare dropped steadily before them to disappear down some long drop, leaving a sickly sweet scent.

In the lingering light as Sprawle's sight returned, it was clear they had come to a small, roughly circular shelf of rock that jutted into a cavernous bottomless amphitheatre, the oddly light air sighing ever so gently on their cheeks. The gigantic door where the three now stood was flanked by columns carved from the jet rock like the façade of some historied edifice. Within the great clash of odours here, of the sea, the aromatic flare, of cold ancient stone, of perhaps a hundred men in various states of cleanliness, the smells of both Master Jack and Viola were strong indeed.

They are here!

A faint light came from somewhere high beyond the great door, and the three edged vigilantly out into the amphitheatre, the sagaars' dance reduced to a pent rocking motion.

High and directly above them was a throne-like balcony cut in the sheer rock. On it stood an arrogant figure, partly luminous in Sprawle's superior vision, face masked behind white striped with four horizontal bars of red. Here at last was the elusive 'Master Jack'. Wrapped in a heavy, fur-collared cloak of the deepest purple, his arms were raised, his fingers twirling odd figures in the lurid smokes that rose from the metal stands at either hand. Crested with a high three-corner hat sporting a ray of five large white feathers, it was apparent he was the grammaticar — the leader — of this degenerate cult. Arranged on either side of their leader upon steps chiselled from bare stone curving from the height of the crested grammaticar down to well below the shelf, stood two lines of pasty forms — maybe three score or more on each side. It was the entire conventicle of helots, every one robed in thick red and masked in white bearing one, two or sometimes three bars. Long sinuous tubes were fixed before them, bending away from their mouths to run down in to the occult darkness of the abyss. Silent now, they too had their bare arms stretched, the flesh there torn and bloodied as they swayed from side to side in practised unison.

None seemed to heed the intruders.

Clearly, in the throes of their 'summoning', the fictlers were not expecting an expedition of rescue.

Succedere, O! Sigilot Magni! Succedere!

The grammaticar cried again, flourishing a flammagon that with a spark and cough of flint and pan, released another perfumed flare.

This time Sprawle shut his eyes in the nick, and in the fading blaze, he could see before him at the very edge of the shelf a high-backed chair of carven stone and he *knew* who he would find seated there. As if to confirm his certainty, a small figure sagged sideways in the seat and there before them was the drooping, insufficiently wrapped figure of Viola Grey.

Before Sprawle could act, a great dread assailed him, rushing upon them all suddenly — adherent and as yet unseen invader alike — up from that gaping abysmal hole, bringing with it a horrid, nigh-maddening fishy stink mixed with the vinegar reek of the sea. Quickly, Sprawle pushed at a slot on the side of his sthenicon to deaden the stench and spare himself its worst. Before him something glistening and loathsome reeled from the pit, something so grotesque as to defy reckoning rising from the infinite depths. Thrice perhaps a man's height, its movements as it scaled the precipice before the sacrificial seat sounded like the slap of wet leather. Surely it had not come all the way from the waters of the Grume? At its appearance the worshippers together began a great ululation of unhallowed joy that shrieked and leapt about the stones of the drear amphitheatre.

Viola in her swoon barely stirred.

A bizarre gibberish — more felt than heard coming from this grotesque thing — smote the party, shrieking in their inner beings of sodden brooding hatred sunken but living still in crushing sightless deeps. With this came dread images printed directly on the mind's eye of the vile inescapable degradation of the human race, whose only escape was to give over yourself and willingly join the horror.

For a flash, Sprawle fought not to throw himself down appalled and grovel to be granted this one slender escape. Could it be that the falsegods did truly dwell in the bleak ocean deeps, brooding and waiting to be freed and then to visit horror upon mankind? How was it possible that such bee-rumours — fantastical folk tales — typically the credo of the credulous and the weak were actually true! *What will Atticus make of such a thing?*

With astounding presence the Pail sisters leapt forward, the elder sagaar seizing the abducted girl.

A sibilant piercing squeal, thick with wrathful frustration, drowned all other noise as the Shiggeloth beast realised its morsel was being stolen from its very grasp.

Spurred into action, Sprawle bellowed wordlessly and fired his heavy hauncet pistol at the rising behemoth come in from the sea.

And with this chaos reigned.

*   *   *

Rueing every degree the sun sank on its meridian, Atticus Wells stood alone upon the bank of the road and peered intently up into the darksome wood. In the interminability of waiting, Door had taken the carriage on to find a place to turn it about so as to be pointing the correct direction for departure and to prevent the horses from becoming too cool and so unable to leave promptly should hurry be needed. Wells had insisted on waiting at the foot of the ambiguous path. His assistant had gone out and only after some time come back with the lentum right-facing and an apology that it had taken him a fair trial to find anywhere roomy enough to turn about, but still Sprawle and the Pail sisters had not returned.

Closing his eyes, Wells listened for any clue of his friends, of anything. There was nought but the jink of harness and thump of hoof, the creak of crooked boughs and sigh of drooping needles. Yet it was too hushed; even the mournful whistling calls of the choughs that had rung so persistently during their journey here were stilled.

A cracking sound above, followed by a clatter of dislodged pinecones and hillside soil. Up in the trees, hurrying forms descending fast towards him. Figures skidded and skipped a dangerous career between the trees, ignoring the winding and safer route, making a more direct path of their own. Gasping great gulps of air, the rescuers slid the last yards and sprang on to the road. Yet only two of the original three returned.

'We must fly!' Sprawle cried, the rescued Viola in arm, the girl barely sensible under the influence of some stupefying draught.

'Where is Paraclesia?' Wells asked hotly. By the strained look on Sprawle's face and the unquiet humours surging beneath his skin, he almost did not dare the question.

'She is ... she is dead,' Cilestine answered, her voice hard and thick, her grief hidden behind egret mask.

Door already flicking the horses to start, the three survivors and their young charge sprang aboard the lentum and the party fled the dismal bastion of Case Nigrise. The horses whinnied loudly in protest at the ferocity of their flight, Door did his utmost to build and keep pace yet not tip the carriage upon its side in the tight turns.

'We uncovered more than our damsel and her captors,' Sprawle explained ominously as they were jostled violently in the hurrying lentum. 'Master Jack and his thralls were in a cavern that must reach even to the sea, calling up some sea-born beastie the very moment we arrived. No doubt this beastie — this Shiggeloth — was to eat poor

Viola but Cilestine snatched the girl from under its very maw as it went for her. Paraclesia leapt to challenge the Shiggeloth and kept it bayed while Cilestine carried Viola away. I shot at the thing and Paraclesia wrestled bravely, yet four times her size it over-powered her. My grenadoes did little to it and we were forced to flee … Men we can face but not some monstrous evil summoned up from the deeps too.' The lurksman pressed his palms against his eyes.

Her mask removed, Cilestine said nothing but clung to the frame of the carriage door and her face set cold, peered back to see if they were pursued.

'What is this Shiggeloth anyway?' Sprawle vocalised his original thought. 'I thought these fools served Sucathës or somesuch!'

'It is, from what little I have read, the famuli of Sucoth,' Wells returned. 'Its servant …'

'So are we to conclude falsegods as real!'

'So it might seem.' Wells could scarcely credit it himself.

As they bounded along, he took a phial from on of the padded pockets hanging from the protecting sash that bound his middle and unstoppering it, waved the open neck under Viola's nose.

The girl grunted, her groggy, wildly rolling eyes snapping into clarity.

'It's hartshorn, m'dear,' Wells said as if by way of greeting. 'Very invigorating.'

She blinked at him uncomprehendingly for a beat, then her whole expression went round with alarm and an agony of horror. Realising she was free, Viola tried to spring away and out of the carriage, but was tumbled from her seat by the precipitous and dangerous careen of the lentum cab.

'Fear not, Viola Grey,' Wells cooed with especial calmness. 'You shall see your mother again.'

The girl stared at him hopelessly, barely grasping his words or her salvation. Already in an attitude of defeat, she capitulated quickly, sagging where she had been thrown.

Suddenly the team's wild nickers turned to shrieks of fright. Door cried out so loud as to be heard over the crash and rattle of their progress. Something unhallowed hissed and jabbered in a loathsome simulacrum of speech. The cabin lurched more violently yet and its occupants realised they were being lifted off the very ground. For a beat the whole fit was suspended then with a mighty shock and the wails of terrified and agonised horses, it crashed back to earth.

Stunned and momentarily immobile, Wells lay on his back, head spinning, realising he was collapsed across the door of the lentum half crushed and tipped on its side.

'Out! Out!' someone cried. 'The Shiggeloth has caught us!'

… Sprawle's voice?

A strong grip seized the sleuth and he was hauled clear of the wreck. Door had him, carrying him now under strong arm like an invalid child, striding as fast as he could up the steep embankment flanking the road. Horses screamed still, and gripped firm in Door's grasp, Wells caught sight of their foe.

They had all seen their share of monsters, yet there was something disconcerting in the frame of this beast: tall as three tall men — big even from one hundred yards — its massively broad shoulders came in sharply to a narrow cylindrical waist, its strange triangular hips from which came *three* long, strong, oddly-jointed legs, and its elongated skull ending in a fish-like fin. Running down the face was a great vertical mouth extending down the what ought to be the chin and thick ropey neck to the midst of its chest. So *this* was the Shiggeloth, devoted servant-monster to Sucathës the Devourer, its very reality portentous with dire implications on the truth of the sunken falsegods. Even as he watched the mighty famuli devoured the last horse, stripping the poor nag's armoured shabraques with its curling arms like a child peeling an orange, its gory perpendicular mouth quivering and yawning perversely as it ate. Swallowing a last mouthful, barrel trunk bloating with this equine feast, the Shiggeloth turned and cast about as if looking. Though it possessed no eyes, it fixed its dire attention upon the tiny fleeing figures of the carriage's previous occupants scrabbling up the further slope and away from Case Nigrise. With a peculiarly sibilant and triumphant hoot, it pivoted awkwardly and strode on tripod limbs to catch them, its long supple arms writhing with the jaunting rhythm of its walk.

A bleakness and hopeless terror took grip of Wells' soul.

Door stumbled and slipped upon the slick of pine needles underfoot, sending his chief tumbling as he sought to catch his fall.

Clutched in Cilestine's arms, Viola screamed.

Despite himself, Wells froze, watching this incomprehensible horror of the deeps stride towards them, and some small, removed part of him wondered matter-of-factly if he was finally done in.

There was a flash and a sharp crack. One of Sprawle's grenadoe detonated with a flat thump on the Shiggeloth's flank, engulfing the creature in a rapidly expanding deep red fizz.

The dark enchantment broke.

Wells scrabbled to stand. Helping Door to do the same, the sleuth made his own way up the cleft in the hill now, forcing his ungainly legs to move at pace with great agonising gyrations of hip, pulling himself along by his arms, too.

With a great whooping, fictlers appeared on the road far to left below, several dozen of them and more still sprinting in their long red robes, catching the party now that they were beset and their transport a ruin.

At the top of the cleft the rescuers found a long ridge that ran off southwest into further gloom. Achieving the higher ground, Cilestine put Viola into Door's care and without a parting word or a second look, veered away into the trees and down towards the fictlers. Regretting this last goodbye, Wells knew her intent, to take the fight to their pursuers and purchase them all some distance.

Its aberrant mouth wide with hooting rage, the Shiggeloth swatted at the foul air as Sprawle threw yet another grenadoe, slowed but coming on still, crashing through limb and trunk as if they were mere twigs in its increasingly maddened career.

From the left — beyond even the chasing fictlers — blared a sudden and shocking roar.

'What new horror has come to defeat us!' Sprawle cried angrily, pivoting, a third caste already in hand to hurl at this new threat.

Bearing down the knotty road, throwing trees of its own aside as it came, loped a second monstrosity half seen through the woods, a horned, bearded giant of hairy terrestrial aspect, heedless of the little fictlers running terrified from under its cruel cloven feet.

'The Gutterfear!' were the cries of the terrified helots of Sucoth.

Bellowing stentorianly like a beast defending its territory from a rival, this shaggy newcomer gave challenge to the smaller Shiggeloth. Thwarted, the famuli did not hesitate but turning aside from its pursuit, sprang nimbly from the height with appalling dexterity in a creature so large, and in that single bound grappled tremendously with the larger Gutterfear.

'Well I never ...' Wells breathed heavily in dread fascination, reprieved and vaguely aware of the reverberations of the shattering struggle quivering through his feet and bowed shins. 'Saved by a monster.'

Barely visible now among the trees, it seemed the Shiggeloth was trying to wrap its great vertical maw about its opponent's long-bearded head as if to swallow it whole. Smaller it might be, but more quick and cunning too, winding its quasi-tentacle arms about its foe, pinning the Gutterfear's arms to its mighty trunk. Staggering and writhing to get an advantage, the shaggy giant barked thunderously in dismay, its tiny glittering black eyes wide and rolling.

With profound yet rapid calm, Door placed Viola in Sprawle's care and kneeling, took aim with his longrifle and fired at the wrestling behemoths, striking the Shiggeloth upon its elongated crown.

The tiny sting of an insignificant wasp, this single frank shot still caused the sea-horror to recoil as if from a much mightier blow, loosing for a beat its grip on the Gutterfear. The shaggy defender took this merest chance and snatched the famuli by its unwrapping arms, tugging the Shiggeloth away. Grasping one of its triplicate legs, the Gutterfear lifted the squirming bulk high, bent it with a foul squelch deleteriously in two, and threw it back into the pines. The half-broken Shiggeloth fell with an astonishing crash that flattened entire trees and sent splinters bursting lethally all about. One such deadly sliver sped straight at Wells, striking him sharply on the right shoulder, and though its needle point was foiled by the excellence of his well-proofed frockcoat, its force smote him to the needle-matted ground. It was the Gutterfear's turn to pounce, scrabbling up the further slope to where the Shiggeloth even now was recovering with preternatural vigour. Pinning its enemy with its brawny calloused knees, the

Gutterfear reached far into the sea-monster's quivering mouth and with an inordinate wrench of his powerful arm, seemed to pull the Shiggeloth's insides out.

The surviving fictlers wailed at the overthrow of their adored one. Yet they were not undone, for even as Sprawle helped him to his feet, Wells could see the feather-crested leader below, rallying scores of his helots about him; he could hear the fellow calling for his brethren to forget their fallen prince and the now-feeding Gutterfear — Sucathës has many such servants — and seek the end of these ignorant defilers. In their raging distress, the fictlers threw themselves up the incline to overrun this arrogant handful who dared thwart the sacred venerations of their unhallowed lord, swarming around Cilestine who, skipping between black trunks, danced destruction amongst them. Despite her ferocity, a great host streamed up through the woods, cackling like crazed things, firing fusils and pistols at their prey.

From the cover of a knot of youthful pines sprouting from a tall statuesque boulder, the three men plied fire down from their advantage of height, felling several fictlers whose places were promptly taken by another, four score or more white masks coming on undaunted.

'We have certainly kicked the wasp's nest, haven't we,' Wells declared over the din, reaching out and firing his own long-barrelled pistol into the massing foe, striking a fictler square in their chest.

Hard hit, the fellow fell forward on hands and knees while his cult-mates stepped around him, shook himself and stood again.

'I think these dullards' humours are charged with more than mere nerves,' Sprawle returned as one of his own targets rose once more to come on. The lurksman tossed grenadoes amongst the advancing helots — one, two, three, popping in cruel gusts orange or mauve, felling maybe a dozen at a time; yet still their adversaries pressed forward, bawling in fury as they came.

At threat of being overwhelmed, Wells and his companions were forced again to flight, hurrying across the easier level of the ridge, the sleuth's legs an agony he could not afford to heed. Twice as they ran, Sprawle pivoted in an almost offhand manner to return fire; twice a fictler fell, never to rise again, while hidden now in the trees far behind and echoing through the hills, they could hear the Gutterfear still bellowing as if to challenge any other sea-born intruders to show themselves. Finally they came to a gap in the thick trees: the summit of another shallow gully, a natural drain for a spring that bubbled out from its subterranean flow and chuckled down to an ancient stone bridge and a proper road that curved away ahead.

'There!' Sprawle insisted, pointing to the cover of the bridge and a large monolith of dark rock to the right of it.

Partners with him on many a quest, his fellow adventurers did not quibble but scurried and skipped down the course of the runnel, while Sprawle held back. Worming a delaying primer into the new cracked neck of a grenadoe, he laid it in the bole of age-ed turpentine a little way down the furrow. Returning to the top of the ridge he made sure to catch the attention of their pursuers then ran off to the left. Some fictlers followed him, but most thought themselves too clever to be so simply fooled and led by their grammaticar continued on the path after Viola and her two guardians.

Scaling the footings of the bridge to the road, Wells and Door — Viola in arms again — took cover as best they could to wait for their comrades; the sleuth would rescue this girl, but not at the complete abandonment of his friends.

Placing Viola in the shelter of the boulder and covering her quaking, inadequately covered frame with his outer coat, Door knelt again in the shadow of the stone to load his longrifle. Levelling it on the gully, he waited. All too soon the fictlers showed themselves, the feather-crested grammaticar directing his minions to range out about him and flank their prey from the heights above the road, levelling their own firelocks to send balls spanging about

Door fired.

In the nick of time the grammaticar must have seen the flash in the pan, for the hateful figure veered sharply, avoiding the shot while a less fortunate helot stepping where he had just been, fell.

A clatter of hoof and cart sounded to the right and scuttling to hide behind the wall of the bridge, Wells aimed his hauncet ready to face whatever came. A simple donkey cart slewed about the acute bend beyond the crossing driven by a rather gaunt fellow with honest eyes but an ill-favoured face whose liniments were currently contorted in a grimace of panic. Under fire from fictlers on the ridge, the driver's battered copstain hat was set flying. *Better hat than head!* The companion who rode precariously beside him was facing the way they had come, flourishing and firing a pistol in each hand, and Wells instantly recognised the heavy drapes of Sprawle's scarlet hood.

Dear Sprawle!

A sudden flash and thudding report. The grenadoe at the summit of the gully detonated, engulfing a mass of fictlers, sending survivors reeling away, silencing musket-shots for a breath.

'The timing of your fuse is as excellent as ever!' Wells cried to his friend and leapt up to grab at the bit strap of the nearest ass as the cart slowed on Sprawle's clear command. 'I see you have brought a jaunty fit to extract us from this stouche!'

The owner of the cart seemed none too pleased with such an arrangement, yet an angry retort from Wells seemed enough to cause him to turn a more agreeable cheek. He was a peculiar fellow, this smudgy cart driver; lies and truth swept in turn over his visage like the swell on a shore, yet his shrewd gaze spoke of a forthright soul.

A shriek from the rise of the gully heralded the return of egret-masked Cilestine, the surviving Pail sister dashing about the spreading fume of Sprawle's grenade, came dextrously down the slope to her comrades. Plainly thinking her a foe, the cart driver drew forth a heavy volley gun of seven barrels, only to be stopped by Sprawle before he could do any more harm. Battered and bleeding, the sagaar returned to them as one come back from the dead.

'There are more,' the sagaar breathed heavily, taking a moment, sipping

'Then let us take this jink out of here,' Sprawle declared, moving to alight in the cart.

In an abrupt act of compliance the cart driver helped Door to lift Viola in his humble transport, making room in the oddly odiferous tray of his cart for them all.

'Well done, sir,' the sleuth declared, introducing himself quickly. 'How is it you are here?'

'Fetching stooks,' the man said — a patent lie.

Despite this Wells let himself be handed hastily to the seat next to the troubled driver. He caught one glimpse of the long notched iron pole, the folded winch-frame and several species of spade in the fellow's cart-tray and fathomed exactly the nature of his trade. Here was a corser. In any other circumstance the sleuth would have avoided such a man, but need drove and whatever qualms he might have, here was not an occasion for them. They did at least among the dark trades, have a code of ethics; their hinge, or whatever it was called.

'Come on, my chums,' Bunting growled, spying white masks skulking yet in the gloom at the summit of the wooded gully. 'I don't want to die out here!'

No sooner were the five clambered aboard than the cart lurched to a start.

'Fear not, my man!' Wells returned with forced flippancy to the cartman as he clutched his hat to head. 'If you're born for the gibbet, you'll never drown.'

With a shake of his head Bunting snorted darkly, flogging poor Hammer to set a better pace for Anvil.

Not a moment too soon. Fictlers dashed across the heights on the left in an attempt to outflank the escapees, firing vigorously on them, balls smacking the frame of the cart and slapping painfully on good proofing.

'How many are there!' Bunting cried.

Too intent on their pursuit, on reloading Sprawle's pistols, Wells did not answer, yet wondered the same himself. White masks were everywhere on the slopes behind, undaunted and unrelenting. *How gravely I have underestimated them*, the sleuth berated himself bitterly. An idiot fringe they might have been in social reckoning, but these fictlers were a genuine and organised threat.

First one ball then another struck Door. He fell back with a huff among the obscured bundles of corpses, his proofing saving him from immediately mortal harm. Shaking himself, the hefty fellow simply sat up, levelled and fired, piercing a fictler sprinting along in plain sight through the eye-slot of his mask. In a patter of returning shot, Door coolly reloaded and fired again, bringing an end to another foe.

Still the implacable fictlers came on.

Leaping abruptly from the cart, Cilestine gave a parting glance to her comrades — there would be no returning for her this time. Rapidly she scaled the ridge to the heights on the right and crisscrossed back through the trees. They lost sight of her in the woods, but her angry screeching shouts rang out through the folds of land over the racket of the dashing cart.

Careering about one turn then another, they picked up pace as the gradient of the road steepened and the pursuit seemed to falter. Bunting kept his donkeys at pace, too far was not far enough from such dire mayhem.

'You always in such straights?' he called over the racket of their haste to the one named Wells, juddering along on the seat beside him.

The stunt fellow seemed a mite put out by this. 'No, as it happens,' he returned rather tightly. 'Today has been especially hard … Do you always venture out to such awkward places to find corses?'

Wells peered over his darkened spectacles and Bunting had a brief sight of the weird blue-on-red eyes of a falseman.

Bunting suddenly felt rather trapped. 'I —'As true as he tried to be to the hinge, it would never be true enough for such a fault-spotting chap as rode with him now. *How low can my days drop?*

Of a sudden, Wells pitched forward from his seat by Bunting, clutching his neck, gore sputtering through the man's oddly elegant fingers. Bunting tried to grab at him without losing grip of the reins but Wells fell from his seat to the road, the hurry of the cart quickly leaving him behind.

Sprawle would have none of this. 'Girl be dashed!' he seethed and sprang down from the back of the cart and ran to his stricken friend.

Glancing about wildly, Bunting caught a glimpse of some grand-looking fictler standing on a rock behind, his thricehigh splayed with gaudy feathers and a musket in hand. 'How did they catch us so fast!' The corser slowed.

'Leave!' Wells barked angrily, sprawled on the dirt, spitting dark thick blood. 'Go, Mister Door! Go! Return her … to her mother … GO!'

Fictlers caterwauled in the trees.

'GO!' the one called Door cried, the agony clear in his stifled voice but obedient none-the-less, urging Bunting onwards.

Whipping reins cruelly, the corser set Hammer and Anvil back to their ungainly gallop, the girl, Viola, cringing in the jumble of stooks and covertly wrapped corses, pressing herself into the corner of the cart-tray below and beside him. Merciless in his fear, Bunting kept his beasts at their jaunting pace, looking back to see Sprawle standing in defence over his friend, throwing a caste high and long at the oncoming fictlers, then stand and deliver with his pistols.

Sobbing, Door loaded and fired, loaded and fired from the back of the cart — each shot a kill, yet to little avail as the massing fictlers jumped from all points along the road and closed about the still flailing Sprawle and Wells surely dying on the road.

Abruptly the road about them erupted in a great magenta cloud obliterating all sight of the rushing foe, and the desperate end of those bizarre fighting men.

Viola shrieked.

A handful of fictlers or more were running along the right-hand bank, keeping impossible pace with the jauntily speeding cart.

'How do they run so fast!' Bunting cried as he lashed his poor team to greater exertions. Long had he striven to preserve his own hide and he was not about to lose it in such a meaningless fashion.

Just as the cart was pulling ahead, the fictlers veered and sprang from the bank at them. Door's musket spoke and one masked adversary fell in mid-spring. Another misjudged and struck hard the side of cart, falling to the road where the right wheel jolted shockingly as it rode over the hapless fellow. Yet four of the mindless cultists had succeeded in their aim, landing in the tray of the cart or gaining a hold on its side. Two collided squarely with Door, the three toppling together onto the bundles of corse and twigs. The franklock twisted mightily in their corporate grip, striking one fictler savagely before being stunned as the second tore the sthenicon from his face and felled him under a whirl of blows of knife and handle.

A white mask loomed all too close and Bunting was clutched rudely about the throat. A pale knife blade danced before his face; 'No one violates the sanctuary of Sucathës the Devourer and lives!'

hissed in his ear. From the corner of his popping flickering vision as the wind was choked from him he could see the fourth fictler struggling with Viola, trying to heave her out of the tray. For a wee lass she put up a prodigious fight.

'I haven't violated nothing, ye hackmillion sprattling!' Bunting spat.

Letting go the reins, the corser grasped the knife-wielding hand and gripped the hold about his throttle[1], and pulled — a life of digging up the dead got you nothing if not great strength of arm. In the scant reprieve, the corser snatched up his heptibus and thrusting its muzzle backwards under his arm into what he presumed was his assailant's belly, discharged all seven barrels at once. The clutching at him vanished as the fictler was flung savagely out of the cart.

Pivoting in his seat, the corser could see that Viola was overcome, the fictler even now lifting her to toss her over the side. Yet the vile fellow's ambitions were brought instantly to nil as the butt of the heptibus stove in the back of his cranium.

As if realising he alone was left, the last fictler looked up, bloodied knife poised above its masked head. With a harrowing growl, Door bloodied and half-broken, snatched the cultist by his collars and with a great heave of his legs, flipped the fellow up and out of the cart, sending him toppling and crashing down the bank of the stream on the left.

'Get her home to her ma,' Door wheezed, pierced by many wounds despite the quality of his proofing, and lying terribly still amongst the morbid wrack.

Needing no second invitation, Bunting drove Hammer and Anvil like a wild thing, the cart shaking violently, tipping dangerously on the sharper bends, driving on and on until the sounds of battle were far behind. Only when they were clear of the darksome knotty path and Viola's shuddering sobs had subsided as she tended the ailing lurksman, did Bunting ease his donkeys' pace. Yet seeing phantoms of white-masked faces in every nook and shadow, he did not stop, not at the descent of evening nor at the fall of night to get in and away from

---

[1] throat

monstrous night-lurking threats as was common practice, not even to find poor Door better care. *Them fictlers could get us yet!* No, he kept steadily on, pausing only to give the donkeys brief respite. It was only when they trod at last in broader downs and more regularly settled lands that he felt that they were properly safe and relented. It was here that he found that the fellow called Door was dead.

A windfall addition to my toll at least, Bunting thought dismally.

'W-what has become of them?' the girl had asked yet again of her saviours.

But Bunting had no reply. Surely the fate of those brave, done-for fellows was clear …

'We should go back!' she persisted.

However right she might have been, they had won free by such slim margins there was scant chance Bunting would actually act on such compunctions. How he wished there was a guide to follow, a set of accepted conduct to ascribe to and ease his misgivings, but there was none that he knew of and the hinge was no use to him here.

Unanswered, the girl lapsed to silence and eventually to sleep.

Still Bunting drove on under a misted veil of silent stars, his mind turning, turning, turning upon the hinge, upon his debt, upon this sorry juncture of his life.

My neck or another's …?

He looked sidelong at the slumbering girl.

Would her parents grant him a prize or other monetary distinction if he passed the girl back to them? That Wells chap had said nothing on it before he was overtaken by doom, and Bunting had had little joy in his dealings with the higher crusts of society. He scratched his chin ruminatively. The final item on his toll turned like an unwelcome song through his thoughts …

1 of the female kind, a child of elder years, scarce beddened.

Curled against him was just such a one.

Shivering even in sleep under the borrowed coat of a man violently dead, Viola Grey could never reckon on her second-hand rescuer's unsmiling contemplations.

In the glow of dawn they approached a thickly wooded junction in the south-running cartway while wagtails in the trees above chortled their welcome to the day. Here, the corser halted in an agony of choice. Head hanging he remained motionless for the longest time, eyes closed, hands clasped in his lap. Finally he looked up and peered at the lightening land.

He had made his choice.

With a flick of the reins, Bunting Faukes, corser and perpetual wayfarer, urged his two faithful donkeys to take a left turn and the road back to Brandenbrass.

AFTERWORD

'The Corsers' Hinge' is set in the very same place in which the Monster-Blood Tattoo series occurs, the Half-Continent. 'Hinge' explores the lives and dilemmas of several ordinary people in, what is for them, their common struggle to live and breathe in such a place where corpse-trafficking and monster-hunting are the norm.

My gratitude to Tiffany, my wife, and Will and Mandii, my friends, for reading drafts, the Clare for joining me in the journey, and Jack and Jonathan for letting me take part.

— *D.M. Cornish*

Ian Irvine is a marine scientist who has developed some of Australia's national guidelines for the protection of the marine environment and still works in this field. He has also written twenty-six novels. Ian's three Australian and UK bestselling fantasy series, The View from the Mirror, The Well of Echoes and Song of the Tears have sold a million copies and are published in many countries and languages. He has also written a near-future eco-thriller trilogy about catastrophic climate change, Human Rites (recently revised), plus twelve books for children in the Runcible Jones, Sorcerer's Tower and Grim and Grimmer series. His next fantasy novel is *Vengeance*, Book 1 of The Tainted Realm.

Tribute to Hell:
A Tale of the Tainted Realm

IAN IRVINE

Greave was sliding between the thighs of his god's forthcoming month-bride, exulting at the conquest, when an icy finger went where no finger had gone before and a wintry voice said, *Have you heard the one about the definition of savoir-faire?*

Greave had often told the joke, smugly implying that he was that very master. An inveterate seducer, he prided himself on his self-possession, but it eluded him now. The irony did not.

Go on, then. Complete the deed.

Not for anything could Greave continue, and now he felt the young woman grow cool beneath him. Then cold. Then freezing; the god had frozen her solid.

Her fate will be echoed by every woman you touch, said his god, K'nacka, *until you have paid for your crime and redeemed yourself. To ensure you do, I hold hostage your little sister, the one person you care about more than yourself.*

'What must I do?' said Greave, fighting to remain calm despite the absurdity of his position. He glanced over his shoulder. The god had the form of a round-bellied man, a plump, jolly little fellow, save for the agate in his eyes.

In the High Temple, on the Altar of the Seven Gods, there is a Graven Casket.

Spikes closed around Greave's fluttering heart. 'The most precious treasure of the temple. You want me to steal it.'

No mortal may approach the casket and live. However, there is one tiny instant of time when this spell fades and a man at the end of his rope may draw near. The day after tomorrow, at precisely the fifth hour after midday, you will open the casket and take out what lies inside.

'The casket is sealed,' said Greave. 'It can only be opened, and then but once, by the touch of a god —'

The touch of a god — but not a god, K'nacka corrected. He tossed down a pair of small bones held together by a silver wire. *These come from the little finger of a dead god. Touch the casket with a god-bone, it will spring open, and you may safely remove the contents.*

K'nacka vanished, leaving Greave frozen in place and knowing that the task was a trap. He had to do it, but he was not going to survive, and neither was his little sister.

Novice Astatine was lying awake, scratching some itchy specks on her stomach, when Abbess Hildy slipped into her cell.

'The gods are weakening,' intoned Hildy, 'while the power of the dark princes swells. Our lost souls wail so loudly that I sometimes recognise their voices — and they all lived *good* lives.'

Astatine shuddered. The abbess's ecstatic visions were always disturbing, but this was the worst yet.

'The more sainted they were in life, the louder they shriek,' Hildy said. 'Something is dreadfully wrong with the world.'

Ice was advancing from all sides on the island of Hightspall, the last surviving outpost of the empire, but that was not what Hildy was talking about. 'What did you see this time?' whispered Astatine.

'The wicked Margrave Greave is planning to open the Graven Casket. You must stop him.'

'Me?' Astatine choked.

'You will journey to the High Temple and prevent this dreadful insult to the gods. Our beloved K'nacka must be weeping at the insult.'

'But I've taken binding vows,' said Astatine, wringing her fingers under the covers. 'The corruption inside me must be cleansed.'

'You take too much upon yourself,' Hildy snapped. 'Your sins are insignificant.'

Astatine bowed her head. The abbess was wise, while she was a foolish, worthless novice. 'Abbess, I've left the wicked world for good; I can't go back.'

'You feel that the world abandoned you,' said Hildy, 'so you seek to escape it, and yourself, in closeted obedience.'

Astatine bit the tip of her tongue to prevent an angry retort. The other novices called her 'the mouse' because she was so timid; they did not realise that she was constantly suppressing the urge to bite. 'I merely serve my god's will.'

'I see a wilful arrogance in your subservience,' said Hildy. 'You seize on every duty, no matter how painful or demeaning, and never rest until it is done to perfection. You take pride in your suffering.'

'I offer it to my god. I merely serve my god —'

'You seek to eliminate your self, because the world is so painful to you that you can only think of escaping it.'

'I don't belong there,' Astatine said plaintively. 'Even here, I feel as though I'm living in the wrong body. The sickness I carry inside me has infected all Hightspall.'

Hildy slapped her face. 'Curb your presumptuous tongue, Novice.'

Astatine clutched the abbess's wrist. 'Tell me that our land is not sick and the common folk despairing. Tell me that the nobility aren't wasting their lives in debauchery because they no longer have hope. Tell me that our gods are strong, and love us.'

After a long pause, Hildy said gently, 'I cannot tell you any of those things. Hightspall *is* sick, the people despairing, our gods dwindling — but it has nothing to do with you.'

'Please, Abbess. If I go outside, I will surely break my vows.'

'Your first vow, and the greatest, is obedience,' said Hildy inexorably.

Astatine lowered her eyes. 'And I obey. But —'

'The vision I saw may also have gone to the Carnal Cardinal, Fistus.'

'He is a holy man of god,' said Astatine. 'He will protect the Graven Casket.'

'If the casket is opened, our beloved K'nacka will be in peril; he may fall.'

'*Fall?*' whispered Astatine. 'But the gods are almighty and everlasting.'

'Then fly! Stop this obscenity before it is too late.'

'Abbess … The Margrave Greave is a powerful man, a warrior who has never lost a fight. How can I stop him?'

The abbess thought for a while, then said, 'At the fifth hour after midday, on the day after tomorrow, you must duel with him and win.'

'He would kill me at the first blow.'

The abbess's eyes rested on Astatine's creamy, almost unblemished skin, her curvaceous form outlined against the bed bindings designed to prevent sins of the night. 'You will duel him with your weapons, not his.'

'I don't understand.'

'Surely you can't be that unworldly …'

A flush crept up Astatine's throat and blossomed into crimson. 'But my second vow —'

'Your vow of obedience comes first. If it is the only way to stop this dreadful sacrilege, you will break your second vow.'

'But … if I were unchaste, how could I come back?'

'Break that vow and you cannot come back.'

'And if I refuse?'

'Those who will not obey have no place here.'

'I'm doomed, either way.'

'You will be serving your god; what more can you ask?'

Astatine was silent.

'Swear that you will stop the margrave,' said Hildy.

'I'll *try* to stop him.'

'Swear that you will stop him, no matter what.'

The task was impossible, but Astatine had no choice. 'I swear that I will stop him. I will serve my god, no matter what it costs me. My life has no other worth.'

'Take this gown, and go at once,' said the abbess.

After Astatine had ridden out on one of the abbey's mules, Hildy said, 'And I pray you do break your vows for, devout though you are, you do carry corruption with you. You never belonged in this House of God.'

Roget came back from the bar with a flagon and poured a hefty slug into a glass. 'Get this down, before you fall down.'

Greave clutched his groin, wincing.

'What's the matter?'

'Frostbite.'

Roget chuckled. 'Even for you, that's a new one.'

Greave's chattering teeth broke a wedge of glass from the rim. He spat it out, gulped the liquor and wiped his bloody mouth. 'More!'

Roget cantilevered a wire-thin eyebrow but poured another large measure. After drinking it from the whole side of the glass, Greave's eyes met his friend's.

'I don't think I'll ever be warm again.'

'Take your time. Was it Satima?'

Greave nodded stiffly.

'I warned you,' said Roget. 'What insane folly sent you after a god's month-bride? And K'nacka is the most jealous of all the gods. But that's why you seduced her, isn't it?'

Greave did not reply.

'You've had the most beautiful women in the land yet you're never satisfied. I hate to say this, but it's time you settled down.'

'What for? The ice advances across land and sea. Soon it will crush Hightspall out of existence.'

'Not in our lifetime.'

'And our gods are declining; they've abandoned us.'

'Don't speak heresy,' said Roget, uneasily. 'Greave, you live for pleasure, but do you ever find it?'

'Life is empty,' Greave muttered. 'The harder I go after anything, the quicker it turns into a mirage.'

'Like I say —'

'All I have left is the hunt. I can't give it up.'

'And every time you take greater risks.'

'I only feel alive when I risk everything. The pursuit is bliss, the act anti-climactic; the hangover, worse each time. I'm like a reluctant drunk — remorseful in the morning but back in the bar every night.' Greave picked up the flagon of raw spirits and, his teeth chattering on the neck, drained it.

'Hey!' cried Roget. 'That's enough liquor to kill a stallion.'

'Yet I'm stone-sober,' said Greave. 'And freezing inside.'

Now Roget was shivering. 'What did the month-bride do to you?'

'The moment I mounted her, she went cold.'

'Probably afraid, poor girl. I hope you took pity and sent her —'

'*Dead* cold. K'nacka froze her solid under me.'

Roget gaped. 'He appeared *in person?*'

Greave dabbed at his bleeding lip. 'And then —'

'No, you've gone too far this time,' Roget grated.

'*I didn't kill her.*'

'The moment you seduced the month-bride of a god, you doomed her.'

'The wench is dead; what does it matter?' Greave said carelessly.

Roget shoved his chair back and stood up. 'You were always reckless and self-centred, but you used to care, deep down. Who will you destroy next?' he said disgustedly. 'My sister? My *mother?*'

A deep, inner pain jagged through Greave; he clutched at his friend's coat. 'Don't go, please. I — I'm desperate.'

Roget sat down. 'You must be, to admit to it. Is there more?'

'*Her fate will be echoed by every woman you touch,* K'nacka said. On the way here, I glanced at a pretty girl in the street — just for a second, I swear — and frost appeared all over her clothes. If I lust after a woman, any woman, she'll be frozen to death. And there's worse.' He told Roget the rest.

Roget paled, glancing over his shoulder. 'The Graven Casket! Greave, I'm not a devout man; my sins are as numberless as the souls screaming in Perdition. But this is too much.'

'What can I do?' said Greave. 'A god has ordered me to open the casket —'

'Which is sealed until the End of Days.'

'Maybe these are the End of Days.'

'He's a trickster. It's a trap.'

'I know, but if I don't do it, my little sister dies. Roget, help me! There has to be a way out.'

'You think you can outwit a god? You're far gone, my friend. I suggest you make amends for your wicked life, then prepare to meet your fate.'

Astatine plodded the dusty track, holding the reins of her mule.

'I'm sorry, noble beast,' she said, rubbing it behind the ears. 'We've still a long way to go.'

Her feet were blistered but she made an offering of the pain, trying to divorce herself from it. Ever since becoming a novice she had attempted to eliminate her recalcitrant self, to become no more than a vessel and servant for her god, but self kept intervening.

A dust cloud appeared ahead and she headed for the trees. The mule resisted.

'Come on. I don't want to be seen.'

It turned its head, studying her with hazel eyes.

'I want no part of the world's temptations,' she muttered. 'My god is everything and I am nothing. I exist only to serve.'

The mule's snort reminded Astatine of the abbess, who seemed to see right through her. She led the beast to a rivulet and bathed her aching feet. Pain is also nothing, she told herself. Yet as she probed her broken blisters, tears sprang to her eyes.

She dashed them away, cursing her weak flesh, and knelt to pray for strength. But, as so often lately, prayer would not come.

'What am I to do?' she said to the mule. 'I can't *duel* this wicked margrave; can't stop him insulting the gods, even if I do break my second vow. He'll use me and I'll be cast out into the awful world, abandoned even by my god.'

She clutched her only possession, the silver prayer medal left in her hand when she had been given to the abbey. It was so worn that she had never been able to identify the god it represented, though she took it to be her beloved K'nacka.

Father, please help me find another way.

Lord, if no other way can be found, give me the strength to break my vow of chastity in your service.

Father, if my sacred vow must be broken, help me to endure the lustful margrave.

I am just your vessel, Lord. I have no worth other than to serve you. Whatever happens to me I will endure it joyfully, in your name.

But it was so very hard.

Greave bit down on a twig to prevent his teeth from chattering. It was a hot afternoon, yet thirty-four hours after the encounter with K'nacka he was still freezing inside.

'Ready?' said Roget. They were trying to look casual as they strolled through the maze of clipped shrubbery surrounding the High Temple.

'No.'

'It's but thirty minutes until the fifth hour.'

'I know. Go through it again.'

'The plan is simple. We enter as the noble pilgrims we are and I'll use my sorcerous arts to make a diversion. You'll run up, open the casket and snatch the contents. Then we run for our lives — and pray my spell holds.'

'There's bound to be a trap.'

'If so, we'll have to deal with it. What are you to do with the contents?'

'K'nacka didn't say.'

'Oh!' Roget said. 'What do you think that means?'

Greave did not answer. 'Hello,' he said, gazing at a small figure limping out from behind an arc of tea bushes. A hot gust blew back the cowl, tumbling her wavy black locks. 'It's a novice, and a pretty one.'

'Ahem,' said Roget.

'What?'

'Not even you would sink low enough to seduce a nun — *would you?*'

'I seduced K'nacka's month-bride. They don't come any lower than me.'

A reckless urge swelled, a lust to possess her no matter the consequences, and even here, *even now*, Greave could not deny it. He checked the sun; there was just enough time, master seducer as he was, to do the business before five. He licked his lips, cast a furtive glance at his friend, then turned towards her, putting on the smile that few women had ever been able to resist.

'Go for a walk,' he said over his shoulder. 'Fifteen minutes.'

'Greave, no!' hissed Roget.

The little novice stopped suddenly, raising one hand to her hair in astonishment, and Greave's inner ice moved south. He ignored it, for lust was searing along his veins and he only felt truly alive when life or death rested on the toss of a coin. Now he felt like a superman and, no matter the consequences, he had to have her.

'Her hair's frosting over,' hissed Roget, jerking Greave back by the collar. 'Look away before you kill her too!'

Greave tried to pull free. 'I don't care. I've got to take her.'

'Even if it costs you your little sister?' Roget snapped.

It broke through the madness where nothing else could have and, with a wrench, Greave turned away. Now he could no longer see the novice, he was sickened by his depravity. 'Let's get on.'

After a day and a half away from her abbey, Astatine felt bruised. The world was strange and uncomfortable, the people unfriendly, the beasts of the forest savage. All she wanted was to fly home, close the great doors behind her and never look outwards again. But she had sworn to the Abbess.

Two noblemen stood in a gap in the maze not far ahead, talking. The tall one turned, staring at her, and her hair crackled — *it was covered in frost.* Astatine stopped, hand on her head, not understanding what had happened. But her time was running out; the fifth hour was almost upon her. She limped towards them, clutching the medal.

Lord, give me strength.

The dark-haired, wiry fellow was scarred like a duellist, though he did not look unkind. The other man — the Margrave Greave — was tall and broad-shouldered. Big feet, big hands. Not handsome; his mouth was too full, his nose a fleshy, sensuous monument …

Father, help me to do this dreadful thing.

Momentarily the medal warmed in Astatine's hand, then cooled again. Her prayers would not be answered.

She rubbed her pale cheeks to redden them, which would, apparently, make her more enticing, then shrugged off the novice's habit. The gown Hildy had given her was modest, yet Astatine's gorge rose at the thought of what she must do, and her vow of chastity burned as if etched into her skin.

The noblemen turned abruptly and headed towards the temple. The hour was nearly upon her: if she could not stop them her god would be profaned, her oath broken, and she condemned to a world she wanted no part of.

'Wait,' she croaked, but her voice did not carry. 'Lord Greave!' Astatine jerked the front of her gown down as far as it would go and ran after them.

They stopped. Greave half turned, his eyes lowered, and Astatine felt frost settle on her hair again. He was a dangerous man.

His friend came down and blocked her path. 'I'm Roget. Can I help you, sister?'

'I must speak to Lord Greave,' she said breathlessly. 'It's urgent.'

'And so you shall,' said Roget, 'after he returns from worship.'

'Now!' cried Astatine desperately, 'before five o'clock!' She darted around him and was running towards Greave, her bosom bouncing, when her breath froze in her throat.

He was staring at her cleavage, lust a forest fire in his eyes, and the cold intensified. As he tore his shirt open, pains like growing needles of ice shot through her toes.

'Greave! Remember your sister!'

Greave choked, spat out bile. 'My soul is black, little novice; I must be shriven at once.' He covered his face, turned and fell to his knees on the sharp rock.

Roget whipped off his cloak and wrapped it around Astatine so tightly that she could not move. The frost began to melt, sending icy trickles down the back of her neck, though she remained frozen inside. She had lost.

'You said *five o'clock*,' he hissed. 'Who betrayed us?'

'I don't know what you're talking about.' Astatine tried to hold back tears of despair.

He touched his sword to her breastbone. 'Who sent you?'

She had always believed that she would be glad to die serving her god, but she so wanted to live.

'The abbess saw Lord Greave in an ecstatic vision. Please, you must stop him from committing this dreadful sacrilege.'

Roget sheathed the sword. 'Who are you?'

'I'm nobody. The Abbess ordered me to stop Lord Greave, and I swore I would ...'

'At the cost of your other vows?'

'No matter the cost.' Astatine blushed.

Roget sheathed his sword, cursing. 'We'll have to take her with us.'

Greave rose, looking the other way. His gashed knees were bloody. 'Send her home, Roget. There's a demon on my back, driving me to have her.'

'If we leave her here, Fistus's priests will torture the truth out of her. Come on.'

As Roget dragged Astatine along, she was frantically trying to think of a safe way to stop Greave. But there was only one way now.

'It's too easy,' Greave muttered as they passed through the open doors. 'Where are the guards?'

Apart from a scatter of kneeling worshippers, the candle-lit temple was empty. The altar was a slab of yellow travertine ten yards by six. The Graven Casket, a tarnished, dirty silver box, sat in the middle.

'I don't like it either,' said Roget, who was a pace behind, keeping Astatine out of his friend's sight. He held her arm. 'You won't make a sound, will you?'

'No,' she whispered.

'Got the bone, Greave?'

He nodded stiffly.

Roget cast a minor spell, forming a billowing halo of mist around them. 'Go!'

Greave ran, knowing that he'd entered a trap of K'nacka's making. He was probably going to die unpleasantly and by the manner of his death ruin his family's noble name, but there was no way out.

'Look out! yelled Roget, drawing his sword. The worshippers had cast off their cloaks to reveal red tunics — warrior monks.

With a despairing cry, Astatine darted for the altar. She must be planning to throw herself upon the casket, Greave thought, sacrificing her life to prevent him opening it.

A pang of remorse struck him, an unfamiliar feeling he had no time to analyse. As she scrambled up the front of the altar he vaulted onto it from the side, landed on his bloody knees and skidded across the polished stone. The hour was five o'clock, so a man at the end of his rope could approach the casket, but if he touched it he would die.

Astatine crouched on the altar, her lips moving in prayer. She looked up suddenly and Greave did too, for the shadows below the high roof were thickening. Something was forming there.

Swords clashed below them; Roget was fighting three monks at once. Another half dozen were advancing on the altar, and from a door to his left a crimson-clad man appeared, the Carnal Cardinal. Fistus's face was hungry, his eyes hooded, and the full-lipped, greedy mouth was as red as his gown.

Greave drew the god-bone from his pocket, but fumbled and dropped it. As he snatched it out of the air, several of the hairs on his arm passed through a milky nimbus surrounding the casket and the pain was like being impaled on a body-length spike. He screamed.

The novice rose, staring at him, but as he met her eyes, frost whitened her hair and gown. Her gaze slipped to the casket, she swallowed, then tensed. Even after witnessing his agony, she was going to do it.

'Use the damn bone!' bellowed Roget.

Under the roof, the shadows continued to thicken — K'nacka was coming. As Astatine tensed, Greave's right arm jerked towards the casket. This is the trap, he thought. The god will get whatever is inside, and I'm going to die in agony.

He flinched and tried to draw back. Better the novice die than him; what did one nun matter, more or less? But his arm kept stretching, his fingers reaching out, and, as she moved, the god-bone touched the top of the casket.

As Astatine dived, K'nacka materialised high above. The temple shook; the ground rumbled and cracks jagged across the paved floor.

The lid of the casket sprang open, sending the god-bone soaring. She was too late. The nimbus went out, then her hands caught the casket and she tried to slam the lid.

She did not die; she felt no pain at all, but the lid would not close and now the casket was bouncing and tumbling beneath her as the altar shook ever more wildly. Astatine tried to hold it, sobbing with terror, but the outside was slippery with soot. She looked into the open casket and froze.

K'nacka arrested in mid-air, plump legs swinging ten feet above her. *Where is the Covenant?* he wailed, then vanished.

Astatine let go. The casket snapped shut and the deadly nimbus reappeared.

Fistus, whose eyes had not left the tumbling god-bone, caught it left-handed. 'Abbess Hildy is behind this sacrilege,' he said to his guards. 'You know what to do.'

Roget raised his hand, the candle flames pinched out, and Astatine bolted. She had broken her oath and let down her god. After she told the abbess, she would be cast out.

Greave pounded through the maze into the forest beyond, running until the full horror of his defeat caught up with him, when he slumped onto the mouldy leaves. There was no way back this time.

'Fistus knew we were coming,' said Roget, panting. 'He was waiting for the god-bone.'

'I've been manipulated from the beginning,' said Greave.

'Don't blame Providence for your own flaws! We'd better get moving,'

'What's the point? I've lost everything.'

Not yet. But you will if you let me down again.

Greave felt that icy finger again, though this time K'nacka was ten yards away, perched on a low branch. His belly was shrunken to a pot, his plump cheeks sagged and his eyes darted like rats pursued by a ferret. But he was still a god; he could snuff out Greave's little sister with a snap of his pudgy fingers.

'What must I do, Lord?' said Greave.

The casket was empty. The novice must have stolen the contents for the abbess. She has insulted the Seven Gods and profaned our High Temple. Swear that you will recover the contents then burn the abbey, with everyone inside it, as a sacrifice to me.

Greave felt sick. He too had insulted a god; he too had profaned the temple, and whether he committed this terrible crime or not, he was also going to die.

Swear, on your sister's life.

He hesitated no longer. His sister was all he had left. Besides, how could he oppose the will of a god? 'I swear.'

When Greave reached the abbey he discovered Astatine in its chapel, kneeling before the icons of the Seven Gods in the semi-dark and praying, with quiet desperation, for forgiveness. Exhaustion had temporarily quieted his lust, so he half-shuttered his lantern and examined her sidelong. He could not allow the curse to freeze her until he learned the truth.

She looked young, innocent and afraid, and his heart went out to her, but he hardened it. Astatine had claimed that she wanted to prevent his sacrilege, then had committed a worse one. She was a liar and a thief, and the choice between her life and his little sister's was no choice at all.

'Where is it, Novice?'

She jumped. 'Where's what?'

'Whatever was in the casket.'

She wrung her interlocked fingers. 'It was empty save for some flakes of ash.'

'Liar! It can only be opened with a god-bone.'

'Someone must have opened it with a different god-bone.'

'If they had, it would not have opened for mine.'

Greave searched her, roughly, knowing he was hurting her, though she maintained a stoic silence, her gaze fixed on the icons. He found nothing, though of course she was only a novice. The abbess would have the contents now.

He picked up the lantern but put it down again. He had sworn to torch the abbey, and could not defy his god, but neither could he bear to think of the little novice being burned alive. Far better that she die swiftly and painlessly here.

As he drew his knife, Astatine turned towards him. Frost had formed all over her, yet her eyes were unflinching in the face of death and it shook him, for he could not have done the same. He cursed; though he was a heartless seducer and a blasphemous oath-breaker, he was not a murderer.

In a frenzy of despair he slashed his chest, spilling his blood before the icons. It was the best sacrifice he could make, though he knew it would not appease K'nacka. He was standing over Astatine, his blood dripping from the knife, when the abbess opened the door.

'And I thought you'd already plumbed the depths.'

The Abbess's voice dripped contempt; evidently she thought he had killed the novice. Hildy limped across and struck at him with her cane, but as he turned to protect himself she stumbled and his knife slid into her side.

Greave felt such a pain that the blade might have pierced his own flesh, but he fought it down. The god had given him an order and he had to obey. 'Where are the contents of the casket?'

'I swear by the Seven Gods that the casket was empty,' said Hildy, holding a hand to the wound. 'Now get out!'

As Greave stumbled away, his lantern shaking, Hildy pulled Astatine close. 'Listen carefully. I've had another vision, a worse one.'

The smell of blood was overpowering; unless the bleeding was stopped, the abbess would die. 'Please, Hildy, sit down. Let me bind the wound.' Astatine tore a strip from her habit and pressed it against the gash.

'Hush, little sister; it's too late for me, but the fate of Hightspall lies in the balance and only you can save it.'

'I'm just a novice. I don't know anything.'

'You're the one person I can trust.'

And yet you're throwing me out. 'W–what did you see?'

In the gloom, Hildy's old face was a crumpled rag, her eyes dying embers. 'A dreadful Covenant between K'nacka and Behemoth, the Prince of Perdition —'

Astatine cried out in disbelief, for Behemoth hated the gods and everything she believed in. But then she remembered K'nacka shouting, *Where is the Covenant?* 'Abbess, K'nacka and Behemoth are the bitterest of enemies — *aren't they?*'

'Oh, yes. Eternal enemies.'

The pad was red with blood. Astatine dropped it and made another. 'What does the Covenant say?'

'I dare not speak the words. Only K'nacka and Behemoth know where it is hidden, but if it is ever revealed, it will be the end of the gods.'

That thought was unimaginable; abandonment multiplied a thousand times. 'The gods are almighty and everlasting,' Astatine chanted.

'If only they were,' Hildy whispered.

'Abbess?' said Astatine, alarmed now.

'Why do you think Hightspall has grown so wicked and depraved these past twenty years; why no one cares any more?'

Because of the corruption I carry inside me, Astatine wanted to say, but that would only earn her another slap. 'Hightspall is the last island left of the old Empire, and the ice is coming to end us.'

'Stupid girl! It's got nothing to do with the ice. The balance has been tilted — the gods are waning, while Perdition grows ever stronger and, if this Covenant is revealed, must soon topple Elyssian.'

Astatine could not come to terms with such talk. The gods had always dwelt in Elyssian, and they were eternal. 'What can *I* do?'

'You must find this wicked Covenant and, without reading it, destroy it. Swear that you will do so.'

'Please don't make me leave the abbey.' Astatine felt as though she was being torn apart.

'By the morning, there will be no abbey.'

The pain grew so bad that she struggled to think clearly. 'But … what if I can't find the Covenant?'

'You must swear,' said Hildy, becoming so agitated that blood surged through the pad.

'I — I swear.'

Outside, people were shouting. Weapons clashed and Astatine heard the roar of fire. She ran to a window, then back to the abbess. 'It's the Red Monks. Fistus is burning the abbey.'

'My time is up,' said Hildy. 'Astatine, when I took you in as a little girl —'

At the far end of the chapel, a window was smashed and blazing sheaves of oil-soaked straw arced in, trailing brown billows. Astatine scrambled to her feet but Hildy pulled her down.

'Abbess?'

'You weren't abandoned on the doorstep, newborn. The abbey was paid handsomely to take you in, and threatened with ruin if I revealed your origins. But now it is lost, you must know.'

Astatine could not take that in. 'What will become of me?' she cried. 'I've nowhere to go.'

'You must make your own way in the world, little sister.'

'But I'll infect it with the sickness I carry around with me.'

'Don't start that again,' snapped Hildy. 'It is a particularly offensive form of arrogance to assume that the world's ill's could come from one so innocent as yourself.'

Astatine bit her lip. 'Where can I go? Hildy, who were my parents?'

'I never knew your mother's name, but she's long dead.' Hildy began to pant. Astatine, trying to staunch the ebbing blood, was afraid the abbess would never speak again, but then she whispered, 'Your father brought you here. He was a demon out of Perdition.'

'No!' Astatine gasped. 'Who?'

'I'm afraid it was … Behemoth.'

Her god's enemy. 'It can't be,' whispered Astatine, choking with horror.

'He brought you here,' said Hildy. 'And because of the link between you and him, if anyone can find the Covenant, you can. Stop whimpering! Before I die I must pass my gift to you. Lean forwards.'

Astatine did so, numbly. How could it be true? Demons were dark, yet she was pale. And she was petite, so how could the mighty Behemoth be her father?

Hildy gripped the sides of Astatine's head, strained, and agony sheared through her skull. The abbess's hands fell to her chest. 'The stigmata —'

Instinctively, Astatine inspected her own hands, though they were unmarked. When she looked up, Hildy was dead.

A hot wind shrieked through the broken window, swirling the smoke around her. Her head was throbbing so badly she could not see. Astatine crawled off, but did not get far before she was overcome by the smoke.

'Once again, Greave, fortune has saved you from damnation,' said Roget as he carried an unconscious Astatine away from the burning chapel. Behind them, a horde of red-gowned monks was torching the abbey outbuildings under Fistus's direction. 'Truly, you must be intended for great things.'

'I swore a mighty oath,' said Greave dully, 'but I was too weak to hold to it.'

'It was an evil oath, made under compulsion. Breaking it proves there is yet some good in you.'

'I seduced K'nacka's month-bride!' cried Greave, sick with self-loathing. 'Now I've let down my god, slain the sainted abbess and doomed my little sister. I'm worthless.'

'Then redeem yourself!' snapped his friend. 'Here, carry the novice.'

'I'll destroy her too.'

'Just don't look at her,' said Roget, enveloping Astatine in his cloak. 'If you do, I swear I'll run you through.'

Greave was thankful for the darkness, for the soft weight in his arms was temptation enough. Had he been able to look on Astatine's lovely face, nothing could have saved her, or himself.

Hours later they hid among the tumbled boulders on a barren hilltop and he lay her down.

'Sleep, little one,' said Roget, putting a minor charm on her.

They sat watching the distant flames until, not long before a chill and windy dawn, the abbey had been reduced to cinders. As the sun rose, the cavalcade of red-clad monks rode away.

'Fistus isn't going back to the city,' said Roget. 'He's heading into the drylands. I wonder why?'

'I couldn't give a damn.' Greave stretched himself on the hard ground and closed his eyes, knowing there would be no sleep for him.

'He's going to work a miracle!' Astatine sat up so abruptly that she whacked her head on the pebbly overhang.

The headache came shrieking back, then the smoke, the crackle of fire and the abbess dying beside her. Astatine groaned and opened her eyes to find herself alone on an arid hilltop scattered with boulders of conglomerate.

Boots grated on grit and Roget appeared, breathing heavily. Greave was close behind.

'Did you call out?' said Roget.

'I saw the Carnal Cardinal,' said Astatine.

'What, here?' Greave said sharply, eyes averted.

'In a dream.' She rubbed her throbbing forehead, realising that she had not been dreaming, for the images remained clear in her mind. 'No, it must have been Hildy's gift.'

Greave swung around. 'What are you talking about?'

Astatine jumped up and moved away, watching him warily. 'Before the abbess died, she passed her gift to me ...' What gift, though? Her ecstatic vision? 'She sees — *saw* things — bad things that might come true.' Like the evil Covenant Astatine had to find and destroy. 'And I just saw Fistus, clear as a raindrop.'

'When he caught the god-bone, he looked triumphant,' said Roget. 'Getting it mattered more to him than our sacrilege. What kind of a priest would act that way?'

'Perhaps one who seeks power for himself,' said Greave. 'What else did you see, Novice?'

'He was on a barren hill.' She looked around. 'A bit like this one —'

'There are a thousand barren hills in these badlands.'

'There was a huge, ruined shrine on top. It looked as though it had been hacked in two by a monstrous axe … one that had cut halfway through the hill itself.'

Greave and Roget exchanged glances. 'The Cloven Shrine,' said Roget, his fingers curling.

'I've never heard of it,' said Astatine.

'The truth was too shocking to be told. Few people know the story.'

'Fistus does!' Greave said darkly.

'The shrine was destroyed when the Great God, the original ruler of Elyssian, was defeated and cast down in the Second Coup. He crashed through the shrine, nearly splitting the hill in twain.'

'And died there?' Worms were dancing along Astatine's backbone.

'The Great God could not be killed,' said Roget. 'He could only die at his own hand and, in despair at being cast out of Elyssian, that's what he did.'

Astatine trembled. She knew about the First Coup, when Behemoth had rebelled, yet, inexplicably and at the moment of victory, turned his back on Elyssian and set up his own rival kingdom, Perdition. Was he behind the Second Coup? Were the gods passing away? Was that why the world was so sick?

'What "miracle" is Fistus planning?' said Greave.

'I don't know,' said Astatine. 'But I don't think he means to honour our gods.'

Assuming, of course, that they were still *her* gods. If she was half demon, maybe she had no gods. Astatine could not bear to think about that. The destruction of the abbey had left her empty and belonging nowhere. If her beloved gods had also been taken away, how could she exist?

She had to find the Covenant.

Dawn was breaking as they crept up the chasm cutting across the cloven hill. Greave kept his eyes fixed above him, for his curse had not abated. Twice the previous day he'd frozen Astatine's hair, and the second time he had only come to his senses when Roget put a sword blade to his throat. At times, Greave wished his friend had used it.

'How dare Fistus pretend to perform a miracle?' cried Astatine. 'Why don't the gods punish him for this insolence?'

Her child-like faith was an insult to his intelligence but Greave kept silent, not daring to further provoke the gods.

'They must be afraid,' said Roget uneasily.

'How can the gods be afraid of a mere man?' said Astatine.

'I don't know.'

'The way up isn't guarded. Do you think Fistus *sent* the vision to me?'

'If he's not afraid of the gods, how could he have any fear of us?' said Roget. 'He probably wants us to see his miracle.'

Greave wondered if the cardinal could be a bigger monster than himself, though it hardly seemed possible.

They reached the top at sunrise, eased behind the mounds of shattered rock and peered over. Fistus, his priests and monk guards had gathered on the far side of the elongated hilltop, before the Cloven Shrine. A ragged arc of believers encircled it, witnesses to the coming miracle.

'The priests are digging a trench,' said Astatine. 'What can they be doing?'

No one replied.

Astatine slipped away between the piled rocks, for Greave's brooding presence disturbed her, and what if his increasingly desperate self-control snapped? She also needed to be alone, to think.

Her faith, already undermined by what the abbess had told her, had been shaken to its footings. How dare the Carnal Cardinal attempt a miracle! If he had set himself above the gods he had sworn to serve, it was no wonder Hightspall had lost hope.

Would things get better if she destroyed the Covenant? Unfortunately, she had no idea where to look for something that a god and a demon had hidden. It could be anywhere.

No, not *anywhere*. K'nacka and Behemoth, being eternal enemies, would not have trusted each other, so the Covenant must have been hidden somewhere that neither could gain access to. Perhaps in the keeping of a third party agreeable to both, such as Fistus?

K'nacka had expected it to be in the Graven Casket, though the casket had not been opened before Greave touched the god-bone to it, and it had been empty … save for those flakes of ash. Black flakes — the way paper burned when it did not have enough air! Yes, for the outside of the casket had been covered in soot; it had come off on her fingers.

The Covenant must have been destroyed from outside, by fire, but by whom? Not K'nacka — he had been shocked to discover that the casket was empty. And what would Fistus have to gain by destroying such a valuable document? That only left Behemoth.

Why would he destroy a Covenant that, evidently, gave him power over a god? He would not — *unless he had another copy.*

'That's it!' she said, rubbing her silver medal furiously, though after Hildy's revelation about her father it gave her no comfort. 'It was Behemoth — Father —'

The air went so cold that it crackled, then with a little *pop* a man appeared, sitting cross-legged on the rocks before her. He was an odd-shaped, awkward-looking fellow not much taller than she was, with thin, short legs and a heavy, muscular body. His skin was dark, his head bald, his nose hooked, and the point of his beard jutted towards her like a javelin.

'You called me, Daughter?' His voice was so deep it might have been formed inside the hill; it reverberated like the throb of an organ pipe.

'You called me *daughter*,' she whispered. 'Are — are you really my father?'

Though she yearned for a father, a demon was the last father she could want. Besides, a mighty demon like Behemoth might have a thousand daughters; she might mean nothing to him. He was her god's enemy and had undermined everything she believed in. Astatine was too overcome to speak.

'You expected some great, hulking brute?' Fire flickered in his raised eyebrow. 'I prefer this form; both enemies and friends underestimate me. What do you want, Daughter?'

'Th–the Graven Casket was empty. What happened to the Covenant?'

'I gave Fistus the power he craved so desperately; in return, he allowed me to destroy it.'

He sounded convincing, but he was the Prince of Deceivers. 'Why, Father?'

'To make mischief.'

Astatine's entire life had been submission and obedience, but neither would serve her now. Dare she challenge the Lord of Perdition? Sweat dripped from her palms at the thought, not to mention that she owed her father respect. Could she put that obligation aside? She must. 'I — I don't believe you. I know you made a copy of the Covenant. Why, Father?'

Behemoth swelled enormously; his black eyes flashed and his left hand shot out, encircling her wrist like an icy manacle. 'How dare you question *me*? You are over-bold, Daughter.'

Astatine had never been bold; the other novices had mocked her as 'the mouse'. She wanted to scream and run, but reminded herself of her oath, and it stiffened her. She would keep her word to the Abbess, whatever it cost. The mouse had to bite.

She caught Behemoth's dark wrist with her pale hands, squeezed hard and, amazingly, he winced.

'You *are* my daughter,' he said, glowering at her. After shrinking to his former size, he resumed his seat.

'Well?' she said, pretending an imperiousness she could not feel.

'Life in Elyssian becomes tedious, when one faces an eternity of it. That's why I left and set up Perdition, though I was no more contented there.'

'But Elyssian is the epitome of perfection,' said Astatine, wide-eyed.

Behemoth rolled his eyes. 'Even reaping the souls of the wicked begins to pall, when one is the wickedest of all. There's no villainy I haven't done, Daughter, and tempting mere mortals into sin lost its joy long ago, In short, I was bored witless. And so, I discovered, was my enemy, your precious god, K'nacka.

'We took to meeting in Hightspall for a game of dice, each striving to best the other, and I won more often than I lost. But without something precious to lose, even gaming's charm fades, and the stakes grew ever higher until, finally, K'nacka had nothing left to put on the table. Nothing save a pound of his own flesh.'

'Father?' said Astatine, not understanding, though a chilly wave of horror surged through her. This was terribly wrong; she did not want to hear it.

'Having nothing else, he wagered one of his balls — and lost.'

'Balls?' Her cheeks grew hot.

'He should have known that *my* dice were loaded.' Behemoth's thick lip curled. 'K'nacka begged for another chance, double or nothing, and I was happy to dice again — as long as he signed a binding Covenant promising to pay tribute to Perdition if he lost the other ball.'

'A tribute of what?'

'A tithe of souls, the most perfect and saintly of all those who enter Elyssian. You can imagine how delightful I found that irony, Daughter. The harder that mortals strove to live good lives, the more likely they'd attract the attention of K'nacka and become part of his tribute to me. Good or bad, I'd reap their souls.' Behemoth grinned savagely. 'And I won. Suddenly, my life had meaning again.'

And this monster was her father? No wonder she felt that she had been carrying a sickness around inside her, infecting the world.

'Hildy said she could hear the shrieks of the saintly,' Astatine whispered. 'Oh, Father, how could you?'

'It's what I'm for. Hightspall needs me, and so do the gods. Without evil, where is the good?'

'But Hightspall is falling apart, and it's your fault. You've got to put things right.'

'I don't do *right*,' he snapped.

'Then why did you burn the Covenant?'

'So K'nacka could not.'

'Where did you hide the copy?'

His smile faded; he seemed to be reassessing her. 'In a place where you can never see it.' Behemoth faded away.

Did he mean that the Covenant was hidden in Perdition? Could she only destroy it, and keep her oath, by dying?

*   *   *

'Fistus looks ready to work his "miracle",' said Roget as they watched the preparations in front of the Cloven Shrine. A hundred red-robed monks stood guard to either side.

Greave ached for a drink. Stone sober, he lacked the courage to do what must be done. 'Can you tell what spell it is?'

Roget focused his spyglass. 'No, but it's no ordinary magic.'

Think of this as another seduction, Greave told himself, the riskiest and most glorious of your life. It got him to his feet, but he felt no thrill — this task was all risk and no reward. 'We'd better move.'

'Taking him on is suicide.'

'I'm dead either way.' Greave headed across the rock-littered hillside. Roget and Astatine followed.

The Carnal Cardinal turned to meet them, his mouth as red as a feeding vampire's. 'You think to challenge *me?*' Fistus pounded his chest. 'I've done a deal with Behemoth himself.'

'And betrayed the gods you swore to serve,' said Greave, only now realising his own hypocrisy.

'They've forsaken us and must be cast down.'

A white object in Fistus's hand reflected the light; something small, pointed and familiar. Ants scurried across Greave's scalp.

'The god-bone,' he said hoarsely. 'That's what you were after all along.'

'I used sorcery to whisper into your mind,' sneered Fistus. 'It was surprisingly easy to heighten your despair and encourage excesses your dull wits could never have imagined.'

'You *wanted* me to seduce K'nacka's month-bride?' whispered Greave.

'I knew he held the god-bone in Elyssian, though there it was beyond my reach. The only one way to get it was by giving K'nacka the means to destroy the Covenant — via a man at the end of his rope.'

'But you'd already allowed Behemoth to burn it.'

Fistus smirked. 'Poor, deluded K'nacka didn't know that.'

'How dare you set yourself up as a rival to the gods you swore to serve!' cried Astatine.

The hooded eyes fixed on her, but dismissed her as insignificant. 'My spells are greater than theirs,' said Fistus, 'yet are they recognised? The gods treat me like a churl.'

'They recognise your true nature,' Greave said recklessly.

Fistus's gory lips thinned. 'Get rid of them,' he said over his shoulder, then turned to a crude bench his priests had constructed from slabs of shrine stone. A large stone chalice stood on top, empty save for a small amount of grey powder. The trench they had excavated was half full of it.

The monks drove Roget, Greave and Astatine back, but did not attempt to harm them. Fistus wanted them to see his might, and despair.

'At least you know that his magic was behind some of the terrible things you've done,' said Roget.

'Is that supposed to make me feel better?' Greave said in a dead voice. 'To discover that I've been manipulated like a mindless fool? Besides, he didn't corrupt me — he only fed the sickness that was already there.'

'Without him, you might have come to your senses.'

'I don't think so,' Greave rasped. 'The hook had already bitten too deep, and there's only one way off it now.'

Fistus dropped the god-bone into the chalice, raised his hands and began the spell.

'Is the grey stuff the dead god's ashes?' said Astatine, peeping through her fingers.

'Gods, have mercy!' cried Roget. 'It's a *Resurrection* spell. But surely not even Fistus would dare —'

A whistling sound arose from all parts of the horizon and raced towards the hill, rising to a series of ear-rending screeches that collided, collapsed, then an utter silence, more unnerving yet, enveloped all.

The chalice quivered and burst, its contents billowing upwards in a grey plume which slowly pulled together to the form of a man, a giant almost the height of the Cloven Shrine, though the skin hung on him and his granite face was fissured with despair. A wound between his ribs ebbed red; the bloody blade dangled from his right hand.

Astatine gasped and fell to her knees. 'The Great God,' she whispered.

'Oh, this is monstrous,' said Roget. 'The Seven Gods must strike Fistus dead.'

As the Great God shambled forwards they saw chains linking his wrists and ankles, yet even shackled and weak from centuries of death he was a forbidding figure. Fistus cried out involuntarily and backed away, eyes darting.

'He's overreached himself!' said Roget. 'The Great God will splatter him like a gnat.'

'Either way, we're done,' said Greave.

Fistus stopped and his lips moved as if exhorting himself to stand firm, then he raised his hands for another spell.

'It's a two-part spell, resurrection and control,' said Roget. 'Now comes the control part. If he's quick, he might just do it.'

'No man can control a god,' said Astatine. Just speaking the words was blasphemous.

She took out her medal and began to rub it furiously but then, recognising the worn image on it as Behemoth, hurled it away. She began to twist her fingers together, then abruptly thrust them down by her sides, but she could not keep them still.

As the Great God attempted to turn aside the spell, he stumbled and it struck him on the right cheek. Howling in rage, he broke his wrist shackles and reached up into the low clouds. Thunder rumbled and the cloud boiled up into a thunderhead, incandescent with lightning. The sky went black. Astatine could not see. Lightning stabbed down at the Cloven Shrine, collapsing half of it; another bolt struck three of the priests dead. The remainder ran for their lives, though the red-gowned monks remained.

Fistus stood firm and cast the spell again.

'This is the end of the world,' said Roget. 'Whoever wins, priest or god, there'll be nothing left.'

'It's my punishment for seducing the month-bride,' said Greave, head bowed. 'And for a lifetime of depravity.'

Suddenly Astatine saw him from the other, tormented side. 'Not a lifetime, Lord,' she said gently. 'Just a time, and it's over now.'

'Too late. No one can undo this.'

There had to be a way but could Astatine, the little mouse, find it? She must — her gods needed help and she could not deny them.

I can't be a timid novice any longer, she thought. Demon's blood runs in my veins; my father is Behemoth, the Prince of Devilry, who once beat the Great God himself, then turned his back on Elyssian. I've got to do this!

'Yes, someone can.' Astatine backed away between the rocks. 'Father?' she called, her voice ringing out between the thunderclaps. 'Help us. If Fistus's spells can control a god, neither Hightspall, Elyssian nor even Perdition is safe.'

Behemoth appeared in the air before her, cross-legged as before. 'Daughter, I cannot interfere.'

'Why not?'

'A sacred compact forbids us. We can cajole, persuade, seduce, even threaten, but neither gods nor demons may act directly in the world.'

Was she to fall at the first obstacle? No; she summoned her demon blood, stood tall and curled her lip. 'I thought you were supposed to be *evil*!' she said, dripping scorn. 'Break the damn bloody compact.'

'I can,' he said, smiling at the mildness of her oaths, 'but would you call demons into Hightspall without the gods to balance us?'

Astatine paled. She had not thought of that. 'Do it!'

As Behemoth faded, she ran back to Greave, who was hunched over as if in pain. 'Lord Greave, you have a link to K'nacka. Call him down.'

Greave turned, his eyes unfocussed. 'K'nacka?'

'Yes, quickly.'

Greave rubbed his face with his hands, then called her god, who appeared at once. Had he been waiting for the summons?

Astatine's heart began to pound so furiously she feared it would tear free of its arteries. Her god, her god! But she had to be calm; there were only seconds left.

'Great K'nacka,' she said, bowing low. 'See what your servant Fistus has done? The Seven Gods must enter Hightspall and stop him before it's too late.'

There is a compact, little nun, said K'nacka.

'Break it!'

The gods do not break compacts. He glared at her as though she were a turd on his pillow.

'Perdition is going to.' She lowered her voice. 'Besides, I know where the Covenant is.'

His head jerked up, wobbling his jowls like twin jellies. *I've been told it was burned in the casket, long ago.*

'I have a perfect copy,' she lied, 'and if you're *afraid* to break the compact, I'll reveal the Covenant. The gods will become a laughing stock — and you will be cast down.'

K'nacka let out such a roar than she was blown tumbling backwards and, by the time she had recovered, he was gone.

'Fistus is taking control,' Roget said, peering over the rocks.

Astatine did not think Greave's head could hang any lower. She pitied him now, but could do nothing for him either. Her efforts had been in vain. Who did she think she was, little mouse, to order immortals about?

'Stamp them out!' shouted the Carnal Cardinal, pointing in their direction.

The Great God stopped, one foot in the air, bundles of lightning bolts clutched in his upraised left fist. Now he swivelled away from Fistus, grinding stone to dust beneath his feet, and hurled a bolt at their refuge.

Astatine dived away as a ravine was blasted through the rock mound, sending fountains of shattered stone arching out to either side. The god swung back towards Fistus, flinging bolts at him, one after another. One shattered the remains of the Cloven Shrine; a second killed dozens of Red Monks. Most of the survivors fled, but Fistus remained where he was, deflecting the bolts with sweeps of his arms.

'His magic is unbelievable,' whispered Roget.

And Father gave it to him, thought Astatine. If he won't put things right, I must. 'Gods, please break the compact!'

Fistus cast the Control Spell again, but neither gods nor demons appeared. The Great God rotated like an automaton, took a step towards their hiding place, and Astatine prepared to die.

She huddled in the lightning-riven dark as smashed rock fell all around. The sky was lit by tremendous energies in black and white and red, then the Seven Gods appeared in the east. A host of demons came howling from the west, led by Behemoth, but both gods and demons stopped and hovered above the Cloven Temple.

The Great God squeezed a dozen bolts into one so brilliant that his flesh could be seen hanging transparently on his bones, then hurled it at his ancient enemy — Behemoth.

Astatine's breath congealed in her throat. 'Father!' How could he survive such a blast?

The bolt hurled Behemoth backwards, lighting him up like a comet, but he wrung the lightning into a clot the size of a snowball and flung it at Fistus. The cardinal leapt to safety as the Cloven Shrine vapourised, its molten foundations cascading like lava down the cleft in the hill.

'Fight!' roared Fistus.

The Great God crushed more bolts together and Astatine knew that, this time, her father must die.

'Together, you fools!' she roared, then clapped her hands over her mouth in horror. Who was she, an insignificant novice, to order her gods about like servants?

The Seven Gods rotated in the air, the force of their combined glares singeing her garments, and Astatine quailed.

A ghostly smile appeared on Behemoth's grim face. 'As my beloved daughter said, *together!*'

Gods and demons, working together for the only time in eternity, attacked the Great God. He blasted a host of demons away, tumbling them like bats in a hurricane, then five blows struck him at once. He toppled; he fell; he slammed into the hilltop with the force of an earthquake.

'Rise!' commanded Fistus, and the Great God struggled to rise.

'He can't be beaten this way,' said Roget quietly. 'The Great God's fate is that he can only die by his own hand.'

Fistus's spell drove the Great God up onto his knees and he attacked anew but, after a titanic struggle, the gods and demons brought him down again.

'He can't take much more.' Astatine was moved, despite everything, by the driven god's suffering.

'Neither can they,' said Roget. The exhausted gods clung to the rocks like moths to twigs, while clusters of battered demons shrieked in the fuming cleft. Behemoth lay on his back, his barrel chest rising and falling, bellows-like.

'The Great God's new wounds are healing themselves,' said Greave, who was standing upright now, jaw set as if he'd come to some terrible resolve. 'If he can rise again, he'll win.'

'No, Fistus will win,' said Astatine.

'The Great God is sitting up,' said Roget.

'And we can't stop him. He can't be killed.'

'There is a way.' Greave exchanged glances with Roget. 'We both know it.'

'No,' cried Roget. 'One speck of a god's blood will slay the strongest mortal.'

'I gave Fistus the means. Only I can undo what he's done.'

'The price is too high.'

'I've already paid the price,' said Greave, 'but redemption still eludes me.'

Greave shook his friend's hand and, to Astatine's surprise, her own. This time, as his eyes met hers, she felt no trace of frost. 'I'm truly sorry,' he said.

He strode off, head held high. As the Great God climbed to his knees, healed save for the self-inflicted wound between his ribs, Greave drew something from his pocket, thrust it arm's length up into the gash, and twisted.

The Great God reared up, writhing with the pain. Greave, his arm trapped in the wound, now swung back and forth fifteen feet above the ground.

'He's failed,' said Astatine. 'He's going to fall.'

Fistus cursed and fired a spell at Greave, who swung in under the god's arm, pulled close, then thrust again. The god stumbled; Greave's blood-covered arm slid free and he fell to the ground, convulsing.

The Great God staggered around, crushing shrubs and monks underfoot, then tripped and toppled head-first into the chasm, dead. Fistus clutched at his head and slumped, writhing.

'What's the matter with him?' said Astatine, gathering her skirts and running to Greave.

'The severing of a Resurrection Spell causes unending agony,' said Roget. 'Though less than Fistus deserves.'

The flesh of Greave's arm was smoking and bubbling, the seething mess creeping towards his heart.

'Roget?' she cried. 'What am I to do?'

'There's nothing anyone can do.'

Greave's arm spasmed and a small white object slipped from his hand. 'Burn this with the body,' he said quietly, 'then scatter the ashes.'

'What is it?' said Astatine, laying her hands on him. Her forgiveness seemed to ease his pain.

'K'nacka gave me two finger bones, but I only used one to open the casket. This is the other.'

'You thrust it into the Great God's heart.'

'He could only die by his own hand.'

'And now you're dying as well.'

'Death feels a lot more comfortable than my empty life.' His eyes closed. 'Look after my little sister, won't you, Roget?'

'I will,' said Roget, gripping his hand, and Greave died.

Fistus was bound and gagged, his staff and magical devices broken, then the gods and demons gathered.

'There must be a reckoning,' said K'nacka, his eyes glinting. 'Behemoth has gone too far this time — seducing our cardinal, corrupting the temple, putting Elyssian, Hightspall and Perdition at risk. He must be curbed, *forever*.'

'I can cause you more grief than you can me,' said Behemoth.

'Isn't this how it all started?' said Roget quietly.

How could they prevent the terrible cycle from beginning again? Astatine had thought of a way, though it required her to sit in judgement on two immortals: the god who had been the mainstay of her wretched life, and the father to whom she owed, if nothing else, daughterly respect.

'How can one so worthless as I presume to pass sentence on my god?' she mused. 'Surely that would put me in the same league of wickedness as Fistus?'

'When our gods fall short,' said Roget, 'we can only rely on our own good sense — for good or ill.'

Astatine's chest tightened until it was hard to breathe, and she felt her panic rising. A thousand times she had been slapped down as an arrogant, ignorant novice, told that she must not think or question, only obey. But unthinking obedience would serve her no longer; for the sake of Hightspall, and the gods, she must take control. If she did not, Greave's noble sacrifice would be wasted.

Breathing became a little easier. She had to do this, no matter if it cost her life. Astatine raised her voice. 'Worshipful K'nacka, beloved Father, would you come with me?'

Neither god nor demon looked pleased at the summons, yet they followed her down the hill and out of sight of the others.

Well, mortal? growled K'nacka, perching his plump buttocks on a pointed rock.

Her heart was galloping now. 'My lord,' she said, gulping, 'Your wickedness led to this disgraceful Covenant, and to the torment of thousands of innocent souls you paid in tribute to Perdition. You are unworthy.'

You blasphemous little slut! cried K'nacka, rising into the air and raising a fist to smite her dead.

Behemoth cleared his throat and K'nacka subsided, muttering.

Her father was grinning. 'Oh, yes, you're definitely *my* daughter.'

'You're just as bad, Father! No, *worse*. How could you do this to me?'

The smile became predatory. 'Make your petty point.'

'Even when I was a little girl, I never felt I belonged, not even in my own body. And all my life I've believed that I carried corruption inside me — that I was responsible for the despair and wickedness in Hightspall.' She met their eyes, trying not to flinch. 'But it came from you, Father — you and him.'

'So?' said Behemoth.

Astatine stalled, unable to see the way ahead. She had thought to shame K'nacka and Behemoth by telling the gods and demons about the Covenant, but without proof they would ignore her. Besides, that would break her oath to Hildy. She sought for another way.

'Lord K'nacka,' she said, 'you have debauched Elyssian and shamed the gods. Either you abdicate, or I'll reveal the Covenant.' She prayed that he would not call her double bluff.

Abdicate! K'nacka's cry started an avalanche down the slope. *Where to?*

'Perdition.'

Show me the Covenant.

Her bluff had been called, and she had lost. Her father was smiling grimly; no help there. The skin of her belly prickled, the dark specks that were always itchy, and Hildy's dying words, 'The stigmata —' resurfaced.

They struck her like one of the Great God's thunderbolts — so that's why she'd always felt that *she* was corrupting the world. Astatine took a deep breath, praying that her hunch was right, and held out her hand. 'Father, your enchanted blade.'

He gave it to her. She opened her habit and made a careful scratch across her lower belly with the tip of the knife, then up, across below her breasts and down again.

'It wasn't my body I did not belong in, was it, Father?' she said, feathering up her creamy skin to reveal a dark inner skin beneath. She peeled the pale rectangle off and held it out, displaying the damning words and signatures on the inside.

'*It was my skin!* When I was a little girl you covered my dark skin with a second, pale skin onto which you'd copied the Covenant on the inside.' She took a step towards Behemoth. 'How could you do this to me? All the ills of the world come from this dreadful Covenant.'

'Not *all* the ills,' said Behemoth, somewhat abashed. 'I don't turn good to evil, Daughter. I merely improve on the evil which already flourishes in humanity.'

K'nacka eyed the Covenant, slowly extending his fingers.

'It's under my protection,' hissed Behemoth.

K'nacka drew back, rubbing his chin. *To give up Elyssian*, he said shrewdly, *I need more. What else are you proposing, demon's daughter?*

'Father will give you back your —' Astatine flushed; no virtuous novice would name those body parts. 'What you've lost.'

I lose Elyssian, and all he gives up are the balls he robbed me of with loaded dice, snapped K'nacka. *It's not enough.*

'Father will also abdicate,' said Astatine, avoiding Behemoth's furious eye. 'Perdition must find a new lord.'

Me? breathed K'nacka.

'Isn't it better to reign in Perdition than endure eternal mockery in Elyssian?'

'Damned if I'll abdicate!' said Behemoth.

'Exactly,' said Astatine, 'and you will return all the unjustly reaped souls to Elyssian.'

'Or?' said her father.

She had not realised how sharp his teeth were, how black his eyes. Astatine swallowed, wavered, but knew she had to go on. 'Or I'll tell your fellow demons that you've been making deals with the gods.'

'I could destroy the Covenant.'

It's under my protection, said K'nacka, raising his fist.

Behemoth turned his way, putting on a patently false smile. 'K'nacka, my old sparring partner, we don't have to put up with this. She's just a slip of a girl. We can take the Covenant off her in a second, and destroy it together.'

Astatine hadn't thought of that, yet they had diced together; they had just fought side by side, and they both wanted the Covenant destroyed. Of course they would take it.

Do you seriously think I'll deal with you again after you cheated me? said K'nacka.

'It was worth a try,' said Behemoth.

Besides, I can't bear the tedium of Elyssian any longer.

'Not even with all those month-brides to comfort you?' Behemoth said slyly.

They were just for show; what use are brides to a codless god? But it'll be different in Perdition. I'm looking forward to the challenge of toppling you. I feel quite alive again.

'So do I, my old enemy,' said Behemoth, his black eyes gleaming. 'So do I.'

After K'nacka had returned to the other gods, Behemoth said, 'You drive a devil of a bargain, Daughter.'

'I learned from the master. Oh, and when you go, take Fistus with you.'

'If he enters Perdition alive, he'll suffer even more cruelly.'

Mercy, vengeance, or retribution? The abbey's teachings, or Perdition's? She had broken her vow and no abbey would take her in, but she would always be a demon's daughter. Besides, mercy would only give Fistus the chance to begin again. 'He has to pay his debts. Take him.'

Behemoth nodded, rose, but settled down again, staring at her.

'What?' Astatine said, afraid he was going to punish her.

'Take off that ugly white skin. Let me see my beautiful daughter as she really is.'

She started, then went between the rocks, undressed and took hold of an edge of her white skin. It sloughed off easily, as if Behemoth had broken the bonds that held it in place. Astatine threw the ugly novice's habit away, put her gown on over the cocoa skin that felt so right, and went back.

Behemoth sighed and, to her astonishment, an adamantine tear appeared in one eye.

'Come back with me,' he said. 'In Perdition you will be a princess. You can have everything you ever wanted.'

Astatine was tempted, but she said, 'Why would I want to be a princess of tormented souls?'

'A nun is a slave to live souls.'

'I can't be a nun; I've broken my vows.'

'No one need ever know. You can go back, if that's what you *really* want.'

'I would know. Besides, someone has to make up for what you and K'nacka have done to Hightspall. I'm going to help put it right.'

'You won't succeed. The world is too far gone.' He grinned wickedly. 'It's mine.'

'Not any more. I'm going to fight the influence of Perdition all the way.'

'I'm sure you will,' he said fondly. 'But the gods are no better, you know.'

Astatine hesitated, now knowing how imperfect the gods were; how capricious. She wasn't entirely sure she believed in them any more, as gods. And yet, perhaps they were needed.

'People have to believe in *something*, Father. If they can't, they'll believe in *anything*. Besides, I believe that the gods reflect who *we* are. If we live better lives, they might, too.'

'Blasphemy!' he growled. 'Well, don't think you're going to corrupt me into goodness.'

'I'm my father's daughter,' she said, smiling sweetly. 'I've already corrupted *you*.'

AFTERWORD

'Tribute to Hell' is set in the Elder Days of a new fantasy world explored in detail in the trilogy The Tainted Realm, which will be published worldwide by Orbit Books from late 2010. The first book is *Vengeance*.

— *Ian Irvine*

John Birmingham's proudest achievement as a writer was being published in the *Long Bay Bay Prison News*. After that it was all downhill. Contributing editor for a bunch of porn mags like *Playboy* and *Penthouse*, sleeping on the couch at *Rolling Stone* while he waited for his dole cheques to clear. Raiding the beer at the cricket and footy while writing for *Wisden* and *Inside Sport*. No wonder he shifted to indie comedy in *He Died With a Felafel in His Hand* and genre writing with the *Axis of Time* series and his current trilogy which kicked off in *Without Warning*, and continues really, really soon with *After America*.

A Captain of the Gate

JOHN BIRMINGHAM

Then out spake brave Horatius,
the Captain of the Gate,
'To every man upon this earth
Death cometh soon or late.
And how can man die better
Than facing fearful odds,
For the ashes of his fathers,
And the temples of his Gods?'

Thomas Babington, first Baron Macauley.

Books like this bear the name of only one author, which is a grave disservice to the many people who bring them into being. My US editor, Betsy Mitchell, and my Australian boss lady, Cate Paterson are both owed a debt I can never hope to repay. So too my agent Russ Galen who first proposed this idea while I was in the US on a Fulbright scholarship in 1998. To them, and to all of the production staff at Random House and Pan MacMillan, I offer thanks.

A number of people from various libraries, universities, research foundations and public and private archives were also embarrassingly generous with their time on this project. I am grateful beyond words to the trustees of the McKinnon Foundation for the unfettered access and unstinting support they provided throughout the research and writing process. The US Library of Congress, the Department of Defense in Washington, the Office of Strategic Services (Archives and Records), the Imperial War Museum in London, the Australian Colonial Office and the Southeast Asian section of the International Criminal Court (War Crimes and Human Rights Division) were all enormously important and supportive of this project.

Finally I must acknowledge the love and counsel of my wife and children who put up with six years of obsessive, irascible, distant and downright unacceptable behavior from me while I brought this book to print.

Branch McKinnon exhaled, and with the hot, stale breath, went some of the tension cramping his arms and shoulders. Not that he *relaxed*. That would have been impossible. But as he saw the end coming, with no chance of escape or redemption, he accepted it for the first time, and some of the fear and the strain of the last few weeks ebbed away.

He waited. The muzzle of his Thompson gun tracked the small group of North Koreans as they cautiously rounded the huge mound of burning rubble at the end of the street. It had been a seafood warehouse, and the stench of burned and rotting fish guts was vile enough to blot out the smells of the harbour city as it died around him. Spoiled meat, slumping piles of garbage alive with carpets of black flies, the unwashed bodies of his platoon, napalm smoke and festering wounds; the evil stink of the warehouse blotted them all out.

Pusan was dying. The little port city that had held out for so long would be overrun, probably in the next few hours, and his small band of brothers was sure to die with her. He was aware, without turning to look at them, of his men in the firing pit next to him. Nate Lundquist was hunkered down over the platoon's thirty cal. Jimbo Jamieson held a belt of shiny cartridges off the rubble and ash. He had another two boxes of ammo and, most precious of all, a spare barrel ready to go. Never taking his eyes off the enemy as they crept closer, he could still sense the rest of the guys. A patch of red hair peeking out beneath the curve of a helmet. The unnaturally straight line of a bayonet. A muted cough in the next foxhole, barely audible under the freight train scream of sixteen-inch shells arcing overhead. As long as they'd had the Navy at their backs McKinnon had felt there might be a small chance of surviving. But even the brightest optimist couldn't ignore how thin the cover from the big guns had grown.

Word was, two of the battlewagons had been sunk in the last six hours. McKinnon had heard more than a dozen different rumours as to how, but he paid none of them a scrap of notice. All that mattered was the stone cold reality of those Koreans, or maybe Chinese, down the end of the street. Even yesterday they'd have been blown to pieces miles away from the edge of town. Now they were right in the heart of it. The docks, where the promised evac had descended into an unholy clusterfuck, were only two miles away. Thousands of people were trapped down there — Americans, Koreans, soldiers and civilians — none of them willing to wait anymore. When the captain had detailed Branch and his men as a rearguard he'd given it to them straight. Everything had gone to shit. Friendlies had turned their guns on each other. ROK forces had shot down women and children to clear a path to the barges for themselves. Marines, our marines, had poured fire on them in turn. It was, said the captain, an unmitigated horror. But what choice did they have? As long as they held the docks, they at least had to try and get some people away. They had to try.

McKinnon found himself shrugging again as he recalled the conversation. The captain hadn't bothered to insult him by pretending any of *his* boys were going to get away.

And then Lieutenant Branch McKinnon was flying. Turning slowly, impossibly through the air, like a Baltimore Oriole. His mind, detached from the dead, stringless puppet of his body pulled free with a discernible tug. He watched himself falling back to earth with bricks and clods of dirt, with the disembodied arms and legs of his friends and enemies, with clattering pieces of steel and burning splinters of wood. Lieutenant Branch McKinnon of Macon, Georgia, twisted oh so slowly through clear air, up so high he imagined could see the entire city below him. The savage close-quarter battle that still raged around the spot where he had been blown clear out of his hole. The burning, ruined block he had been tasked with defending. The hundreds of communist soldiers running towards his position. And beyond that. He could see the Nakdong River curling its way around the mountains within which the city nestled. The beaches, on which thousands of people had gathered like dumb migrating animals, waiting to step off into the water. The port at which thousands more clawed at each other with hands and teeth for a spot on the handful of barges pulling away to sea. He could see the surviving ships of the US fleet as they poured on speed to escape the ignominious end.

Branch McKinnon saw all of these things. Or thought he did before he fell back to earth and into darkness.

01

The Grave

To watch a city die is a rare and terrible thing. Great capitals rise and fall across the long arc of history, but relatively few men attend their last hours. Fewer still have witnessed the death of more than one, and for the most part such men are found in the service of tyrants and conquerors. Branch McKinnon, firstborn of Elsie and Lester, a humble son of the great state of Georgia, served no such master, but he was well acquainted with their kind. He fought them for most of his fifty-nine years, and saw them consume one city, one country after another.

Pusan did not kill him. Nor did Saigon, or Jakarta. Having survived the taking of the Imperial Palace in Tokyo in 1946, he would have been entitled to call that his lot and to retire from the field. Millions of others did. In a sense, the whole country shrank away from any more violence after Tokyo. McKinnon was a keen carpenter and sometimes spoke of the quieter life he might have lived building schoolhouses and barns and children's toys back home. Instead he was drawn to those places where things fall apart and men contend with each other to do their worst. He died, famously, in Singapore, another fallen city, but for once a loss that meant something; one that actually changed the world for the better.

He rests now in Arlington, probably content, if not quite at peace. Each day brings a new host of mourners to disturb his repose and they come in numbers rivalling those visiting the Kennedy and Eisenhower memorials. A visitor who knew nothing of American history might still understand why two popular Presidents both cut down in their prime would each day attract many hundreds of people wishing to pay their respects. But McKinnon's simple marble headstone, buried in a mound of flowers that often spills over to cover the graves that surround it, could well confuse them. They might imagine that only a great man could command such affection, but surely a great man would not be interred so humbly, not if he were the favored son of such a proud and powerful republic.

McKinnon, a great man by any measure, flawed as are all men, celebrated and reviled, a creator-destroyer of the first order, lies beneath a simple tombstone because he demanded it be so. He is with his friends, and they lie as they fell: together. It is all too easy, away from the insensate horror of battle, to glorify the deaths of otherwise ordinary men, to forget that death in combat is always squalid and mean, and worse, to view their lives through a prism in which they were only ever brave and wise. McKinnon, like every other man and woman buried at Arlington, had his moments of bravery and wisdom, more so than most. But he was mortal and while it is true that his courage never failed him, at least on the battlefield, his wisdom and his judgment sometimes did.

When pressed for introspection he invariably described himself as 'just a free man', but he chose to fight for his freedom and for others' in a time when that made him unusual, if not unique. During the long years when America withdrew from the world, flinching away from confrontation, Branch McKinnon sought it out. It made him in turns a pariah and a hero. He was famously denounced on the floor of the Senate as a murderer, a fraud and, most painfully of all, as 'a traitor'.

But times will change, as Dylan sang, and when President Clinton spoke at the dedication of the Singapore Memorial he undoubtedly did so for all Americans when he said, 'When these men fought, they saved the world.'

And so the world comes to pay homage.

On an unusually bleak October day one year and one month after the atrocity of 9-11, with a cold rain threatening, and an ill-tempered, contrary wind jagging through the long rows of headstones, a line of mourners wound down from the small, tree-covered knoll in Section 1 of the Arlington National Cemetery, a short walk from the grand colonnade of the Memorial Amphitheatre. At the somewhat ragged start of the line, maybe three hundred yards away from the first gentle rise of McKinnon's Hill, a regular smattering of new arrivals joined those who would spend the next hour shuffling forward to say a prayer, lay flowers, or just stand quietly with their heads bowed. There is a point about a hundred yards from the grave where everyone stops talking as though they have entered the nave of a church. No marker signals exactly where this transition is made, and no instructions are ever issued to the visiting public, but those soldiers of the 3rd Infantry Regiment who tend the gardens of stone avow that every day the same thing happens. People fall silent at about the same point as they approach the hill.

Back down on the road, however, where the queue began on this unremarkable day, most folks were chatting quietly and possessed of good if not high spirits, given the solemnity of their surroundings. A few muttered darkly about the anniversary just passed. Two young men, cousins studying at the Catholic University, discussed the war in Iran with a young, pretty woman wearing an FBI windcheater. But mostly conversation never strayed far beyond private concerns, as strangers swapped details of their hometowns, their journeys and, more often than not, their family connection with the National Cemetery.

Some had distant ancestors buried there, men and women who died in the Civil War. Daytona Anderson, a young archaeology graduate at George Washington had come to visit her great, great, great grandmother, one of nearly four thousand former slaves and residents of Freedman's Village who are buried in the cemetery. Anderson felt that while she was there, she should also pay her respects on McKinnon's Hill.

'My Auntie Desire served with Admiral Houston,' she said, by way of explanation for the detour.

Others had come to acknowledge great grandfathers who fought with Pershing during World War One, and uncles and fathers lost on the Kanto Plain, in the bloodbath of Tokyo, or later at Inchon and Pusan. Like Anderson, they too had felt the need to make a show of public reverence in addition to whatever private calling had drawn them to Arlington. Separated from the Singapore Memorial by the vastness of the Pacific, they had chosen to visit what is now an accepted 'unofficial' site for those wishing to commemorate the South East Asian War, McKinnon's Hill.

Other mourners, whose loss was more immediate, and whose grief was still raw, spilled quiet tears onto the freshly clipped grass for sons and daughters lost in what very nearly became the Third World War. Ruth Ramshaw of Boise, Idaho, used one gloved finger to trace gently over a photograph of her only son, Michael, whose life ended thirty thousand feet above the South China Sea when the Chinese jet fighters he had drawn away from Admiral Houston's relief force finally put three missiles into his F-16, long after he had spent the last of his munitions, and two minutes before he would have run out of fuel. On either side of her, supporting a woman they had not met until today, Frank and Karen Muesburger of Council Bluffs, Iowa, had spent the morning at the Tomb of the Unknowns. Their son, Master Chief David Muesburger, is officially listed as Missing in Action, but Frank and Karen have laid him to rest in their hearts. He was a Navy Seal, working the island chains in the northern reaches of the former People's Democratic Republic of Indonesia, operating with Sumatran freedom fighters — or 'pirates 'n' cutthroats', as Frank Muesburger, himself a 20-year Navy man, calls them with a wry grin

'He never came home,' said Frank, clutching a handful of letters from his missing child. 'And he won't. Ever. We know that. But he's our boy and we love him every bit as much now as on the day the Good Lord sent him to us.'

Ruth, Frank and Karen would stand patiently for most of that morning, protected from the elements by cheap, collapsible umbrellas and thin plastic rain slickers, shuffling forward in their old Hush Puppies and trainers, talking quietly with each other and with those around them, supporting anyone in need of a strong shoulder, and perhaps taking comfort and solace themselves when necessary. Given the day's dreary, inclement conditions you could understand why they might have taken leave of Arlington beforehand. Ruth Ramshaw had already visited the grave of her own son, and the Muesburgers had laid a wreath at the memorial dedicated to the spirit of their lost boy. But they did not leave. Like hundreds of others they waited unhurriedly to wind their way up the gentle climb to the Hill, there to exchange whatever private thoughts they might have with the man who, in any analysis, had played a large part in precipitating the war which claimed the lives of their children.

A cynic might shrug off such dedication as the inevitable result of myth making by the champion cynics of the former Reagan and Bush Administrations. The increasingly shrill, partisan tone of national politics will not admit to high ideals on either side of the great divide, and the legacy of a figure such as McKinnon, who at times inspired extreme feelings and rhetoric from both left and right, will always be contested. Undeniably though, he remains admired and even loved by the many Americans who visit his grave every day, and even more tellingly by those who have travelled even further, across tens of thousands of miles, to pay their respects.

Salted throughout the line of mourners at Arlington were visitors from much farther afield than Council Bluffs or Boise, Idaho. Not five steps from where Frank Muesburger stood talking with a former Marine of comparable vintage was a most remarkable sight, two Papuan chieftains in full ceremonial dress, attended by expensively suited diplomats from the State Department and the Australian Colonial Office. Chiefs Somare and Wingti, resplendent in cassowary feathers, bone necklaces and penile gourds, stood motionless and utterly silent, stirring only when a pulse of movement passed along the queue, requiring of them one or two steps in the direction of their goal. Their presence elicited some comment and a considerable degree of curiosity, but not nearly as much as those confronting penile gourds demanded.

Branch McKinnon was known to millions of Americans indirectly, through the stories they read of him, or the news bulletins in which he featured. People from some of the farthest corners of the globe knew him personally and, to hear them speak of it, owed him a blood debt. The Papuan Chiefs were not alone in having travelled so far to make good on the balance. A little further up the queue stood four elders of the Kayan people of Borneo, while two Laotian monks waited under an oak tree about halfway up the hill to take their turn at the graveside. Less ostentatious, but no less sincere in wishing to pay homage were nearly two-dozen visitors from a broad fan of nations and peoples, among them ethnic Chinese businessmen from Java, three nuns from Luzon, and one stooped and white-bearded gentleman from Nippon, Yuki Moritake.

Supported by two granddaughters, one on each arm, the former Japanese Army officer stared resolutely forward as he approached his destination in hobbling fits and starts. His deeply lined face, seemingly carved from oil-stained teak, remained largely hidden beneath the brim of a Chicago Cubs baseball cap. His granddaughters, Miko and Satomi, tried to keep him dry beneath their own umbrellas, but never quite settled on a suitable arrangement of the cover, allowing the drizzle that built up over the morning to soak him through.

Moritake was unusual, if not unique that morning. A former enemy who became a close and treasured friend of McKinnon, he had once been sworn to kill the American and all of his comrades. He labored mightily towards that end but failed, a cause of unutterable shame at the time, but now a reason for contentment if not celebration. McKinnon was the first American he had ever seen in the flesh, the first and last he ever met in close combat, and, according to the stooped and frail grandfather who had long ago led the defence of the Emporer's inner sanctum, a man of *giri*.

The personal story of Branch McKinnnon does not begin with their meeting of course. He arrived in the world in 1925, born at a quarter past five in the afternoon, following a twenty-hour labor, during which his mother, Elsina Grace McKinnon, nee Wilmott, half bit through one of her husband Lester's old leather belts. Baby Branch was a big boy at 10.3 pounds, and he took his own good time in getting here. He enjoyed an unremarkable, if straightened childhood, his daddy always managing to find just enough work to see the family, which soon enough grew to three children, through the hardest days of the Great Depression.

We'll return to Macon, Georgia, in due course, and spend a little time with the McKinnon clan, but it is Branch's public life, his American story, to crib from the title of his own, unfinished memoir, which most concerns us. For in that life, so violent, so conflicted and chaotic at times, we find a parable of what might have been these past years, if only we had not shied away from the world and all its discontents.

Is there a point in time of which one can say, there is where it started to go wrong?

It's impossible to know with certainty, but had the Manhattan Project delivered the atomic bomb in time to use before the invasion of Japan it's most likely that half a million Americans would have lived, instead of dying in the dreadful meatgrinder of Operation Downfall. What then might have been different? What life might McKinnon, and millions of others have lived? But these are questions for those privileged to live a soft existence, away from bomb burst and rocket fire. They were a long way from McKinnon's thoughts on March 1st, 1946, as he rode an armoured landing craft toward Buick Beach, Sagami Bay, twenty-five miles southwest of Tokyo.

02

THE EARTH MY HELL

The invasion was never going to be a surprise. Operation Olympic, the allied attack on Kyushu, five months earlier, had not caught the Japanese unaware. They had known it was coming for more than a year, and had prepared as best they could. Indeed, they had prepared a much more formidable defence than anyone on Douglas MacArthur's staff had thought likely. While the Japanese could only guess at the forces that would come upon them, they were intimately familiar with the terrain upon which battle would be joined, in southern Kyushu, below the line of the central ranges. The *gaijin* were constrained in their choice of landing site, almost certainly having to come ashore at Miyazaki and Ariake Bay, and more than likely on the Satsuma Peninsula near the town of Kushikino as well.

The Japanese had known that the Allies would amass the greatest fleet ever seen, far larger even than the armada that accompanied the D-Day landings in 1944. And so it had been. On November 1, 1945, more than 500 warships had appeared over the horizon to the south of the home islands, among them forty-two aircraft carriers, twenty-four battleships and hundreds of cruisers and destroyers. Behind them came even more vessels, troop transports and supply ships. Thousands of aircraft filled the skies, flying from bases in the Ryukus. British Bombers, protected by Australian fighters, pounded dozens of hastily constructed airstrips all over Kyushu. US Navy Corsairs flew in dense blue swarms above the slow moving fleet, ready to throw themselves at the waves of sacrificial *kamikaze* that the Allied high command knew would form a lynchpin of the defense.

And still the losses had been horrific. Eleven carriers sunk, including the venerable *Enterprise*, and that had been the least of the damage. Eighty-nine troop transports had been struck by suicide bombers. Nearly 43,000 men had died without setting foot on Japanese soil. When the landing had been forced, those losses spiralled up to 100,000 inside two weeks. The optimists on MacArthur's staff had argued that there were unlikely to be more than eight divisions opposing the lodgement. The pessimists thought ten. In the end, there were fourteen, all of them fighting to the death. Of the 140,000 Japanese soldiers massed in these divisions, only 1902 were captured, almost all of them rendered incapable of resistance by their wounds or shell shock. Every other man gave his life for the Emperor.

The American soldiers and marines who fought on the beaches and across the plains of southern Kyushu drank from a deep well of horror which even their comrades who had liberated the Nazis' concentration camps had not known. For not only did they fight against the men of the Imperial Japanese Army, but every step of their advance was resisted by the Japanese people themselves. An 80-year-old farmer, a small schoolboy, a pregnant woman, any one of them might suddenly spring at you from the door of a hut armed with nothing more than a sharpened stick, or a farming implement. The official history of the campaign, published in 1954, listed Staff Sergeant Tom Rilke as the first recorded casualty of just such a 'non-combatant' attack. After a firefight in a small hamlet outside of Kushikino, Rilke had been trying to lure a schoolroom full of frightened children out into the open with an offer of chocolate, when he was set upon and inexpertly beheaded by their teacher, a nineteen-year-old girl wielding an awl. After hundreds of such attacks General Walter Kreuger, commandant of the US 6th Army, sought and received presidential approval for one of the most controversial orders in American military history. As of March 13, all civilians in the Kyushu theatre of operations were deemed to be combatants unless they immediately surrendered upon being challenged to do so. Entire villages were razed by artillery and aerial bombardment when the occupants refused to show themselves.[2]

---

[2] The policy was credited with saving thousands of American lives but it remains a sticking point in relations between the two countries, with some ultranationalist Japanese politicians still demanding fifty years later that the US apologise for its 'war crimes'. Throughout the 1970s some American diplomats maintained that they could tell how difficult any given set of trade negotiations were likely to be by the fervour with which, in the weeks beforehand, the Japanese Foreign Ministry pressed the issue of 'reparations' to make good civilian losses during Operation Downfall.

By the end of major combat operations more than a million Japanese, both civilian and military, were dead. American losses stood at nearly one hundred and twenty thousand killed in action. The second half of Operation Downfall, the invasion of Honshu, was infinitely worse.

McKinnon missed Kyushu. He arrived in Japan as the lieutenant in charge of the second platoon, A Company, 3rd Battalion, 24th Infantry Division. It is a truism of popular fiction that all lieutenants are gangly, thin-limbed, and wet behind the ears, barely able to find their own asses with a good map in a small, well-lit room. Their men merely tolerate them, grizzled non-coms work around them, and they almost inevitably die in the first ten seconds of any engagement, leaving the real men to get on with the business of war. It works well as a dramatic device, but if it held true as often in real life as it does in Hollywood, all battles would quickly devolve into chaos and madness as any semblance of command disappeared. Branch McKinnon was not a green officer, wet behind the ears, and awestruck in the presence of his senior NCOs. He had been promoted from the ranks. Fighting with the 3rd Battalion through the Indonesian archipelago, in the Philippines at Breakneck Ridge where he won a Silver Star and his third stripe, and on Luzon where he was commissioned in the field after the savage hand-to-hand combat at Zig Zag Pass.

The men he led into battle on the Kanto Plain were likewise, for the most part, survivors and veterans of MacArthur's island hopping campaign that took the Allies from their last bastion in Australia all the way to the inner sanctum of Emperor Hirohito's Imperial Palace in Tokyo. The Battalion, McKinnon's home for the previous three years, had suffered close to 4000% casualties in that time. Indeed, it is likely McKinnon would have stepped onto the Kanto Plain as a company commander or possibly even a battalion level officer had he not spent at least 18 months of those three years recuperating in hospital from his various wounds. It is also possible, of course, that had he not been out of action for so long and so often, his name would have been etched into the Battalion's honor roll as yet another of the glorious dead.

* * *

We know from McKinnon's own unfinished autobiography that he was not a commander who played favorites with his men. Although there were three men in the second platoon, with whom he had fought since the Battalion's first operations in New Guinea, he was no more mindful of their safety or care that he was of the freshly minted privates who had joined the platoon straight out of basic training, two days before the Division shipped out for Downfall. In a letter written to his mother on the eve of the invasion, McKinnon worried more about his untested charges and what might befall them in the meat grinder of Tokyo,

'It would be such a terrible shame, Mom,' he wrote, 'if anything were to happen to those kids this late in the game. I just don't know that I could forgive myself.'[3]

Given the much greater casualty toll of the first phase of Downfall, everyone involved in Coronet, the second half of the operation, from President Truman to the humblest foot soldier, had reason to fear what was waiting for them on Honshu. The geography of the island virtually wrote the operational concept for the Allied planners. That same geography could be read by its Japanese defenders, of course. Estimates varied on both sides with, for instance, British and Australian military authorities advising their respective War Cabinets to expect Allied casualties of nearly 2,000,000, and Japanese casualties of a staggering 10 to 15,000,000, depending on the extent to which strategic bombing and unconventional weapons such as gas and germ bombs were deployed, an option the new British Labour Party government ruled out within a week of being elected. It remains a matter for conjecture how the following sixty years may have played out had Churchill's conservative government retained office in 1945. Declassified documents from the Imperial war office (see appendix 1) indicate that Sir Winston was solidly behind a USAF plan to carpet bomb the

---

[3] McKinnon had ample chance to find out whether he could forgive himself over the next two weeks, as three of the four new recruits were killed. Pvt. Andrew Forster, from Delaware, stepped on a mine less than a mile from the beach where the platoon disembarked from their landing craft. Pvt. Michael Hall, Sioux Falls, was cut down while approaching a Japanese pillbox on the outskirts of Tokyo. And Pvt. Greg Beck, Kansas City, was cut down by a pitchfork wielding gardener in the grounds of the Imperial Palace.

urban area of greater Tokyo with a mix of incendiary, high explosive, biological and chemical warheads. A War Cabinet memo from February 1945 went so far as to authorize Bomber Command to begin planning to shift strategic assets to the Pacific Theatre in August 1945 with this very plan in mind.

At that stage, of course, nobody outside the very highest councils of the Allied command had any idea of the failure of the Manhattan Project. It was not until 1964, nearly a full decade after the first successful atomic test was carried out in New Mexico, that the US government released any information related to the Allies' wartime atomic program. While Truman's frustration with the lack of progress at Los Alamos has been well-documented by his biographer, Stephen F. Murphy, he was not the only American, or indeed the only person on the Allied side, praying for deliverance via the agency of a miracle weapon. The archives of all the victors contained many examples of correspondence from private soldiers and junior officers such as McKinnon, fervently hoping that an invasion of the Home Islands might be made unnecessary by the unveiling of some super weapon. McKinnon himself made reference more than once to news articles he had read about the German rocket program and how rumors had spread through his platoon that the Navy had developed massive 'rocket barges as big as aircraft carriers' but carrying no planes, only hundreds of V2-style missiles.

'I don't believe it for a minute myself,' he wrote to his sister on Christmas Eve 1945, 'but the boys have been very excited this week by talk that the whole show might be called off because Halsey and Nimitz are planning to steal MacArthur's thunder by parking hundreds of these things offshore and just raining them down on top of Tokyo until there's not enough of the nips left to scrape up and put in a bucket.'

Unfortunately for Second Platoon there would be no deliverance from above. A Company were lucky to avoid the fate that befell the first wave of attackers on Honshu, where casualties in some units topped out at 90%. By the time McKinnon and his men came ashore on March 3, 1946, fatigued and seasick from having sat in the heaving, untidy swell and cross chop of Sagami Bay for two days, the lead elements of the Eighth Army had pushed the beachhead in six miles. The dreadful wrack and ruin of modern industrial-scale slaughter had not been cleared away, however, and the platoon were greeted upon stepping ashore with a hellish mound of disembodied arms, legs, heads, torsos and various slabs and chunks of unidentifiable human refuse piled into a huge funeral mound for burning by the Army Corps of Engineers later that day. McKinnon's platoon sergeant, Elmore Greaves of Flagstaff, Arizona, one of those three men who had been with the young officer from the very first days of the war, roared abuse at anybody who stopped to stare, but was himself delayed on the beach by having to take a minute to vomit up the remains of the tinned fruit he had had for breakfast on the armored landing craft.

The Battalion history records the first casualty as occurring less than 15 minutes later when Pvt. Forster was killed by a 'Jumping Jack' style mine a few hundred yards in from the high water mark. Forster receives just that one line acknowledgment in the official documentation, but McKinnon recorded the incident in some detail in his notebook later that day, expanding on it at some length in the manuscript of his unpublished memoirs[4] a few years later.

'We could clearly hear the rumble and thunder of the frontline a few miles away,' he wrote.

'The Navy was still sitting close in shore, hundreds of destroyers and cruisers and even a couple of big battle wagons like the *Missouri* and *Tennessee* punching giant 15-inch shells twenty miles inland. They screeched overhead like birds of prey and landed only God knew where somewhere up ahead, probably in the middle of some Tokyo suburb. Planes roared overhead constantly, fleets of heavy bombers, British Lancasters by the look of them, US and Canadian Liberators and Flying Fortresses, and hundreds, maybe thousands of small buzzing fighters. Australian Spitfires. US Corsairs and Mustangs, some of them loaded out with rockets and bombs under their wings for ground attack missions and close support.

---

[4] *The Fall of Giants*, unpublished manuscript, McKinnon, B. 1953. Original copy held by The McKinnon Foundation, Washington DC.

'Perhaps there was too much going on. There was so much traffic in the landing zone, so many thousands of men moving to and fro. Trucks and jeeps and tanks everywhere. Sergeants bellowing at privates, officers yelling at each other. For some of the boys in my platoon it was overwhelming. They just didn't have their mind in the game. But I should have, and I didn't, and Forster died because of that. We were walking in single file up a steep valley that had been clearly marked out with white stakes by the engineers. As long as you stayed between the stakes you were safe. But, as Elmer told me later, Forster wasn't paying attention. He was too busy gazing up into the heavens, hypnotized by the vapor trails which crosshatched the sky like thousands of woolen threads. I was leading from the front of the column, trying to get a signal back to Battalion on our new radio. It was on the fritz of course. Damn thing seemed to be out of action more often than not. I had assigned each of the new guys a buddy from one of the older hands in his squad, and Forster was supposed to be teamed up with Bob Whitelock, who'd been with us for over a year. Unfortunately, Bob had the sea sickness something terrible and at the very moment Forster wandered off the marked trail, his buddy was bent over about 25 yards back, up chucking into the sand.

'Even with all that noise and chaos on the beach, I recognized the click click sound off one of the Jumping Jack mines the Japanese had developed from the famous German 'Betty' design. I was already dropping to the ground with the words 'take cover' at the back of my throat when it detonated. The blast seemed louder than I remembered, but then I hadn't been in action for a few months. The ringing in my ears faded after a few seconds and all I could hear was Forster screaming that his legs were gone. He screamed for less than a minute until Doc Waters got the morphine into him and put him to sleep. That was the only thing for it unfortunately. It wasn't just his legs he lost. Half of his innards had splashed out over the rest of the platoon. He had no chance ...'

The platoon was delayed between the sand dunes for all of ten minutes before the demands of their timetable saw them leave the mortally wounded soldier behind in the care of two Navy corpsmen. McKinnon's men met up with their sister platoons at the rendezvous point a mile inland, at the site of what had been a small fishing village. First Platoon had been sniped on the way in, but without casualties. Their radio was working fine and they called in close air support from a pair of P-51 Mustangs which unloaded a volley of rocket and cannon fire on the small hill from which the fire was judged to have come. Third Platoon, by way of contrast, came up five minutes behind McKinnon and reported no incidents at all.

With the Company gathered together at its first staging point, McKinnon and the other platoon commanders wanted to press on, but had to wait for orders from Battalion HQ before they could move any further inland. The situation across the southern reaches of Honshu was still in violent flux. In contrast with the operation at Normandy, which involved twelve divisions, the invasion of the main Japanese island required twenty-five divisions, two separate US armies, the Eighth and the First, and a Commonwealth Corps made up of forces from Great Britain, Canada, Australia and New Zealand under the command of Lieutenant General Leslie Morshead. The British Empire forces, in-line with a strong recommendation from Gen. Douglas MacArthur, had trained in the United States for six months before the operation and deployed using only US equipment and logistics. They came ashore with the US First Army at Kujukuri Beach on the Boso Peninsula. Even so, there were significant and occasionally calamitous breakdowns of communication between the armies.

Over one million Allied troops were ashore and engaged with the enemy by the time McKinnon's platoon disembarked from their armored landing craft. Opposing them were 800,000 Japanese soldiers, many brought home from the occupation of China in the previous six months. Allied planning had allowed for an opposing force of up to 600,000 men, up to half of whom were expected to be low-quality personnel from home defense units. The disparity in these numbers was one of the great intelligence failures of the Second World War and as a direct consequence the casualty figures for Operation Coronet skewed wildly towards the upper limit of the worst-case scenarios, in spite of all the lessons learned on Kyushu.

Complicating matters at a tactical level were hundreds of thousands of Japanese civilians who abandoned their noncombatant status. As before, they were not organized in any sense that a military mind would recognize. No poorly trained, poorly equipped regiments of home defense troops or civilian militia joined their uniformed colleagues on the frontline. Rather thousands of Allied soldiers died at the hands of women, children, the old and infirm who had been wired up with explosives and left behind as human bombs. After the Allies changed tactics on Kyushu and began engaging any civilian who did not immediately surrender, the enemy responded by having its civilian kamikaze do just that, before blowing themselves up as their surrender was taken.

Of course not every civilian was 'booby-trapped' in that way, but the uncertainty created a tactical nightmare for the advancing Allies, who never knew whether the small child or aged refugee crying out for assistance with their hands held high was swathed in a bomb belt, packed with ball bearings, rusty nails, scrap metal and even handfuls of gravel. Every single human being they encountered thus became a potentially lethal adversary. Add to that the efforts of the main force Japanese military, which included not only the Army units returned from China, but thousands upon thousands of 'special units' trained and equipped for more 'conventional' kamikaze operations, and the utter chaos and insensate savagery of those first days of combat become a little clearer. Ten thousand Allied Naval personnel alone died as Japanese pilots, their fragile, obsolete aircraft packed with high explosive, threw themselves on the invasion fleet. Over a dozen capital ships, including three aircraft carriers, succumbed to attacks by 'suicide submarines'.

'Thou camest on earth to make the earth my hell,' quoted Admiral Fraser, Commander. of the British Pacific Fleet as he witnessed near simultaneous detonations of underwater kamikaze beneath the keel of the *USS Iowa* at the very moment that Lieutenant Branch McKinnon back on shore ordered Sergeant Greaves to gather the men and prepare for a double time march to the frontline where the Battalion was urgently needed to bulk up a collapsing flank.

The men of Second Platoon, still daubed in the remains of Private Forster, shouldered their packs and weapons without complaint, but with a grim and somber frame of mind as they prepared to push deeper into their own small corner of the earth, their hell.

Afterword

This is an idea I had a few years ago, that I'm still working on, for an alternate history of the Cold War. There were a couple of what-ifs in the back of it. What if the A-Bomb didn't work, at first? What if the slaughter of invading Japan pushed America back into isolationism? What if, and this my favourite, the Domino Theory then came true? ASEAN becomes the Association of Socialist East Asian Nations, a third communist bloc. The fag end of the British Empire is wheezing along as the world's policeman. And then Ronald Reagan gets elected and everything changes. The idea was to write the history of the period via a biography of one of its players, an adventurer by the name of Branch McKinnon. If I ever go ahead and do it, a big if, it would look exactly like a work of non-fiction, with footnotes, apprendices etc, but of course, it'd all be total bullshit.

— *John Birmingham*

Jennifer Fallon, is the international bestselling author of the Hythrun Chronicles, the Second Sons trilogy and the Tide Lords quartet. She has also co-authored books and short stories for the *Stargate* TV series. Her short stories have been published in magazines and a number of anthologies, including *More Tales of Zorro, Baggage*, and *Chicks in Capes*. She shares her house with a very large Mastiff who is afraid of, well, everything, a little old Maltese afraid of nothing, three psychotic cats who are undoubtedly plotting the takeover of Planet Earth and a collection of pewter and crystal dragons from all over the world, who seem content to do nothing more than collect dust.

The Magic Word

JENNIFER FALLON

CHAPTER I

Every morning the High Princess of Hythria sprinkled crumbs on the sill outside the living-room window of her borrowed apartment in the Medalonian capital, the Citadel, for the small brown bird that flew down to greet her.

Every morning the little bird would land on the very edge of the stonework, tentatively approach the crumbs, tweeting softly, as if debating aloud the wisdom of accepting this unexpected bounty ... and then he would snatch up the fattest crumb and fly away, disappearing amidst the shining white spires of the city with his prize.

Every morning. The same bird, the same time, and, Adrina was starting to suspect, the same damn crumb.

'Didn't we do this yesterday?' she said, climbing awkwardly to her feet as her winged visitor dived and swooped away toward his nest somewhere high in the white towers of the city.

Damin glanced up from the scroll he was reading by the fire. He always got up before she did. And she always found him by the fire, which was odd, because, as a rule, Damin wasn't the sitting-by-the-fire type.

'Did we?'

He sounded distracted. No, worse than that. Utterly disinterested.

'I feel like I've been pregnant forever.'

'*Tell* me about it.'

Adrina glared at her husband — sitting there sipping mulled wine as if he didn't have a care in the world. 'So says Damin Wolfblade, the wastrel who spends his days swanning around the Citadel with the Lord Defender, pretending he's important.'

He grinned. 'I'm the High Prince of Hythria, Adrina. I *am* important.'

'And my job is to do nothing more than sit here incubating your precious Hythrun heir?'

Damin put down his wine and turned to study her. 'I rather thought you *liked* the idea of being here in Medalon. You kicked up a big enough fuss about coming along.'

'I know ...' She sighed and stretched her aching back. 'But don't you ever feel as if we've been here in the Citadel *forever*?'

Damin's face creased with a thoughtful frown. 'I never really thought about it.'

'Why doesn't *that* surprise me?'

'All right,' he said, smart enough to know when he was approaching the edge of a precipice. 'Now that you mention it, it does seem like we've been here a long time, but I was under the impression we're still here because we're waiting for you to *deliver* my precious Hythrun heir before we can travel again. If you're sick of being in Medalon ... well, any time you're ready, sweetheart.'

The nearest thing to hand was Adrina's empty wine goblet. She hurled it across the room, scoring a hit squarely over Damin's left ear. The empty clay goblet fell to the ground, shattering as it landed.

'Ow!' Damin exclaimed, jumping to his feet as he rubbed his wounded head. 'What was that for?'

'For blaming me. It's not my fault we're stuck here.'

He glared at her, still rubbing the lump on his head. But if he had a glib answer, he wisely kept it to himself. Assuming a much more sombre expression, he asked, 'Do you seriously think it's something magical keeping us here? Something to do with the Harshini, maybe?'

'I don't know. Perhaps we should ask Shananara. I can't really explain it, though, so I'm not sure what we'd ask. I just have a feeling, that's all, and it's *not* indigestion brought on by pregnancy that's causing it. Gods, I even feel like we have this conversation every morning.'

'I'll speak to Tarja.'

'Which is your answer to everything, lately,' she complained. 'Can we go riding today?'

'Won't that be bad for the baby?'

'Maybe it'll bring the wretched creature on.'

Nodding, Damin walked toward her. 'Let's ride then, and see if we can't hurry this mighty prince's entrance into the world.'

Adrina glared at him, annoyed at the assumption she was having a son. Before she could say so, however, there was a knock at the door to their apartment — a suite once the luxurious quarters of a senior Sister of the Blade. Adrina didn't know which sister had lived here and didn't care to know. They all made her uneasy, so it hardly mattered anyway.

'That'll be Tarja,' she muttered as Damin crossed the sitting room to open the door.

He opened it and stepped back to allow their visitor into the room. Adrina sighed. Sure enough — as she had known it would be — it was Tarja Tenragan.

The tall, dark-haired Lord Defender bowed politely to both of them. 'Good morning, Damin. Your highness.'

'Good morning, Tarja,' Adrina said, with a distinct lack of enthusiasm. It wasn't that she didn't like Tarja ... she was just sick of seeing him. She was sick of everyone here. She really *did* feel as if she'd been trapped here in Medalon for years, not just the month or so it should have been. 'Did you want something, Tarja? Damin and I were just about to go riding.'

'Of course,' The Lord Defender said with a smile. 'I'll order your horses saddled …'

The small brown bird flew down to eat the crumbs Adrina sprinkled on the sill outside the living-room window of her apartment. He landed on the very edge of the stonework, tentatively approach the crumbs, tweeting softly, as if debating aloud the wisdom of accepting this unexpected bounty … and then snatched up the fattest crumb and flew away, disappearing amidst the shining white spires of the city with his prize.

The same bird, the same time, and, Adrina was becoming convinced, it was the same damn crumb.

'Didn't we do this yesterday?' she said, climbing awkwardly to her feet as the sparrow dived and swooped away, as he always did, toward his nest somewhere high in the city.

Damin glanced up from the scroll he was reading by the fire. As usual, he was up before she was, by the fire reading. As usual, Adrina thought it odd, because Damin wasn't the sitting-by-the-fire type.

'Did we?'

He sounded as distracted as Adrina remembered. No, worse than that. Utterly disinterested.

'I feel like I've been pregnant forever.' The words were out of her mouth before she could stop herself.

'*Tell* me about it.'

Adrina glared at her husband — sitting there sipping mulled wine as if he didn't have a care in the world, wondering why it felt like they'd had this argument so many times before. 'It's all right for you, Damin Wolfblade. You're the wastrel who spends his days swanning around the Citadel with Tarja, pretending you're important.'

He grinned at her. Even before he opened his mouth, she knew he was going to say, 'I'm the High Prince of Hythria, Adrina. I *am* important.'

'And what?' she couldn't help responding. 'My job is to do nothing more than sit here incubating your precious Hythrun heir?'

He put down his wine and turned to study her. 'I rather thought you liked the idea of being here in Medalon. You kicked up a big enough fuss about coming along.'

'I know.' She sighed wearily and stretched her aching back. 'But don't you ever feel as if we've been here in the Citadel *forever?*'

Damin's face creased with a thoughtful frown. 'I never really thought about it.'

'Why doesn't *that* surprise me?'

'All right,' he said. Now that you mention it, it does seem like we've been here a long time, but I was under the impression that's because we're waiting for you to *deliver* my precious Hythrun heir before we can travel again. If you're sick of being in Medalon ... well, any time you're ready, sweetheart.'

Adrina picked up the nearest thing to hand — her empty wine goblet — and hurled it across the room, scoring a hit squarely over Damin's left ear with the unerring skill of a well-practised throw. The empty clay goblet fell to the ground, shattering as it landed.

'Ow!' Damin exclaimed, jumping to his feet as he rubbed his wounded head. 'What was that for?'

'For blaming me. It's not my fault we're stuck here. You're the one who put me in this condition.'

He glared at her, rubbing the lump on his head. But if he had a glib answer, he kept it to himself. Assuming a much more sombre expression, he asked, 'Do you seriously think it's something magical keeping us here? Something to do with the Harshini, perhaps?'

'I don't know. Maybe we should ask Shananara,' she said, deciding that today she would *insist* they speak to the Queen of the Harshini, and not just suggest the idea. 'Although I can't really explain it, so I'm not sure what we'd ask her. I just have a feeling, that's all, and it's *not* indigestion bought on by pregnancy that's causing it. Gods, I even think we have this *conversation* every morning.'

'I'll speak to Tarja.'

'Which is your answer to everything, isn't it?' she complained. 'Can we go riding today?'

'Won't that be bad for the baby?'

'Maybe it'll bring the wretched creature on.'

Nodding, Damin walked toward her. 'Let's ride then, and see if we can't hurry this mighty prince's entrance into the world.'

Adrina glared at him, annoyed at his insistence she was having a son. Before she could say so, however, there was a knock at the door to their apartment.

'That'll be Tarja,' she muttered as Damin crossed the sitting room to open the door.

He opened it and stepped back to allow their visitor into the room. Adrina sighed. Sure enough, it was Tarja.

The tall, dark-haired Lord Defender bowed politely to both of them. 'Good morning Damin. Your highness.'

'Good morning, Tarja,' Adrina said, with a distinct lack of enthusiasm. It wasn't that she didn't like Tarja ... she was just sick of seeing him. She was sick of everyone here. Adrina was becoming obsessed by the idea she was trapped here in Medalon for years not just the month or so it should have been. 'Did you want something, Tarja? Damin and I were just about to go riding.'

'Ah ...' Tarja said, glancing at Damin. 'I was hoping to borrow Damin for a while, your highness. I have a bit of a problem and I thought he might be able to help.'

Adrina stared at Tarja in shock.

'I beg your pardon?'

'I have a bit of a problem and I thought Damin might be able to help,' he repeated, looking at her oddly.

This was different. Adrina couldn't say why, but it felt *very* different. 'What sort of problem?' she demanded.

'Interrogating a prisoner.'

'You can't interrogate a prisoner on your own?'

'This man is proving ... difficult.'

Damin closed the door, not nearly so excited by this break in their normal routine as his wife. 'Why not just have one of the Harshini read his mind?'

Tarja glanced at Damin and shrugged. 'They have prohibitions against that sort of thing.'

Adrina was still surprised, but suspicious, too. The Defenders were by no means gentle interrogators. It was hard to imagine any prisoner resisting them for long. 'And what do you suppose my husband is going to be able to extract from this prisoner that your Defender bullies can't?'

'It's not that he won't give us any information, your highness,' Tarja explained, as much to Damin as Adrina. 'It's what he's telling us.' To Damin he added, 'And I *have* spoken to Shananara. She's already spoken to him and in her opinion, he's telling the truth, even though what he's telling us is ridiculous.'

'What's he saying?' Damin asked. Adrina could tell he was already getting caught up in Tarja's latest folly. It was more proof they had been here far too long.

'He's claiming,' Tarja announced, 'that the world is about to end.'

CHAPTER II

Tarja's harbinger of doom proved something of a disappointment. Adrina expected a wild-eyed lunatic dressed in rags with fiery eyes and crazy, uncombed hair that stood on end, spouting incomprehensible prophetic verses while banging his head repeatedly against a wall.

What she discovered — when she invited herself along to the cells at the back of the Citadel's Defenders' Headquarters with Tarja and Damin — was a slender youth of about nineteen or twenty. He seemed calm, had a pleasant, if unremarkable face — albeit somewhat bruised and battered — dark hair and a perfectly lucid manner. The lad was rather the worse for wear but his cuts and bruises didn't seem to bother him overly much.

The stone cellblock was dimly lit, the only daylight coming from the narrow windows at the top of each cell with bars set into the thick granite blocks. Dust motes danced in the infrequent light, stirred into frenzy by their passing. The young man claiming the world was about to end stood up from his pallet as they approached the bars of his cell, his expression filled with hope and expectation.

'My Lord Defender —'

'Don't start,' Tarja warned the young man. He turned to Damin. 'Did you want some time alone with him?'

Damin studied the battered and bruised prisoner with a frown. 'I'm not sure there's much more I can do, Tarja. Your lads appear to have worked him over quite thoroughly.'

'Not that it got us anywhere. He's sticking to his story.'

The prisoner took a step closer to the bars. 'You don't need to torture me, my lord,' the young man insisted with a reassuring smile that split his lip afresh and started it bleeding. 'I told you already —'

'And I told you to shut up,' Tarja warned.

Without knowing why she spoke up, Adrina stepped forward. 'Let me talk to him.'

Damin and Tarja turned to stare at her. 'What?'

'Let *me* talk to him. I'll find the truth for you.' *And for me*, she added silently. Truth be told, anything was better than a day where the highlight was a sparrow stealing crumbs.

Her husband shook his head. 'If you think I'm going to endanger my heir by letting you anywhere near a dangerous prisoner ...'

'He's not dangerous,' she said. Adrina addressed her next words to the young man. 'You're not dangerous, are you?'

'No, my lady.'

'There, you see. He's not dangerous.'

'Adrina,' Tarja began in a patient and vaguely patronising voice, 'I know you're bored, but this isn't the way —'

'To amuse myself?' she cut in. 'Thank you, Tarja, but I was going to suggest that as torturing this boy clearly hasn't achieved anything, you might as well try something different. Like treating him in a civilised manner. It's a well-known sign of insanity, you know ... doing the same thing over and over and expecting a different result.'

Tarja didn't seem pleased by her observation, Damin even less so, but her husband knew her better. For all he gave the impression he was uninterested in anything that didn't involve him having a good time, Damin Wolfblade was smarter than most people gave him credit for. He studied the prisoner for a moment longer and then, much to Adrina's relief, he nodded.

'Fine. Do it your way.'

Tarja was appalled. 'You can't be serious!'

Adrina looked at her husband for a moment and then turned to Tarja with a bright smile. 'No, Tarja … I think you'll find that's his serious face.'

The Lord Defender stared at his Hythrun guests and then threw his hands up. With an unhappy sigh, he signalled the guard to come forward with the key. 'Be it on your own head, then,' he warned, 'if something happens to Hythria's High Princess and her unborn heir.'

'No need for keys,' Damin said, holding his hand up to forestall the guard unlocking the cell. 'Just a chair will do.'

Adrina opened her mouth to object, but Damin never gave her the chance. 'Tarja's right, Adrina. It's too dangerous. You can talk to him, if you must, but you're not going to do it anywhere within reach of him. You can chat from out here in the corridor through the bars.'

'But Damin …'

'It's that or we forget this and go riding.'

Adrina glared at her husband. She didn't think she was in danger from this young man, but her husband had a point, because there was really no way to be certain. 'Oh, very well.'

Tarja nodded to the guard and he hurried off to find Adrina a chair. She turned to the prisoner with a reassuring smile. He looked a little bemused, but had wisely done nothing threatening; nothing that would give either the Lord Defender or the High Prince of Hythria cause to change their minds about letting him talk to the princess.

A moment later, the guard arrived with a straight-backed wooden chair, which he placed on the cobblestones in front of the prisoner's cell, well out of arm's length of its occupant.

Damin unsheathed his sword and handed it to Adrina. 'If he makes a move toward you, cut him down.'

It seemed a ridiculous precaution, but she accepted the blade as she sat down, a little annoyed her back was already starting to ache. *Damn this being pregnant forever.*

She glanced over her shoulder. 'I'll be fine,' she assured both of them, straightening her skirts as she turned to face the prisoner. 'Now go, and leave us in peace. I'll tell you all about it when we're done.'

Neither Damin nor Tarja seemed too pleased by her command, but they did as she bid, retreating up the hall out of earshot. Adrina put them out of her mind and turned to the cell. 'Now, as for you, my lad,' she said, shifting a little on the uncomfortable wooden chair, 'why don't you tell me how you got Tarja Tenragan believing your arrival heralds the end of the world?'

Chapter III

'The Lord Defender doesn't want to believe me, my lady,' the young man said, taking a cautious step closer to the bars, one eye on the bare sword only a few feet away. 'If he did, he'd give me the help I need, not make me the feature attraction of the morning matinee for bored princesses looking to relieve the tedium.'

Adrina stared at the young man in surprise. 'I could call my husband and the Lord Defender back, you know. They might be able to torture some *manners* into you, if nothing else.'

The young man seemed to realise his mistake. He bowed apologetically, brushing the dark hair out of his eyes. 'I'm sorry. It was not my intention to offend you, your highness.'

'Do you have a name?'

'Of course.'

Adrina glared at him silently.

'Oh … I mean yes, yes … Dirk Provin.'

'And where are you from, Dirk Provin.'

'Ranadon.'

Adrina's brow furrowed for a moment. 'I do not recall ever seeing or hearing any reference to a country called Ranadon.'

'That's because it's not a country, your highness. It's a *world*.'

'I don't understand.'

He dabbed at the blood leaking from his split lip with the edge of his sleeve. 'I come from an entirely different world, your highness. We don't even share the same sky. On my world, we have two suns.'

'And yet we speak the same language.'

'We all come from the same Creator.'

'How did you get here?' Adrina asked, thinking she should have listened to Tarja. This glib boy was talking nonsense.

'The veil between our worlds is breaking down. I crossed into your world near a place on my world called Omaxin. I came out east of your citadel and found my way here, where I was arrested for … well, I'm not exactly sure what I was arrested for. All I know is that when I asked to speak to someone in charge about the threat to both our worlds, they locked me up and started beating the crap out of me, mostly, I gather, because they don't like what I'm saying.'

Adrina couldn't help but smile at his wounded tone. If he was making this up, he was a very good liar. 'Don't people on your world draw the wrong sort of attention for suggesting the world might be about to end?'

He shook his head. 'Not as a rule. Generally they start religions.' He smiled then, as if his comment was a joke only he understood. 'I'm sorry … the answer to that question is the reason I'm here. When we realised the problem on our world, I came to yours, looking for the solution.'

'You say *we*, as if others on your world know of this impending doom. Were you able to convince the rulers of *your* world, then, that your preposterous story is true?'

'Yes.'

'They must have a great deal of faith in you.'

'On my world, I am a religious leader.'

'You're very young for such responsibility.'

A small self-deprecating smile flickered across the young man's battered face. 'It kinda helps that the most powerful prince on Ranadon is a cousin. And that he owes me a favour.'

'*You* are a prince?'

Her question gave Dirk pause. He thought about it for a moment and then shrugged. 'Well, technically. I find it's much more useful to be Lord of the Suns. That way I've got everything covered.'

Adrina was beginning to regret volunteering to talk to this seemingly harmless youth. He was toying with her. 'You have about one minute left to start making sense, young man, before I call my husband and the Lord Defender back and let them do with you what they will.'

He took a step closer to the bars, close enough now to grip them. His fingers were bloody and swollen, but seemed to be intact. 'Let me ask you a question, first, your highness. Don't you ever get the feeling there is something wrong with your world? Something not quite right with it?'

Adrina paused for a moment before answering, the boy's question chillingly close to the uneasy feeling she'd had for some time. 'I don't understand what you mean.'

He thought about it for a second or two and then said, 'All right, let me put it another way. Don't you ever get the feeling you're just marking time? That nothing in your world is progressing the way it should?'

Adrina rose to her feet, suddenly nauseous. 'Explain what you mean by that.'

'I mean, your highness, your world and my world and all the other worlds touching them have stopped. Worse, they may soon disappear.'

'What other worlds?'

'The other worlds of the Creator,' he said.

'You mean the gods?'

He shook his head. 'No, I mean the one who *created* the gods. And the goddesses. And you, and me, and this place, and my world, and your world, and everything else we see, and hear, and feel.'

Adrina took a small step back from him, bumping into the chair. Her experience with Xaphista's followers had left a bad taste in her mouth and a deep suspicion of all monotheistic religions. 'You believe in one god? Like the Kariens and their worship of Xaphista?'

'Your highness, I don't even know what a Karien is. Or a Xaphista, either, for that matter. I'm just convinced everything comes from one Creator and I think something has happened to the Creator, which is why the veils between our worlds are failing. It's how I can be here. It's why I *came* here.'

'For what?' Adrina asked. 'We've never even heard of this Creator of whom you speak. How do you suppose anybody here can help you find him?'

'Magic.'

'Magic?' She repeated with a frown. 'What's so special about our magic? Surely your own magic is powerful enough?'

Dirk shook his head. 'Well, there's the rub. You see, on my world, there is no magic. And much as it irks to admit it, your magicians may be the only ones who can find him.'

'You mean the Harshini?'

'Are the Harshini like the woman with the black eyes they brought here this morning to see if I was telling the truth? Her name was Shannon ... or something like that.'

Tarja had mentioned that Shananara had already been here to see the prisoner. 'Yes ... she is Harshini. But what do you expect of them?'

'I'm not sure yet. But the Creator must have given them powers for a reason, so we might as well avail ourselves of their skills.'

'In that case,' Adrina said, shaking her head, wondering what Shananara had made of this strange boy, 'you don't need the Harshini, Dirk Provin. If what you say is true — and I'm not saying I believe a word of your ridiculous story, mind you — then you may need something far more powerful. You may need the Demon Child.'

'You believe me,' the young man said, sounding surprised. He studied her with his disconcerting, metallic grey eyes.

'I never said that.'

'You do. Otherwise you'd have handed me back to the Defender's torturers, by now.'

'I may yet,' Adrina said, moving the sword so she could use it like a walking stick. Damin would be outraged to see her damaging the tip so carelessly, but gods, her back was aching. 'Explain to me how you've come to the conclusion this Creator of yours even exists.'

'Because we've stopped.'

'Stopped what?'

'Everything.'

Adrina rolled her eyes. 'I said proof.'

'I could show you proof, but it's mathematical and you wouldn't understand it,' he said patiently. 'So, let me ask you a question instead, your highness. How long have you been pregnant?'

'I'm due to give birth any day now.'

The young man nodded. 'Fine. Leave me here to rot. But humour me, if you would, my lady. Start keeping a tally of the days from now. Come back when you have the proof for yourself.'

'What are you suggesting? That I'm *not* nine months pregnant?'

'For all I know, you're nine *years* pregnant.'

That tallied so closely with what Adrina had been feeling for a while now that she paled at the thought of his seemingly absurd suggestion. 'That's ridiculous.'

Dirk Provin studied her with those unsettling, metallic grey eyes that saw right through her hollow rejection of his theory. 'But you know I'm right.'

'What you're suggesting is impossible.'

'So is the idea I crossed into your world from another world. But it's true, my lady, and if you want your world to go on, then we have to do something about the Creator.'

Adrina shook her head. 'This is nonsense.'

'The Lord Defender doesn't think so.'

'Of course, he does,' she said. 'That's *why* you're locked here, fool.'

'If the Defenders thought I was merely some village idiot having delusions, then I'd have been out of here hours ago. I'm still in prison because he fears I might be telling the truth, my lady. He doesn't want me out there spreading seditious suggestions that we're in trouble.' He gripped the bars even tighter, pleading with his eyes as well as his words. 'Don't you see? That's why he brought you and your husband here. And that Shannon woman … She told him I was telling the truth. He just doesn't want to believe what I'm saying and is hoping you'll tell him he's right and I'm wrong.'

'Is that a fact?' Adrina smiled sceptically. 'And how do you know that?'

'Because I died today, my lady.'

'You died?'

Dirk nodded. 'Been three times now, Lord Tenragan's Defenders have tortured me to death trying to force a more palatable truth from me. And because I'm *not* going to lie to make them happy and because I'm not of this world, I keep coming back.'

'I don't believe you.'

Dirk pointed to the sword. 'Then try it yourself, your highness. Run me through.'

'I'm not going to help you kill yourself!'

'But I won't die, don't you see? And until you believe that, I'm going to rot in here and you're going to ...'

'Feed crumbs to the same sparrow every morning,' she finished, mostly to herself.

He looked at her strangely. 'Sorry?'

'Nothing,' Adrina said, hefting the sword in her hand. Being Damin's sword, it was long and heavy and built for a man of considerable strength and stature. Adrina could barely lift the damn thing.

She managed it nonetheless. Dirk Provin didn't even flinch as she approached, intending to call his bluff. She was convinced he would back away at the last second, certain the lad was thinking no woman — and a pregnant one at that — would have the mettle to do anything so insane as run a prisoner through.

It took a special sort of insanity to kill a man in cold blood — which was unfortunate for Dirk Provin, because Adrina was being driven more than a little bit insane by being stuck here in Medalon, feeding that same damn sparrow every morning, waiting for a child who — if this boy were to be believed — would never be born.

Grabbing the hilt with both hands, she raised the blade, pointing it at Dirk's chest and took another step closer. 'Are you sure you want me to do this?'

Rather than pull away, the boy gripped the bars even tighter. 'Just don't miss,' he said, with a grimace, as he braced himself for the impact. 'This is going to hurt. I'd hate to suffer all that pain for a flesh wound that proves nothing.'

The lad's bravado was impressive, but Adrina was still certain it was motivated by his belief in her cowardice, more than his belief in his own immortality. She stepped even closer. The blade was growing heavy in her arms. She rested it for a moment on the cross-piece of the barred cell door, the tip only inches from the boy's chest.

She hefted it a little higher. Dirk Provin closed his eyes and looked away. The blade was trembling in Adrina's hands. It had occurred to her that this lad might simply be trying to avoid any further suffering at the hands of the Defenders by arranging for someone to kill him, because he lacked the wherewithal to take his own life. But somehow, she knew that wasn't the case. And it appalled her a little to realise that even if it was, she was prepared to take the risk, because she needed to be certain, one way or another, that he was lying.

At least, that's what Adrina told herself as she thrust the blade forward, squeezing her eyes shut. The blade was sharp and heavy. It caught for a moment on the young man's ribcage, and then he cried out as it slid, almost without resistance, into his heart.

Chapter IV

'You said you were going to talk to him!' Tarja shouted at her. 'Not kill him!'

'I didn't kill him,' Adrina pointed out calmly. 'The boy is fine.'

'You ran him through, Adrina.'

'And no sooner did I pull the blade out than he jumped to his feet, as right as rain.' She turned to her husband. 'You're going to think I'm insane —'

'No! *Really!*'

'Don't you take that tone with me, Damin Wolfblade!'

The Queen of the Harshini, ill-equipped to deal with any sort of emotional extremes, stepped between Damin and his wife. 'Adrina's action, shocking as it is, your highness, leaves us little choice but to believe the boy's tale,' she said.

'It's crazy,' Tarja said. 'He's crazy.'

'Then how do you explain how he keeps coming back to life?'

Damin's eyes widened in shock. '*Keeps* coming back?'

'I didn't run him through on a whim, Damin. Tarja's heavy-handed thugs have killed the boy three times already. And now for a fourth time, he's come back to life. He claims we can't kill him here because he doesn't belong in our world.'

'And, naturally, you couldn't resist trying to prove him wrong?' Damin turned to Tarja. 'Is that true?'

'It is,' Shananara said, before Tarja could deny it, lacing and unlacing her fingers. For a woman denied emotional extremes, she was very unsettled.

'Then Dirk Provin *is* telling the truth?'

Everyone looked to the Queen of the Harshini for the answer, but she simply shrugged. 'I can tell you only that he believes what he claims is true, and that his gift for resurrection would seem to support his claim. Beyond that, I can tell you nothing for certain.'

'Well, for what it's worth, I believe him,' Adrina said. 'I don't know if what he's saying about a Creator is true, but I know in the very core of my being we *have* been here far longer than we should, and I am damn sure I should have given birth ages ago, too.'

'Even if it is true,' Tarja said. 'What are we supposed to do about it?'

'I think the first thing we need to do is confirm the rest of his story,' Damin suggested.

'You mean running him through and having him survive the experience without a mark didn't convince you?' Adrina snapped impatiently.

'I mean finding this break in the veil between worlds he claims to have used to get to our world.'

Adrina perked up at the idea. 'Will it take us long to get there?'

'I'm not letting you anywhere near this wretched veil, Adrina,' Damin said, looking a little panicked.

'Why not?'

'I imagine he doesn't wish to endanger his heir, your highness,' Shananara said with a faint smile.

Adrina shrugged. 'I'd say his precious heir is in far more danger from me staying here waiting for something that's never going to happen.'

'That's a valid point,' Tarja said, surprising Adrina with his support. The Lord Defender looked thoughtful, making Adrina wonder what else he was concerned about. Whatever it was, he wasn't planning to share it with them now. He rose to his feet and announced decisively, 'I'll make arrangements for us to leave this afternoon. They picked Provin up not far from the Citadel, so I don't image his magical veil between the worlds — assuming it exists — is too far off the beaten track.'

'He's playing a prank on us,' Damin warned. 'He's probably laughing himself silly at the idea we're falling for this.'

'Yes, dear,' Adrina agreed. 'The way he faked his recovery from the mortal wound I inflicted on him was simply hysterical.'

Damin wasn't amused. 'It would make me feel better if you stayed here in the Citadel.'

Adrina pushed herself awkwardly to her feet. 'Why do you think that, right now, I am interested in doing anything to make you feel better, Damin Wolfblade? Besides, if Dirk Provin keeps coming back to life because he doesn't belong here, what possible harm can any of us come to, if we cross into his world?'

CHAPTER V

The expedition to visit the site of Dirk Provin's supposed veil between worlds was deliberately small. The High Prince of Hythria seemed convinced they were simply pandering to this prisoner's flights of fantasy and it was foolish in the extreme to play along with him. He could do little to argue the case, however, given the determination of the Queen of the Harshini and his wife, who — having witnessed Dirk Provin's resurrection — were both adamant the young man's story should be taken seriously.

They left after lunch, mounted in a small group with only two of Tarja's red-coated Defenders as an escort. Adrina was thrilled to be out of the confines of the Citadel and gave her horse its head as soon as they were over the bridge and on the main road south. Damin caught up with her quick enough, and demanded she slow down, but even the brief spurt of speed seemed to blow the cobwebs out of her head, although her child protested the jostling with a few well-placed kicks, hard enough to make her grunt.

'See, even the child thinks you're a lunatic for galloping off like that.'

Adrina glanced over her shoulder at the others rapidly catching up behind them. 'I don't let *you* dictate to me, Damin. Why would I listen to your child?'

Damin had no chance to answer before the rest of their party arrived. Shananara's face creased with concern as her unbridled horse came to a halt without any visible effort on her part. 'Should you be galloping like that in your condition, your highness?'

'I don't see why not,' Adrina said. 'If Dirk Provin is right, I'm not going to give birth. Ever.' She turned to the young man mounted on a borrowed Defender's horse led by Tarja. As a precaution his hands were tied to the pommel of his saddle. 'Isn't that right, Master Provin?'

'I assume so, your highness.' The lad seemed reluctant to be drawn into making a definitive ruling on the matter. Despite being bound, he sat comfortably on the horse, clearly used to being in the saddle, but his manner seemed ill at ease.

'Let's not take that as a given,' Damin suggested, frowning at the young man. 'How far out of the Citadel did you say this world-bridging veil of yours is supposed to be?'

Dirk looked around uncertainly. 'I thought it was east of the Citadel. We were in a forested area. Although it was dark when I arrived, it took me less than an hour to find the road.'

Tarja glanced at one of the guards, who nodded and pointed confidently east. 'That would make it the woods around Bottleneck Gorge. That's the only wooded area within half a day's walk of the city.'

'Bottleneck Gorge it is then,' Tarja said, turning his mount east. He tugged on Dirk's horse's lead rein, pulling the young man behind him. Adrina fell in beside Damin and Shananara, with the two Defenders behind them, and they headed toward a veil between two worlds that was, in all likelihood, not there.

It was an hour or so later, once they were well into the tree line, that Adrina heard the noise. It was a rhythmic pounding like nothing she had ever heard before, so foreign to her senses that at first, she thought she might be imagining it. A moment later all doubt the strange noise was nothing more than a figment of her imagination vanished as the ground shuddered with the impact of a massive explosion somewhere ahead of them.

The horses reared in fright.

'What the hell ...' Tarja turned to Dirk as he fought to bring both his own mount and the one he was leading, under control. 'Founders! What was that?'

'Why are you asking me?' the boy replied, clinging to the pommel of his saddle with grim determination. 'When I came through the veil it was like a mist. There was nothing burning. Nothing exploding, either.'

Adrina circled her mount a few times to settle him, and then turned to look in the direction of the detonation. The acrid black smoke — unlike the wood smoke Adrina was used to — billowed into the clear morning sky like an evil black tower tottering on its foundations.

Tarja dismounted, and drew his sword. 'Get down,' he ordered the prisoner. 'We'll go on foot from here.'

Dirk lifted his tied hands the few inches the slack in his bond would allow. 'Love to,' he said, 'soon as you let me loose.'

Tarja waved one of the Defenders forward, drawing his sword. Damin and Adrina — with some difficulty — dismounted as the guards released Dirk Provin. The second Defender took up the reins of their mounts. Dirk shook his hands in an attempt to restore their circulation.

'Stay here with the horses,' Tarja ordered the Defenders, and then shoved Dirk none too gently to get him moving. 'You go first.'

The lad shrugged. 'You think I'm leading you into an ambush?'

'Well, if you are, they'll take you out first, won't they?'

Dirk shook his head, smiling ever so slightly at Tarja's unforgiving tone, and then headed off into the trees in the direction of the acrid-smelling smoke. The rhythmic pounding had stopped, but the source of the explosion remained a mystery. Damin offered Adrina his hand, which she accepted gladly, more exhausted from the ride than she was prepared to admit.

'Do you still think he's lying?' Adrina asked Damin and Shananara in a low voice as they followed the Lord Defender and this interloper from another world, leaving their somewhat bemused escort back at the edge of the tree line with the horses.

'I'm of two minds,' Shananara admitted. 'But there's something burning up ahead and I don't think it a bonfire.'

They hurried forward through the trees and the unnaturally silent forest until they reached a narrow clearing bordering the edge of a steep gully. Although they couldn't see the water, they could hear it tumbling over the rocks below. Nobody paid any attention to it, however. Their eyes were fixed on the strange machine that lay mangled and burning on the ground and the two men climbing from inside the belly of the mechanical beast, singed and shaken, but apparently unharmed. Smoke belched from the wreckage like a dragon spewing forth all the ills of the world. Adrina's eyes watered as she stared at the spectacle, unable to find the words to describe what she was seeing.

'By the gods,' Damin exclaimed, coming to a halt beside her. 'What is this thing?' He turned to Dirk Provin. 'Is this what brought you here? This ... metal monster?'

Dirk shook his head, as gobsmacked as they were. 'I ... I have no idea ...'

'It's a helicopter,' one of the men climbing from the wrecked metal contraption announced in a matter-of-fact sort of tone. He winced in pain and then turned to glance at his companion, but made no move to help him. The man turned back to look at them. He was tall and dark-haired and — except for his hair colour — shared more than a passing resemblance to Damin. 'What? You all look like you've never seen a chopper before?'

'I don't think we're in Kansas any more, Dorothy,' the other man grunted, still trying to extract himself from the wreckage with some difficulty. Finally, he clambered out of the burning wreck and looked around, examining each of their group with a wary eye. His companion seemed equally disturbed. 'I'll lay you odds we're not even on Earth any longer, Rodent.'

The man named Rodent frowned. 'It's not possible,' he said. 'We just ditched the crystal in the Mariana Trench. There's no way Lukys has had time to find it and open a rift. Besides, it's not High Tide yet.'

The two men from the wreckage of the metallic machine looked at each other oddly. 'There's no Tide at all,' the Rodent said. 'Can you feel it? It's gone.'

'High tide?' Damin asked, his hand on his sword hilt. 'We're nowhere near the coast here.'

The taller of the two men turned to Damin, looking at him curiously. 'I'm sorry … can you tell us where we are?'

'Medalon. You have come through the veil.'

'Shut up, Provin,' Tarja said, pointing his sword at the two newcomers. 'Who are you? Where are you from?'

'My name is Declan Hawkes,' Rodent said, holding his hands up to indicate peaceful intentions. 'This is Cayal Lakesh. We appear to have …' His voice trailed off and he turned to his companion for help.

The other man simply shrugged.

'Actually, I have no idea what we've done. A few minutes ago, we were flying over the Pacific Ocean, patting ourselves on the back for outwitting Lukys.'

'Seems like Lukys got the last laugh,' Cayal Lakesh said, slapping out a small flame on his sleeve as he came to stand beside his companion. 'Who are you people?'

'I am Her Serene Highness, Princess Adrina.' Someone had to take charge here. 'This is my husband, Prince Damin, High Prince of Hythria, Tarja Tenragan, the Lord Defender of Medalon, Shananara, Queen of the Harshini, and Dirk Provin, who claims to be a prince and a religious leader on his world of Ranadon.'

'Well, at least they sent a welcoming committee worthy of us,' Cayal remarked to his companion. 'Where did you say we are?'

'Medalon,' Tarja said, taking a step forward, his sword still held out threateningly in front of him.

'Never heard of it.'

'Nor have you yet told us where you came from. Or what that metallic beast is. Or how you killed it.'

Declan Hawkes glanced over his shoulder at the smouldering, twisted metal heap behind him and smiled. 'More like it tried to kill us. But somehow you — armed with nothing more than a sword and a bad attitude — managed to bring it down. How did you do that, by the way?'

'The Lord Defender didn't bring your machine down,' Dirk said. 'You've come through the veil between worlds.'

'You don't know that …' Damin began, but Dirk shook his head and pointed at the wreck and the two strangers.

'They are not of this world, your highness, any more than I am. Look at their machine. Their clothes. They are not from your world, and they're certainly not from mine. That leaves only another world we know nothing about.'

'Do you have any idea what these people are talking about, Rodent?' Cayal asked his companion.

Hawkes shook his head and turned to Tarja impatiently. 'Are you going to stick me with that thing? If not, would you mind putting it away?'

'Not until you explain —'

'Look!' Dirk Provin cut in, pushing himself between Tarja and the stranger before the two men could come to blows. 'It's obvious what's happened here. These men and their machine came through the veil the same way I did. There is no point threatening them, Lord Defender, because if they're not from this reality, you won't be able to kill them, anyway.'

'Actually, he's not going to have any luck killing us, whatever reality he thinks we're from,' Cayal remarked, as Tarja somewhat reluctantly sheathed his blade. 'Can someone please tell us what's going on? And how a ragtag bunch like you lot were able to destroy a world?'

'Destroy a world?' Shananara asked, looking a little puzzled. 'Nobody has destroyed anything.'

'Where we come from, my lady, when you start jumping between worlds, you leave piles of rubble in your wake.'

Dirk Provin seemed rather rattled by that prospect. 'Do you know that for certain?'

Declan Hawkes nodded. 'Absolutely. What I don't understand is how you were able to activate a Chaos Crystal when there's no sign of the Tide.'

'We're nowhere near the coast here,' Damin said, a little impatiently. 'I told you that already.'

'I don't think he's talking about ocean tides,' Adrina said, wondering what a Chaos Crystal was. It sounded like trouble. 'And we used no crystals to bring you here, gentlemen. If we are to believe young Master Provin here,' she added, indicating Dirk, 'you fell into our world, much the same way he did.'

The two strangers glanced at each other. 'Then how do we get home?'

Everyone turned to look at Dirk. Adrina found that interesting. Although they all professed to doubt his theory, they seemed to assume he had the answers about what to do next.

As if suddenly realising the weight of expectation he was being asked to shoulder, the young man threw his hands up and took a step backward. 'Why are you all looking at me? I have a theory about what's causing this. I never said I had the solution to the problem.'

'What is the problem, exactly?' Cayal asked.

'Dirk Provin believes we all live in different worlds created by a single entity — hence the reason we all speak the same language,' Adrina explained. 'He also believes something has happened to the Creator and that's the reason the walls between our worlds are breaking down.'

'It's worse than that,' Dirk added glumly. 'I suspect that if we don't do something, we'll all cease to exist.'

'I see ... so you think *God* brought us here?' Hawkes asked carefully.

'I think the Creator *created* God,' Dirk corrected.

Cayal glanced at Hawkes. 'I think the natives here have been smoking something trippy.'

Dirk didn't understand the reference, but he got the patronising tone in which it was spoken clear enough. 'You can believe me or not,' he said. 'Have fun finding your way home.' He turned to face Tarja and held out his joined wrists to the Lord Defender. 'Back to the Citadel and my cell, then, my lord? I think we're done here.'

'Hang on,' Damin said. He seemed concerned. Adrina wondered if that meant he was starting to believe Dirk Provin, or he just didn't like the idea of leaving these two decidedly odd strangers to their own devices. 'Let's assume you're right, Provin. Let's assume we were all created by this being you speak of, and you're right about something happening to him. You must have some idea how we can fix this. You'd not have crossed the veil from your world otherwise.'

Adrina nodded in agreement. 'He's right ... you would have stayed at home. Aren't you a religious leader? If you thought you couldn't stop the end of the world, you'd be at home comforting your flock, not standing here trying to convince us to do something about it.'

'I have no idea what you're talking about, but it sounds perfectly reasonable to me,' Cayal said. 'Particularly if it means you haven't destroyed Earth and we can get back there some time before the sun goes supernova.' He turned to his companion and added sourly, 'You'll be sorry we chucked that crystal in the drink when *that* happens, Rodent.'

Damin ignored the aside, probably because very little of what the handsome stranger said made any sense. He kept his attention on Dirk Provin. 'Well ... what do we do now?'

Dirk lowered his arms and shrugged. 'I'm not sure. Really ... I'm not. But ...'

'But what?' Tarja asked, his hand still on the hilt of his sword.

'Well ... I think we need to find the Creator and speak to him ourselves. I mean ... he may not even be aware of what's going on.'

'Find the Creator?' Declan Hawkes asked. 'How?'

'That's obvious,' Shananara said. 'We have to go through the veil.'

CHAPTER VI

While they were arguing Adrina noticed a mist gathering that nobody else seemed aware of. It wasn't until the storm of argument Shananara's announcement unleashed was in full swing that Adrina realised the mist was thickening so rapidly the trees around the clearing had faded into nothing. As Damin and Tarja, Dirk Provin, and the two strangers, Declan and Cayal, argued about the merits of crossing this imaginary barrier between worlds, the barrier overtook them.

'Damin ...'

Her husband ignored her. He was busy disagreeing with Tarja, while Dirk tried to defend his position, and the two newcomers made snide comments to each other that seemed to indicate an ambivalence in their relationship, reminding Adrina of two teenage boys comparing the size of their manhood.

'Damin!'

'*What, Adrina?*'

'It doesn't matter any longer. Look around you.'

Damin looked up and gasped as he realised they were now almost completely swallowed by the mist.

The others finally noticed it, too. They fell silent as the mist thickened to a silent, impenetrable fog.

'Founders!' Tarja swore, looking around wildly. 'Where did this come from?'

'It's the veil,' Shananara said. She looked at Dirk for confirmation. 'Isn't it?'

The young man nodded, looking around with something more akin to curiosity than fear. 'I expect so. But it wasn't this thick the last time. And it didn't linger like this.'

'It's similar to the cloud bank we flew through just before we crashed,' Declan Hawkes said.

Cayal nodded in agreement. 'Told you not to go there.'

'You did not,' Hawkes said, shaking his head. He turned to Dirk. 'If we've been swallowed by a veil that takes us into other worlds, where are we now?'

'I don't know,' Dirk said. 'I don't even know how many worlds there are. We could be anywhere.'

'More to the point, how do we get back?' Adrina asked, as it occurred to her that if they couldn't find a way out of this fog, they may well have left their world behind forever.

'I'm not sure if we *can* go back,' Dirk said. 'Maybe we can only go forward.'

'We're not actually going anywhere at the moment,' Cayal remarked, 'in case you haven't noticed. It's more like we're being sucked in.'

'The mist *is* getting thicker,' Adrina said, wondering if the slight edge of panic in her voice was as obvious to the others as it was to her.

Damin must have noticed. He turned to her, put his arm around her shoulders and drew her close. 'It'll be fine, Adrina.'

'And you know this from your vast experience being sucked through veils into other worlds, I suppose?'

'Are you sure we're in another world?' Declan asked. The fog had thickened so much there was nothing around them but the roiling white mist. 'This looks like we're caught in a cloud with a floor made of cotton wool.'

'What's cotton wool?' Adrina asked.

'Who cares?' Tarja said, reaching out to feel the fog as if it was a tangible thing. 'How do we get out of it?'

'You can't.'

They all turned at the new voice. Adrina gasped as a figure resolved out of the mist ahead of them. The man was tall, dark-haired and black-eyed and dressed in dragon rider's leathers. He was Harshini, obviously, but Adrina didn't realise who it was until Shananara — she who was incapable of human emotions — exclaimed in surprise, 'Brak!'

So this was the legendary Brakandaran. Interesting that he was here. Particularly as he was supposed to be dead.

'Are we in one of the Seven Hells?' Tarja asked, staring at Brak warily.

Brak shrugged. 'I'm not sure if there really is a Hell, actually. This place is more like … Limbo.'

'What's that?' Dirk asked. He had no inkling what this was. No way of appreciating the devastating impact the sudden reappearance of Brak would have on the people of Adrina's world. Tarja, in particular, was looking pale. Adrina could imagine what he was thinking, and it wouldn't be about a minor thing like falling through a veil between worlds.

'It's the place we all come to await our future,' Brak said. 'I can't really explain it any better than that.'

'A future decided by this Creator of yours, I suppose,' Declan said, looking at Brak with deep suspicion.

'Creator?' Brak asked, eyeing the man curiously. 'Are you a follower of the one god, Xaphista?'

'I thought R'shiel killed Xaphista?' Damin said.

'She did,' Brak agreed with a shrug. 'But he still has his adherents.'

'I've no idea what any of you here are talking about,' Declan said, shaking is head in confusion.

'Where we come from,' Cayal added, 'we're the gods. Immortal, actually. Tide Lords. You've never heard of us?' He glanced at his companion. 'Tide must have been out a long time here, Rodent. They've forgotten us again.'

'It matters little who you are here,' Brak told him. 'In this place, you are not what you were, or what you might be. You simply are.'

'Even if you're dead?' Damin asked pointedly, staring at Brak. His arm had tightened subconsciously around Adrina when Brak appeared and he still hadn't let her go.

'Am I dead?' Brak asked.

'You were the last time I checked,' Tarja said, as disconcerted by Brak's appearance as Damin.

Brak turned to Adrina. 'I'm dead?'

'I suppose …' she agreed uncomfortably. 'But Death took you body *and* soul, so we always thought that meant you'd be back.'

Dirk seemed to be listening to the conversation with great interest, but like Cayal and Declan, he was unaffected by the implications of the miraculous resurrection of Brakandaran the Halfbreed. His mind was obviously on more immediate concerns. 'Your machine crashed, you say. Does that mean you died in your world, too?' he asked.

'Highly unlikely, son,' Declan said. 'Immortal, remember?'

Dirk turned to Brak. 'But *you* died in *your* world?'

'Apparently.'

'That's excellent!'

The others looked at him askance, particularly Brak. 'Well, I'm glad you think so.'

'No … I don't mean it's good that you died. I mean it's good you're here. It means we're getting closer.'

'Closer to what?' Tarja asked, frowning suspiciously.

'To the Creator.'

'He's a religious leader, did you say?' Cayal asked Adrina out of the corner of his mouth. 'Clearly, a true believer.'

Dirk heard the aside and turned on Cayal. 'This is nothing to do with religion. This about survival. If the veil is breaking down to the point where we can interact with people from other worlds, even people long dead from their own worlds, then one of two things is happening. We're getting closer to the Creator or things have degenerated so far we've all become one mixed up hodgepodge of a world that makes no sense to anybody.'

'Let's be optimists,' Shananara said, 'and assume this mist is bringing us closer to the Creator.'

'I hate to be the harbinger of doom, Shananara,' Brak said, 'but I think the hodgepodge theory may be closer to the truth.'

'How would you even know?' Cayal asked.

'I meet people here sometimes,' he said with a shrug. 'People not of my world. Some of them are as solid and real as you are … others are more … ephemeral. As if they're not fully formed.'

'What do they look like?' Dirk asked, with the shameless curiosity of a child. The more bizarre this got, the less bothered he was by the end of all life as they knew it, now he'd been presented with an even more intriguing enigma.

Brak shrugged. 'Faceless, transient things. They look human, and sometimes they solidify into actual people.' He turned to study Dirk for a moment. 'You know … I think I've seen you before. A long time ago. But you were much less substantial then.'

'I've been here before?'

'Probably,' Brak said. 'How did you get here, anyway?'

'*Here* sort of came to us,' Cayal said, turning to Dirk, who appeared to be the only one with even a workable theory, let alone an answer for their current predicament. 'You say you're looking for your Creator?'

'Not just *my* Creator,' Dirk corrected. 'I'm looking for the man who created us all.'

'Why do you assume he's a man?' Adrina asked.

Dirk shrugged. 'Well … I don't know. I never really thought about it. But whatever he … or she … might be, I think something has happened to … him … her … and that if we don't do anything to stop it, we'll all cease to exist, along with our worlds.'

Brak seemed happy to accept the young man's ludicrous theory more easily than anybody in Medalon had done. But then, Adrina figured he'd had time to adjust to the idea. It was still very new to the people from her reality.

'So what do we do now?' Adrina asked, as Damin seemed to relax enough to let her go. It was all well and good to stand about theorising, but their current predicament wasn't going to be resolved by talking about it. They needed to do something concrete.

'Follow the light,' Brak said, pointing into the mist.

'What light?' Tarja asked, following the direction of Brak's pointing finger with a puzzled expression.

'After a while here, you start to notice the mist isn't evenly lit,' the Halfbreed explained. 'And the closer you get to the light, the more ghosts you meet.'

'Ghosts?' Shananara asked, sounding curious, rather than afraid.

'The beings that haven't formed yet,' Brak explained. 'Or maybe they have formed and now they're fading away. I don't know. I just know there are more of them the closer you get to the light. At least there used to be.'

'Used to be?' Dirk asked, looking around, probably for the lightest part of the mist. Although Brak was pointing in one direction, Adrina couldn't really pick the difference. It all looked disconcertingly similar to her.

'Lately it's been flaring and then dimming for a while each day ... if you can call the time here days.' He shrugged apologetically. 'It's kind of hard to explain.'

'I don't understand what you mean by flaring,' Declan said, looking confused. 'How can it —'

His words were cut off by a loud buzzing noise, which was followed almost immediately by a flash of bright light so intense, so terrifying, it sundered the mist and Adrina felt herself falling into an abyss that seemed to go on forever.

Chapter VII

When Adrina finally became aware of her surroundings again, she was on her hands and knees. The ground was squelchy and soft beneath her fingers, the light green and filtered through a thick canopy of vegetation that afforded no hint of blue sky.

She had no idea where the swamp had come from. It was like nothing she had ever experienced before. She had certainly never experienced anything like this in person. Gone was the white mist, the deep penetrating cold of Limbo.

And everyone else. She was alone.

'Damin!'

Adrina waited for a response, but in her gut she knew she was alone. She had fallen through the veil — maybe they all had — and landed … somewhere.

She had no idea where this new world was, nor who inhabited it.

The princess was certain of only one thing. She was alone and the only way out of here was back through the veil.

If she could find it.

The world surrounding Adrina was nothing but greenery and the chirruping of a million unseen insects. Her skirts were soaked by the muddy ground. The muggy air tasted so moist and loamy she feared she was in danger of drowning with the intake of every breath.

A splash behind Adrina made her spin around in fright. 'Damin? Is that you?'

She knew it wasn't, just as she decided calling out like that was probably a stupid thing to do. This new world could be full of danger. And even if, like Dirk Provin, she couldn't die on a world other than her own, she *could* be hurt. The agonised scream Provin let out when she'd run him through readily attested to that.

Adrina pushed herself to her feet as the insects fell ominously silent.

She heard the soft splash again and this time wisely said nothing. There was something about the splash that alarmed her. It wasn't the sound of someone tramping through water looking for dry land — assuming there was such a thing in this place. It was the soft splash of something trying to conceal its presence. The furtive splash of a hunter looking for prey.

The sound seemed to be coming from her right. That left Adrina only one direction in which to run.

Picking up her skirts, Adrina turned and headed away from the water as fast as her bulk and the thick vegetation would allow, wondering how slow and lumbering a creature she could outrun. The ground sucked at her feet, as if deliberately trying to hold her back, but she pushed on, not sure if she was imagining the sound of someone crashing thought the jungle behind her, or if her fear was really starting to get the better of her.

There was also the problem of the direction she was running.

Suppose I'm getting further and further away from the veil, instead of running toward it?

Another crash in the undergrowth behind her, this one much closer than the last, spurred Adrina on, the decision about the direction she was running taken from her by whatever large scaly thing was pursing her. Adrina didn't know if it was actually something large and scaly. It might be large and hairy. Whatever it was, it *was* large and it was definitely getting closer, close enough now that she could hear it grunting.

The crashing behind her grew louder. Adrina could no longer hear herself think over the sound of her own laboured breathing and the heavy panting of whatever was running her down, and probably planning to make a meal of her.

The child bounced uncomfortably in her womb as she stumbled ahead, objecting to the rough ride. Adrina grunted and stumbled in response to a particularly savage kick, just in time to discover her fears about the type of creature pursuing her were well founded. She fearfully glanced over her shoulder as the monster burst through the trees behind her.

It was huge, much taller than a man, reeking of rotting vegetation, dripping with green pond scum and — as she had suspected — covered in mottled brown scales. She screamed as it opened its mouth wide, its massive teeth ready to tear her head from her shoulders …

… when the buzzing noise started up again, followed by another flash of intense light and once again, Adrina felt herself falling into the abyss.

CHAPTER VIII

When she came to this time, Adrina was relieved to find an unpolished wooden floor beneath her hands rather than a squelchy smelly swamp. The floor was splintered and dusty and badly in need of cleaning. She looked around. She was in a storeroom of some kind, cluttered with the abandoned detritus of what appeared to be several lifetimes.

How she'd fallen through a mist and landed here remained a mystery. Even where 'here' might be was not clear. And she was still alone. Damin, Tarja, Shananara, Dirk Provin, Brak, and the two self-proclaimed immortal Tide Lords, Declan Hawkes and Cayal Lakesh, were gone.

'Is anybody here!' Adrina climbed to her feet with some difficulty. Her call faded into the haunted shadows of the attic, where even the dust motes seemed content to hide.

'Anybody?'

Adrina looked around, wondering where the door might be. A shaft of sunlight filtering down from a small circular window high above the rafters provided the only light. She couldn't see an exit immediately, but she wasn't worried.

I mean ... who builds a room without a door?

'I don't think any of the rooms here have doors.'

Adrina squealed and spun around to face the girl who'd answered her unspoken question.

And whom she was absolutely positive wasn't standing behind her a moment ago.

'Gods! Where did you come from?' she gasped, stumbling backward, recognising the newcomer immediately. It was R'shiel — the Demon Child herself — dressed the way Adrina had last seen her, in those distracting, skin-tight dragon-rider's leathers.

'I could ask you the same thing.' R'shiel smiled, as she reached out to help Adrina up. 'Her Serene Highness, Adrina, High Princess of Hythria, isn't it?' she said and then glanced at Adrina's swollen belly and gasped, 'Founders! You poor thing, you're still pregnant!' R'shiel sniffed the air and frowned. 'And you smell awful. What's that on your skirt?'

Adrina glanced down at her protruding belly and swamp-stained skirts, then sighed. 'Yes … well, I'm afraid the baby is out of my control, and the gunk … well, that's a souvenir of an encounter with something large and scaly who thought I was lunch. How did *you* get here?'

'I'm not sure,' R'shiel said with a shrug. She was taller than Adrina remembered and prettier too. 'I went looking for Brak …'

'It would be too much to hope you found the Creator, instead?' she asked. That would solve most of Adrina's problems, right there.

'Who?'

'The Creator. It's what Dirk Provin calls the … being, I suppose … who created all of us.' She laughed — albeit a little hysterically. 'When you appeared out of thin air, for a moment there, I thought it was you!'

The girl frowned as she glanced around the dusty attic, and seemed much older for it. 'Who is Dirk Provin? Founders, for that matter,' R'shiel said, suddenly turning back to Adrina, 'how can you be here talking to *me*?'

'We came through the veil.'

'The veil?'

Adrina frowned. 'The veil between worlds. Dirk Provin says it's breaking down. That's how he got to our world. And how the others —'

'What others?' The Demon Child began to circle her curiously.

'The Tide Lords in the metal machine. Cayal and Declan.'

R'shiel reached out and poked Adrina on the shoulder, quite painfully. 'And what *are* you doing here, while we're on the subject of imaginary friends.'

'*I* am not imaginary,' Adrina protested. 'I happen to be as real as you are, thank you very much.'

R'shiel looked around and caught sight of her reflection in a dusty mirror leaning against a stack of old papers. 'I have to say, I'm not even sure *I'm* real, any longer. That doesn't look like me.'

'What *do* you think you look like?' Adrina asked.

'Not what I think I do, obviously.' R'shiel caught sight of something else behind the mirror. She reached over and pulled it out. It was a stuffed toy, but nothing like any animal Adrina had ever seen before. 'Look at this.'

'Excuse me?' Adrina was a little miffed by R'shiel's short attention span. Several worlds were at stake. They didn't have time to reminisce over childhood toys.

The girl smiled at the stumpy-legged creature, with its large nose, flat face and fluffy ears, and then put the toy down and began to poke around some of the other accumulated junk. There were abandoned toys lying about — a pair of pink satin shoes with long ribbon ties and square toes poking out from beneath a pile of dusty books, a wheeled, metal contraption. There were other items that might have been sporting equipment. Or weapons. Adrina really wasn't sure. In her reality, they were one and the same.

'This place feels like nobody has been here for years. I wonder who this stuff belongs to.'

'I'm sure, once we get my little problem sorted out, there are many happy hours ahead of you rummaging through ... well, whatever this junk is. In the meantime, young lady, as you clearly know your way around this place, you must take me to the Creator.'

R'shiel looked up from a box she'd found containing what appeared to be a set of children's coloured blocks. 'I don't know who you're talking about.' Something else caught her eye and had her rummaging through dusty boxes. 'Founders, there's a whole lifetime belonging to someone in here.'

'That's wonderful, I'm sure,' Adrina said, rolling her eyes. 'You have to help me find the one,' she added, opening her arms to encompass the cluttered, doorless storeroom, 'who created all this. We need to fix this veil problem, R'shiel, so we can all get on with our lives.'

'What veil problem?'

Before R'shiel could answer, the loud buzzing noise came back.

This time, Adrina was ready for the flash of intense, terrifying light. She reached out just in time, grabbing R'shiel's arm as the floor gave way and once again, Adrina felt herself falling.

CHAPTER IX

The room was gone. Adrina had landed in a field of lush emerald grass, the undulating fields rolling away toward a line of misty hills in the distance. The sky was overcast, a gentle misty rain was falling and when she finally gained her feet, she discovered behind them a series of tall standing stones arranged in a circle.

R'shiel had fallen with her. She also climbed to her feet and looked around, but she seemed intrigued by where they'd landed, rather than alarmed by it.

'Any idea of where we are now?' Adrina asked, shivering in the sudden chill of the misty rain.

'I'm not sure …' R'shiel studied their surroundings for a moment. 'I've seen it before, but the horizon seems further away every time I come here.'

Adrina was starting to despair of ever getting any sense from the Demon Child. Maybe the Provin lad was right about something happening to the Creator — only the problem wasn't that something *physical* had happened, but that he was going mad and his first victim was R'shiel. 'So you know this place? What is it?'

The girl shrugged. 'I don't think it has a name yet.'

'Do you know what that buzzing noise was? And the light?'

The Demon Child shook her head, squatting down to feel the texture of the grass. 'It started a while ago. About the same time as the voices.'

Wonderful! Now she's hearing voices.

'And what did these voices of your say?'

'Gibberish mostly,' she said, running her hand through the damp grass without looking up. 'They were very odd … they sounded like they were giving instructions. Things like, *lie down, ma'am, wrists on seven … ninety-eight degrees north by north-west of the nipple … can we have your date of birth please?*' R'shiel stood up, breathing in the aroma of the rain-soaked grass with an appreciative sigh. She smiled. 'This place is amazing.'

Adrina wanted to stamp her foot with impatience. R'shiel was speaking nothing but nonsensical claptrap. 'What about *our* world?'

'What about it?'

'*What about it?*' Adrina repeated incredulously. 'While you're here chatting with the voices in your head and admiring the scenery, my girl, our world — your world too, you might recall — is falling apart. Have you forgotten that?

'No ...'

'Then have some mercy, at least. I've been pregnant forever!'

The Demon Child glanced at Adrina's swollen belly. She reached out and placed her hand on it for a moment, smiling apologetically. 'I wonder if you'll have a boy or a girl.'

'I'm beyond caring, to be honest.'

R'shiel removed her hand and studied Adrina thoughtfully. 'Do you *want* a girl? Or would you rather a boy who grows up to be like his father?'

'Hah! That would imply you're going help me do something about my child growing up at all, doesn't it?'

Her tone seemed to wound the Demon Child. 'This is not my fault, you know.' She looked past Adrina, her attention suddenly elsewhere. 'Did you see that?'

'See what?'

'I'm not sure.' R'shiel seemed puzzled. 'I think I saw something moving, which is odd, because there's never been anything alive here before.' R'shiel pushed past Adrina and broke into a run, heading for the standing stones. She disappeared inside the circle. A moment later, something emitted an angry squeal, like a puppy caught in a trap, and R'shiel reappeared clutching a strange creature by the scruff of its neck. It looked like a large, animated doll dressed in an odd red suit, with tiny leather boots and jaunty green scarf tied around his neck, which R'shiel was using to maintain her stranglehold on its squirming body.

The creature wiggled furiously, trying to escape the Demon Child's firm grasp, cursing at her in a variety of languages, his little face wrinkled with angry malice.

'Gods!' Adrina said. 'What is that?'

'I have no idea,' R'shiel said. She lifted the creature to look him in the eye, keeping him at arms length to avoid his wildly flailing limbs. 'What are you?'

'I am ye death!' the little man screeched. 'I am ye worst nightmare! Put me down, woman, or I'll smite ye where ye stand!'

R'shiel smiled. 'Smite away, little one. I am the Demon Child. I smite back, you know.'

The little creature suddenly went limp, his anger forgotten. He hung in her grasp, eying R'shiel curiously. 'Ye are the Demon Child?'

'In the flesh. Who are you?'

'*What* are you?' Adrina added with a frown, fearful this might be the Creator. They were in serious trouble if it was.

'I be one of the Lairds of the *Leipreachán*,' the little man announced as proudly as he could while dangling by the scruff of his neck. 'My name is ... well, it's none of ye damned business, actually.'

'Well, Lord None of Ye Damned Business,' R'shiel said, 'we're looking for the Creator. Do you know where to find him?'

The *leipreachán's* eyes narrowed slyly. 'I might. What do ye need her for?'

'Our worlds are in danger,' Adrina explained. 'Falling apart. The veils between them are breaking down.'

The little old man sniggered. 'That's because ye are the old worlds. The Creator is done with ye.'

'How do you know that?' R'shiel demanded, shaking him to emphasise her point.

'Because this be the new world,' the *leipreachán* said with a smirk, opening his arms wide to indicate the rolling green hills surrounding them. 'The old worlds will fade into nothingness as the Creator forgets all about ye.'

'How do we stop the Creator forgetting about us, my lord?' Adrina asked politely, wondering if R'shiel's intimidation tactics were actually making things worse.

'Ye have to know the magic word,' the *leipreachán* said.

'And just what, exactly, is the magic word?' R'shiel asked.

Before the *leipreachán* could answer, however, the loud buzzing noise started up again.

As if he knew what was coming, the little man started wriggling again with renewed vigour as the intense light blinded all three of them. R'shiel lost her grip as the rolling, misty hills disappeared and once again, Adrina was falling.

CHAPTER X

Every morning, a small brown bird flew down to eat the crumbs the High Princess of Hythria sprinkled on the sill outside the living-room window of her borrowed apartment in the Medalonian capital, the Citadel. This morning was the same as every other morning. The small brown bird flew down to eat the crumbs on the sill outside the living-room window of her apartment. The little bird landed on the very edge on the stonework, tentatively approach the crumbs, tweeting softly ... and then snatched up the fattest crumb and flew away, disappearing amidst the shining white spires of the city with its prize.

The same bird, the same time, and, Adrina was certain, the same damn crumb.

'We did this yesterday,' she said, climbing awkwardly to her feet as the sparrow dived and swooped away.

Damin glanced up from the scroll he was reading by the fire. As usual, he was up before she was, by the fire reading. As usual, Adrina thought it odd, because Damin wasn't the sitting-by-the-fire type.

'Did we?'

As usual, Damin was distracted. No, worse than that. Utterly disinterested.

'I've been pregnant forever.' The words were out of her mouth before she could stop herself.

'*Tell* me about it.'

Adrina glared at her husband — sitting there sipping mulled wine as if he didn't have a care in the world. 'It's all right for you, Damin Wolfblade. You're the wastrel who spends his days swanning around the Citadel with Tarja, pretending he's important.'

He grinned at her.

'I'm the High Prince of Hythria, Adrina. I *am* important,' she said in unison with her husband.

Damin stared at her in surprise. 'How did you know ...?'

'What you were going to say?' she finished for him. 'The same way I know the next thing I should say is something about how I've nothing to do but sit here incubating your precious Hythrun heir.' She held up her hand before he could interrupt, adding 'To which you will reply that you rather thought I liked the idea of being here in Medalon because I kicked up a big enough fuss about coming along.'

Damin was studying her as if she was going a little bit mad.

'I know ...' Adrina sighed wearily as she stretched her aching back. 'You think I'm crazy. So I'm going to ask you if you ever feel as if we've been here in the Citadel *forever*? You're going to tell me you never really thought about it. And we'll go back and forth, talk about going for a ride and such for a while until I lose my patience and throw something at you.'

Damin still couldn't think of anything to say, although he looked like he was wracking his brain for something that wouldn't land him in trouble. He was saved by the knock at the door to their apartment — precisely on cue.

'That'll be Tarja ...' she said as Damin crossed the sitting room to open it, still looking at her like she'd suddenly sprouted a third eye in the middle of her forehead.

He opened the door and stepped back to allow their visitor into the room. Sure enough, it was Tarja.

The Lord Defender bowed politely to both of them. 'Good morning Damin. Your highness.'

'Good morning, Tarja,' Adrina said. 'Shall we go visit your prisoner?'

Tarja stared at her in surprise. 'I beg your pardon?'

'That's why you're here, isn't it? You're hoping to borrow Damin for a while. You have a bit of a problem and think he might be able to help.'

'I beg your pardon?' he repeated, looking at her oddly.

'Adrina seems to have acquired the ability to predict the future,' Damin explained, closing the door with a decidedly worried frown. 'It's more than a little spooky, I have to say.'

'I'm not prescient, Damin,' she said, rolling her eyes. 'We've been here before and I just want to save time. So take me to Dirk Provin. Now.'

Tarja glanced at Damin. 'How could she know about Dirk Provin?'

'I have no idea,' Damin said. 'I don't even know who he is.'

'He's the prisoner,' Tarja said, looking even more rattled than Damin, 'claiming the world is about to end.'

Chapter XI

The stone cellblock was dimly lit as usual, the only daylight coming from the narrow windows at the top of each cell with bars set into the thick granite blocks. Dust motes danced in the infrequent light, stirred into frenzy by their passing. Dirk Provin stood up from his pallet as they approached the bars of his cell, his expression filled with hope and expectation.

'My Lord Defender —'

'Don't start,' Tarja warned the young man. He turned to Damin. 'Did you want some time alone with him?'

'Damin doesn't need time alone with him,' Adrina declared, pushing her way forward. 'All he's going to tell Damin is what he's been insisting all along: he comes from an entirely different world. His world has two suns and we speak the same language because we all come from the same Creator.'

Dirk Provin stared at Adrina with a look very similar to the one her husband and Damin had treated her to, earlier this morning.

'How do you know that?' he asked.

'It's a long story,' Adrina said, 'but to save time, let's just agree that the veil between our worlds is breaking down and you crossed into your world near a place on your world called … well, truth is, I can't remember what it was called, but it doesn't really matter.'

'Omaxin,' Dirk said, looking very unsettled. 'It was near Omaxin.'

'Well, there you go,' she said, turning to Damin and Tarja. 'Release him.'

'Excuse me?'

'Release him,' she repeated.

Damin asked what everyone was obviously thinking. 'Why?'

'Because we have to meet up with the others.'

'What others?' Dirk asked, even more puzzled than Damin and Tarja, who'd had a short while to get used to the fact that she seemed to know everything that what was going to happen next before it happened.

'The two Tide Lords who are about to come crashing through the veil in a large mental monster that makes no sense to anybody. If we're going to figure this out, we're going to need them too, I suspect.' She turned to Dirk. 'You came out of the veil east of the Citadel, didn't you?'

He took a step closer to the bars, close enough now to grip them. His fingers were bloody and swollen, but seemed to be intact. 'You know about the veil?'

'I do,' she said.

'How?' Tarja asked, not attempting to hide the scepticism in his tone.

'Because this has happened before, Tarja. And it *keeps* happening, only like Dirk Provin says, the veil is breaking down, so some of us are beginning to notice.'

Damin and Tarja seemed unconvinced, but Dirk was positively excited. 'You've met people from other worlds?'

'They called themselves Tide Lords. I think they have magical powers of some kind, so we'll need their help.'

'With what?' Damin asked, looking at his wife as if she had gone completely mad.

Adrina paused for a moment before answering, and then shrugged. Either Damin was right and she'd lost her mind, or this was their only salvation. Right now, instinct told her the latter was her best option.

'Because,' she said, 'they are magicians and the only way to fix this is to find the magic word.'

Chapter XII

The expedition to visit the site of Dirk Provin's supposed veil between worlds was small. The High Prince of Hythria seemed convinced they were simply pandering to Adrina's flight of fantasy. He could do little to argue the case, however, given the determination of his wife and Shananara, the Queen of the Harshini, who was adamant Adrina's prescience should be taken seriously.

They left after lunch, mounted in a small group with only two of Tarja's red-coated Defenders as an escort — as they had the last time they undertook this journey. Adrina gave her horse its head as soon as they were over bridge and on the main road south, out of impatience as much as anything. Damin caught up with her quick enough, and demanded she slow down, something she was reluctantly forced to do when her child protested the jostling with a few well-placed kicks, hard enough to make her grunt.

'See, even the child thinks you're a lunatic for galloping off like that.'

Adrina glanced over her shoulder at the others only a few paces behind them. 'I don't let *you* dictate to me, Damin. Why would I listen to your child?'

Damin had no chance to answer before the rest of their party caught up to them. Shananara's face creased with concern. 'Should you be galloping like that in your condition, your highness?'

'I don't see why not,' Adrina said with a shrug. 'Unless we find the magic word, I'm not going to give birth. Ever.' She turned to the young man mounted on a borrowed Defender's mount led by Tarja, his hands tied to the pommel of his saddle. 'Isn't that right, Master Provin?'

'I assume so, your highness.' The lad seemed a little reluctant to make a definitive ruling on the matter. He sat comfortably on the horse, clearly used to being in the saddle, but he was ill at ease.

'Let's not take that as a given,' Damin suggested, frowning at the young man. 'How far out of the Citadel did you say this world-bridging veil of yours is supposed to be?'

Dirk looked around uncertainly. 'I thought it was east of the Citadel. We were in a forested area. It took me less than an hour to find the road.'

Tarja glanced at one of the guards, who nodded and pointed confidently east. 'That would make it the woods around —'

'Bottleneck Gorge,' Adrina said, before the guard could answer. 'That's the only wooded area within half a day's walk of the city.'

'Bottleneck Gorge it is then,' Tarja said, turning his mount east with a shrug, apparently not convinced, but not so certain Adrina was insane that he could ignore her, either. He tugged on Dirk's lead rein, pulling the young man behind him. Adrina fell in beside Damin and Shananara, with the two Defenders behind them, and they headed toward a veil between two worlds that only Adrina and Dirk Provin believed was there.

It was an hour or so later, once they were well into the tree line, that Adrina heard the rhythmic pounding she'd been waiting for; a noise so foreign to her senses that the first time she'd heard it, she thought she might have imagined it. A moment later, the ground shuddered with the impact of a massive explosion somewhere ahead of them.

The horses reared in fright.

'What the hell ...' Tarja turned to Dirk as he fought to bring both his own mount and the one he was leading, under control. 'Founders! What was that?'

'I have no idea,' the young man said, clinging to the pommel of his saddle with grim determination. 'When I came through the veil it was like a mist. There was nothing burning. Nothing exploding, either.'

'It's the Tide Lords,' Adrina said as she circled her mount a few times to settle him, and then turned to look in the direction of the explosion and the acrid black smoke billowing into the clear morning sky.

Still looking sceptical, Tarja dismounted, and drew his sword. 'Get down,' he ordered the prisoner. 'We'll go on foot from here.'

Dirk lifted his tied hands the few inches the slack in his bond would allow. 'Love to,' he said, 'soon as you let me loose.'

Tarja waved one of the Defenders forward, drawing his sword. Damin and Adrina — with some difficulty — dismounted as the guards released Dirk Provin. The second Defender took up the reins of their mounts. Dirk shook his hands in an attempt to restore circulation to them.

'Stay here with the horses,' Tarja ordered the Defenders, and then shoved Dirk none too gently to get him moving. 'You go first.'

Adrina pushed her way ahead of them. 'Gods, Tarja, you'd think he was leading you into an ambush.'

'Well, if it is, they'll take him first, won't they?'

Dirk shook his head, smiling Damin offered Adrina his hand, which she accepted 'Come on,' she said. 'We don't have much time before the veil closes in on us.'

They hurried forward through the trees and the unnaturally silent forest. Adrina could feel the unspoken scepticism of her companions and ignored it. When they reached the narrow clearing bordering the edge of a steep gully, they stopped, staring at the strange machine that lay mangled and burning on the ground and the two men climbing from inside the belly of the mechanical beast. As it had the last time Adrina was here, smoke belched from the wreckage like a dragon spewing forth all the ills of the world. Her eyes watered as she stared at the spectacle, tapping her foot impatiently.

'By the gods,' Damin exclaimed, coming to a halt beside her. 'What is this thing?' He turned to Dirk Provin. 'Is this what brought you here? This ... metal monster?'

Dirk shook his head, as gobsmacked as they were. 'I ... I have no idea ...'

'It's a helicopter,' Adrina said as one of the men climbed from the wrecked metal contraption.

He winced in pain and then turned to glance at his companion, but made no move to help him. The man turned back to look at them. 'What? You all look like you've never seen a chopper before?'

'They haven't,' Adrina announced, stepping forward. 'Well, no actually, they have. They just don't remember it. You're Declan Hawkes, right? And that is Cayal Lakesh?'

'I don't think we're in Kansas any more, Dorothy,' Cayal grunted, still trying to extract himself from the wreckage with some difficulty. When he was free, he clambered out of the burning wreck and looked around, his curious gaze fixing on Adrina. His companion seemed equally disturbed. 'I'll lay you odds we're not even on Earth any longer, Rodent.' He studied Adrina curiously for a moment. 'How do you know who we are?'

'We've met before, although you probably don't remember it. You just ditched some crystal you're trying to hide in something called the Mariana Trench and believe there's no way your friend Lukys has had time to find it and open a rift. Oh, and it's not High Tide yet.' She turned and added to her husband. 'I know … we're nowhere near the coast here. Just trust me on this, Damin'

The two men from the wreckage of the metallic beast stared at her with concern. 'Where are we?'

'Medalon. You have come through the veil. I am Her Serene Highness, Princess Adrina. This is my husband, Prince Damin, High Prince of Hythria, Tarja Tenragan, the Lord Defender of Medalon, Shananara, Queen of the Harshini, and Dirk Provin, who is a prince and a religious leader on his world of Ranadon.'

'Well, at least they sent a welcoming committee worthy of us,' Cayal remarked to his companion. 'Where did you say we are?'

'Medalon,' Tarja said, taking a step forward, his sword still held out threateningly in front of him.

'Never heard of it.'

'Nor have you yet told us where you came from. Or what that metallic beast is. Or how you killed it.'

Adrina slapped Tarja's blade away impatiently. 'We don't have time for any of this idiotic male posturing,' she said. 'The veil will envelop us soon and before it does, we need to find the magic word.'

'*Please?*' Cayal ventured with a tentative smile.

Adrina wanted to stamp her foot with impatience at these foolish men, but she knew she didn't have time. The clearing was already filling with a haze which she suspected was more than just the result of the metal machine crash. The veil was taking them over once more. Any minute now, the loud buzzing would start up.

She didn't want to do this over and over again.

'What do you want us to do, your highness?' Dirk Provin asked. He seemed to understand her impatience. And believe her when she claimed this had all happened before.

'Believe what I'm telling you, that would be a good start,' she snapped. 'I know you all think I'm losing my mind, but this has happened before. Who knows how many times? I've been through the same veil that brought you two here,' she explained, pointing to Declan and Cayal, 'and you,' she added to Dirk. 'I have seen other worlds too, and I met Brak and R'shiel and a *leipreachán*.

'What's a *leipreachán?*' Damin asked.

'It's an Irish fairy,' Declan replied, looking around with a frown. 'Are you *certain* we're not on Earth?'

'I don't even know what Earth is,' Adrina said, annoyed at the interruption. 'I only know the *leipreachán* said the Creator has lost interest in us, and that to save our worlds we need to discover the magic word.'

'You do know *leipreacháns* are sneaky little buggers who like to play tricks on people, don't you?' Cayal said, clearly doubtful of her sanity.

'I believe her,' Dirk Provin said.

'You would,' Tarja snapped, rolling his eyes.

'Well, on the balance of things, your story is no crazier than anything else that's happened today,' Declan said with a shrug. 'Exactly how did you meet this *leipreachán* anyway?'

Adrina wasn't sure she had time to explain. The mist seemed to be getting closer. As quickly as she could, she told them her story. About how she was certain she'd lived this day over and over. How she'd met Dirk before and how they'd come here to find the Tide Lords. She told them about the loud buzzing noise and falling through the veil; about meeting Brak and R'shiel and the *leipreachán* and his insistence that the secret to their future was to discover the magic word. They listened to her in silence, giving Adrina no hint as to whether they believed her or not.

She never really got a chance to find out if they did believe her story. Adrina had barely finished her tale when the buzzing noise started. Reaching for the nearest person, the bright light blinded her as she began to fall through the veil, with no idea where she would land, or who was falling with her.

Chapter XIII

Every morning, a small brown bird flew down to eat the crumbs the High Princess of Hythria sprinkled on the sill outside the living-room window of her borrowed apartment in the Medalonian capital, the Citadel. This morning was the same as every other morning. He landed on the very edge on the stonework, tentatively approaching the crumbs, tweeting softly … and then flew away squawking in fright at the appearance of a small man dressed in a red woollen suit, who was suddenly and inexplicably perched on the windowsill.

Adrina stared at the *leipreachán* and then glanced over her shoulder at Damin, who was engrossed in the scroll he was reading, and utterly disinterested in his wife's preoccupation with taming the birds who inhabited the high towers of the Citadel.

'How did *you* get here?' Adrina asked, turning back to the *leipreachán*.

'Same way you got to my story, I imagine,' he said, looking past Adrina to examine the room curiously. 'Is that ye husband?'

'If I answer you, will you tell me the magic word?'

The *leipreachán* laughed. 'Ye've not had any luck finding it then?'

'I wouldn't be here feeding sparrows if I had,' she pointed out grumpily.

The little man seemed to find that terribly amusing. He crossed his arms and his legs and looked out over the tall white towers of the Citadel for a moment with a wistful sigh. 'Seems a pity this is all going to fade away soon. All for want of one little word.'

'And what word would that be?'

'Ah … now that's *ye* problem, dearie. Not mine.'

Adrina reached out to grab the little man, but he disappeared over the edge of the sill before she could reach him. For a moment, the idea of him plummeting to the ground where someone would have to scrape him off the pavement with a shovel was very satisfying, but then she realised the *leipreachán* probably couldn't die here, because he wasn't from her world …

'We have to see Tarja's prisoner,' Adrina announced abruptly.

Damin looked up. 'Sorry?'

'When Tarja gets here,' she said impatiently. 'We have to see his prisoner.'

'Ah … when Tarja gets here?'

Precisely on cue, there was a knock at the door to their apartment.

'That'll be Tarja …' she said, looking unavoidably smug as Damin crossed the sitting room. He opened the door and stepped back to allow their visitor into the room. Sure enough, it was Tarja.

The Lord Defender bowed politely to both of them. 'Good morning Damin. Your highness.'

'Good morning, Tarja,' Adrina said. 'Let's go.'

Tarja stared at her in surprise. 'I beg your pardon?'

'I need to speak to Dirk Provin,' she said, picking up her shawl. 'Don't worry, you can explain who he is to Damin on the way.'

'I beg your pardon?' he repeated, looking at her oddly.

'Adrina seems to have … lost her mind, actually,' Damin said, as she headed down the hall. Adrina didn't care what he thought. The end of the world was at stake.

The stone cellblock was dimly lit as usual, the only daylight coming from the narrow windows at the top of each cell with bars set into the thick granite blocks. Dust motes danced in the infrequent light, stirred into frenzy by their passing. Dirk Provin stood up from his pallet as they approached she bars of his cell, his expression filled with hope and expectation.

'I was expecting the Lord Defender —'

'Do you know who I am?'

Dirk shook his head. 'Should I?'

'I suppose not, but it would have simplified things if you remembered. You're Dirk Provin, right? You come from an entirely different world. Your world has two suns and we speak the same language because we all come from the same Creator.'

Dirk Provin stared at Adrina with a look very similar to the one her husband and Damin had treated her to, earlier.

'How do you know that?' he asked.

'It's a long story,' Adrina said, 'but to save time, let's just agree that the veil between our worlds is breaking down and you crossed into your world near a place on your world called … well, truth is, I can't remember what it was called, but it doesn't really matter.'

'Omaxin,' Dirk said, looking very unsettled. 'It was near Omaxin.'

'Whatever … the point is, I know how to fix things.'

'You do?'

'We need the magic word.'

'Well, naturally,' Dirk said in a tone that said he was humouring her and probably thought her barking mad. 'And how do you know we need … the *magic* word.'

'Because I've met people from other worlds besides you.'

Dirk's expression abruptly changed from scepticism to relief. 'You believe me, then?'

'Of course I believe you. But I need to you to explain something. You say you come from another world?'

He nodded. 'It's called Ranadon.'

'This other … man, I met. He didn't call his world a world. He called it his story.'

'You hesitated when you said man.'

'Well, I'm not sure he was a man, come to think of it. He called himself a *leipreachán*. Declan Hawkes says that is some sort of Irish fairy.'

'Then perhaps story means to him what world means to us?' Dirk ventured, looking a little uncertain.

'But why would it?' she asked. 'You said it yourself. We all speak the same language because we all come from the same creator. Why wouldn't we use the same words to mean the same thing?'

Dirk thought about that for a moment and then nodded. 'So you think the Creator is —'

'Creating stories, not worlds,' she finished for him, his measured tones too slow for her excitement. 'It makes perfect sense, don't you see? We're not separate worlds, we're separate stories, and the new stories, like the one with the *leipreachán*, are taking over from the old.'

'And one single word is going to save us?'

'Of course!' she said, almost bouncing up and down with excitement. 'Don't you see? What's the one word that will continue our stories? That will keep our worlds and the people in them alive?'

Dirk stared at her with the dawning light of comprehension. He shook his head as the sound of Damon and Tarja running down the dimly lit corridor in pursuit of her grew louder and louder.

'It can't be that simple,' he said, shaking his head.

'Why not?' she asked, as Damin skidded to a halt and pulled her roughly away from the bars and the man he undoubtedly considered a dangerous prisoner.

'Are you hurt, your highness?' Tarja asked a moment later as he arrived. Dirk wisely stepped back from the bars. Tarja glared at the young man warningly and then turned to Adrina. 'Did he hurt you?'

'Of course not,' she said, shaking free of Damin's grip. 'Let him go.'

'I can't let him go!'

'Why not? At worst, he's a lunatic, at best he's telling the truth. Trust me, Tarja. If you let him go and escort him back to where you found him, he'll leave. Forever.'

'How could you possibly know that?' Damin demanded, caught between confusion and anger.

'Because he knows the magic word,' she said, looking at Dirk with a smile. 'And he's going to tell it to the Tide Lords, too, on his way back through the veil.'

Chapter XIV

Adrina heard the rhythmic pounding ahead as she pushed through the trees. A moment later, the ground shuddered with the impact of a massive explosion somewhere in front of them.

The horses reared in fright.

'It's the Tide Lords,' Adrina said, before anybody could ask and then turned to look in the direction of the explosion. The acrid black smoke billowed into the clear morning sky as Tarja dismounted, and drew his sword. 'Get down,' he ordered Dirk. 'We'll go on foot from here.'

Adrina hurried through the trees and the unnaturally silent forest. She could feel their unspoken scepticism, and ignored it. She was excited now, wanting to get this done. When they reached the narrow clearing bordering the edge of a steep gully, she stopped, ignoring the strange machine that lay mangled and burning on the ground, focussing instead on the two men climbing out of the mechanical beast. As it had the last time Adrina was here, smoke belched from the wreckage like a dragon spewing forth all the ills of the world. Her eyes watered as she stared at the spectacle, tapping her foot impatiently.

'By the gods,' Damin exclaimed, coming to a halt beside her. 'What is this thing?' He turned to Dirk Provin. 'Is this what brought you here? This … metal monster?'

Dirk shook his head, as gobsmacked as they were. 'I … I have no idea …'

'It's a helicopter,' Adrina said as one of the men climbed from the wrecked metal contraption. 'You're Declan Hawkes, yes? And Cayal Lakesh?'

'I don't think we're in Kansas any more, Dorothy,' Cayal grunted, still trying to extract himself from the wreckage. When he was free, he clambered out of the burning wreck and looked around, his curious gaze fixing on Adrina. His companion seemed equally disturbed. 'I'll lay you odds we're not even on Earth any longer, Rodent.' He studied Adrina curiously for a moment. 'How do you know who we are?'

'We've met before, although you don't remember it. You just ditched some crystal you're trying to hide in something called the Mariana Trench and there's no way your friend Lukys has had time to find it and open a rift. Oh, and it's not High Tide yet.' She turned and added to her husband. 'I know … we're nowhere near the coast here. Just trust me on this, Damin.'

The two men from the wreckage of the metallic beast stared at her with unease. 'Where are we?'

'Medalon. You have come through the veil. I am Her Serene Highness, Princess Adrina. This is … well, you know, I don't think it matters who we are. All you need to know is that you're not in your world, you don't belong here, and the only way back is the magic word.'

'*Please?*' Cayal ventured with a tentative smile.

Adrina knew she didn't have time to berate the Tide Lord for his flippancy. Every time they did this, the gap between the veil's appearance seemed to grow shorter. The clearing was already filling with smoky mist. The veil was taking them over again. Any minute now, the loud buzzing would start up again.

She was fed up with doing this over and over.

'Just tell them, your highness,' Dirk Provin suggested. He seemed to understand her impatience. And he believed her when she claimed this had all happened before.

He was smiling. Probably because this time, he knew, he'd be going home.

Adrina considered that excellent advice. As the buzzing noise started yet again, she reached for Cayal and whispered the magic word to him. A moment later, the bright light blinded her as she began to fall through the veil, only this time she wasn't frightened.

Adrina knew the magic word.

CHAPTER XV

Every morning, a small brown bird flew down to eat the crumbs the High Princess of Hythria sprinkled on the sill outside the living-room window of her borrowed apartment in the Medalonian capital, the Citadel.

Every morning the little bird would land on the very edge of the stonework, tentatively approach the crumbs tweeting softly ... and then snatch up the fattest crumb and fly away, disappearing amidst the shining white spires of the city with its prize.

Every morning. The same bird, the same time, and, Adrina was sure, the same damn crumb.

Didn't we do this yesterday? Adrina thought about asking, fearful the words would provoke a replay of the day's events yet again.

'Didn't we do this yesterday?'

Adrina spun around and stared at Damin in shock, forgetting all about the dull ache in her back that had bothered her since she woke this morning. It seemed to intensify as she climbed awkwardly to her feet. Her daily winged visitor dived and swooped away toward his nest somewhere high in the white towers of the city.

Damin glanced up from the scroll he was reading by the fire.

'Didn't we do this yesterday?' He sounded distracted. But no longer utterly disinterested. 'It feels like you've been pregnant forever.'

'You've noticed.'

'Well,' he said grin, 'it's kind of hard to miss ...'

'I don't mean me being pregnant,' she said impatiently. 'I mean you noticing that we keep doing this over and over.'

He nodded thoughtfully. 'We do, don't we? Why is that?'

'It's because our worlds are stagnating. The veils between them are breaking down. It's something to do with the Creator being either too distracted or too busy creating new worlds to care about us. The only way to save our world and set things to rights is to use the magic word. Trouble is, even though I know what it is, I don't know what to do with it.'

Damin put down his wine and studied his wife for a moment before answering. 'You know, only about every third word you said then makes any sense at all.'

'I know,' she said in frustration. 'But when Tarja gets here to tell us about Dirk Provin, we can fetch him, and then speak to the Tide Lords and see if any of them know how to use the magic word.'

'What do you mean, when Tarja gets …?' Damin's question was interrupted by a knock at the door — precisely on cue.

'That'll be Tarja,' she said as her husband crossed the sitting room to open it, staring at her as if she'd suddenly sprouted a third eye in the middle of her forehead.

He opened the door and stepped back to allow their visitor into the room. Sure enough, it was Tarja.

The Lord Defender bowed politely to both of them. 'Good morning Damin. Your highness.'

'Good morning, Tarja,' Adrina said. 'Shall we go visit your prisoner?'

Tarja stared at her in surprise. 'I beg your pardon?'

'That's why you're here, isn't it? You're hoping to borrow Damin for a while. You have a bit of a problem and think he might be able to help.'

'I beg your pardon?' he repeated, looking at her oddly.

'Apparently, our worlds are stagnating,' Damin explained, closing the door. 'The veils between them are breaking down because the Creator is either too distracted or too busy creating new worlds to care about us. The only way to save our world and set things to rights is to use the magic word. Trouble is, even though Adrina knows what it is, we don't know what to do with it.'

Adrina stared at Damin in shock.

'What?' he said, a little defensively. 'I said you didn't make any sense. I never said I didn't *hear* you.'

Tarja glanced at Damin. 'How could she know about the prisoner?'

'I have no idea,' Damin said. 'I don't even know who your prisoner is. I just know … well, I'm not sure what I know. But I trust Adrina's instincts. I think we should do as she says.'

'And what is it you want us to do, you highness?' Tarja asked her, more than a little dubious.

'We have to ask Dirk Provin and … the other people we'll meet later today, what to do with the magic word,' Adrina said, trying to be patient. In truth, she wanted to bolt down the stairs in search of the solution to this endless, repetitive existence, but she knew she had to contain herself. It would do no good to lose Tarja's cooperation at this point and have to go through all this again tomorrow, and the day after … and how ever many days after that until someone believed her.

'I see,' Tarja said, with the care of a physician coaxing information out of a lunatic. 'And what exactly is this "magic word", your highness?'

'Sequel,' Adrina said, savouring the power in the magical word. 'We need to bring forth a sequel.'

AFTERWORD

This story is, in part, the result of countless emails asking me what happens to the characters in my books after they end, to which I always want to respond: *when I know that, I'll write the sequel.* It's also partly in response to a comment one of my daughters made about what the voices in my head are doing on a day to day basis …

— *Jennifer Fallon*

Cecilia Dart-Thornton was 'discovered' on the Internet after she posted the first chapter of her unpublished trilogy to an Online Writing Workshop. Subsequently an editor contacted her, and within a few weeks Time Warner (New York) had bought her three-part Bitterbynde series. On publication the books were acclaimed in Amazon's 'Best of 2001', *Locus Magazine*'s 'Best First Novels of 2001' and the Australian Publishers' Association Award: 'Australia's Favourite Read of 2001'. In Australia they reached the top of the *Sydney Morning Herald* bestseller list. They have also received accolades in the *Washington Post*, *The Times*, *Good Reading Magazine*, *Kirkus Reviews* and more.

Cecilia's books, including the four-part Crowthistle series, are available in more than seventy countries and have been translated into several languages.

The Enchanted:
A Tale of Erith

C ECILIA D ART-T HORNTON

CHAPTER ONE

Don't you go down by the river, my darling,
Nor through bluebell woods to the old ruined mill.
Those are the haunts of the strangers, my darling,
As ancient as starlight, they linger there still.

As evening drew nigh, Mazarine stood in the bay window of the library, looking out across Kelmscott Park. Sweeping lawns rolled down to the lake, which lay like a shattered mirror fallen from the sunset sky, reflecting clouds as red as flame. Unseeing, the young woman gazed out through distorted panes, past the distant chimneys of Clover Cottage, towards wooded hills stitched with glimmering streams, where clandestine trees, long-shadowed, bowed darkly before the wind.

The oaken panelling of the chamber in which she stood had been polished, over the years, to the sombre glow of antique amber. Floor-to-ceiling shelves upheld vellum-bound volumes; chartreuse, tawny, sable, their spines embossed with gilt lettering. On the mantelpiece the inner cogs of the mahogany clock went *click!* as a ratchet alternately caught and released a gear that unwound the spring and moved the hands. Ticking clocks, the sombre glitter of old gold, the gleam of polished wood — these were the trademarks of Kelmscott Hall.

Mazarine had not lived long at the Hall — only since the demise of her parents last Uainemis, at the beginning of Summer. Having no siblings with whom to commiserate, she mused longingly on her lost family, clutching to her breast the tilhal-locket on its necklace chain which held their portraits in miniature: her mother, who had taught her the lore of eldritch creatures and, sitting by the fire on long Winter evenings, related thrilling legends of immortal Faêran knights sleeping for centuries beneath some long-forgotten hill; her father, who had often taken her riding through the woods near Reveswall, identifying every herb and flower, bird and beast they had encountered. Now both those dear ones lay beneath the green turf — sleeping the *other* sleep, that which is a gift belonging only to mortal beings. The tenet that had carried Mazarine unscathed through loss and catastrophe sprang from the conviction that somehow she and her loved ones would all meet again, never to be separated.

Until she came of age to inherit her vast fortune, she must perforce dwell here at Kelmscott, in this remote backwater of Erith far from her childhood home in northern Severnesse, under the guardianship of her mother's distant cousin, the Earl of Rivenhall. Though the circumstance carried its own drawbacks, she was determined to make the best of it.

Beyond the library window two figures moved into view on the lawns, one small, one hulking — the under-gardener's young apprentice, followed by the Chief Steward, Ripley. In Mazarine's opinion, Ripley was nothing but a bullying ruffian, but her guardian held the fellow in high esteem, having given him leave to dwell, rent-free, in a small house on the grounds; an abode far superior to the cottages of the gamekeeper and the gatekeeper. The young woman watched in consternation as the man gesticulated threateningly, while the under-gardener's boy quailed. Presently Ripley cuffed the lad over the side of the head, knocking him down. An involuntary cry escaped the watcher's lips, but before she had time to throw open the casement and give voice to her indignation the lad had picked himself up and run off. Ripley turned on his heel and went swaggering away in the opposite direction.

If the Chief Steward was repulsive to Mazarine, she found his master, the Earl of Rivenhall, equally so. To compensate, there were five creatures hereabouts — other than the gentle horses and the enthusiastic hounds — that made life bearable and even enjoyable. These included the Wilton family who lived at neighbouring Clover Cottage, and two others. A door creaked on its hinges as one of those others now entered the library.

'The master will be late, but someone nears the gate,' said a high-pitched male voice. 'Beneath the leaves so green, 'oo rides to Mazarine?'

'Oh, Thrimby,' said Mazarine, turning toward the shadows from which the voice had emanated. 'You are up early.' Barely distinguishable in the twilight gloom cast by tall, carved bookshelves, the eccentric servant's spare, shrunken form was clad in ragged breeches, a patched waistcoat and a threadbare jacket. Mazarine wondered how long it took him to compose the little rhymes of which he was so fond. Thrimby was never seen during the day — and rarely at night, either, for he was reclusive. It was his wont to rise after the rest of the household had retired to their bedchambers, and to steal away at cock-crow to wherever it was he made his own bed. Mazarine could only assume that her guardian tolerated Thrimby's odd habits because of the exceptional service he provided. Every morning the entire mansion — and it comprised a veritable warren of rooms — would be shining spick and span from chimney pots to cellars, largely due to Thrimby's unsurpassed exertions. Day in, day out, he accomplished the work of a whole bevy of chambermaids, scullerymaids and footmen; moreover he never complained and never seemed to tire. A gem indeed. Mazarine strongly suspected he was not human. At his announcement of a visitor, her heart had begun fluttering like a trapped butterfly. 'Why will my guardian be late?' she asked. 'And who is coming here?'

A triumphant smile gleamed out of the dimness. 'Wielder of the Kelmscott seal will be late for evening meal, for 'is carriage lost a wheel. From the tower's top we saw bird that 'overs over moor, lame and weary and footsore.'

The heart of Mazarine jumped more wildly.

'A wheel came off the earl's coach?' she said, endeavouring in vain to keep her voice steady. 'I hope he remains hale,' she added without conviction. 'How do you know these things, Thrimby?'

She heard the servant sigh. Perhaps he found it an effort to keep composing jingles on the spot. Or perhaps not — it might come naturally to such an unusual fellow as Thrimby.

'We spotted it just as 'e drove away,' he replied. 'We knowed it would come off by end o' day.'

'I see. I daresay it was too late to tell the coachman by the time you noticed it.'

Silence, save for the faint moaning of the wind outside in the machicolations.

'Thrimby, would you mind asking after the under-gardener's boy on my behalf? I fear he has lately suffered at the hands of our Chief Steward.'

'Aye.'

There was nothing more that Mazarine could do for the under-gardener's boy. The earl never took heed of her pleas for better treatment of the servants. Privately the young woman decided that in the morning she would bring the buffeted lad a parcel of food from the kitchens. Presently she cleared her throat and broached the subject uppermost in her mind, which she had been saving until last.

'And you indicate that Lord Fleetwood is coming home?' *Bird that hovers over moor* could only mean one person. Hawkmoor, Lord Fleetwood, officially lived at Kelmscott but was often absent for two or three days, overseeing his estate almost three miles away on the other side of Somerhampton.

'Aye.'

Thrimby's conversation had dwindled. Possibly he was working on another few lines of doggerel.

'Thank—'

The servant's hands flew to his ears. 'Don't say it!' he cried sharply.

'Oh!' Mazarine exclaimed. 'Forgive me, I forgot. Habits are hard to break. I should say, *I appreciate your bringing me these tidings, kind Thrimby.*'

Thrimby's status was unique among the staff in that his deference was neither expected nor demanded. An abhorrence of being thanked was another of the servant's foibles. By this, Mazarine was almost certain he was no mortal creature, but a wight of eldritch, a beneficent domestic brownie. For some unknown reason no-one in the household ever acknowledged this possibility however, so to avoid causing conflict she never mentioned it either — not after the first time. Once, soon after she had arrived at Kelmscott, she had diffidently asked her guardian, 'My lord, do you suppose perhaps Thrimby is a brownie?'

Instantly she was aware she had made a mistake. The look he had given her, of cold scorn, made her wither like a flower blasted by frost.

'A what?' he had barked, thrusting his face close to hers.

'A brownie, sir,' meekly she repeated, stepping backwards.

'What nonsense! I have no idea what you are talking about. Get your mother's tales out of your head, you silly girl.'

And that was the end of it. A second suspicion was growing on Mazarine — she had never seen her guardian actually speak to Thrimby, or even occupy the same room. She wondered whether he knew the servant existed. Perhaps he thought it more expedient to feign ignorance of the enigma dwelling right under his nose.

In the kennels the hounds were belling joyously. Their cacophony barely disguised the sound of hooves beating on the gravel of the wide terrace that ran along the front façade of the mansion. A rider was cantering up the drive to the marble portico. It would be *him* — the only one of Mazarine's five favourites who dominated her thoughts almost every waking moment; the only one who could make her feel as though she were walking on air, or make her blush and become awkwardly self-conscious, although plainly he never intended to have such effects. Hastily she rang the bell for a footman and requested that he tell the housekeeper to ensure that supper would soon be ready. Then she brushed down her vespertine skirts of mourning silk, prodded ineffectually at her hair — a lavish mane of bronze curls, coiffed that morning by her personal lady's-maid — and rushed out of the library toward the front drawing-room, glancing anxiously in the flashing multitude of wall-mirrors as she passed.

In the drawing-room a footman wearing Rivenhall livery was lighting the lamps against the drawing in of darkness, and an upper housemaid knelt on the hearthrug before the fireplace, coaxing life into a pile of kindling. She cupped her hands and blew on the reluctant flames, whose leapings were being combated by fitful gusts blasting down the chimney. Mazarine tried to compose herself to meet the newcomer, but could not bring herself to sit still on any of the velvet-upholstered armchairs or divans, and instead paced back and forth. The last roseate rays of the sinking sun slanted through the drawing-room's recessed window, striking sparkles off the gold braid on the windowseat cushions, setting afire the brass lamps, the candlesticks and the fire-irons. She heard the uneven sound of Hawkmoor's boots on the marble tiles as he crossed the portico and entered the vestibule, and could contain herself no longer, but glided out to meet him.

Stripping off riding gloves, a tall figure stood illumined in a shaft of late sunlight that raked through the open doors. A swirl of dead leaves had blown in when he entered, and now eddied at his feet. Beyond those doors a groom could be seen leading a black horse away toward the stables. Heat and cold raced through Mazarine's person, swift on each others' heels, and she could not take her eyes off the newcomer. Limned in that rose-gold light, he appeared to her like a painting of some marvellous Faêran lord. More than perfect was he; unbearably beautiful, lean and lithe. He was dressed in Dainnan uniform; leather leggings and a shirt of high quality wool with voluminous sleeves, beneath a sleeveless suede tunic reaching almost to his knees and slit down both sides along the length of his thighs. At each shoulder, the Royal Insignia was embroidered — a crown above the numeral fifteen, flanked by the runes J, the hook and R, the sail. At his side his hunting horn swung from a green baldric, and a sheathed dagger was attached to his belt. His hair was Feorhkind brown, like Mazarine's, but much darker; so dark it was like a swatch of midnight. The long locks, gathered in a black ribbon behind the neck, fell to his waist. Handing his gloves to the head footman, he glanced up. His expression, which had been stern, softened.

'Good evening, Mistress Blythe.'

'Good evening, Lord Fleetwood.'

Lord Rivenhall, Hawkmoor's sire, was also Viscount Fleetwood. As the eldest son of an earl, The Right Honourable Hawkmoor Canty was entitled to use his father's highest lesser peerage dignity as his own, though he remained a commoner until such time as he inherited the title.

'You were not expecting me, I understand,' said Hawkmoor. 'Perhaps there will be some supper in any case.'

'Most certainly!'

'Cottrell,' the young man said to the head footman, 'will you ask Goodwife Strood to have supper served in the conservatory this evening?'

'Very good, m' Lord.'

'For it is a fair Autumn evening,' Hawkmoor continued, directing this comment to Mazarine, 'and I would fain enjoy it.'

This was true. During the last four weeks of Autumn, the Windmonth — Gaothmis — was unseasonably balmy, still tinged with the lingering warmth of Summer. In the conservatory, oranges and limes glowed like spherical lamps on the trees, and ginger plants thrust fragrant leaves from their pots. Ripe figs and grapes dangled from above, although the last of the peaches and cherries had been plucked and preserved for Winter use, and most of the strawberries were gone.

A table was set — according to instructions — for two. Generally the earl, Mazarine's guardian, took his meals in the lower dining room, a formal and formidable chamber. Mazarine and Hawkmoor preferred the airy greenery of the conservatory, through whose glass walls one could look out, during the day, at the gardens. At nights the view dwindled to orbs of candlelight, but the servants would light the strings of tiny stained-glass lanterns that festooned many of the garden trees. In Mazarine's opinion these resembled the faerie-lights, or possibly glow-worms, strung through hedges by the *siofra* when they held their miniature revels.

The *siofra* were tiny human-like beings dressed in snail-shells and spiderwebs and seedpods. As a child living in the village of Reveswall in the north of Severnesse, Mazarine had often beheld such woodland folk. By contrast, few such entities could be glimpsed in her new home. It seemed that here in the remote south-eastern shires of Severnesse, far from the trading and passenger routes of the flying Windships and the aerial pathways of Relayers on their sky-horses, eldritch wights — numerous everywhere in Erith — were more adroit and sly at hiding themselves. It made the wild and haunted places seem both emptier and more dangerous. Even the eerie shang-wind seldom blew in this backwater; people hardly bothered to wear protective taltry-hoods, though the law decreed they must carry them at all times.

Folk did, however, adorn their necks with amulets; and some planted rowan trees around their homes and hung bells upon the harnesses of their horses or employed other wards against malign forces. Children were taught the ancient chant cataloguing wight-repellents:

'Hypericum, salt and bread,
Iron cold and berries red,
Self-bored stone and daisy bright,
Save me from unseelie wight.
Red verbena, amber, bell,
Turned-out raiment, ash as well,
Whistle-tunes and rowan-tree,
Running water, succour me ...'

Nonetheless these precautions were taken chiefly from force of habit and tradition rather than fear of imminent peril.

Together Mazarine and Hawkmoor seated themselves at the white-clothed table beneath the orange trees in the conservatory, and held converse as they dined. Delighted to be the subject of the undivided attention of her distant relative — if indeed they were related at all — yet somewhat nervous lest she say or do anything to mar the occasion, the young woman felt, at first, awkward. It was a rare chance, that they could be alone together. It seemed her guardian continually exerted himself to make certain it seldom happened. The earl would only take himself to town if Hawkmoor was away for several days on business. When his son was in the house he never went out, or if he did, he demanded that Mazarine accompany him.

Mazarine and Hawkmoor had never met during their childhood days, and in those old times she had only encountered his father on three or four occasions, for the Blythes and the Cantys had rarely mixed. She retained vague memories of a well-dressed, aristocratic visitor grabbing her by the chin and forcing to tilt her face up to his for his examination, and of a voice murmuring low, so that her parents could not overhear, 'Gad, you are a plain little thing, aren't you! What an Ugly Gosling. Cheer up girl, perhaps you will grow up to be a swan after all!' At the time she had felt crushed, as if she had failed a test she'd had no idea she was undergoing. On subsequent occasions she'd tried to avoid him.

It was a sheltered life Mazarine had led in such a remote neighbourhood, with a governess to tutor her, and few friends. When she was orphaned, her parents' executors contacted her last remaining relatives. Though consumed by grief, she had briefly wondered whether, when he encountered her once more, her new guardian would consider she had evolved into a swan or remained a gosling. He had, however, made no comment at all about her looks.

Since her arrival at Kelmscott Hall a few weeks earlier, the orphan had formed a friendship with Laurelia Wilton, an unwed damsel of her own age who dwelled in nearby Clover Cottage with her parents. Professor Wilton was a poor but respectable apothecary whose livelihood depended on selling his home-made galenicals, simples and other pharmacopeia to physicians and chirurgeons in nearby Somerhampton. He occasionally took in boarders to supplement his meagre income. The warmth of Laurelia's family soon secured them a place in Mazarine's affections and sometimes she felt as if she had known them for years. Though the earl never invited the Wiltons to Kelmscott Hall, his ward visited them as often as possible, learning more about them as time went on. She was also beginning to be further acquainted with the earl and his heir, and the more she discovered about the latter, the more she wished to know.

'I trust your farming establishment is thriving, sir,' Mazarine said shyly, before tasting a spoonful of kale soup.

'In sooth, the harvest has been bountiful this year, Mistress Blythe,' Hawkmoor replied, with a warm smile that had the effect on his companion of a draught of strong wine. 'The corn was of the highest quality, and commanded an excellent price at market. I am fortunate that my land is rich and fertile. The King has been generous.'

The earl's sole heir possessed an independent living, for he owned an estate of two thousand acres, presented to him by the King-Emperor of Erith as a reward for saving his life. Mazarine was aware that when she was thirteen years old Hawkmoor, then aged eighteen, had joined the famous brotherhood of the Dainnan. When they dwelled at the King-Emperor's court these elite warriors were royal bodyguards; when they roamed the lands of Erith they were peacekeepers, and always they were ready to fight as soldiers in times of war. The Dainnan name bestowed on Hawkmoor was 'Rowan', and he had served with the brotherhood for six years. By the time he turned twenty-four he had risen to the rank of captain, commanding his own company of a hundred and eighty men. That was a year ago.

'Pray tell me,' said Mazarine, 'how did it happen that the King's life came into danger and you rescued him?'

'He was travelling through the countryside with his retinue, and I was among them,' said Hawkmoor, breaking bread onto a porcelain plate adorned with the Rivenhall coat of arms. 'It was a Summer Progress.'

'I am not familiar with such an event.'

'Few natives of Severnesse would be acquainted with it, because His Majesty has never voyaged to these shores. As you know, he keeps mainly to the lands of Eldraigne and Luindorn and Finvarna. It is his wont, in Summer, to travel from country estate to country estate, staying for a few weeks at each. The peers vie for his patronage — some even build magnificent new wings onto their mansions, purely to provide attractive accommodation. Anywhere the King-Emperor lays his head is afterwards titled the King's Bedchamber, or the Royal Apartments, and only a select few are permitted to sleep therein, or no one at all ever again, and the hosts will boast of the royal visit for generations to come, as they boast of the King's father, and his grandfather before him.'

'It is a wonder there is any grand house left without a King's Bedchamber, if the d'Armancourt dynasty is so keen on journeying!'

'His Majesty Progresses only once a year, and stays long at each place. I believe there is no fear of a glut!'

They both laughed.

'So you were on this Progress, sir?' Mazarine prompted.

'Indeed, and we had halted at twilight — it having being a warm day and the King-Emperor needing refreshment — to swim in a cool, clear pool in the shadow of a ferny cliff some twelve or fourteen feet high. It was a fair scene, framed by flowering sedges. Slender waterfalls were hanging down the cliff's face like silver chains. Dragonflies darted amid water lilies. The Dainnan of course entered the water first.'

'In the manner of the Tasters at the Assaying before a feast, I daresay,' said Mazarine, ' — those men who are employed to eat the food before the King is served, to provide a warning by their demise, should it be poisoned.'

'Precisely! We tested the water in case of danger to His Majesty's person — in case this fair pool was the haunt of a drowner or some other fell incarnation. We swam, we dived and we sought among the blue-flowering pickerel weeds that grew in the depths, looking for signs of any malicious being such as the Bocan or the dreadful waterhorses, or the emaciated drowners with weed-green hair, such as Peg Powler or Jenny Greenteeth or the Fideal, who can drag a man into the depths with terrible strength. But we found none. What's more, our horses walked down fearlessly to the edge to drink and that was an encouraging sign, for beasts are generally the first to scent danger. Then we deemed it safe, and all of us left the water while His Majesty plunged in.'

Hawkmoor paused to drink from a chased silver-gilt cup.

'Our King-Emperor carries with him always,' he continued, 'an artefact of special value — the Coirnéad, it is called — a silver-clasped hunting-horn, white as milk. Legend says it is of Faêran craftsmanship, and that if ever the sons of the House of D'Armancourt in dire need should sound the horn, help will come. Yet in preparation for bathing His Majesty left this treasure in the keeping of my second-in-command.

'For myself, I donned my raiment, girded myself with my weapons-belt and climbed to the top of the cliff to watch over my liege-lord, though my warriors arrayed themselves about the brink. His Majesty was swimming among the lilies when all of a sudden there reared up from the black-shadowed water a monstrous figure, twice the height of a man and dripping wet. It was, in fact, one of the powerful fuathan; not merely a minor wight to be repelled with simple chants or handfuls of salt. The thing must have been lurking in a lair burrowed into the side of the cliff, underwater, else we would not have overlooked it.'

'By the Powers! Was it Cuachag himself?' cried Mazarine. 'Cuachag, the most terrible of fuathan?'

'I think not,' said Hawkmoor, replacing the cup on the table, 'for had it been he, I doubt whether I would have lived to tell the tale, for what can a mortal man do against one of the Nightmare Princes?'

Mazarine shuddered.

'Yet if not Cuachag, then something close,' said Hawkmoor. 'Something potent.'

And he described the ensuing events so evocatively that Mazarine felt as if they were unfolding before her eyes.

Water sluiced from the fuath's brawny shoulders and from the grassy mane that grew right down its back. The face was ghastly in appearance, for where the nose ought to have been there was only a punched-in hole, like a miry puddle. This manifestation was clad all in ragged green garments that looked to be fashioned of waterweeds. Waist deep, it raised its enormous arms, splaying webbed fingers, and thrashed the water with a spiked tail. Clearly it was intent on doing harm to the King-Emperor, who perceived his danger. He knew he had no chance, but faced the monster bravely, prepared to wrestle it with his bare hands undaunted; ready to die like a true monarch.

It all happened quickly. As soon as the wight appeared, the Dainnan guards had dived into the pool. In that space — an eye's blink — Hawkmoor perceived that the rescuers could not swim to the King in time, so he sprang to his feet and made a great leap off the cliff onto the fuath's shoulders. The water-giant began to bellow and sway like a forest tree in a storm, but the young warrior wrapped both his legs about its neck and one arm about its great slimy skull. He hung on, though being jerked hither and thither like a fish flapping on a hook, meanwhile trying to draw his dagger from its sheath, for the banes of the fuathan included cold steel, which would vanquish them instantly.

At the very least, Hawkmoor's object was to purchase more time for his men to reach the King. But as he pulled the knife from its scabbard, the fuath swivelled its head and sank its toxic fangs into his calf. He did not know if he uttered any sound — they told him later that he shouted with rage as he plunged the dagger into the wight's eye socket, but he had no recollection of it. The creature collapsed, generating huge waves that almost swamped the men, but some reached the King and bore him safely to land, and others swam to the Dainnan leader as the waters were closing over his head, for he was drowning, half-insensible, still hanging onto his foe as if clinging to his very life, and its inky, eldritch blood was swirling through the gleaming waters. They could hardly prise their leader away from the monster, though it was dying, or metamorphosing — for those immortals could not perish, only diminish. Presently the fuath shifted into the shape of an insignificant water-spider and scooted away, leaving its vanquisher at death's threshold.

They dragged Hawkmoor from the water. The King's Chirurgeon tended his wounds, but advised there was scant hope the patient would live beyond a day. He lived, nonetheless, to make the journey back to court on a litter, and there he lay on his sickbed for three months in fever and agony, and it was beyond the power of the best chirurgeons and carlins to say whether or no he would pull through.

Hawkmoor laughed without humour. 'Be that as it may, you know the outcome, Mistress Blythe,' he continued. 'I did live, but only as three-quarters of a man, for when I healed I was,' — he paused an instant — 'as you see me now.'

'Fie! I beg you, do not do yourself such discourtesy, my lord!' cried Mazarine.

'Afterwards, the heart went out of me,' Hawkmoor said quietly, 'for now that I can no longer leap over a stick the height of myself, and stoop under one the height of my knee, and take a thorn out from my foot with my nail while running my fastest, or barely even walk straight, being forced to limp askew, like some old gaffer, I no longer wished to be Sir Rowan of the Dainnan brotherhood. They asked me to stay as an instructor and tactician, but I refused to be relegated to that status. I want the life of active service or nothing.'

'Yet you live,' Mazarine said earnestly, 'and that is sufficient.'

'Do you think so?'

'Indeed! Besides, your lameness is so slight it is hardly noticeable.'

'Hardly noticeable to you, perhaps, but not so slight.'

She understood, then, that it was with great effort and pain that her companion forced himself to walk straight, so that none should perceive what he considered to be his weakness. At the same time she felt grateful and elated that he had allowed her to see past the bluff — it signified that he placed great trust in her; that he believed she would not betray his confidence by letting anyone else know what agonies it secretly cost him to play the part of a man who was fully hale.

'As some compensation,' she said, 'you won Southdale Farm for your courage and quick thinking.'

'Which allows me independence,' he said. He did not need to add, *from my father*. Mazarine was well aware — for it was common knowledge — that there was no love lost between the earl and his heir.

The earl had, on occasion, declared he would cut off his son's inheritance. This threat, however, had never exerted any effect on

Hawkmoor, who desired only a roof over his head and food on the table. Jewels and gold held no allure for him. As for the titles, for which he cared scarcely a whit, they would always remain his by right as long as he was considered his father's progeny, and who could prove otherwise?

Hawkmoor did not resemble the earl at all in appearance or manner. Mazarine had once overheard the servants whispering that the two were not, in fact, related by blood — a rumour which might have cast aspersions on Hawkmoor's mother, had public sympathy not been largely on her side.

'Little wonder she strayed, if stray she did,' people murmured. 'Such ill-treatment she received at his hands! Poor creature — no surprise she died so young.'

'Some say the first Lady Rivenhall was forced to take a lover to fulfil her husband's desire for an heir! He wanted to keep his title from going extinct!'

'Really? What a scandal!'

'For the master is barren, they say, barren as a mountain peak forever under snow. He could not get a child on any of his other wives, could he!'

'Aye, and what happened to those wives, that's what I've always wondered! It can't be pure chance, to be made a widower three times.'

'Hush! If Ripley should hear you — or worse, the master himself — your own husband will soon be widowed, I'd warrant!'

'Well, who's young Fleetwood's real sire, d'ye think?'

'I wouldn't hazard a guess. Nobody knows. Nobody ever will, I s'pose.'

Mazarine banished the stale hearsay from her thoughts. A footman was stalking through the foliage of the conservatory, bringing another course on a silver-gilt salver, and the sour-faced butler was pouring more wine. Half-heartedly she wished he would not — she was unaccustomed to such quantities and it was going to her head, but it seemed to take the edge off her nervousness. Indeed, she felt flooded with delight to be in the company of this handsome young gentleman, whom she had quickly come to admire, trust and love as no other.

He was saying something about Thrimby, in response to which she said, 'How I envy Thrimby his ability to make up rhymes on the spot! It is clever of him, to be sure!'

'Do you have a desire to speak in rhyme, Mistress Blythe?' her companion bantered.

'Perhaps not to speak rhymes, but at least to write them. I used to compose poetry ...' Mazarine broke off.

'But no longer? Why not?'

'I —' The young woman wrestled with a sudden upwelling of sentiment. She could not trust herself to speak, being afraid that if she confessed the reason, she might burst into tears, and tried to mask her fragility by pushing a piece of glazed parsnip around her plate with her fork. Presently she regained control. 'Forgive me.'

Her dinner companion gazed upon her with infinite tenderness. 'Pray, let us speak of nothing that discomposes you, Mistress Blythe. Behold, I brought you a gift!' From his pocket he took a small parcel, which he handed to her. 'I purchased them from a passing pedlar on my way here. Is the colour permissible for those who wear mourning?'

Grateful to be distracted from her sorrow, Mazarine unwrapped the parcel. Out spilled a handful of shimmering silken hair-ribbons. Their colour was deep purple, like a stormy sky.

'Indeed, I have often seen this lovely colour combined with mourning-dress,' the young woman said with shy delight. 'Gramercie, sir! I will wear them tomorrow! Now in return for your kindness I will answer your question, for I have regained my composure. Writing poetry was once one of my favourite occupations. On that fateful day when my parents set off to call on a friend whose company I found excessively tedious, I begged to be spared the outing so that I could stay home and work on my latest epic. My mother and father met their deaths on that drive.' She need not explain the manner of their passing; Hawkmoor knew the details only too well. As their carriage was crossing a bridge, a wheel hit a large stone lying in the road. The equipage overturned, toppled over the parapet and fell into the fast-flowing river. 'Now,' Mazarine concluded, 'guilt prevents me from writing any more.'

'Guilt?' interposed Hawkmoor with a puzzled frown.

'I cannot help wondering — what if my presence in the carriage had somehow been able to prevent the accident? My weight — slight though it be — might have balanced the equipage and stopped it from tipping over, or perhaps I would have been more alert than they, and foreseen the collision that was about to happen and warned the driver to swerve in time.'

Her companion shook his head. 'You are too harsh on yourself, Mistress Blythe.'

'Be that as it may, sir, since that day I have locked my books of writings in a chest. I will no longer be a poet.'

Clearly Hawkmoor perceived her returning distress, for he embarked on a more light-hearted topic. Their discourse grew more animated and playful, until by the time dessert was served, Mazarine was so exhilarated by the fragrance of the spice plants, the wine and the enchanting proximity of Hawkmoor, that she abandoned herself to jocosity.

'It is your turn to talk,' she said. 'I am eating raspberry pudding. No, pray do not make me laugh — I have a mouthful. No please, that's so cruel while I am eating!'

'It is *your* turn, I insist upon it!' Hawkmoor said amusedly.

'Not at all! You see, the reason why our friendship is so amicable is because it is based around me eating while you talk.'

'Really?'

'Really. And you see, I eat raspberry pudding every day. That is why you will just have to make certain we are together every day!'

Mazarine's supper partner was just about to frame a reply when a commotion from the direction of the kennels heralded a new arrival at Kelmscott. Abruptly, all gaiety ceased.

'Who is coming in, Cottrell?' Hawkmoor demanded, throwing his serviette down on the table. His features had settled into their former stern expression.

The head footman bowed. 'I cannot say, m'lord. Methinks it is likely to be Lord Rivenhall.'

The imminent approach of Mazarine's guardian was like a dousing of icy water upon the young woman's mood. For a short while, in the company of Hawkmoor, she had managed to divert herself from the sad mood that had attended her since her bereavement. It had not been so long ago, after all, that the loss of her parents had changed her life forever. She started up from her chair, but Hawkmoor said, 'Pray do not be disturbed on my sire's account, Mistress Blythe. Let us finish our meal.'

She thought he spoke angrily, and if any of her merriment had remained, it now fled. Hesitantly she resumed her seat, though she could not eat or drink, or even speak, and in silence they waited. At length the rumble of voices and the clatter of boots announced the earl's advent, and the man himself approached, shouldering past the branches of the orange trees, his valet and two of his bodyguards in his train.

He doffed his travelling cloak and threw it aside for the valet to retrieve. A gentleman of middle age, he was elegantly attired in a long, pleated surcoat split at the sides, dark blue cross-gartered hose, and a heavy coat, sumptuously embroidered. His head was ornamented with a rondelle hat of blocked felt, brimmed by a stuffed ring of cloth, gold-netted, tied beneath his chin with thin black ribbons. From beneath the hat a profusion of glossy brown ringlets cascaded over his shoulders. The earl was quite the fashionable dandy. His person, however, failed to match the gorgeousness of his coiffure and garments, for his face was heavily jowled, the flesh blotchy and veined in the places where his cosmetic powder had rubbed off, and his belly, though corseted in a stomacher, was swollen, through over-indulgence, to a solid paunch.

His eyes squinted at Hawkmoor from between flabby folds of flesh. 'What are you doing here?' he snapped, without preamble or greeting. 'I thought you were to be absent for three more days!'

'Good evening to you too, sir,' Hawkmoor said calmly. 'I finished my tasks early. And you? You seem a trifle ill at ease — you are well, I trust? You come late.'

'And you have dined without me,' said the older man. 'You could not wait.'

'For that I must apologise,' said Mazarine, repressing her resentment of the intruder's rudeness for courtesy's sake and starting up a second time. 'The fault was mine —' Her guardian turned his attention to her.

'Ah, Mistress Blythe,' he said, grasping her hand and favouring the back of it with a moist kiss before she knew what he was about. He bared his flawless teeth in a smile. 'Come, let us to the drawing-room. This wilderness is not a fit place for a man to recover his powers after the excessively provoking string of events to which I have been subjected this evening.' Without further ado he propelled his ward away, his plump fist pushing at the small of her back, so that she had no choice but to go where he directed. She heard Hawkmoor striding unevenly in their wake, cursing under his breath.

As soon as they reached the drawing-room the earl dismissed his bodyguards. He bade his valet pull off his coat for him, remove his shoes and loosen the laces of his stomacher, though he kept his hat on, as was his wont. 'The cursed coach broke down on a lonely road through the forest!' he fumed, slumping in a chair before the drawing-room fireplace and throwing one stout leg over the arm of it. To a hovering footman, 'Where is the mulled wine, for Providence's sake? I called for it hours ago. And bring me my evening robe!' To the chamber at large, scowling: 'How such a mischance could occur I know not. Something came loose. As head coachman, Ogden ought to have seen that all was in order before we departed. It was his responsibility. Since he was not worth his pay I dismissed him and sent him packing as soon as we arrived home. Fleetwood, I charge you to hire a better scrivener than this idle coachman you got for me.'

'I never hired him in the first place, sir. That was Ripley's achievement, if you recall.'

'Do not mince words with me, pray. I am ill-used enough as it is. To top off my woes, while I was waiting half the night for the acorn-headed footmen to screw the wheel back into place and make some repairs, we were assailed by a troupe of gypsies!' The earl stared about the room with an air of baffled contempt.

'Gypsies, my lord?' asked Mazarine, who felt she ought to make some sort of response to fill the ensuing void of silence.

'That is what I said, is it not? A great gaggle of 'em in the moonlight, hopping about like fools to the hideous squeakings of their fiddlers. Gypsies near the borders of my land! I shall have them run off the estate if they dare set foot within my bounds!'

A butler entered with a jug of mulled wine on a tray. He poured some into a goblet while his master snapped his fingers, 'Hurry up! Hurry up!' after which the peer proceeded to refresh himself with deep draughts.

'What did they look like, these gypsies?' Hawkmoor asked. Mazarine glanced sharply at him. It was unlike him to contribute to a conversation with his sire unless forced by necessity.

'Why would you want to know?' the earl retorted gratingly. 'They looked like all the rest of their kind, of course — half-sized, ragged folk, their hair long and straggling and greasy, clinking with silver bracelets and hoop earrings, limping and hopping as if they were all lame as three-legged frogs, ha, ha!'

Mazarine saw Hawkmoor wince at this remark, but he merely said, 'They drove no covered wagons?'

'Did I say they had wagons?'

'You did not, sir. Which makes me suspect they may not have been gypsies at all.'

'What do you mean?'

'By your description they were trows.'

'Zounds! Sir, do you not have ears to hear? How many times do I have to repeat myself? Amershire is free from all sinister wights! Trifling oddities such as griggs and harmless types of waterhorses might hang around in certain places, but mere tricksy tom-fools, nothing perilous. Unseelie things simply do not come this far south-east. Any half-wit knows that.'

Mazarine wanted to interject, 'You are deluded!' She lacked the courage, however, to speak so forcefully, being a comparative newcomer in the earl's household. Furthermore, she was alarmed to perceive that Hawkmoor was swiftly losing patience with his abrasive sire, and might at any moment cease to tolerate his uncouthness. If that should happen, bitter words would pass between the two, and she lived in dread of Rivenhall's heir being banished from the house. Life at Kelmscott Hall would be far less bearable without him.

Fortunately, at that point her guardian's valet hastened in carrying his master's evening robe, a voluminous affair of carmine velvet edged with ermine, which he helped him put on. The earl slumped back into the chair, swallowing more wine.

'Now I return to my own domicile,' he said, 'only to find my heir engaged in an intimate dinner with my ward. What am I to think, eh? Perhaps you have been sweet-talking her, eh Fleetwood? Trying to worm your way into her affections? Well, I shall have none of that nonsense, do you understand?'

To her horror, Mazarine saw Hawkmoor turn pale with wrath. He glanced briefly in her direction and his glance intimated silently, 'For your sake, I will leash my anger — but only for your sake.'

'Good night, Mistress Blythe,' he said. Without another word he spun about and strode from the room, his gait studied, perfectly even and precise, regardless of the price in pain.

CHAPTER TWO

When those we love have ceased to tread the earth
And, wingèd, flown beyond our mortal ken,
Then wither poetry, music and mirth,
And only love can bring them back again.

Hawkmoor kept his distance from his sire whenever possible. He and Mazarine formed a tacit agreement to limit their meetings to times when the master of Kelmscott was elsewhere. Ever since he had discovered them dining together, the earl had made it clear that he strongly disapproved of their forming an attachment, and derisively voiced his scorn of such a possibility at every opportunity. When Hawkmoor was out of earshot he would disparage the young man to Mazarine. She began by defending him, but ceased as soon as she understood that this merely provoked her guardian to outbursts of greater vehemence.

Nevertheless, by dint of quick thinking and the earl's intemperance, they did manage to steal moments together in the presence of none but Mazarine's lady's-maid. The earl had a habit of late-night carousing with such of the local land-owners as shared his fondness for inebriation. On mornings when he lay late abed, inconvenienced by over-indulgence on the previous night, Hawkmoor and Mazarine enjoyed hours to themselves. On one such morning they sauntered arm-in-arm through the walled herb garden.

'Tell me of your home in the distant north.' Hawkmoor suggested, idly toying with a plucked stem of tarragon.

'Why, you yourself, sir, have travelled through lands as far-flung as any!' the young woman replied, laughing.

'Aye that is true, but I have never visited Reveswall, so tell me, pray!'

'Well, it is a fair land, though anyone who travels along a country road at dusk might spy slanting eyes, emerald or topaz, watching furtively from the hedges and winking out as quickly as they appeared; or hear the sound of laughing and sobbing, or shrill voices talking gibberish, or high-pitched singing, or the faint strains of music played on bagpipes, thin reed whistles or fiddles.'

'Ah, yes. Such phenomena are observed everywhere in Erith. Go on!' Hawkmoor prompted, observing his dinner companion's enthusiasm with evident pleasure. 'What was one of the oddest things you ever saw?'

'Once, when walking home along a familiar path through the meadows at evening, my father and I spied a thing a thing like a donkey's head with a smooth velvet hide, hanging on a gate. We knew not what to make of it. Cautiously my father approached this peculiar incarnation, but suddenly it turned around, snapped at his outstretched hand and disappeared! I cried out, startled, and asked my Papa what it was.

'"I believe," he said, clearly somewhat rattled though unhurt, "it was something called a Shock."

'"What do Shocks do?" I enquired.

'"As far as I am aware, they merely hang on gates," said Papa. "They are seldom seen. Little is known of them."'

'I have never heard of such a creature,' said Hawkmoor, shaking his head. 'There are strange things in Erith more numerous than can be catalogued by humankind.' They talked on, drifting from subject to subject, and eventually he said, 'Next week I must interview applicants for the position of scrivener and book-keeper to my father. He has demanded this of me, insisting that it is my duty to perform such tasks for him.'

'Scrivener? Does he not already employ a scrivener?'

'No. He has always looked after his own accounts — which is why his finances have fallen into a chaotic state.'

'That is hardly imaginable!'

'To all appearances my sire is wealthy, Mistress Blythe, but he is not as well off as in years past. He has a growing number of creditors, for he spends considerable amounts of money on a variety of pleasures whenever he goes to town.' The young man twirled the sprig of tarragon in his fingers.

'Forgive me if I sound presumptuous, my Lord, but why should you be the one to find him a scrivener?'

'No forgiveness required, Mistress Blythe. My sire will not bother himself with sifting through the applicants. He has faith in my judgement of men, at least, for it was I who engaged the services of Tom Glover, the truest of men, the most honest and capable manager for my own estate. Southdale Farm thrives under his direction.'

'How many have applied for the scrivener's position?'

'Six-and-twenty.'

'Then you will indeed be kept busy! I daresay you have a hundred matters to attend to at Southdale, yet you will be forced to remain here, interviewing book-keepers. Perhaps you will find it tedious.'

Hawkmoor's gaze met hers in the sunlight, and she saw her face reflected in his dark eyes. So handsome was he that it was thrilling to look upon him.

'I can no longer find it tedious in this house, Mistress Blythe.' And in case she had overlooked the message he added, 'Not since you arrived.'

Stars were stabbing ice-white fractures into the dusky heavens beyond the glass roof. Mazarine found herself at a loss for words. Hawkmoor had quite unexpectedly bestowed on her a compliment, which was uncharacteristic of him — his manner was usually quite reserved. She tried to cover her delighted confusion by bending down to examine a patch of blue-flowered rosemary. What could he mean by it? Surely she was ascribing too much significance to his words — after all, she was no beauty, and he, achingly beautiful, was a kind of lodestone attracting all the eligible young ladies of the district.

Straightening up, she regained her composure and the two of them began to conjure ways to make tedious interviews with book-keepers interesting; inventing scenarios that became more and more far-fetched, until at length each comment, no matter how trite, set off another peal of laughter.

In the second week of Gaothmis, Hawkmoor kept his promise to his sire. Ensconcing himself in his book-lined study, he interviewed the two dozen applicants for the position of scrivener.

On another morning when the earl was still snoring abed, Mazarine and Hawkmoor were taking the air in the shrubbery, their elbows linked. As usual they were accompanied by Mazarine's lady's-maid Odalys, who trailed after them, deliberately shuffling her feet through the fallen Autumn leaves to make them rustle, for she liked the sound. Lost in some reverie, she was humming an ancient tune called 'Bogles in the Hedges'.

'I wish that your coming-of-age would befall tomorrow, Mistress Blythe,' said Hawkmoor as they strolled. At unguarded moments like this, he allowed himself to limp; it eased the torment of wrenched and poisoned sinews that had healed awry.

'I too!' Mazarine replied. 'The third of Sovrachmis is but six months away, yet it feels like six years. I am more than ready to assume responsibility for my life and my fortune on my twenty-first birthday.'

'I can hardly wait for that day,' said Hawkmoor

'Why?' Mazarine asked nonchalantly, feeling her pulse accelerate.

'Oh the bogles in the hedges,' tunelessly sang Odalys at their backs, 'the drowners in the sedges, the warners in the mountains and the asrai in the fountains …'

Mazarine could not help laughing at her maid's rendition, and Hawkmoor joined in, both trying to smother their hilarity so as not to cause offence.

'I do believe she learned that lamentable ditty from Thrimby,' said Mazarine.

'Ah, the matchless Thrimby!' said Hawkmoor, with a smile of such marvellous comeliness that it thrilled his companion to her very fingertips. Amongst the brilliantly coloured foliage of the crimson glory vine that crept upon a stone wall, a blackbird began to sing. By then the companions had lost the thread of their conversation.

'I must leave you soon,' Hawkmoor went on, gazing thoughtfully down at Mazarine — for he was a good deal taller than her, being two inches more than six feet in height. 'I can see the day's first applicant approaching along the driveway.'

Mazarine had witnessed some of the comings and goings of the hopefuls. Unexpectedly she now beheld, walking around the side to the servants' entrance, a young man with a scholarly air, whose face and form she knew well. 'Wakefield!' she cried. Releasing her escort's arm she ran up to the newcomer, through the fading glory of the golden abelias whose cast-off leaves were strewn upon the footpaths like handfuls of shining coins. 'Master Squires! What a wonderful surprise!'

The new arrival stopped in his tracks and regarded Mazarine with astonishment. 'Mistress Blythe!'

A comely young man in the sober dress of a clerk — dyed in shades of dark blue and slate — and a soft grey cap with a rolled woollen brim, the applicant turned out to be an old friend of Mazarine's, her companion of early years when she and her parents had lived in the north. Overjoyed to see him, the young woman took his arm with artless eagerness, enquiring as to the health of his parents who, he assured her, were quite well and still dwelling in their old abode.

'Fleetwood, where are you?' Mazarine cried, turning back with shining face. 'This is a childhood friend of mine, Master Wakefield Squires! I have not seen him these six or seven Winters, since he left Reveswall to travel the world. Master Squires, pray allow me to introduce you to my cousin, Lord Fleetwood.'

Hawkmoor had caught up with them. He stood gravely regarding the newcomer, who bowed. 'At your service, sir,' he said, to which Hawkmoor responded with a murmured courtesy. Mazarine was about to launch into a happy exploration of the events in their lives since last they parted, when she recalled the object of her old friend's visit.

'I daresay I had better leave you to conduct your business,' she said, 'but afterwards, Master Squires, will you oblige me by taking refreshment in the front drawing-room?'

'I would be honoured, Mistress Blythe.'

'Splendid! I will have Odalys conduct you there at the conclusion of your interview. Fleetwood, will you join us?'

Hawkmoor shook his head. 'Five other appointments await me this morning,' he replied. 'Besides, I am certain you two have many reminiscences to mull over, and my presence would only be an intrusion. Delighted to meet you, Master Squires — shall we proceed indoors?'

Wakefield stood aside to allow Mazarine and her cousin to enter at the side door, before bring up the rear with Odalys. Above their heads, unnoticed, a scowling face peered down at them from a second storey window.

Over the next few days Mazarine was unable to secure more than a few brief moments alone with Hawkmoor, for as usual the earl created obstacles to their companionship at every turn, and besides, the young man was fully occupied with numerous tasks. After an intensive week of interlocution Hawkmoor narrowed down the list of applicants to three young gentlemen, one of whom was Wakefield Squires.

Late one night at the end of the week Hawkmoor was leaning on his elbows at the desk in his study. The window in front of him gave onto a view of the ornamental lake. In its depths on nets of constellations hung the moon's reflection, like a giant platter of polished pewter. The rest of the household was abed — all save one.

A pattering, as of mice's feet, roused the young man from his brooding. 'Thrimby, is that you?'

The servant moved into a shaft of starlight. Though he was a small fellow, and wizened as though ancient in years, he carried cleaning implements on his shoulder as if they weighed nothing, and moved nimbly, like a youth. Hawkmoor had no notion of his age. Thrimby had been at Kelmscott ever since he could remember, quietly busy at his nocturnal chores, always wearing his ragged clothing and his worn-out slippers. His old nursemaid had warned her charge never to offer the servant new garments. 'For,' she had cautioned, 'if you do, he will go away and never come back.'

'Why?' the child Hawkmoor had wanted to know.

'Because he is a brownie, though some refuse to acknowledge the fact. Brownies depart forever if you thank them or give them clothing. If Kelmscott Hall were to lose its brownie it would be much the worse for the family.'

His old nurse was always right, so he had heeded her advice.

'What can I give him to show gratitude?' he had asked.

'A bowl of fresh, creamy milk each day, a hunch of soft bread. Sometimes a handful of herbs. That is all. Oh, and domestic wights such as brownies approve of mortal folk who are tidy and hard-working. They despise slovenliness and loathe being spied on. Therefore be diligent and allow him his privacy, I dread to think what would happen if we were to lose him!'

She had died of old age in her dreams, his nurse, and been buried in the local graveyard, having been the closest approximation to a mother he had ever known. His father's next two wives had not been permitted to show interest in the lad; they had to put forth their charms exclusively for the earl.

'Aye 'tis Thrimby 'ere, young master,' said a voice like the swivelling of rusted hinges. 'Ye be sleepless, eh?'

'I am.'

'Pinin', no doubt.'

'Pining? What makes you say so?'

'Blind Freddy could see it.'

'Well, and small wonder if I am.'

'She returns your affections,' said Thrimby, whisking a few token motes of dust off the top of a pile of books with a bouquet of plumy feathers.

Presently Hawkmoor replied, 'Your comments are of a very personal nature, Thrimby.'

'And why should they not be? I've knowed ye since ye was a little 'un, young master. I know all that goes on in this 'ouse, and I tell ye, she returns your affections, is owt wrong wiv that?' Screwing up his odd little face the servant squinted at the young man.

'Nothing is wrong with it,' said Hawkmoor, shrugging.

'Wot's wrong wiv *you* then?' Thrimby lifted a corner of the hearthrug and swept furiously under it with a straw besom.

''Tis true, I am heavy of heart. I flattered myself that she would accept my offer of marriage once she turned twenty-one,' said Hawkmoor. 'Now I am not so certain of the future.'

'Don't let the old master stand in yer way!'

''Tis not him.'Tis Squires.'

'Wot, that bookish young gentleman? I can't see it, meself.'

'She dotes on him, Thrimby. She has invited him to take elevenses with her twice this week. That makes three meetings in the space of seven days.'

Vigorously rubbing a brass lamp with a polishing rag, Thrimby said, 'In that case, send 'im packin' young sir. 'Tis your call. A master never need *explain* to those who serve in 'is domain, for he may 'ire and fire at whim and nobody can gainsay 'im. And if a servant fails to please by causing damage or unease, 'e'll find 'imself outside the door among the starving and the poor.'

He subjoined, rhyme-less, 'But you don't 'ave to 'ire 'im in the first place!'

'Very good!' said Hawkmoor in a brief flash of admiration for the spontaneous jingle. 'It is indeed my "call", as you put it,' he continued. 'I wish only for Miss Blythe's happiness, and so I shall do what I believe is best.'

Thrimby stared at the young man for a long moment, sighed profoundly, scratched his head and resumed his housework.

Hawkmoor recommended to his sire that Wakefield Squires be hired.

Whereupon that young scholar was grilled by Chief Steward Ripley, regarding his ability to keep his employer's affairs to himself, and his willingness to sign an Agreement of Secrecy whose stipulations, Ripley assured him, would be pursued vigorously, were the signatory ever to break his word. This brawny thug gave the young man to understand that he meant 'vigorously' in a very physical sense, in consequence of which Master Squires had second thoughts about taking on the position, and said so, causing the earl to step in, saying he was satisfied that only a gentleman who took the contract *seriously* would consider throwing away such a lucrative and highly sought-after situation, and this was *precisely* the kind of employee he had been looking for, and Ripley must be excused for his exaggerations because we are all civilised creatures, and Lord Rivenhall would *never* countenance ruffianly behaviour from his staff.

Subsequently Master Squires reconsidered, for the earl could be both charming and persuasive when it suited him. The young scholar took lodgings at Clover Cottage with the Wiltons, thereafter commencing to appear at the earl's side door early every morning and work all day in his study in the west wing. Assiduously he dedicated himself to writing letters and keeping the books or, to be more accurate, sorting them out, for he discovered the accounts to be in an almost inextricable state of chaos.

Mazarine was pleased to have her childhood friend so close at hand, although a niggling doubt prompted her to ask Hawkmoor whether he had hired Wakefield for her sake.

'Not at all,' said Hawkmoor. 'I assure you, Miss Blythe, he was the best candidate.'

And instantly Mazarine regretted having asked such a question, for it would appear to cast doubts upon Hawkmoor's integrity. He must have supposed she believed him capable of disloyalty to his father, a breaker of his promise to choose the featest man for the job. Yet it was too late and the thoughtless words could not be unsaid, though she apologised, which only seemed to make matters worse.

From the time of Master Squires's engagement, Hawkmoor no longer appeared as warm towards Mazarine as before, but cold and formal. She wondered whether she had done anything else to upset him, and agonised over it, and felt, as when they had first met, uncertain in his company.

Fully cognizant of the reason for his heir's reserve and revelling in it, Lord Rivenhall continually invited Master Squires to dine with the family. Mazarine was amazed that such an arrogant swank as her guardian would invite an employee to dine at his own table, but Hawkmoor grimly understood, and took his meals in subdued silence, leaving the chatter to Wakefield and Mazarine who, encouraged by the earl, indulged in recalling their childhood adventures.

Once or twice after dinner Mazarine quietly asked Hawkmoor if he were in good health.

'I am indeed. Gramercie,' he merely replied, and walked away with symmetrical poise.

If the young master kept himself aloof from Mazarine, he confided his inmost observations to industrious Thrimby, on the nocturnal occasions when that mysterious personage made himself apparent.

'I find myself in constant turmoil, Thrimby,' said he, sitting once again at his desk by the window, 'restraining my sorrow and wrath. I can assure you, it goes hard with me. I would leave this house, if not that I crave to be near *her*, under the same roof. Yet it is torture knowing she is infatuated with another, and my father slyly adds to that torment with his teasing.'

'I tell you, 'tis you,' insisted Thrimby, frenziedly scrubbing the hearth with an enormous brush of boar's bristles. '*You*, she fancies.'

'Why then does she spend so much time with *him*?'

'They share memories of 'appy child'oods, that is all!'

'She is more often in his company than in mine.'

'Because the master contrives to separate the two of you.'

'I am not convinced!'

'Suit yourself, young master.' Dunking the brush zealously in a pail of rinsing-water, Thrimby continued,

'When jealous thought uplifts its 'ead, it crushes trust until it's dead,
And tortures love's reality. Then joy and satisfaction flee.'

He resumed scrubbing. Soap bubbles flew up like flocks of tiny birds.

'To be honest I am not jealous, Thrimby,' replied Hawkmoor. 'I merely wish to make Mistress Blythe happy, and if she would be happier with him than with me, then that is how it must be.'

''Tis true enough that ye be not the jealous kind, young master. As blind, deaf and dumb as a mole wearing ear-muffs mayhap; as self effacin' as a snowman jumping into a frying pan, maybe, but not the jealous kind. As sacrificial as a worm wot offers itself to a blackbird to save the other worms ... '

'Yes, yes, Thrimby, much obliged; that's enough. I do comprehend your rather insulting point. But I will not be persuaded otherwise.'

When Wakefield was working on the accounts and Hawkmoor was away at Southdale, Mazarine occupied herself with her hobbies — watercolour painting, sketching, collecting foliage and flowers for pressing, and writing letters to the friends she had left behind in northern Severnesse.

Most often the earl was in his study in the west wing, arguing with Master Squires, or closeted in the library with his Chief Steward, plotting recondite strategies, or out shooting game with some of his louche companions — country gentlemen from around the district, or sleeping off the effects of a night's carousing in his own halls or the halls of his hunting companions.

Unexpectedly one afternoon, the earl summoned Mazarine to his side.

'It is my wish to conduct you on a progress through this house, my dear,' he said, offering her his arm in its brocaded sleeve. 'It occurs to me you have not yet viewed all its glories. I think you will be pleased with what you see!'

Bemused, she capitulated, passing her hand through the crook of his elbow. They strolled leisurely from chamber to chamber, along galleries, up and down staircases wide and narrow, through 'secret' passageways behind the walls and out along balconies and roof-walks. The house's interior décor seemed to include an inordinate number of mirrors and, as they passed them, Mazarine's guardian took every opportunity to glance at his image, whereupon he would adjust his latest millinery acquisition — all feathers and jewelled brooches — or rearrange his luxuriant shoulder-length ringlets or pick at his gleaming teeth with a silver toothpick he kept in a tiny ivory box in some inner pocket of his sleeve. Mazarine, in rustling black silk, walked calmly by his side. At length they arrived at the Long Gallery, whose row of tall windows provided extensive views of the grounds. The rear wall was decorated with paintings of the current earl from boyhood to manhood, captured in various magnificent attitudes; winged and graceful, flying in the clouds; sternly commanding, standing at the helm of a Windship; courageous and dauntless, galloping into battle on a white charger; sensitive and poetic, reclining beside a pool, trailing his unrealistically slender, pale fingers among the waterlilies.

In front of the latter work of art, the earl paused and, turning to face his ward, grasped both her hands in his.

'May I speak to you candidly, my dear?'

Nonplussed, dumbfounded and suddenly anxious, Mazarine nodded. She tried not to meet his eyes, which resembled two pools of half-cooked albumen congealing in pink bowls.

'You see, my dear,' the earl said earnestly, 'it is an unfortunate fact that, despite what blandishments your fond parents have no doubt lavished upon you, your physical attractions are, shall we say, limited. To be frank, your features are plain, your character is dull and you possess few accomplishments. One tries to be optimistic, however I am afraid that in the normal course of events you cannot hope to attract a husband of any worthwhile status. Due to our family connections I am, nevertheless, prepared to overlook your dearth of charms and, if you are careful to continue pleasing me, I might one day offer you — yes, you — the title of Lady Rivenhall!' He paused to survey the effect of this good news, but when there was none — no doubt because the young lady was overcome with appreciativeness — he continued, 'Being raised to such high estate would benefit you in numerous ways. You would be able to make the most of your ordinary looks with fine raiment, cosmetics and coiffure, because I, being widely acknowledged as a paragon of style, would condescend to teach you myself.'

Mazarine, who had kept her eyes cast down throughout the entire monologue lest her guardian detect that she had begun to feel unwell, was trying hard to mask her reaction. *The preposterous old fool!* she said to herself, *How could he so much as dream I would accept him? I fear I must feign gratitude at this ludicrous proposal. I must keep the peace in this house for my own sake, until I am twenty-one — then I shall be free!*

'I know what you are thinking,' said her guardian. At these words a cold wire threaded itself along Mazarine's spine. He had it wrong, however. 'You are thinking that Fleetwood, who has tried to flatter his way into your good graces, might undergo a fit of apoplexy if he does not get his way. Yet fret no more on the matter, my dear — the boy's peevish tantrums can be taken care of. You understand of course that he feels no real attachment to you. It is merely that without your compliance a cripple such as he has small chance of snaring himself a wife. By rights he ought to be wheeled around in a bath chair. He feigns straightness of limb, but his tricks fool nobody. Everyone knows of his wry gait, and eligible young ladies of good breeding and fortune find such skewedness unacceptable, there is no doubt of it.'

Hold your tongue! Mazarine told herself desperately. *Let him rant. They are only words … do not let him provoke you!*

'Dear uncle,' she forced herself to say at last, 'how generous you are. Pray excuse me, I am so overwhelmed by your kind offer that I find myself indisposed.' With that she hurried away, one hand plastered to her brow as if she were suffering some malaise of the head.

'I shall send whatsername your maid to your chambers,' her guardian shouted after her, turning away to glance in the closest mirror.

Instead of going directly to her suite, Mazarine detoured by way of her uncle's study. She knocked at the carved oaken door, pushed it open cautiously and peered inside.

'Do come in, Mistress Blythe!' said Wakefield, replacing his quill in the pen holder and jumping to his feet. Piles of papers and ledgers towered around him, burdening the desk, the cabinets and the floor. 'I have not yet taken a break for elevenses, so I may interrupt my work for a few minutes, at least. My word, you do look downcast! Pray take a seat on the divan. Shall I ring for your maid? Or some cordial?'

'No, no! I would rather speak with you alone,' cried Mazarine. Once she was seated beside her friend she said diffidently, 'Wakefield, I know I can confide in you. The thing is, I am in love with Fleetwood.'

'I know,' the young clerk said cheerily. 'I have known since the moment I first saw you together, and I am uncommonly happy for both of you, for I feel certain that that worthy gentleman returns your sentiments!'

'Perhaps,' Mazarine replied dubiously. 'Perhaps not. For, you know, it might be difficult for anyone to love me in that way, because I am —' she hesitated, embarrassed, and averted her face '— it must be admitted, I am not very pretty …'

'Not pretty!' cried Wakefield, half rising from his chair, 'Not pretty? Where in Aia did you get that idea?'

'I have always believed …'

'What nonsense!' Wakefield plumped himself down again and leaned forwards. 'If you will pardon my bluntness, Mistress Blythe — Mazarine, if I may presume on our friendship — in my humble opinion you are one of the most beautiful creatures in Erith!'

'You are trying to reassure me, Master Squires. It is most kind, but —'

'Say no more on the subject!' Wakefield said with mock severity. 'I can see you are deluded. One good stare into a looking-glass should tell you of your beauty, but clearly you are blind to it. Nevertheless accept my word, and believe in your mind if not your heart, that you are indeed extraordinarily comely! If you will not be convinced, try asking your house-brownie. Eldritch wights cannot tell lies, so perhaps you will place confidence in him!'

'Oh, so you have glimpsed Thrimby?'

'Yes, why not?'

'I suspect my uncle never has.'

'Perhaps Thrimby will not let him!'

They both laughed. It was a relief for Mazarine to converse mirthfully and freely with her friend after the unpleasant rhetoric to which her guardian had recently subjected her.

'Now that you have entrusted your romantic secret to me, Mistress Blythe,' Wakefield murmured, waggling his eyebrows, 'I have a similar arcanum for your ears alone!'

'In sooth? Tell on!'

The young man leaned closer and began to whisper in Mazarine's ear. It was at that moment that Hawkmoor chanced to pass by the study door — which Mazarine had left ajar — his footsteps muffled by the thick carpeting of the hallway. He glanced inside. The two confidantes were positioned out of view, but one of the earl's ubiquitous mirrors — a vast, shimmering expanse, like a frozen skating-pond in a heavy gilt frame, fastened to the wall above the mantelpiece — revealed their reflected images; the two heads bent together in a most intimate pose as they whispered together. That single glimpse was enough for the heir of Rivenhall. Despairing, he hastened away.

Meanwhile Wakefield was murmuring, 'Mistress Wilton and I are troth-plighted!'

Mazarine's chime of delighted laughter smote Hawkmoor like a blow as he retreated along the passageway. In the study, the next few minutes were given over to Mazarine's congratulatory utterances and her showering of praises upon the person of Laurelia Wilton.

'Keep the news to yourself, pray, dear Mistress Blythe,' said Wakefield. 'Laurelia and I cannot be wed until I have scraped together a little more capital to ensure our financial security.'

'The matter is safe with me!' Mazarine assured him. 'But hush! I hear my uncle's voice. He is coming. I would rather avoid him!' Taking her leave of the clerk she flitted noiselessly out of the study through a secret passage that opened behind a hinged bookcase — a way she had discovered by herself, and which she was fairly certain the earl was unaware of.

CHAPTER THREE

Misunderstanding leads to jealousy
Or hate or anger — sometimes to all three.
Our motives, though of high integrity,
Are lost if not presented limpidly.
Through etiquette, reserve or courtesy,
We misconstrue good purpose constantly.

After the earl's declaration Mazarine found it more difficult than ever to catch a moment alone with Hawkmoor. She wished only for an opportunity to ask him why he had become so distant, and whether she had inadvertently caused any offence, but it was as if Steward Ripley, the bodyguards and most of the other servants — including even the under-gardener — were spying on her. Any time she believed she was on the verge of being able to converse with Hawkmoor unobserved, whether indoors or out, some member of the household would appear casually around a corner, supposedly labouring at an important task — re-pointing the masonry, inspecting the beams for woodworm, hunting for truffles, searching for the earl's lost snuff-box — always just within earshot.

'Prithee, take yourself elsewhere!' Mazarine would beg.

'Alas, mistress, his lordship appointed me to this task. I cannot disobey!'

In exasperation Mazarine would suggest to Hawkmoor that they move to a more secluded spot. If he could be persuaded to do so, it was only to be surprised by yet another employee appearing at their elbows. There was no privacy to be had at Kelmscott Hall. Furthermore, the earl would not hear of his heir and his ward going off together on any jaunts outside the estate. He came up with a remarkably ingenious set of excuses to thwart such excursions and, since he was master, his word was law. Besides, to make matters worse it began to dawn on Mazarine that Hawkmoor, too, was avoiding situations likely to bring them together.

Away over the hills thunder grumbled. The wind was rising. As evening drew in, a storm was rapidly approaching from the distant coast. Mazarine, passing through the darkening galleries of Kelmscott in the west wing, heard the echoes of men's voices. Drawing near to her guardian's study she stopped outside the closed door. The utterances were muffled. Mazarine, however, had not paused to eavesdrop; she merely wished to ascertain who was within, for Hawkmoor was due to arrive home at any time, and if the earl was preoccupied she intended to seize the opportunity to speak in private with the object of her affections. At length she was satisfied that the room did indeed contain the earl, deep in conversation with Ripley. Doubtless the two connivers would be conducting their vigorous discussion for a good long while, for by the gravity of their tones it sounded as if they dwelled on serious matters, probably pertaining to the series of disasters Master Squires was uncovering in the earl's ill-kept records of monies owed and monies due.

Hastening to a window overlooking the driveway, Mazarine gazed out. The evening skies hung heavy and sullen, bruised with rainclouds.

A flash of white light briefly illumined the figure of a horseman on the avenue, between the outlines of tall cypress trees stencilled against the sky. Hawkmoor was here already! Picking up her skirts the damsel rushed along the gallery at speed. Down the stairs and out the door she flew, finally intercepting the new arrival as he let his horse walk to the stables beneath an arbour dripping with the magnificent amber, gold and ruby leaves of the climbing plant known as 'crimson glory-vine'.

At Mazarine's appearance the rider halted. He turned towards her with a look of sad enquiry, holding the reins of his steed loosely in his right hand. As so often, his masculine beauty struck the girl with force. Momentarily, she became tongue-tied. *She who hesitates, loses*, her mother used to say, and abruptly it was true, for a groom appeared from the stables, and the moment was lost. Hawkmoor dismounted — without betraying the slightest evidence of any twinge, so well had he schooled himself — but denied the reins to the servant and stood holding them, while his horse nodded its long head and chewed on the bit. The groom waited, eyes respectfully cast down.

'Mistress Blythe,' Hawkmoor said. With his other hand he swept off his hat. She noticed that his heavy hair was working loose from its band at the back of his head. The wind, stronger now, was whipping strands about his face. Her skirts billowed in the gusts, and coloured leaves came showering around them both, like a carnival.

'I wish to speak with you,' she stammered.

'I am at your service.'

'A little more privacy would be fitting …'

'Certainly.' Hawkmoor dismissed the groom, who bowed and trotted away. Together Hawkmoor and Mazarine walked towards the stables. The horse was eager to get to his haybox, and tugged on the reins; Hawkmoor caressed the steaming arch of the animal's neck and soothed him with gentle words.

Diffidently, Mazarine endeavoured to order in her mind the best way to broach the subject she dreaded. Presently she drew breath and opened her mouth, but once again she had left it too late. The keening of the wind and the low mutter of thunder running back and forth across the horizon had masked the sound of boots crunching on gravel.

'*What?*' bellowed the well-known voice of the earl, and in another few strides he was with them, Ripley close at his shoulder, and a couple of bodyguards loitering ominously in the background.

'What passes here? Do my eyes deceive me, or do I see my own heir consorting with my ward, behind my very back? Do I deserve such thanklessness as this, that as soon as I look the other way the two of you are colluding secretly together? Mazarine, I hold you not responsible, for you are but a child, but *you* sir, have you no respect for your sire, no sense of filial devotion?'

The earl's flabby face was empurpled with emotion. Mazarine felt the heat of shock and indignation burn her own cheeks. Her companion, however, remained cool.

'I may converse with whomsoever I wish,' Hawkmoor said icily. 'Your view is unreasonable.'

'Do you dare defy me, you halting ingrate?' the earl's voice rose in pitch until it became a squeak. 'Insubordinate pup! You itch only to take my place and inherit my money and title. 'Tis true is it not? Eh?'

Hawkmoor regarded his sire expressionlessly without deigning to reply, which attitude provoked the earl to greater wrath. He clenched his fists, quivering as if he longed to smite the calm and self-contained young gentleman who confronted him.

Placing her hand beseechingly on her guardian's arm Mazarine said, 'I beg you sir, do not be angry with Fleetwood! He has done nothing amiss. I only asked to speak with him, that is all.'

'Oh, so that is how it stands between you two, eh?' The earl rounded on her. 'She tries to protect her favourite, while he hides behind her skirts like some cringing cur!' Pushing his face close to Hawkmoor's, the earl snarled, 'Go, sir! Get out! From this hour forth you are banished from my house. I disinherit you, as I ought to have done at your birth, for your slut of a mother was faithless. All that is yours will be thrown out upon the sward — let your servants pick up the pieces if they will.'

Mazarine uttered a gasping cry.

'Gladly will I go,' said Hawkmoor. He bowed curtly to Mazarine, leaped upon his steed with extraordinary agility, and galloped away.

As if to emphasize the drama of the moment a clap of thunder split open the skies overhead, and rain came sluicing down in torrents.

Desolation enfolded Mazarine.

The skies wept all night, as did the earl's ward, alone in a deep armchair in the library. She was barely aware of the occasional noises of energetic housework emanating from different parts of the building, generated by Thrimby attending to his tasks. Before sunrise next morning the servant popped in and said without preamble, "'E were somewhat envious o' the bookish chap, were the young master.'

'Fleetwood? Envious of Master Squires?' Mazarine looked up and dabbed at her eyes with a lace-edged handkerchief.

Thrimby, obsessively whisking a bunch of feathers in a cloud of dust over by the bookshelves, said, 'Aye.'

'Surely not!'

'Aye, but 'e woz, mark ye. Thought ye liked Squires more'n 'im.'

'I had no idea! In that case I must send him a message assuring him of my truest affection!'

Immediately Mazarine fetched paper, ink and quill, and penned a note which she sealed with red wax and gave to her loyal lady's-maid, with instructions to have it delivered swiftly and in utmost discretion to Southdale Farm. The reply came back that afternoon — Lord Fleetwood had not rested the previous night at the farmstead but had tarried there only for long enough to change horses. Declaring that he would catch the next post-chaise heading for the west coast, he had galloped away to town. Whither he had gone, no one could say — out of Amershire, certainly; possibly out of the country. The household at Southdale knew of no way to contact him and had no notion of when he would return.

After this precipitate departure the earl's behaviour towards Mazarine became conciliatory in the extreme, as if he wished to curry favour with her, to make amends for his outburst.

'Let us dine together more often, my dear,' he would say, 'without the intrusion of any of these young pups. Let us ride out together in my coach! Poor creature — you do look downcast. Allow me to cheer you up! Come to town with me and I shall buy you a new hat, or a lap dog!'

For Mazarine the only consolation for these trials was that the earl, aware that Lord Fleetwood had gone far away, allowed his ward to make daytime excursions without him at her side. It appeared, too, that he had got wind of Master Squires's attachment to Laurelia Wilton, and felt reassured that there could be no intrigue between Mazarine and the clerk. Often, Mazarine and her maid, escorted by one of the Kelmscott equerries, would ride over to Clover Cottage. Filled with foreboding, she unburdened herself to her most trusted confidantes.

'Soon, I am certain,' she said to Laurelia Wilton on one such visit when they were alone together, 'my guardian will ask me to be his wife. I shall refuse — but I fear what will happen next, for he is a ruthless man!'

'Surely he would not use violence against you!' Mazarine's friend was horrified. Pinned loops of light brown hair, straight as corn silk, framed her heart-shaped face as she sat in the parlour working at her embroidery. Her gown was pale blue, her favourite colour.

'I am not certain ...' said Mazarine.

'Thrimby bides in Kelmscott Hall. He will see that you come to no harm.'

'Ah yes, the illustrious, industrious Thrimby. But I do not know the extent of his powers.'

'He is an eldritch wight, is he not? A faerie-creature of the seelie kind?'

'Perhaps. Who knows? Even if he *is* of that race, he is not of the powerful ones. Domestic wights may be lightning fast and expert at cleaning — also good at eavesdropping and spying — but I would not wager on their winning a battle with the master or any of his hired thugs.'

'My dear Squires tells me your guardian's finances are in disarray,' said Laurelia. 'He is close to ruin! If he can no longer pay these hirelings, he will have to let them go.'

'I do not believe he is quite that desperate, yet.' Mazarine sighed and added, 'He professes affection for me, but I fear he is only after my inheritance.'

'Nobody is in any doubt of *that*,' Laurelia retorted tartly, 'which is no insult to *you*. I only mean that the earl is incapable of love for any creature other than himself.'

'He shall not lay his hands on any more of my parents' money!' cried Mazarine. 'Already the executors pay him a sizeable pension for my upkeep. Oh, it has been odious beyond belief, this misunderstanding with Fleetwood. I only wish he would return swiftly! Where can he be? How I long to undeceive him! How I long for his support!'

Hawkmoor, nonetheless, did not return.

Weeks passed. During Nethilmis, the first month of Winter, itinerant strangers were glimpsed on several occasions, roaming in Kelmscott Park. On each occasion when Ripley and his henchmen got up a posse to throw the 'gypsies' off the property, they had already disappeared.

'Not gypsies, I am certain of it,' Wakefield said to Mazarine and Laurelia one evening as they took their ease by the parlour fire at Clover Cottage. 'As sure as Thrimby is a brownie, they are trow-folk — or hilltings, or Grey Neighbours as they are sometimes called. Trows, roaming abroad from their hidden lands beneath the hills.'

'People around here believe that trows seldom stray into these parts,' said Laurelia.

'Then they had best be careful,' said Wakefield, 'for he who remains ignorant of the ways of wights puts himself at risk.'

'Why?' Mazarine asked. 'I do not know much about trow-folk myself. Though other kinds of wights aplenty haunt Reveswall, trows are rare. Are they so unseelie?'

'Not unseelie in the way the fuathan are unseelie,' Wakefield replied, 'for they are not destroyers of humankind, but neither are they always seelie. For the most part they neither help nor hinder human beings. Sometimes the trow-wives enter people's homes by night, in search of a basin of clean water in which to bathe their babies.'

'I thought wights had to be invited to cross the thresholds of humankind,' said Laurelia.

'At some time in the past,' Wakefield answered, 'a householder must have given them permission to enter that particular abode, and being immortal, they may keep that permission for generations of men until someone revokes it. The trow-wives depart by cock-crow, without doing harm, and might even leave a silver sixpence behind if they are pleased with the cleanliness of the establishment. They must be gone to Trowland before sunrise, else they will become *Erithbund* and forced to roam aboveground until sunset. On occasion whole tribes dance by moonlight, and on other occasions they take it into their heads to steal.'

'Steal what?'

'Silver ornaments. They love silver. And milch-cows, sometimes, for the cream. Or people.'

'*People?*'

'Indeed,' said Wakefield, 'and when they carry people off to live with them in Trowland, they leave a replica in their victim's stead — a crudely carved post or log, which for a few hours remains wrapped in Glamour's illusion. When the enchantment wears off, it can easily be seen that the replica is nothing more than a piece of wood.'

'Do the trows hurt the stolen ones?'

'No. They keep them as servants, bound by invisible, intangible chains. Those who are thus enchanted may never return to the lands of the sun.' After a solemn hiatus he amended, 'In almost all cases.'

'What do you mean *almost all cases?*' asked Mazarine, leaning her elbows on her knees. 'Is there any chance people who are trow-bound can escape?'

''Tis not impossible,' said Wakefield, 'though 'tis unlikely.' And he told the story of Katherine Fordyce, a woman who had died at the birth of her first child. 'At least, folk thought she had died,' said the storyteller, 'but she had, in fact, been taken by the trows, and an effigy left in her place. You see, her family and friends had forgotten to *sain* her when her child was born, which was how she fell into the power of the trows. She dwelled quite comfortably among the Grey Neighbours but the enchanted cannot escape Trowland unless some human creature chances to see them and has presence of mind enough to repeat the phrase, *Güde be aboot wis.* The only mortal man ever to spy Katherine again was a man named William Nisbet, who was walking up a slope near her old home when it seemed as if a hole opened in the side of the hill. He looked in and saw Katherine sitting in what he described as a queer-shaped armchair, and she was nursing a baby.

There was a bar of metal stretched across in front to keep her a prisoner. She was dressed in a white gown which folk later knew, by William's account of it, to be her wedding dress. Nisbet thought she said to him, "Oh, Willie! What's sent you *here?*" and he answered, "And what keeps *you* here?" to which she replied, "Well, I am hale and happy, but I cannot get out, for I have eaten their food!" William Nisbet was so taken aback that, alas, he forgot to say "Güde be aboot wis". Katherine, being enchanted, was unable to give him any hint, and in a moment the entire scene disappeared.'

'And has no one glimpsed her since?' enquired Mazarine.

'No.'

'How long ago was she stolen?'

'About five hundred years.'

This sobering fact reduced the company to silence. They sat pondering the story's significance while in the hearth, a log went up in sparks and collapsed in cinders.

Nethilmis, the Cloudmonth, ushered in the Winter of 1038. Bands of 'gypsies' were seen more frequently in the district as the cold weather deepened. Across Severnesse, and indeed across the whole of Erith, the populace was preparing for the midwinter Imbrol Festival with traditional celebrations that would farewell the old year and welcome in the new. Plum puddings wrapped in calico were boiled in cauldrons. Choirs rehearsed the old songs that told of holly and ivy and sleigh rides, and huge logs burning in hearths.

Three months remained until Mazarine's twenty-first birthday, and the earl dedicated the first weeks of Winter to paying court to his ward. She remained adamant in her rebuffs. Perceiving that she was not to be convinced he appeared to become increasingly desperate, particularly when the bailiffs came knocking on his door brandishing letters of demand. It was highly embarrassing for a gentleman in his position, he cried indignantly, not to mention insulting, to be subjected to petty demands from commoners. Nonetheless the bailiffs would not be dissuaded, and put him on notice to pay his dues or suffer the consequences.

Soon afterwards a liveried messenger rode out from Kelmscott Hall under escort by a heavily armed guard. He carried a sealed package containing a letter of utmost importance. No one save the earl and his chief steward knew to whom this significant missive was addressed, or what instructions it conveyed. Even Thrimby had not managed to discover anything about it.

Mazarine continued to avoid her guardian, desiring only that time would swiftly bring her the day of freedom. She bade her lady's-maid tie Hawkmoor's purple ribbons in her hair every morning, and every evening she laid them out carefully on her dressing table. At nights she lay awake for hours.

Two days later, her fragile equanimity was once again shattered.

CHAPTER FOUR

Let those who would their loved ones keep
Sain them, and be well-planned,
Lest they be taken while you sleep,
To that Enchanted Land.

Early one bleak morning when snow-clouds were gathering in the skies, a new messenger came cantering with brisk determination along the avenue of cypress trees flanking the driveway. The rider was arrayed in the livery of the District Court. He bore a notice, addressed to Mistress Mazarine Blythe of Kelmscott Hall, and insisted on being present in the front drawing-room when she unrolled the scroll, which had been tied with official red ribbon and imprinted with the waxen seal of the Judiciary of Severnesse. After deciphering the contents, Mazarine let fall the parchment, swaying as if she, too, were about to drop to the floor. Her face blanched like paper. Master Squires, hovering concernedly at her side, supported her, helping her onto a nearby stool.

'May I presume to look at this dispatch, Mistress Blythe?' he murmured.

Too faint to utter a word, Mazarine nodded weakly. Master Squires picked up the scroll and read it to himself.

'Severnesse Shire Court, East Riding, Amershire.

21st Nethilmis 1038.
To Mistress Mazarine Blythe,
Kelmscott Hall,
Borough of Breckmouth.
East Riding, Amershire.

Regarding Your Agreement with The Right Honourable The Earl of Rivenhall.

Madam,
The Purpose of this Letter is to give formal Notice of the Breach of your Verbal Promise of Marriage to The Right Honourable The Earl of Rivenhall, dated 1st Nethilmis 1038.
Please be advised that due to your Failure to honour this Agreement, the Plaintiff is entitled to claim Damages and asserts he is left with no choice but to refer this Matter to the Court of Severnesse. You are required to attend a Hearing at the Somerhampton Law Courts on 14th Dorchamis, 1039.
Signed: A. C. Sotheby,
Clerk of Courts.'

'By the Powers!' Wakefield exclaimed, throwing down the scroll, 'There must be some mistake!'

'No mistake,' said the earl peremptorily, bursting into the room with his usual entourage in tow. The court messenger bowed politely; the earl returned the salute with a nod. 'Mistress Blythe made her vow of marriage to me before witnesses, and on that premise I based the planning of my finances. Now that she has gone back on her word I face ruin. I would forgive her, soft-hearted fool that I am, were she to honour her vow, but should she fail to return to her senses, I must demand recompense, as anyone in my position has a right to do.'

Mazarine, pallid and shocked, looked upon her guardian. 'Never would I have believed that anyone could be so black-hearted,' she said in a trembling voice. 'I have done nothing to harm you. How you could drum up these lies to wrong me is beyond comprehension.' Rising to her feet she added, 'I cannot stay a moment longer beneath your roof. This day, this very hour, I will depart, whether or not you give your leave. I have done with you.'

'You may not depart!' shouted the earl. 'You are under my jurisdiction!' and he stepped forward, lifting his hand as if to strike the girl.

Instantly Wakefield Squires blocked his path. 'Recollect, if not your honour as a *gentleman*, then the presence of the agent of the Judiciary,' he said, shielding Mazarine with his body, whereupon the earl backed away. His bodyguards glowered, glancing sideways at their master as if hoping for an order to lay rough hands upon this upstart. The earl, however, was too canny to display mob violence in the sight of the messenger.

'You are discharged forthwith, Squires,' he said, 'and be careful I do not have you served with a claim for damages, for you have foully mismanaged my accounts.'

'Threaten away,' said the young man. 'The law is greater than you, and justice will be done.' He offered Mazarine his arm and together they left the room.

So it happened that Mazarine and her maid departed with haste from Kelmscott Hall, in the company of Master Squires. They took refuge at Clover Cottage, where Professor Wilton and his wife insisted that Mazarine dwell until she came into her inheritance.

That night, it began to snow.

Dorchamis, the Darkmonth, brought with it Winter Solstice and the traditions of Imbrol. The first day of the month was New Year's Day, also called Littlesun Day. Right across the lands of Erith uproarious celebrations ushered in the new year, 1039. Enormous bonfires like burning palaces blazed on snowy hilltops. Indoors, garlands of red-berried holly adorned the rafters, green ivy festooned inglenooks, sprigs of mistletoe dangled above the doors and wreaths of fir and spruce needles encrusted with pine cones decorated the tables. The human populace exchanged presents, feasted on rich fare, danced, imbibed large quantities of various beverages, sometimes quarrelled and occasionally fell down.

Wakefield Squires was fortunate enough to be offered a position in the mayor's office in town. The remuneration was better than that which he had received at Kelmscott Hall, and he accepted the job with delight, commuting daily on foot through the snow.

Midwinter was the season when some Erithan maidens, inquisitive about the possibilities that lay beyond the boundaries of mortal knowledge, deliberated on the alarming and intriguing feasibility of venturing into the wild places during the long nights of Dorchamis, to find out whether the Caillach Gairm, the eldritch blue crone as ancient and fierce as Winter, should decide to appear and present them with a coveted Staff of Power in exchange for whatever mortal asset she might wish to take for herself — the colour of their hair and eyes, their power of song, a finger or a toe, or more … If the girl felt that the consequences were too onerous, she would refuse to strike the bargain, yet it was a terrible decision to make, knowing that never again would she be offered that opportunity.

Neither Mazarine nor Laurelia craved the power of a carlin's Wand. Laurelia floated with her beau on joyous clouds of romance, but Mazarine's heart ached. She had lost the one she loved, and now, to compound her misery, she had been wrongfully accused, and faced a trial. Her friends comforted her, and in return she tried her best to appear cheerful as she joined the Imbrol festivities.

'Will you obtain the services of a lawyer?' Laurelia asked Mazarine, as the entire family sat around the fire in the parlour of the cottage, sipping mulled wine. Professor Wilton, a doughty gentlemen with grizzled whiskers and a receding hairline, occupied a rocking chair. His wife, a small woman in a gown of brown kersey, sat near the fire toasting crumpets on a long-handled fork, while his daughter nestled close to her betrothed on the divan. Mazarine's maid Odalys was mending petticoats while the Wiltons' maid-of-all-work, Tansy, perched upon a hassock alternately sewing buttons on a shirt and caressing the ears of the two pet dogs that lay stretched out on the rug. It was unusual for employers to mix so familiarly with their servants, but both Odalys and Tansy were considered to be almost part of the family.

'No,' said Mazarine. 'I am innocent — that is defence enough, surely? I will speak the truth and the truth will prevail.'

'My dear girl!' Professor Wilton exclaimed in dismay. 'Pardon my presumption, but surely you cannot consider demeaning yourself by speaking in court! A gentlewoman of noble birth …'

'Nonetheless, sir, I will do it.'

The apothecary sighed. 'Perhaps you will think better of it eventually.'

'I thank you for your solicitude, Professor Wilton, but I see no reason to change my mind. Besides, I cannot afford such expenses until I come into my inheritance. Until I am twenty-one, there is only a meagre income supplied to me, for keeping Odalys.'

'We could find some way of borrowing the money,' suggested Laurelia. 'It could be repaid as soon as you reach your majority.'

'Gramercie, dear friend,' said Mazarine, 'but I am convinced that hiring a lawyer will not help me. Before Lord Fleetwood went away, our discussions used to range over many topics, including the judicial system of Amershire. Three magistrates preside at Somerhampton Law Courts, so he said, and it is generally held that verdicts are largely influenced not by one's lawyer, but by which judge is allotted to one's trial. The allotments are chosen by ballot, so the outcomes are partly dependent on the luck of the draw, and partly on the merits of the case.'

'That does not seem fair!' exclaimed Laurelia.

'Nevertheless, Mistress Blythe is right. That is the way it works,' her father said.

'What of these three magistrates?' Wakefield wanted to know.

'The best of them all is Judge Innsworth,' said Mazarine. 'She is wise, strictly impartial, and fair in her sentencing. Most folk hope to go before her. I hope I shall.'

'Most folk? Why not all?' asked the young clerk.

'Because she is strictly impartial!' said Mazarine.

'The worst judge, for Mistress Blythe in particular,' said Professor Wilton, courteously inclining his head in Mazarine's direction, 'would be Hackington-Cluny, for he is a crony of her guardian's; a hunting and gambling companion and an oft-times visitor at Kelmscott Hall. There is not a drop of impartiality in that fellow's blood. I suspect he can be flattered, bought or cajoled into doing or saying anything at all. No doubt he owes the earl a few favours.'

'I fervently pray that Mazarine will not have to be tried by such an immoral character!' cried Laurelia, scandalised. 'If this is common knowledge, why do the authorities not relieve the rogue of his post?'

'He wields influence over many citizens in high places.'

'What an outrage! And the third magistrate?

'Judge Rotherkill falls into a class somewhere between the other two,' her father replied, 'for he is neither as perceptive or just as Innsworth, nor as corrupt as Hackington-Cluny. Indeed, as far as I know he is not at all corrupt. His judgements and sentencing, however, leave a lot to be desired, in my opinion.'

'I have no fear of Rotherkill,' said Mazarine. 'As long as it is not Hackington-Cluny who holds my future in his hands, I will not be afraid.'

'Yes, that gentleman is indeed a formidable threat,' said Goodwife Wilton, breaking her silence and looking up from her stitching, 'but to my mind there is one to be even more wary of, who has even fewer scruples and a greater propensity for violence, and that is the earl himself!'

Two weeks after the Imbrol Festival, Mazarine, in the company of Laurelia, Professor Wilton and Master Squires, boarded an enclosed sleigh borrowed from a wealthy neighbour of the Wiltons. The neighbours' coachman, Tofts, rode postilion on the near horse of the pair. He blew the coachman's signal for 'start' on his coach-horn, being rigorous in observing these formalities — whereupon the horses lunged forward, the tiny bells on their harness tinkling, and off they glided over the frozen road to the Somerhampton Law Courts.

It was just before sunrise. Peering through the thick glazing of the window, Mazarine observed the shadowy countryside through which they passed; woodlands and meadows whose snow-dusted shapes were just beginning to be picked out in glitter by the pre-dawn light. Largely uninhabited by mankind, save for the odd, courageous woodcutter or lime-burner, the vales and hills of Amershire were the secret haunts of countless unhuman, immortal incarnations, elusive and rarely seen. One had to be cautious of them, however, if one wished to arrive safely at one's destination. There, for example, in that breeze-rattled, leafless hazel thicket, might dwell Churnmilk Peg, eldritch guardian of the ripe nuts in Autumn, who would burst out angrily at you if you tried to steal her harvest. Or that grove of wild apple trees, their black boughs now snow-laden — might be guarded by a colt-pixy who would chase away an apple-thief and curse him with '*cramp and crooking and fault in his footing*'. Winter, too, had its preternatural manifestations; in particular the sullen Brown Man of the Muirs and the blue-skinned crone, the Caillach Gairm, who roamed abroad at this, her season of greatest power.

A farmer's sledge approached out of the gloom from the opposite direction and Tofts blew the call for 'Near Side', meaning that he would keep to the left and the sledge should pass on their right. The farmer looked mystified but tipped his hat convivially as he went by, and Tofts gave him a condescending nod.

Dimmed by a range of clouds along the distant hills, the sun's glow was broadening when the sleigh came to the stone bridge that spanned Tybeck Stream and slid to a halt. No beast would cross this bridge without intervention, for it was under eldritch guardianship. The horses shivered, tossing their heads and prancing nervously between the shafts. The presence of wights always made animals excited or uneasy. As for any human pedestrians who set foot on the bridge — if they were not careful to observe formalities they would find themselves being flung over the parapet into the icy water. Standing up in the stirrups, Tofts called out authoritatively, 'Riverside Dan! Riverside Dan! Let us cross the Tybeck Span!'

Bubbling water gurgled around the granite stanchions. A curlew whistled. After a protracted moment the sleigh lurched into motion again; the horses, sensing some kind of release beyond human ken, trotted briskly across the bridge.

Close to the town of Somerhampton some churls on the way to market had carelessly overturned a sled of winter root vegetables in the middle of the road. Imperiously, Tofts sounded 'Clear the Road' on his horn, as if he were the driver of the King's Royal Coach. Rolling their eyes and shaking their heads, the peasants, well-muffled in coats and gloves, righted the sled and piled their worts back into it while Tofts waited impatiently.

At last they bowled away once more. Tofts signalled 'Slacken Pace and Steady', as they passed through the gates of the town, and finally 'Pull Up' outside the Law Courts. By this time the passengers' ears were ringing with all the coachman's blaring signals.

The building that housed the Somerhampton Law Courts was as majestic and solemn as befitted the proceedings that took place therein. Up and down the exterior colonnade milled an army of bespectacled scribes making copious notes on sheets of paper, and a bevy of stern guards keeping the peace. A few idlers and loafers had positioned themselves at the arched entrance portals, stamping their feet and huddling into their scarves, their breath condensing like smoke on the cold air. They ogled the new arrivals.

'Ooh, who's that?'

'I believe 'tis the earl of Rivenhall's ward! What an enchanting young creature! I wonder what she is doing here.'

'Perhaps she has been called as a witness in some trial.'

'Look down the road — here comes a dashing turnout! Whose is the coat of arms blazoned on the doors?'

'Why, 'tis the earl himself!'

Mazarine and her companions were conducted inside to a cold, lofty chamber large enough to accommodate fifty persons but containing two sentries, a clerk, a junior clerk, a hunch-backed usher and a cluster of be-wigged gentlemen in black robes, solemnly clutching vellum-bound documents, who turned out to be the earl's legal advisors.

'Yours is the first case of the morning, m'lady,' said the usher with a bow. The stench of stale beer drifted from his garments. 'Where is m'lady's defence counsel, if I may be so bold as to enquire?'

'I have none. I speak for myself.'

Giving a resigned shrug that expressed a certainty of doom, the usher guided the newcomers to their seats, where they waited in trepidation to discover which magistrate had been allotted to their chamber. A mild disturbance at the other end of the room accompanied the appearance of the earl and his steward.

Presently the bailiff announced the arrival of the magistrate.

'All rise. The Honourable Judge Sir Lupton Rotherkill, presiding.'

A sigh of mingled relief and disappointment passed through the company as they stood up.

Judge Sir Lupton Rotherkill seated himself at a high bench behind a counter of polished walnut, and peered at the defendant from beneath a white wig. Weatherbeaten was his visage, the mouth turned downwards at the corners. A pair of gold-rimmed spectacles perched at the end of a pointy beak of a nose. As everyone resumed their seats Wakefield murmured, 'I mislike the look of this character. He has the world-weary air of a man who believes he has seen all and knows all, and whose jadedness has worn away any genuine sentiments he might once have felt.'

'Methinks you are too discouraged,' said Professor Wilton.

'The man seems an automaton!' Wakefield insisted. 'I'll warrant he will not judge the case on its merits but merely apply the formula he uses for all lawsuits of this ilk!'

'Let us hope the formula is wise and just,' said Mazarine, who was tightly clutching the back of the bench in front of her.

'Silence!' warned the clerk of courts.

The session commenced with the allegations against Mazarine being read out by the clerk. The plaintiff's chief counsel was given to opportunity to speak, which he did, employing his eloquence so cleverly that for one absurd moment Mazarine herself was on the point of wondering whether she was, in fact, in the wrong. 'And furthermore,' the lawyer appended, 'Mistress Blythe has absconded from beneath my client's roof without permission and, by law, ought to return home immediately!'

This was an unexpected sting in the tail of his oratory. Catching Laurelia's indignant eye Mazarine mouthed the word, *Never.*

The defendant was then permitted the right of reply. She stood up, as graceful and dignified as a young willow tree, but a shudder passed through the court officials and the earl's counsel, who considered it indelicate for a gentlewoman to thus make a spectacle of herself — not to mention unfair for depriving worthy legal gentlemen of their livelihood.

Summoning her courage, Mazarine spoke clearly and concisely, presenting her version of the facts and explaining her innocence of the charges. She answered all questions straightforwardly and with such an air of honesty that it seemed clear to her friends that there could only be one verdict — she must be exonerated. When she sat down and all the giving of evidence was over, quietude reigned, overlaid by the scratching of quill-pen nibs on paper.

'Well done!' said Laurelia, giving her friend's hand a squeeze. Mazarine smiled, then glanced sideways at the earl's coterie. They looked smug.

Judge Rotherkill, expressionless, appeared to be deliberating. The waiting seemed intolerable.

Some imperceptible signal must have passed between the magistrate and the clerk of courts, for presently the latter intoned, 'All rise for the judge's decision.'

Respectfully, the chamber's occupants obeyed, though the earl's coterie managed to make it look as if they were about to stand up in any case, and the order had simply happened to coincide with their own inclinations.

'Humankind,' pronounced Judge Sir Lupton Rotherkill, leaning forward and gazing at the court over the top of his spectacles, 'unlike eldritch-kind, is capable of telling lies. Not only capable, but adept. In a disagreement such as this no man can be certain who is telling the truth, for it is one person's word against another's. The question of who is in the right must be decided by Providence. Therefore I *bynde* both the plaintiff and the defendant to this command: that to decide the issue they, or their representatives, must fight a duel with swords.'

Expressions of shock rippled through the audience. The earl looked angry and Mazarine felt stunned. A clamour of voices broke out in the courtroom.

'Silence!' roared the clerk, whereupon the hubbub subsided.

'If the defendant or her representative wins,' continued the magistrate, 'Providence will have decreed that her version of events was the truth, whereby the plaintiff must pay her one thousand golden guineas as recompense for the inconvenience, in addition to court costs. If the plaintiff wins it proves he told no lie, and the defendant must honour her promise by marrying him. She will also pay costs.

'According to common law,' he added, 'women, the elderly, the infirm of body, and minors may name champions to fight in their stead. On the allotted day the combat is to begin before noon and be concluded before sunset. The litigants must be present in person. Before fighting, each litigant must swear an oath disclaiming the use of gramarye for advantage in the combat.

'Whoever wins the contest,' Judge Rotherkill concluded, 'wins the case. Until the matter is decided in this manner, the plaintiff and the defendant must neither see nor speak with each other. The duel must be fought before the end of this month — Dorchamis the Dark. If it fails to take place, both parties will be held to be in contempt of court and fined accordingly. If one party fails to appear and field a champion, they will lose the case.'

There was no time to collect one's thoughts; the judge had spoken, and the usher hurried both groups out of the courtroom so that the next candidates might enter.

In the overcast skies the clouds were pressing down as if more snow was threatening. Mazarine and her companions were keen to depart with all speed from the town, where knots of gawkers and loiterers stared at them inquisitively as they exited the building. They repaired to the sleigh without delay.

'Swords!' Professor Wilton exclaimed disgruntledly as he stepped into the vehicle. 'Swords! Trials by combat at common law in Erith are generally carried on with quarterstaffs!'

Wakefield closed the door, Tofts blew his horn officiously and off they slithered once more. As Laurelia unwrapped parcels of bread and cheese and Professor Wilton handed around small bottles of cider, Mazarine said without hope, 'I cannot afford to hire a skilled swordsman. My guardian will win.'

'Not at all!' said Professor Wilton. 'We will find a champion for you, dear lady. Never fear!'

'We have two weeks!' said Wakefield. 'We shall begin the search straight away!'

'That Judge Rotherkill is an utter beast,' said Laurelia feelingly. 'Fancy leaving it to *fate* to decide, and so *brutally*!'

'At least he did not order me to go back to Kelmscott,' said Mazarine.

The journey home proceeded uninterrupted save for the obligatory halt before Tybeck Span, and they returned to Clover Cottage before noon.

CHAPTER FIVE

True justice is elusive, caught in truth and falsehood's dance;
But equity is rarely found when all is left to chance.

That night at Kelmscott House, the earl and seven of his cronies reclined by an enormous blaze in the Long Gallery, discussing the day's proceedings. After doing justice to an eight course meal, they settled in for a long night's drinking. Two butlers were kept busy running up and down the stairs to the cellar, fetching more bottles and firkins. No music or singing was called for; the earl was not partial to such entertainments, but there was much bragging and telling of bawdy jokes until the small hours of the morning. So intent on their carousing were these merry gentlemen that they failed to notice certain scufflings and shiftings in the wainscots and corners, but when at last they lost consciousness, sprawled in various undignified positions across the furniture with legs akimbo and open mouths dribbling, the strange little servant Thrimby appeared from behind a tapestry wall-hanging and, by the light of the dwindling fire, regarded them with some disdain. To himself he muttered,

'You pukin' fools wot snore like drains,
With milk for blood and bone for brains,
Think ye that Thrimby will stand by
Submissive? Nay! I prophesy,
As Mazarine doth seek strong arms
For to defend her from your harms,
Then will I find the one she needs
And ye may rot like blighted weeds!'
With that, he scooped some ashes from the hearth and strewed

them over the person of the senseless earl. For good measure, he also removed one of his master's shoes and threw it on the fire before leaving the room. As it blazed it sent stinking fumes into the room, making the snorers cough in their sleep.

One person had borne witness to this from an ill-lit corner. A young laundry-maid, though exhausted from her day's labour, had been unable to sleep. She was worried by the presence of the drunken louts on the premises. Once, late at night, not long ago, one of the earl's inebriated cohorts had barged into the servant's quarters and tried to molest her; she had managed to escape and hide, but the memory, the fear, was indelible. She felt miserable, too, without Mistress Blythe in the house. Well-practised in silence she stole through the house in Thrimby's footsteps, to see what he would do next.

The wizened creature proceeded to the side door, then out through the conservatory — plucking a few weedy leaves here and there as he passed — to the stables. There, curled up in a pile of straw against the warm body of a sleeping horse, lay the under-gardener's boy. Peeping through a chink in the walls the laundry-maid saw the youngster awaken and sit up, while Thrimby spoke to him. She strained her senses to catch his words.

'Ye must repeat the message three times,' Thrimby was instructing, 'then drop in these sprigs of wormwood and dandelion and sweetgrass. Now speak up loudly, mind! None of yer mumblin'! Afterwards depart, and make it quick, and make no sound and do not look back. Can ye do this?'

Clearly terrified, the boy emitted no sound.

'If you do not go, no one will,' said Thrimby, 'for it goes hard wi' me to leave these premises. Do not be afeared! If ye do as I say, naught will 'arm ye.'

'What is the message?'

'Say this: 'I call thee, Lord Fleetwood, wherever ye stray.

Your love be in danger on this very day

She needeth a champion as never before

Make 'aste, never sleep till ye ride to 'er door.'

The boy nodded tightly.

Thrimby took a small flask out from the tattered depths of his clothing and thrust it roughly towards the lad. 'Take this. If ye feel cold the drink will warm ye. Go now.'

'Now? At night?' The lad stared, aghast.

'The best time.'

'But 'ow will Lord Fleetwood be found?' asked the boy. 'No one knows where 'e bides!'

'Leave that to me and mine,' said Thrimby. 'There be ways o' finding folk. There be ways o' sendin' messages across Erith. Fear not. Play your part and word will get through.'

Shivering with cold or fright the lad scrambled to his feet, wrapped his woollen coat about him and disappeared into the night.

The laundry-maid felt a sweet sleepiness stealing over her; reassured, now, by the notion that Thrimby had matters in hand. Yawning, she made her way to her pallet in the attic.

Next morning she could hardly wait to snatch a moment alone with the under-gardener's boy.

'I saw you with Thrimby. Where did you go last night? What did you do?'

The lad paled, and shifted restlessly. 'I went through the snow to the pool in the dell, down past the old apple-orchard,' he murmured, 'and there I knelt at the brink and leaned my head over. There was bits of ice floating in the black water. It was like a broken looking-glass. I could see me face starin' back at me.'

'Sain thee!' said the laundry-maid, drawing back and gazing at him round-eyed, as if she had never beheld him before. ''Tis a wonder you did not catch your death o' cold!'

'I had to say a rhyme that Thrimby made me learn,' said the boy, 'and I threw in some leaves. That were all.' He looked troubled, and fidgeted with his fingers.

'That was not all was it? What else happened?' The girl edged closer, glancing warily over her shoulder in case of eavesdroppers.

'I shouldn't ha' turned around. It gives me evil dreams.' After hesitating a moment, the lad continued, 'As I walked away, all I could think of was, *Don't look back! Don't look back!* But at the last moment I *did* look back and I saw something rising from the water, but oh!

I cannot speak of such a sight, beautiful as a dream but so queer and wrong-like that I knew in me 'eart it were perilous to look any longer! I wanted to scream but knew I must not make any sound, so I ran home as fast as me poor tremblin' legs would carry me.'

'Sain thee!' the laundry-maid repeated. 'I ain't never going near the apple-orchard dell again!'

'Me neither,' said the lad.

The day of the duel was set for the last day of the month, the thirtieth. Mazarine had requested that the period of preparation be extended to its furthest limit, to allow her enough time to find a champion. She had, however, failed in that quest. Possessing only a mere pittance of an income, she could not afford to hire any swordsman at all, let alone a skilled and famous mercenary from the outlands such as the earl had employed, claiming that he himself was too infirm of body to participate in the contest.

'When the time comes,' Mazarine said to Wakefield, 'will you speak for me on the field of honour and avow I have no representative?'

'I will if necessary,' said Wakefield, 'but instead, allow me to be your champion. I am a passable swordsman.'

'I will not allow it!' said Mazarine. 'Meaning no disrespect to your prowess, Master Squires, but what chance has any citizen against a professional swordsman? You and Laurelia are to be married, and that's an end of it. What a foolish notion, though kindly meant!'

'Yet if you have no champion you have no hope,' said Wakefield.

'There is always hope,' replied Mazarine, though she did not believe it. In truth she was resigned to her fate, a state of mind which bestowed upon her an air of serenity. It was obvious that Lord Rivenhall would win the contest by default and she would be forced to marry him one dreary morning, thus putting her entire inheritance in his hands. Before nightfall of her wedding day, she decided, she would dress herself in beggar's rags and trudge on foot all the way to her old home in the north, where she would find work as a nameless kitchen maid — an honourable profession, if a lowly one.

Unbeknownst to Mazarine and her friends, while they had been searching for a champion who would risk his life for little or no fee,

Steward Ripley — henchman to Mazarine's erstwhile guardian — had by flattery and ruse, managed to gain the confidence of Tansy, the maid-of-all-work employed in the Wilton household.

Tansy was a simple lass who loved her employers. In her breast a slow fire of anxieties smouldered and Ripley knew how to fan them all to flames. She wondered: Might she, Tansy, be replaced by the lady's-maid Odalys if Mistress Blythe's stay were lengthened? Would Laurelia be arrested for harbouring a fugitive who should by rights be dwelling beneath her legal guardian's roof? Would Miss Blythe's presence bring the entire household into disrepute? Would Master Squires fight a duel and be killed, leaving Laurelia forever bereft of her true love?

The masterful Steward Ripley could sweep away all the causes of Tansy's qualms, he told her, if only the maid could secretly keep him supplied with information concerning Clover Cottage and everything that went on there, until the day of the duel. There might be one or two other ways in which she could help, as well.

After much persuasion, half relieved, half scared, Tansy agreed to comply.

The appointed hour swiftly approached.

A wintry gale came blowing across the crystalline landscape, roaring in a thousand voices. To fight the bitter cold, enormous fires heated the Long Gallery of Kelmscott Hall where, on the night of the twenty-eighth the earl was imbibing grape brandy and playing at dice with his cronies.

'I say, Rivenhall,' said one gentleman, 'that ward of yours seems pretty cool and confident.'

' Indeed, Cluny? I had not noticed. I never see the minx, y'know. It is against the court's edict.'

'She appears a self-assured wench, though. What d'ye make of it?'

'Why, I make nought of it. What is your meaning?'

'My meaning is, surely she would not be so unruffled if she had not hired, in secret, some swordsman whom she believes will defeat your man, Henry what's-his-name.'

'Henry Ide of Knightstone. My man is famous, Cluny, surely you have heard of him!'

'Quite. And I'd warrant your wench has found someone equally as famous, else why so smug?'

The earl laughed forcedly, dismissing the suggestion as ludicrous, but after that moment he fell quiet and sat staring broodily into the fire, cradling his wine cup in his hands. The jovial gentlemen were still carousing at midnight when without explanation their host left them, summoned his Chief Steward, and shut himself in the library with him. Dozing or inebriated, his cronies hardly missed him; those who noticed his absence cared little, as long as they could continue to drink his brandy.

Next day Ripley passed a secret message to the Wiltons' maid, Tansy. On the eve of the duel the girl, with pounding pulse, followed his orders and mixed one of the apothecary's galenicals with the dogs' supper. Named *'Wilton's Surpassing Remedye for Sleeplessnesse'*, it was made from agrimony, cinquefoil, elder, linden, passionflower, poppy, purslane and hemlock …

That night at Clover Cottage the wind rattled the doors and moaned in the eaves. The entire household was asleep in bed when the window to Mazarine's bedchamber was quietly opened from the outside, and the earl climbed in. Though tipsy, he was sufficiently in control of his faculties to be able to move stealthily. The dogs, motionless in deep slumber or death, failed to hear or scent the stranger.

Mazarine woke with a start when the intruder clapped a hand across her mouth. Leaning so close to her that his ringlets and the ends of his hat-ribbons tickled her face he whispered, 'Now hear this, you little fool. First thing tomorrow morning you must officially agree to this cursed marriage, or your friends will suffer. There is no need for this duel. Do you understand? Nod and I will let you speak. Cry out and I will hurt you.'

Mazarine pretended to be too dazed with sleep and fright to comprehend, though her cunning adversary saw through the ruse. He commenced to make further threats, his murmurings muffled by the wind's shrieks and lamentations, which masked, too, the hoof-beats — faint at first — of a rider drawing near.

At the rear of the cottage Ripley, lurking in wait with the earl's horses, heard nothing over the creaking of bare branches and the soughing of icy airs; neither did he see the young man on the far side of the building, who flung himself down from his steed's back and strode with uneven gait to the threshold.

In the grip of her captor, Mazarine struggled. Just then there came a loud hammering at the front door.

'Hold your tongue!' the earl whispered, clamping his hand more firmly over Mazarine's mouth. 'Do not give me away! My men are surrounding this house and at my order they will set upon anyone I choose to name!'

Over the sighs of the wind Mazarine, frozen in her captor's grip, heard Professor Wilton's footsteps as he trotted along the passage to the door, then the click of lock and latch and the sound of his voice jovially raised in greeting:

'Lord Fleetwood! Unlooked for and heartily welcomed!'

On hearing this name pronounced, Mazarine felt her blood race.

'Come in, pray!' cried the apothecary. 'How odd — I wonder why the dogs did not announce your visit! By the Star — they are still sleeping, the lazy creatures!'

Under his breath the earl cursed. 'If you betray me, Mistress Blythe, I will give the signal for my fellows to kill your leman,' he said softly. 'That is, if I do not slay him myself. Do you understand?' This was worse than any other threat. Fearful for Hawkmoor's life, Mazarine nodded. The earl subtracted his paw from her mouth and, drawing his sword, stood facing the closed door of her bedchamber.

A moment later Professor Wilton rapped on the other side of the portal.

'Wake up, Mistress Blythe! Lord Fleetwood is here to see you!'

The earl touched his finger to his lips and shook his head warningly.

'Tell him I cannot,' Mazarine called out weakly from amongst her pillows. She climbed out of bed and stood shivering on the floor in her bare feet, her nightdress ruffled by cold gusts from the open window.

A brief consultation took place outside her door, followed by the beloved voice of Hawkmoor saying, 'Mistress Blythe — Mazarine! Pray come out to me, for I have ridden hard this night to reach you!'

Again the earl shook his head. Mazarine nodded vigorously to signal acquiescence, in an attempt to forestall him from suddenly flinging open the door, rushing at Hawkmoor and running him through.

'Mazarine!' Hawkmoor called.

His life hung in the balance. All that protected him from the earl's blade was the door itself, and her wits.

She had to save him. Her heart was breaking.

Opening the door half an inch only, Mazarine said, through the aperture, 'Go away. I will not meet with you.'

'I do not believe it,' said Hawkmoor, and the pain in his voice was as sharp as a blade of ice. Over and over she tried to dissuade him from entering the room but he was persistent. Eventually, in desperation, she forced herself to declare in the most convincing tones she could muster, 'Lord Fleetwood, I detest you. How can I speak more plainly? I wish you would go away and never return.'

This proclamation was greeted by deep silence from beyond the bedchamber, during which Mazarine suffered Hawkmoor's unspoken agony as deeply as her own. It was as if her heart had been torn open and thrown down to bleed on the floor. Outside the cottage, the sad songs of the wind were fading as it fled east across the snowscapes. Soon afterwards the young man swung himself onto his horse and rode away, but the household was stirring and the intruder made his escape through the window before he could be found out.

CHAPTER SIX

'Where did you go last night Johnnie? Where did you go last night?'
'I went down to the orchard pool, mother, but I'll never go there
more.'
'What did you see in the water, Johnnie? What did you see in the
water?'
'I saw my face in a mirror, mother, but I'll never go there more.'
'What more did you see last night, Johnnie? What more did you see
last night?'
'Only shadows or vanities, mother, but I'll never go there more.'

As soon as the earl had galloped off with his servant and Mazarine was certain he was clear of the place, she ran weeping from her room and told the Wiltons — who had heard with some puzzlement the hoof-beats of two riders hastening away after Hawkmoor's departure — everything that had happened.

'What?' roared Professor Wilton, scandalised. 'That blaggard under my very roof? By the Powers, if I were a younger man I'd punch him in the nose!'

'Are you hale, Mazarine?' Laurelia enquired solicitously, 'did he harm you?'

'I am unhurt!'

'Why, the courts should be informed of this outrage!' fumed Laurelia's mother. 'Just fancy, that reprobate sneaking into our very home!'

'No, pray! I will never have to do with the courts again if I can help it!' said Mazarine feelingly.

Her revelations were followed by a teary confession from Tansy, hanging her head in shame, who confessed that the dreadful episode was entirely her fault and declared she must leave the Wilton's employ instantly. The dogs could not be roused and she shrieked in horror that she had accidentally killed them, until the professor assured her that the dose she had administered was less than lethal, and prevailed upon her to remain in his employ.

Wakefield announced that he would saddle up the professor's old hack and ride immediately for Southdale farm —'For that is where Lord Fleetwood is staying, I'll warrant!' — to inform Hawkmoor of the news and bring him back. The family protested —'No man should go galloping out alone on such a cold and windy night! The weather is bad enough but 'tis the least of the perils one might encounter in the darkness! Wait until morning, and we will send a messenger.'

At length good sense prevailed and he agreed to abandon the scheme. Nonetheless no one went back to bed that night. They huddled over a meagre fire listening to the fading sighs of the breezes in the chimney, until the stillest of dawns rinsed the sapphire-pale meadows and woods with a tincture of honey melted through amber.

The messenger was duly sent, but he returned with bad news. Hawkmoor was not at Southdale Farm. He had not visited there since his banishment from Kelmscott House. No one at the farm knew anything of his whereabouts.

Wraith-like clouds came swarming across the sky, and in the misty half-light snowflakes drifted down like swans' feathers.

'I do not believe,' Mazarine said brokenly to Laurelia, 'that anyone could feel more wretched than I.'

There was, nonetheless, no time to mourn. The duel was set to take place that very day. The outcome was a forgone conclusion; Mazarine must conceded defeat, for she had no champion.

In the middle of the morning the snow ceased to fall. Clouds tore themselves into long shreds and floated away in the path of last night's wind. The landscape sparkled gorgeously. Trees with salt-white foliage of snow were stamped like cut-outs against a deep blue sky, their shadows flung across a carpet of white velvet all powdered with diamond-dust.

According to tradition the combat was to be held at Firgrove, the ancient 'field of honour' — a forest clearing surrounded by rank on rank of ancient snow-laden fir trees more than a hundred feet tall. In this spot gathered Sir Lupton Rotherkill, several other members of the legal profession, the litigants, their seconds and supporters, constables, marshals and numerous members of the public who were prepared to brave the cold and the perils of the forest for the sake of a spectacle. It was a day to witness blood spilled on the snow.

Slender mists drifted between the trees and the frosty morning was dull. Several folk carried lanterns on poles, whose light flowered out with golden petals. Men were efficiently shovelling the snow aside, freeing a space for the combat to take place. This would be a relatively clandestine event, because the King-Emperor in far-off Caermelor disapproved of duelling to the death, and had all but banned it throughout Erith. In various backwaters such as Amershire, the practice endured, though it was never advertised. It was a strange, silent gathering in a still, majestic setting illuminated by glimmer and pale snowlight.

To add to the weirdness, a shang wind began to rise.

Rarely did the preternatural wind blow in the south-east of Severnesse, and when it did, there were few tableaux to be seen. As soon as most people sensed — by a prickling at the nape of their necks — the beginnings of an unstorm, they were quick to put on the taltry-hoods whose fine mesh lining of talium metal insulated human thoughts and passions from the ghosting-effect of the shang. This eerie effect could draw upon the energy of human emotions to imprint upon the atmosphere translucent images of events involving intense passions such as love, joy, fear, sorrow, wonder. Each time the shang wind breathed across the land, those same scenes would be revived like silent reflections upon the air, and play themselves out again, over and over. When the shang winds wafted, then would appear dreamlike visions. Century after century the visions hung in the air, gradually fading to nothingness — battles, suicides, lovers' trysts, celebrations, partings … it was too much to bear, which was why the laws of Erith decreed that all must wear the taltry hood when the unstorms rose, on pain of dire punishment.

In the forest surrounding Firgrove there remained three tableaux still substantial enough to be descried. There was the Pinned Lad — a woodcutter's lad upon whom a tree had fallen, transfixed without his taltry when the unstorm rose, crying out for help in agony as his leg was crushed. There were the Runaway Lovers — two young people eloping by moonlight, in their haste forgetting to take their taltries; the unstorm had caught up with them as they ran away hand in hand, ardently in love. Their wind-painted story had a happy ending; so too did the tableau of the Swinging Child, an innocent sweeping back and forth joyfully upon a rope-swing its father had made for it, heedless of needing a protective hood. Long ago the tree that once supported the swing had died and its fallen limbs had been carted away for firewood. The phantom-child swung in mid air, eternally young, eternally ecstatic, quaint in its old-fashioned costume.

Further away on the main road to Somerhampton the Highway Robbery, generated sixty years earlier, repeated itself. In the town square the Mayday Dance around a be-ribboned pole flickered dimly into view, dating from six centuries before, and in the forests more distant there was the phantasmic Burning Cottage from about a hundred years ago.

And on the gravel driveway of Kelmscott could be viewed the Homecoming of the Third Earl, an ancestor of the current proprietor. So delighted was the reckless young man to be returning home after a long sojourn overseas that he leaned bareheaded from his carriage, waving and singing, while the unstorm blew. What song he sang, no one now could recall, for he had long lain in the graveyard on the hill, but his misty coach-and-four regularly bowled up the driveway when the shang wind stirred.

Too, the unstorm made the edges of real things glitter — leaves, icicles, footprints — as if all was spangled with faerie-dust. It was a beautiful event to behold, though bizarre and unsettling. After it passed, it left no mark — unless anyone had been unwise enough to go without the taltry and allow passion to rule.

There was passion aplenty at the field of honour, where everyone was hooded. The face of Mazarine — who stood with her friends — was as colourless as the newly fallen snow that lay along the fir-needles. She could see her guardian on the other side of the cleared space — which was mushy with foot-ploughed ice crystals — shoulder to shoulder with his cronies and Ripley and a few cowled strangers, amongst whom, doubtless, was the famous swordsman everyone had been talking about. The earl was splendidly arrayed in gorgeous raiment, with peacock plumes fountaining from the hat beneath his taltry, his expertly curled hair dangling in spirals to his shoulders.

The eldritch wind sprinkled rainbow scintillants on the snow.

When all were assembled, the Master of the Field shouted out, 'The defendant is a woman. Who stands forth to represent the defendant?'

As agreed with Mazarine, Master Squires was to reply, 'The defendant has no champion,' whereupon the Master of the Field would call out his question twice more, the third call being the final one. Then the plaintiff's champion would be thrice summoned, and when he appeared, the day would be declared in favour of the plaintiff. It was all a formality, but it had to be undergone.

Master Squires moved into the clearing. To Mazarine's surprise, the young clerk made no answer to the first call. A second time — 'Who stands forth to represent the defendant?'

'I do,' said Wakefield, saluting the Master of the Field. Throwing off his cloak he revealed the metal plates he was wearing beneath. The armour, battered and rusty, looked as if it had been borrowed from some aged knight whose glory days were long past.

After a moment's shocked pause, Mazarine and Laurelia ran forward and took the young man by the elbows, Laurelia whispering urgently into his ear. The crowd was murmuring excitedly.

'This gentleman appears for me against my wishes!' Mazarine cried loudly. 'I will not have him fight on my behalf!'

'He has volunteered,' said the Master of the Field, 'and you must accept him, unless another offers to take his place. Then, if there is argument, the law will decide.'

No matter what they did or said, Mazarine and her friends could not dissuade the young man. 'For, surely Hawkmoor will come soon,' he said. 'Then he can take my place.'

'Hawkmoor has no knowledge of this duel!'

'I'll warrant you do not give him sufficient credit.'

The earl and his cronies, meanwhile, were laughing behind their hands.

An ink-stained clerk against a mighty warrior …

With a sigh the unstorm swept away, its jewellery glints fading. The atmospheric charge dissipated.

'The plaintiff has pleaded "infirm of body". Who stands forth to represent the plaintiff?' then demanded the Master of the Field.

All heads turned toward the earl's coterie. The public was eager to set eyes on the eminent swordsman. A tall man stepped forward, throwing back his taltry-hood. Dark hair spilled forth, tied back with a band. The cloak fluttered to the ground, revealing fluted scallops of armour with a golden sheen. The watchers gasped.

This was *not* the famous mercenary from the outlands everyone had expected. Instead of Henry Ide of Knightstone, there stood the earl's own heir.

Half-hidden amongst the crowd, Mazarine felt as if her breath had been snatched away. *This was impossible.* As the onlookers gaped in amazement Hawkmoor drew out his sword and ceremonially raised it vertically in front of his face, saluting the judge, the Master of the Field and the earl.

'The mercenary, Ide, has been paid to depart,' he said with composed certitude. 'I am the heir of Rivenhall; therefore it is only fitting that I represent my sire. It is a matter of duty and honour.' He sheathed the weapon.

'This man has volunteered,' the Master of the Field said to the earl, 'and you must accept it. Unless,' he added ceremonially, 'another volunteers to take his place.'

A clamour arose from the onlookers.

Mazarine's erstwhile guardian began to rage and bawl but he could do nothing to alter the situation.

Steward Ripley said in his master's ear, 'Providence appears to be generous, sir. The clerk is clearly no fighter, and when he is slain, you will win the hand and property of the fair damsel. That is the likeliest outcome, since Fleetwood, though lame, is proficient in the arts of war.'

'He has undermined and betrayed me!' fumed the earl. 'He dismissed my champion without my permission or knowledge! And why? And why? That is what I would like to know!'

'If any other champion is to volunteer for either side, let him step forward now!' announced the Master of the Field. He looked about expectantly. Silence and stillness greeted his words. No man in the crowd dared moved so much as a toe, lest it should be deemed they were offering themselves in combat. Three young lads whose lack of years made them immune to this danger ran around the edges of the clearing, sprinkling handfuls of salt as a ward against wights.

'Why indeed?' murmured Ripley. 'Perhaps he has tired of his infatuation with the wench and wishes to see the family estate preserved for his future use. For, surely he is aware that the property will have to be sold if you do not get the girl's money to pay off the creditors.'

'More likely he has done this to spite me,' fumed the earl, 'and to show off. It's as much as to say, *I with my useless leg am a better man than your best mercenary —*'

He broke off as the Master of the Field proclaimed, 'No other swordsman having appeared for either side, the combat must now begin!'

A short scream pierced the air. Mazarine, distraught in the arms of Laurelia's mother, was overcome by horror that two of her dearest friends were to be set against each other. 'Fleetwood believes I have renounced him. He still supposes I love Master Squires!' she gasped.

'Then he will slay Wakefield!' cried Laurelia, sinking into her father's arms.

'I know him better than that,' Mazarine cried brokenly. 'He will do the opposite. I fear his intent is to sacrifice himself for my sake. I cannot let him die without knowing the truth. I must tell him!' detaching herself from the embrace of her protectress she called out, 'Fleetwood! Fleetwood, hear me!'

Her voice, however, was drowned by the hubbub of the throng, and it was too late, for the duelling-space had been cleared and the marshals pushed the crowd back. Grim-faced, the two competitors faced one another inside the circle and the contest must begin.

'There is some plot afoot,' the earl growled in a low voice. 'No doubt the clerk has some tricksy gramarye working on his behalf, else why would he be so bold? Against eldritch powers a mortal man cannot compete.'

'Not so!' said Ripley. 'To use enchantment is to cheat. It is forbidden.'

'Forbidden maybe, but who's to prove it and what would be the use after the limping pup is cut down and I am ruined?'

As if in response to the earl's doubts, the Master of the Field ushered forward a carlin, a woman of wisdom and power, robed in Winter's shades of blue and grey. Her forehead was adorned with a painted blue disc, and an embroidered stag's head decorated her left sleeve. The carlin, whose slight stature and middle age belied her abilities, scrutinised the combatants through the hole in a self-bored stone, an artefact that possessed the power to unveil the disguises of gramarye.

'I see no Glamour on either of them, nor on their weapons,' she said, before withdrawing with a scowl to the hindmost ranks of the crowd. Patently she disapproved of such bellicose goings-on.

'If Fleetwood is slain you will be well rid of him!' Ripley muttered to his master.

'And none too soon!' agreed the earl, who was too preoccupied with suspicion and indignation to notice that the under-gardener's boy, inconspicuous among the gathering, was bestowing upon him a look remarkable for its vehement and speculating character.

'So,' whispered the lad, so softly that none could hear him, 'you would see your own son slain for your greed, would you, you old wretch? I shall know what to tell the rhymer!'

Trials by combat at common law in Erith were carried out on a duelling ground of sixty feet square. Each litigant was allowed an iron shield, and could be protected by armour, provided that they were bare to the knees and elbows, and wore only leather shoes on their feet. Both combatants were properly clad.

Into the hush the Master of the Field bawled, 'The combat is to begin upon my signal, and conclude before sunset. Before fighting, each litigant must swear an oath disclaiming the use of witchcraft for advantage in the combat.' He stated the oath, which both men repeated after him: 'Hear this, ye justices, that I have this day neither eat, drank, nor have upon me, neither bone, stone, ne grass; nor any enchantment, sorcery, or witchcraft, whereby the law of mortal man may be abased, or the law of eldritch forces exalted. So sain me.'

'Either combatant may end the fight and lose his case by crying out the word "craven", which acknowledges "I am vanquished". The party who does so, however, whether litigant or champion, will be punished with outlawry. Otherwise fighting will continue until one party or the other is dead. The last man standing wins the case. Champions, before I give the signal, do you have any final requests?'

'I do,' said Hawkmoor.

'What is your will?'

'I wish for a private word with my adversary.'

'Granted, but first you must both lay down your weapons.'

Both champions did as the master of the field ruled, and met one another in the very centre of the field of honour. There Hawkmoor bent his head and whispered something to his opponent, whereupon the latter, whose stricken countenance was ashen pale, now took on an expression of dazed puzzlement.

They parted, walked back to their positions, and took up their swords.

Laurelia whispered, 'Mazarine, what can you mean? Why do you believe Lord Fleetwood will sacrifice himself?'

Her friend was sobbing. 'He wants to save me. Knowing I could not afford to hire a skilled swordsman, he had two choices; either he could volunteer as my champion and risk losing the fight to a mercenary who had the advantage over a crippled man, or he could represent the earl and throw the fight. He chose the latter ...'

'Oh! But surely —' Laurelia was prevented from saying more, for the Master of the Field raised his right hand.

'Champions,' he shouted, 'Lay on!'

The duel began with the contenders circling one another warily, weapons at the ready. Hawkmoor was a skilled swordsman — far better than Wakefield, who handled his blade as clumsily as if he had hardly so much as touched a weapon in his life. This inequity was plain to the watchers, to whom the outcome appeared so inevitable that they had ceased betting on it. They waited, downcast, for Hawkmoor to win. Their mood was low; they had expected a close fight of fire and fury, between two worthy adversaries — not the slaughter of a well-meaning but misguided pen-pusher by one who was infinitely his superior. Some turned their faces away, unwilling to witness the sad death of such a courageous young man.

Steel chimed on steel. The snow slid treacherously underfoot and both combatants were hard put to keep their balance. Wakefield flailed his weapon as a thresher might beat at a stook of corn. Plainly, Hawkmoor could have finished off his opponent at any time, had he chosen to do so.

'Leave off! Leave off!' Mazarine screamed, struggling to break free from the restraining grasp of her friends. They would not let her approach the duelling-circle, which was patrolled by marshals whose job it was to shove all would-be trespassers unceremoniously out of the way. 'Stop the fight!' Mazarine cried. 'Hearken — *I will marry Lord Rivenhall.* There is no need for this!'

Summoning every ounce of effort she shook off her well-meaning captors, ran through the crowd and burst into the cleared space. At that moment Wakefield had his back turned, but Hawkmoor, who was facing her, had her in full view. The combatants had just mutually disengaged to take a brief respite from their efforts. Both were breathing hard; Wakefield staggered as if he were about to topple over. Having torn a purple ribbon from her hair Mazarine flourished the streamer aloft, calling Hawkmoor's name aloud. In that instant the young lord's gaze met hers and his eyes flashed, as if in recognition or farewell. He drew his sword into the vertical position, point upwards, and bowed in formal salute. One of the marshals seized Mazarine by the arms and pinioned her, but from the moment Hawkmoor had set eyes on the damsel he stood motionless. She stared, uncomprehending, as his opponent, half blinded by sweat, unaware of her presence and delirious with exhaustion, resumed his unskilled swiping. Hawkmoor did not move so much as a finger, nor did he flinch when Wakefield, who had been stabbing wildly at the air, chanced to strike him hard below the ribs.

Blood gushed. The crowd gave a mighty, gasping shout: it was a mortal blow.

Lord Rivenhall's champion sank to the ground, which now seemed thickly strewn with bright rose petals. The marshal released Mazarine, who ran to the wounded man and fell to her knees, cradling his head in her lap. Like a black swan against the crimson snow she drooped over him in her mourning raiment, while Wakefield stood dazedly by, swaying unsteadily, his sword arm hanging limply by his side.

The dying man's blood-soaked hair fanned out across Mazarine's skirts. 'I love you,' she sobbed, her lips close to his beautiful face. 'I love only you. I was forced to send you away from the cottage because Rivenhall had broken into my bedchamber and vowed to kill you if I betrayed his presence.'

Hawkmoor, his handsome face as pale as the marble of a tomb, looked up at her one final time, sighed once, and swooned.

Wakefield uttered a hoarse shout of horror. The sword fell from his hand. 'He told me he would permit the death blow,' he moaned. 'I would not believe him!'

The Master of the Field crouched beside Mazarine. He felt for the pulse of the fallen man, and put an ear to his chest, then shook his head and rose to his feet.

'I declare,' he said, 'that the victor is the champion of Mistress Blythe!'

CHAPTER SEVEN

Over and over old battles are fought,
Dearly — so dearly was victory bought
Centuries earlier. Yet in these days,
When the shang wind blows the conflict replays.
Over and over wraith-lovers must part;
Fond kisses, sad looks and a desolate heart.
Over and o'er the dim shipwreck plays out –
Seen, but unheard, drowning sailor-ghosts shout.
Triumph and sorrow, delight and regret,
Are printed on winds that can never forget.
That which time's passing forsook and let go
Returns in a vision when unstorm winds blow.

Without delay the constables moved in to take charge of the earl who, the moment his representative was unexpectedly struck down, had made a desperate attempt to fight free of the crowds and make good his escape.

'You're for the shackles, my lord!' said the Chief Constable smugly, bustling him away. Steward Ripley made no attempt to impede the instruments of the law but stood by, grimacing.

'Liar! Liar!' the crowd jeered as the earl was escorted from the clearing. Evidently they considered that Providence had ruled accurately. Rivenhall was a deeply unpopular citizen.

Laurelia's father supported Wakefield as he tottered from the scene, and the body of Hawkmoor was borne away on a litter.

'Put him in my sleigh!' cried Mazarine, her voice raw with pain. 'As his nearest free living relative I claim him!'

Through the wintry landscape Mazarine's hired sleigh drove, and on the way her tears fell upon Hawkmoor like pearls, half-frozen. It was not until they had almost reached home that she thought she noticed something that made her spirits leap with a mighty lurch. Was that a tiny flicker of his lids?

'Professor Wilton,' she gasped, hardly daring to shape the words lest they prove to be unfounded, 'I believe Fleetwood lives yet!'

And it was true. Extraordinarily, by the slimmest of threads, a thread that unravelled by the minute, the young man still clung to life.

At the cottage Laurelia's father devoted all his energies to ministering to the patient. On a bed Hawkmoor lay, hovering between life and death, while Mazarine nursed him. All that night she kept vigil at the patient's bedside. Her friends took turns to keep her company, praying to Providence that Hawkmoor would be saved. Despite all efforts he remained without consciousness; unspeaking, unmoving, his lashes dark against the waterlily pallor of his skin. At length Mazarine dozed, dreaming that her sweetheart lay dead upon a catafalque. When she wakened, weeping, he still lived, the slightest of pulses beating in his temples.

Come morning, Professor Wilton said, 'There is no hope. I am sorry, Mistress Blythe. He will soon cross death's threshold.'

'As long as he breathes I will continue to hope!'

On the second night Mazarine sat drooping by Hawkmoor's bedside when all others were abed. In his slumber he now twisted and struggled, as if doing battle with an invisible foe, and his skin was hot to the touch. The wind, blowing from the direction of distant Somerhampton, carried the notes of the town hall's bell tolling the stroke of midnight. As the note faded from memory Mazarine gave a start, for someone stepped towards her from the shadows and the stillness of the house, and it was none other than Thrimby.

'Fear not,' said the withered creature, laying a small paw-like hand gently on her arm.

'My friend!' exclaimed the young woman, trembling. 'I supposed you never stirred from Kelmscott Hall. How came you here?' for she had heard no sound of his approach — no footsteps, no knock at the door. Even the dogs, though fully recovered from their dose of hemlock, had stayed silent.

'Never mind,' said Thrimby, glancing about the room. 'Alas, the young lord chose to slight good Thrimby's sound advice. Instead he chose to throw the fight, and now he's paid the price.'

'Did you send for him, Thrimby? Did you ask him to fight on my behalf? He wanted to be certain Rivenhall lost the duel, so instead of following your suggestions he allowed himself to be struck down. He is terribly ill … oh, it is too much to bear!'

'Ye must be swift to outwit death,' said Thrimby, 'for there's one way to save,' he paused for effect then went on, 'your love who's near his final breath, and keep him from his grave.'

'Save him?' Mazarine gasped. 'How?'

'Be strong, have courage and take heed. Trows hold a healing spell — so you must seek them with all speed if you would make him well.'

'I would indeed make him well,' Mazarine said vehemently. 'Tell me what I must do, dearest Thrimby! How shall I find the Grey Neighbours and how should I entreat them to help?'

'Thrimby knows where to find them!' The shrivelled fellow leaned even closer to Mazarine, so that she could smell the strange scent of him, like the leaves of wormwood after rain, and he told her what she must do.

'Tomorrow eve the moon shines bright
Upon the winter snow,
Then you must face the threats of night
And solitary go.

Beside the frozen forest pool
They'll hold their revelry
Where wind and stars and wild things rule;
But you must fearless be.

Bring silver as the promised fee,
But wear no warding charm.
Show courage, truth and courtesy
And they'll do you no harm.'

He told her more, then sat at her feet with his arms curled around his bent knees and sang an odd little song. Mazarine's head began to nod and she fell into another doze. When she awoke Thrimby was gone. She looked out of the window but all footprints had been obliterated by the gently falling snow.

Somehow Hawkmoor clung to life throughout the following day. Mazarine informed her friends of what had passed, and told them she had made up her mind to follow Thrimby's directions. '*Beside the frozen forest pool* can only mean Coome Pool, which lies on the other side of Firgrove,' she said.

They tried to persuade her not to attempt such a foolhardy enterprise. Wakefield Squires, once he had rested a day or two, was barely troubled by the bruises he had sustained during the duel. 'To ask you to wear no wight-repellent charm, in the dead of night?' he exclaimed. 'No talisman, no iron, nothing of the colour red? What is Thrimby thinking of?'

'To go alone into the forest at midwinter? What are *you* thinking of, Mazarine?' cried Laurelia.

'How can you be certain they are truly trows, these creatures Thrimby has found in the forest?' asked Professor Wilton. 'If they turn out to be gypsies, then they are not bound by the same codes as immortal beings. Gypsies, being humankind, can tell lies and break promises. Even if these folk prove to be the Grey Neighbours, you will not necessarily be safe. Quite probably you will be throwing your life away!'

'I would rather be dead than watch *him* die,' declared Mazarine. 'It is perilous, but I will dare! And no one who is my friend will gainsay me!' She gathered together all her silver ornaments — filigree bracelets, rings, chains — and exchanged all her gold coins for silver, then placed the entire hoard into her jewel-casket, closed the arched lid and locked it.

That night, against all advice from her companions, she borrowed Professor Wilton's grey mare and, wrapped in her warmest cloak, rode out alone, according to Thrimby's instructions.

By the radiance of the full moon she entered the dim forest and travelled along the narrow winding paths. When she came close to

Coome Pool she dismounted as Thrimby had bidden, tied the mare to a tree-bole and continued on foot, carrying the casket. The air nipped and slapped at her face. Fear set her trembling; with every step she expected to be set upon by unseelie agencies of the night, and torn apart. Every shadow might harbour some malignant incarnation waiting to pounce.

Presently the faint strains of fiddle music came to her ears, so thrilling yet hair-raising that it was as if the fiddler sawed upon the listener's very nerve-strings. As she climbed to the top of a rise she witnessed a throng of figures dancing beside the pool.

Mirror images of the tall, glacial fir trees that in places crowded to the water's brink hung suspended in the broad expanse of ice. Through the boughs brilliant moonshine struck in glinting lances. Half a dozen bonfires flamed from the snow like flowers of crimson glass. In the night sky the lunar orb hung close to the horizon; a gigantic disc, palely shimmering, against which the dancers were silhouetted in black.

The quaint folk moved clumsily. Some cavorted in a bounding, ludicrous style, others danced artistically, with elaborate though irregular steps. By the silver radiance of moon and the red glow of flame they danced to a thin music like the piping of reeds, backed by a boisterous beat made by rattling snares and the deep, rhythmic thud of a bass drum.

The human watcher stopped a little way off, in the shelter of the trees. The revellers kept up their antics without appearing to notice her, and she dared to edge closer, dreading that they might suddenly disappear, for if they were wights then they would loathe being spied upon, like all of their kind. Though she moved slowly across the hummocky snow she made no secret of her approach, so as to avoid being accused of stealing up to catch them unawares.

The closer she came to the dancers and musicians, the more clearly she perceived them. Surely they could not be gypsies, for they were too outlandish to be human! Like children, they were small and slight in stature. Their heads were large, as were their hands and feet. Their long noses drooped at the tips and their drab hair hung in lank strings. Each and every one of them stooped and limped to varying degrees. All were clad in rustic raiment dyed several shades of grey, or else weathered and washed to greyness, and the women — or trow-wives — wore fringed shawls tied around their heads. In counterpoint to their plain clothing, silver metal glinted like starlight at their wrists and necks, their ears and ankles.

Mazarine was not more than twenty yards away when the music stopped in mid-flight and, as one, the revellers turned to stare at her. When a figure started up from a hummock close at hand she jumped, and almost dropped the casket.

'Whit be dee after, ma vire, whinkin' here sae brauely ootadaeks?' said a deep voice.

The speaker confronting her on the low mound looked like a dwarfish man, though bigger than the rest, and fiercer looking. A silver fillet encircled his greasy locks and he was wearing a cloak embroidered with silver thread. By his size and relative magnificence he looked to be their leader, or their king. A heavy ornamental chain chinked and swayed about his thick, short neck, and earrings like polished coins dangled from his lobes. Inexplicably he carried in his hand a large silver spoon with a curved handle and a deep bowl, rather like a soup ladle. His dialect resembled the common language of Erith, but not so closely as to be fully intelligible.

Mazarine barely comprehended his meaning but, falling to her knees in a deferential pose, she stated her case, begged for his help and offered the gift of the casket, unfastening the lid. The others gathered around, speaking in some unfamiliar language. The young woman was terrified, yet at the same time she could not help feeling something akin to both pity and liking. There were children amongst these folk, and some of the wives carried babies in their arms. These strange, shrunken people seemed innocent and simple yet, in some unfathomable way, dangerous. Above all, there was that about them which felt *alien*; something indescribable and incomprehensible in human terms.

Solemnly they looked at the silver objects in the open casket; picked through them, held them up shimmering in the snow-shine and examined them. They had a discussion amongst themselves. Then the king pointed to Mazarine's treasure and spoke again.

'It be lang-banks-gaet tae bring yon Laird Fleetwood back frae da verra t'reshold o' deat'. We'se doe what du axes us, ma hinny, bit faith we maun hae a gud koab. Dis be niver eno' siller.'

'Not enough silver? But I can get no more. What else would you have from me? I will give anything that is in my power to give!'

A broad smile stretched the little fellow's mouth. As soon as the words had left Mazarine's lips she regretted them, for once a promise is made to wights it must be kept, or severe retribution is exacted upon the tergiversater.

Once more the little people conversed with one another. At length the king turned to the damsel and said, 'We will tak' dy furst brun bairn.'

'My what?'

'Aye, dy furst brun. Dat's da teind.'

A kind of coldness began in the core of Mazarine and burned along her veins to her fingertips.

'But sir, I have no child.'

'Ane day ye might.'

'If I ever do, and if I give my first born child to you, what would you do with him or her?'

'We'd treat em kind and raise da bairn tae be oor servant.'

'Your servant in Trowland? Or on your gypsy wanderings?'

At this question the king merely laughed, and his subjects followed suit.

I may never bear a child, Mazarine though feverishly, *even if my love, by any miracle of fortune, should live and we should be wed. If he dies, I will never marry. Besides, I have given my word to these people, and I fear — perhaps without cause — that my loved ones might be made to suffer in some fashion if I break it.*

The little king crossed his arms in front of his chest and cocked his head to one side, fixing Mazarine with a bright and beady eye. 'What say ye?' he demanded.

The situation is urgent. In desperation I am forced to agree, for Hawkmoor may not survive another night.

'Very well then,' she said at length. 'Let the bargain be struck!'

One of the fiddlers resumed his scraping and the stunted

merrymakers began again to prance and leap excitedly, as if in celebration of this news, yodelling and whooping in shrill tones. Some gathered any scattered coins and dropped them back into the casket, before closing the lid and bearing their treasure swiftly away.

'We s'll come this verra nicht tae do our wirk,' the little king announced. 'Noo mun du gie us dy strik alang!'

'I do not understand, sir!'

'Dy consent tae cross dy t'reshold!'

It was vital to use caution when conversing with eldritch creatures. Words had immense power; they were binding contracts. Careless phrases could be fatal. 'Very well. You may cross the threshold of Clover Cottage,' said Mazarine, carefully choosing her words, mindful of Thrimby's advice. As if they had caught her meaning and welcomed it the dancers leaped higher, shouting gleefully.

'Leave da hoose doors unlockit,' the Trow-king instructed the damsel, 'and tak awa' a' da charms. Leave da krankin' man laenerly and blow oot da lamps. Stir-na from der böls and tie up da yalkie-dogs.'

Mazarine stood hesitating while the little king expertly twirled the silver spoon in his hand. She would rather these peculiar beings had given her some medicine to take back to the sick man in the cottage, than have them pay him a visit themselves.

'Whyfor be dee a-solistin', ma hinny?' asked the king, glancing at her slyly. 'Be ye o' a mind to jine da dancin'?'

'No sir! I was wondering whether you might entrust me with the healing unguent, or philtre, or whatever it may be that you would bring to Lord Fleetwood. I could administer it myself and save you the trouble.'

'Ach!' exclaimed the wight, grimacing hideously as if he had just been insulted. 'Away wi' ye, awa' wi' ye noo. Fare dee well!'

With that the Trow-king appeared to dismiss his human petitioner, who felt it would be discourteous, not to mention perilous, to stay longer. Recalling Thrimby's warnings she strove against her inner desire to throw herself sobbing at the feet of the quaint little monarch and beg him to hand over a miracle cure on the spot. Instead she bowed respectfully, expressed her gratitude without saying 'thank you', hastened to where Professor Wilton's doleful mare waited, and rode away through the snow.

Laurelia and Wakefield ran out of the cottage to meet the rider, their faces glowing with relief that she had returned to them. 'Does he live?' Mazarine called out as soon as they were within earshot, and they assured her that yes, the patient still clung to life.

It was not yet midnight. As soon as the damsel set foot indoors she hurriedly explained to the household what must be done, as far as she could interpret the Trow-king's instructions, and quietened their protests by saying, 'We have no choice. If we cannot save him by other means we must try any chance, no matter how outlandish it seems.'

Therefore, as the curious little king had ordered, they left the doors unlocked, tied up the dogs, removed all the charms about the premises, left the sick man alone and blew out the lamps. Then they shut themselves into their bedchambers, climbed into bed, pulled up the covers and waited in the dark. The night was windless and completely still. In the hearth the fire burned low. Not a sound came through the gloom besides the steady drip-drip of melted snow running off the chimney. Hours seemed to drag on without end. Across miles of snow came the far-off chimes of the Somerhampton town bell striking twelve, but it was long past midnight when the edges of hearing were brushed by soft cluckings as the cooped hens stirred in the yard, and the patter of light footsteps on the doorstep, and the faint squeaking of hinges.

The floorboards creaked.

Suddenly the iron hand of fear gripped Mazarine. *What if I have been tricked into letting in a pack of gypsies who might harm him, or rob us, or both?* Quelling the notion as a mere folly she steeled herself to remain beneath her coverlet and make no sound.

Presently the floor-planks creaked again, the hinges complained and the hens clucked sleepily. When all had been quiet for what seemed a lifetime, Mazarine could wait no longer. She jumped out of bed, lit a lamp with shaking hands and ran into the sick-room on her bare feet. The other members of the household were not far behind. She held the lamp close to the pillow. Golden lamplight washed across the attractive countenance of Hawkmoor. He was sleeping peacefully at last, healthy colour tinging his skin in place of the ghastly pallor. Mazarine and her friends glanced at each other, scarcely daring to hope.

While Mazarine resumed her place beside the sick-bed, Goodwife Wilton and the maid Tansy scoured the house, checking to see whether anything had been taken. All was in its proper place.

'Nothing has been stolen,' said Laurelia's mother. 'I am convinced something excellent has happened here this night!'

In the morning Hawkmoor opened his eyes for the first time.

They brought him water and gruel. When he had sipped he fell back against the pillow. 'Mistress Blythe, where are you?'

'I am here, Fleetwood!'

'I had a strange dream,' he whispered. 'I thought I saw children crowding around this bed. Upon my eyes and mouth they let fall raindrops, glistening with a sweet white light.'

'By all that's extraordinary,' said Professor Wilton in astounded joy, 'I declare, the patient is recovering!'

Then all trouble and woe fell away from Mazarine and a blissful sense of peace enfolded her. Hawkmoor would live. He had survived the duel but there would be no legal consequences, despite the rule that the outcome was to be decided by the slaying of one of the combatants. On that fateful day he had been declared dead on the field of battle and Master Squires had been officially proclaimed the victor — nothing could change that proclamation, not even this miraculous recovery.

Even as she rejoiced Mazarine said to herself, *I will not tell anyone of the terrible bargain I made. There is a chance it may never need to be fulfilled, and to confess would be to cause unnecessary anguish.*

Fleetwood remained extremely weak. All that month he lay abed, with Mazarine never far from his side. Inevitably, during this time they confirmed their love for each other and cleared up all misunderstandings. Happiness acted upon the young man like a tonic. As he grew stronger he began to look for diversions and one day he asked a favour of her.

'Will you read some of your poetry to me? For I would fain have the honour of hearing what none have heard before.'

For a single moment only, Mazarine hesitated. With a smile she said, 'I can refuse you nothing!' and went to fetch her books of writings. From that juncture, she sat beside him and read to him every evening, and it was not long before she began to write once more. Then she knew at last that love had brought her back from the lands of sorrow.

Miraculously, as Hawkmoor convalesced, the old fuath-stricken wound on his calf began to heal. By Winter's close when he had fully recovered, all the scars had vanished and, to the joy of everyone, he was no longer lame.

CHAPTER EIGHT

Limping, lumping, tripping, thumping,
Clumsy dancers in the night.
Don't be tricked; though they seem graceless,
Trows can move as fast as flight.

By the first month of Spring, Sovrachmis of the Primroses, Wakefield Squires and Laurelia Wilton had become man and wife. Hawkmoor employed the young scholar as his own scrivener and bestowed on the couple life tenure, rent-free, in the best cottage at Southdale Farm. No longer would Wakefield have to trudge to Somerhampton to work in the mayor's office.

With the change of season celebrations again broke out across Erith, marked by the traditional symbols — coloured eggs and candles, a procession of ewes decked in garlands of green leaves tied with pale yellow ribbons, and weddings. Mazarine ceased to wear mourning. She celebrated her twenty-first birthday on the third day of Sovrachmis, and on the twelfth day she and Hawkmoor were married. Henceforth the damsel would be known in society as Mazarine Canty, The Right Honourable The Viscountess Fleetwood.

For two years and one month the earl must serve his sentence in Somerhampton Jail where, in respect for his station, he received better treatment than the majority of the prisoners. He was quartered in the well-appointed section of the jail reserved for those aristocrats who, for various reasons, had not succeeded in bribing their way out of their legal difficulties. Ever the dandy, he remained as much preoccupied with his cosmetics and curls in prison as he had been outside, and as unpopular. To satisfy his creditors he was forced to sell Kelmscott Park. With the money from Mazarine's inheritance the newly-weds purchased the estate.

After their wedding Lord and Lady Fleetwood went to live at the Hall, where Thrimby greeted them hospitably, as if he were the true owner, which Mazarine sometimes felt he was. Hawkmoor dismissed Ripley and his cohorts, but provided liberally for the servants who had proved themselves faithful and true. Those who had spied on the couple in the early days were not penalised, for they had been driven by fear, not greed, and they begged forgiveness. As for the young laundry-maid and the under-gardener's lad, they received promotions and a significant increase in wages. Thrimby, on the other hand, declined to discuss wages, behaving as if insulted when the topic was mentioned.

Now that the heavy burden of care had been lifted from their shoulders, the young bride and her friends rejoiced. Those who had been separated were finally united; the sick had been cured, the steadfast rewarded and wrong-doers punished. It seemed, at last, that all was well. Often the young bride looked upon her handsome husband and recalled how she had almost lost him. She treasured every moment they spent together. Their days of bliss together flew past on wings of sunlight and apple blossom, but after half a year, the merriment faded from Mazarine's demeanour. She became withdrawn and thoughtful.

'What ails you, my love?' Hawkmoor would ask, putting his arm around her waist. 'Tell me, that I may put it right!'

'It is nothing,' she would say, brightening. 'Nothing at all.'

At nights she lay awake staring at thin spindles of moonlight slanting between the curtains of the great, canopied bed.

A child was on the way, and she knew not what to do.

As time went on her misery deepened. Already she loved the unborn child more fiercely than life itself, and her every waking moment was spent trying to plan an escape from her predicament. Soon, she knew, her condition would become apparent to others and there would be no hiding the truth.

At length she revealed the news of the child to Hawkmoor, whose wonder and pride knew no bounds. His happiness, however, was short-lived, for no sooner had she told him than she began to weep. He held her in his arms until the sobs died away, then questioned her. 'I made a bargain for your life,' she confessed. 'I promised to give our first-born child to those who saved you!' She dared not look at his face, for the shock and sorrow she would read there.

Presently her husband said calmly. 'Be comforted, my love. We will find some way out of this plight. If they were gypsies who dared to ask this monstrous thing of you, then unless they break in and steal our child, they shall never touch him. He shall be guarded day and night.'

'I believe them to be trows. 'Tis unlikely they were human.'

'If they were wights,' said Hawkmoor, 'that is another matter — for I fear they will take what is due to them, no matter what barriers are thrown in their path. Yet do not despair! There is always hope.'

Thrimby greeted the tidings of the expected child by performing a jig on the drawing-room hearth-stone, during which he stumbled over his ragged hose and had to kneel down to straighten them. While still on his knees he glanced up, an enlightened expression brightening his pinched features as if an idea had just struck him. 'Well, sain my bones!' he exclaimed. 'Now who would ha' thought! So this is what 'tis like to be short!' — whereupon he resumed his little dance, still on his knees, as if to sample being a dancer of low stature. After falling over and bruising his elbow he stood up. 'That's enough of that!' he said, 'I'd rather eat my hat!'

'Gentle Thrimby,' said Mazarine, 'you have rescued us from dire straits twice before — once when you sent a message to Lord Fleetwood bidding him return home, and once when you told me how to save his life. We ask your help a third time, and I hope 'twill be the last.' After entreating the servant to make himself comfortable in the drawing-room with herself and her husband, she explained the terrible bargain she had made.

When she concluded her tale Thrimby shook his head sadly, and with some vexation. 'T'was trows, not gypsies that ye saw,' he said with a snort, wriggling uncomfortably on his tapestry-upholstered armchair, 'and if ye should withhold the payment ye 'ave promised, or try substituting gold, or silver, or the wealth of kings, this bargain to evade, ye'll not succeed. A life was pledged. Yer promise has been made. And if ye try to 'ide yer child they'll find 'im without doubt. Though 'e be under lock and key the trows will steal 'im out. They'll carry 'im away into their kingdom underground, which he can 'ardly leave, for with enchantment 'e'll be bound.'

The notion rendered the listeners speechless with dismay.

'At all costs we must stop them from taking our child,' Hawkmoor said presently.

'It may not be possible,' said Thrimby, so intent on thumping at a lumpy cushion he found irksome that he forgot his rhyming. 'If 'tis possible, 'twill will not be easy. Trows is a formidable force. It is said that they possess a smatterin' o' governance over the weather, and that some 'ave mastered the art of makin' weed-stems fly, or old ploughbeams, or bundles of twigs or grasses, so that they can climb aboard and go ridin' through the air! 'Ave ye 'eard them stories?'

'Not I! Tell us, pray!' said Mazarine. 'If we are to thwart the trows we must know as much as possible about them!'

'All right', said Thrimby, and tucking up his outsized feet to sit cross-legged in the armchair, he began. 'One night after sunset a gentleman saw a band o' trows go by in a cloud of dust, and they was shoutin',

"Up horse, up hedik,

Up we'll go riding bulwand,

And I know I'll ride among you."

'The gentleman thought this scene so wondrous that 'e repeated the words, and straight away found 'imself up in the air in the middle o' the band, seated sideways on a mugwort stem. They flew along until they 'lighted on the roof of an 'ouse. Luckily for 'im, the Grey Neighbours paid 'im no attention. The gentleman 'eard them sayin' that a woman was in labour within the 'ouse, and that when she were delivered, she would sneeze thrice, and if nobody *sained* her they would exchange 'er for an image and take 'er with 'em. So when she sneezed the gentleman said, "May the Star *sain* you," whereupon the trows vanished in the blink of an eye. The man climbed down and entered the 'ouse, where 'e was received with cordiality, but the story goes that the 'illtings raised a gale, so 'e weren't able to get 'ome for a week.'

'They were angry with him for cheating them!' exclaimed Mazarine. 'It seems they are powerful enough to stir up the very winds!'

'*Some* o' them may be powerful enough,' said Thrimby.

'Which ones are *we* dealing with?' asked Hawkmoor. 'The weak or the strong?'

Thrimby shook his head once more. 'Alas,' was all he said in reply.

The three conversed together throughout the night until cock-crow, and much was said, and much was planned. At the close of discussion, however, when a wan gleam of dawn trickled through the shutters and they were about to wend their weary way to bed, Thrimby uttered a grim warning that echoed in Mazarine's mind ever after —

''Tis risky,' he said grimly. 'There's no knowin' if the deal can be undone.

Ye must not 'ave false confidence this battle can be won.

Remember as ye rock yer babe and sing yer cradle-song,

Trow gramarye is ancient as the 'ills, and thrice as strong.

Prepare yerselves to face the worst. Ye owe the trows their due.

'Tis likely they will take their fee no matter what you do.'

Said Hawkmoor sharply, 'In that case, I will make preparations forthwith.'

And so it passed that within two sevennights all plans had been laid. The couple, dressed in disguise and accompanied by their entourage, boarded a white-sailed seaship at the Port of Raynemouth. In secrecy their ship weighed anchor and headed down the coast. Turning west she passed through the strait separating Severnesse from the cold southern land of Rimany, where dwelled the Arysk-folk whose hair and skin was the colour of rime. Thence to the southernmost cape of Eldaraigne the vessel journeyed, though her progress was slow, for it seemed the wind was ever against her. During a brief sojourn in Eldraigne to take on supplies, neither Mazarine nor Hawkmoor set foot on shore, and their servants were forbidden to mention their names, or their port of origin or their destination.

From there the captain set course north-west along the passage between Luindorn and Eldraigne. Far in the distance on the starboard side the passengers could see the walls and towers of the great city of Caermelor. Onwards they sailed up the coast of Luindorn. A hundred nautical miles away to the east, they knew, lay the Royal Isle of Tamhania, veiled in its enchanted mists. None could make landfall there without knowing the password that would part those vapours and allow vessels to reach safe harbour. The ship was not bound for Tamhania, however, but for Finvarna, that western land of rugged coastlines and cloudy heights; of deer with giant antlers, and red-haired warriors in kilts who could recite entire sagas from memory, and who held contests in games, feasting and 'having the last word'.

In the far north of Finvarna, Lord and Lady Fleetwood's party at last disembarked. The seaship sailed away, while the party travelled on by carriage and wagon, into the west. Finally, when they had arrived at the loneliest castle in the most remote outpost of Finvarna they rested. Atop a gaunt cliff the stronghold stood, overlooking ocean waves that roared as they smashed themselves to pieces against jagged rocks. Gulls wheeled, mewing, through the granite battlements and turrets. Here the party remained, incognito, until Mazarine's time should come.

In the Spring of the year 1040 a comely, healthy boy was born in the castle by the sea. When he was three months old Mazarine and Hawkmoor publicly named him 'Richard'.

After the naming ceremony at Castle Creig-Ard, local guests congregated in the formal gardens to drink to the baby's health. Harpists were playing melodious airs and folk were conversing cheerfully, when in the midst of the celebrations a curious little figure popped unexpectedly out of the gathering, right next to the spot where Mazarine stood holding the baby in her arms. The stranger was robed in grey, and his deep hood partially obscured his visage. Before the proud mother could comprehend his purpose, he lightly touched her child's left palm with a bony finger, leaving a small dot, greener than emeralds. 'Richard Canty be marked fur wis,' he said clearly, 'and whan he be twall munts and ane day auld, we will av him.'

Having made that vow he bowed, walked away and somehow vanished among the assembly. 'Stop that fellow!' Mazarine shouted in horror, trying to wipe off the mark with her handkerchief. The baby began to wail. A hue and cry was got up, and people began running to and fro.

In a moment Hawkmoor was at his wife's side. 'What's amiss?' he asked.

'A stranger has put a mark on our darling's hand, see?' Mazarine held up the tiny pink-and-white hand of the baby, displaying the emerald dot in the centre of the dewy palm.

'A strange stamp indeed,' said Hawkmoor, examining it closely.

'I tried to scrub it off,' said Mazarine, with tears starting in her eyes. She showed him the square of white linen, whose centre was stained light green. 'But to no avail. It seems indelible!'

'Keep the handkerchief in a safe place,' said Hawkmoor. 'I'll take a guess it might be of some use to Thrimby when we ask him what to do.'

'Thrimby? But he is not here with us!'

'Aye, but now that we have been discovered we must return to Kelmscott Park. Clearly there is nowhere in Erith the Grey Neighbours will not find us. We will be better off at home, where at least we will have Thrimby to advise us.'

'Of course!' Mazarine agreed. 'You are right.' She choked back tears.

Though Lord and Lady Fleetwood made light of the event to their guests, their hearts weighed heavy. For them, the very sunlight had drained out of the day. Retainers searched high and low, but the mischief-maker could not be found, and the celebrations concluded early.

As soon as travel arrangements could be finalised the family voyaged back to Severnesse. On the first night at Kelmscott Hall, Lord and Lady Fleetwood took the child and hurried to the kitchens in search of Thrimby. They found him in the scullery, zealously polishing a frying pan.

'Good master and good mistress, I be glad,' he said, 'ta see ye safely back here with the lad. A bonny 'un, clean-limbed and bright of e'e! And did ye do with 'im as I told ye?'

'We did, Thrimby,' said Hawkmoor, 'but an appalling thing has come to pass. The Grey Neighbours tracked us down. They have daubed our boy with a mark, and no amount of soap and water will remove it!'

Thrimby dropped the frying pan with a crash that startled the child and set him bawling.

'By the Powers!' the domestic squeaked, too aghast to form a rhyme, 'The mark o' the trows!'

'I tried to rub it off before it dried,' said Mazarine.

'Ye did? What did ye rub it with? Quick lass, I must know!'

'A handkerchief—'

'Did ye keep it? I must see it!'

Mazarine produced the cloth, which she carried in the aulmonière hanging from her waist-belt. Thrimby stared at it then folded it up and placed it in one of the patched, ragged pockets of his threadbare coat. Solemnly he gazed up at the young mother, who was endeavouring to console her baby.

'I'll keep this now.' he said. 'Ye did right, master and mistress. Ye did all that can be done. The mark will never come off until the 'illtings 'ave been paid full price. Did the one who marked the little 'un say anythin' to ye?'

'He said they would come for our son a year and a day after his birth. That is all. What should we do? Where can we go to hide?'

'You cannot 'ide. 'E's been marked. There's nowt for it now but to wait.'

So they waited, the entire household, and the seasons of that year rolled by too quickly, and the child grew.

Also fast approaching was the date of the earl's release from prison after the completion of his sentence. The young couple had no wish to associate with the man who had made their lives miserable in numerous cruel ways. Now a pauper, Lord Rivenhall was friendless; nevertheless Hawkmoor made arrangements for his future accommodation at a cottage on the edge of the Southdale Farm estate. 'After all,' he said, 'no matter what ill deeds he is guilty of, he is still, I suppose, my father. I owe him shelter, at least.'

On New Year's Eve the earl was walking through the prison yard on his way to bed after partaking of a celebratory evening meal, when he fell down insensible upon the cobblestones. Deeming him intoxicated the warders carried him off bed, but next morning he awoke lopsided. His left side was paralysed and he slurred his words, though he still retained the power of speech and his faculties of reason.

'He has suffered the elf stroke!' the prison chirurgeon diagnosed. 'Elf-archers have hit him with their elf-shot!'

The warders searched half-heartedly in the prison yard for flint arrowheads. It was said that if the barb that had caused the stroke was found, the victim could be cured. No tiny stone chevron, however, could be discovered. Unable to walk, the earl was confined to his bed and chair. On hearing this news, Mazarine and Hawkmoor pitied him and resolved to care for him under their own roof when he was discharged.

Early in the year 1041 Lord Rivenhall was set free. Hawkmoor sent a carriage to bring him to Kelmscott Hall, where Mazarine had engaged nurses to take care of him. Still fussing with his appearance the earl uttered no word of gratitude on his arrival, but commenced to demand attention night and day. He was surly and argumentative, and refused to take off his cap even when being bathed. His once-gorgeous curls lost their lustre and became as tangled as a rat's nest.

At Mazarine's request, Professor Wilton attended the patient twice weekly.

Once, having returned to Clover Cottage after such a visit, the apothecary found that one of his galenical phials was missing. In hindsight he was unsure whether he might have forgotten to replace it in his medicine case, and sent a messenger to the Hall to ask whether a small glass bottle had been found. Mazarine enquired among the household servants, but no one had seen the container and the matter was eventually forgotten.

*   *   *

That year the dying days of Winter were bitingly cold. At Kelmscott Hall, servants kept the hearth-fires well-stoked. When evening fell, Mazarine and Hawkmoor entertained a company of friends in the drawing room, while their child crawled freely about the floor. He was growing stronger and bonnier day by day, though he had as yet not a tooth in his head, and the fine bronze filaments of hair that had rubbed off on his mattress after his birth had, so far, not reappeared.

Silent in his wheelchair by the fire the earl sat huddled in a shawl. With his head sunken between his shoulders and a severe black cap tied over his straggling ringlets he appeared more like a grotesque, maned vulture than a man.

The tables were arrayed with wine and dishes of sweetmeats. Merry was the company, and at length the lady of the house arose to take her place at the harp so that she might sing to them, when the child, in his efforts to pull himself to his feet, took hold of the leg of a small marquetry table. The table teetered and Hawkmoor's wine goblet toppled, spilling its crimson contents upon the carpet. Laughing, the mother scooped up her child, but some of the scattered droplets splashed onto her hand.

Picking up a hand-bell she rang for a servant.

'My darling, we must watch you every minute, mustn't we!' said Mazarine, fondly kissing her child's brow. A housemaid appeared with basins and cloths to clean up the mess, but before she had begun her task Mazarine started to scream.

'My hand is burning! Oh, it is on fire!'

Quickly she placed the child in his nursery-maid's lap and bent double, clutching her hand to her breast. 'Cold water! Bring cold water!' she cried, tears streaming down her cheeks. The housemaid offered her the basin and, gasping, she plunged in her fist. 'Do not touch the wine!' Mazarine cried, and the servant backed away from the slowly spreading red pool on the floor. By this time all those present, save the earl, had sprung to their feet. They watched, appalled, as the red pool fizzed and steamed, and all colour bleached from the carpet in that spot.

'Hush, hush bonny Richard!' said the nursery-maid, rocking the whimpering child in her arms to placate him.

Hawkmoor placed his arm protectively around his wife's shoulders. 'I shall send for Professor Wilton!'

'No need,' she replied. ''Twas but a few drops, swiftly washed away. The water has soothed the hurt.'

'The wine was poisoned,' exclaimed Hawkmoor, whereupon all heads turned and all eyes regarded the earl with suspicion.

Revealing his perfect teeth in a grin like a death's head he said in rasping tones, 'I cannot walk. How could I do it?'

Said Hawkmoor harshly, 'Enough, sir! I have had my fill of you and your tricks. I will not suffer my family to endure a viper in our midst.' And so saying, he banished the earl to the east wing; the most remote and secluded apartment in the house.

It was with apprehension that Lord and Lady Fleetwood quietly celebrated their son's first birthday. Their every waking moment was plagued by dread of what might befall next evening at the appointed hour, a year and a day from the moment of his birth. Their minds were somewhat eased by the fact that trows — or gypsies — had not been seen in eastern Severnesse for twelve months, and Hawkmoor was inclined to believe his son was safe. Thrimby and Mazarine opined otherwise.

'Away they'll steal 'im,' Thrimby muttered pessimistically. 'In 'is place they'll leave a carvin' of 'is face and body on a stock of wood. Their call no mortal e'er withstood.'

'We have nailed charms over every door and window,' Hawkmoor reminded him.

'They will avail ye nought, my lord,' Thrimby said. 'When trows come seekin' their reward no charm can stop them — neither lock, nor bar o' iron or wood or rock.'

'Yet we cannot just sit back and do nothing!' Mazarine retorted. 'We must try, even if we are doomed to fail!'

'Ye've done all that I asked of you,' said Thrimby, 'so far, but there be more to do, in preparation for the hour of doom when wights put forth their power. Be brave and follow my advice to cheat the 'illtin's of their price, but know that if ye thwart the trows their vengeful wrath ye will arouse!'

'We care nothing for what revenge they might wreak upon us,' said Mazarine, 'as long as our child is secure!'

'In that case,' said Thrimby, 'this is what you must do.
If we cannot defeat them, then at least
We'll make full sure their access is decreased!
Tomorrow night bar ev'ry path and gate,
Seal ev'ry window on the whole estate,
Stop ev'ry cranny, lock and bolt each door,
Strew salt in handfuls round about the floor,
Tell servants to be quieter than a mouse —
No sneeze or whisper must disturb the house.
No matter what occurs, do not cry out —
All will be ruined by a single shout!
Upon the precious child put ample charms.
His mother must retain him in her arms,
And when all these amendments are in place,
The father should hold both in his embrace.'

'When will they come?' asked Hawkmoor.

'Not till the darkness falls, you can be sure,' replied the eccentric fellow, 'For though the sun's bright blaze they can endure, they do not like its touch, and shun the day. To move by moonlight is their chosen way.' Regarding the listeners earnestly he said, 'Think well of Thrimby — this is all I ask! Now, are you braced to undertake this task?'

'Of course we are!' said Mazarine.

Raising one hand the servant added dramatically, 'Mark ye, if you take this step you can never go back!' His audience stared at him in awe and some fear, whereupon he relented, saying, 'Don't mind me, I were just tryin' to add some theatrical spice to the situation.'

The young couple smiled, comprehending that he had merely tried to invoke a little mirth to ease their minds, but Mazarine said, 'Dear Thrimby, I believed you incapable of lying. How, then, are you able to exaggerate?'

'It all depends what you make of it,' he answered,
'And how you make the words and meaning fit.
For never mind what step you take, or when,
You never can go back and start again,
Unless you hold Time's keys within your hand
That past and future flow to your command!'

CHAPTER NINE

Remember as you rock your babe and sing your cradle-song,
Trow gramarye is ancient as the hills, and thrice as strong.

Wakefield and Laurelia had been admitted into the secret of the bargain with the trows. On the fateful night they insisted on staying at Kelmscott Hall with their friends, to provide what support they could.

After calling the servants together Hawkmoor addressed them, saying, 'Grave peril will surround Kelmscott Hall this night, so heed my instructions, for lives depend on your compliance. Until sunrise you must all remain indoors. Do not allow yourselves to be lured outside, no matter what occurs. Neither door nor gate nor window must be opened. Seal yourselves in! Stopper your ears and your mouths too, for you must speak no word during the dark hours and indeed, make no sound at all — not so much as a whisper or a sneeze. Nobody in the household should cry out, under any circumstances. Those of you who feel daunted by this prospect have my permission to depart from this house for the night and we will think no ill of them. Those who remain must swear to adhere to these directions.'

Every member of the household staff vowed to comply, and sombrely went about their tasks.

After an early supper Hawkmoor and Wakefield patrolled the premises with Goodwife Strood, the chatelaine, and the new Chief Steward, making certain that every door and window, large or small, was locked and barred — including the portals in the lonely wing where Lord Rivenhall sulked.

'What if the old master calls out?' asked Goodwife Strood. 'He would do it, methinks, just out of spite, beggin' your pardon, sir.'

'Never fear,' said Hawkmoor. 'Every evening he demands one of the apothecary's sleeping draughts, quaffs it to the last drop and snores till morning. His nurses will see to it that this night is no different.'

At day's end family and friends gathered in the drawing-room, prepared to keep vigil throughout the night. Footmen built up the fire and lit as many candles as possible, but no brightness could dispel the sense of disquiet charging the atmosphere. Outside in the western sky, clouds of scalding gold were melting in a flood of blazing rubies. One of the upper housemaids went about closing the shutters, blocking out the last glimpse of the sunset. To Mazarine it felt like being locked in a cell.

Flames licked at the logs in the fireplace, throwing out wraith-like shadows that writhed curiously on the wall hangings. Up and down the solemn quietude of the great house, long corridors, cavernous galleries echoed every creak of contracting wood, every whisper of sifting dust. Those who waited in the deepening evening strained their senses in an effort to detect what was brewing, unseen, in the surrounding darkness. Out there, evening mists would be rising from the lake, curling in stealthy streamers through the shrubbery and around the house. From beyond the walls came no sound. All was as quiet and still as if the world had ceased to exist. No breeze blew, no night-owl called; no leaf rustled, no twig scratched on a windowpane.

Only in the drawing-room was there any noise; the whisper of flames, the ticking of a clock, the low breathing of the people there assembled and the occasional sigh. When a log in the fireplace fell in with a crash, everyone jumped. A footman quietly added more fuel to the burning pile.

Hours passed.

Mazarine, in rose-pink silk, sat with Hawkmoor at the centre of a circle of salt thickly strewn upon the floor. They remained wide awake, every nerve stretched to its utmost. Bedecked with little charms of amber and rowan-wood, the child slept in his mother's arms. The lace collar of his dove-white frock framed his apple-cheeked face, soft as velvet, abandoned to dreaming.

At midnight there came a soft knock at the front door; *rap-rap-rap*.

Those who had fallen asleep in their chairs awakened with a jolt. The child opened his eyes. Without a word Mazarine gently clasped him in a firmer embrace. Her husband encircled them both with his arms.

'We are here for Richard Canty!' The low-pitched, resonant command seemed to penetrate to the very foundations of the premises.

The baby began to fret.

'Bring oot Richard Canty! Richard Canty, come!'

Those who stood guard in the drawing-room gave no answer. They listened, they waited, they scarcely drew breath. Their hearts hammered.

Once more the voice called out and received no reply. Presently, through the taut silence, the listeners could clearly hear the clatter of footsteps departing from the door, and straight away the dogs in the kennels began to howl and bark furiously, as if disturbed by an intruder. Their tether-chains rattled and cracked as they hurled themselves forward to their limits.

Still nobody spoke.

It was the child who broke the uncanny hush in the drawing-room. Suddenly he was squirming and writhing in his mother's grasp, as if trying to wriggle free, wailing at the top of his lungs. Mazarine held him more tightly, with Hawkmoor's strong arms encircling her.

Creamy clouds of cooing arose all around, and a mighty flapping of wings from the courtyard, as flocks of birds erupted from the dovecote. Out in the stables the horses began to neigh. A series of crashes and loud bangs erupted as they pranced and plunged, trying to kick down the walls. Next came the whoosh of ignition and the roar of flames; evidence of an inferno being kindled in the stables. The horses shrieked, striking out with their hooves, as if endeavouring to escape a conflagration. At this, Hawkmoor closed his eyes and buried his face in his wife's hair, for he loved his horses as his best friends, and it cost him dearly to refrain from rushing to the door.

The child was struggling to wrench himself from his mother's hold. He, alone of the company, gave voice. He cried and squirmed until he was red in the face, but Mazarine, tears streaming down her face, would neither speak nor let him go. Meanwhile, outside in the kennels and stables the tumult increased.

All at once Mazarine felt herself seized by paralysis, as if crammed into a narrow iron coffin. With a scream of rending metal, every door and window in the house flew open.

A deep voice bellowed, 'Richard Canty!' The awful summons was like the roar of measureless waters plunging through caverns that had never known the sun. 'Comes da call, Richard Canty! No midder's airms be strang eno' tae hold dee! Bearin' wir mark, bald and toot'less, if dee canna traivle, krieckle tae wis!'

Desperately, Mazarine held on to her child. The other watchers in the room were bound to the spot by the same invisible chains that constrained her. Nobody besides the infant could move. A powerful suction seemed to be dragging at the interior of the house, like the pull of a tidal wave; so intense that had they not been made as rigid as stone they could not have resisted it. Mazarine's gown billowed as if blasted by a hurricane; her hair tumbled from its pins and whipped about her face. Her arms ached from holding so tightly to her precious bundle, and she felt her husband's limbs tremble as he strove to keep his embrace intact. Minute by minute — or hour by hour, they strove against the terrible pressure.

At last every door and window slammed shut simultaneously and immediately they were free to move again. The child ceased to wail. Total silence clamped over the house. The fire had gone out and even the clock had ceased to tick. Time hung in suspension.

''Tis over,' said Thrimby.

'Yes,' whispered Mazarine, peering at him through her tangled locks, 'yet I am more afraid than ever, now that we have tricked them of their fee. Their vengeance will be severe.'

Hardly had she spoken when the eaves almost lifted off, and the house was rocked by a sudden gale, threaded by wild laughter. Boomed the voice, 'Richard Canty bald and toot'less! Tae be oor servant in Trowland, ane life be as guid as another!'

Thrimby rushed to the nearest window, reached up and threw open the shutters. 'Look!' he shouted.

Save for Mazarine, who would not allow her child near any aperture, the company joined him at the fenestrations. Looking out across a landscape illumined by fading stars and the pale, waxing, pre-dawn glow, they beheld none other than Lord Rivenhall himself, in his velvet robe, crawling and rolling down the lawns towards the shrubbery, where indefinable shapes milled in the dimness. Away went he, bald-headed without his wig of ringlets, shrieking indistinctly from his gummy mouth, his false teeth abandoned on the grass like the washed-up skeleton of some odd sea-creature. Despite all his effort and will, he was obeying the summons of the trows.

Said Hawkmoor, his voice rough with mixed emotions, 'Oh. It comes to me now. His name is Richard Canty. Had I known it was for this reason that Thrimby bade me pretend to name the child after his grandsire, I would not have done so with such blitheness.'

On all fours the earl scrambled into the shrubbery, whereupon the laughter and the wild wind swirled once about the walls, then swept away towards the distance.

'Thrimby, what have you done?' Mazarine asked the servant-poet, who now stood before her hugging himself and rocking back and forth on his toes, as she rocked the child.

'I took yer 'andkerchief, as 'twere some charm,' he said he with a grin, 'and rubbed the trow mark on the master's palm.'

Dumfounded, Mazarine grasped the full meaning of Thrimby's deed. For the first time she permitted a spark of hope to awaken in her spirit. 'Will they not be angry and seek vengeance for the substitution?'

'Nay, I'll warrant they will not wrathful be. They found it droll, and laughed full merrily!'

'But what does it mean, '*if dee canna traivle, krieckle tae wis*'?'

'It means *if you cannot walk, then crawl!*' cackled Thrimby. 'Aye, crawl like a babbie, or like the old master, on 'is bony knees!' He scowled. 'That stingy wretch, that hairless grasping fop who primped and preened himself from toe to top, who laughed on Firgrove's field, and felt no pain to think his heir, young Hawkmoor, would be slain. Bah!'

Far off a rooster crowed. Behind the horizon the sky was paling.

'Now comes the dawn-sun's fiery brand,' said Thrimby, 'and trows must flee into their land beneath the 'ills, else they'll be bound on Er'th till sunset comes around.'

Or perhaps someone else said it, for when Mazarine looked around, Thrimby was nowhere to be seen.

The peaceful radiance of the springtime sun spread its blessing across the land. Everyone burst into conversation, exclaiming over the night's events. The doors were unbarred, whereupon Hawkmoor accompanied by Wakefield and a retinue of household staff hastened outside to survey the damage to the premises. Others stepped out, their joy tempered with awe, to greet the new day. An under-housemaid re-kindled the fire while Mazarine paced around the chamber, too on edge to feel sleepy. In her arms, worn out but secure, the child slumbered.

'What has happened to us on this strange night?' Laurelia asked wonderingly, walking beside her friend. 'I confess, I am bewildered.'

'My darling boy's true name,' said Mazarine, 'is not Richard but Westwood. We named him twice, as Thrimby advised — once in a secret ceremony at Creig Ard, then in public, in case the trows had got wind of our whereabouts. It is the name first-bestowed that is the true one. By such tricks as this we tried to keep our son safe from the trows, but we could not guess that they would take Lord Rivenhall instead! Away in the east wing he was struggling, I daresay, against their summons as my darling was struggling in my arms — yet we could not know what was happening to him, and would have been powerless to prevent his leaving in any case.'

'I could scarcely believe my eyes when I saw the earl's bald head!' said Laurelia. 'Now it is clear why he always wore those hats. I daresay the cap tied beneath his chin was holding his wig on.'

'Bald?' echoed Mazarine.

'Indeed, and toothless, too, as bald and toothless as your bonny babe here, yet nobody ever knew, because the earl's vanity would not let him admit to it!'

Presently, a shout was heard from one of the courtyards. Soon afterwards Hawkmoor re-entered the room, followed by the stable-boy and the master of hounds, who was carrying what appeared to be a small log of wood.

'All is well!' Hawkmoor cried. ''Twas all Glamour; neither beast nor fowl nor outbuilding has been harmed or damaged — but look here! We found this limb of moss-oak leaning against the wall of the kitchen gardens.'

The wood had been cut to his son's exact height, and crudely carved into the shape of an infant resembling him.

'A trow-stock!' exclaimed Hawkmoor in disgust, and he bade the servants fling the wightish effigy on the drawing-room fire, where it burned fiercely until it fell to ash.

From that day forth the earl was never seen again — except, possibly, once. After seven years the laws of the land decreed that he was extinct, and his titles then passed to his heir. The new Lord and Lady Rivenhall enjoyed a long and happy life together with their seven children, but ever after, their first-born son Westwood Canty, Lord Fleetwood, was curiously drawn to the wild places.

When he was eighteen years of age — tall and strapping, the very image of his father — Westwood was walking home along a sunken road one Summer's evening when he sat down on a milestone to rest. The last twinkle of the sun's rays had just vanished below the tree-tops and an eerie afterglow suffused the landscape. The road clove between two hills, with steep, leafy banks rising on either side. Seated on the stone Westwood happened to glance up. He jumped to his feet, astonished at what he saw. On the other side of the road an opening ran into the hillside. He felt certain it had not been there a moment earlier. In that hollow place stood a speckled cow, and if he was not mistaken she was Southdale Farm's very best milch-cow, which had died a year ago. Even more impossible was the figure that squatted on a three-legged stool, milking the cow into a wooden pail; a shrunken, shrivelled old man with a pushed-in mouth and a head as bald as an egg. A metal bar extended from one side of the opening to the other, as if to prevent his exit. This apparition, who was wearing fine clothes with a dirty lace collar and cuffs, looked up at young Westwood and grimaced, but cordially grunted something that might have been 'Good evening', had his lips not flapped indistinctly over toothless gums.

Westwood bowed and wished him the same.

The ancient gaffer seemed to be waiting for him to say something more, and Westwood thought about an old phrase his mother had taught him during his boyhood years, in case he ever chanced upon someone who was trow-bound, which seemed to be the case here. While he scratched his head and tried to recall the exact words the old man filled up a cup with frothy milk and offered it to him with a gummy smile. Westwood took the vessel, put it to his lips and was just about to drink when he remembered that those who eat or drink trow food become trapped in Trow-land forever. Aghast, he threw down the cup. As the contents splashed across the road the old man shrieked and the entire scene disappeared.

Westwood hastened home without pausing until he reached his door. Afterwards he recalled the phrase his mother had taught him, but he was never sure whether what he had seen that evening had been real, or whether he had fallen into a doze, there on the milestone, and it had all been no more than a dream.

AFTERWORD

'The Enchanted' takes place in Erith, the setting for my Bitterbynde series. It was a joy to return to that fantastic yet familiar world after so long an absence — to the shang winds, the towers of the Relayers and the flying ships. Not least, it was a delight to revisit the myriad seelie and unseelie wights of Erith; in particular the trows, that interesting race from the folkloric traditions of the Orkney and Shetland islands.

The idea for the story came to me some while ago. Whenever I have a story idea I jot it down for future reference, and wait until the time is right for it to become fully fledged. Kelmscott Hall is, of course, titled in honour of William Morris. The name 'Mazarine' simply arrived with the protagonist, but it refers to a beautiful, deep shade of blue, one of my favourite colours.

— Cecilia Dart-Thornton

Notes on the Text of 'The Enchanted'

The Shock appears in *County Folk Lore Vol. I* 'Gloucestershire', ed. ES Hartland 1892, 'Suffolk' ed. Lady EC Gurdon 1893, and *Leicestershire and Rutland*,, ed. CJ Billson 1895. It is also mentioned in *The Bitterbynde Book 1: The Ill-Made Mute* by Cecilia Dart-Thornton, Tor, 2001.

The Tale of Katherine Fordyce is told in 'The Home of a Naturalist' by Edmonston and Saxby, in *County Folk-Lore Vol. III*, Orkney and Shetland Islands, pp. 23-5, Folklore Society County Publications, 1901.

Trows, being creatures from the folklore of the Shetland Islands, speak a Shetland dialect.

'Up horse, up hedik' is based on an anecdote in *Shetland Folk Book Vol. III* ed. TA Robertson and John J Graham, Shetland Times Ltd., Lerwick, 1957. Also mentioned in *The Bitterbynde Book 1: The Ill-Made Mute* by Cecilia Dart-Thornton, 2001.

The Trows Come for Their Payment was inspired by and partially quoted from 'Sandy Harg's Wife', in R.H. Cromek's *Remains of Galloway and Nithsdale Song*, London, 1810, p. 305. Another version appears in *The Crowthistle Chronicles Book 2: The Well of Tears* by Cecilia Dart-Thornton, Tor, 2005.

Jack Dann is a multiple-award winning author who has written or edited over seventy-five books, including the international bestseller *The Memory Cathedral*, which was 1 on *The Age* Bestseller list, *The Rebel: an Imagined Life of James Dean*, and *The Silent*, which *Library Journal* chose as one of their 'Hot Picks' and wrote: 'This is narrative storytelling at its best ... Most emphatically recommended.'

He is the editor of the groundbreaking anthology *Dreaming Down-Under* (with Janeen Webb), which won the World Fantasy Award in 1999, and *Dreaming Again*, which *Bookseller+Publisher* chose as their 'Pick of the Week'. *B+P* gave it five stars and wrote: 'Here are stories that engage with the building blocks of our culture and others that give shape to our shared darkness and light. *Dreaming Again* is at once quintessentially Australian and enticingly other. If you read short fiction you'll want this collection. If you don't, this is a reason to start.' Dann lives in Australia on a farm overlooking the sea and 'commutes' back and forth to Los Angeles and New York.

His website is jackdann.com.

Jonathan Strahan is the two-time Aurealis Award winning and Locus Award winning editor of more than forty books, including *The New Space Opera* (with Gardner Dozois), *Eclipse Three*, and *The Starry Rift*.

Three times nominated for the Hugo Award, he is also the editor of the 'Best Science Fiction and Fantasy of the Year' and 'Eclipse' anthology series, *Swords and Dark Magic* (with Lou Anders); *The Locus Awards* (with Charles Brown); *Mirror Kingdoms: The Best of Peter S. Beagle*; *Ascendancies: The Best of Bruce Sterling*; *The Best of*

Kim Stanley Robinson; *Fritz Leiber: Essential Stories*; four volumes of work by Jack Vance; and many more. In the 1990s he co-founded the groundbreaking Australian semiprozine, *Eidolon*, and edited *The Year's Best Australian Science Fiction and Fantasy* anthology series. He is currently the reviews editor for *Locus: The Magazine of the Science Fiction and Fantasy Field*. Strahan lives on the west coast of Australia with his wife and two daughters, and visits the United States regularly.

His website is www.jonathanstrahan.com.au.